SKAGBOYS

SKAGBOYS

IRVINE WELSH

W. W. Norton & Company

New York • London

For information about permission to reproduce selections from this book,
write to Permissions, W. W. Norton & Company, Inc.,
500 Fifth Avenue, New York, NY 10110

For information about special discounts for bulk purchases, please contact
W. W. Norton Special Sales at specialsales@wwnorton.com or 800-233-4830

Manufacturing by RR Donnelley, Harrisonburg, VA
Production manager: Anna Oler

Library of Congress Cataloging-in-Publication Data

Welsh, Irvine.
Skagboys / Irvine Welsh. — 1st American ed.
p. cm.
ISBN 978-0-393-08873-1 (hardcover)
1. Young men—Scotland—Fiction.
2. Drug addicts—Scotland—Fiction.
3. Edinburgh (Scotland)—Fiction.
I. Title.
PR6073.E47S57 2012
823'.914—dc23
2012018043

W. W. Norton & Company, Inc.
500 Fifth Avenue, New York, N.Y. 10110
www.wwnorton.com

W. W. Norton & Company Ltd.
Castle House, 75/76 Wells Street, London W1T 3QT

1 2 3 4 5 6 7 8 9 0

In memory of Alan Gordon, 'the leader of the team',
and Stuart Russell and Paul Reekie,
the real leaders of the opposition in England and Scotland

'There is no such thing as society.'

Margaret Thatcher

'That Calvinistic sense of innate depravity and original sin
from whose visitations, in some shape or other, no deeply
thinking mind is always wholly free.'

Herman Melville

Contents

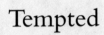

Tempted

Prologue: Notes from Rehab Journal

Journal Entry: Concerning Orgreave

Even the plank-stiffness of this old, unyielding settee can't arrest my body's slink into deliverance. It reminds me of the university residences in Aberdeen; lying in the dark, basking in exalted freedom from the fear that coalesced in my chest, like the thick phlegm did in his. Because whatever I hear outside, cars scrunching down the narrow, council-house streets, sometimes sweeping their headlights across this fusty old room, drunks challenging or serenading the world, or the rending shrieks of cats taking their torturous pleasures, I know I won't hear that noise.

No coughing.

No screaming.

No thumping sound: doof doof doof . . .

None of those urgent, raised whispers which, by their panic levels, enable you to calibrate just how sleepless your night will be.

Just the dozy, relatively silent darkness, and this settee.

Nae. Fuckin. Coughing.

Because it always starts with a cough. Just one. Then, as you will him to settle down, your quickening pulse tells you that you've subconsciously been waiting for that bark. Then the second one — the worse moment — when your anger shifts from the source of the cough onto those who would assist him.

Just fuckin leave it, ya cunts.

But, of course, you hear the disturbance from behind the paper-thin walls; a weary sigh, the sharp click of the light switch, the skittish footsteps. Then the voices, cooing and pleading, before the grim procedure starts: the postural drainage.

Doof . . . doof . . . doof . . .

. . . doof . . . doof . . . doof . . .

The dread rhythm of my father's big hands pounding on his thin, crooked back, insistent, even violent. Such a different sound and beat to my ma's timorous taps. Their hushed and exasperated encouragement.

I wish they would leave him in the hospital. Just keep him the fuck away. I'm not going back to that house until he's gone forever. It's so wonderful that from this haven you can forget all that and just let your mind and body dissolve into sleep.

'C'mon, son! Up! Move it!'

Awakening sore and stiff, to the gravelly voice of my father. He's standing over me, his thick brow furrowed, naked from the waist up, his chest a forest of blond-grey fur, as he brandishes a white toothbrush. It takes me three full seconds, each measured in an eye blink, to remember that I'm on my gran's couch in Cardonald. I only got to sleep a few hours ago and it would still be pitch black except for the small table lamp he's clicked on, oozing a fatigued aquamarine glow across the room. But he's right, we have to go: to make the bus at St Enoch's Square.

~~I know that once I get moving I'll be fine, even though I'm a little untidy~~ FUCKIN DAEIN IT AGAIN!!

Ah <u>ken</u> *that once ah git movin ah'll be fine, even though ah'm a bit scruff order and ask tae borrow Gran's iron; just tae get the worse creases oot ay the navy Fred Perry before ah pill it ower ma thin, white, goosebumped body. Dad's huvin nane ay it but.* 'Forget it,' *he says, waving his toothbrush, marching tae the bathroom across the hall, clicking oan the overhead light as he goes.* 'It's no a fashion show! C'moan!'

Ah dinnae need that much encouragement; the adrenalin's leaking intae me, buzzing us up. There's no way ah'm missing this yin. Granny Renton's up tae see us off; small, white-heided in her quilted dressing gown, but robust and ever-alert, peerin at us ower her glesses, duffel bag in her hand. She gapes at us for a second, makes some kind ay gesture, then she's off fussing eftir ma dad in the hallway. Ah can hear her soft sing-song voice. 'Whit time's the bus go . . . where does it leave fae . . . whit time will ye get there . . . ?'

'Go back . . . tae yir . . . bed . . . Mother,' *ma dad garbles in between moothfaes ay toothbrush and spit, as ah take the opportunity tae quickly pull oan ma clathes; shirt, jeans, socks, trainers n jaykit. I'm looking at the framed pictures of my Granda Renton on the mantelpiece. Gran's taken oot the four medals he got in the war, including the VC, which I think was fae Normandy. He wouldnae have liked them being on display like that; he kept them in an old baccy tin and always had tae be cajoled intae showin us them. Fair play tae him, he told us from the off, me n*

4

ma brother Billy, that it was aw bullshit. That some brave men got nae medals for their heroics, while wankers could get decorated for nowt. Ah recall, one time when we were aw oan holiday in the guest hoose doon in Blackpool, ah was pressing him, 'But *you* were brave, eh, Granda, charging up that beach, ye must have been brave.'

'I was scared, son,' he'd telt me, his face sombre. 'But most of all ah wis angry; angry at being there. Really angry. I wanted tae take it out on somebody, then go hame.'

'But that man hud tae be stoaped though, Faither,' my dad had implored, 'ye said so yirsel!'

'Ah know that. Ah wis angry that he wis allowed tae git started in the first place.'

The two pictures ay Granda R offer subtle contrast. In one he's a cocky young gadge in a uniform that lends him gravitas, aboot tae swagger off oan an adventure wi his mates. The second, more recently taken, shows him wi a deep smile, but different tae the other presumptuous grin. It's no exactly false, but it looks set and hard-won.

Ma gran returns, catching me at the pictures. Perhaps she sees something in us, in profile; a hint ay the past, because she sidles up tae me, puts her airm roond ma waist and whispers, 'Gie the bastirts hell, son.' Gran smells fragrant but old, like she has a soap naebody uses any mair. As my dad comes through and we prepare tae leave, she adds, 'But watch yirsel and look eftir ma laddie,' meaning him. It's weird that she still thinks ay him that wey, wi him being ancient, no far offay fifty!

'C'mon, pal, the cab's here,' he says, maybe a bit abashed at her fussing, as he looks through the curtains ootside tae the street, before turning and kissing my gran on her foreheid. Then she grabs my hand. 'You're the best ay them, son, the best ay them aw,' she whispers in urgent confidence. She's said this every time ah've seen her since ah wis a bairn. Used tae make us feel great, till ah found oot she said it tae aw her grandchildren, and her neighbour's kids! Ah'm sure she means it at the time, but.

The best ay them aw.

She releases the grip and hands Dad the duffel bag. 'Dinnae you be losin the Thermos flask in that bag, David Renton,' she ticks.

'Aye, Maw, ah telt ye ah'd keep an eye oan it,' he says sheepishly, like he's become a surly teenager again. He starts tae go, but she stops him. 'You're forgettin something,' she says, and goes tae the sideboard and *produces three small glesses, which she proceeds tae fill up wi whisky. Ma dad rolls his eyes. 'Maw . . .'*

She isnae hearin him. She raises a gless, forcing us tae follow, although ah hate whisky n it's the last thing ah want this early in the morning. 'Here's tae us, wha's like us — damn few n thir aw deid!' Gran croaks.

Dad knocks his back in a oner. Gran's has already gone, by some kind ay osmosis, as ah didnae even see her pit the gless tae her lips. It takes me two retching gulps to get it doon. 'C'mon, son, yir a Renton,' she chides.

Then Dad nods tae me and we're off. 'She's an awfay wumin,' he says with affection, as we climb intae the big black taxi, ma stomach burning. Ah wave back at her small figure, standing in the doorway in the murky street, willing the daft auld bat tae git back inside, intae the warm.

Glasgow. That was how we learned tae spell it at primary school: <u>Granny Likes A Small Glass Of Whisky.</u>

It's still pitch dark and Weedgieville is spooky at four o'clock on a Monday morning, as the cab creaks and rumbles intae toon. It's minging in here; some dirty fucker's puked fae last night and ye can still smell it. 'Jesus Christ.' The old boy waves his hand in front ay his neb. Ma dad's a big, broad-shoodird sort ay gadge, whereas ah take mair eftir my mother in build: sticklike and rangy. His hair can genuinely be called blond (even though it's now greying), as opposed tae mine which, however ah try n dress it up, is basically ginger. He's wearin a broon cord jaykit, which ah have tae say is quite smart, though ruined by the Glasgow Rangers FC lapel badge, pinned next tae his Amalgamated Union of Engineering Workers yin, and he fairly reeks ay Blue Stratos.

The bus is waitin fir us in the empty square behind Argyle Street. Some pickets are being harassed by a change-scrounging jakey whae keeps staggerin oaf intae the night then returning, always reprising the same routine. Ah climb oan the bus tae get the fuck away fae the pest. This cunt disgusts me; he's nae pride, nae politics. His deranged eyes roll and those rubber lips purse in that purple face. He's been beaten tae a pulp by the system, and aw the parasite can dae is try tae scrounge offay people whae've goat the bottle tae fight back. 'Wanker,' ah hear masel snap.

'Dinnae be sae quick tae judge, son.' Dad's accent is mair Glaswegian; stepping off the Edinburgh train at Queen Street does that. 'Ye dunno that boey's story.'

Ah say nowt, but ah dinnae want tae ken that minger's tale. Oan the

6

bus, ah sit beside Dad and a couple ay his auld mates fae the Govan yards. It's good, cause ah feel closer tae him than ah've done in a while. It seems ages since we've done something thegither, just the two ay us. He's pretty quiet n thoughtful though, probably worried cause ay ma wee brother, oor Davie, being taken back intae the hoaspital.

There's plenty bevvy oan the bus but naebody's allowed tae touch it till we head back, then we'll celebrate stoapin they fuckin scab lorries! Stacks ay nosh but; Granny Renton has made loads and loads ay sannies on white, spongy Sunblest bread: cheese and tomatay and ham and tomatay, like it's a funeral we're gaun tae!

Mind you, oan the bus it's mair like a fitba match than either boneyerd procession or picket; it has a big Cup Final vibe tae it, wi aw they banners hingin in the windaes. Half ay the people on oor coach are striking miners, fae pits in Ayrshire, Lanarkshire, the Lothians and Fife; the other half trade unionists like the auld man, and assorted fellow travellers, like me. Ah was delighted when Dad telt us he'd got us a seat; the politicos at the uni would be as jealous as fuck that ah wis oan one ay the official National Union ay Mineworkers' buses!

The bus isnae that far out ay Glesgey before the night fades away intae a beautiful summer sky ay early-morning greeny-blue. Even though it's early, a few cars are on the road, some ay them blaring their horns at us in support ay the strike.

At least ah'm getting some conversation out ay Andy, whae's ma dad's best mate. He's a wiry, salt-ay-the-earth Weedgie boy, an ex-welder and lifelong CP member. His bony face has this almost translucent, nicotine-yellay skin stretched ower it. 'So, that'll be you back at the uni in September, eh, Mark?'

'Aye, but a few ay us are gaun oaf oan the InterRail acroas Europe next month, eh. Been back graftin at ma auld job as a chippy, tryin tae get some shekels thegither.'

'Aye, it's a great life when yir young. Make the maist ay it, that's ma advice. Ye got a girlfriend at that university?'

Before ah can answer, Dad's ears prick up. 'Better no have, or that wee Hazel'll be daein her nut. Lovely wee lassie,' he says tae Andy, then turns tae me n goes, 'Whit is it she does again, Mark?'

'Windae displays. At Binns at the West End, the department store, likes,' ah tells Andy.

A big contented crocodile smile spreads across my dad's pus. If the cunt knew what Hazel and me's relationship wis like, he widnae be sae keen tae bang oan aboot her aw the time. ~~A terrible~~ But that's another story. The auld boy's just chuffed tae see us wi a bird, worrying fir years ah was a possible buftie boy due tae ma musical tastes. Ah hud an aggressively glam-rock puberty, and was a teenage punk. ~~Then there wis the time that oor Billy caught me wank~~

Another story.

We're makin good time, n it's still aw cool when we git ower the border tae England, but as we get near Yorkshire and oantae the smaller roads, things git a wee bit weird. Thaire's polis everywhere. But instead ay stoapin the bus every few yards for nae reason at aw, as we expect, they just wave us oan. They even gie us helpful directions as how tae git tae the village. 'What the fuck's aw this aboot?' one boy shouts. 'Whaire's aw the usual roadblocks n harassment?'

'Community policing,' another gadge laughs.

Ma dad looks oot at a row ay smiling coppers, one ay whom waves at us wi an ear-tae-ear grin. 'Ah dinnae like this. This isnae right.'

'As long as they dinnae stop us gettin they scabs sent back,' ah goes.

'You'll keep the heid,' he warns us in a low growl, then frowns. 'Whae's this mate that yir meetin up wi then?'

'Just one ay the boys fi London ah used tae stey in the squat at Shepherd's Bush wi. Nicksy. He's awright.'

'Another wan ay they dippit punk rockers, ah'll bet!'

'Ah dinnae ken what music he's listenin tae now,' ah tell him, a bit irritated. He can be a daft auld fucker sometimes.

'Punk rock,' he laughs tae his mates, 'another fad he got bored wi. What's the latest yin, this aw-night soul stuff? Gaun doon tae Bolton Casino n drinkin Cokes!'

'It's _Wigan_ Casino.'

'Same difference. Some night that must be! Cans ay juice!'

Andy n some other boys join in n ah jist take the slaggin cause it's pointless arguing wi dozy auld fuckers aboot sounds. Ah feel like telling thum that Presley and Lennon are wormfood and tae git the fuck ower it, but naw, it's a barry vibe oan the bus, and as ah say, nae point arguing.

Eventually, wi the help ay the polis, we get intae the village n park the bus in the main street, in a line wi aw the others. It's weird, cause it's that early, the

8

sun's still warming up as mair people assemble. The auld man slopes off tae a payphone, n ah kin tell by the expression oan his coupon what the gist ay the conversation is, n that it's no good news.

'Awright?'

'Aye . . .' he says, then shakes his heid. 'Yir mother wis sayin that the wee felly hud a terrible night. They had tae gie him oxygen, the lot.'

'Aw . . . right. Ah'm sure he'll be okay,' ah tell him, 'they ken what they're daein.'

Fuck. Even doon here that little cunt has tae spoil it aw . . .

Dad says something aboot how he shouldnae huv left Wee Davie as my ma doesnae dae the postural drainage right, n he worries that the nurses at the hospital are too busy tae spend enough time oan it. He shakes his heid, pain nippin his pus. 'They cannae afford tae lit that fluid build up in his lungs . . .'

Ah cannae listen tae this same crap again. We're in Yorkshire n the atmosphere's still brilliant but it's like the Cup Final feeling's changed intae a sortay music festival vibe. Everybody's upbeat as we march tae the field where the pickets are massed. My dad even cheers up n gits talking tae this Yorkshire boy, then swaps his AUEW badge for the gadge's NUM one, baith ay them proudly pinnin the other yin's button oantae his chest like it wis a medal.

We can see the coppers assembling ahead ay these barriers they've pit up. Thaire's fuckin loads ay them. Ah eyeball the white-shirted cunts fae the Met; a boy oan the bus said they dinnae want tae use too many Yorkshire polis oan the front line, in case ay any divided loyalties. On oor side there's banners fae every trade union and political group ah've ever heard ay joining the gathering. But ah'm startin tae feel edgy: thaire's still mair polis. For every load ay pickets that swells oor ranks, the polis force seems tae increase tae correspond, and then some mair. Andy gies vent tae the growin sense ay trepidation in the air. 'They've been preparing fir this for years, since the miners done ower Heath.'

Ye cannae miss the plant we intend tae blockade; it's dominated by two huge phallic chimneys, risin out ay a series ay industrial Victorian buildings. It looks ominous, but the polis have goat us aw herded intae this big field on its north side. Then thaire's a sudden stillness in the air as the chants fade away; ah look at the plant and it feels a bit like Auschwitz and for a second ah get the queasy notion that we're gonnae be corralled _intae_ it, like thaire's gas ovens

9

thaire, because no only are the polis outnumberin the pickets, they're now positioned oan three sides ay us, and we're cut off oan the fourth perimeter by this railway line. 'These bastards know what thir daein here,' Andy shakes his heid ruefully. 'They led us right here. Something's gaun oan!'

Ah sense he's no wrong, cause up ahead there's aboot fifty polis oan hoarseback and quite a few mair wi dugs. Ye kin tell they mean business, cause thaire wisnae a WPC in sight. 'You stick close tae us,' ma dad says, suspiciously clockin a group ay thickset boys wi Yorkshire accents, whae seem like they want tae get steamed in.

Suddenly a roar ay applause ripples through the crowd, as Arthur Scargill appears tae a rock star's welcome, and the 'Victory to the Miners' chant starts up. That comb-over hair ay his flaps in the breeze, and he pulls oan this American baseball cap.

'They say that there's been a lot ay MI5 infiltrators doon here,' this gadge called Cammy fae our bus is sayin tae Andy, as we bunch forward tae git a view ay Scargill.

Ah disliked that kind ay talk, cause ah preferred tae think ay British Secret Service cunts as bein like Sean Connery, decked oot in tuxedos in Monte Carlo, no sad fuckers snoopin roond pit villages in Yorkshire, pretendin tae be miners and grassin every cunt up. Scargill's got the megaphone and he launches intae one ay his trademark rousin speeches that tingles the back ay ma neck. He talks aboot the rights ay working people, won through years of struggle, and how if we're denied the right to strike and organise, then we're really nae better than slaves. His words are like a drug, ye feel them coursin through the bodies aroond ye; moistening eyes, stiffening spines and fortifying hearts. As he wraps up, fist punched into the air, the 'Victory to the Miners' chant reaches fever pitch.

The miners' leaders, including Scargill, are up arguing wi the top coppers, telling them that we're no getting tae stand where we fuckin well need tae, in order tae properly picket, n we're penned intae this field which is way too far fae the plant. 'Might as well be in fookin Leeds,' a big gadge in a donkey jaykit shouts at a pork-chop-sideburned copper in full riot gear. 'You're a fookin disgrace!'

The cunt stands impassive, lookin ahead, like he's one ay they guards at Buckingham Palace. But the mood suddenly changes again, the tension seeming tae dissipate as a fitba gets kicked intae the crowd n some ay us get a game started up, using miners' hard hats for goalposts. A surge ay euphoria comes ower me as ah clock that nippy wee cockney cunt, Nicksy; he's on the baw, giein it loads, mouthing off, so ah steam in wi a dirty two-fitted tackle on him. 'Take that, ya English bastard!' ah'm shoutin as he goes doon, then he springs up howlin: 'You farking MI5 or what, you farking Jock cunt?!'

The boys around us stop playin, as if anticipating a showdown, but instead we start laughin.

'How goes it, Mark?' Nicksy asks. He's a wiry, busy-eyed wee gadgie, wi a floppy fringe and hooked nose, whae looks and moves like a lightweight boxer, perpetually shuffling and swaggering. The boy has some fuckin energy.

'Awright, mate,' ah say, lookin ower tae the lines ay polis. 'Heavy stuff here the day but, eh?'

'Too farking right. Came up ta Manchester on the train Friday, got a lift through here this morning. Place was farking crawling with Old Bill.' He nods to the coppers' lines. 'Some of them divs was trained in new riot tactics after Toxteth and Brixton. They farking want it.' His head whips round to me. 'Who ya here with, san?'

'Ma auld boy. Came doon oan the Scottish NUM bus,' ah explain, as the baw flies ower our heids and we make a half-ersed attempt tae get back intae the game. But as mair numbers are assembling oan baith sides, the tension starts tae mount again. People stop chasin the baw as somebody shouts that the scab lorries are due soon, and we're too far away fae the road tae stop them. Some boys mob up and start chuckin stanes at the polis, whae respond by bringin forward a cordon ay long-shielded polis in front ay the ordinary coppers. A cheer goes up as one polisman takes a healthy skelp on the coupon wi a bit ay brick. I feel sickness in the pit ay ma stomach, but there's an electricity in me, overriding it, as a roar goes roond that the scab lorries are here tae pick up the fuckin coke fae the plant!

Every cunt steams forward tae try and get through the polis lines, n ah'm propelled right intae it aw, airms pinned tae ma side for a scary minute, and ah lose Nicksy n ah'm wondering in panic where ma dad is, suddenly rememberin what Granny Renton said. A space opens up and ah move intae it, then the mounted polis charge us and every fucker runs back. It's like a row at the fitba, but it's made room fir the lorries tae pass and we're aw gaun fuckin mental! Ah'm shoutin right in the face ay a young copper, ages wi me, 'WHAT YE FUCKIN DAEIN, YA SCABBY NAZI CUNT?!'

There's another surge forward, but when the horseback polis charge again, the whole polis lines are right behind them. Stanes are hurled through the air at the cunts and a pig oan the tannoy warns that if we dinnae retreat a hundred yards, they're gaunny steam in wi full riot gear. We can see them, gettin ready, wi their helmets, short shields and batons.

'This is outrageous,' one old Yorkshire miner says, eyes seared with rage, 'they ain't used riot squads against pickets in this coontry!'

'Them fookin small shields,' another gadgie shouts, 'they're for aggro, not fookin defendin their sen!'

The boy's called it right, cause as we stand our ground, the bastards charge forward and it's fucking mental. Maist people are wearing ordinary clathes, a few have thick donkey jaykits, but naebody has weapons tae protect themselves and when the polis attack, waving their batons, there's mass panic among the strikers, as it aw goes oaf. Ah git hit oan the back, then the airm, which makes me feel sick, then smacked in the temple. The blows feel different tae bein punched or kicked, ye kin feel them daein damage under the skin, but the adrenalin is the best anaesthetic, and ah lash oot, stickin the boot against a shield . . .

FUCKIN USELESS.

It's fuckin no fair . . . it's no fuckin right . . . whaire's ma shield? . . . whaire's ma fuckin bat, the crappin cunts? . . . it's fuckin no right . . .

Ah'm punchin n kickin against the perspex, tryin tae brek through but it's fuckin useless. Fuck this; ah turn back and run intae space n blooter a copper fae behind, a cunt whae's stooried past us in pursuit ay a striker. He stumbles, lookin like he's gaunny go doon, but keeps his footing and carries on after the gadge, completely ignoring us. Ah see one boy's doon and gettin battered tae fuck by three polis. They're bendin ower him, thrashing at him with their sticks. A lassie, about ages wi me, long, black hair, is screaming at them in appeal: 'What are you doing!'

One of the cops calls her a miner's slag and pushes her. She stumbles and faws oan her back, n gits pilled away by this aulder boy, who takes a stick acraos the shoulder for his trouble. Every cunt's screamin and shoutin n ah'm standin, paralysed between thought and action, just _jammed_, and an aulder copper looks at me, glances at the younger polis, then barks right in ma face, 'GET THE FUCK OUTTA HERE NOW, OR YOU'LL GET FUCKIN KILLED!'

The concern scares us mair than the threat; ah find masel movin away,

forcing through the confused, shrieking crowds, tryin tae find my dad and
Andy, or even Nicksy. It's crazy everywhere ye turn; one huge, brawny gadge
wi long biker's hair n leathers is smashing the fuck oot ay a copper; even
though the pig has a short shield and baton, the big gadge just overpowers
and pummels the stupid cunt wi his huge sledgehammer fists. One gadge's
staggering around wi blood skooshin oot his heid, like he cannae see
anything. Ah feel a sickenin thud acroas ma back n ma guts rising, but ah
fight it and turn and see a panic-faced cop wi a stick n shield move away,
as if ah'm a threat tae _him_. Everything is slo-mo now and ah'm pulsing
wi anxiety aboot the auld boy, but at the same time revelling in the buzz,
pumped up tae fuck. Thankfully the polis draw back, and the battered
pickets reassemble and we move forward, eftir picking up stanes fae the side
ay the field. Ah grabs a rock, reasoning that these radges are taking nae
prisoners n ah fuckin need some sort ay weapon. But what ah really want
right now is tae find ma dad.

  What the fuck . . .

  Suddenly, these searing wails ay rage are rippin through the air, people
sounding so agonised that for a second ah think the polis have sprayed
ammonia or somethin intae our eyes; but it's the scab lorries; they're starting
tae leave the plant, full ay the coke. Another push, but we're repelled by
the polis, and Scargill walks in front ay the polis lines, shoutin through the
megaphone, but ye cannae make it oot, it's like a British Rail customer
announcement. The scab lorries recede tae diminishing jeers and boos as the
fight just drains oot ay everybody. Ah feel something hard and horrible freeze
solid in ma chest, and ah'm thinkin, game over, and ah keep lookin for ma
faither.

  _Please let him be awright proddy god pape god muslim god jew god
buddhist god or any gods please let him be awright . . ._

  Some ay the pickets head oot the field taewards the village wi their
injured comrades, but others just lie oot in the sun, looking that casual, ye
couldnae believe they'd been involved in a mass brawl just minutes ago.
Ah'm no like that; ma teeth hammer thegither n ah'm shakin like ah've
goat a small motor stuck inside us. For the first time, ah can feel where ah've
been hit, wi hard throbs in ma heid, ma back, and ma airm, which hings
limply by ma side.

  FUCKIN . . .

  Ah feel like ma dad looks: a worrier. Like he looks now, no in the younger pictures ay him. Ah once mind ay askin him aboot it, why he eywis seemed that worried these days.

'Children,' he'd replied.

LET HIM BE OKAY!

Ah'm ready tae head back tae the village tae find the bus; ah supposed that the auld man and Andy would've gone there; but the next thing ah ken is that the polis riot squads are advancing taewards us, drumming oan thair short shields wi thair batons. Ah cannae believe it, cause it's game over, the fuckin lorries are away! But they fuckin well charge right at us, we're unarmed and heavily outnumbered, and ah'm thinkin: *these cunts really want us deid*, and the only thing tae dae is nash like fuck n scramble doon the embankment oantae the railway line. Every step jars ma fuckin back. Ah catch ma jaykit oan a fence and hear it tear. Oan the track beside us, thaire's a chunky auld guy wi a rid face, whae's limpin, and he gasps in this north ay England accent: 'That's . . . that's . . . they're tryin ter fookin murder us!'

Whaire's ma fuckin dad?

We cross the line and ah'm helpin the auld gadge climb up the other bank. His leg's fucked, but ma back's giein me gyp, n it's a struggle cause ma airm's totally fucked n aw. The boy's rabbiting in ma ear, in shock. He sounded northern tae me, but tells me his name's Ben n he's actually a striking Notts miner. He took a bad whack oan his kneecap.

My pain has been displaced by a sickness comin fae deep in ma belly. Cause fae the other side ay the track we're witnessing this terrible carnage; the pickets that are left are bein clubbed like seals and lifted by the polis, some are game as fuck and still fightin back in spite ay it aw. A boy in a red lumberjack shirt, oan his knees, tendin tae his decked mate, gets smashed across the skull fae behind by a riot copper and collapses oan top ay his pal. It's like an execution. At the overhead bridge a few pickets have grabbed stuff fae a scrapyard and are flingin it at the polis. Some boys have dragged a car fae the yard, and they pull it across the road and set it alight. This isnae about policing or containment, this is a war against civilians.

War.

Winners. Losers. Casualties.

Ah leaves the Ben gadge n gits back tae the road and ah'm relieved tae see my faither. He's standin wi this boy whae looks weird; it's like he's wearin Batman's cowl. Ah git closer n realise it's aw rid-black blood, completely

14

covering his face tae the extent ah kin only see the whites ay his eyes n teeth. I'm shocked when ah tipple it's Andy; his heid's been stoved in, big time. The polis are still advancin and they half chase, half herd us back intae the village. We get oan the bus, n a lot ay the boys look well fucked. Ma dad has a cut hand. He says it was fae a broken bottle ~~thrown~~ flung by a picket that didnae clear the lines. Andy's in a bad way and needs treatment, but a polis cunt in the escort tells us that anybody stoaping at a hoaspital is liable tae arrest and that we should jist go hame. The arrogant, hate-filled faces: so different tae the beaming coupons that greeted us oan the way in.

The cunts set us up.

We've nae reason tae disbelieve the copper, but ah want tae get oaf n see if Nicksy's awright. 'My mate,' ah tells ma auld man, but he shakes his heid and goes, 'No way. The driver's shut the door n he's no openin it for anything.'

The bus starts movin, n Andy's goat some boy's shirt tied roond his heid tae try and staunch the bleedin. Ma dad's sittin wi an airm roond him, makeshift bandage oan his hand as poor Andy mutters, 'Never seen nowt like it, Davie . . . cannae believe it . . .'

Ah'm sittin thaire, lower back nippin in the seat, wonderin how far up this goes; the Chief Constable, Home Secretary, Thatcher . . . whether they gied the orders or no, they wir complicit. Anti-union laws and big pay rises for the polis when everybody else in the public sector's dosh and conditions are getting cut back . . . the cunts fuckin primed them for this . . .

It's like a morgue oan the bus as it slithers oantae the motorway. Eventually the bevvy being dispensed n consumed wi a vengence starts tae kick in, and the defiant chants ay 'Victory to the Miners' gather force and conviction. But it doesnae feel glorious tae me. It feels like we've been cheated, like coming back fae Hampden and the referee's gied the Old Firm club a nonsense last-minute penalty. It's really hot ootside, but the bus has been blowin cauld air and it's freezing in here. Ah'm sitting wi ma heid burrowed intae the windae, watchin ma breath steam it up. Ah'm feeling really sair now, particularly my airm, n every inhalation is like a punch tae that fuckin spine.

These boys at the back ay the bus start stampin thair feet n singin these Irish Republican ballads of defiance, then a couple of pro-IRA chants come into the mix. Soon they're exclusively belting out Irish Republican ballads.

15

Ma auld man's sprang up oantae his feet, pointin at them in denunciation, his hand bleedin through the rag wrapped roond it. 'STOAP SINGING THAT SHITE, YA DIRTY IRA TERRORIST BASTARDS! THAT'S NO A SOCIALIST SONG, N IT'S NO A TRADE UNIONIST SONG, YA FUCKIN FENIAN SCUMBAGS!'

A skinny wee gadge gets up and starts shoutin back at him, 'FUCK OFF, YA UVF TORY HUN BASTARD!'

'AH'M NO A FUCKIN TORY . . . ya fuckin . . .' Ma auld boy's stormin doon tae the back ay the bus like a bull, n ah'm up in pursuit and grab ah hud ay his airm wi ma good yin. We're the same height, but ah'm much punier and thank fuck Cammy's up and helpin me restrain the auld radge. My faither and the cunts at the back are shoutin at each other, but they're being urged tae calm doon, and me and Cammy are pullin him away, a spasm ay cripplin pain comin fae ma back makin ma eyes water, as the bus wobbles oantae a slip road.

Fuckin Weedgies, they cannae dae nowt without bringin thair fucked-up fitba and Ireland shite intae everything . . .

We get him settled doon, n fair play, one ay the radges immediately comes up and apologises. It's the skinny cunt, he's goat practically nae chin and big, uneven teeth. 'Sorry aboot that, big man, yir right, wrang song, wrang place . . .'

My faither nods in acceptance as the gadge passes him a bottle ay Grouse. The auld boy takes a conciliatory slug fae it, then at Beaver pus's prompting, passes it tae me, but ah wave it away. Fucked if ah'm takin a drink ay anything oafay these cunts, let alaine that shite.

'It's awright, emotions runnin a wee bit high,' ma faither goes, noddin tae Andy, whae looks doolally, like he's in shock.

Then they start talkin aboot the events ay the day, n soon thair airms ur roond each other's shoodirs like they're best mates. Ah'm feelin fuckin nauseated. If there's one thing that's even sicker than those sectarian cunts at each other's throats, it's when they start cosyin up thegither. Ah cannae sit here wi this fuckin back. Ootside ah sketches the road signs for Manchester, n no really kennin what the fuck ah'm daein, ah suppose half thinking aboot Nicksy, ah stand up. 'Ah'm gettin oaf here, Dad.'

Ma auld boy's shocked. 'Whit? You're comin hame wi me . . .'

'Ye dinnae wahnt tae git oaf the bus here, pal,' his new Chipmunk-

choppered best china unhelpfully intervenes, but ah studiously ignore the cunt.

'Naw,' ah goes tae ma Dad, 'but ah said ah'd meet some mates at Wigan Casino,' ah lie. It's a fuckin Monday at noon, and the Wigan Casino shut a few years back, but it's aw ah kin think ay sayin.

'But yir gran's expectin ye back at Cardonald . . . wir gaunny git the train back tae Embra later . . . yir brother's in hoaspital, Mark, yir ma'll be worried sick . . .' ma auld man's pleadin wi us.

'Ah'm oaf,' ah tell um, n ah nip doon tae the front and get the driver tae pull up at the hard shoulder. He looks at us like ah'm a radge, but the airbrakes hiss and ah jump oaf the coach, ma back jarrin in sudden pain. Ah look back tae the hurt, uncomprehendin expression oan ma dad's face as the bus moves away and ebbs intae the traffic. It hits me that ah huvnae goat a fuckin scooby what ah'm daein here, walkin by the side ay this motorway. But the back feels better wi me movin: ah just had tae get the fuck oot ay there.

The sun's pummellin doon and it's still as warm as fuck, a really beautiful summer's day. The cars shoot past us headin north, as ah rip the COAL NOT DOLE sticker fae ma denim jaykit. The tear oan the sleeve isnae too bad; it kin be stitched nae bother. Ah lift ma airm, stretchin it oot through the nagging ache in my shoodir. Ah climb up the bankin oantae this overpass, n look ower the railins doon the motorway at the cars n lorries ripping by underneath me. Ah'm thinkin that we've lost, and there's bleak times ahead, and ah'm wonderin: what the fuck am ah gaunny dae wi the rest ay ma life?

I Did What I Did

Eight birthday cards arrived this morning: all from girly-wirlies, and that ain't counting my mother and sisters. Sweet as you fucking well like. One from Marianne, with a sad 'call me' plea, after the desperate showboating of foxy love notes and kisses. Probably taking stock ay the fact that she's becoming a crushing bore; aw this 'come to my sister's wedding' guff. Dae ah look like Consort-at-a-Schemie-fest material? Still, she's back in the fold, and therefore most serpently getting pumped with prejudice later.

Of course, the upbeat mood is spoiled by a filthy brown envelope fae the dole, inviting me tae a job interview for the plum garage attendant's post at Canonmills. Thrilled to bits they're thinking of Simone, but I must respectfully decline, with a wee word tae my mate Gav Temperley at the dole office about this unwanted intrusion. Working chappies fail to under-stand the minds of men of leisure. I am not employed through *choice*, you fucking cretins; please dinnae mistake *me* for one of those hapless drones who wander around town in a trance, searching for non-existent labour.

Garage attendant. Not in this fuckin life, Milksnatcher and Bike Boy. Get the Billionaire Playboy cairds up in your shitey offices, then I just might be interested!

But the best present comes in the form of a phone call. Happy twenty-second birthday, Simon David Williamson; Cunty Baws has finally left the building! I'm taking the news, conveyed by my sister Louisa, in one breathless, gasping utterance, with a triumphant punch in the air. A quick look at the dictionary, it's an 'M' day today, and I decide my new word is:

MYOPIA, noun, nearsightedness. *lack of imagination, foresight or intellectual insight.

Then ah'm heading right doon tae the Bannanay flats!
Ya fuckin beauty!
As ah hit the foot ay the Walk it starts tae pish doon; cauld, skin-stinging rain, but I crack a smile, stretching my bare, T-shirted arms out,

18

and raising my head to the sky on this beautiful day, letting the bounty of the good Lord cool my skin.

Tae the business at hand; ah get up tae the Williamson rabbit hutch on the second floor of this systems-built warren that dominates the old port proper, not the shite south ay Junction Street and Duke Street, which ah refuse tae acknowledge as *real* Leith. — Simon . . . son . . . my mother pleads, but ignoring her and Louisa and Carlotta, I immediately go tae the parental boudoir, tae check that the vain, posturing prick has emptied the jackets and shirts fae his wardrobe. A sure sign that he's *genuinely* flown the coop rather than this all being a device for future manipulative leverage. My heart races as I pull the creaky door open. Yes! All gone! YA FUCKIN BEAUTY!

God, after all he's put her through, you'd think she'd be delighted, but Mama's sitting on the couch sobbing and cursing the skanker that's stolen his brass heart. — That hoor that'sa brainwashed him!

Non capisco!

She should be thanking the demented muppet for taking that dirty, slimy leech off her hands. But no: Lousia, my older sister, is sobbing with her, and my younger one, Carlotta, sits at her feet like a daft wee lassie. They look like an Amsterdam Jewish family, who've come back tae find the man ay the house carted off tae the camps!

He's only fucking well kipped up wi some minger!

Ah sink doon on my knees beside them, holding my mother's chubby hand, still wi his poxy rings on it, stroking Carlotta's long, dark locks with my other paw. — He cannae mess us aroond any more, Mama. It's the best move for everybody. No sense in being myopic here.

She sobs into a hanky, displaying the grey roots in her inky-dyed and stiffly lacquered hair. — Ah cannae believe it. Ah mean, ah always kenta he was-ah sinner, she says in her halting Scheme-Eyetie accent, — but ah never-ah thoughta he'd dae this . . .

Ah came doon here tae provide support, practical if necessary, fuck, ah wis even ready tae help the prick pack, but he'd blissfully gone. If ah kent it was all gaunny be that smooth ah'd have broken the bank and bought some Moët Chandon! I *ultra* want tae celebrate. Twinty-fuckin-second! All I get here, though, is gloom, despair and greeting puses.

Fuck that. I stand up, and leaving them bubbling away, head ootside onto the landing for a cigarette. Ye almost have tae admire the bastard for the iron hold he has ower them. My father: David Kenneth Williamson. Ah've seen the pictures of the old girl when she was young; a dark, sultry Latin beauty, before the pasta kicked in and she mushroomed to her current HGV proportions. How the fuck did she faw for that shifty-looking spunkbag?

The rain has stopped and the sun's back out strongly, removing any evidence ay the shower's existence save for a few puddles in the uneven paving stones on the concrete of Schemesville below. That's what ah should dae, go through the hoose and remove all lingering traces of that cunt. Instead, ah take a deep, satisfying inhalation on my Marlboro.

Looking down over a sunnier-than-ever Leith, I-spy-with-my-little-eye Coke Anderson and his wife and kids getting oot ay a motor. The missus, Janey, is an old banger for sure, defo a looker in her day, and still worth one at a push. She's arguing wi Coke, who's lurching behind, pished again as usual. The daft cunt hasnae had a sober day since the docks pensioned him off on med retirement, back in the day of Our Lord fuck-knows-when. Ah feel sorry for the young boy, Grant, he's about eight or nine, as I know how mortifying an auld felly who refuses to shape up can be; though with mine it was generally women rather than bevvy that provided the embarrassment. But heh-low . . . *ride alert, ride alert* . . . the daughter has turned oot a right wee fuckin belter! Probably be a baboon-morphed bloated slag by the time she's eighteen, but I *certainly* wouldnae mind getting a wee taste ay that sweet, sweet honey before it goes oaf!

Ah hear their verbal conflict continue as they mount the stairs, Coke's nasal apologetic whine, — But, Ja-ney . . . ah jist met a couple ay the boys, Ja-ney . . . nice tae be nice, but, eh?

What's the daughter's name again . . . come tae Simon . . .

— Change the record, for God sakes, Janey moans, turning the stair bend and looking briefly at me before rubbernecking back tae Coke, — jist stey oot, Colin! Dinnae bother us, eh!

Ah acknowledge the wee Grant felly's beetroot coupon with an empathetic smile. *Feeling your pain, Sonny Jim.* And the daughter is behind him, pouting with sulky teen lips like a model who's just been told there's *one more* outfit change and another catwalk prance before she can indulge in that much needed line ay charlie and a vodka martini.

— Simon, Janey says curtly as she passes me, but the wee honey, Maria, her name is, gies me the snooty treatment. Very blonde and tan, I believe they're no long back fae a family holiday in Majorca (where Coke inevitably disgraced himself), the skin tone brought up by that tight black skirt and light yellow top.

And suddenly that name . . .

That'll be the last ever family holiday that wee yin goes on. It'll be viva Fucksy Central wi a bunch ay mates or some lucky, lusty local lad fae now on in. And Simon David Williamson here might just be putting himself in the frame for *that* particular vacancy. Louisa used tae babysit her, n ah should've taken mair interest, just on the off chance she'd turn oot a stunner. But who could have forecast that plain wee podger would have evolved intae a catwalk creamer in the space ay six months?

Coke is lurching up behind them all, and finally, wheezingly turning onto the balcony, befuddled pus glaring in appeal, palms upturned, — Aw but, Ja-ney . . .

The wife and kids trudge inside their designated council hutch and Coke lurches past me, looking scarecrow-daft in profile as the door slams in his coupon. He stands there for a second or two, before turning back tae me in bemused shock.

— Coke.

— Simon . . .

Ah don't fancy going back inside to hear Mama and *mie sorelle* snivelling mindlessly over the departed bastard, and Coke seems *Scotland Yard* from his place. I've only been away for a year, but the transformation in wee Maria in that time is nothing short ay breathtaking. More info needed for the detailed files. — Fancy a pint? It's ma birthday!

The prospect of mair pish briefly lifts Coke's jakey spirits. — Ah'm a bit short . . .

Ah consider this for a second. What's in it for me? A possible parental intro tae the family estate, and the opportunity tae woo the delightful Maria. It's an investment, and Old Baxter's rent money will just have tae wait a wee bitty. Besides, my gainfully employed ginger-heided buddy is moving in, tired with family strife at Chez Renton. Well, Rents will be rent boy this month. — My shout, buddy. The birthday boy's in the chair!

Blackpool

Saturday Lunchtime

The radio's blaring away as me, Dave Mitch, Les and Young Bobby the YT chant along wi Nik Kershaw at the top ay oor voices: — WOO–DINT IT BE GOOOOD TO BE IN YOUR SHOES, EE-VIN IF IT WAS FOR JUST ONE DAHY . . . as Ralphy Gillsland, drawing the plane along a stretch ay wid, screws his face up.

Ah've been a bit jittery after a few peeves too many in Leith last night and ma posture's that awkward wi this fucked-up back, ah vernear took the top ay ma finger oaf trying tae chisel the lock fitting intae this door. Thought the blood widnae stoap, but ah staunched it wi a bandage ay cotton wool n gauze.

Fuck, ye can *taste* the weekend, cause it's Saturday morning and we're excluded, but no for long! Apart fae this OT, which is good cause we're in the toon, oot ay the workshop, refitting this gutted boozer in Tollcross, it's been a decent enough week. Ah missed the shitein competition on Monday through being at the Yorkshire picket, so Sandy Turner, the driver, has deposed me with a fifteen incher, which Les pointed out tae us twice aleady this week, lying on top ay a soggy *Daily Record*, oan the flat roof ay the garage at the back ay the factory. The minging gulls have drawn some attention though. The van hire boys in the unit ower the road can witness their squawking rooftop feeding frenzy, and in the hot weather the smell rises n wafts back up intae the shithoose. It's jist a matter ay time before the gaffer tipples.

Mind you, Ralphy's far fae chuffed anywey, cause he wants us tae work late oan these bar units. As much as ah'm enjoying daein proper custom joinery again, it's Saturday lunchtime so it isnae gaunny happen.

Ralphy hus mibbe the maist grotesquely unfortunate coupon in the universe. He sports these huge jowls that look like vagina flaps, and this aquiline hooter Les describes as 'an outsized clit'. Tae make things worse his mooth runs north–south instead ay east–west. Les once dubbed him 'that fanny-faced cunt'. It's true; that's how he looks! And he goes rid tae, as if he's just had a fair auld pummelling, the image completed wi his thinnin hair cut badly oan top like it's a Brazilian. He's whingeing like

fuck through that clit neb and aw ah can think aboot is the impending
Northern Soul all-nighter at Blackpool. — Ye have tae finish cutting they
skirtings, Mark, they need tae be done the night soas Terry and Ken can
pit them in the morn's morning. That's a cert.

Aye, right.

Ah'm only a fucking temp here, but Ralphy's pittin everything on me.
As if ah fuckin well care aboot what he deems 'a cert'. The 'cert' is that
he's a moaning-faced straightpeg, the kind ay small businessman Thatcher
loves; a grasping, spiritually dead, scab-minded cunt whae continually
trumpets on aboot 'how hard he works for his family'. The inference is
that we're all meant tae stand aside and be contendedly shat upon for this
greater good. What the cunt forgets is that you've *met* his family: the fat,
money-grubbing, chasm-souled, muck-bucket ay a wife, and their charmless, mutant offspring. So we're thinking: *fuck* your family, ya fud-faced
bag ay Barry White; your family are *fuckin vermin* who should be exter-
minated before they can cairry oan your work n make this world an even
mair intolerably boring n evil place than it already fuckin well is. So git
the fuck oot ay here wi that garbage, ya greedy bastard.

Ah intend tae fully exploit the charmed position ah'm in wi this summer job at my former employer, before swanning back tae academia. —
Ah'm knocking off now, Ralphy.

— Me n aw, Davie Mitchell says, following up. — Goat stuff tae dae,
eh.

Well, that sets oaf a fair auld wobble in these facial folds. Ralphy's eyes
light up in pain. It's like he's just seen us swipe the McCain's oven chips
offay the plate ay his sausage-fingered *kinder*.

— Entitled tae a peeve on a Saturday, says Les helpfully. Les is a fat
cunt ay aroond ma faither's age, wi thinnin fair hair n a ruddy, boozy
complexion. He's constantly ripping the pish oot ay everything. — Even
young Boab here's goat a date movie lined up, eh, Boab?

Bobby has a smile on his custard-spotted coupon, and his dark, girlish
eyes burn wi mischief, when ye can see them under that big fringe.
— Too right. Ah'm giein this burd the stinky pinky, he laughs, a powerful, shoodir-shakin, hee-haw, which never fails tae get the rest ay us going
and leave Ralphy utterly dismayed. Ye can see him checkin oot Bobby's
filthy nails, imaginin them rippin through his teenage daughter's hymen
in the back row ay some fleapit.

— Aw, c'mon, lads, he wails, aw high and conciliatory over that taut,
beautifully *final* sound ay tools being downed. — Youse can at least stey
another hour!

23

We're aw lookin at the flair as we pack away oor gear. Les is singing, Sinatra-style, — . . . *to walk away from some-one who, means ev-ray-thing in life to you* . . .

Ralphy stands wi his hands oan his hips. — Mark, he appeals, — you usually never lit me doon, pal . . .

Ah *always* let the cunt doon, though my absence at Aberdeen for a year has made the hert grow fonder. But his pathetic, transparently manipulative appeal fails miserably. He forgets thit when ah telt him ah wis taking Monday off tae join the picket, he said: 'That's typical ay you. Go away tae support layabouts whae dinnae want tae work when there's plenty work here needin done.'

Well, fuck you, fanny-flaps, ah've made up ma ooirs n ah'm off. — No go, ah tell him sadly, then protrude my choppers, go bug-eyed and pit oan a George Formby singing voice, — Ah ave ter be in luv-er-lee lit-tle Lan-ca-sheeeerrrr . . .

Les n Bobby join in oan the air ukuleles, and we enjoy a brief jam, but *dae we fuck* stay another hour. Gleefuly abandoning the whingeing cunt, we hit the boozer at Port Hamilton. Just a quick couple for me then it was hame tae git changed n meet the boys.

So Tommy, Keezbo, Second Prize and me are heading doon tae the all-nighter at Blackpool in Tam's motor. Ah've made up a tape, n Otis Blackwell is giein it loads wi 'It's All Over Me'. Ye cannae beat a bit ay Northern, and the Wigan Casino ay our teen years is sorely missed. This should be a good night though, it's being pit oan by some ay the original Blackpool Mecca boys. Tam's at the wheel aw the wey, wi that outrageous seventies fitba guy's haircut; ah'm at the back wi Keezbo, sittin funny, cause ay this fuckin back, tryin tae keep the weight oan ma left erse-cheek. It's no exactly the maist sought-eftir locale as that fat cunt takes up aw the room, his hands spread across his gut, like a ginger-heided Buddha. Second Prize, heid shorn in a number-one cut which makes him look harder than he is, by bringing oot his tight features and the sharp angles ay his skull, is riding shotgun. Him n Keezbo ur drinking, him heavily, n ah'm pretending tae but keeping my tongue in the bottle ay voddy as it comes roond. Ah umnae mad keen oan voddy neat, n ah want tae stay straight tae enjoy the dancing n the buzz ay the Lou Reed.

Keezbo's fat, doughy neck, spotted wi freckles, seems tae swell oot ower his shoodirs like Darth Vader's helmet. He's goat barry ginger hair but, the bathbrush-thick variety, that'll never thin or recede, no wispy like mine. He's wearing those chinos wi the big high waistband, no a great idea for anybody, but disastrous on a fat cunt. Tommy's already made a wee comment aboot 'Gorgie fashion'. Predictably Keezbo wants tae stop fir chips, when we're barely ootside Edinburgh. — Ah'm starvin, Mr Tommy . . .

— No way, no till Blackpool. Want tae catch the fitba oan telly.

Keezbo grabs two folds ay fat in his hands. — Ah'm wastin away tae nothing here. Tell them, Mr Mark, he pleads, ginger brows rising ower the top ay the thick, black frames ay his specs.

— Keezbo's lookin seriously malnourished, Tam. You contributed tae the Biafra appeal, ah say, then pit oan the voice ay ma auld racist neighbour fae the Fort, Mrs Curran, — Let's look eftir our ain people first!

— Awright, but Kendal services just, says Tommy, sweeping his hand through that Rod Stewart mess on his heid. — What happened tae your finger? he asks.

— Chisel. Cunt's got us that de-skilled wi jist knockin panels thegither, ah've loast the touch when ah go back tae real work, ah say as Keezbo mumbles something in complaint. — Think you can hold on, buddy? ah ask him.

— Ah'm burnin fat big time, Mr Mark. It'll be touch n go. If Mr Rab wid pass the voddy back, it might help tae take ma mind oaffay it . . .

— Mmmgh . . . Second Prize reluctantly growls, and Keezbo's pudgy paw goes up tae collect the Smirnoff.

Despite lookin like a coconut pit oan its side and turned inside oot, Keezbo rivals Tommy as our best dancer. Ah tend tae stand there like a twat oan the sidelines, wishing ah kent how tae dance, till the speed kicks in. Then ah wished ah kent how tae stop. Once ah got too carried away at the Casino n fucked ma back tryin tae dae a flip. Trust that copper tae find that exact fuckin spot wi his stick! Cunt'll be sittin at hame in some Barratt box, watchin telly, frigid wife, ingrate kids, oblivious tae the fact that he's destroyed the dance for the boy Renton. Thank fuck fir par-acetamol. But Keezbo though, for such a bloated cunt he's something else. Must be the drummer's rhythm. Too podgy for the flips, aye, but he can hit that deck like a fat, ginger sex machine.

We get tae Blackpool and dump the car. The smell ay fried food, diesel and the sea air pits us in mind ay September weekends long gone. Ah mind ay comin here wi Ma, Dad, Billy, Wee Davie, Granny and Granda Renton. Me, aw self-conscious and gangly oan a scabby donkey, Davie being raced up alongside us in his wheelchair by Granda Renton, them aw shoutin, 'HE'S BEATIN YE, MARK!'

Me wantin tae heel the stoical beast in its ribcage; tae ride the fucker galloping intae the Irish Sea, just tae be free ay the embarrassment. Ah

mind being that mortified, ah sloped oaf tae see *Oliver!* six times oan ma
tod at a local cinema. 'Ye cannae want tae see that again, son. We were
gaunny go tae the Pleasure Beach,' muh ma would moan. 'Aw, gie him
the money and let him go, he'll only huv that face oan aw day,' Dad's
heid wid shake. And ah'd greedily take the cash, craving the beautiful
solitude ay the cinema in the dark, and the taste ay ice cream taken at
leisure, away fae Billy's pigeon-hawk eyes, wi the phrase *so long, suckers*
deliciously reverberating in ma heid.

. . . *never before has a boy wanted more . . .*

We hit the Golden Mile and get tae that big, mad boozer under the
Tower. It's rammed, but we get some drinks in, just in time tae see
Platini score the winner against Portugal.

— That cunt's decent, eh, Rab, ah say tae Second Prize, whae has a
pint and double voddy and is startin tae enjoy himself, but he doesnae
want tae talk fitba. — Northern Soul? he asks, soundin like ma faither.
— What is it but, Mark? What the fuck's it aw aboot?

— You'll see, mate, Tommy laughs, as a fat boy next tae us opens a
bottle ay Beck's, which shoots ower him as his mates chortle. Ah'd clocked
them giein it a shake when he wisnae lookin. — Yawl fooking coonts,
he says, in a West Midlands accent.

— Nae luck, buddy, Tommy smiles, patting the boy's back.

— Look don't coom into it with these coonts, he moans. Every group
has a fat mate; some have several. It's the Tower Bar in Blackpool, and if
you're in the right frame ay mind and in the right company, it's one ay
the greatest places oan Planet Earth.

Ma best mate is possibly Tommy. Cares aboot things, aboot people;
maybe just a wee bit too much for the kind ay world we're compelled
tae live in. Despite being one ay the hardest and best-looking cunts ah
ken, wi his solid light-heavyweight boxer's build, Tommy's basically a very
humble sort ay gadge.

We start talkin aboot what we like in lassies, and ah mention that ah
prefer smaller-breasted girls, which is a sacrilegious comment tae these
cunts. Eftir bein called everything fae a poof tae a paedophile, Keezbo
shakes his heid n goes, — Naw, Mr Mark, ah like a good pair ay knock-
ers oan a bird.

— Liked them that much ye grew yir ain, ah goes, grabbin his beer
tits.

But this wee exchange tells us that as perfect as the Tower is for the
moment, the moment tends tae go pretty quickly. Fitba n lads has tae
surrender tae dancing n lassies, so we drink up n make oor wey tae the

club. Headin doon the prom, ma memory suddenly rushed like warm water ower frozen moments ay the past. Ah could hear Ma reading tae us fae the chair between our beds, Billy's n mine, her furry tobacco voice rising and falling as her heid turned fae one tae the other. Books aboot dugs and bears and hoarses. Aw ay us enjoying the story but tensely waiting fir Wee Davie's next bark tae pull the curtain doon oan our precious, borrowed time.

The club's in the function lounge ay a big hotel, further up the prom. We get in, n it's buzzin. There's a record oan ah dinnae recognise but ah'm no wantin tae gie Keezbo the satisfaction ay askin him, so ah sing along, lip-syncin the lyrics as we shuffle through the busy crowd. Second Prize looks tae us, then the bar, then the Pepsis, in raw panic. He realises that the gaff isnae licensed. — Thaire's . . . thaire's nae fuckin peeve . . .

— Aye . . . Tam grins.

Second Prize fuckin explodes, his coupon bursts florid like he's havin a fit. — Whit's aw this aboot? YE TAKE US AW THE WEY DOON HERE N THAIRE'S NAE FUCKIN PEEVE, YA CUNTS!

Ah thoat he wis gaunny lash oot at one ay us, cause he's hyperventilatin, but he just turns n storms oot ay the nightclub.

— Fuck sake . . . what a state . . . ah'll go eftir him, Tommy says.

— Leave um, ah goes. — How fuckin ridic is that?

— He likes a drink but, Mr Mark, Keezbo says.

— We aw do, but imagine no bein able tae go fir a few fuckin hours withoot Christopher Reeve, ah laugh, — that's worse than a fuckin junky! He could've hud some Berwick wi us!

So we have a look around, pleasantly surprised by the amount ay decent fanny in the house. Ah love ma Northern, but some club nights could be bit laddie-orientated. Suddenly ah hears that pianny tinkle introducing the Volcanoes classic '(It's Against) The Laws of Love' n ah'm right oan that flair, back or nae back. Ah shout tae Tommy, — C'mon, Tam, 'Laws ay Love', but then ah'm distracted, as ah catch sight ay a wee gadgie wi a bandaged heid oan the dance flair. It's Nicksy.

I am reviewink, the sit-u-ay-shun . . .

Ah'm watchin the cunt strut his stuff for a bit, his patter is abysmal, n ah'm finding a wee groove masel as ah close in on him. Tommy n Keezbo are still lurkin oan the sidelines. Ah'm aboot tae get up thaire n say hiya tae Nicksy, but 'Skiing in the Snow' comes oan, and ah'm straight oaf the dance flair cause it's the Wigan's Ovation's version rather than the Invitations' original. Fat cunt that he is, that tasteless Jambo wanker Keezbo gets right up thaire, n starts giein it big licks.

27

Fae the bar, as we eye up the girls, aw lookin the part, whether it's sleeveless dresses (magic!), vesty tops n short skirts (ya cunt ye!), or tight troosers n blouses (barry!), Tommy's asking us aboot this trip tae Europe oan the InterRail. — You're gaun wi a mate n two birds, right? Tidy.

— Aye.

— Ye ridin one ay thum?

— Naw, ah tell him, suddenly thinking ay Fiona Conyers, one ay the girls, how barry she is, just a totally brilliant lassie. Comes fae Whitley Bay. Committed socialist. Long, straight, inky-black hair, a big toothy smile, and a chest that demands your attention. An odd wee cluster of tiny spots on her foreheid, a greasy patch the Clearasil cannae contain. Ah'm suddenly gripped by an urge tae gie her a wee tinkle. It's probably jist the speed diggin in, but.

Keezbo's no fuckin aboot, he's groovin oan that flair tae big cheers. Everybody likes tae see a fat extrovert gaun fir it, shakin that flabby erse. They reason that if he can pull they can, and he must piss so many cunts off when he walks away wi a dolly at the end ay the night and they go hame tae bed wi a gutful ay peeve and a fistful ay that best friend whom they've let doon yet again. N ah ken cause ah've been one ay them often enough. But ah cannae knock a fellow ginger, especially as me and Keezbo play thegither, me bass and him drums. Can never keep up wi the fucker, but.

Tommy's in his yellay Fred Perry, trying tae look smooth, biding his time till mair lassies hit the space. We're aw pretty desperate for a ride, eftir aw it's the fuckin weekend, but ah think Tam mair than maist; dinnae think he's hud a sniff since he split up wi Ailise at Christmas.

Ah close up behind Nicksy, whae's loosely dancing away wi some Manc lassies but generally sniffin aroond the dance flair like a polis dug in an Amsterdam warehoose. Grabbing his shoodir heavily, ah go, — I'm arresting you, Brian Nixon, for assaulting the truncheon of an officer of the law . . .

— MARK RENTON! He plants a kiss on my foreheid. He's well gone, but the lassies and some other cunts look at me like ah'm some kind ay superstar, cause Nicksy's a bit ay a face on the Northern scene.

— How's the noggin?

— Some filth cunt walloped me. Couldn't go to the hozzie, they was just lifting every fucker. It was farking crazy, eh?

— Aye, no half. Cunts smashed up the Fleetwood Mac. Strugglin oan the dance flair.

— Any excuse, he laughs, then points tae his nut. — Yeah, six stiches, but your farking Graeme Souness tackle hurt me loads more, you cahnt, he smiles, bending to rub his ankle, then looks to the exit. — Who you dahn with, sahn?

— Three mates. Well, two now. One cunt left a bit sharpish when he saw thaire wis nae peeve. Believe it or no, it's Rab, the boy ah wis telling ye aboot that was once on Man United's books. Now he cannae go ten minutes withoot a swallay.

— Is Matty here? he excitedly enquires.

Ah want tae tell Nicksy that Matty's no quite the same boy that he kent back in that Shepherd's Bush doss in '79, but ye dinnae want tae slag off one mate tae another. — Naw, failed a late fitness test. Shirley, the bairn n that.

— Shame, I ain't seen that cunt in years.

— Some other chaps for ye tae meet, but. And here's a wee felly . . . Ah pull a couple ay blue pills fae ma jeans watch poakit and slip yin tae Nicksy. We down them, and cheerfully rant at each other. Brian Nixon, ma first buddy in that squat that Matty n me pertied oor wey intae. Monday, Tuesday, happy days. Ah mind ay Nicksy sayin he hated his real name cause ay the association wi Richard Nixon. Ah like ma real name: wish cunts would use it mair, instead ay that Rent Boy shite. So we rap oot some stuff at each other, gaun ower auld times, aboot the strike and the class war. *Good fuckin speed . . .*

Wir tanning the Orbit sugar-free as ah introduce Nicksy tae Tommy and Keezbo. They're right ower when they see that he's in largely female company, two Manc lassies called Angie and Bobbi. Nicksy's known here cause it's rare tae find somebody comin up fae London tae the provinces and, fair play, the fucker has some moves on that flair. He tells me that he's no interested in any ay the lassies though. — Loved up, n I?

— Nice one. She here?

— Nah, she won't leave London. Tell ya wot, ain't half missing her. She don't mind me taking off though, cause it ain't like we never see each other, she lives in the same flats, just up the stairs.

— Never shit where ye eat, gadge.

— Cheeky cunt, he says. — Nah, mate, this one's special. The muver of my kids.

— They aw are wi you but, geezer, ah retort, getting intae an auld game. — Mind that lassie in the squat at Shepherd's Bush? Lorraine. Fae Leicester. She broke your hert. You faw too hard, buddy, that's your problem.

— Entirely different scenario, he grins, — and a bird in the flat is worth two in the bush, didn't they teach ya that at school, sahn?

It's great tae see the cunt again, and properly catch up aboot auld times. He tells me that Chris Armitage fae Salford, another ex-London punk buddy, will probably be along here at some point. It's shaping up tae be a good yin. So as Nicksy blethers tae Tommy, ah start chatting tae Bobbi girl.

Can a fellow be a villain all his life?

She's a serene wee dark-broon-heided honey, her name short for Roberta, but Tommy's being a pest, n asking loudly, — Does Hazel ken that yir gaun tae Europe wi two birds?

— Hazel and me are auld news, Tommy.

— Aye, for ten minutes, then it's business as per usual.

— No this time, ah say, hoping that Roberta gets the point. Ah decide ah prefer Roberta tae Bobbi, cause ah didnae want tae think aboot a bird huvin the same name as Young Bobby fae the work.

Ah get oan the flair wi her for a bit as Frankie and the Classicals' 'What Shall I Do' starts up. Roberta's chunkier than ah thought or that ah normally go for, well, no exactly chunky, but has a bit mair meat roond the thighs and erse than her face, shoodirs and smallish breasts pushing against that tight rid-and-white squiggled top wid lead ye tae think. Her longish brunette hair's barry, and she has a pretty face. So basically, ah've opted for a policy ay steyin tight oan her, rather than zonal marking. Ah'm serenading her by reciting the refrain, — Huh, baby, what's happening wit choo? Nothin? Ah, that's too bad. Hey, jist came around to see what was happenin wi choo, to see if there was any new party. Ah, c'mon, you can do bettah than that now, uh . . .

— You're mad, you are, she goes, aw encouraging girly-giggles, the sort that fizz n bubble in yir guts like champagne. Then she clocks ma hand and asks, — What happened t' yer finger?

— Industrial accident. Ah gie her a wink.

The gig ends in total euphoria as the DJ lays doon that old Wigan Casino signature climax track, Dean Parrish's 'I'm On My Way'. Then, sadly, we are. We stand ootside the club and it's nippy, as we're faffin aboot for too long as Tommy's still worried about Second Prize, n tae be honest, ah kind ay am n aw. Nicksy and Roberta suggest a party back in Manchester, at somewhere called Eccles, and ah'm as keen as Colman's finest, though trying tae play it cool. — What aboot Rab?

— He'll have headed back tae the motor, Mr Mark, Keezbo says, — he'll no get a drink at this time.

Ah realise it's actually a still, mild summer night and it's the Lou Reed that's spreadin the chills. Ah catch Roberta's teeth chattering n she gies me a cheeky smile, pushing her hair back. There's nae sign ay Second Prize at the car. — He'll have gone tae Manchester, ah say unconvincingly, — he's still goat mates thaire fae the fitba.

— Too right, Mr Mark, says Keezbo, who's been firing intae Angie, this big tall bird wi long, dark hair, and he doesnae want the night cut short. Aye, for a Fat Ginger Specky Cunt, Keezbo's pretty outstanding at getting his hole. He makes lassies laugh, comin ower as a cheerful, cuddly teddy bear, whae's nae real sexual threat. There's probably been a few who've asked, durin a moment ay clarity, 'What am I daein wi an obese sweaty cunt oan top ay us, his fat ginger knob pistoning away intae ma fanny?'

So we pile intae the motors; ah'm in Nicksy's car, a messy rust-bucket full ay auld newspapers, takeaway cartons and empty beer cans, in the back wi Roberta and this other lassie, no Angie, n ah'm in nae big hurry tae get tae our destination as Nicksy's goat a good Northern tape oan and the Tomangoes are giein it loads wi 'I Really Love You' and me n Roberta and this other lassie, whae ah think's called Hannah, are singing along and gently shoodir-chargin each other in the back. A lassie wi collar-length, straight blonde hair sits in front wi Nicksy. When we get tae the Eccles gaff it's stowed wi people fae the Blackpool gig. Ah'm suddenly overwhelmed by the realisation that it feels great tae be me; a young, smart, working-class boy fae these beautiful islands. How blessed could a human being possibly be?

Roberta and me sit oan this battered couch, and talk aboot travelling. Ah reckon that eftir Europe ah'm gaunny dae the States next summer, get on that BUNAC thing fir the visa, teach fitba tae American bairns, then just fuck off and tour aroond till the poppy runs oot. The others are in this kitchen and spillin oot intae the wee backgreen, dancin tae they Northern Soul records, aw proper waxins like the International GTO's 'I Love My Baby', and we've sat doon, sharing this room wi these dirty-looking cunts, who're smokin smack offay some tinfoil. Ah'm watchin them and one gadge, he's goat lank hair n big dark circles under his eyes, looks at us wi a grim smile n cauld eyes. — Wawn summer dis? he slurs in a Scouse accent.

Mingin cunts daein that fuckin crap at a Northern perty . . .

— Naw . . . yir awright, ah say, waving the pipe and foil away. Roberta looks a bit cross and does the same. The minging gadge shrugs and giggles n passes it tae his mate who burns the underside ay the foil wi a lighter and sucks up a load ay smoke through the pipe intae his lungs, gaun aw stunned and heavy-eyed as it hits him.

Stupid cunt, turning intae a fuckin zombie oan that shite when thaire's aw this fun tae be hud . . .

— I wanna get out of here, Roberta says. — Let's go and find t'others.

Ah gets up wi her, and we head taewards the kitchen, tae see if Salford

Chris has showed up. Ah'm making for the back gairden when Roberta intercepts us n says, — Ah were kinda thinking that we maht go back t'mine.

— Sound, ah go, in cool delight, tippin Keezbo the nod as the do-do-do-do-do-dos announce the start ay that Invitations classic 'What's Wrong With Me Baby?'. And ah'm thinkin, this Roberta better be some ride, pullin us away fae this, as ah shout ma buddy the rendezvous instructions, — The Swinging Sporran in toon, Sackville Street at the Arndale, the morn at twelve bells.

Keezbo's wi this Angie bird, n he nods ower tae Tommy, whae's talkin fitba battles wi some Man City lads. — Two—nil tae the Fort Ginger Rhythm Section, Mr Mark, and he smiles a grin as long and oily as the River Forth.

— Go on, the Section, ah gies him the thumbs up back, — toughest skiers aroond!

As we depart, the sun's comin up ower west Manchester's red-brick buildings, but we're still speed-chilly as Roberta takes my airm. Ah decide tae stick it roond her shoodirs and she curls satisfyingly intae ma side. — It ruins yer lahf, she says, talkin about they heroin junky cunts, as we head back tae hers, — ya get addicted after joost woon go, lahk. Glad ya got more sense.

— Too right, ah tell her, all sniffy and virtuous, but now ah'm thinking, ah really have tae try that shit. In fact ah'm cursin ma cowardice n the shabby pretence it was some sort ay coolness or intelligence or experience.

Ah fuckin bottled it like a pansy, pot-smoking student wanker, and those boys saw that and fuckin well knew it. Is that what ah'm becoming? A smug, fucking insipid student cunt?

But ah can never huv a bad thought too long oan speed, n ah'm ootay my box ranting about the brilliance ay the Minds' *Sons and Fascination* album, how it's much better than *New Gold Dream* (no tae say *NGD* is a bad album) and aw ah can think aboot is removing Roberta's clathes, and ma ain of course, n the world is a pretty fuckin okay place.

Monday Morning

My heid's nippin eftir that weekend, n see this fuckin Fleetwood . . . At least yon Roberta lassie was a dark horse; ah've never been gammed like that before, n she didnae seem tae bother aboot the ginger pubes. We had a good laugh n aw. She goes: 'I don't normally sleep with somebody I've only just met, you know.' 'Neither do I,' ah said, 'naebody usually lets us.' She looked angry for a second, then laughed and hit us with a pillay. Ah fucking love Manchester! We spent maist ay Sunday eftirnoon in the pub; first the Sporran, then oantae the Cyprus Tavern wi Roberta n her mate Celia, and Keezbo, Angie, Nicksy – Chris Armitage (whae finally showed), till Tommy swung by wi some Man City Kool Kats, and issued the Fort Ginger Rhythm Section an ultimatum: lift hame now or make yir ain wey back. So ah reluctantly left ma new and auld pals, lookin forward tae hooking up wi them again. As we'd staggered oot the boozer, pished n stoned, n went tae find the motor, we saw some sacked miners handin oot leaflets in Piccadilly. Ah couldnae look at them; ah steered every cunt ower the road oan some crap pretext.

Roberta and me exchanged numbers. Whether we never see each other again or end up star-crossed lovers is totally irrelevant. The key was that we had a barry time n neither ay us regretted a single minute.

But regrets are for Monday mornings and now ah'm back under the harsh strip lights ay the workshop, sweatin like a blind dyke in a fishmonger's. Our insubordination oan Saturday, up at the cushy number in the pub, has been punished and we've been taken oaf that job n pit back tae the two-slice: the monotony ay factory work. So it's knocking house panels thegither then nailing ties onto them, so they can throw up mair cheapo Barratt slums-tae-be oan the last toxic fields in between Edinburgh n Glesgay.

POOKOW go the nail guns, attached tae long tubes oan a circuit that blows continuous compressed air, smashing the six-inch nails intae the wid like bullets.

POOKOW.

POOKOW.

Monday morning; cunting, evil, degrading, spunk-guzzling Monday morning. Aroond thirty staff oan duty and ah cannae talk tae one single fucker. Not one. Gillsland is the one cunt tae dae well oot ay the recession, moving oot ay high-end shopfitting wi six men, tae low-end house-panel construction and thirty employees. The labour costs are aboot the same, mind you, the tight cunt.

Bank accounts don't grow on trees, you gotta picka pocket or two . . .

POOKOW.

POOKOW.

But ah didnae care how monotonous n de-skilled the job wis, ah just wanted tae keep my heid doon, hide in some solid graft, build a few panels, sweat oaf the toxins fae the weekend's drink and speed, and work through this mashed vertebrae and mean depression till brek time.

Then at the silent brek, three cups ay black coffee go doon. Ah see Les looking at us. Ye ken what's coming next. — Right, lads . . .

Ah could've done withoot performing in the bogs and ah hudnae really expected victory. It was Les's ritual though, n tae be fair tae the cunt, it certainly kick-started the week.

The six ay us assemble: Me, Davie Mitch, Sean Harrigan, Barry McKechnie, Russ Wood and Seb (that's Johnny Jackson's nickname — he once went oot wi this ride called Sonia, so we call him *Sonia's Ex Boyfriend*, that being the cunt's only claim tae fame). We go tae the lavvy, hittin an aluminium cubicle each. Les issues each ay us the last week's *Daily Records*, Monday tae Friday, and one *Sunday Mail* fae yesterday, which he eywis brings in tae make up the numbers. This is where Les is in his element. A frustrated comedian, he compères at the Tartan Club and the Dockers' Club. It's an obvious tears-ay-a-clown job; his wife left him years ago n his daughter, whae he nivir sees, lives in England. Life has its disappointments, but Les grabs his crapulent fun where he can. He's also a man tortured by piles tae the extent that he creams his erse *before* he goes oot drinking.

We each spread oor papers oantay the flair in front ay the toilet pans; ye can hear the rustling fae the other traps. Then ah lower ma keks n boxers, squattin ower the papers.

Stey relaxed . . .

The key is tae make sure that the shite comes out in a oner, wi nae breaks. That means you have tae get close tae the flair and be deft enough tae move forward so that it disnae coil in a pile but straightens oot in a line oan the newspaper.

Smooth action . . .

Ah'm daein nicely here, ye can feel it comin oot at an even pace, in a solid flow, and ah feel it touch the flair so ah start tae slide forward in a slow, steady movement while maintaining the excretion . . . the fuckin back . . . giein us gyp . . . keep gaun . . .

Ya beauty . . .

Splat . . . ah hears it fawin oantae the paper like a darted ape oot ay a tree. Then ah arch myself back oantae the pan, grateful tae take the pressure off the lower back, and shite oot the dregs before wiping ma erse. This is the trickiest part ay the shitein operation, disposin ay the afterbirth, as Les calls it. As ye generally eat before ye peeve, the afterbirth is usually mair sloppy and drink n drugs toxic n burny than the broon bairn, but it's mission accomplished, n ah clean masel off, n admire ma work. The log sits steamin oan the flair in front ay us, a thing ay beauty; solid, broon, unbroken, wi that lovely smooth coat where it slid oot wi nae cling-on at aw. This baby hus tae be a contender. Real Scots shite ower the *Record*.

Ah exit and wash my hands, swallayin another two paracetamol. Sean Harrigan, a Weedgie exile dumped in Livvy, is already oot, a sure sign that he's done the business. Barry McKechnie is next, followed by Mitch. Then Seb; ah cannae see his yin being unbroken. Finally Russ Wood shows, with an unhappy shake ay the heid.

So we slide the fruits ay oor labour out oantae the flair in a neat row while Les goes tae work wi his measuring tape. He commentates as he judges aw the shites: — Barry McKechnie: a poor effort, son. What sort ay a weekend did you huv? At hame in front ay the telly?

— Win some, lose some, Barry says wi a shrug. He's a new boy, didnae work here back when ah wis full-time, but he seems sound enough.

— Seb: no bad, mate. That's coiled a bit but, Les observes. Poor Seb's destined tae be perennial bridesmaid; a bit too fat tae balance right n git the proper technique gaun. It requires a certain athleticism. — Davie Mitchell: excellent.

— Aye, ah hud a curry oan Saturday and an all-day session eftir the Hibs game at Falkirk.

Livvy Sean slides his paper out. There's a big, ugly, steaming, black-and-tan tortoise on that *Record*. — Sean Harrigan: a beauty! Les declares, — as tar-brushed as the Princess Royal's first bastard. The yin ye never hear aboot.

— Ah wis oan the Guinness at Baird's in the Gallowgate.

— Be mastered by nae Orange bastard, ma soapy chum, Les smiles. — Worked a treat for ye, Sean. Russ Wood . . . He looks at Russ's skittery wee effort.

— . . . C'mon, Russ . . . that's a poor show.

— It's the wife wi this diet and veggie nonsense. Shite like a trooper. Ah hud tae go earlier, it was a cracker n aw.

— Aye, right, Sean says.

— Honest, Sean, Russ protests, — it's this high-fibre diet. First thing every morning a drop a log the size ay big Morag in the canteen's thighs.

— Ye need tae change the diet if you're serious about playing wi the big boys, Russ, Les dismisses. — Right, Marky. He looks at me, then at ma offering which lies steamin oan top ay Aberdeen's Gordon Strachan. — Excellent result, coming in at fourteen and a quarter inches n the undisputed winner. No a weak link in it, nice and compacted but sliding oot intae a nice straight line.

— That boyfriend ay yours packin the fudge nice n tight again, Rents? Sean laughs, jealousy in his mean, tight eyes.

Ah wink at him. — Ah'm ewyis the postman rather than the letter box, Sean, you should ken that mair than maist.

Sean's aboot tae say something back, but Les beats him tae the punch. — Ye'd want a condom before ye'd go near a mingin Weedgie's hole!

— Ya cunt, ah'd want a fuckin diver's suit!

— Shoatie, Young Bobby hisses, his gangly frame bent roond the door, — Gillsland n Bannerman!

We pick up the papers, open the windaes and fling oor bombs oot oantae the flat roof as Barry heads back oot wi Bobby tae stall the gaffer. They didnae hud them back for too long, cause we're just shuttin the windaes n makin fir the wash handbasins, when ye hear that nasal mewl. — What's aw this then? Gillsland moans. — Thaire's a joab needs daein! What yis hingin roond here like a bunch ay queers fir?

— We wir waitin oan you comin in n showin us how tae gie a proper gam, Ralphy. Les pushes out his cheek with his tongue, making a cock-sucking motion. — Blew the whole Jubilee Gang ootside the Granton chippy one night, eh, Ralph? Swallayed ivray time, they tell us. Went hame n licked the missus oot tae prove thit eh swung baith weys, then retched up aw ower her muff. Nine months later she hud a bairn that looked like every cunt in Granton, eh, Ralphy?

— What are ye talking aboot? Gillsland says indignantly, then retorts, — Takes yin tae ken yin!

— Ah, those summer nights ay love doon old Granton toon, ah well-a, well-a, well-a, well, tell me more . . . Les muses, sliding into song, as we ignore Ralphy and Bannerman, who, registering the creeping stench, waves his hand in front ay his face, and we head back oot oantae the tedious job.

POOKOW.

POOKOW.

POOKOW.

Sean and Mitch are asking us aboot ma weekend. — Blackpool. Northern night. No bad, but it'll never be another Wigan.

POOKOW.

WHEEEESSSSSHHH . . .

THOK.

Never saw it coming, but it whistled past Sean's heid at bullet velocity, embedding a good two inches intae a plank in the woodpile behind him. Ma blood ran cauld for a church-length second, presumably Sean's did tae, before he dived behind a pile ay frames stacked up oan pallets. Ah wasnae far behind, and a good thing n aw; another whistle and a THOK and another six-inch nail wedged into the wood in front ay us.

— YA FUCKIN WEE BAM! NEARLY FUCKIN WELL KILT US! Sean roars, ower at Bobby, who's blasting off aw ower the place with the high-powered compressed airgun.

— Gonna blow your brains out, muthafuckah, Bobby grimaces, sending another couple ay bullet nails ower into the widden pallets in front ay us.

— FUCKIN COOL IT, YA DAFT WEE CUNT! Les shouts at him. This wee fucker is oaf his fuckin heid and he's gaunny kill somebody. He loves that gun, standin thaire wi the idiot grin across his coupon. But he's stalled now cause Les never usually halts a prank.

— Hi, Bobby, ah goes, standin up, — c'mon, buddy, git that fuckin safety catch back oan! If Gillsland comes in wir aw fucked. C'mon, mate, screw the fuckin nut, eh?

Bobby looks ower at us n ah *think* ah see him discreetly click the catch oan, but fear gobbles up ma spinal column as he turns the compressed airgun at us and fires . . .

Fuck sakes . . .

Of course, nowt happens, except ah almost defecate again, in spite ay the empty bowels. — You're fuckin nuts, Bobby. C'mon, pal, lit's git they ties sorted.

So Bobby starts firing into the ties, using the airgun for its true purpose, but Sean isnae chuffed at aw. — That wee cunt's fuckin well away wi it, he says, screwing his finger into his heid. — Tellin ye, Mark, he's no fuckin real. See if the cunt does it again, Gillsland's gittin tae hear ay it!

— Ah'll huv a blether wi um. Dinnae say nowt.

— Ah'm no a grass, Mark, n ah'm no wantin nae cunt tae lose thair joab, but he's no right in the heid. He shouldnae be daein a fuckin joab like this!

It was true. Bobby was the open-moothed, slack-jawed, drooling, fearless superstar ay the outfit; a deranged youth whae'd come intae oor humble midst via a rehabilitation scheme ay some sorts, the speculation ay the nature ay which got mair and mair outlandish in concert with his nutty deeds. We aw loved this laddie dearly, he brightened up the drab monotony ay the factory, but we kent that he could completely fuck us up at any minute, dragging us oan a crazy whim intae the abyss ay unemployment or serious industrial injury. It was times like this that ah was glad ay the escape hatch ay university; this was gaunny end in tears.

The clock says yon time, so ah slap Young Bobby on the back, and we down oor tools and head fir the canteen. — Ah kent what ah wis daein, Mark, he protests, — ah wisnae gaunny shoot any cunt, like.

— Fair enough, Bobby, ye got tae watch though, mate.

Bobby nods apologetically. He likes me; all psychos seem tae. Ah'd long accepted the universe as a rough, tangled and flawed place, so ah never judged, at least publicly, and generally indulged the capricious foibles ay the bam. They made life interesting. We walk across the forecourt tae the canteen adjoining the warehouse that services several businesses oan the industrial estate. Sean was still a bit shaken, maintaining a discreet distance fae Bobby, as if the cunt was still tooled up in some wey.

The canteen is pretty basic. They'd started tae dae pies and sausage rolls wi beans and chips or filled rolls, but maist ay the boys still brought their ain pieces. Big Mel, an oil tanker ay a lassie, was oan her ain the day withoot her sidekick Morag.

— Awright, Mel doll?

— Hiya, handsome.

— Nae Mozzer, Mel? ah enquire, as me Sean, Les, Bobby n Mitch join the queue.

— Naw, Mark, she's took a day oaf . . . oan the sick. She lowers her voice as Ralphy Gillsland comes in with Bannerman and wee Baxy. We hated those cunts, Fanny-Flaps, Bannerman, the gravel-voiced foreman, and Baxy, his sooky wee sidekick.

— Steel's order done yet? Bannerman, the big box-like cunt wi the square body and heid, shouts doon the line at me.

Ah resent talking tae Bannerman at the best ay times, especially when ah'm oan ma fuckin brek. — It went oot oan the van this mornin, ah took great delight in telling him. That was maistly doon tae Young Bobby. Deranged he might be, but that troubled son ay Niddrie Mains certainly kent how tae work that gun.

— Good, Bannerman mutters sourly.

Ah dinnae even look back at the miserable cunt. While Ralphy, in spite ay ma antipathy tae him, seems tae perversely like me, Bannerman was my enemy fae the start. The cunt loathes me even mair since ah went oaf tae uni. Ah turn tae Mel. — Still seein that felly, Mel? She's been humping this big fermer's boy fae West Calder.

— Him! No way, she replies, blowing air out the side ay her mouth wi the force of Bobby's gun.

— Big laddie but, Mel, Les says suggestively.

— Tiny wee fuckin welt oan it but, she scoffs. — That's nae use tae me!

Ah ponder this fir a bit. — Right enough, Mel, ye want tae git yirsel one ay they dwarf boys. Huge knobs oan these cunts . . . or so they tell me.

— Ah, ya dirty fuckin dwarf-shaggin cunt, Les dives in. Bobby flashes a smile full of teeth and snickers his wheezy, shoulder-shaking laugh.

— Ah've been sucked oaf by a few ay they in ma time, ah swivel my hips, — ideal height, nae need for knees, but ah've nivir gie'd yin the message. Ah'm relyin oan you fir the details thaire, Lesbo.

— Aye, you can fuck off, ya cunt, Les says. It isnae much ay a retort, but that's Les. Barry gadgie, but despite his stand-up pretentions, nae Oscar Wilde: even less so in wit than in sexuality.

Young Bobby is dribbling again as he stares at Melanie's breasts. She clocks him and throws a sulky yin. — Bobby, cut that oot. Ah slap him playfully roond the heid as he shoots me that gurgling toddler smile. Even though he's only aboot five years younger than me, Young Bobby definitely brings oot some latent paternal instinct in us, which makes me feel a bit uneasy. — Listen, Mel, Boab here's yir man.

— That skinny wee laddie? Ah've seen mair meat in one ay they pies!

For a split second ah think that Young Bobby is gaunny blush. But then he just winks and twists his lower lip downward. — Any time, any place, baby.

Melanie lets oot a horsey laugh n whacks some mashed tatties oan a plate fir Mitch. — They say that aboot skinny guys. Aw prick n ribs, Les ventures. — Frank Sinatra weighed only a hunner n thirty pounds, but Ava Gardner goes, 'A hunner ay that wis cock.' Mel hilariously tries tae look a bit demure, but ah clock her shootin Bobby the glance a closing-time drunk gies a fish supper. Ah wag my finger at her as ah'd been the only cunt tae catch this, n she grimaces back at us.

Mel dishes up pie, beans n mash fir me, then does the same for Young Bobby, who picks up the plastic bottle and covers every square centimetre ay tattie and pie wi broon sauce till it farts oot the dregs. Nane left for the approachin Bannerman! — Wasted aw the fuckin sauce, he growls in outrage, clocking Bobby's plate as he huds up the empty boatil. — Ye couldnae have wanted aw that fuckin sauce!

Bobby thinks aboot this, then announces, — Ah wis jist feelin . . . he sweeps his hair back tae show a furrowed brow, — . . . saucy! Then he waltzes tae the table as Les, Mitch and me cannae help chortling away. Even Sean's lightened up. Wee things like that seem trivial but those were the kind ay glorious mini-victories Bobby effortlessly specialised in. It made getting shot at worthwhile.

After work ah sees Sick Boy at the Fit ay the Walk, standing at the bus stop, large eyes scanning this waiting lassie, as he rubs his pointed five-o'clock-shadow chin in contemplation. Ah watch his expression shift in a heartbeat fae baleful, like a baby animal throwing itself oan yir mercy, tae cruel and arrogant. He's just ready tae make his move. His black, collar-length, mod-cut hair has a glossy sheen to it, and he's wearing a white V-neck shirt tae highlight his dusky Mediterranean skin, inherited fae his Eyetie ma. He's got broon canvas troosers wrapped roond legs that seem a wee bit too long for his body, and he's wearing decent trainers for a change – he usually wears expensive Italian shoes, always knock-off. Sick Boy's constantly on the pull, and ah disturb the cunt just as he's aboot tae pounce. — Rents . . . he says irritably, nodding at the lassie, — . . . I was *working* . . .

— Take a brek, n come for a beer, ah tell him, cause ah need tae talk aboot movin intae the gaff in Montgomery Street.

— If you're buying. Too many baboons in this neck ay the woods, anywey, he moans. Baboons are what he calls lassies wi bairns: *Brat Attached, Bugger Off Onto Next.*

We go intae the Central and start chewing the fat. He collapses oantae a bar stool, while ah elect tae stand. Sick Boy's doing his usual: running doon Leith, telling us that he's meant fir better things. — I know things are hard, but there are just so many pusillanimous fuck-ups in Leith.

— What?

— Pusillanimous. It means lacking the will or courage to go on. Moaning. Whingeing.

An auld cunt wi a bunnet and nae teeth, whae's been standin at the bar next tae us, chips in. — A loat ay people widnae like ye sayin that, he warns, eyes fired up.

— Ever heard ay the term *private* conversation?

— You ever heard ay the term *public* house?

Sick Boy raises his brows, seems tae consider this, then goes, — Fair fucks, you've got me bang tae rights, boss, and he shouts up another round including the old boy, who pulls up a bar stool, glowing wi a sense ay privilege. However, the auld cunt takes it as an opportunity tae tell us the story ay his life, makin it oor cue tae guzzle up n escape.

As we emerge intae the warm sunlight ay the fading summer night, that nosy saw-faced auld cow fae the Fort, Margaret Curran, is comin up the road, wi her big bag ay washing. She scowls indignantly as she spies a Paki family, well, ah shouldnae really say that cause thir mair likely tae be Bengali, waitin at the bus stop.

— Why is that poisonous minger always carrying a bagful ay washing? Sick Boy asks as she comes closer.

— She goes up the laundromat aw the time, jist soas she kin hing oot wi her mates, ah tell him, mimicking her voice: — Ah always take it up the Bendix, son.

— Oo-er, missus! Sick Boy goes.

Mrs Curran passes us and ah cannae resist it, n go, — Ye been takin the dhobi up the Bendix again, Mrs Curran?

— Aye, Mark, every day. It's a never-endin struggle, even wi Susan movin oot tae get mairried. Ma Olly n Duncan get through a lot ay washin.

— It must be a bit sair, Sick Boy says, the bad bastard, — ah mean, a big load up the Bendix *every single day*.

She looks dumbfounded and hostile, her mooth curling doonwards, heid jerkin back like it's oan an invisible chain, as if she's tippled.

— Ah mean, yir hands n yir airms n that, he qualifies.

Ma Curran relaxes. — Naw, son, ah git a walk up thaire, n chat tae ma pals, n ah take the bus back tae the Fort, she explains, then looks at me in hostility. — So how's the new place?

— It's no that new. We've been thaire four years now.

— No bad fir some, she says bitterly. — They've goat thaime on D Landin now. She turns tae the Asians, climbin oantae the 16 bus. — A whole faimly, n the Johnstones' auld hoose. She purses in disgust. — The smell ay that cookin makes ye seek. Bloody seek tae the gills, n it stinks the dryin green right oot. That's how ah take it up the Bendix sae much.

— Any excuse, ah chide, noting that Sick Boy's lost interest in the game and is now checkin oot this passing lassie; coupon, tits, erse, legs, but maist ay aw, handbag.

— Nae excuses aboot it, this country isnae fir the white people thit made it any mair. Mrs Curran shakes her heid, then turns and continues her goose-step up the Walk.

Sick Boy's also oan his heels. — Listen, Mark, huv tae go, catch ye later, he says, off in pursuit ay the lassie. Ah watch him for a bit and he soon falls intae first step, then conversation, wi her. Cunt. If ah tried that wi some bird, she'd huv the polis right oan us in a second. Naebody could accuse him ay bein pusill-whatever-the-fuck-ye-call-it.

So ah'm left on ma tod, but ah'm quite chuffed aboot it. The sun comes oot and ah test ma back by grippin the bus shelter roof, n daein a couple ay pull-ups, before headin oaf doon the road.

Notes on an Epidemic 1

At a national referendum on 1 March 1979, the people of Scotland voted by a majority to reinstitute a parliament. This would restore some degree of sovereignty to their country, after almost three hundred years of undemocratically imposed union with England. George Cunningham, a Scottish, London-based Labour MP, put forward an amendment to the Devolution Bill, which rejigged the rules so that this parliament would not be automatically offered to Scottish citizens.

The Conservative Party, led by Margaret Thatcher, came to power in May 1979. With a meagre percentage of the Scottish vote, it was thus argued that they had no democratic mandate, but they steadfastly opposed and vetoed the setting up of the Edinburgh parliament.

Too Shy

— That's the fuckin tragedy ay Scotland. Frank 'Franco' Begbie, heavyset, with a number-two cut, tattoos on his hands and neck inching towards the light, makes the declaration from a bar stool in an austere Leith Walk hostelry, one never destined to feature in any Edinburgh Pub Guide. For emphasis he punches Spud Murphy's thin biceps, the casual sledgehammer blow almost knocking his friend off his seat. — Nae fuckin qualification fir the European Nations Cup again!

In evidence Franco points to the television mounted in the corner of the pub, above the jukebox, which, through blazing luminous colours, shows two sets of Continental footballers taking the field. Tommy Lawrence tenses his tight, muscular frame, arching his neck towards the screen, and even lazy-eyed Mark Renton does too, because it's Platini time again. They scrutinise the lines of alert players in mid-shot as the camera pans along their ranks, looking for clues as to how the game might unfold. From the shabby bar they find themselves in – nicotine-stained walls, cracked floor tiles and battered furniture – they're wondering how it feels to be up there, chests expanded, mentally focused, ninety minutes away from at least some kind of immortality.

Spud, dirty-blond hair sticking up in tufts, grimaces, massages his injury, trying to dissipate that insistent throb Renton and Tommy knew so well. Regarding his near-tearful expression, Renton is moved to affectionately consider that if *Oor Willie* grew up in the Kirkgate, wore washed-out Fred Perry shirts, shoplifted and took loads of speed, he and Spud would be dead ringers. Apart from the Dudley D. Watkins scribbled golden smile, Spud has two expressions: totally-scoobied-as-to-what-the-fuck's-going-on and the constantly-on-the-verge-of-tears look he is currently deploying. Assailed with self-pity and self-loathing, regarding his folly in sitting next to Begbie, he glances around. — Aye . . . it's bad, likesay, he concedes, wondering how he can manoeuvre into another seat. However, Tommy and Renton particularly, himself suffering with an injured arm and back, are determinedly keeping Spud in between themselves and the animated Franco. Staring down the lighted barrel of Frank Begbie's Regal King Size, the tip blazing like a third eye as inhalation hollows the smoker's cheeks, an overwhelming sense of 'what the fuck am I doing here?' descends on Renton.

Tommy, meantime, takes in that bull-like neck and stocky frame. Franco isn't that tall, about the same height as Renton, just shy of six foot, and thus smaller than him, though he's brawny enough, his dense body seeming to aggregate the mass of the bar's other occupants. He's wearing a leather bomber jacket, which Tommy notes is a dead ringer for Renton's, though he insists on getting complimented for it. — Aye . . . fuckin barry jaykit but, eh . . . suave as fuck, he announces yet again, as he hangs it carefully on the back of the stool.

Spud scans the twisting cables of Frank Begbie's biceps and forearms, unravelling from under the sleeves of his white Adidas T-shirt, marvelling at their power in comparison to his and Renton's thin, milky limbs. Tommy coldly eyes the expanse of Begbie's ribcage, thinks of the pivoting right hook that would open it up and send Franco sprawling to the floor. The execution of such a blow is well within Tommy's capabilities, and the follow-up of boot to head also inside his emotional and martial lexicon. But it was no-go, because with Begbie, that's when the real problems would start. Besides, he was a mate.

A belligerent nod from Begbie to Mickey Aitken behind the bar, and the old boy moves like an oil tanker in a cardigan, picking up the handset and attacking the TV, ramping up 'La Marseillaise'. Platini, a man-of-destiny glint in his eye, is giving it the big one as Keezbo's ample frame swaggers jauntily into the pub. Tommy, Spud and Renton all share a solitary, unacknowledged thought: *Maybe that fat Jambo bastard can sit beside Begbie and take the pummelling.* In the sparsely populated boozer Keezbo instantly registers his friends at the bar, then Lesley the barmaid, who has emerged from the office to commence her shift. Forget Platini, she's the obvious attraction here, with her ratty good looks, collar-length blonde hair and substantial cleavage, although it's the tight jeans and exposed midriff that catches the sly eye of Mark Renton.

Keezbo takes in a more generic sweep of the barmaid before asking, — How's the light ay ma life?

Lesley returns his evaluating look, though limits her scope to Keezbo's strangely stirring pale blue eyes, framed by his black specs. Trying to ascertain where he is on the joking/flirting matrix, she keeps her tone pleasantly neutral. — No bad, Keith. Yirsel?

— In the pink, now thit ah'm feastin on your beauty, Miss Lesley.

Lesley's smile contains that genuine flash of coyness that Keezbo often manages to kindle, even in the most seasoned girls about town.

— Sack it, ya fat cunt, Begbie says, — she's mine but, eh, Lesley?

— In yir dreams, son, Lesley tells him, her buoyancy and swagger rallying after Keezbo's wrong-footing.

— And wet as fuck they ur n aw, Begbie laughs, close-shorn head looking as hard as a crane's wrecking ball.

Keezbo orders up a round of lagers. For a better view of the screen, they take seats near the corner, in a crescent-shaped booth of slashed leather seating, which spills its foamy guts around a Formica table. Renton has found an old wrap of speed in his jeans pocket and passes it round; each of them, except Begbie, whose eyes are still trained on Lesley, taking a dab. — She's no shy, he observes on behalf of the company. There's a big grin on Keezbo's face as he comes over with the pints on a tray, his beaming expression conveying the eager glee of a man with an obsession to share. Setting the drinks down on the table, he takes his dab of amphetamine, moistened by fraternal gob. Wincing under the salty tang, he washes it down with a mouthful of beer. — Mr Mark, Mr Frank, Mr Tommy, Mr Danny, what about this yin: Leo Sayer versus Gilbert O'Sullivan?

Begbie looks to Renton in anticipation; in the relocation they've somehow ended up next-door neighbours. Renton goes to say something, then thinks better of it. Instead, he looks to Tommy, as he takes a sip of lager made even more rancid by the dregs of sulphate powder clinging to the back of his throat.

— It's a good yin, Tommy concedes. Keezbo habitually invents imaginary square-go scenarios between unlikely participants. This time they seem well matched.

— Gilbert O'Sullivan wrote that fuckin nonce song aboot beastin bairns, Begbie suddenly snaps, — that cunt deserves tae fuckin die. Mind ay that? That fuckin video?

— Eh, 'Claire', aye, but ah didnae see it that wey, Franco, Spud ventures, — it wis jist a song aboot babysittin a wee lassie he kens, likesay.

Begbie dispenses him a trademark paint-stripping stare. Spud instantly withers. — So you're the big fuckin music critic now, eh? Is it fuckin natural for a grown man tae write a fuckin song aboot a wee lassie that isnae even his ain? Eh? Answer us that if ye fuckin well kin!

Renton has learned over the years that the worst thing you can do is to make Frank Begbie feel isolated, so he feels it politic to join in on his side. — You've goat tae admit, Spud, that it is a wee bit fuckin suspect.

Spud looks crestfallen but Renton can detect the phantom gratitude in his eyes for the out he's just given him. — Come tae think ay it, ah suppose so . . .

— Too fuckin right, Begbie sneers, — listen tae this rid-heided cunt. He points at Renton. — Cunt kens mair aboot music thin any cunt roond this fuckin table – him n Keezbo. The cunts wir in a band wi Stevie Hutchison, he contends, looking around to see if there's any arguments. No takers.

— What d'yis think but, boys, Keezbo asks again, moving things on, — Leo Sayer or Gilbert O'Sullivan?

— Pushed, ah'd have tae go for Sayer, Renton ventures. — Thir baith light wee gadges, but Sayer's a dancer, so he's nippy on his feet, whereas O'Sullivan usually jist sits behind a pianny.

They ponder this proposition for a few seconds. Tommy thinks back to the days at Leith Victoria Boxing Club with Begbie and Renton, how it had been not enough for one and too much for the other, but just right for him. Dropping the fifteen-year-old Begbie in the ring after 'mermaiding' him; rendering his opponent apoplectic by tempting him out into deep water in pursuit of his would-be prey, before he tired in impotent frustration, unable to get past that cutting jab and catch Tommy. When he ran out of steam he was picked off, a street fighter given a lesson in the sweet science by a boxer. Tommy had thought at the time he'd pay dearly for that victory, but instead he'd gained Begbie's respect, though his opponent took the opportunity to stress that any conflict outside the ring would be an entirely different scenario.

And Tommy, who with some regret had chosen football over boxing, had no reason to doubt this. He'd come to admit that Begbie was a more accomplished pavement warrior. Tommy could focus on one foe in the ring, but panicked in the hurly-burly of the urban rammy, where good peripheral vision was required to read what was happening with possible multiple opponents. Frank Begbie thrived on imposing himself on that sort of chaos. — It's what Rent fuckin well sais, he decrees, — it's a flyweight's fight, n that usually goes oan speed. Sayer tae pummel the nonce in three. Tam?

— Aye, sounds aboot right tae me.

— Sayer, they toast, raising their glasses, with Spud adding, — The show must go oan.

— Well, if this show hus tae fuckin well go oan, you git up n git a fuckin round in, ya Jewish cunt, Begbie says, killing his pint in one extended swallow, forcing the others to keep up.

Spud pulls a sullen, petulant expression but complies. He's still working in the furniture deliveries, though his employer has sold off one lorry, and there's been talk of further redundancies. But he consoles himself with the fact that he's been there since he left school: a good, reliable worker. Surely he's safe. Keezbo hasn't been so fortunate; he tells them he's been made redundant from the building firm he works for as a brickie. — Ah'll still dae some casual work for um, but he cannae afford tae send us tae Telford College tae finish ma City n Guilds.

— Whaire the fuck's Second Prize? Begbie asks. — Heard the cunt goat a doin. They tell us he's no sayin whae fuckin well did it.

— He'll no mind, he went intae the club mingin eftir bein oan the peeve aw weekend. Dunfermline sacked him, freed the cunt. He went oan a bender n he's been oan it since, Tommy explains, looking at Keezbo and Renton. — We shouldnae huv left him in Blackpool.

— He left us, as ah recall, Renton says.

— Mark's right, Tommy. Keezbo takes of his specs and rubs at his eye. — Ye cannae nursemaid the boy.

— Cunt's turnin intae a fuckin alkie, Begbie scoffs.

—Yir no wrong, Mr Frank, Keezbo nods, scoring the air with his specs to make the point.

As the conversation turns to wasted talent, Renton takes his chance to move. Almost to his disappointment, the speed is kicking in, everyone is gabbing with nobody bothering about the game. So he asks Mickey tae turn down the commentary for a bit, which he reluctantly does, but only after looking to Begbie to get the okay. The heads of some silently disgruntled drinkers pivot round to the other screen in the far corner by the entrance to the bar. Then Renton hits the jukebox and puts on Kajagoogoo's 'Too Shy'. Thinking of the line *Modern medicine falls short of your complaint*, he finds it amusing to consider Frank Begbie sporting a haircut like Limahl's. As the refrain strikes up he flutters his lashes, like a roaring twenties chorus girl, at the back of Begbie's bullet head, drawing nervous, pained expressions from the others.

Something seems to register on Franco's psycho radar and he turns quickly, almost catching Renton out. — Seen Sick Boy?

— Aye, bumped intae him in the Walk jist the other day. Had a quick beer in the Cenny on the wey hame fi work, Renton responds coolly. — Movin in wi him up at Montgomery Street.

— What aboot the game? Keezbo moans.

— We can still watch it, pit the commentary back oan fir the second half. Ah jist fancy some sounds, Renton's moved to explain, noting that Tommy's not too happy either.

Begbie won't be shifted from the subject of Sick Boy, until his point is made. — Cunt's eywis oan aboot bein too fuckin good fir the Bannanay flats, but ah hear he's been hingin aroond his fuckin ma's bit aw the time.

— That's cause his auld man fucked off wi that younger bird, Renton says.

Keezbo has his glasses off again, and is polishing them on his Clash *Combat Rock* T-shirt. It's XXL but it strains across his gut. — That's right, Mr Mark. Ah saw him up the toon wi her. She's only aboot twenty-five or something. Goat a bairn, ah hear.

Renton turns away to the screen. *Fuck shagging somebody that's had a bairn.* It was bad enough thinking about another guy's cock having been up the bird you were cowping, but their bairn being pulled through her fanny . . . no fucking way, he thinks, and gives a shudder to shake off his squeamishness.

— Tidy, is she? Tommy asks.

— No bad, Keezbo admits, — ah'd gie her one.

— Dirty, lucky auld cunt.

— You jist need tae git yir fuckin hole, Tam, Begbie says, then turns to the table. — Saw um tryin tae fuckin chat up that Lizzie McIntosh at the Fit ay the Walk the other day.

— Jist sayin hiya, Tommy shrugs.

— Punchin above yir weight wi that yin, Mr T, Keezbo laughs.

Tommy responds with a calculating smile, while Spud reminisces. — Ah spoke tae her once. She wis paintin, like wi an easel n that, doon the Shore. Barry paintin n aw. That wis what ah sais tae her: barry paintin. She's at the art college, eh, Tam?

— Aye.

— Wee snobby fanny, Begbie says, — ah mind ay her fae school. Yill git nowt oafay her, Tam. Should come wi me tae the Spiral, met this bird thaire last week. She wisnae fuckin shy!

Renton grinds his teeth, recollecting a school incident with Begbie that he considers bringing up, and then decides against it. Instead he recalls Lizzie from the O-grade art class. A ride and a half, though that class was rammed with them, he considers: it still made up about fifty per cent of his wanking material.

— Lizzie isnae really snobby, but. She swears like a fuckin trooper, Tommy says. As the words spill from his mouth, his own cowardice and that of all them around the table suddenly shames him. They'd all experienced that chance encounter with a girl like a long-absent sun, calling you out of a dark place, opening you up, rendering you as helpless as any blossoming flower.

48

—You are right on the money wi the McIntosh honey, Renton smiles, discreetly squeezing the bone and cartilage of Tommy's knee. — She gies off that aloof vibe that a lot ay shaggable rides dae, but it's basically just a defence mechanism tae stop radges chatting them up. She's awright when ye get spraffin wi her.

The others seem to accept this contention; all except Begbie. — Aye, bit swearin's aw fir fuckin show wi they snobby cunts, they dinnae jist fuckin swear naturally like normal cunts fuckin well dae.

For some reason that eludes him, Renton's suddenly beset with a great love in his heart for Franco, dispensing him an acknowledging wink. — You ain't wrong thaire, buddy.

Begbie bristles vaingloriously, sitting back, almost purring in contentment. Then his face alters dramatically and paranoia swamps Renton, as he thinks: *I've misjudged what's gaun oan in this moody cunt's heid!*

Then he realises that Begbie's focused on something *behind* him, so he spins in his seat to see a skinny, angular-framed girl, around eighteen years old, with spiky mousy-blonde hair, shaved short at the sides. Ignoring Lesley at the bar, she advances towards them, stopping a few feet away, her arms folded across her slight chest. They register her one by one as Begbie sits back with a belligerent set to his face. — What are you fuckin well wantin?

— Tae talk, she says.

Renton immediately thinks the girl looks interesting. *Actually mair my type than Franco's. He usually prefers a bit ay meat on dem bones dem bones dem dry bones.*

—Talk aw ye want, Begbie scoffs, shrugging off her attentions, — fuckin free country!

— No here, she says, glancing poisonously at the others, who look back to the screen, except Tommy, who gives the girl an anaemic smile, then nods hopefully to Begbie and the door. Franco seems to consider this, then rises and heads across to an adjacent table with his pint, compelling the girl to join him. The others note that he isn't offering to buy her a drink.

— This does not look good, Tommy muses, as Renton's other choice, 'White Lines' by Grandmaster Flash and Melle Mel strikes up on the jukebox.

— Cause ah ken it's yours! they hear her screech on top of the beat in high, adenoidal tones, as, on-screen, Platini sweeps a silent effort over the bar.

— Aye, so you fuckin well say, Begbie retorts, sitting back in the seat, composed, now evidently enjoying himself. And the rest of them are too; they are all ears.

— It could only huv been you!

Begbie thinks of the silky distraction of the girl's clothes that night, the delicacy with which she stepped out of her shoes. How those fleeting memories held sovereignty in his head over any images of her nakedness. He liked her in clothes. Although it was summer, it had gotten nippy outside. She shouldn't have come out without a jacket. It could get cold down in the port. — Listen, if ye go oot withoot a fuckin jaykit whin thaire's fuckin snaw flying aboot, ye kin git a fuckin cauld, right?

She stares at him, agog, then bursts into an incredulous shriek: — What the fuck ur ye talking aboot? Jaykit? Snaw?

On the television, Dominique Rocheteau deflects a free kick which sails just past the post. Renton glances from the screen back to Begbie and the girl.

As the record urges Get Higher Baby, so too Begbie's voice rises. — Ye go oot without a fuckin pill whin thaire's fuckin spunk flyin aboot, ye git up the fuckin stick!

Lesley raises an eyebrow to Renton as she pretends tae clean the glasses. Mickey Aitken looks over at a couple of curious customers who turn back to the other TV.

The girl examines Begbie in silence for a spell, biting on her bottom lip. Eventually she urges, — So?

— So fuckin well deal wi it. It's your fuckin problem, no fuckin mine, and Franco Begbie shakes his head, takes a long drink, then sets his glass down carefully on the table. He thinks that the flecks in the Formica look similar to those on an egg he recalled finding in a bird's nest as a kid. — Ah said tae ye: 'Gie's a fuckin ride.' Ah nivir sais: 'Gie's a fuckin bairn.' How? Cause ah'm intae rides n ah'm no intae fuckin bairns!

The girl stands up, shouting, pointing at him: — YOU'VE NO FUCKIN WELL HEARD THE LAST AY THIS, SON! Then she turns n heads across the pub for the exit as the half-time whistle goes on-screen and the players troop off the field. So far the Spaniards have given a good account of themselves, but it's France who've come the closest.

— HI! Begbie, on his feet, roars back. — YOU'RE FORGETTIN THAT AW THE BOYS WIR THAIRE N AW! He gestures to the others. — THAT FUCKIN LINE-UP THIT YE DID!

The lassie stops abruptly. She turns and looks at them in horror, then shouts to Lesley at the bar in appeal: — HE'S TALKIN SHITE! Lesley looks to Mickey and shrugs, as the girl turns back to Begbie. — YOU'RE FUCKIN WELL GITTIN IT, SON!

— AWREADY FUCKIN HUD IT! he shouts back at her, making the cross with his arms. — N IT WIS FUCKIN SHITE N AW!

Renton watches her cringe in humiliation as she exits through the swinging doors of the bar, her thin, white shoulders the barest he's ever seen, as if they would only ever need the night as a shawl. He imagines another world, where she was not impregnated with the seed of Begbie, and going after her, walking with her, perhaps placing his jacket over her lissome, delicate back.

Frank Begbie downs his pint, shouts up another round and comes over to rejoin his company. — If this yin goes up tae the fuckin coort ah've goat youse boys tae back us up n say youse wir fuckin well in thaire n aw. Every cunt kens thit wi share n share alike doon the fuckin port!

— They kin tell wi blood tests, Franco, Tommy goes.

Renton is tempted to mention what he'd read about this new DNA testing in the *Scientific American*, up the Central Library, but then remembers that he's in a pub on the Walk, not the students' union at Aberdeen, where a smart cunt's conjectures are less likely to be appreciated.

Begbie's lips pull back over his teeth. — Ah ken aw that, Tam, fir fuck's sake, he snaps, then his expression warms, — but it'll keep the slag away fae the fuckin coort if she thinks half ay fuckin Leith's gaunny be aboot, claimin thuv been in thaire pumpin away oan Franco's sloppy fuckin seconds, ya cunt!

Through their laughter, the rest of them are starting to feel sorry for the girl. Particularly Spud. *Too many Bicardi n Cokes, a horny flush, one slip-up and yir bringing up a Begbie for the rest ay yir life. Doesnae matter if the burd's a wee bit dippit, naebody deserves that.*

The second half resumes and Platini, with an air of inevitability, puts the French ahead. The pub goes crazy, at least the other corner does, and Begbie is visibly riled by the commotion, casting silencing glances down the narrow bar. Tommy wonders if he would ever stand up to Franco again, considers what circumstances might compel him to do so.

The afternoon spins by in another couple of rounds of drinks. Up on the screen, Platini has reached a personal sporting pinnacle, and in triumph holds aloft the European Nations Cup. Renton and Keezbo are surprised to see that it was two–nil; they hadn't noticed the other goal. Amphetamine, adrenalin and their own dramas had got in the way.

— Dinnae even ken her fuckin name, Begbie sais meaning it in a barbed, disparaging way, but it somehow coming out, to his surprise and that of the others, as something between an accusation and a lamentation. For a few moments he thinks of that flecked bird's egg: unsure of whether he smashed it or left it alone in the nest.

First Shot: Just Say 'Aye'

Perversity and obstinacy are integral tae the Scottish character. Since ah said 'no' tae these cunts back in Manchester, ah've been obsessed wi heroin. Ah sometimes wish ah'd said 'aye', then ah might be mair inclined tae leave it alaine. Also, it's meant tae be a good painkiller, n this back still nips, especially at night. The doaktir thinks ah'm at it, n they paracetamols are fuckin useless.

It's an open secret in oor circle that Matty, whae gets maist ay oor speed, has been skag-happy for donks. Through him ah ken that Johnny Swan, an auld fitba mate ay mine, gets good gear. Ah huvnae really hung oot wi Johnny in ages, no since we played thegither fir Porty Thistle. He wis a decent player. Ah wis shite but applied masel like fuck tae get oot ay gaun tae the boxing club wi Begbie n Tommy.

It's time that friendship was re-established.

In the flat in Monty Street, ah tell Sick Boy aboot it and he's in. — Sounds fuckin excellent. Ah fancy some ay that shit, have for ages. He starts crooning the seminal Velvet Underground song, about sticking the spike into ma vein . . . come to Simone, he says, his jaw juttin oot, as he puts doon the dictionary he's been thumbing through.

— But jist a wee bit tae try, cause mind wir meetin Franco up toon the night.

Sick Boy batters his heid wi the palm ay his hand. — I am pig-sick tae the back teeth ay that cunt making arrangements on my behalf. I just don't *need* it. Having tae listen aw night tae whae's gittin killed and whae's gittin stabbed . . .

— Aye, but a wee bit ay smack'll mellow us oot, n then we'll go n see him up in Mathers.

A shrug ay the shoodirs, and he gets up and yanks the cushions oaf the couch, prospectin for coins and shoving the meagre booty deep intae his poakit. — I should get a bigger allowance from the state, he grumbles. — I'm tired ay mooching oaffay chicks tae supplement my income.

We head oot and dive oantae a 16, bound fir Johnny's pad at Tollcross. It's a blindin hot day so we sit doonstairs at the back for a better view

53

ay the passin fanny. Back top deck wi Begbie, tae intimidate wideos, back bottom wi Sick Boy tae leer at lassies. Life has its simple codes.

— This is gaunny be so much fun, Sick Boy says, and rubs his hands thegither. — Drugs are *always* fun. Do you believe in cosmic forces, destiny n aw that shite?

— Nup.

— Me neither, but bear one thing in mind: today was a 'T' day.

— What . . . ? ah ask, then it dawns on us. — Yir dictionary thingy.

— All will be revealed, he nods, then starts talking about heroin.

Smack's the only thing ah huvnae done, ah've never even smoked or snorted it. And ah must confess that ah'm fuckin shitein it. Ah wis brought up tae believe that one joint ay hash would kill me. And, of course, it wis bullshit. Then one line ay speed. Then one tab ay acid; aw lies, spread by people hell-bent on self-extermination through booze and fags.

But heroin.

It's crossing a line.

But as the boy said, anything once. And Sick Boy doesnae seem concerned, so ah bullshit tae keep ma front up. — Aye, ah cannae wait tae dae some horse.

— What? Sick Boy looks at me in horror as the bus growls up the hill. — What the fuck are you talking aboot, Renton? *Horse?* Dinnae say that in front ay yir dealer mate or he'll laugh in yir face. Call it skag, for Papa John-Paul's sake, he snaps, then stares oot at a short-skirted lassie meandering wi seductive intent up Lothian Road. — She's a peach . . . far too carefree in bearing and expression tae be a baboon . . .

— Right . . . ah feebly respond.

We get tae Johnny Swan's place, and even though the stair door's got an entryphone, it hings open like a daftie's mooth. We climb the steps, instinctively knowing that it'll be oan the top flair. It's the only flat wi nae name oan the scabby black door. Johnny greets us wi a smile, though a wee look passes between him n Sick Boy. — Mr Renton! It's been a long time . . . come in . . .

— Aye, a couple ay year at least, ah acknowledge. Ah wis at a perty up here back then. Wi Matty. Eftir we came back fae London. Swanney still has the fair hair, but it's longer n mair straggly now, and these piercing blue eyes, but his choppers are a mass ay green n broon. Wi his permanent look ay surprise and always seemin oan the verge ay outrage, he reminds us ay Ron Moody, who played Fagin in *Oliver!* A rancid smell like stale sweat hings in the air, emanating fae either tenant or dwelling, and intensifying as we follay him inside. Sick Boy, who ah intro, catches the whiff and makes nae attempt tae disguise his distaste.

One windae is boarded up, darkening the front room. The others have big, viney plants wi green tomataes oan them, hogging maist ay the remaining light. There's still fuckin lino oan the flair, though it's topped wi some distempered rug. Oan the waw, above the fireplace, there's a barry poster ay Siouxsie Sioux, naked fae the waist up.

We faw doon oantae a leather couch. A sick joke ay a budgie, greasy feathers, shuffles along a spar in a cage, looking like Richard the Third. Eftir quickly catchin up aboot auld times, Johnny gets doon tae business. — Matty Connell tells us you're still daein the Northern Soul thing. Ah take it yir lookin fir some speed?

Ah glances at Sick Boy, then back tae Johnny, tryin tae be aw cool. — Actually, we heard that you've goat some nice skag.

Swanney's eyebrows arch, n he puckers his lips. — They aw want it now, he grins. — Ivir done the skag before? he asks, rolling up the sleeve ay his shirt. Ah kin see rid marks poking up like angry plukes. — Ah mean, banged up?

— Aye, ah lie, no lookin at Sick Boy, — back up at Ebirdeen.

Swanney reads it as such but doesnae gie a fuck. He pulls oot a wooden box fae under a glass coffee table, upon which sits a barry blue-n-gold vase, a Scotland World Cup 82 mug, a candle half melted intae one ay they blue-n-white ringed plates every cunt's goat, and a tin ashtray fill ay cigarette butts. — Ye want a hit?

— Aye.

He opens the box and puts some white powder fae a wee placky bag intae a spoon and sucks water fae the mug intae a hypodermic syringe. He squirts the contents intae the spoon, which he heats up under the candle, stirring it wi the needle as it dissolves. Catching Sick Boy staring, he spits a cheeky grin ower his shoodir, squeezing one ay they wee Jif things fill ay lemon juice intae the water. Still stirrin wi the needle tip, he then sucks it back intae the barrel ay the syringe.

Ah sit back, entranced by his preparations. Ah'm no the only yin: Sick Boy's like a nerdy science student scrutinising his mentor. Johnny looks at me, sitting thaire open-moothed like a spare prick at a hoors' convention. He gits the score. — Ye want me tae dae it fir ye?

— Ta, ah nod. Sound cunt Swanney, sparin ma embarrassment like that.

He sharply tugs ma airm towards him, like it's a Christmas cracker, resting it on his thigh. Johnny's jeans are minging and sticky oan ma wrist, like he's spilt honey or treacle oan his leg. He ties a leather strap round my biceps and starts tapping at ma veins. Ma back throbs wi a phantom truncheon strike, as a shiver spreads through me.

Ah know that this is crossin a line.

Ma heart pounds. Ah mean, really pounds. We're meant tae meet Franco for a peeve n aw, tae watch the Euro 84 fitba, and he hates gittin stood up!

Say no.

Johnny tap-tap-tappin at my airm and me distracting masel by lookin at the dry flakes ay skin on his scalp jist at the hairline.

Begbie. Goat tae meet Begbie at nine!

Ah'm thinking aboot shoutin 'stop' but ah ken that ah could never turn away at this point. If smack is as addictive as they say, then ah'm already aw the junky ah'm ever gaunny be.

Say no.

Ah'm thinkin aboot university; ma studies, the philosophy module and free will versus determinism . . .

Say no.

Thinkin aboot Fiona Conyers in the history classes, sweeping her long black hair aside, her wide pale blue eyes and white teeth as she smiles at me . . .

Say naw.

Johnny still tap-tap-tappin like a patient old prospector looking for gold. He looks at me and shoots us a cracked smile. — You've goat shite veins.

Not too late! No too late tae make an excuse, he gied ye an out thaire, say no, no, no . . .

— Aye, ah cannae gie blood.

Say something else . . . say fuckin naw . . .

NAW, NAW, NAW . . .

— That might be just as well, he smiles as he stabs the needle intae my airm. Ah look at him petulantly, upset at the sharp pain, the intrusion. He smiles wi those rotten teeth and sucks some ay ma blood back intae the syringe. The word 'dinnae' briefly forms on ma lips but he pushes and empties the contents ay the barrel intae me. Ah look at the empty hypo. Ah can't believe he's just put that shit *inside me*.

Fear rises up ma spine like mercury touched by heat up a thermom-eter. Then it's gone. Ah smile at Johnny. Just as the thought forms: is that aw there is tae it? ah get a sudden rush and a glow, then ma insides, body and brain, are like a fruit pastille, melting in a huge mooth. Suddenly everything that was burning in ma heid, every fear and doubt, just dis-solves, ah can just feel them receding intae the distance . . .

Aye, Aye, *Aye*, *Aye*, AYE, *AYE*

In my mind's eye, ah've goat an image ay ma brar Billy, when we were walkin along Blackpool prom, crossin ower the road n turnin intae a side street ay red-bricked guest hooses. It's a hot summer's day n ah'm eatin a 99 ice-cream cone.

Johnny says something like, — Good shit but, eh?

— Aye . . .

Aye . . .

Ah'm overwhelmed wi the sense that everything is, was and would be, completely okay. A state ay pure fuckin euphoric bliss passes through us, like sunshine ower shadow, makin things no only right, but *just* right.

Aye . . .

A sudden nausea curdles in my gut and ah feel this moist sickness risin up intae ma throat. Swanney sees me dry-retching and passes ower a sheet ay newspaper. — This shit's strong, forgot ye were a novice, deep breaths . . . he says.

Oh aye, but nae fear now, Swanolito, ah'm fuckin flyin . . .

Ah swallow it back doon, ridin it oot, and ah feel great, propping maself up against the back ay the couch. Ah dunno what ah'd expected, mibbe acid-like hallucinations, but there's nowt like that, everything is as it eywis wis, but it no sae much *looks* as *feels* beautiful, welcoming and just *damn fine*, like aw the sharp edges in the world have blurred and smoothed. Ma stiff and jagged spine is now like a bendy piece ay rubber. A polis baton would bounce right oaf it, smashing the cunt right back in the chops . . .

Oh aye.

— Good, mate, eh? Swanney says.

— You did something . . . interesting . . . there, John. Ah feel the words tumble slowly oot n we're laughin softly thegither.

Sick Boy is next up, and watching me in wonderment. Then the tourniquet is oan his airm, and Johnny's spike is gaun intae his big, dark vein.

— This is the best, ah say, as ah watch it hit him, and feel him slump against me, as warm and soft as a big stuffed toy.

— Oh . . . ya fuckin beauty . . . he gasps, then throws up onto the newspaper. When he sits up, he fixes me in a dopey smile. — The word . . . the 'T' word . . . ma dictionary . . . wis tourniquet . . . by the . . . by the Holy Papa's sweet, low-swingin nutsack . . . that's fuckin cosmic . . .

— Cosmic . . . ah parrot in slow laughter. We're gaun naewhaire, we've scored a gram fae Swanney, which Sick Boy's pocketed, and we're sitting here for a wee while longer in the deep, dozy silence ay afternoon heat, broken only by a kid's shout or passing car horn ootside. Swanney pits oan a Doors album. Never liked that shite before but ah'm sortay gittin it now. Maist ay aw ah'm enjoyin the slow stream ay delicious talk, wise and daft, posturings and retorts, and how ah'm baskin in the hypnotic afterglow ay 'Riders on the Storm', even as ah luxuriate in the track on the first side he's pit back oan. As the darkness presses in tight around us, ah feel great. Fuck gaun intae toon, and the mean backstreets, where edgy club bouncers spar verbally wi sly, have-a-go drunks, cheered oan by underdressed, goosefleshed lassies wi cries as shrill as seagulls. I've nowt but a withering disdain for it all. Disnae matter if it's Mickey Platini or Franco Begbie, they will aw just have tae wait.

Family Planning

Belle Frenchard heard the retching sounds coming from the bathroom, as she advanced up the stairs with a cup of milky tea for her daughter. Instantly, she prayed that it wasn't Samantha making those noises. *Please let it be Ronnie, Alec or George, they were aw oot last night. But no Samantha.*

When her daughter, grey and frail, emerged to face her, they exchanged a dark, slow acknowledgement, and Belle just knew. The words tumbled from her slack mouth. — Yir in the family wey . . .

Samantha didn't try to deny it. She felt herself stiffening up as she faced the bull-like figure of her mother. She thought about the life growing inside her, and was startled by the absurd truth that she herself had emerged from Belle's doughy, sweaty frame.

That wee bastard Sean . . . The first notion Belle settled on quickly crumbled. — But Sean's been in the fuckin army for six fuckin months . . . she thought out loud, before demanding, — Whae's is it!

Samantha glared back into Belle's deranged eyes, wanted to truculently proclaim, 'It's mine.' But all that spilled from her was a limp, — What d'ye mean?

— What the fuck d'ye think ah mean? Belle stood, hands on her hips, veins bulging in her neck. — WHAE'S THE FUCKIN FAITHER?!

At that point Ronnie, who had been slowly lumbering up the stairs, nursing a brutal hangover, shot into higher animation. A heavy-muscled gym rat, he rarely drank, and was glad of the rush of adrenalin supplanting the lethargy of the booze still clogging up his system. Cold eyes in tight focus, he asked in low, threatening tones, — What's aw this?

— Tell um, Belle insisted, crossing her meaty forearms. — Tell us whae the fuckin faither is!

— It's nowt tae dae wi youse!

— Aw aye? If it's gaunny be livin under this fuckin roof it's goat plenty tae dae wi me! Belle stridently trumpeted. — Thaire's nae money comin intae this fuckin hoose! George's idle; he's idle. She pointed at Ronnie who felt a rage burn inside him. He hated the way his mother used that term for his employment status. — Alec's idle!

59

And now George, lean-framed, with the piercing eyes of his older brother, and Alec, heavier, slower and softer, were up the stairs, lining up behind their mother, the judge, and brother, the sheriff, of the posse that had already decided it was a lynching party. Samantha felt the oxygen being sucked out of the air. — Ye dinnae ken um. He's fae Leith.

— If we dinnae ken um, we soon fuckin will, dinnae worry aboot that, Ronnie said, voice low wi threat, tensing the muscles in his arm and back, enjoying the power he felt surge through his frame.

— He's takin responsibility, whaever he is, Belle rasped, head shaking, hand squeezing the banister, then was suddenly zapped by an incredulous afterthought. — How the fuck did ye faw fuckin pregnant in this day n age?

Samantha chewed on her bottom lip, swallowed hard. — Ah wis oot drinkin with Wilma and Katie. Ah forgoat tae git ma faimlay plannin . . . wi Sean bein away . . . She cringed at the thought. — Ah met this felly. Wi goat pished, n then . . .

— Sean's gaunny dae his nut, George said in malicious glee, savouring the thought, like a connoisseur does a drop of good wine, then added, — but ye ken that, eh?

Samantha half turned into the wall. Sean was not a comforting thought.

— What's his name? Ronnie demanded.

Samantha's thin jaw shot defiantly forward. — He's goat a lassie, he's no interested in us bein thegither, n he doesnae care aboot the bairn, she said in a righteous burst, feeling the sway and impact of her information. — Sais if ah try n claim it's his he'll git a dozen ay his mates tae stand up in coort n say they wir aw wi us n aw, she blurted out, then began to cry.

— Ye surely didnae . . . Belle couldn't stop herself.

— COURSE AH DIDNAE! Samantha wailed at her mother. — What dae ye take us fir?!

— Well, this felly'll huv tae stand by ye, Belle mumbled, a little guilty.

— He's no gaunny but! He telt us!

— We'll fuckin well see aboot that, Ronnie said in soft, measured fury.

Belle's rage cooled, and she put her arm around the girl, all the time perfectly aware that her daughter was manipulating her. — There, there, darlin . . . we'll git through this.

Ronnie, though, his huge muscles pumping up with blood, right in front of her, was like a superhero in transition. The way that Franco bastard had treated her had been an insult to him as much as her. He had ripped the pish out of her in that pub, and now he was going to fucking well get it. — Ah'm no gaunny ask ye again, Ronnie said in a low wheeze. — What's his name?

— Francis, she said softly, — Francis Begbie.

The brothers looked to each other. — Dinnae ken um. Ronnie turned to George, estimating that his younger brother was more likely to be a peer of this boy who had disgraced their sister.

— He's a wide cunt, George conceded warily, now concerned that he would be the one delegated by Ronnie to take revenge. He looked into his older brother's murderous eyes, then considered the growing reputation of this Francis Begbie boy. Estimated the potential squeeze of being caught between those two forces.

George's silent younger brother, Alec, who, due to his prematurely thinning hair, was often taken for the senior of the pair, suddenly spoke. — He's a deid cunt, if he disnae dae the right thing by oor Sam.

— Too fuckin right, Ronnie snapped. — Youse two go and pey this Francis Begbie cunt a wee visit. Pit him in the picture. Sort it oot. Jist tell um he disnae want *me* comin n seein um!

With her mother's arms around her slender body, Samantha unleashed another cataract of sobs, even as she cracked a smile, unseen and buried in that meaty bosom.

Way of the Dragon

We fucking well shat ourselves this afternoon, the Rent Boy and me. We're in the flat, me sprawled over my two corded black beanbags, Renton spreadeagled oan the couch, discussing the barry time wi the skag the other night; puffing Denis Law and watching Bruce Lee and Chuck Norris's climactic fight scene in *The Way of the Dragon*. This gram bag wi goat fae Swanney's fair burning a hole in ma pocket, but Rents wants tae leave it for a bit n we've made a pact that we're daein it thegither. I'm about tae broach the subject again when there's a hammering on the door. Then a voice, booming through the letter box down the hall: — Youse cunts! Open the fuck up!

We look at each other and the thought flashes between us: *It's Begbie! We stood the cunt up!*

Neither ay us are in a hurry tae move. Renton can get it and take the blow across the chops. But he's thinking the same thing. — We ignore it, ah whisper.

Rents eyes widen. — He's probably heard the telly, but.

— Fuck! Right, we'll both go. You talk . . . naw, I'll talk . . . naw, you talk!

— What's it tae fuckin well be!

— You talk!

We get up and head tae the door, mentally preparing excuses, and ah snip it open, and Begbie, excited, pushes past us intae the flat. He's carrying six tins ay lager. — Sorry tae fuckin well stand yis up the other night, boys, a wee pressy tae fuckin well make it up likes, he says, as we follow him back intae the front room wi a glance ay bemused relief passing between us. Franco collapses oantae the couch. — Bruce Lee . . . fuckin barry! Aye, ah met this fuckin burd, eh? Mind ay that June, June Chisholm fae Leithy? Wisnae much back then but see the fuckin tits oan it now, ya cunt! Wisnae fuckin shy, tell yis that fir nowt . . .

— Aw aye, Rents sais, tentatively standing next tae him and springing a can. He chucks me one ower and ah crack it open, even though it's

Tennent's pish, which ah cannae drink as the inside ay ma mooth instantly tastes like the tin. I slump back onto the bags.

— Hud that yin in ma fuckin sights fir donks, ya cunt. Franco rubs his baws through his jeans and treats us tae a pelvic thrust. — Saw her up the fuckin Spiral oan Friday night n ah jist fuckin well gits up n fires right in thaire! Anywey, been fuckin well nailin it aw weekend. Fill hoose, the loat. Wisnae even gaunny gie us a fuckin gam at first. Ah goes: 'Ya cunt, giein us a fuckin gam's the least yuv goat tae worry aboot!' Aye, wisnae that fuckin shy once ah goat her gaun! And he thrusts forward on the couch, hudin his can up for clinking, so it's toast time again. I stretch over tae oblige. I recall that Chisholm slag: a baboon-in-waiting. Our Francis is surely the man to help her fulfil her sordid destiny.

— You're on a molten streak right now, Franco, Rents goes.

— Too right. Youse two probably ended up fuckin pished n shaggin the lovely 'Pam' again, he waves a hand in the air, — whin ah wis fuckin pulverisin that June's pussy aw weekend. He slams his fist repeatedly intae his open hand. — Stick wi me, ah'll git yis yir fuckin hole awright, ya useless cunts!

Ah force another slug ay what tastes like rancid, liquid aluminium. — I feel inspired by your success, Frank, I grin, rising and secreting the can and its vile contents onto the windae ledge behind the curtains. — I've a couple ay prospects so ah'm gaunny leave you boys and check them oot. Don't wait up, Mark.

Poor Rent Boy. Not only have ah lumbered him with Begbie, he also has his video ruined at its climax. Fuck watching kung fu movies wi Franco, it's as dangerous as it gets as he tries to demonstrate his versions ay the moves, usually on you. As Renton has moved into this flat, he can share the entertainment and hosting duties.

I'm off to see *mama mia* and, of course, our good neighbours Coke and Janey. I've been doing my fair share ay hingin oot down the Bannanay flats, and it ain't just been for some of Mama's home cooking. Yeah, life at the old place is better *sans* Cunty Fud, and my ma has heard the great news that she's finally got that new Housing Association gaff in the South Side she's been eftir for years. That will seeken his pus!

Enthusiastically trotting down the Walk to my old power base, I elect tae body-swerve Mama's homestead for my neighbours' identical abode. Janey, wearing a flattering blue top and tight black leggings, beckons me in and settles me doon in an armchair. Another Mogadon saga of *Corona-*

tion Street, the British brain-dead's perennial drug of choice, seeps intae the magnolia walls ay the Anderson household.

But Simone is finding it rather hard tae stay cool with Maria sitting opposite on the couch. My leg beats out an insistent rhythm as I sneak glances at her; blonde hair pinned back, but fringe cascading forward into those big blue eyes. With the heavy lids, long lashes and that hair flopping into them, they have a sleepy aspect that screams 'bed'. That delectable honey-coloured flesh revealed as she's wearing a backless one-piece brown dress, properly displaying that slender neck and strong limbs, covered in the faintest of downy blonde hair. The dress comes just above the knee, her long shapely legs tapering down to painted toenails and gold flip-flops. Then a sudden mock fight with wee Grant erupts; her magazine dropped and retrieved, the manoeuvre briefly exposing a sliver of white panties, so electric against those Majorca-tanned thighs that I almost cream on the spot.

Quit mitherin! Deirdre says on the box.

Those big full lips . . .

Thankfully, *hatefully*, Coke turns his wizened coupon tae me, chomping at the bit. — Ah'm thinking it might be time for a wee drink. Ye comin doon the boozer, Janey?

Am ah eckers like, rooster-puffs Ivy Tilsley, as Janey, curled up like a cat in the big chair, says, — Nah, I'm steyin in and catching up oan ma soaps. If ye go oot, bring us back a fish supper.

— Mince pie supper for me, wee Grant says in squeaky enthusiasm.

I look to Maria, buried in her magazine, ignoring everybody.

— You no wantin anything back fae the chippy later oan, hen? Janey asks her.

She looks up from the mag. That sweetly contemptuous pout: my God, I'm closer than I've ever been to love. — Nup.

Coke raises his eyebrows, and signals for me tae rise. And so we depart. — Teenagers, he muses as we turn intae the stair.

— Aye, it must be hard, bringing up kids, like. Wouldnae be me, ah can tell ye. It's aw my ma wants but; me, Carlotta and Louisa wi stacks ay bairns tae bring roond tae her place and spoil.

— Naw, stey young free and single for as long as ye can, Coke advises. — No that ah've any regrets, he qualifies stridently, though I know I'll hear a fucking shedload of them in the pub once the drink starts to flow, — cause Maria's a crackin lassie, never gied us a minute's trouble. And the wee man, he's brand new n aw.

Do you actually know how phenomenally fucking rideable your daughter is?

We emerge from the grey stairs intae blinding sunshine and take a stroll

doon tae the Bay Horse in Henderson Street. Inevitably, Coke starts gabbing once the alcohol goes down. He has two moods: sober, morose and
quiet, then drunk, slavering and noisy. — Heard that boy, the fitba player,
your mate, took a bad doin in the Grapes.

That cunt Dickson again, I'll wager. Still, it's probably the one occasion
it was warranted. — Rab McLaughlin. Second Prize, we call him, on
account ay the number ay kickins he's had. Always wants tae row when
he's pished. I'm sure he no only asked for it, but begged, I inform Coke,
thinking that it's only a matter ay time before he and Second Prize meet
up and become best mates. I can see them now down at the hostel, swap-
ping jakey tales of woe.

I'm getting a bit antsy. I should have called in at my mother's, and I'm
thinking ay daein some ay that gear ah got fae Johnny Swan. Rents made
me agree we should wait a few days and shoot it together, but he'll be
stuck on the pish with Begbie now and probably heading for the cells in
Queen Charlotte Street or the High Street with that psychotic wretch in
tow. Now I'm wanting tae get shot ay Coke, but without alienating him,
as I need tae maintain the open-house policy. That wee Maria is a frosty
chicky, and I reckon it'll take something special tae get intae those snooty
wee keks. A case of the ugly ducking who becomes the swan overnight
and starts tae sense her power. I see a Kathleen Richardson or Lizzie
McIntosh No. 2 in the making; she needs tae get a taste of SDW meat
before she develops the same cock-teasing habits. The fear that I might
have missed the boat suddenly overwhelms me, and makes me think of
how tae up my game.

So we trawl the pubs, heading towards the river, then going in a circle,
ending up in the fucking Grapes. It's against my better judgement, but
I'm bursting for a pish, so needs must. By this time Coke is half blootered
and hanging onto the bar, railing against some perceived injustice or other.
I head tae the lavvy, now definitely tempted tae shoot up some mair ay
that shit I got fae Johnny Swan. The barrel-like figure of the heathen
Dickson stops me en route: — Get him oot ay here, okay?

— He's no botherin anybody.

— He's botherin me. Get him the fuck oot!

— Aye, awright, geez a minute. I turn and go intae the bogs.

That Dickheid is as wide as fuck, so ah resolve tae dae some ay this
magnificent gear on the cunt's premises. I have tae develop some expertise in cooking up and fixing, cause you know that sure as fuck Renton
will be all anal about it. That cunt will have read everything on heroin
by now, and be talking as if he invented the fucking stuff. So I sit on the

bog, bolting the door and go through the ritual: lighter, spoon, cotton balls, Jif, water in small screw-on container, syringe, needle and, above all, gear. I don't load up too much before whipping off my belt, daein ma airm the wey that Swanney creep showed us. Slide it in, like a plane landing, rather than jab it, like a helicopter. Ah find a vein easy, some ay us have fucking oil pipes in our airms, no wee lassie's wiring like Rent Boy.

He shoots home . . . whae-hae-hae . . . this rush is going through me, but it's probably just the adrenalin . . .

Fuck . . .

Is it fuck the adrenalin . . . ah'm being broiled fae the inside . . . surging up tae glory, glory . . .

Jesus fuck, it's strong gear and ah'm fucking melted! Ah feel the sweat beading on my forehead n ma pulse racing. Ah have tae stey parked on the seat for a while. Some mutant bangs the door. Again. But fuck them; this feels so good. Let them shite their fusty pants; minging cunts ought tae have defecated before they fucking well went out.

Sky rockets in flight . . . ooh ah!

Although I could quite happily sit here all day, I force masel tae rise.

When ah get out, there's nae sign ay Coke, so I sit in the corner, at one with this lovely world, though part of me is realising that drawing attention tae yourself by being junked up in an ex-polisman's bar wi a bagful ay skag might no be such a good idea, especially as I've nae drink in front ay us.

So I rise and glide across tae the bar where two mutants are standing. One ay them bears that strange smile where ye cannae tell if the cunt's a sweetie wife or a psychopath. — Dickson's taken yir mate through the back for one ay they special wee chats ay his.

By the sweet-smelling baw bag of the Holy Papa himself, I think it might be time for me tae leave. There's little tae be gained in trying tae stop Coke fae getting the same treatment as Second Prize, especially in this fucking state wi shite in ma veins and the best part ay a gram in my pocket. But Dickson suddenly comes back in, and he looks shaken tae fuck. The Big Man mantle has definitely fallen and I'm thinking: surely *Coke* hasnae put the shits up him? The chunky ex-pig approaches me wi a scared and apologetic hang tae his face. — Yir mate . . . he's through the back. Ah never touched him, we were just arguin n he fell ower the barrel and dunted his heid, and Dickson's face is flushed as his lips tremble. — It looks a sair yin. He shakes his head, sucking his lip under his front teeth. Every grotesque expression on his face seems slowed doon, it's like being in a zoo, but one where you're observing your own species in their minuscule behaviour. Then his voice ascends in petition tae the assembled bar: — Ah never laid a hand oan him!

Ah go through tae the back with this big cunt called Chris Moncur, where we find Coke totally fucking prone and battered. I'm down by his side, shaking him, and he's deadweight, ah cannae get any response. — Coke . . . Coke!

Coke . . . aw naw . . .

His face is swollen, and his mooth is burst open. — Thought he fell ower a barrel, Moncur says, kneeling alongside us, looking up accusingly at Dickson. — Did eh faw forwards?

— Chris . . . c'mon . . . he jist cowped ower, he wis pished, Dickson says, now really shitein it.

— Looks tae me like it wis a bit mair thin him jist bein pished, some other wide-lookin cunt says, his hands on his hips. Dickson was daft enough tae think those wideos were his mates, but naebody loves ex-bacon, and it's evident they've just been waiting patiently tae turn on him.

But Coke . . .

He's gone. Ah'm standing ower the cunt, regarding his rubbery slavering mouth and ah look up at Dickson's fearful face, turned away in profile. — He's away, ah say, standing up.

Another boy wi a red nylon jerkin crouches over him. — Naw, he's still got a pulse, he's breathing . . .

Thank fuck for that . . .

Ah go back tae the bar: ah'm fucking well right out ay here. A couple ay the boys follow me through, one gadge dialling 999 on the payphone, asking for the police as well as an ambulance. Dickson has come after us and is still totally crappin hissel. — The boy wis pished, just fuckin out ay it. He was telt tae go!

I'm heading, but big Moncur sees me sneaking out and shouts, — Hi! Simon! You'd better stey here!

— Most serpently, I groan, and there's nothing ah can dae, wasted and wi a G ay gear on us, as the ambulance and polis arrive. The paramedics try tae resuscitate Coke, while the polis take statements. One young cop, a country simpleton by the look and sound ay him, gapes at me and asks us if I've been smoking 'wacky baccy'.

— Naw, I'm just a bit pished, been oot aw day, ah tell him. He moves onto some others while an aulder polisman quizzes Dickson. The paramedics have loaded an oxygen-masked Coke intae the back ay thair van. I feel the gear rubbing at me, in ma system and in my pocket, so ah slip

the fuck away from this sordid drama, heading up tae Junction Street where I jump in a cab up tae the Infirmary. I'm sitting in the A&E, feeling great, waiting for Coke, but I drift into a doze and when I snap out of it the clock on the waw says it's forty minutes later, and there's a gungy taste in my dry mooth. It takes ages but ah manage tae locate the ward Coke's been admitted tae. When I get up there, Janey, Maria and Grant are sitting outside in a cul-de-sac waiting area. — What happened? Janey gasps, rising.

For a perverse second I think of the chips Coke never brought back. — Dunno, ah wis in the bogs, and when ah came oot he wis gone. Then they said he wis through the back wi Dickson. He was unconscious when we found him lying there. We called the polis and the ambulance. What did the doctors say?

— Head injuries; thir runnin tests. But he's no woke up, Simon. He husnae woken up! And I feel Janey's full, ripe body against me, see wee Grant looking wacko and the tears condensing in Maria's eyes, tears ah want tae lick dry, and ah'm telling them all, — It's awright . . . he'll be fine . . . they ken what they're daein . . . he'll be fine.

And I know it's just not the case, but ah'm hugging Janey and thinking about how much a life can change in the time it takes tae fix up.

68

Held Out

The visit tae the parental home was a mistake. Once you've vanished it's best tae stey that way; tae return is tae rematerialise intae the madness of others. Ma and Dad gab urgently aboot Wee Davie in the hospital, pressing me tae visit him. *I cannot stand* my mother's fantasy that he 'asks after me' when the poor wee fucker scarcely has a scooby as tae whae's in the room. Ah felt like screaming: try tellin some cunt whae gies a fuck.

— You ken how he goes, son, you ken how he says: Maaarrryyyk . . . and she obscenely imitated that scary chant he does in the early evenings.

Wee Davie gets aw the expert attention he needs fae the NHS. He not only has chronic cystic fibrosis, he's also been diagnosed with muscular dystrophy *and* extreme autism. The odds ay aw these conditions occurring in the one person have been estimated at aroond four billion tae one by a senior medical examiner at Edinburgh University, tae whom my wee brar is somethin ay a celebrity.

Just when ay thoat the beer-swilling discussion roond the kitchen table couldnae get any worse, it sure as fuck did, as my ma and dad, succumbing tae mild drunkenness, started ludicrously talking aboot Emma Aitken, a lassie fae ma primary school. — Aye, he ey liked that wee Emma. Took her tae the school qually, Dad teased.

— What did ye git offay her? Billy asked wi leering malevolence.

— Fuck off, ah bit back at the contemptible clown.

— Ah'm sure he was a perfect gentleman. My ma idly ran her fingers through ma hair, making us pull away, as she turned tae Billy. — Unlike some.

— You're no telling me that ye didnae go fir the tit, Billy laughed, then guzzled oan his can ay Export.

— Git tae fuck, you, ya bam.

My auld man's index finger swings between Billy n me like a clock's pendulum. — Enough, youse pair. This conversation's for the pub, no the hoose. Show a bit ay respect tae yir mother.

So it was great tae relaunch back up tae Montgomery Street. Despite his name bein on the rent book (or maybe because ay it) Sick Boy's seldom here. The gaff's in a perfect location: at the Walk end ay the street, just in between Leith and Edinburgh. It needs some new furniture, but. There's an auld couch in the front room and a couple ay beanbags n these two auld wooden chairs by a nasty-swaying table. In the bedroom you've goat a shitey divan n an auld cunt's wardrobe. There's a wee box bedroom n aw, but it's fill ay Sick Boy's clathes. The kitchen has another wee table n two dodgy chairs sittin oan these broken flair tiles that trip ye up in the dark, n a cooker ye cannae see cause it's that covered in grease, while the fridge makes these scary rattlin noises. The bog . . . enough said.

A knock at the door and it's the landlord, Baxter. A bit ay a mumpy-faced auld cunt, but if ye mention Gordon Smith, Lawrie Reilly or any bygone Hibs stars, his coupon fair lights up. — They say Smith was the best ever, ah volunteer, as he pulls oot a tatty auld rent book, his emphysemic wheeze like an auld diesel train grinding intae Waverley Station.

Only one ay Baxter's eyes works. The functioning lamp blazes wi imposing luminescence. The other yin looks like a shaved twat in *Penthouse*, crusted ower wi fanny batter. — Matthews, Finney . . . he croaks wistfully, settling doon intae a rickety chair at the kitchen table, as he licks his thumb and turns the book's pages, — nane ay them were in same league as Gordon. Ask Matt Busby who wis the best player he ever saw!

Second Prize?

There's nae real wey tae respond tae that, so ah gie the auld cunt an inane smile n soak up his reminiscences.

Auld Baxter eventually departs, banging on about Bobby Johnstone as he goes. He'll get tae Willie Ormond by the time he hits the Fit ay the Walk. Wi the place tae masel, ah consider huvin a J. Arthur Rank but ah'm too fucked eftir that shift at Gillsland's the day. At least we were oot ay the factory, daein real joinery, fitting oot another pub, this time in William Street. Ah cannae wait tae go back tae the uni. Ah enjoy the crack wi the boys, but ye bring a book in there n every cunt's takin the pish, except Mitch, but he's packin it in, so thi'll soon be nae cunt left tae talk sense wi. But before that it's the InterRail, wi Bisto, Joanne and Fiona. Of course, that's if the lassies show up and it isnae aw jist talk.

I'm watchin a *World in Action* programme aboot Ugandan Asians in Britain, and Sick Boy comes in, eyes rid, face colourless, lookin like he's seen a ghost. As it happens, that isnae too wide ay the mark. — It's Coke. He's deid.

— Coke Anderson? Fae your bit? Yir jokin!

Fuck me, a sombre shake ay his heid tell us he isnae. — He was in a coma and they pulled the plug this morning.

Apparently Dickson fae the Grapes panelled Coke and smashed his heid in. That boy's a cunt; wis chucked oot the polis for daein people ower in the cells. Every copper does that, n fair enough, maist drunken radges that git banged up for a night would rather take a couple ay skelps fae some inadequate fascist, and be turfed oot in the mornin, than face the hassle n expense ay a coort appearance. Dickson got really overzealous though, n wis asked tae leave, or so the story goes. They say it wis him that panelled Second Prize eftir he went oan that bender when Dunfermline freed him: that could have been any cunt though. Poor Coke but; Sick Boy tells us the lights went oot and never came back oan. Thaire's a coroner's report next week. That is beyond fucking brutal.

Sick Boy keeps running his hands through his hair, then shaking his heid. The occasional 'fuck' explodes fae him in a gasp. — Janey and the kids are devastated, he says, lookin roond the flat like he's just stepped in it for the first time and doesnae like what he sees. — I'm goin doon thaire . . . Cables Wynd House . . . lend a bit ay moral support.

Ah ken he's in shock cause ah've never, ever heard him call the Bannanay flats 'Cables Wynd House' before, unless it's tryin tae impress some rich festival bird fae oot ay toon.

— Thing is . . . he looks away, then ruefully back to me, — . . . ah goat a bit skagged up when it was aw gaun on . . .

— What?

— Ah banged up in the lavvy in the Grapes, the stuff we goat fae Swanney. When ah came oot, next ah kent, that pig cunt hud blootered Coke.

What the fuck . . .

— Right . . . ah goes, unable tae hide ma disappointment, cause we'd made a pact tae dae it thegither back here. Ah've goat tae admit ah wis tempted eftir spending the evening wi Franco. The cunt kept gaun oan aboot what a barry ride that June is, in between tellin us his ain personal version ay the Duke ay Edinburgh Awards; whae wis getting chibbed, and the poor unfortunates that merely had a burst mooth tae look forward tae.

Sick Boy forgets aboot Coke for a second; turns keenly on me. — Did you dae any?

— You've goat the stuff! How could ah huv fuckin well done any?

— Ye might've sneaked up tae Johnny's.

71

Ah realise that if Begbie hudnae dragged us oot n filled us fill ay pish, ah probably would've. — Naw, ah tell him, — ye goat tae watch that stuff . . . then ah panic. — You've still goat it, right? Ye didnae dae it aw?

— No way, only a wee bit. Thaire's still nearly a fill gram left, he says, hudin up the placky bag, showing me the main bean's intact and maist ay the crumbs are still there.

— Ye wantin some, likes?

— Naw . . . ah'm takin it easy.

— Aye, ah hud the heebie-jeebies a wee bit, Sick Boy admits. — It's a bit fuckin rough when it leaves yir system, so that's me oaf it for a while. Goat tae respect that shite; ah'll stick tae speed right now, he says, stubbin oot a cigarette in the McEwan's Export ashtray oan the shoogly table, and producing a wrap and taking a dab. — Wantin a bit?

— Naw, ah'm just gaunny sit in front ay the box, ah tell um.

— Right, see ye. He gits up.

— Ah peyed the rent. Baxter came roond.

— Good man, ah'll square ye up later oan. Catch ye in a bit, he goes, and the cunt's oot the door.

Nae point in pressin him for poppy eftir the shite he's hud tae deal wi, and anywey, it feels good tae be oan ma ain. Ah decide tae have a wank eftir aw, visualising this skinny lassie wi big teeth that works in this baker's up in Aberdeen. Once ah've shot ma duff ower the threadbare broon couch, ah feel a bit low, n realise that um thinkin aboot gear. Ah should've took that skag oaffay Sick Boy. *Cunt*. That wis barry, the other night thaire.

Ah call Johnny, but the phone's jist ringing, so ah grab ma jaykit and head doon tae Matty's. He answers the door, pasty-faced n wi spiky black hair, blow-dried off tae the sides tae hide slight premature recession at the temples. His swivel-eyed suspicion only slightly abates whin he sees thit ah'm oan ma tod. A rivulet of snot runs fae his nostril acroas his gaunt cheek like a duelling scar. Fae the angle ay it, he's been lyin oan the couch in a semi-doze. Matty has the demeanour ay a man destined tae scavenge the remnants ay some other cunt's feast. Beckoning me in wi a twist ay his heid, he promptly vanishes intae the kitchen, leavin me in the tiny front room. It's goat this obscenely huge telly dominatin the place, the biggest ah've seen.

Matty's bird Shirley comes ben, a pretty lassie wi an oval-shaped face and big pools for eyes, figure a bit wrecked since havin the bairn, Lisa, whae's in her airms, dressed in a one-piece romper suit. It's sortay like Shirl's *still* huvin a bairn. As ah sit doon oan the couch, Lisa climbs oan

72

toap ay us. — Hiya, pal . . . terrible twos, eh? ah nod tae Shirley as the bairn goes fir a tug ay ginger hair.

— Tell us aboot it. So how's university life? Shirley asks. Despite the extra pounds there's still something sexy aboot her. It has tae be they big hazelnut eyes, eywis pregnant wi pathos.

— First year wis great, Shirl, looking forward tae gaun back, ah say, takin evasive action as Lisa's goat what looks like a Farley's rusk in her hand and seems determined tae wedge it intae in ma coupon, — Thanks, pal, but ah ate awready . . . Ah turn back tae Shirley. — Ah'm enjoying working back at Gillsland's for the break, the crack wi the boys n that, ah tell her.

Ah've goat tae say that the flat is fuckin mingin, n it's no jist the bairn wi the nappies n that. It's like Matty's dragged Shirley doon tae his level; she wis nivir a scruff at school. Ah ken Matty's a mate n his dad wis an alkie, but it hus tae be said that the cunt is, eywis wis, n will eywis be, a fuckin tramp.

— Still seein Hazel? Shirley asks, in that coquettish but interrogative wey lassies have.

— Naw, no really, just as mates. Met a lassie doon in Manchester a few weeks back, said ah'd go doon tae see her. Been workin too much though, tryin tae get money for this trip tae Europe.

— Very nice. Wish ah could go tae Europe. Nae chance ay that now. She looks wi rueful affection at the bouncing bairn, jumping up and doon oan ma lap. — Maybe when she gets bigger, she says, then asks, – How's yir brother?

— Fine . . . ah say, unsure ay whether she means Wee Davie or oor Billy.

— Any word oan gittin him hame?

Wee Davie. — Naw.

— Funny man! Lisa shouts at us.

— That's right, pal. Sound judge ay character, ah smile at Shirl, liftin the bairn and makin fartin noises against her belly, which she laps up.

While this weird wee domestic scene is gaun oan, weird for me any roads (it's scary that cunts actually live like this), ah clock boaxes ay snide goods piled up in the corner, behind the big chair. Kennin Matty it'll be cheap shite, n ye kin see it in the toap yin that's already opened; there's a nylony-style bomber jaykit in a placky bag that looks better quality than the merchandise it contains. You could buy togs oan Junction Street that wid be high-end fashion in comparison. Shirley chuckles as Lisa renews her rusk assault on me, but ma threshold for this shite hus been reached.

Take this bairn oot ay ma fuckin face now.

Matty comes oot fae the kitchen, n makes a face at Shirley whae's gettin up and headin in, leavin me wi Lisa. Ah can hear raised whispers fae behind the door and Shirley doesnae seem chuffed. Matty eventually appears in time tae save Lisa gurgling mair bits ay rusk ower us n sais, — Cunt, let's nash.

Shirley isnae happy as she lifts the bairn. Ah'm sayin nowt, n she's no lookin me in the eye.

Despite huvin the appearance ay a demented leprechaun n snufflin like he's goat a bad cauld, Matty fair bounces doon that stair like a man possessed, tae the extent that it's hard tae keep up wi um. Was ey a fast cunt at school n back in the Fort. No that much skill oan the fitba field though, but plenty pace. — What gruesome fuckin knock-off have you goat in they boaxes, Connell?

— Usual shite, he cheerlessly informs us. — Nae room in the bedroom, n Franco's moanin aboot us pittin too much in the lock-up. Cunt, you goat poppy fir a taxi? he asks.

— Nup, ah lies. Ah shelled oot oan Sick Boy's fuckin rent n ah've goat this Europe trip tae pey fir, so sometimes ye huv tae caw canny.

— Fuck, he goes, — cunt, huv tae be the bus.

— Whaire we gaun?

— Muirhoose.

— Telt ye ah saw Nicksy a while back, eh?

— Aye . . . London?

— Naw, Manchester. He wis askin eftir ye.

— Aw.

We gits oan a 32 at Junction Street. Matty's as quiet as a corpse as the bus chugs along. Like he's tuned oot everything.

— Things okay? ah ask.

He jist smiles, exposin a bank ay yellay teeth. Mingin cunt, takes five minutes a day tae brush yir choppers. — Birds, he rolls his eyes. — We finally goat offered a hoose offay the cooncil.

— That's awright. The flat's maybe a bit wee fir youse *and* truckloads ay squirrelled chorrie.

— Aye, but they offered us Wester Hailes. Cunt, ah'm no gaun oot thaire.

Wester Hailes is aboot as far away fae Leith as it's possible tae git n still be in Edinburgh. A soulless, Jambo-infested scheme. — Shirley's no too chuffed ah take it?

— Naw . . . well, tae tell the truth, it's this fuckin skag. Cunt, ken how

74

she's a bit ay a straightpeg but, eh? Well, ah suppose she's goat the bairn n that . . .

— Makes a big difference, eh?

— Ah suppose, he goes, wiping away some snotters oan his sleeve. — It's a barry hit, but see huntin it doon . . . Swanney just takes the pish, vanishes oaf the face ay the earth whin it suits the cunt. Cunt, ah went up tae his at Tollcross last night n the light wis oan in his hoose, ah jist saw it fae the street, ah could tell thaire wis some cunt in, but he widnae fuckin well answer. The stair door wis loaked, so ah rang another buzzer n goat in. Cunt, ah looked through his letter box n ah fuckin well saw the radge; just walkin acroas the hallway fae the kitchen tae the front fuckin room, Matty's eyes bulge incredulously. His freckles look like they've been painted oan that pale face. — So ah batters the door n starts shoutin through the letter box. Guess what? The cunt *still* fuckin pretends he's no fuckin well in!

Ah strike what ah think is a sympathetic expression, but ah'm finding this quite funny.

Matty isnae. He's now animated, like a puppet operated by an epileptic; hands that jerky that if he tried tae have a wank he'd tear his foreskin tae shreds. — So ah goes n phones um up this morning n the bastard still hus the brass neck tae claim he wis oot. Ah tells um, 'Beat it, ya mongol, ah fuckin well *saw ye*, Johnny!' Cunt turns roond n sais: 'Ye didnae see me, chavy, ye must huv been hallucinatin,' but his voice was that wey . . . Matty pauses a bit, then looks harshly at us. — Ye ken when some cunt's really jist rippin the fuckin pish oot ay ye?

Ah make a feeble protest on Johnny's behalf, but Matty cuts me off.

— Ah ken he's an auld mate ay yours, but fuck um! Wir gaunny meet Goagsie n Raymie at Mikey Forrester's. Cunt, he's goat this shootin gallery, wi aw bang up thegither wi they big twinty-mil syringes. Like blood brothers. Matty suddenly smiles, warmed by the thought. — Ye ken Forrester?

— Ken the name.

— Lorne Street originally. No bad cunt, total tea leaf, kin be a bit ay a wideo.

— Did Begbie no kick his cunt in a while back?

— Aye, Matty says, — Lothian Road, but that wis donks ago, he adds, a bit embarrassed.

The story fae Begbie (which ah've had tae endure many times) was that he and Matty wir in Lothian Road and they met Gypo, this prick fae Oxgangs, who wis wi this Forrester gadge, and got intae some drunken argument wi them. Matty backed doon but Begbie didnae and ended up battering them baith. He wisnae too chuffed wi Matty for no bailin in. Anyway, the mention ay the story puts Matty back in silent mode. Eventually he breaks the hush and asks, — Seen that fat cunt Keezbo?

— Aye, wis oot wi him the other night.

Matty isnae fond ay Keezbo, cause he once went oot wi Shirley. It was long before Matty, but some cunts never let go ay things like that. Also, Keezbo kin actually play the drums, whereas Matty's shite oan guitar. No even good enough for us, n that's what it's really aw aboot.

— Jambo cunt, he says under his breath.

Ah say nowt, cause me n Keezbo are the best ay buddies, like me n Matty used tae be, when we wir punks n went doon tae London.

We git oaf at Muirhoose, cutting through the deserted shopping centre past units that exhibit only graffiti oan thair steel shutters, n headin for this five-storey block at the back ay the prefabricated library. Schemes like this, Wester Hailes or Niddrie, thaire's nowt roond thum but mair scheme. Mibbe a wee patch ay crap shoaps selling tinned goods and some rotting, overpriced veg and a murderous pillbox ay a bar. At least in Leith, if ye live in a scheme, yir surrounded by pubs, bookies, cafes, shoaps n loads ay shit tae dae.

Matty tells us that since the bastards shut the needle exchange in Bread Street a few years back, injectin equipment's been hard tae come by, but he sais this Forrester gadge gets these big syringes fae a hoaspital contact. Sick Boy's already went and sorted oot his ain works fae this nurse he kens, cause he doesnae like the idea ay sharing needles, but it doesnae bother me. He says he'll sort me oot wi some n aw, but.

We climb a few flights ay stairs n chap the door, and a figure forms on the other side ay the dimpled wire gless. It opens up tae reveal a tall but chunky-faced gadge wi thinning blond hair. He looks doubtfully at us, then clocks Matty. — Mathew . . . come in, pal ay mine.

Ah follay Matty inside, tae a front room wi scabby faded rugs slapped on toap ay the oil-black flair tiles. Posters adorn the otherwise bare waws. Thaire's a nice Zeppelin yin wi the four symbols, and a barry, ginormous Jam *Setting Sons* but the rest are ay shite bands no even worth mentioning in passing. A burst couch, two identical teak coffee tables, a brutalised armchair and a pair ay grubby mattresses comprise the room's furnishings. The place seems solely used fir the consumption ay drugs, wi the possible exception ay the odd gang bang.

Best bit is that it's decked oot wi some kent faces. Goagsie fae Leith's thaire, as is Raymie, Swanney's sidekick, and as they vouch for us, Forrester relaxes a bit. Ah'm surprised tae see LA Woman (as Spud calls her), Alison Lozinska, whae ah went tae school wi, and who briefly (in a taste lapse on her part) went oot wi oor Billy. Blondie Lesley fae the boozer's present, wi a lassie called Sylvia; tall, thin, wi collar-length blondish-broon hair. Two boys are introduced tae me; a guy called ET (which ah git telt is short fir Eric Thewlis) and this aulder gadge, American Andy, whae's cookin up gear in this big metal spoon under a Calor gas burner, so nae prizes for guessin whae's oan first dabs. Naebody intros these two other gadges. One looks well dodgy, a hard-faced salt-n-pepper-heided cunt wi a bad Mars bar across his coupon, n whae stares at us till ah look away. The other boy is wee, n hus an awfay big heid, no quite a dwarf, but *like* a dwarf. Forrester seems awright, a bit hostile at first, probably cause ah'm new, but grins when ah produce the readies, tipplin that ah'm no here tae try n ponce or queue-jump fir ma shot.

Ah sit oan the mattress beside Alison. She says hiya, n kisses me platonically oan the side ay the cheek.

There's a load bein cooked up intae this big syringe n it's comin ma way. Ah'm tryin tae get the vein up, ma belt roond ma airm, the wey Johnny did for us, but nowt's fuckin happening. The syringe goes fae this American Andy, tae ET, tae Mikey, tae Goagsie n thir fawin like dominoes n ah'm next but ah'm still tap-tap-tappin like a ballroom dancer. Ah see Raymie cookin separately on his ain works n fixin hissel a shot, while Ali, Lesley and the Sylvia bird look on, rolling joints, declining all skag offers. Ah'm no lookin at Matty but ah kin hear um snappin at us,

— Cunt, c'mon, we've no goat aw fuckin day!

Thaire's nowt ah kin dae but pass it on tae the moanin fucker. Ah gie up n pick up a foil pipe fae one ay the tables n start tae amateurishly burn some gear, tae the contempt ay the others. — Wastin fuckin good gear, Forrester moans, running a hand through his thinning quiff.

— Fuck sakes, Renton, wee Goagsie's mooth snaps like a pedal bin.

— Aye, sort it oot, ya radge, Matty's spiteful campfire voice, as a wasted Forrester, who at first looks like he's playin pin the tail oan the donkey, manages tae inject him.

— Well, yis urnae fuckin hudin oot oan me! Ah peyed ma fuckin dough, ah snaps back. — Swanney fixed us, he kens how tae git a fuckin vein up . . .

— Beat it, ya mongol . . . Matty's snake-like contempt, as he crumbles, the junk slapping him back intae the couch.

THESE CUNTS.

— Chill, Mark. C'mere, Alison goes, beckonin me closer tae her n

Lesley n this Sylvia bird, n thir passin a foil pipe roond. — Yir embarrassin yirsel, n that's pittin it mildly, she chides.

— Didnae ken youse were intae this, Ali, ah says tae her.

— Everybody is, darling. She chews on some gum. — Jist chasin it like, widnae go near needles!

She lights the underside ay the sheet ay foil, n the gear oan it starts burnin, n ah'm moppin up the smoke.

Fucker . . .

Ah takes a big couple ay dunts intae ma lungs. Ah hate smoking *anything*, n ah'm fightin no tae go intae a coughin spasm, though ah'm wincin n bucklin n ma eyes are gushin like a broken hydrant . . .

Ya cunt, ye . . .

Ah feel somebody gently take the foil sheet n pipe fae ma hands . . .

— Smokin wit de laydees . . . Matty says derisively, in a mock-Jamaican accent, face as pallid as white heather. Forrester adds something aboot the girls being okay, and wee Goagsie laughs n aw. Ah turn roond n say, — If youse cunts . . . Ah cannae finish the sentence, the gears hittin us like a marshmallow sledgehammer. Ah'm too wasted tae care aboot thir shite, besides ah'd rather be stuck wi the lassies than these fuckin spazwits . . .

Wanky fucked-up twats . . .

Alison's a bit bombed, mooth slack n eyelids heavy, but she's rabbitin oan aboot some new joab she's goat that she's startin the morn, savin fuckin trees. Then she's tryin tae tell us aboot this poetry group she goes tae. Ah kin believe it, cause she wis eywis bright at school, hud that prefect blazer wi the pipin roond it . . .

— Emily Dickinson, ah lean intae her, — . . . that lassie could write a fuckin poem . . .

— Ye know, Mark . . . Ali forces her features intae a thick smile, — we should huv a proper conversation . . . like whin we're baith straight . . .

— We did . . . yonks ago. Zeppelin versus the Doors . . . in the Windsor that time. Mind?

— Right . . . but ah wis oan mushrooms then . . .

— Aye . . . ah might huv been oan acid . . . ah recall, but ah'm watchin Forrester withdrawin the big syringe fae Matty's thin airm, noticin weepin track marks for the first time. That cunt's a minger: eywis wis. He catches us starin at him. — Naebody wis haudin oot on ye, Mark . . . cunt, ye wir haudin oot oan yirsel . . . he sais, now in a contented smirk. — Git some proper wirin, man . . . then he flops back. Ah start crawlin ower, n pill masel up tae sit next tae him oan the settee. — Sorry, man . . . he goes, n we share a wee snigger n hud each other's hand like we wir gaun oot thegither.

The big syringe goes tae the two scary fuckers, Sergeant Salt n Pepper and his Ventriloquist Doll, n the cunts are soon disintegrating. Ah think it's mibbe time tae git away fae them, but the lassies scurry ower tae us n Ali's propped herself up against ma legs, ah kin feel her back restin oan ma shins. Her braids ur that black n shiny ah huv an urge tae touch them, but ah resist, smilin instead at that Sylvia burd wi her sharp, keen, white features. Goagsie's gaun on tae a spilled Sergeant Salt n Pepper aboot how Motörhead are really a punk instead ay a metal band, and people start hudin conversations wi themselves, as the sun goes doon n dark shadows start tae faw across the room.

Ah doze off for a bit, then ah feel ma throat constrictin n jerk awake wi that fawin sensation, like whiplash fae a car suddenly stoapin. Matty's conscious next tae us; the cunt's eyes are open, starin straight ahead. He's sweatin, clenchin his hands, diggin his fingernails intae his palms, like he's oan so much junk he's cravin again awready. Fuckin radge, ah'd never let masel git messed up like that oan a poxy drug!

Forrester's ower, crouchin beside us, n he's chattin tae the lassies, but in a sleazy wey. Thank fuck they two creepy fuckers ower by are spangled; Sergeant Salt n Pepper's nearly asleep. The dwarfish fucker's heid lollin around like it's gaunny faw oaf his shoodirs. — Naw bit, how long bit . . . ? Forrester slurs at the girls.

— How long what? Ali says, in wasted indifference.

— How long should a gadge n a lassie be gaun oot thegither before they go tae bed?

Ali turns disdainfully away tae Lesley sayin something that ah dinnae catch, but it sounds like, — Chop them doon before they infect everybody, n Forrester looks up like a mumpy bairn tae register ma reaction. Ah try tae keep ma expression neutral. Probably realisin he's nae chance gittin intae Ali's or Lesley's keks, he persists wi this Sylvia lassie. — Naw, how long bit?

— Wi you, ah'd say forever.

— What?

— Even here, Mikey, naebody's gaunny sleep wi ye, and she blows some cigarette smoke right in his face. — Even. Fuckin. Here.

— Dinnae count on it, Raymie says, standin up n pullin oot a big, white cock, then comin ower and wavin it in Mikey's coupon. — Get them roond this then, gadgie, c'mon honeybunch!

— Fuck off! Mikey shouts fae his hunkers, pushin him away as we aw start chucklin.

Raymie thankfully complies, floppin back oan a mattress, tellin us ay his youthful amateur gymnast days, when he practised obsessively until he was able tae perform self-fellatio. — Ah kin still git the bell-end n even a bit ay the shaft oan a good day, but no a proper right-tae-the-back-ay-the-throat gam.

— Tragic, Lesley says.

— Agreed. So if any ay you fair damsels would like tae help oot . . .

Nae takers, as the Sylvia lassie gets up, then forces herself doon next tae us on the couch, makin us bunch along n push up against Matty, whae mumbles something vaguely hostile. Sylvia's chewing gum but ah cannae mind if she chased some skag like me n Ali n Les. A John Lennon song plays fae a shitey tape deck but ah'm hummin that Grandmaster Flash yin in ma heid . . .

— If ah could dae that ah'd nivir leave the hoose . . . Goagsie says tae Raymie.

— You never do anyway, Gordon. You are one housebound, helmet-suckin, hamster-chopped harridan . . .

Everybody has a wee chuckle at that, cause Goagsie is a bit ay a baw-faced cunt.

— Cunt, Matty laughs, and he sounds a bit like his auld self, — ah'd be telling masel a hud a heidache eftir a couple ay weeks!

— You're a new face, this Sylvia's sayin tae me, — A nice yin tae.

Ah ken she's just flirtin wi us tae wind up Forrester, whae's takin aw this in, but ah get intae it. Eftir a bit ay wasted small talk we start snogging. Her lips feel numb on mine, but her proximity is comforting and ah've never felt so relaxed neckin a bird before. Ma tongue is probing every crevice in her mooth, gaun ower her teeth n gums, but despite the intimacy it feels more detached than sexual. It obviously doesnae look that wey fae the ootside, cause we hear a shout: — You're a cunt, Sylvia, a total fuckin cunt!

We breks off tae see Forrester standin ower us, lookin well pissed off, hand goin through his sparse hair.

— That's no a very nice thing tae say tae a lady, ah interject. And it isnae, ye kin call a *gadge* a cunt, but it isnae very congenial tae say that tae a *bird*.

— You fuckin well keep oot ay this.

Fuck . . .

Ah'm tryin tae get up but ah'm wedged in between Matty and Sylvia, and wi the gear in ma system ah kin hardly move. Ah push up but ma hand's oan Sylvia's thin black leggings and Matty's filthy jeans, and he twists away wi a curse like ah wis tryin tae molest him.

— You're nae good, Sylvia. Always the fuckin slag. Never been any good. Anywhere. Have ye? Forrester taunts in a low, creepy voice.

— Aye, right, she goes.

Ah squeeze her thigh n shout at him, — Steady, ya fuckin choob.

— Aye, fuckin well calm doon, you, eh? Ali says.

— Whae the fuck ur you? Forrester ignores her, challengin me.

Ah grips Sylvia's leg again. — Bruce Wayne, ah goes, n that gits some laughs. In frustration, Forrester kicks the sole ay ma trainer, n ah lunges in slo-mo tae ma feet n squares up tae the cunt n we're right in each other's faces.

— Ladies, please. No handbags, Raymie lisps, — I beg of thee.

— Neither ay you boys is much ay a fighter. N yir baith skagged up, wee Goagsie helpfully reminds us.

Forrester and me baith have the grace tae look embarrassed, as a mutual tremor ay wary acknowledgement passes between us. Then our host looks witheringly back at Sylvia. — Fuck who ye like, ya daft bitch, he says, turnin oan his heels and headin oot, slammin the door shut behind him. As ah faw back intae the couch, ah hear his feet gaun up the stairs.

— Thanks very much, she shouts back at him, then turns tae the room in appeal. — Like ah need *his* fuckin permission? Last ah looked he wisnae ma faither, n ah dinnae mind ay mairryin um!

— Ah nivir bother askin ma faither whae ah kin shag, ah idly observe.

— Gled tae hear it, Sylvia says in clipped tones as Ali stifles a giggle.

— Me neither . . . groans Matty, — . . . unless it's muh ma.

— That's only good manners, ah shrugs.

Raymie looks at the Eric Thewlis gadge, n his face goes straight and he says, — You really should gie yir ma a bell, n eftir a puzzled silence, every cunt tipples n laughs. A daft round ay shite talk starts up, but aw this effort has knackered me n ah'm driftin back intae a semi-crash. Ah kin vaguely hear Goagsie arguing wi one or baith ay these dinguls in the corner aboot people ah dinnae ken, n one gadge called Seeker, whaes name's been bandied aroond a lot lately. The next thing ah ken is ah'm ootside blinkin in the cauld n gittin in a taxi wi Matty, Goagsie, Lesley and this Sylvia bird, headin back tae Leith.

— Did you ken that Ali's ma's dying? Lesley goes.

— Aye? Fuckin hell . . .

Sylvia's hand on my thigh.

— She's goat the big C.

81

— Cancer? ah goes.

— Aye . . . Lesley cringes, as if hearin the word exposes ye tae the disease. — It wis in her breasts. Hud a double mastectomy, but it's no done any good. It's terminal.

— A double mastectomy . . . cunt, that's where they cut baith the tits oaf, right? sais Matty, and ah cannae help glancin at Lesley's ample cleavage. Lesley shivers and nods. — Sair yin, Matty goes, — especially as it never worked. Cunt, how bad would that be, tae go through gittin yir tits cut oaf n still telt yir gaunny die? he speculates in noxious cheer. Then he says, as if inspired, — Cunt, Fat Keezbo's ma, Moira Yule, she hud that, eh, Rents?

— Aye, but she wis awright, they goat it in time, ah goes as Sylvia whispers tae me that ah've goat a nice erse.

— She went fuckin scatty but. They fuckin budgies, Matty laughs.

Ah gie him a harsh look tae tell um tae shut up, then rub Sylvia's thigh. Keezbo's ma did go a wee bit doolally wi gittin that aviary in the hoose, but ye dinnae start talkin aboot a mate's faimlay business like that. Fair play, the wee cunt doesnae make a meal ay it. — Where is Ali, anyway? ah goes, suddenly worried that she's no wi us.

— Cunt, she went wi Raymie tae Johnny's, Matty goes.

Goagsie's melted intae the windae n makes a sort ay groan. — Tryin tae tell me aboot Seeker . . . he mumbles, — ah ken fuckin Seeker . . .

Ah've goat the tweakins ay a semi in ma troosers. — Ye game? ah whispers in Sylvia's ear, catchin the smell ay fags n cheap perfume.

— If yir huntin, she smiles back harshly.

The rest disembark at the Fit ay the Walk, n me and Sylvia carry on doon Duke Street n up tae hers at Lochend. She calls it 'Restalrig' but it's pure Lochend. And ah hate Lochend. It's beyond wide. The place teems wi psychic assassins ready tae burst yir mooth. Normally ah'd be twitchin anxiously at shadows up here at this time ay night, especially as ah'm aboot tae bang one ay their birds, but as the taxi pulls away and a group ay swaggering wideos are lopsidedly winding towards us, ah strangely feel nae fear whatsoever.

The leader ay the pack gies Sylvia a gelid smile, carving concern oantae her coupon, then ah git the same treatment. — You're Begbie's mate, eh? Billy Renton's brar?

Ah've never met this cunt before in ma puff but ah ken fae Franco's obsessions exactly whae he is. — Mr Charles Morrison.

— What? Ah get a hollow-moothed, limp-jawed stare as his lips crawl back fae his teeth and his eyes bug oot.

— A pleasure to make your acquaintance. Your reputation precedes you.

Morrison looks briefly bemused. His expression is leaden and pained, wary of conspiracy. A heavyset sidekick pipes up, — Whae's this cunt?

Ah'll never fuckin look at the others, far less talk tae them. Only Cha is important and ah don't take my eyes off him for a second. His face is chalky, but it possesses a strange dignity and feral beauty, underneath the orange sodium street lamp. Then his features crease and a throaty chortle emerges and ah start tae get worried for the first time as he announces, — Ah like this cunt's patter!

And it seems he does. So ah'm spraffin wi these radge-gadges for a bit, then ah feels Sylvia's tug oan ma sleeve, a gesture that doesnae go past Cha. — You'd better go, mate. Duty calls, eh? he sniggers complicitly. — See yis.

Dismissed by Cha, we head intae Sylvia's stair, and the refuge ay the flat. Ah've impressed her the night by standing up tae Forrester (no really a big danger) then fronting it wi Cha Morrison (a risky undertaking by aw accounts). — You're feart ay nowt, you, she says in admiration.

— Naw, ah'm feart ay *everything*, ah tell her, which, when acknowledged, probably yields pretty much the same outcomes. Still, ah've done something right, cause she's no fuckin aboot, guidin us intae the bedroom. Ah've never seen so many clathes; oan the flair, hanging oot ay cupboards, spillin fae suitcases and holdalls. But they're thrown off the bed and ah'm on her and we're snoggin again, then gettin oor kits oaf. Sylvia briefly huds up a yellay nightdress, frayed at the helm, as if she's considering pittin it oan, but then wisely dismisses the idea. She isnae a shy lassie, though; she grabs ma cock and watches mesmerised as it stiffens in her hand. Pulls back the foreskin tae let ma cherry surge gratefully intae the light. My fingers glide ower that sweet fur, parting her dark, moist crack, and when she lets go ay ma knob it takes the place ay ma hand, and ah push, heart racing with that appreciative jolt ay *completion* as it slides home.

So we're banging away like fuck. She doesnae seem skagged but ah'm numb n ah'm no being very creative, just gettin intae ma stride n tryin tae hump and sweat the junk oot ay ma system. It's barry, cause ma back feels awright. Maybe it's the gear, but although ah'm sustainin the erection, ah cannae seem tae blaw ma muck, even when she 'positively gushes' as Sick Boy would say.

The lady was positively gushing.

Eventually, ah dae something that ah never thought ah'd dae, n ah fake an orgasm, groanin, then makin my body tense. She'll probably be able tae tell thaire's nae stuff inside her cause we never bothered wi a flunky.

In a joltin chill ah suddenly think aboot Begbie and that mad wee Pilton biler in the boozer. Even though ah've shot nowt ye kin still git undetected traces ay spunk and 'it just takes one' as our auld science teacher Mr Willoughby used tae say. — You're . . . ehm . . . awright, ah ask, — ah mean, the pill n that?

— Aye, but it's a bit late tae ask aboot that now, son.

— Sorry, should've checked it oot before. Passion ay the moment, eh?

She rolls her eyes doubtfully and sparks up a snout, offering me yin. Ah decline n she gies us a brief, uncomprehending look. The lighter illuminates her pinched, sharp face. Coupons like hers ah always think ay as auld persons' puses. She'll eywis look the same. — That Mikey can be jealous if ah talk tae anybody else. He's obsessed. It's creepy. Ah dinnae fancy him, n ah've made it fuckin plain enough.

Forrester's an arsehole, but naebody likes a cockteaser and ah can tell that this bird's been delightin in giein the radge the runaboot. There's nae fun tae be had in listenin tae somebody rabbitin on aboot their fixation wi a party *they arenae even fuckin*, so ah get my clathes oan and head off intae the night, citing the excuse ay work in the morning.

When ah git back tae the flat, Sick Boy still isnae back. Ah start tae strip oaf again n look at ma body in the full-length mirror. Ah systematically tourniquet and tap up ma veins, finding oot where the best yins are. There's better ones in ma legs, a good yin on the crook ay ma arm, and one oan the wrist that ah just might be able tae get up oan demand. Ah'm fucked if ah'm gittin left oot again.

The door goes and it's awfay late, aboot two o'clock, n ah answer it in ma Ys, thinkin it's Sick Boy, n the cunt's left his keys. But it's Spud; wi a cairry-out. He's semi-pished and tells us he's been peyed oaf fae the removal firm the poor cunt's worked at since he left school. — Fancy a beer, or mibbe gaun up the Hoochie fir the last bop, likesay?

Hate tae say it but ah 'm bored with the Hoochie. A bad sign: the Hooch and Easter Road are the only temples ay spiritual enlightenment left in this city. Ah tell him ah'm skagged up, n besides, by the time wi get up thaire it'll be game ower.

He follays ma eyes tae the works oan the table. He shakes his heid n blaws oot heavily fae puckered lips. — Ah've done the lot, man, but ah draw the big broon line in the sand at Portybelly beach wi the smack, likesay.

— Ah jist chase it, but, ah inform him. — Ye dinnae git addicted that wey. It's barry, man, like nae other feelin oan earth. Ye jist dinnae gie a fuck aboot anything; everything is just so damn fine, ah tell him.

— Ah pure want tae try it.

No exactly a hard sell. So ah git oot the gear n a foil pipe (ah've practised makin tons ay them) n we huv a blast. Ye can feel the aluminium particles wi the dirty smoke stickin tae yir lungs, but the heid starts tae feel weighty and a euphoria creeps intae my soul expanding through us like a burst ay sunlight. Spud, wi his crooked smile and heavy eyes, looks like a reflection ay me and we share a solitary thought: *Everything else can go n fuck itself.* Sittin back oan the couch, ah tell um, — Ye see, Spud, this is aw just a big adventure before ah clean up for gaun tae Europe, n back tae uni.

— An adventure . . . he rasps, fightin back the urge tae puke, then succumbin, as thick yellow vomit splashes from him oantae the flair, where the cairry-oot sits, untouched.

Dutch Elm

She was late, and knew that wasn't the way to make the desired impression on the first day of her new job. Going out yesterday had been a bad idea, but following that visit to her parents', Alison had wanted to obliterate everything. The terrible moment her mother had coughed that viscid blood into her hanky. The way they'd unravelled; her mother, father and her, as they sat transfixed on the dark red stain in her mother's hand. But the real horror had been in the mask of guilt on Susan Lozinska's face. She'd *apologised*, fretfully saying to her eldest daughter and her husband, Derrick, — I think it's back.

It had been Alison's afternoon off, a break from finishing up at the pool, before she started her new job. She'd popped her head into the parental home to salve her guilt about not seeing her folks as often as she perhaps should, since moving out a couple of years ago. Her younger siblings, Mhairi and Calum, weren't around, and she'd been glad of that. Her dad's tense, white face as he tried to get some defiance into his voice: — We'll get the tests done, and if it is, just saying like, if it is, we'll get through it, Susan. We'll get through it thegither!

Alison had felt the room spinning and the world seemed to sink through her. She'd stayed a while, responding in kind to their thin voices, which seemed muffled, as if coming from another room. Her mother, now looking so wrecked and stricken, and her dad, a thin, mustachioed man, who'd been just about holding onto a spruce and spiffy sense of himself in middle age, visibly dwindling in solidarity with his wife at the onset of this terrible news. *It's back.* Then Alison had left, walking up to her flat in Pilrig. Unable to settle, she'd quickly headed out into the early evening. In Lesley and Sylvia, she'd bumped into two girls she didn't know that well. They'd gone to some drug party in Muirhouse, after which she'd ended up at Tollcross on Johnny Swan's couch.

Johnny had wandering hand trouble and had tried to feel her up in the night. Through her befuddled narcotic and emotional confusion, she'd sprung to animation and told him to fuck off; she wasn't *that* blootered. Then he'd begged her so much for sex, to the point where Alison almost felt like *she* was the abuser for refusing to fuck him. For a second she'd almost relented, just to shut him up, before it dawned on her exactly how horrible that would have been on every level. Eventually, he gave up and left her, grumbling his way back to the bedroom.

Leaving in the early-morning light, she'd returned to her Pilrig flat, showered, then staggered up to her new job, and the conference at the City Council Chambers.

During her mother's long illness, Alison had grown used to filling her life with distractions. The Edinburgh Women's Poetry Group was a good one. It had the added advantage of being a male-free zone. She'd gone along to the EWPG with her mate Kelly, till the latter's boyfriend Des felt threatened and, through his sneering derision, put a stop to her friend's involvement. It wrecked her head to see Kelly, such a happy and outgoing soul, develop this brittle exoskeleton when Des came into the company. It was the refuge she'd habitually slither into, from where she'd hang on every inconsequential word that came out of his mouth. Still, that was her choice, and Alison's had been to keep going to the poetry group.

She wasn't enamoured with all the girls there. Plenty had an obvious sexual agenda, while a few really hated men, generalising from their personal bad experiences. But Alison could tell some hadn't internalised the lesson, and were thus destined to find their next equivalent, the misogynistic semi-alcoholic who brooded bitterly from the bar stool about the last bitch who'd taken him to the cleaners. There was a Des for every one of those girls; it really was such a pity he was with Kelly. Then there were those that Alison considered the worst members of the group: the ones who actually thought they were decent poets.

Most of the women, though, Alison liked. It had been an experimental time in her life. She learned a little about verse structure and haikus, and that after going to bed with this girl called Nora, she could never be a lesbian. When Nora went down on her it was enjoyable for a bit, but then Alison had started thinking, *Right, fair enough, but when's the fuckin tadger comin along?* But obviously it wasn't and she'd started to feel irritated and tense, like she was wasting her time. At least Nora wasn't selfish cause she got the message, lifting her head out the turf, conceding, 'This isn't really working out for you, is it?' Alison had to confirm it wasn't. And she felt bad that she wasn't moved to reciprocate: Nora's somewhat heavy, musky scent had made her think of her own menstruation.

Nora was nothing if not persistent, however, and the next week she told Alison she had 'a solution tae our problem'. Couching it in those terms was disconcerting enough, but Nora had brought a dildo round, a strap-on. It was certainly formidable, but when she'd attached it to herself Alison had instantly erupted in laughter. Then she was besieged by the notion that if a dildo could crumble into a semi, then by Nora's expression you'd have thought that had just happened. But she tried and Alison could say, hand on heart, that she didn't have a sapphic bone in her body.

As she entered the oak-pannelled Chambers, weighed down by the close heat from outside, Alison was set on edge by the presence of all those busy, purposeful bodies and the foul waft she caught rising from her own armpits, in spite of the attention of both shower and roll-on deodorant. *Yuck. Drug and alcohol sleaze. You keep washing it away. It keeps coming back.*

She made her way to the back of the two-thirds-full hall and sat down. Her new boss, Alexander Birch, was heading to the podium, positioning himself behind the lectern. With his light grey suit, and hair fashionably styled, Alison found herself disconcertingly impressed by her new boss. He had a gay man's grooming, but with the slightly combative edge of the sporty heterosexual.

— I'm Alexander Birch, and I was drawn to working with trees for some reason that eludes me, he began, to the inevitable polite laughter. He'd long since learned to use the potentially embarrassing coincidence of surname and profession as a business tool. Allowing the mirth to subside, he then restarted, steely-eyed and deadpan. — I don't want to sound melodramatic, he looked around at the quieting, settling mass of bodies, — but I'm here to talk about a terrible plague that threatens to change our beautiful city beyond all recognition.

The rustling abruptly stopped, and he had everybody's attention, even Alison's, who was wondering if such irony was sailing a little close to the wind.

Her view was quickly revised when Alexander's longish face remained set in earnest concentration over a slide projector. He clicked on the frontal view of a dark-looking insect. With its extended legs, it seemed to be challenging all in the room to a square-go. — This is the elm bark beetle, or *Scolytus multistriatus*. This creature spreads a fungal disease fatal to all elm trees. In an attempt to stop the fungus from spreading, the elm responds by plugging its own tissue with gum, which prevents water and other nutrients getting to the top of it, and then it starts to wither and die.

He isnae jokin!

Again the drum spun, sending a second slide clicking onto the screen. It showed a tree yellowing from the top down. — The first symptoms of infection are the tree's upper branches beginning to wither and shed leaves in the summer, giving the diseased tree an unseasonal autumnal hue, Alexander solemnly explained. — This spreads south, eventually going into the roots of the tree, which subsequently atrophy.

Alison had settled down in her seat at the back of the Chambers. Crossing her legs, she sidetracked herself with carnal thoughts, which came easily in the squalid hangover and, indeed, was the only way to eke any enjoyment from it.

Going south. To the root.

Then suddenly, with an involuntary shudder, she wondered what they could do with her mother. The tests. More chemo. Would it work this time? Probably not. Would they take her to the hospice, or would she die at home, or in a hospital?

Mum . . .

Her breath caught. In panic, she pulled raggedly on the stale hot air in the room. A sequence of slides flashed up, some cityscape shots of Edinburgh, ranging from the recognisable Princes Street Gardens and the Botanics, to the hideaway corners of the city. — Edinburgh is a city of trees and woods; from the magnificence of the natural woodlands at Corstorphine Hill or Cammo, to the huge variety of splendid specimens in our parks and streets, Alexander argued, a pleasing flourish to his rhetoric. — Trees and woodlands have an inherent biodiversity value, whilst providing opportunities for recreation and environmental education. Our objective is to maintain a multi-aged treescape with a wide range of species that will achieve a balance of the physical, economic, social and spiritual needs of the city. Edinburgh has over twenty-five thousand elm trees: they are an integral part of our city's treescape.

As Alexander looked around at the forest of faces in the audience, Alison visualised her new boss as a little boy lurking hesitantly on the edge of the woods. There was nothing shrinking about him though, as he went on: — Failure is not an option. We've lived with this nightmare since it was discovered here back in 1976. We've already lost 7.5 per cent of our elms. Now we have to intensify our efforts on sanitation felling, even if it means accepting that we're now moving into a post-elm Edinburgh.

That was what her mum felt. Failure. Stricken by that horrible disease and she blamed herself. *She feels like she's abandoning us, as if she's failed.*

The next slide showed a group of overall-clad, power-saw-wielding workmen, engaged in the act of felling trees. To Alison, Alexander looked sombre, as if he was mourning the passing of an old friend. Another shot, this time of some trees piled up and blazing, a thick black cone of smoke billowing into the air against a blue-white sky. Alison thought of the last funeral she was at. It would have been Gary McVie from school, who'd died on Newhaven Road, driving home a stolen car while drunk. He was a young, popular and good-looking boy, and there had been a big turnout. Now she imagined his smashed body blasted to bone chips and dust, down in that furnace they'd lowered the coffin into. Matty, who'd briefly worked at Seafield Crematorium, had cheerfully told her that the incinerator didn't completely reduce bodies to ash, the attendants had to put them through this crushing device to grind down the stubborn skeletal larger bones: the pelvis and the skull.

Mum . . . oh Mum . . .

Alexander's messianic gaze fell on the assortment of councillors, officials, staff and pressmen, then swept upwards to the smattering of concerned citizens in the public gallery. — The intensification of Dutch elm disease control, through a sanitation policy of the felling and burning of elms, is absolutely vital in order to keep the disease at a manageable level and allow us to gradually replace the elms with other species.

Alison was now thinking of her mother playing with grandchildren, the kids she supposed that one day she, Mhairi and even Calum might have, as Alexander clicked on a slide of trees being planted. Suddenly, he was upbeat once again. Did he have kids? Alison thought she recalled him saying something in passing to that effect. After the interview, when she'd been appointed and came to see him and they'd had a coffee and an informal chat.

— This policy of ruthlessly culling diseased trees and renewal through planting is the only way to preserve our treescape, thus our cityscape, he contended, winding up the presentation on that positive note, graciously thanking the audience. It had seemed to go well, even if was intended more as a 'hearts and minds' session, as he'd previously described it to her. The recreation committee had already passed the policy and it would go through the formality of going to the full council next week, as extra resources had to be sought from the Scottish Office. As he climbed down from the platform, Alison gauged Alexander's smile; terse and businesslike, warm and inclusive, yet some way shy of frivolity, accepting with ease the admiration for the way he'd formulated this policy and was now preparing to enact it.

When she finally caught his eye, Alexander was in the company of a late-middle-aged man. He had an implausibly red face, as if it had been spray-painted, this startling effect heightened by his silver hair and a bright yellow shirt. — Alison . . . Alexander smiled, as she moved over to them, — this is Councillor Markland, chair of the recreation committee. He then turned to the belisha-beacon man. — Stuart, Alison here's our new admin support for the unit. She's been seconded from the RCP.

— How's things at the Commie these days? Councillor Markland asked her.

— Fine, Alison smiled, warming to the councillor for using the punter's colloquialism for the Royal Commonwealth Pool, rather than the bland councilspeak Alexander had deployed. — I've just started this job with Alexander today, on secondment for a year.

— Come and grab some lunch with us, Alexander said, — then I'm going to take you on a wee drive round some of the Dutch elm disease hot spots.

They left the Chambers, heading in hazy heat across the Royal Mile to a wine bar. It was the last day of the festival and the narrow street was packed with crowds watching performers do their things on the cobblestones. By the time she got across, Alison had flyers for eight different shows pressed into her hand. Alexander took a couple, but Stuart Markland waved away the proffering young students with a low, gruff burr, displaying the intimidating bearing of a man who'd seen it all before. But he ignited as they stepped inside the tavern, literally rubbing his hands with glee as they were shown to a table in the corner.

Though far more appreciative of the wine than the food — her stomach seemed to have shrunk — Alison nonetheless forced her way through it, mindful that she'd eaten little over the last two days. Stuart Markland seemed to be enjoying both. He grinned wolfishly at them as he shovelled some chicken Kiev into his mouth, then wiped it with his napkin.

Alexander, nursing one glass of red, made a serious point. — I don't like the way some people are deploying the acronym 'DED' in council correspondence. I've made this view known to Bill Lockhart. If the papers get a hold of that and start adopting it, it gives off a ghoulish, defeatist impression. We have to avoid own goals, Stuart, he said, compelling the councillor to give this point his attention.

— For sure, Markland barked.

— *Dutch elm* sounds more robust. Alexander stabbed the air with his fork. — The press will be a huge part of this campaign, so let's make sure we're all singing from the same song sheet as soon as possible. Alison, you might like to monitor the correspondence relating to the unit, and Dutch elm disease in general, and perhaps diplomatically issue a wee note to concerned parties to that effect.

— Right, Alison said.

What the fuck is he on aboot?

Markland seemed to be considering something, lowering his busy brows. For a few seconds, Alison thought it was the wine he was savouring, before he asked, — So when does this felling and planting policy start coming intae action?

— I've got a squad out right now. Down in darkest West Granton, by the gasworks. Started yesterday, Alexander said, stopping short of smug in his self-satisfied confidence. He knew he'd bent the rules and jumped the gun by sending them out before the policy was rubber-stamped, but he was anxious to appear dynamic.

He studied Markland's booze-beaten face for a reaction, feeling palpable relief when it crumpled into a smile. — You dinnae let the grass grow under your feet, the councillor said, adding, — no pun intended, and to Alison's delight and Alexander's obvious discomfit, he waved across to the bar, ordering a second bottle of wine.

When the bottle came round, Alexander put his hand over his glass, and looked up at the waiter. — I'm driving.

Markland reminded Alison of an illustration of the Cheshire cat from a book she'd had as a child, as he turned to her. — Great, aw the mair for us! Here's tae the new unit, he toasted.

Alison in Wonderland, Mum used to say.

By the time she left the bar with Alexander, Alison was more than pleasantly groggy to the extent that she had to be careful as she lowered herself into the passenger seat of his Volvo. She thought there was no point in trying to conceal her state. — Wow . . . I'm not used to afternoon drinking, she said. — I have tae admit, I feel a wee bit sozzled n that's pittin it mildly!

— Yes, thanks for taking one for the team, Alexander nodded, starting up the car, apparently genuinely pleased at her for drinking what was the best part of a bottle of wine.

Barry fuckin job this . . .

With yesterday's excesses, the lack of sleep and the early-afternoon effect, she was certainly feeling it. — S'awright . . .

— Don't get me wrong, Stuart Markland's a great guy, Alexander said, turning onto the South Bridge, — but he's very much of the old school.

Alison was about to say that she had no objection to that, but quelled her talkative instinct. *You're at work*, she kept reminding herself. But it didn't feel like that, sitting in this upholstered car, the windows down, the sun blasting in. Alexander was a bit of a wanker, but he looked good in that suit, and she felt like flirting with him. She stretched her legs out, her gaze going down her shin bone to the red-painted toenails, jutting out her strappy flat summer shoes. The impression that Alexander's eyes had made the same journey beset her, but as she turned quickly, they were firmly on the road.

— This is a very, very sad sight, he frowned, as they drove up West Granton Road. They pulled up outside the big, blue gasworks tower, and as they stepped out of the car, Alison saw the squad of men chopping away at a tree with cutting equipment, like a moving version of the slide Alexander had shown earlier.

— This one was exhibiting signs of infestation, he said, squinting in the sun, pointing out another stricken tree, which men were busy digging out. Then his arm swept over to a mini-forest on the other side of the gasworks tower. — These guys are still healthy. Well, for the time being. This really is the front line.

I want you up me, Alison thought to herself, first just as an intoxicated subversive and vaguely malicious impulse. Then the growing kernel of lust, which seemed to flare up after she'd allowed herself that trangressive notion, both surprised and excited her, as they stepped off the tarmac onto the grass.

Along this stretch of foreshore, reclaimed from the river, two chopped trees were being hauled away to join some others in a pile. Although it was hot, the ground was growing mushier and Alison felt a cold, wet squelching in her feet. They moved close to a man two-handedly chucking splashes of petrol from a large rectangular can over the ruined trees. He was about to set them alight when Alexander shouted, — Wait!

The man looked up at him with a hostile frown. A second, authoritative-looking guy, with close-cropped black hair and thickset features, whom Alison assumed was the supervisor, stole menacingly over and growled, — Jocky, git these fuckin things burnt, glaring at Alexander in challenge, his jaw thrust out.

Alexander shot out what he hoped would be a disarming hand. — You must be Jimmy Knox. We've spoken on the phone. Alexander Birch, Dutch Elm Disease Control Unit.

— Aw . . . right, Jimmy Knox responded without a hint of deference, only taking the proffered hand with some reluctance. — Well, we've goat tae get these bastards burnt before the fuckin beetles in them git

93

airborne. Then wir aw fucked, and he looked at Alison, who had raised her hand to shield her eyes from the sun, adding, — pardon ma French, doll.

— Of course, Jimmy, I just wanted to show Ms Lozinska . . . Alison here . . . Alexander ushered Alison close, and she stepped gingerly, unable to avoid sinking into another patch of wet turf. — Alison, Jimmy Knox. He and his guys are doing great work here at the coalface, and I don't want to hold them back, he shook his head emphatically, — but I must show you the top of this tree. Please bear with us one second, he urged the bemused-looking foreman. — Look at this bark, and he bent over and grabbed a yellow handful of tree. — Rotten. Come closer, he implored Alison. — Look. All rotten, he declared again, his eyes misting.

Alison didn't really want to get closer, but felt duty-bound to comply. As her right foot sank into some mud, she stumbled and almost fell, correcting herself, but kicking over the petrol can. Jimmy let out a semi-audible curse and Alexander jumped forward as it splashed against his back trouser leg. – It's okay, he cooed as one of the men picked up the can, and planted it firmly into the soggy ground. At Alexander's prompting, Alison's hand reluctantly sank into the spongy bark, experiencing the same sensation as her feet in the sodden grass.

They stepped back to let the man ignite the trees. There didn't seem to be much moisture in them, as the branches went up quickly, and the bark caught, sending a twisting curl of black smoke into the air. Alison watched the burn and crackle of the fire and was mesmerised by it. She was aware of Alexander, standing close to her, as the waves of heat flickered across her face. She could have stayed there forever, even though her feet were cold and submerging further into the soggy ground.

She heard Alexander stage-clear his throat, breaking the fire's spell, and and they said their goodbyes to the crew. As they turned to leave, Alison could hear derisive laughter from Jimmy Knox and some of the men. She looked to Alexander, but if he had registered it, he evidently wasn't bothered. She found it strange to be cross on his behalf, and also annoyed at him.

— These guys are all pretty pissed off, Alexander remarked, as they approached the car. — They were all taken on from the long-term unemployed register through the Manpower Services Commission's Community Enterprise Programme. Now the government are changing the rules and making all the jobs part-time, on the reasoning that you can take twice as many people off the employment roll for the same costs. He looked at the groups of workmen. — Still doesn't change the fact that there isn't enough work to go round. Now these guys will have to either accept part-time wages or go back on the dole.

Alison nodded, thinking about a report in the evening paper, which noted that the Lothian Health Board had been forced to increase the waiting time between screenings for cancer patients in remission, due to central government funding cutbacks. It had arrested her, an article she would have previously passed over as mundane nonsense, put there to fill a local rag.

— I wonder where it's all going to end up. Her boss shook his head as they climbed back into the Volvo. Alexander prodded his keys into the ignition, but rather than start up the car, seemed to think of something. He hastily turned to her, making strong eye contact. — Listen, what are you up to now? I mean, later?

— Nothing . . . how? She heard herself blowing out the women's poetry group. For what? Why? She didn't want to go home, to deal with the dark messages that would litter her answerphone. It was important to stay out.

— There's a barbecue on at my mother's place in Corstorphine. It's her sixtieth birthday. It'll be dull beyond words, but we don't need to stay, just pop our heads in. I fancy dumping the car and getting a couple of beers. I don't mind admitting I was a little jealous of you and Stuart with that vino, he smiled, eyes sparkling.

— Sure, why not, she replied in fake breeziness, actually wanting to listen to Alexander talk about trees a little longer. And all the time she was aware that the day, whatever it had been, had now become something else.

They headed into town and out past Tollcross where Alison thought about Johnny. How his eyes had glazed over and his mouth shrunk to a tight slit when she'd rebuffed his advances. Like he'd absented himself from his own body and she'd had to shout him back inside. On Dalry Road, Alexander suddenly braked, and pulled up. — That's my brother, he said, and she looked over and saw a shorter version of him, also suited, swagger jauntily into what looked like a run-down pub. — He's certainly slumming it, Alexander read her mind. — Let's go in and say hello. I can leave the car here and we can all cab it out to Corstorphine together.

The Dalry Road pub was a standard working men's dive bar, similar to many that straddled Leith Walk. Alison felt she'd been undressed a dozen times during the short walk from door to bar. Alexander, shifting uncomfortably in his suit, glanced into an alcove at the back of the pub, where his brother, Russell, sat with a man dressed in overalls.

95

Michael Taylor was still and silent as he looked at Russell Birch. His stare was hard. It seemed to Alison that the two men had been arguing.

— Hi. Mind if we join you? Alexander tentatively asked, picking up the vibe.

Russell's eyes popped, first registering the shock at seeing his brother, then looking piercingly at Alison. — Mike . . . eh, my brother. He briefly looked at his perplexed drinking companion, before turning back to Alexander. — Be my guest. So, he asked, pulling up a chair, — how's the forestry business?

— I've moved from the Commission to the District Council, Alexander said, sitting down and sliding over another stool for Alison.

— I heard. How's that working out? Russell asked. Alison was aware that he was checking out her legs and sat down with care, smoothing her skirt across her thighs.

— The job's good, but this Dutch elm catastrophe is killing us. What about the pharmaceutical business?

— Booming. Everybody wants something for the pain, Russell smiled, turning to the man beside him. — This is Michael, he's . . . Russell hesitated, the word 'colleague' seemed to play on his lips before he looked to the boiler suit, — he works beside me.

— Ditto Alison here, Alexander responded. — You heading to the old girl's?

— Yeah. Just going. He shook his pint glass.

— Driving?

— No.

— Let's have another and get a cab, Alexander said, pointing at Michael's drink. — Lager?

Michael shook his head. — Not for me, thanks. I have to go. He got up, leaving about a quarter of his pint. — Russell, I'll see you later.

Alexander watched him leave in mild bafflement, then went up to get a round of drinks.

— So what's my brother like to work with? Russell asked Alison when her boss was out of earshot.

— Aye . . . it's good, she said awkwardly, — it's just my first day but.

On Alexander's return, the brothers began catching up and Alison felt herself drifting out of the conversation. She watched a skinny young guy with red hair come into the bar. For a split second she thought it was Mark Renton, but it was just another product of that white-skinned ginger factory they had somewhere in Scotland.

She'd never quite known what to make of Mark. He was okay now, but he'd been a cruel little bastard back at primary. She remembered that nickname he'd casually given her: *the Jewess*, which had made her self-conscious about her nose. It was strange to think of him now at university, and Kelly probably heading there too. Alison looked at the successful Birch brothers, tried to contemplate what they had that she didn't. She'd always been good at school, even if she had fucked up her Highers. That had been when her mother was first diagnosed. But she could retake them. If only she could concentrate. It seemed that gift of staying power had been taken away from her: that crippling loss of cerebral stamina. Life now seemed a constant quest for the next fleeting distraction. She wondered if that focus would ever return.

The sour miniatures of cooking wine the grotty pub sold were almost undrinkable after the quality lunchtime tipple in the wine bar, and Alison was relieved to be in the back of the taxicab with the Birch brothers. It dawned on her she was with two men she didn't really know, yet she was heading for their mother's birthday party. And they seemed so competitive with each other. — You stink, Russell gracelessly said to Alexander.

— Spilled some petrol down my leg at work. I'll get cleaned up properly at Mum's.

They reached Corstorphine, and a prodigious, red sandstone villa. Its enormous gravel driveway was already full of cars, with more parked outside on the street. When they got round to the back garden, a large space with a stone perimeter wall and established bushes, trees and flower beds, people had assembled awkwardly on the patio and lawn in small groups. Alexander and Russell's father, a weary-eyed man with grey hair and loose folds of skin hanging around his face and neck, stood barbecuing sausages, burgers, chicken parts and steaks.

As Russell circulated among the clusters of neighbours, relatives and friends, Alexander introduced Alison to his father, Bertie, who responded with perfunctory manners. Leaving him to his task, Alexander explained that his dad was fifteen years older than his mother. Alison discerned an isolated old man, work contacts frayed, a busy Rotary-Club-and-coffee-mornings wife off involved in her own activities, preoccupied children hitting the hectic self-absorption of middle age, with elderly golfing partners dead or dying. His eyes, shifty and flinty, seemed to indicate a spirit looking to escape the ponderous residue of its body.

Bored by the crowd, Alison instead enjoyed the assortment of kids running around a paddling pool, growing increasingly feral in each other's company. Of the adults assembled, one couple stood out. A full-mouthed woman with ineptly dyed blonde hair threw her head back in raucous laughter at something said by her companion: a big, muscular, shaven-headed man in a badly fitting suit. Then her face froze in silence as she punched him squarely in the chest, before breaking up into hysterics again.

Bringing her over a glass of wine, Alexander saw where Alison's gaze was, and introduced her to the blonde, who was his sister, Kristen. — Nice tae meet you, she grinned. — This is Skuzzy, Kristen announced, turning to Alexander. — You've no met Skuzzy, eh no?

— No. Alexander warily shook the man's hand.

— Our Alexander's in *horticulture*, she said, making a face.

— Well, not exactly –

— Ye can take a whore tae culture, but ye cannae make her read a book, Alison said, then added, — That was Dorothy Parker that said that.

Kristen gave her a bamboozled look for a second, then a high cackle flared from her, as she turned to Alexander, — I like her! Good tae see ye wi a lassie wi a sense of humour for a change!

— Alison works beside . . . he began in protest, but Kristen was already running down his absent wife, as their mother arrived, nodding curtly in pucker-mouth acknowledgement at Alison, as she pulled Alexander aside.

In Rena Birch, Alison saw a hawk-faced woman with bulging eyes, trained with some potency on her eldest son. — You bring a young girl to my birthday party when your wife is at home with your children, broken-hearted! What kind of a man are you?! I've had Tanya on the phone, and the children, begging for their daddy to come home, and you bring along a drunken – her eyes swivelled to Alison, — *young woman* to my party . . .

— Ah'm no, Alison protested, then immediately had to put hand to mouth in order to silence a hiccup.

— . . . instead of my grandchildren, Rena barked at her son. — How does it look, Alexander?!

Alexander responded with a louche shrug. — I couldn't give a toss how it looks. He glanced at Alison, who realised she'd taken a backward step towards Kristen, his gesture conveying exasperation and mild apology. — Firstly, Alison's a colleague. Secondly, Tanya kicked *me* out of the house. It was her idea that I leave, in order to, and Alison felt herself cringe as Alexander made a quotes sign in the air with his fingers, — give her space to sort things out. So I did. Now I'm supposed to be at her beck and call? Not a chance. She said a lot of hurtful things about wanting me out of her life. Well, be careful about what you wish for, cause that's exactly where I am. And I'll tell you something right now, for you to tell her, if you so wish: I'm in no hurry to go back into it, because I'm having the time of my fucking life!

— You have *child*ren! Rena cawed.

Alison, her arms folded, glass in her hand, was starting to enjoy herself. She smiled as Kristen ranted on to her, though she strained to listen to her boss face his mother's scorn.

— Ken what he sais tae me? Kristen was asking Alison, while shooting a malevolent gaze in the direction of another crusty-looking relative. Perhaps it was her mother's brother. — He goes, 'What do you do?' Ah felt like sayin back tae him, 'What? What d'ye mean, what dae ah do? Ah make love. Ah watch telly. Ah go for a drink.' How dae people eywis huv tae assume that when they ask that, that it hus tae mean *a career*?

Alison shifted her gaze to the barbecue, watching the flames rise and lick at the grease around the sizzling sausages. Enjoying the frown of concentration on Bertie's face, as he loaded chicken breasts onto the grill with his tongs. Though her senses were pleasantly dulled, she was aware that Alexander was raising his voice, cognisant of those assured, workplace tones. — And you think it's better for my children to live in one house with two parents who hate each other, or live in two normal households with sane people?

As Bertie Birch turned his bangers, the flames slithering around the hissing, spitting meat, Alison sensed he was quietly savouring the public spat between his wife and eldest son. For him, Kristen's lowlife suitors and relentless downward mobility, Russell's fatuous but wounded demeanour, and Alexander's ecological arrogance had probably come to embody exotic, mystical qualities.

Even Kristen had fallen silent, now also engrossed in the swelling disputation, inching closer, compelling Alison to follow suit, as Rena raised her voice shrilly: — So this is really about me and your father, is it? Well, have the spine to say it! Poor little you; the Stewart's Melville fees we could barely afford, the summer camps in Bavaria and Oregon to look at your precious trees –

A high shriek suddenly erupted from Alexander. It alarmed everyone. It seemed to have no context, even within the growing storm of his argument with Rena. To Alison, it looked as if he was having some kind of seizure; his hands started flailing wildly in the air and he ran, stumbling into his father and the barbecue. Just as she realised that Alexander had been stung or was at least being pursued by a bee or a wasp, the next thing Alison saw was a sheet of flame flashing in ignition up the back of her boss's legs.

People froze in the gaping horror of disbelief as Alexander ineffectually flapped at his blazing trousers. Russell reacted first, dragging his brother over to the paddling pool, which Alexander fell gratefully into, rolling in a way that reminded Alison of a child at the beach. He sat up in the water, gasping, a black, charred patch visible up the back of his jacket. As if suddenly realising where he was, he quickly stood up, and stepped out of the rubber pool, in mortification rather than shock. He resisted all attempts to call an ambulance. — I'm fine, he asserted, and though his suit was ruined, he miraculously seemed not to have suffered any significant burns.

— I'm going home to change, he said, shaking off the storm of fuss around him. He made his point by stiffly marching his soaked, blackened legs and arse outside. His mother was now arguing with Kristen, and Alison could hear Skuzzy saying, — Leave it, it jist causes arguments, repeatedly, as if on a demented loop. Heading out after Alexander, she saw him striding down the street. She had to run to catch up with him, calling his name as she drew closer. He stopped, evidently embarrassed to see her approaching.

— I'm really sorry, that was my fault, she said, — it was the petrol n that.

— It's okay, it was an accident. It was all down to my own clumsy panicking . . . the wasp . . . a double accident. He suddenly laughed, and she found herself joining in.

When that moment passed, he said forlornly, — I'm really sorry I brought you to such a scene.

Alison immediately thought of her own family, where so much had been left unsaid since her mother's illness. The tension was often insufferable. At least here everything seemed out in the open. — It was kind of exciting, she confessed, then, mindful of his distress, raised her hand to her mouth.

Alexander shook his head. — I don't like bees and wasps. That's why I was trying to stay beside the barbecue, for the smoke. I was stung as a kid and nearly died, you see.

Alison didn't understand how anybody could nearly die from a bee sting, but felt compelled to make the appropriately jolted reaction.

— Yes, it turned out I had a severe allergy and went into anaphylactic shock, he explained, and in response to her nonplussed look, added, — I fainted and they slung me in an ambulance. My blood pressure had dropped dangerously, and I went into a coma for a couple of days.

— God! Nae wonder ye were scared.

—Yes, I feel such a wimp, making a scene like that over an insect, but I'd rather risk being burnt than —

— Shush, Alison said, stepping forward and kissing this still-smouldering man in the suburban street.

Falling

InterRail

Ah first met Fiona Conyers in the economic history seminar. A stand-ard teaching room; small, wi a U-shaped range ay tables and white-board along one waw. The felt pens never worked; it was the one thing that bugged the lecturer, Noel, an otherwise phlegmatic gadge, ubiquitously clad in a scuffed black leather jaykit. There wis aboot a dozen ay us in the group. Only four were chatty: me, Fiona, a tall, aulder boy fae Sierra Leone called Adu, and a plumpish, sweet-faced Iranian lassie, Roya. The other eight were beyond mute: socially retarded tae the point ay being terrified ay gettin asked *anything*.

Fiona wis confrontational wi Noel, challengin every orthodoxy, but in a cool way, no strident like a lot ay the politicos. Her accent was educated Geordie, which became thicker as we grew closer. Like ma ain Edinburgh yin, ah suppose. Ah wis instantly attracted tae her. No only was she gor-geous, but she had a voice. Maist lassies ah'd been wi back hame were silent, wily and formless, precisely, ah realised, because that's exactly how ah wis wi them. But nowt happened wi Fiona and me — ah've eywis been shite at kennin if a bird fancies us. Ah thoat her mate, Joanne Dunsmuir, fae my English lit class last year, wis game; but ah wisnae interested in her. She wis a nosy Weedgie bird, no proper Weedgie, but fae somewhere near thaire. Unlike a lot ay Edinburgh punters who disdain them as tramps, ah've nowt against Soapdodgers, cause ay ma faither being yin. But thaire wis a fussy, domineering air aboot Joanne that ah disliked. The type ay lassie who went tae uni tae look for a felly she could boss aboot forever.

Back hame ah was a waster; frivolous and fucked-up, always looking for some sort ay adventure. Getting wasted, screwin hooses, trying tae screw lassies. Here ah wis the opposite. Why not? It made perfect sense tae me. Why go away, jist tae dae the same shite that ye dae at hame? Tae be the very same person? Ma reasoning is ah'm young; ah want tae learn, tae add tae masel. At uni ah'm deadly serious, and most of all, hard-working and disciplined. Not because ah wanted tae 'get on'. As far as ah was concerned ah already was *on*. Sitting in the brightly lit library, sur-rounded by books, in total silence, that was ma personal zenith. Nothing in the world made me feel better. So ah studied hard: ah wisnae at Aberdeen tae make friends. Maist weekends in first year, ah headed back tae Edinburgh for the fitba or tae go tae gigs or clubs wi ma mates or my on–off girlfriend, Hazel. But ah made one good pal, Paul Bisset, an Aberdonian gadge. 'Bisto' wis a workin-class boy fae Torry, quite short but stocky, white-blond hair, looked like he worked on a farm even though he was a townie. He ran wi the thug element at A'deen, lived at hame wi his ma and, like me, put in a proper shift workwise. Another bond was that we'd both had proper jobs (he was a printer) and kent how shite that wis, and appreciated bein at uni mair than the punters who came straight fi sixth year at school or some poxy college.

Bisto and me had planned a trip tae Istanbul. Ah'd eywis wanted tae travel. Ah'd only been abroad twice, tae Amsterdam wi the boys for some teenage japes, and before that tae Spain, for a family holiday. That wis barry; it wis just me, Ma, Dad and Billy, cause ma Auntie Alice wis lookin eftir spazzy Wee Davie. Dad wis happy, but Ma worried aboot Wee Davie, and spent a fortune phonin hame. Ah lapped it up, it wis the best holiday we'd had, nae freak tae embarrass Billy n me.

When Fiona and Joanne heard aboot our proposed trip, they jist sortay invited themselves along. First it was a joke, then it became mair serious. Even when phone numbers were exchanged and concrete plans made, Bisto n me were still like: aye, well, we're gaunny believe it when they show up.

Eftir the final class oan the last day ay the term, Fiona, Joanne n Bisto wanted tae get pished in the students' union. Ah wis game, but first ah hud tae see the English lit boy, Parker. The cunt had gied us 68 per cent for ma essay oan F. Scott Fitzgerald. That wis nae fuckin use tae me: it was the first time ah'd dropped under 70 per cent for a marked assignment, n ah wisnae happy. Ah mind ay Joanne sayin, — You're mental, Mark, 68 per cent is goooood!

Fuck good; ah'd grafted, and set fuckin standards. Ah wanted a first-class, joint honours degree in History and Literature; well, history, having dropped the literature component this year. Analysing novels meant ripping oot their soul and it destroyed my enjoyment of them. Ah couldnae allow masel tae be trained tae think that way. Only by refusing tae study literature was ah able tae maintain ma passion for it. Ah was also thinking about changing my major fae history tae economics. But ah usually topped every class, only African Adu rivalled me in some, him and Lu Chen, this scarily focused Chinese lassie. So ah tore off, aw ready tae dae battle wi the tweedy Parker, a snotty wee gerbil in a bow tie whae acted like he wis an Oxford don or something. He'd insisted in his notes back that this wis ma weakest essay, that ah'd misunderstood F. Scott's life and work, and the character ay Dick Diver in *Tender Is the Night*.

So when ah got there this cunt's sittin back in his padded chair. His wee office is stowed wi books and papers. It had shelves aw the way up tae the ceilin and a pair ay ladders tae get at the high-stacked dusty auld books. Aw they books, crammed intae this cosy wee hidey-hole. And he had one ay they Rolodex things for aw his contacts, which ah pretend tae hate but secretly think is as cool as fuck. Ah envied the bastard huvin this space; somewhere ye could just lock yourself in, read and ponder. The realisation that ah kent this cunt and the likes ay Frank Begbie, Matty Connell and Spud Murphy astonished me. Parker cultivated that detached, slightly superior look, wi his gold-rimmed specs resting oan the bridge ay his neb, and when he deigned tae focus on ye, it wis in that interrogative polis wey, like ye'd done something wrong. So ah put ma case forward, but he wis unrepentant. — You're missing a key element, Mark, he goes, — which I must confess somewhat surprises me.

— What element? ah said, casting my eye oan what looked like a really auld copy ay *Jane Eyre*, oan the shelving tae the side ay the windae.

— Read the book again, the critical essays, and also the supplementary biog of F. Scott, he offered, standing up in response tae some cunt's tap oan the door. — Now, if you'll excuse me . . .

As he turned his back and went tae investigate, ah took ma chance n reached ower, swiftly slippin the copy ay *Jane Eyre* intae ma holdall. He ushered in some postgrad twat, dismissing me in the same extended sweep ay his airm. Ah left his office bilious, but buzzed at having taxed the bourgeois cheat oot ay his vintage wares. Hittin the bar, ah told Fiona, Joanne, Bisto and some others aboot the conversation, omitting ma virtuous retaliation through the act ay 'resource reallocation' as Sick Boy and me call theft, lest they misinterpreted it. — Wants us tae read it again, cheeky bastard, ah moaned, raisin the lifeless lager tae ma lips.

— You'll be able ter read it on the trains in Europe, Fiona said wi a cool smile, takin a heart-stopping drag on her Marlboro, as Joanne giggled, making me mair convinced than ever that they were takin the pish. When ah goat back tae Edinburgh, however, Bisto called tae say they were definitely coming, they'd bought the InterRail tickets. Ah telt him ah'd believe it when ah saw it.

And fuck me, when the day came roond, ah did a double take when ah first clocked Joanne at Waverley Station, sitting in the big hall. She was reading *Life & Times of Michael K* by J. M. Coetzee, inevitably cause it had won some poxy prize and people like her, despite their free-thinker affectations, would eywis need tae be telt what tae read. We boarded the slick InterCity in an uncomfortable mutual antipathy; like me she wis probably wondering how the fuck we were gaunny stand each other's proximity for four weeks. Thankfully, Bisto was waiting on the train, having got oan at Aberdeen, and he had a cairry-oot. We drank a beer or two each en route tae Newcastle, me electrified at the prospect of seeing Fiona, then forcing nonchalance when ah spied her at the platform, getting oan the train. Joanne suddenly screamin in that Weedgie voice, — Fiona, wur heee-ur!

Fiona looking so gorgeous, rubbing her tongue in concentration against her small, even front teeth, as she slung her bag oan the luggage rack and came towards us. Her presence and series ay movements casually ravaged everything inside us. — Hi, she said directly tae me, and ah'm sure ma skin went as rid as ma fuckin hair or the Aberdeen fitba strip Bisto wis wearin, wi the white pinstripes and 1983 ECWC crest. Aw ah could dae was tae coolly raise a can in a stagey toast, when ma insides were like chopped liver. She had on a black leather jacket turned up at the collar, and removed it tae display a *Gang of Four* T-shirt, while sweeping her hair back. Ah'd never fancied anybody so much in ma life.

We were on the road: London–Paris–Berlin–Istanbul.

Whaire else but Paris? Sittin at this pavement cafe in the Latin Quarter drinking Pernods wi chunks ay ice. It was warm and heady and we were getting rapidly pished. There was a flirty, sexy vibe in the air. Fuck knows how, but a daft drinking game started up, where we passed these chunks ay ice mooth-tae-mooth tae each other. This precipitated the performance ay deep kisses; Joanne and Fiona, tae me n Bisto's open-moothed awe, then Joanne and me, and Bisto and Fiona as ah wept inside, then me and Bisto (we pushed stiff, closed mooths against each other, hamming it up), tae the cheers ay the lassies, then a quick bit ay musical chairs and ma heart poundin as me and Fiona looked at each other and in a suspended moment flashed a contract: *I'm yours, your mine,* before going at it. Eventually aware, wi the cheers turning tae groans, that the ice had melted, and it wisnae the only thing. Our faces stayed welded together as we ignored Bisto's jocularly nervy comments and the controlling Joanne's shrill protests. We'd gone and spoiled it aw for her. She wanted tae meet foreign boys, enjoy a splurge ay Continental cock before hooking some spotty bam at uni for life. Later on, Fiona even telt me she'd said, — This isnae how it was meant tae happen! Loved up, Fiona and me were an embarrassment tae Bisto and Joanne. They had nae interest in each other, but we were rubbing their faces in it, withoot meanin tae.

Like fuck.

Ah loved rubbin it in! It wis obvious that when we got back tae the hotel, near Gare du Nord, that we'd be sleeping thegither. It wis an Algerian grot-hole, but tae me the last word in sophistication. It was like livin wi a bird, but in Europe, which it was really. Growin up wi two brothers, a lassie's simple domestic proximity fascinated me. Ah marvelled at her oan the edge ay the bed, in the surprisingly smart towelling robe they provided, sitting on the frayed and threadbare candlewick bedspread. Stepping oot ay the robe and intae the bath and shaving her legs. No just brushing her teeth, but daein something called flossing, wi this twiney stuff. Sittin at the table in front ay the mirror, putting oan make-up or idly filing nails, her wet hair wrapped in a towel.

Ah even took Parker's advice and reread *Tender Is the Night*, fantasising about Mark Philip Renton and Fiona Jillian Conyers as a modern Dick and Nicole Diver, a bohemian couple travelling through Europe enjoying interesting adventures and making urbane observations oan the world at large. It was a big step up for me. My sex life had generally been a series ay bitter, sly and exceptionally swift copulations in stairs, family bedrooms or under grubby duvets in noisy squats. This wis pure decadence and it meant that poor Bisto and Joanne had to share the adjoining room wi its twin beds.

Then Berlin, and more of the same. Ah fuckin loved Berlin. There was this barry bit oan Line 6 gaun tae Friedrichstrasse, where the U-Bahn train went under the Waw, whizzin through a couple ay spooky abandoned stations on the Commie side that had been shut since partition, before re-emerging intae the western sector. Fiona and me sneaked away fae the others (we did that a lot) and got ower tae East Berlin proper, ah wis desperate tae see it. It wis much better than West: nae billboards disfiguring the beautiful auld buildings. A ginormous three-course lunch, fir thirty pence. A blow job in the park; clandestine spice added by the nearby presence ay armed guards. Almost missing the curfew, as we'd gone in through Friedrichstrasse and tried tae return via Checkpoint Charlie, clueless that we hud tae go back the same wey we'd gained entry.

Later, we sat in a cafe, drinking black coffee, as the sounds of the city – electric trains, car horns and people – buzzed around us, creating a strange but beautiful mood of relaxed excitement. Fiona's eyes twinkled and wonderment leaked from her. — When we wur in Noel's class, remember how white that room was?

— Aye, it always caught the light, and that blind was knackered.

— I mind one time when it was dazzling, it was in your eyes and you had your hand up to yer face n you were arguing wi Noel about the formation of capital in mercantile Europe.

— Eh . . . aye . . .

— I really wanted ter shag yer so badly . . .

Ah felt both elated and in despair at this revelation. — That wis six months ago . . . we could've been daein this for six fuckin months . . .

But we headed east with gusto, kite-aloft oan cheap wine and the buzz of our group. My heart was in a perpetual, turbulent riot, and Fiona's was the same. We constructed this ineffable, giddy universe of celebration around us, pulling everyone and everything in our paths into it; singing the Istanbul and Constantinople song in cheesy American accents on the trains that rolled us through Europe.

> *Why did Constantinople get di woiks?*
> *Ain't nobody's business but dem Toiks'.*

By night, on our return to the hotel, blitzed by the sheer intensity of our togetherness, we'd gratefully fall into each other's arms, coming explosively alive for another day's sublime finale. Her sumptuous massages ay ma lower back, loving fingertips palpating that maltreated vertebrae, kneading out the pain inflicted by the state. We made up nicknames for each other; she called me her Luxuriant Leith Laddie, as ah loved tae steep in a bath. As we crawled into Turkey, Bisto and Joanne eventually cracked and goat oaf wi each other. There wis a gallows aspect tae it aw; they didnae really vibe n wir pushed intae it by the circumstances.

Istanbul was barry, full ay menacing squads ay uptight bams whae patrolled around lookin like they'd never seen a lassie before; it was just like Leith. Ah kept Fiona within airm's reach. Wi ordered some mad stuff in a restaurant. The Aberdonian came out in Bisto when they put a plate ay *koc yumurtasi*, or ram's baws, in front ay us; the cunt didnae ken whether tae eat thum or stroke thum.

The wildest time was crossing the city ower the Bosphorus by boat tae Besiktas pier. A fierce, punishing early-afternoon sun had sneaked centre stage, oppressing and saturating through a heavy haze ay cloud. Ma Fred Perry stuck tae me like a second skin. We decided tae droap this acid oan the way back, which ah'd scored fae a boy in a nightclub the previous evening, basically tae avoid buying the skag he'd offered me, which had tempted the fuck out ay us. The trip hit us like a ton ay bricks oan the deck ay the boat. It got tae me that we were crossing *continents*, leaving Asia and heading for Europe. As soon as that awareness kicked in, the boat's narrow dimensions expanded beyond the range ay ma sight, which encompassed only Joanne. Ah couldnae see Bisto or Fiona, but she was attached tae me, ah could feel her, we were like a beast wi two heids. Her breath and blood pumping through us as if we were sharing veins, lungs and a heart. My life, past, present and future, seemed spread oot in a spatial panorama ower the extended deck; the bedroom in the Fort segueing intae the yin in the Housing Association gaff by the river, which suggested the Bosphorus, and ah turned back intae the East Terracing at Easter Road, then our Montgomery Street front room, which opened up into new vistas and nameless streets, which ah wis excited tae ken that some day ah'd walk doon . . .

— Will walk or have already walked in a previous life, ah whispered tae Fiona who was laughing loudly then saying repeatedly, — Fleegle, Bingo, Drooper and Snork.

Ah minded telling her that my ma called me, Dad, Billy and Wee Davie that, eftir the Banana Splits oan telly. *Makin up a mess of fun*, we thought in unison, as we regarded, now fae a single eye, Joanne having a shitey trip, and pleading constantly, — Ah'm tired ay this, when's it gaunny stoap? When's it gaunny stoap?

Ma one, sudden overwhelming insight that hit me like a baseball bat: *Parker was right*, as several books, flapping like birds, floated in front ay ma vision, mocking *trompe l'oeils* announcing his victory. — Ah get it aw now, ah conceded tae masel, my airm roond Fiona, as Bisto comforted Joanne wi 'fit likes' while the sea took oan the colour and texture ay a giant Hibs strip blowing in the wind, — ah understand how it's aw fucked.

Fiona laughed again, an oddly mechanical sound like some device jamming, as ah pushed her hair tae the side and whispered, — Tender is the night, intae her ear, then locked ma numb lips oantae hers. The acid only complemented my love; lawless, winged, unconfined, crumbling the narrow barriers of my mind.

— When's it gaunny stoap? Joanne kept moaning. — Ah dinnae like this any mair. Ah wahnt it tae *stoap*. When's it gaunny *stoap*?

A gadge wi fantastic ink-black hair wi vivid blond tips, spiked up like an exotic Barrier Reef sea anemone, approached us. He wore mirror-lens shades that ah saw the Fiona-and-Mark Monster reflected back in. It had two zany heads wi protruding tongues, coming fae one body. The gadgie pointed tae the pier that had suddenly materialised at the side ay the now empty deck. — Are you not going to get off the boat, my friends?

Wi the trepidation ay pirates condemned tae walk the plank, we staggered,

111

rubber-legged, doon the gangway tae dry land. — Fuckin . . . fuckin . . . amazin trip, min . . . Bisto gasped at me.

— No bad, ah conceded.

— A mezzur furn . . . Fiona purred.

— When's it gaunny *stow-oh-ohp* . . . ? Joanne bleated.

The answer was, like aw good things: too fucking soon. It was time tae return; our joyful sorrow ricocheting through the railway compartments across Europe as we headed back tae London town, fill ay song. 'Istanbul and Constantinople', 'The Northern Lights of Old Aberdeen', 'I Belong to Glasgow'. (Delivered with surprising uninhibited gusto and not a little soul fae Joanne, who explained there was nae song for Paisley.) Ah wished there was yin for Leith, even Edinburgh would've done. But best of all, Fiona's cheerful version ay 'Blaydon Races'.

The sickening downer as the train crept closer tae hame; Fiona in my airms, heavy bombs ay tears rolling down her cheeks at Newcastle Station. Kissing her oily wee forehead. Feeling in utter despair when she got off the train, wanting tae take her back hame wi us. But no tae a gaff wi Sick Boy in it, and never tae the parental hoose. Instead saying, as the red-faced cunt blew his whistle, — It's only two weeks tae uni! Ah'll come doon tae Newcastle next weekend!

We mouthed 'I love you' at each other like two goldfish through glass as the train separated us wi a slam ay its doors, then implacably removed me fae her, splittin us intae our separate daft wee countries.

— Aw, love's young dream. Joanne's bottom lip curled oot in couthy passive-aggressive bitterness as we headed north, a depleted trio. Then Joanne and me alighting at Edinburgh, leaving Bisto on his tod tae Sheepland. About tae issue her a cool goodbye salute at Waverley, but her lookin distressed and saying tae us, — Ah don't wahnt everybody saying that Paul and me are gaun oot!

Ah departed wi a non-committal smile, and my holdall full ay minging clathes. Actually no . . . it didnae quite happen that wey, but that's another story.

Is it? Be fucking honest.

Be fucking . . .

Enough.

Instead ay walking tae Montgomery Street, ah picked up an *NME* at the newsagent's. It always made us think, wi some guilt, ay Hazel. Then ah jumped on a 22 bus tae get doon tae the old girl's and dump off some washing. We didnae have a machine in Monty Street, and unlike Mrs Curran, ah hud nae desire tae take it up the Bendix.

When ah got hame, ah was so submerged in my own thoughts, it took us a while tae register that my mother was in tears. She sat doon oan the couch and let her heid faw intae her hands. Her thin shoodirs started shakin wi sobs. Ah knew. Instantly. But ah hud tae ask. — What's wrong, Ma? What is it?

Ah looked tae Billy, sitting at the table. He gied us an enervated glance and said, — Wee Davie died in hoaspital. The night before last.

Ah felt a violent, jarring shock, at the finality ay it. The mantra *it's over* playing in ma heid. *A mess of fun. Lots of it for everyone.* Snorky's gone, from my ma's Banana Splits, the silent yin. Fleegle the Hun, Billy Bingo and me, dear, dear Drooper, the cool but slightly socially inept lion, are aw still here. Ah felt a paralysis ay emotion as time stretched out. A pervading numbness was setting in, like a dentist's anaesthetic, spreading through ma body. Then my faither emerging fae the kitchen: me, my ma and Billy aw suddenly looking up like a teacher had disturbed us daein something bad. Baith parents turning tae me, then tae Billy, then me again. Me just noddin back in slow acknowledgement, wi nothing tae say tae them. Never, ever having anything tae say tae them.

Misery Loves Bedfellows

I've been helping my mother and sisters move intae their new South Side home in Rankellior Street, and, in the absence of the bold Marco Polo (and for all his substantial flaws, he's the only cunt roond here on the same wavelength as me), hanging out at Janey's place, hoping tae provide a bit ay support tae her and the kids. And also tae avoid the increasingly clingy Marianne. She told me that her friend April and some radge called Jim were now 'going steady', looking at me wi hopeful, needy eyes as she delivered this completely superfluous information. *Going steady.* A phrase guaranteed tae make ye run for the fucking hills!

So on this dull, dead, supposedly late-summer teatime, ah've arranged to take Janey tae see ma Uncle Benny at the Dockers' Club. Ah find her mired in her perpetual daze, drinking heavily, a fuck-off glass of cheap red vino in front ay her. It's almost like she feels closer tae Coke this way. Her face looks haggard under a feather cut which needs a stylist's loving touch, and her eyes are dull and faraway, as she sits in faded grey tracky bottoms and a yellow T-shirt wi plastic lettering showing some bingo numbers around a bold slogan stating: *I had the Full House at Caister Sands.*

Janey has every reason tae be miserable. Officialdom has excelled in what it's traditionally good at in Britain: screwing the lower orders. They closed ranks very fucking sharpish; the family wanted a murder conviction for Dickson, but that was quickly blown oot ay the water, and now he's no even been done for manslaughter! The pathologist's report had noted severe cranial injuries sustained in a fall as the likely cause ay death. They skated ower the wounds oan Coke's face, focusing instead on his level ay intoxication. So Dickhead will be tried for serious assault, which carries a maximum sentence of two years (out in twelve months) if he's found guilty.

With an offhand pull ay her cigarette, Janey drops a fucking bombshell on me, telling me that Maria has gone wi Grant tae her brother's in Nottingham. — The kids are taking it awfay bad. Grant's in a daze and Maria's just gone bloody crazy! Keeps talking aboot killin Dickson. Ah hud tae git her away.

That wee beauty was in Simone's fucking sights and now this daft auld hag has gone and ruined everything . . .

— Ye can understand her point ay view, I say, lamenting her absence so deeply ah feel like a wound has been carved right intae ma fucking chest.

— Will ye come tae court wi me next week? Janey begs, eyes big and expectant.

Objection! Defence is emotionally blackmailing the witness!

Objection overruled.

— Of course I will.

Her big concern now is that she'll lose Coke's medical pension. Ah've checked it out with Benny, my dad's older and better brother, an auld TGWU stalwart. Janey vanishes intae the bedroom and returns transformed; her features picked out by make-up as she wears a knee-length gold-and-black dress wi dark nylons, which I guess are tights but I'll think ay as stockings. Impact-wise, it's pretty devastating. I can't believe I'm getting this horny vibe off an old baboon! Ah feel like we're on a date, as we head down tae the architectural mishmash of Victoriana and seventies prefab that is the Leith Dockers' Club, a building which encapsulates the area perfectly.

If my father exudes a repellent roguishness fae every pore, Benny is the polar opposite. He looks fifteen years younger than he is and drinks nothing stronger than Lothian's tap water. He's made it his life's work representing others and he takes his role very seriously. — Sorry for your loss, hen, he says. Then, over pints ay Tennent's lager for us and H_2O for him, he expounds the gist ay the situ. Apparently, the Forth Port Authority rules stipulate that any pensions paid get reassessed when the relevant party passes away, not automatically passed on to the next of kin or the dependants. This was recently changed; every cunt is jumping on the Thatcherite cost-cutting bandwagon, particularly when applied tae ripping off the proles. It means that Janey'll still get something, but it'll be reduced tae almost zilch.

She takes this latest defeat on the chin and gracefully thanks a sombre Benny. Ah take her back up tae the flat and we're soon settled doon on the pish, her in the couch, where she kicks off her shoes, me in the armchair opposite. When the vino's tanned, we start drinking neat Grouse whisky. There's a heavy, close atmosphere in the room, as the darkness falls in around us.

Janey's silence is a little disconcerting, but ah'm enjoying the warm glow ay the whisky and the burn it leaves in my throat and chest. — Dinnae tell them he's gone, ah suggest tae her, basically tae put some sound intae the eerie void. — That's my advice, they willnae ken if nae cunt tells them.

— But it's fraud, she says, briefly alarmed, her eyes slightly widening. She reaches over and clicks on a small table lamp.

— What *is* fraud, but? I ask, enjoying her animation within the cocoon of golden-brown light, as ah warm tae ma theme. — Let's get away from state control, and talk fuckin *morality* here. Look at what cunts like Dickson get away wi. *That's* fucking fraud. Murdered a man and he's still doonstairs pullin fuckin pints like nowt's happened!

— Right enough. Fuck them, she spits in defiance, raising the glass tae her lips and taking a sip. — What's the worst they kin dae tae me now, anywey? She falls back intae a lament. — Ah'm no sayin Colin was a saint, Simon, ah'm no sayin that at aw. Ah mean, he could've been a better husband, a better faither . . . and she crosses her legs, smoothing doon the dress as it clings tae the static ay her nylons.

— He was a damn sight better than ma auld man.

This manifestly obvious news seems tae take her by surprise. — But he always seemed nice, your dad.

— Aw aye, ah scoff, he'd be nice tae *you*. A good-looking woman, he'll always be very, very nice tae, ah explain, watching her flush in spite ay herself. — It's his ain family he's no very nice tae.

— What dae ye mean?

Remembering that misery loves bedfellows, ah fix her a glum expression. — When ah wis a bairn he used tae take me out n leave me in the car wi Coke and crisps, while he saw tae his fancy women. Our secret wee messages, he used tae called them. As soon as ah sussed oot what he was up tae, he stopped taking me, in fact he lost interest in me aw thegither.

— Surely he wisnae . . . ah mean, he widnae huv done that tae a wee laddie . . .

— Aye, right. You dinnae ken the half ay it! I'll tell ye a wee story that sums up everything about him and our relationship. My faither's such a cunt that he once took back a watch ah bought him for Father's Day. The money was chorrie, aye, but that's beside the point. It was the fucking thought. But naw, the bastard went back tae Samuel's in St James's Centre wi the receipt ah had tae keep for guarantee purposes in case it fucked up.

— I never thought he'd dae anything like that . . .

— Aw aye, the shitebag went up there and even refused goods, insisted that he wanted the cash back, ah spell it oot, enjoying her puzzled but hostile reaction. She lifts the whisky tumbler tae her mouth, and scratches at an itch on her knee, lifting her dress on one side to show a thigh that has remained pleasingly muscular. I get that familiar twinge heralding the start ay a hard-on as ah take another sip ay Scotch. — N that ain't the half of it. Boasted tae me, and I lean forward, drilling my thumb intae my chest, — and ah was fifteen at the time, fifteen, for fuck's sake, ah shout wi a full-on, traumatised gape intae her eyes, — . . . that later on he went doon tae Danube Street for a decent hooker, then tae the Shore for a curry and a few lagers. Telt us he still had enough for a gam oaffay a scabby streetwalker later. 'Eywis get peckish eftir a ride n horny eftir a scran,' he fuckin laughed at me, patting his flabby gut. That was the cunt *trying to fucking bond*, ah shake ma heid in recall. — Ah think about that saint ay a woman he married and what any ay us did tae deserve him!

— But you're no like him, Janey says hopefully, as she crosses her legs again, and more and more I see her daughter in her, making me think: *How the fuck did Coke pull that?* — you take mair eftir yir ma. She's such a lovely woman. And your sisters are n aw.

— And I thank God for that every day ay ma life, I tell her, and glance at the oak-framed clock on the sideboard. — Right, ah should really be heading off.

This seems tae strike panic in Janey, as she hugs herself and looks around the cold, empty tomb of a flat. Her eyes enlarge and her mouth tightens in appeal. — Dinnae go, she half whispers.

— Ah have tae, I find masel pleading back in the same voice.

— Ah cannae be oan ma ain, Simon. No now.

I raise my brows, push myself out of the chair, and move over tae her. Looking deeply intae her wrecked eyes, ah take her hand and she rises and ah'm leading her intae the bedroom. Ah stop at the bottom ay the bed and whisper, — Are you sure you're awright with this?

— Aye, she says softly, kissing me on the lips, the scent ay spirits and baccy on her breath. Then she turns away from me, but only tae plead in a croaky voice, — Unzip us.

I watch the fastener pull apart under my tug, slicing the gold-and-black dress in two. She lets it fall, steps out of it, then sits on the bed, arching her body to pull off her tights and underpants, giving me a glimpse of a forest of bush, before slipping under the covers.

Ah pull off my gear and get under with her. Slide smoothly into her awaiting embrace. Her body's warm and a lot firmer than ah would have thought for a woman who must be *at least* thirty-five. She's shivering and her teeth are banging together, but I'm hard as fuck and ah ken ah'm gaunny be up her all night and that Coke and regrets will be kept at bay till the morning.

Funeral Pyre

The knocked-off pub mirror shows up the kitchen behind us tae its mankiest effect. Ah'd love tae gless the taunting pus ay the inscribed McEwan's Lager Cavalier. Nae wonder he's aw grins n toasts; getting people tae *pey dosh* tae drink that tepid, poisonous pish. Another erse-up wi that scabby black tie: ah yank it oaf for aboot the tenth time. — Shite!

Sick Boy's at ma shoodir, providing succour. He gets the tie right first go. — There we are, he coos, makin me feel aw baba biscuit-erse. — You should git some breakfast.

Eat something in this midden? No ta. — I'll git somethin at my ma's. There's nowt here.

— I made some lasagne. He points tae the oven.

— It's shite, ah tried some ay it last night. Ah did tae, eftir a quick drink wi a couple ay gadges fae Gillsland's turned intae a bit ay a sesh.

Sick Boy places his hands on his hips. — That was my mother's recipe, ya cheeky cunt, he pseudo-bellows, lightening things fir ma benefit.

— Ah've hud yir ma's lasagne, — and that shite in thaire, ah nod tae the oven, — is nowt like it. Ye obviously never follayed her recipe; for one thing lasagne isnae meant tae huv lumps ay tuna in it.

— I was making use ay the resources available. You get doon the Co-op once in a while, *then* you can critique the culinary skills of others.

Cheeky bastard him. Two words stick treacly in the noggin: rent and money. But fucked if ah kin be ersed arguin wi the cunt right now. — Right, ah'm offski. Ah reach fir ma jaykit, hingin oan a nail at the back ay the door.

— Okay, ah'll see ye at the cremmy at two o'clock, he goes, then suddenly steps forward and hugs me. — You okay?

— Course ah ah'm, ya radge, ah tell him.

He breks his grip, but lets his hands rest on ma shoodirs. — It'll kick in, ye know, the grief, he declares, dropping one hand. — But play the stoical Scot aw ye want. My advice though: the Italian way ay mourning is the best. Open up. Feel the burn inside. Let it oot. He flattens his other hand and gies us a couple ay affectionate gent*lish* slaps across the chops.

119

— Aye, right, ah say, then ah'm out the door.

Ah check the time and start heading doon the Walk. The sun's oot tae play as far as Pilrig, where some big manky clouds appear, tae muscle him fae the frame. Ah get tae Junction Street, narrowly escaping a summer soaking as it starts chuckin.

Ma and Dad are like zombies. Literally. Glazed eyes and bumpin intae things. Ah cannae believe thir still in shock aboot the demise ay somebody whaes death wis signposted since the day he wis born, n by every medical expert in the UK. Did they not understand the term 'short life expectancy'? Did they believe that by beating the fluid offay Wee Davie's lungs they could preserve him forever?

Now they've nane ay the tension ay listening for his breathing, nane ay the doof-doof-doof and the hack-hack-hack ay the postural drainage sessions, following which Wee Davie wid collapse intae exhausted sleep as his creaking lungs filled up wi air. Meanwhile, the rest ay us waited in nervous dread for it aw tae start up again. That's aw gone. Why are they no kind ay relieved?

It's gone *forever.*

Ah leave them holding white-knuckled oantae the worktops in the cramped, dull kitchen they seem perpetually stuck in. In the front room's light, the air is thick with cigarette smoke. Billy and his bird are ripping through them; nae Wee Davie, so nae need tae sit at the bedroom windae blowin the fumes ootside. Now we can *all* have our lungs decimated. My eyes sting and leak; it takes a few seconds fir them tae clear enough tae see Billy shoot me his 'you fuckin weirdo' look, making us conscious ay every step ah take. Ah feel like we've regressed about a decade.

You have the advantage of me, Tobacco Boy.

Sharon's a ride, in a trashy, chain-store boutique sort ay wey. She's got the tits, erse, blonde wedge cut and slender waist that pushes male buttons, everything apart fae the pins, which are a tad shortish n stumpy. An evaluating shrewdness in her eyes engenders speculation that she might be worth spraffin wi ootside ay Billy's stultifying proximity. She's havering oan aboot a lassie called Elspeth, n ah'm inclined tae hear mair cause it's probably Begbie's cute sister (thankfully she looks nothing like him), but the smoke and Billy's mean vibes have a throttling impact, squeezing oot valuable oxygen. A quote fae the Schopenhauer gadgie asserts itself, namely: almost all of our sorrows spring oot ay oor relations wi other people.

Did you not realise, Tobacco Boy, the detrimental power of your evil smoke, disguise it though you might, on the enfeebled lungs of your younger sibling?

120

Ah snatch the *NME* ah left oan the sideboard the other day. Mark E's ironic grin reminds us ay the Fall tape in ma room that ah'd made up for Hazel, who's sure tae be at the funeral. Ah decide ah'll bring it along, and ah'm aboot tae decamp tae that fusty auld den ay music and masturbation, when the phone explodes in a shrill ring, shattering every cunt's pianny-wire nerves. It's relentless, but naebody's movin.

Mein bruder Wilhelm, master ay the accusatory glare: — Is some cunt gaunny answer that fuckin phone?!

I sense your dilemma, Tobacco Boy. Answering the phone would mean having to speak into the mouthpiece, thus depriving yourself of a few precious seconds' inhalation of nicotine, which you so desperately crave!

— I'm sure it'll happen, ah declare, grinning at Sharon, — Ah mean, some day, likes, n ah'm rewarded wi the faintest ay smiles back.

— Dinnae start gittin fuckin wide, Billy threatens, — no the day!

This bam is big-time nippy, and ah'm guessing he's recollecting the time he caught me chugging Wee Davie off. A tough sell explainin tae them aw that it wis solely fir the poor wee cunt's ain benefit; ah certainly derived zero pleasure fae said act. You can operate fae the purest ay motives but some fuckers will eywis misconstrue it tae fit their ain twisted agenda. But ah ken the mood Bilbo's in, and tae be honest, ah'm a wee bit scaredy-cat. — It'll no be for me, ah protest.

We hear the phone being snatched up, my ma saying a few words, then joining us tae augment the dense smoke further wi her B&H. We could aw be cramped in this poky room and still play a passable game ay hide-n-seek. — Mark, it's fir you.

Billy's eyes narrow: annoyed and vindicated at the same time. The latter wins and, eftir hudin the stare for a second, we baith start tae laugh: loud, tension-releasing sniggers. Don't like that lairy cunt, never have; but tae ma extreme discomfit ah'm sometimes compelled tae remember that ah sort ay love him. However, this is Chez Renton; as soon as one cunt gets onside, so another is alienated. — What's fuckin funny? Ma screams. — Ah dinnae find anything funny!

That lingo will see you in hell, Mater. Another set ay Hail Marys chalked up tae some nonce in a frock later!

Ah upturn ma palms in surrender mode. — Ah'll git the phone, and ah head through tae the perennially draughty hall where we keep the blower, fixed tae the waw. — Hello?

— Mark, is that yur?

— Aye. Fi?

— How are yur, pet?

121

— No bad; aw the better for hearing your voice, but.

— Listen, Mark, I'm at the Waverley. Ah wannar come to your brother's funeral with yur.

First emotion: elation. Second: unease at the plethora of potential social embarrassments that loom. *Hazel and Mark E's tape. Ah well.* — Great, eh . . . thanks, that's brilliant, ah go, fiddling aroond in the drawer in the feeble wooden stand under the phone. There's an empty spec case my ma uses for her auld reading glasses. That'll dae for they works that Sick Boy gied us. Ah stick it in ma jaykit poakit.

— Ah'm getting a taxi now, pet. Wor shall ah meet yur?

— Ask the driver tae take ye tae a pub on Leith Walk called Tommy Younger's.

— Okay. See yur in ten minutes.

My mother's evidently been on surveillance, emerging intae the hallway in gunfighter stance. Her thin frame shakes, the cigarette twitching in her hand. — Yir no meeting anybody in nae pub! The car's ordered! We're leaving fae here! We go *as a faimlay*!

— Ah'm meeting my, ehm, muh girlfriend, fae the university.

— Girlfriend? she gasps, as Dad steps oot behind her. — Ye never says nowt tae us aboot nae girlfriend, she accuses, before her big eyes narrow tae slits. — Bit ye widnae, wid ye, Mark, cause it's aw bloody secrets wi you!

— Cathy . . . my dad soothes, his hand on her shoodir.

Her heid lashes roond violently, eyes devouring him. — Well, it is, Davie! Mind that wee lassie we heard greetin in the stair? He wisnae gonnae let her intae the hoose!

That wis a cringer . . . fuckin needy minger followin us hame eftir ah'd cowped her up the goods yerd . . . them bringin her in n makin a fuss ay her, insistin ah sat up n drank fuckin coffee wi her in the kitchen when ah wanted tae die die die . . . or thaime tae aw die die die die, ya huns . . .

As ah feel my neck n ears flarin rid in recall, Billy's oot now, suddenly interested. — Whae wis this?

— Never you mind, my dad sais, and ah remain silent as a hatchet-wound grin splits Billy's coupon.

— Bring her here, Ma appeals, flicking some falling ash fae the sleeve ay her jaundice-yellay cardigan, — we'll huv room in the cars.

— Naw, eh, ah'll just see yis aw doon there. It might be a bit too heavy fir her being in the funeral party, when she doesnae ken anybody, likes, ah explain, as Sharon appears alongside Billy, cocking a waxed eyebrow.

— Ye mean too heavy fir *you*! my ma accuses. — He's *still* embarrassed by us, by his ain faimly! She turns tae the others in appeal. — Well, *he's* away, now, *he* cannae embarrass ye any mair . . . that wee sowel that never hurt a fly . . . that wee angel . . . and she sparks up again.

— Cathy . . . my auld man says, still in a conciliatory mode, — lit um go.

— Naw, she says, eyes again shockingly fish-protuberant. — How's he no gaunny bring the lassie back here? This lassie naebody even kens aboot! He's never even mentioned her! It's aw big bloody secrets, as usual! He's ashamed! she accuses. — Ashamed ay his ain faimlay!

Billy Boy dragons oot some smoke and gies us a feculent glower. — Feelin's fuckin mutual, ah'll tell ye that for nowt.

Your powers of smoke inhalation are impressive, Tobacco Boy. Far more so than your cryptic remarks.

Ma looks ceilingward. — Holy Father . . . what huv ah done . . . ?

— Dinnae start now, no the day, Dad plea-threatens. — C'moan, everybody. Simmer doon. Show some respect for the wee man. Mark, go and meet this lassie, this . . . he stalls on the word like it's a moothfae ay exotic food he's no quite sure aboot, — . . . girlfriend, but dinnae you be late for the cemetery. And you'll be in that front pew wi her, alongside me, yir mother, yir brother and Sharon. Got that?

Aw that fuckin fuss n drama ower whaire some cunt sits . . .

Ah gie a slight nod, instantly aware this action will be too minimalist for him.

— Ah sais *got that*?

Suspicion confirmed. — Aye, nae worries, ah tell um, skippin doon the hallway, oot ay the archaic, reeking fug intae the respite ay stair n street, and oantae Junction Strasse. A peckish Joe Baxi rumbles doon the road n ah flag him, and we tear up the Walk tae TY's.

Inside the big cavern of a pub, ah git a nod fae Willie Farrell and Kenny Thomson, a couple ay aulder boys ah vaguely ken. It's scary, the wey they epitomise Leith gadges; you bar-hop till ye eventually come tae rest in one dive and then just grow auld there. You'll ken where tae find them in ten, twenty years' time. Thankfully, Fiona's only a couple ay minutes eftir us, her appearance liftin me tae the heavens. — Mark . . . so good ta see yur, honey, she says, then her tongue caresses those top pearly white teeth. She's fucking enchanting.

Newcastle Station . . . Waverley . . . fuck that . . .

We embrace, me no lookin at Willie and Kenny, n Fiona puttin ma stiffness doon tae grief. We settle intae a quiet corner wi two lagers. Ah tell her how difficult it's been wi ma family. She says it'll be a hard time fir everybody. Ah agree. What ah decide tae dae is just forget aboot aw the bad, stupid, weak shite. Make like it nivir fuckin well happened. Cause it's her n me now, that's how it's gaunny be and the rest is just a pile ay irrelevant fuckin nonsense.

We down our pints, n ah get another shout in. It's right again. Ah swarm ma senses wi her; touching, looking, kissing, hugging, but when ah try tae talk ah'm aw tongue-tied and cliché-bound. — It's okay, Mark, she says, and as she holds me, a choking ball ay refluxed gut acid comes up but ah force it back doon. Ah feel ma Adam's aypil bobbin as ma cauld palms frame her face. — It is just *so fucking good* tae see you.

— Oh, Sweet Vanilla, she says as we get up, me a bit para in case any ay they cunts at the bar have heard the nickname she's gied us (cause ah look like a vanilla ice cream wi raspberry on toap), then exit oantae the Walk. Ah flag doon an approachin Joey, takin us tae the crematorium.

People are filing intae the chapel ay rest, but we're no late, we're just eftir the hearse n coffin, so they make wey fir us. There's a few ghouls who love this part ay the proceedings, but maist writhe uncomfortably inside their ill-fitting black garments in nervous anticipation ay the peeve tae follay. My ma and dad baith look massively relieved tae see me, as we get intae the seats kept for us, in front ay the Glasgow and Midlothian relatives and assorted friends n neighbours. A drooling simpleton doesnae make a busload ay sentient chums but naebody likes tae see a young cunt stiffed and there's a healthy turnoot. Ah can see ma mates; Begbie, Matty, Spud, Sick Boy, Tommy, Keezbo, Second Prize, Sully, Gav, Dawsy, Stevie, Mony, Moysie, Saybo and Nelly, as well as Davie Mitchell, Young Bobby and Les fae Gillsland's. Nae Swanney. Ah clock Hazel, she's wi Alison, Lesley, Nicky Hanlon and Julie Mathieson, another old tape-trading pal, who had a bairn wi some gadge, and whae's lookin like two big eyes oan a stick. There's grandparents, uncles and aunties and some mair auld relatives ah cannae quite recall, aw locked intae a grim, formless dotage. Sometimes a set ay fiery eyes within a puffy or scraggy white heid offer a clue as tae their previous identities as *real people*; but Schopenhauer was right: life has tae be aboot disillusionment; stumbling inexorably towards the totally fucked.

The service is conveyor-belt pish; the radgeworks God-botherer half-heartedly saying something aboot mysterious ways, as ah clock him glance at his watch a couple ay times. Then ah find ma eyes locking oantae the sealed coffin; even with the attentions ay physios and Ma and Dad's maist sterling efforts, Wee Davie had spazzed up that much that they'd have needed tae brek his airms n spine in a couple ay places tae get him tae assume the position in thaire. Nae wonder the auld boy drew the line at the open-casket pape ceremony the old girl craved.

Some strange things happen, but. On the wey oot the chapel, headin tae the cars in the drizzling rain, eftir pressin cauld, bony flesh wi the mourners, my dad kisses us oan ma cheek. It's the first time he's done this since ah wis at early primary school. The whiff ay his aftershave and his big gravelly chin against ma skin is infantilisin. Then, when we get in the motor tae go along Ferry Road tae the do at the Ken Buchanan Hotel, my ma crushes my hand and sais, through a blindin mask ay tears, — You're ma wee baby now. Ah put it down tae grief talkin, but part ay me is thinkin: *This woman is fucking insane*, as resentment and tenderness battle inside me.

At the hotel, as ah drink a whisky and eat a gut-blistering sausage roll, Hazel comes ower tae me and Fiona. Something seems tae flash between the lassies, but this time ah'm too deflated tae feel awkward. — Hi, Haze. Ah kisses her chastely on the cheek. — Thanks for comin. Eh, this is Fiona, then ah add, in stupid, ham-fisted formality, — Fiona Conyers, Hazel McLeod.

Hazel shakes Fiona's hand. — I'm a friend of Mark's, she sais. Whatever passes between them is dignified, almost touchin, and ah feel masel briefly openin up inside. Ah take a hard swallay ay the burnin whisky tae snuff the emotion.

Fiona said what people always say under these circumstances: it's nice tae meet you but it's a pity it has tae be under these circumstances. Circumstances. Ah've goat Hazel's Fall tape in ma poakit, a mix ay ma fave tracks fae *Slates*, *Hex Enduction Hour* and *Room to Live*, and aye, ah was planning tae gie it tae her. But it disnae seem right in front ay Fiona. Schopenhauer said male relationships are defined by a natural indifference, but female ones typified by antagonism. Then again, he wis a really cynical cunt.

The Hazel tapes.

Hazel and me were friends fae school. Since second year. We listened tae music thegither; Velvets, Bowie, T. Rex, Roxy, Iggy and the Stooges, Pistols, Clash, Stranglers, Jam, Bunnymen, Joy Division, Gang ay Four, Simple Minds, Marvin Gaye, Sister Sledge, Wire, Virgin Prunes, Smokey Robinson, Aretha Franklin, Dusty Springfield and *not* Beatles, Stones, Slade, Springsteen, U2, OMD, Flock of Seagulls, Hall and Oates, thegither, in our respective bedrooms. Ah liked her, but fancied other girls; sluttier yins, ah suppose. Girls wi high shrieking laughter who said 'beat it, son' or

125

'dinnae bother us' when ye made yir move. Whae gied ye measured looks and said 'mibbe' when ye said 'you n me then', like ye were offering them a square-go. But even though it was an obvious imperative, ah never wanted tae just plunge ma cock intae a lassie. Ah was always looking for something mair complicated; possibly drama, mibbe even love, whae the fuck kens?

My mates refused tae believe that Hazel and me wirnae fucking. She's good-looking, in a depressive sort ay way. A goth in spirit, if one wrapped in straight disco-girl clothing; those incongruously bright pastels ay Top Shop on weekdays, pushing the boat oot tae Etam at the weekend. Then one time ah was playing her a Stranglers album, *Black and White*, and we started necking. Ah think ah initiated it, maybe ah was fed up wi the doss cunts' assumptions, or it could be ma mind is playing tricks oan us as it often does. Perhaps the Stranglers lyrics gied us a sense ay entitlement. But whoever started it, it stoaped when ah tried tae go further. She had what could only be described as a panic attack, and the ferocity ay it shocked us. She went intae these convulsions, couldnae breathe for a bit, n started gaun rid. It was like an asthma attack ay the sort Spud used tae get, or Wee Davie, spazzing oot . . .

Postural drainage . . . doof-doof-doof, like strength-sapping body punches intae the big bags at the Leith Victoria gym.

As those teen months progressed, ah tried a few mair times, oddly, usually at her instigation. But the same thing happened. She would just freeze up, then have a violent reaction; it was as if she had a physical allergy tae sex. She wouldnae even gie us a blow job, though she did J. Arthur me off, focused oan ma cock like a scientist conducting an experiment. Once, when ah shot ma duff, the spunk went in her ear and oan her hair at the side ay her face. When she touched the stringy paste, she said, — That's horrible, that mess . . . and started mair convulsive heaves, before gaun away tae wash her face. When she came back her hair was wet, she'd washed that n aw. Ah mind ay really desirin her then, wantin tae ride her so bad, just seeing her standin there wi the wet hair. And I'd only just blown a wad.

But there wis nae wey.

When we eventually did shag, it was grim, but that's another tale. Nowadays we dinnae see each other for yonks, then end up back thegither oan the pretext ay gaun tae a gig or listenin tae some sounds, and have bad sex. Really bad sex. We baith think 'never again' till one ay us, usually her, picks up the phone.

Stevie Hutchison and his bird are talkin tae my ma n dad. He comes ower in that kind ay shufflin walk, shiftin weight fae one leg oantae the other, n pits his arm roond ma shoodir. — Bearin up, bro?

— Awright, Hutchy, aye, jist huv tae git oan wi it but, eh? How's you?

— Seek tae fuck, he goes, his big eyes burnin. — Peyed oaf fae Ferranti's. Applied tae Marconi's doon in Essex. Thaire's fuck all up here. Anywey, ah fancy giein London a wee crack. Mibbe git involved wi a band doon thaire. He glances at his bird, Chip Sandra, whae's chattin tae Keezbo. She's quite a bam, nae way good enough fir Stevie, n ah sortay blame her a bit for brekin up oor auld band, Shaved Nun. — She's no keen tae go, he says wi a crinkly smile. — Elbay time, ah reckon, he winks.

Ah smile back. *Aboot time n aw.*

— What's up, Stephen? Chip Sandra goes, pickin up the vibe.

— Jist music talk, you ken us. Stevie winks at me again, turning tae her. — C'mon, lit's git a peeve, n he steers her away tae the bar wi the vickies placed against her back soas ah kin see thum.

Chip Sandra goat her name cause she wis eatin chips while gittin rode by Matty in a knee-trembler up the Goods Yard. That wis yonks ago. Embarrassing yin fir Matty, huvin a burd eatin chips ower yir shoodir, while you're banging her up against a waw. Even mair so when aw the boys came filin past. Ah cheekily asked Sandra fir a chip n she extended the packet tae us, so ah took yin. Matty wis shoutin, — Fuck off, Renton! Ah didnae ken that aw ay thum – Begbie, Nelly, Saybo, Dawsy, Gav n some others – hud formed a queue n wir helping themselves tae chips as perr Matty thrusted hopelessly oan, his bare erse poking ootay the shadows. Ah mind ay Saybo sayin tae us, lickin the broon sauce fae his chops as we exited oantae the Walk, — Best line-up for the boys that cow's ivir done, ya cunt!

Franco and that June Chisholm bird he's riding are ower, and she's talking tae Hazel. The Beggar Boy digs us in the ribs wi a jab fae the fore-knuckles ay his chunky fist; that yin'll leave a bruise the morn, although it's meant in affection. — Git this doon ye. He hands me a large whisky. You fuckin well hudin it thegither, mate?

— Aye, ah tell him, takin a sip.

My auld man shoots us a glance as if tae say, 'Bad form, with these two ladies, old boy.' The disapproval is tinged wi qualified relief as ah can see that, in his eyes, ah've just gone fae possible buftie boy tae philandering rogue.

Franco looks tae Fiona, then turns tae me. — Introduce us then, ya rude cunt.

— Fiona, this is my mate, Frank Begbie. Or Franco.

127

Or Beggars. Or the Beggar Boy. Or the Generalissmo. Or Psychotic Bullying Prick. I was the bony bag that took those strength-sapping body punches at Leith Vic. Doof-doof-doof . . .

— Hello, Frank. She goes tae shake his hand but is rewarded wi quite a sophisticated peck oan the cheek. The cunt can occasionally pull oot a welcome (non-violent) surprise. Nice one, Beggars. — Mark talks about yur a lot.

The nutter's para glint ignites in Begbie's eye. — Aw does he now? He gazes right intae ma soul, or what's left ay it.

— In very complimentary terms, I might add, Fiona says, wi relaxed grace.

Begbie's coupon softens and humanises in a light smile. Fuck me, she's even managed tae charm that cunt. He drapes an airm roond ma shoodirs. — Well, wir best mates but, eh, Mark? Kent him since fuckin primary. Five years auld.

Ah smile tightly, takin a good blooter ay whisky back, n feelin the burn. — One ay the best, this man, and caught in the moment, ah totally believe it as well. Enjoying a certain licence, ah pump a reasonably heavy dig intae his chist.

Begbie doesnae even notice; he's in his element, particularly good at funerals in the way a lot ay psychopaths tend tae be. Ah suppose if bringing death and despair is yir life's work, then being somewhere like this must feel like a result; the job's already done and you can just kick back and relax. He tightens his grip oan us, n pushes his face psycho-affectionately intae mine, his hot, dark, smoky essence assailing ma senses. — Ye nivir come roond fir us, tae go oot fir a fuckin peeve, jist the two ay us like wi fuckin well used tae.

Because you eywis end up batterin some cunt. — Ah'm in Ebirdeen maist ay the time, Frank.

— No aw the fuckin time, but. It's probably cause wi eywis end up batterin some cunt!

What d'ya mean 'we', ya fuckin bam?

— Naw . . . we eywis huv a barry laugh whin we go oot, the two ay us, like.

— Too right wi fuckin well dae, he announces tae Fiona, then sweeps an airm roond the room, huggin me tighter wi the other yin. — Nae cunt's git oor sense ay humour, eh, no, Rents? Ye cannae fuckin explain it tae maist cunts, pardon ma French, he apologises, then indeed does attempt tae elucidate tae her this unique style ay jocular absurdity that only he and I share.

128

Hazel's heard it aw before n turns tae us. — Ah made you a tape ay that live Joy Division album.

— *Still?*

— Aye.

— Barry, thanks. Ah hear there's a great version ay 'Sister Ray' oan it, ah smile in gratitude. Ah've hud the album since it came oot but ah'm no gaunny tell her. Wi made-up tapes, despite what Sick Boy says aboot it bein a covert act ay aggression and egotistical mind control, it's the kindness ay compiling that counts. In my mind's eye ah can see it written oot oan the index caird spine ay the cassette in Hazel's neat handwriting:

Joy Division: Still

An awkward moment passes between us as ah smile n kill the whisky, while Hazel blinks, lowering her heid demurely, excusing herself and headin tae the buffet table. Ah catch Fiona's eye and we circulate, me pickin up another nip, talkin first tae Keezbo's ma n dad, Moira n Jimmy, then some ay Ma's relatives, the Bonnyrigg–Penicuik crowd, who comfort her.

Ah see Alison headin tae the buffet table and intercept her. — Ali . . . really sorry tae hear aboot yir ma. How bad is it?

— This is me getting intae practice. She gies us a Stanley-knife smile. — No be long now, ah think. Thanks for askin, but, and she sidles oaf taewards the bar, whaire the rest ay the lassies are standin. Then she seems tae think ay something n turns. — Kelly sends her commiserations, she's sorry she cannae be here, but she's got exams aw next week.

— Sound, ah goes, watchin her depart, makin her wey taewards Matty n Gav. Ah see Fiona's talkin tae Tommy and Geoff, so ah sits beside my ma. She's wearin a daft hat as she husnae dyed the grey-broon roots ay her hair in a while. As she pulls oan her tab, sweaty, peroxide locks cling tae her foreheid and her make-up's been running wi her tears. Grief's weight n chain-smoking have gied her a stevedore's rasp. — Ah sometimes think it's God's wey ay punishin me, she sais.

— For what?

— Ah turned against ma faith tae mairry yir faither.

A beam ay smoke streams fae her puckered lips. Her hollowed-oot cheeks and wild stare suggest mental derangement. — Ye honestly believe God's punishing ye cause yir a Catholic that mairried ootside yir religion?

— Aye. Aye, ah do, she says emphatically, her eyes aw pupils. She's nipped

129

we never had a service at St Mary's Star ay the Sea. She'd ey take Wee Davie there when he was younger and easier tae cart aboot.

— What aboot Dad? The auld man's wi Andy and his Weedgie family, Granny Renton and his brothers Charlie and Dougie. Ma whisky's tanned in and ah dump the empty gless oan the table. — He's a Protestant and Wee Davie's his son n aw. So that means at least God's even-handed: he hates yis baith.

— Ye cannae say that, Mark, dinnae say that . . .

— Or mibbe, jist mibbe, he couldnae gie a flyin fuck aboot either ay yis. Ever thought ay that yin?

— No! she shouts, as ah'm thinking, how barry would a God like that be; one that hates fucking Christians, Muslims, Jews and any other cunts that bother Him. And even, or especially, these caste-system justifying cunts: the fuckin Buddhists. But my wee outburst has been picked up and ah've inadvertently created a display ay Christian unity. — C'mon, Mark, shape up, son, Kenny goes, n ma dad and his brothers are right ower wi Billy. Dougie's no sae bad but Charlie's a vacuous, toxic bigot; it was him that got oor Billy intae aw that Orange shite, and ma faither kens it tae. He scowls at me like ah'm the filth of Hades; ah'm sure Billy's telt him the story ay Davie's hand job. They start tae circle roond like vultures. Ah'm lookin for Franco, but he's ower at the bar wi June. Then Fiona's by ma side, makin excuses, effortlessly charmin them all. — He's upset. How, pet . . .

Upset my hairy ersehole. It's this shite that upsets me. The proddies and the papes; the lowlife rump ay losers, distilled fae the dregs ay European Christendom's two most blood-simple white tribes. Sneering, rabid vermin who intuitively know they're at the bottom ay the trash pile at the scabbiest end ay a bunch ay frozen rocks in the North Sea. Aw they can dae is think ay whae tae scapegoat for thair shabby plight, and when the monster that was ma brother came along, it was a (Christian) God-sent opportunity fir them. The fact escaped them that Wee Davie was probably the nadir that only those sectarian spastics could ever have produced, because whatever pigeon-shit colours they drape aroond their slopin shoodirs, or the crappy one-note ballads of loyalty or rebellion they sing, they're aw cut fae the same manky cloth ay noxious idiocy.

Ma lettin me n Billy help her make chocolate cake, in that upstairs kitchen at the Fort. Us aw huvin a barry laugh. Then Wee Davie's screams; aggressive, demanding, violating. Me n Billy lookin at her as if tae say 'leave him', but first her, and then us, hopelessly remembering whae we were. The slow surf ay oor breath drawing in unison as she tore doonstairs. Our fingers gaun intae the chocolate mix in bitter consolation.

Wee Davie's death doesnae upset me. When ah think ay him, aw that comes tae mind is the monstrous, the grotesque. The thing was that he looked like me; sandy rid hair, boatil-white skin, wild blue eyes. Ah used tae think that people just said it tae take the pish, but it was true. Tae poor Billy's Orangeman shame, it was him who looked like the squat, dark-heided, mono-browed Connemara farm boy transported tae the Midlothian pits, just like aw the male papes oan my ma's side.

As a boy ah used tae beg tae get taken tae Porty open-air pool wi Wee Davie, Billy and Dad. Porty wis eywis fuckin freezin and ah hated it n Billy's bullyin seemed tae reach mair psychotic levels there, but gie me that any time before the humiliation ay bein seen oot wi them at Leith Vickie baths.

Ma starts shouting at Margaret 'Bendix' Curran, our embittered ex-neighbour, whae believes that we used Davie tae get the Housing Association place wi the main door, then dumped him in a residential care centre for the handicapped. — Aw ah'm sayin is thit thaire wis others oan that list before you, Cathy . . .

— We never pit um in a care centre! Eh died in the hoaspital, in the Infirmary!

— But now that he's no here, ye should be giein that hoose up, that's aw ah'm sayin, n at that point she clocks ma mate Norrie, whae works for the Housing Department. — Aw aye, what's he daein here? It's no what ye ken, it's who ye ken, right enough!

— Get away fae me! my ma shouts, and my auld boy n Olly Curran, the thin racist whae looks like an undertaker, are ower and joining the argy-bargy, as ah skip across tae the bar where Spud queues up tae buy us a pint. Ah eywis like tae avoid other people's social conflict; ah much prefer tae start ma ain trouble. As ah watch Spud trying tae get the barman's attention, ah feel some airms around me, circling us fae behind. At first ah think it's Fiona, but ah can see her chattin tae relatives, and then ah wonder that circumstances might have made Hazel uncharacteristically tactile. Ah look round n it's Nicola Hanlon. — I just wanted tae gie ye a wee hug, she says, pecking us oan the cheek.

Ah'm thinking, fuck me, could that wee cunt Davie no have checked oot last year? Ah'm attached now n the fanny are queuing up! — Thanks, Nicky, ah appreciate it.

Spud's ower with a pint for me; he's been following Nicky around like a puppy she's just reprieved fae the cat and dug hame at Seafield.

— Cheers, bud.

— Tough yin, Mark: dig in, catboy.

Ah wink at him, then feel somebody grab ma erse, n ah'm thinking, how good can this get? But it's only Sick Boy fuckin aboot. — Wee Nicky's totally hot for you, he whispers, as ah see Billy and Sharon huv got in between Ma n Dad n the Currans. — Ah'd ride her, if only tae upset Spud, he offers, whae we note is back off in hapless pursuit ay her.

Ah ignore Sicko, looking across at Fiona's profile. She's gorgeous and ah just want tae be alone with her. But the cunt persists, so ah tell him, – Aye, ah think ah'm gettin the sympathy shag vote the day.

— Sympathy for the deceased handicapped brother only tells part ay the story. The crucial element is that you already have a bird.

— What dae ye mean?

— The incumbency factor. Lassies see you wi Fiona, tidy by the way, Rent Boy, punching above your weight a bit, he says, lookin ower at her placatin ma mother n faither as the Currans take their leave, — aye, they witness you being a nice, attentive suitor, and they're drawn tae ye because they think ay the negligent creep they were last out wi.

Ah cannae believe this cunt's actually complimenting me. — So it's cause they see me as a good boyfriend?

— Most serpently, but they dinnae realise it's still the honeymoon period. You'll become that negligent creep soon enough; we all do. So strike while the iron's hot; when you get a new bird you're crazy aboot, that's *exactly* the time ye should be riding everything else in sight.

Something thuds in my chest. Ah hear ma voice gaun thin. — But ah dinnae want tae, ah jist want Fiona.

— Of course, he says smugly, picking up a mini sausage roll which has been sweating oan his paper plate, before deciding against it and setting it back doon. — It's a paradox. You can only fight through it using force ay will and trusting in the standing prick, which must be obeyed at all times. Allow it tae override any concerns you have, young Skywalker. Fuck, he says in sudden realisation, — I should be getting peyed fir this advice, I shouldnae be giein it free tae another gadge. Thankfully, you'll be too pished tae remember aw this in the morning.

Ah realise that this cunt really is light years ahead ay us aw. We're just daft wee boys. — How the fuck dae you ken aw this?

— Just through being a keen student ay the game. Experience and observation. I look and I listen, and ah'm prepared to run the gamut of emotions, he declares, throwing back his drink and swanning off. I'm thinking it must be a 'G' day for him, as Norrie Moyes comes up and goes on about the Currans. It seems he hates the cunts as much as me, as they're apparently constantly up at the Housing Department, hassling him. We hatch a revenge plot and start laughing merrily at the prospect.

Then ah catch Billy, abhorrent glare in his eye, bounding ower. He's been talkin tae the Weedgie side n seein off Margaret and Olly Curran. Norrie catches the look and sidles away.

— How goes it, bro? ah quip.

Billy's reeking ay whisky. — You'll be lookin for a new boyfriend now then, eh?

A controlled rage combusts inside me. Ah roll ma eyes. — Pittin yerself in frame, likes? Keep it the family!

We baith notice that Fiona and slimy Geoff fae Bonnyrigg are approaching. If that cunt's been chattin her up . . .

— Ya fuckin pervy wee cunt . . .

— You're fantastic, ah tell him.

— What are you sayin? Eh! he shouts.

Everybody's heard and they gather closer. — Nothing, ah say nonchalantly. — Ah'm just saying that you're brilliant.

— Mark . . . Fiona implores, grabbing my arm.

Sharon's asking Billy, — What's wrong, Billy, why are ye shouting at Mark? It's Wee Davie's funeral, Billy!

— Dunno what he's gettin so steamed up aboot, ah protest in wide-eyed innocence.

Begbie approaches; his static magnetically tightens the slack features of drunks into temporary sobriety and reason. A reprimanding scowl silences Billy. Charlie and Dougie usher big bro away, Dougie looking back at me wi that sad, forlorn shake ay the heid. It makes me want tae laugh in his stupid coupon. Instead, winking at a tight-faced Franco (do ah love that gadge? Yes I do!), ah grab a biro fae the bar, jump up on a seat and tap the pen against my gless. — Can I have everybody's attention, please?!

Eyes swivel in both directions, checking aggravators are onside, then fall oantae me in silence, and the flair is mine. — Wee Davie and I . . . ah look tae ma bemused parents and ma seething older brother, — despite his profound handicap, had a *special* relationship. Ah lit ma smile settle oan an incensed Billy for a couple ay beats. — My mum and dad gave him the best possible life anybody could, and they never, ever stopped loving him, caring for him and, in spite ay everything, hoping for the best for him. And he never ceased tae bring joy and laughter intae aw our lives. He'll be so badly missed, n ah pause tae watch the sobering faces and see

133

thick traces of shame drip fae Billy's coupon. And ah suddenly feel dizzy up here. The peeve. So ah draw a deep breath and raise ma gless n declare, — Here's tae Wee Davie!

The faces in the house briefly sag with sadness and drink, before galvanising for a chorus ay: — Wee Davie!

Ah'm happy tae git doon offay the chair intae Fiona's arms, and fuck me if ah'm no battling back burgeoning tears, as the pride and love radiates through the woebegone eyes ay ma mother and faither.

Notes on an Epidemic 2

Under the Labour government of James Callaghan (1976–79), inflation and unemployment began to rise to post-war record levels.

The Conservative Party produced a zeitgeist election poster, featuring semi-dejected people waiting in a dole queue, with the slogan 'LABOUR ISN'T WORKING.'

Following the election of Margaret Thatcher, in the spring of 1979, unemployment levels tripled from 1.2 million to 3.6 million in 1982, and would stay over the three million mark till 1986.

The same period saw an increase in the number of long-term unemployed to over one million.

It was estimated that thirty-five people were chasing one vacancy.

This interval also saw a replacement of full-time employment by part-time work and (often part-time) college courses, supposedly for 'retraining', to meet the requirements of the new economic order.

Over this period, government statistics became more politicised than ever before; twenty-nine changes in the way unemployment figures were calculated effectively made the real total impossible to determine. Hundreds of thousands of people were removed from the unemployment register by making it progressively harder for people to obtain benefit, then counting only those who were in receipt of benefits, rather than claimants, as genuinely unemployed.

Through all the political squabbling during this era, one factor remains incontrovertible: hundreds of thousands of young, working-class people in the UK had a lot less money in their pockets and a lot more time on their hands.

Love Cats

Bored oot ay ma skull, man. Walkin they streets so long, singing the same auld song, ken every dirty crack oan the pavements ay Pilrig . . . Life's been shite since gettin peyed off fae the removals, been thaire since ah left the school. Thoat it wid be Lou Macari tae be a free man, but ah miss it; the boys, the travel, gaun intae aw they big hooses wi furniture, seein aw they different lives . . . Now it's aw gone.

N it wisnae fair, it wisnae right. Ah couldnae believe it when Eric Brogan sais tae us, — Sorry, Danny, wir gaunny huv tae lit ye go.

Aw ah sais wis, — Aw . . . aye . . . n ah goat ma stuff.

Ah should've says, how me but? Donny n Curtis huvnae been here as long as me. N ah kent it wis that Eleanor woman; her man that grassed us up. Pushed us intae the front ay the queue fir the redundancies. N aw ah wanted tae dae wis tae help her n be nice, when ah saw her greetin n that. Cause she wis that sad when she telt us aboot her son. When ah came roond that big hoose in Ravelston wi the invoice fir the flit, ken?

— Sit down and have a drink with me, Danny, she said, her eyes aw full ay tears.

— Naw, Mrs Simpson, ah cannae . . .

— Please, she actually begged us, but; this smart, tidy, posh woman, really sortay pleaded wi me, ken? What wis ah meant tae dae? — Call me Eleanor, she goes. — Please, Danny, just one drink. I could get you a sandwich?

What could ah say? Ah'd just kent her tae say hiya tae n ah'd listened for a bit when she talked aboot things. Jist bein polite, likesay. She'd opened a boatil ay wine n thaire wis another yin awready empty, but she didnae seem drunk, jist likesay sad.

N aw wi did wis talk. Well, she talked n ah jist pure listened again. Aboot her son, takin his ain life, only seventeen, and how naebody saw it comin.

Then he came in, her man. Started shoutin at her, then at me, n she started greetin. So ah jist sais, — Ah'd better go, likes . . .

He looked at us and says, — Yes, I think you better had.

N ah wis too ashamed tae try n explain tae Eric. But ah pure kent the Simpson boy hud belled um, kent by the wey Eric wis taewards us eftir it. N now ah'm oot. Walkin n wanderin. Up the Walk, doon the Walk. Tae Leith Library, then right up the toon. Miles every day. Gaun intae the jobcentre, but there's nowt thaire. Still go every day, but. Gav Temperley says he'd keep anything decent back fir us, but aw ah goat wis a computer course.

Ah sees Sick Boy, standin at the bus stop. There's a dude whae never does a day's George Raft but seems tae ey have poakits fill ay pretty green, ken? Bet yir life thit it aw comes ootay some chick's purse, but. Ah follay his line ay vision ower the road tae this big poster, one ay the yins the government's pit up tae git people tae grass each other up, like in Nazi Germany, whaire they encouraged the bairns tae gie away thair mas n faithers:

CALL US UP BECAUSE WE'RE DISCREET . . .

AND WE'LL CALL TIME ON THE BENEFIT CHEATS!

N thaire's a big hotline number tae phone. Sick Boy's back leg is gently kickin the grey bus-shelter panel. He sees us comin, n goes, — Spud.

— Awright, Si, ah goes, cause ye kin call um 'Sick Boy' in a crowd, but it feels a bit bad-mannered likesay on yir tod, ken? — How goes it?

— The usual. Bird worries.

— Me n aw, man, in so far as thaire's nane bitin, ken?

He laughs wi a big, open face. It's yin ay they smiles that makes ye see how chicks dig the sick cat. When it gits turned oan ye, ye pure feel thit you're the chosen yin. — Cannae live wi them, cannae live withoot them. I should've stuck wi the project when ah wis altar boy at St Mary's, n joined the priesthood. Would've been the Holy Papa's number two by now. A lifetime ay contemplation n serenity, aw given up for chicks who dinnae appreciate it. So how's you? Nae work prospects?

— That'll be the day, ah goes. — Totally brassic n aw. They sent us tae this computer trainin place likes, but ah wis shitein it that ah'd pure brek the computers, by pressin the wrong buttons n that, ken?

— No my thing, he shakes his heid.

— Naw, me neither. It's a bit ay a fad, man, ah cannae really see that sortay stuff catchin oan . . . ah mean, cats like the human touch. Ken?

— Aye, he sais, but ye kin tell he isnae really convinced.

Ah looks back up tae that poster. It seems tae be sayin: we can make you intae bad people. — Shockin but, eh? Ah points ower the road. — Encouragin people that have goat next tae nowt tae grass each other up. It's like *Nineteen Eighty-Four*, ah goes, then realises, — Ah mean, ah ken it sortay *is* 1984, but ah'm talkin aboot the book likesay, no the year.

— Ah catch yir drift, he sais, lookin doon the road as the bus lumbers up the Walk. He pills a five spot oot ay his poakit. — Here's ma bus, see ye, he goes, n tae ma shock, crumples the note intae ma mitt.

— Ah wisnae tryin tae tap ye up, ah'm pure protestin, cause neither ah wis, but, well, it's sound ay the boy, likesay.

— Nae worries, mate, he goes, wi a big wink, climbin oantae the bus.

— Ah'll gie ye it back next week, ah shout as he heads inside and the bus pills oaf. Sound gadge, Sick Boy, one ay the best.

So ah'm back doon the Walk wi a wee bit mair ay a spring in the step, Sick Boy's gesture reviving the faith in the two-legged species. Ah pill intae the shop tae git ma paper n some fags fae Mrs Rylance, n she looks at us wi a big smile as ah pit ma change intae the yellay plastic CAT PROTECTION LEAGUE boax. — You're a gentleman, Danny son, she goes, they dirty big dentures hingin oot tae dry.

— Well, ye goat tae look eftir oor feline pals, Mrs R. Four legs good, but mibbe two legs likesay no sae bad either, but, ken?

— That's right, son. Ye see, the thing aboot animals is that they cannae tell ye when something's wrong. Ah think the aulder ah git, the mair ah prefer animals tae people.

That is one auld catgirl supreme. — Ah kin sortay see that, Mrs R, cause they dinnae start wars, the likesay that Falklands fiasco, n jist as ah'm aboot tae vacate the premises, hello, hello, another catchick appears, this time it's LA Woman, Los Angelos, Alison Lozinska, wearin a beret n a white jean jaykit, n lookin like a total sex kitten. — Hi, Ali.

— Hi, Danny, what ye up tae?

— Hingin oot oan the mean streets ay Leith, nae changes in this cat's MO, so tae speak. Yirsel?

— Meetin Kelly n the rest ay them ower in the Percy, she says, buying some tabs fae auld Mrs R. — Tryin tae pack these in, she goes. — My ma . . .

— How is she daein? Ah likesay heard offay Mark n Si.

— Nowt they kin dae, just a matter ay time, Ali sort ay snuffles. Ma hand kind ay hovers ower her back, n she sees it, smiles, and touches ma wrist. — You're sweet, she goes, then pills hersel thegither. — Aye, meetin the girls in the pub, then wir hittin the toon. It's Sally's birthday. Comin along for one?

By Sally, she must mean Squiggly. Spells problemos for the boy Murphy. Squiggly n me dinnae exactly see eye-tae-eye, but getting an invitation tae Chick Central does not happen every day, man, so ye dinnae refuse in such a situ, ken? So ah sticks the *Evening News* in the inside jean jaykit poakit as we heads doon Puke Street n ah'm telling her aboot Mark up at Aberdeen, n she goes, — Never thought he had it in him. Ah ken he fancies himself as an intellectual, but I'm surprised he actually managed to get intae uni. He was eywis crap at school.

Ah think aboot this. — We aw were.

— Speak for yersel, ah wisnae.

— Aye but it's different for lassies. Ah'm talking aboot the boys, likesay, ah goes. Ah kin mind ay seein Ali in that prefect blazer. Whoa, man, telling ye, they things should be banned. Pure filth.

Ali laughs and pits her hand tae her mooth. She's goat those cute lace gloves oan, fir the sake ay fashion rather than function, ken? — Danny, you were never at school long enough tae be good or bad at it. And ye were expelled fae two!

— Aye, ah agree, n as we pass Leithy, one ay my alma maters along wi Augies n Craigy, — but mibbe school isnae the best environment for some cats tae learn. Ah mean, maist animals learn by play, ah wink, — n we dae plenty ay that oan they dirty wee streets doon this auld port!

That wis me likesay tryin tae flirt but it bounces oaf the chick like bullets fae Superman's chist, ken? Suppose, though, that this catgirl's goat other things oan her mind. Bit mibbe she's oot tae git away fae aw that. N somebody wis sayin she's seein a gadge; supposed tae be some lucky aulder dude fae her work. Whae kens?

We hits the Percy and it's lassies everywhere; Kelly, Squiggly, Claire McWhirter, Lorraine McAllister, that sexy Lizzie McIntosh supergirl fae the auld school, Esther McLaren, n man, wee Nicola Hanlon (the loveliest sex kitten ay them aw, man, ah amnae kiddin likesay) n many mair besides thit ah dinnae ken, cause it's Squiggly n this lassie Anna's twenty-first, so aw the Leith Lovelies are gaun oot fir a big blow-up in fair Edina.

Squiggers looks soor-faced at ma arrival, cause ah pure gied her that nickname years ago: Sally Quigly = Squiggly Diggly, eftir yon octopus that used tae be oan the telly when wi wir sprogs. Never kent what happened tae that cat, fae the same Hanna-Barbera stable as Top Cat, Yogi Bear n Huckleberry Hound, but never really stuck in the public's consciousness in the same wey, ken? Aye, Squiggers didnae like it but, even if it wis only a bit ay retaliation for her daein that 'Scruffy Murphy' crap.

Ah lashed oot cause ah suppose ah *wis* a bit ay a scruff at school, money bein too tight tae mention at Chez Murphy back in the day, ken?

Otherwise, though, the vibes are better than sweet, n ah'm pure thinkin: forget the boys, forget hearin aw that cack aboot fitba n music n whae's claimed whae n whae's battered whae, n whae's been a radgeboy oan the peeve. Aye, ye cannae beat bein collapsed intae a big chair, just likesay sittin here surrounded by beauty n totally engagin the senses, man:

— . . . so what dae you think, Danny?

Ah think you rule, catgirl. — Well, Nicky, ah dinnae think ye kin go wrong wi the Hoochie. Everywhere else in Edinburgh is such a meat market, ken?

— What if you're wantin some meat, but? she says, the cheeky wee vixen, and it's breakin ma hert cause the likes ay Sick Boy, Tommy or even Rents or Begbie would say something like, 'Well, in that case, jist stick wi me, babe.' But this isnae the kind ay talk that comes oot ay ma mooth, n ah jist smiles at her, thinkin aboot the cruelty ay the world, wi aw that beauty bein wasted oan someone that disnae care, that sees this lovebird as jist another bedpost notch. Ah pure jist want tae say, 'Fancy gaun oot for a bite tae eat sometime? There's a smart new Chinky opened up in Elm Row,' but ah'm no a man ay commerce n a lassie that works fir the Gas Board wid never consent tae go oot wi a common dole mole. N ah bet this dirty, lucky auld boy thit Ali's seein fae her work, ah kin sortay hear her mentionin a gadgie's name tae Squiggers, aw that coy wey, ah bet ye he's goat tons ay spondoolays. It's aw unfair, man, aw pure unfair.

Then thir finishin thair drinks, oan Squiggly's instructions, n movin away, n Nicky looks sadly at me, n says, — Ah feel bad us leavin ye here, Danny –

— C'mon, Nicky! Squiggly shouts.

— It's awright, ah'll catch up wi the boys ower oan the Walk, thi'll be in the Cenny or the Spey or the Volley or somewhaire like that, inching upwards taewards toon and oblivion, man. You ken, the usual circuit.

She smiles, n her n Ali baith sais cheerio. They aw head oaf, leavin ma hert in a million pieces. It's shite when birds take a shine tae ye, but *as a mate.* Happens tae me aw the time; pure cast in the role ay the *nice guy that they dinnae want tae ride.* Ah'd love tae play the *bastard that they bang senseless,* but the likes ay Sick Boy's goat that market sortay cornered in this neck ay the woods, ken?

So ah'm headin doon Gordon Strasse tae cut fae Easter Road oantae the Walk, and as ah'm crossin ower the grand thoroughfare ah clocks two boys leavin the Volley n headin up the street quite sharpish. Next thing ah ken is that Begbie's ootside behind them, shoutin eftir them, — Youse cunts want a fuckin photae?

Uh-aw . . . puppies, kittens n bunnies . . . puppies, kittens n bunnies . . .

The boys turn roond n look the Beggar Boy up and doon. One's a bit feart, he's a chubby boy, n young, but still sortay spamy-heided. The other gadge's goat the swagger, but, wi this killer glare comin oot fae under that that flouncy light broon hair. This laddie isnae a closet poof, frontin it fir aw he's worth; thaire's evil intent in they eyes. — You wir muckin ma sister aboot . . .

Domestic affairs, man. So ah've crossed the road n ah'm alongside Begbie. Goat tae at least provide moral support likesay. The Beggar Boy's ma mate; besides, ah huv tae see him nearly every day, unlike those stranger dudes. Baith the feral and fat domestic cat glance at us, n baith seem tae decide that ah'll mibbe no make much ay a difference. Cannae sortay really argue wi that likes.

No that the Beggar Boy's actin like he needs assistance. — Ah've mucked a few cunts' sisters aboot, he laughs. He turns tae me n goes, — If thir game thir gittin banged, right? Then back tae the boy, — You goat a fuckin problem wi that, cunty-baws?

Well, ye kin see that this cat really hates his sister at this point in time, man, wishin that the lassie had gied her hole tae anybody but Franco or hud swallayed the auld Jack n Jill wi her cup ay English Breakfast that fateful mornin, ken? Fair play tae the gadge but, he takes a step forward n says, — Ah dinnae think you ken whae yir fuckin aboot wi here!

Aw naw, man, ah feel ma eyes quiver n water like thaire's grit in thum. Ah'm wonderin: whaire's the rest ay the boys?

But Franco stands his groond, in fact ye kin tell he's chuffed tae fuck, cause that cat jist loves a row n they boys huv sortay played intae his swipey, swipey paws. — See the fuckin jealousy ay some cunts, eh, Spud? Ah've jist been gittin you boys' sloppy seconds, or so yir hoor ay a sister fuckin well says!

That does the trick: the radge boy flips oot n runs up n swings at Franco, hittin him on the shoodir. Begbie gits a hook in at his side, and the boy thinks he's been punched, but ah see the glint, n his next blow's square intae the laddie's gut, which stops um in his tracks. As he looks doon at the blood soakin his blue shirt, the gadge's face is frozen in horror. Begbie's pocketed the blade but he's jist standin thaire, coolly appraisin his work, like a foreman oan a site checkin the quality ay the job. The chubby boy comes forward n ah'm movin slowly taewards him, but wi ma hands oot, cause it's a square-go n thaire's need for us tae go at it . . .

141

Uh-aw . . .

But now Tommy n some ay the boys have come oot, and Tommy runs up and smacks fatboy in the chops. — Git the fuck up the road, fir yir ain good, he sais, then as the boy staggers away, hudin his burst mooth, Tommy looks at the other gadge bleedin, n jumps oot intae the Walk and flags doon a taxi.

The cab stops and Tommy is sortay escortin the chibbed psycho boy intae it, telling um, — Git that seen tae right away, the gut's no that bad, but the side yin, he might huv hit an organ, and ah'm worried, man, now thit ye kin see the fear oan the boy's face, he disnae look mental now, jist a scared laddie, as Tam's shuttin the door behind um, n the cab speeds oaf.

The chunky, spammy gadge is staggerin up the Walk, hudin his face as he looks back. We're aw laughin, then git back intae the pub. Ye kin tell, though, that Tommy's pissed oaf wi Begbie. Eventually he says, — What wir ye fuckin thinking aboot, bringin oot a fuckin chib in the Walk? Thaire wis nae need. They came in here, clocked us, n they didnae fancy the odds.

— Wisnae gaunny go swedgin wi the cunt in the fuckin Walk, wis ah? Franco sneers. — So ah jist plunged the radge a couple ay times, gie um something tae fuckin well think aboot oan the wey hame, eh?

The gadge makes it aw sound so reasonable.

Tommy's bitin doon oan his bottom lip. — Well, we'll huv tae move oan and you'll need tae sling that chib in case the polis come roond.

— It's a fuckin barry chib but, Franco protests, — best bit ay Sheffield ah've hud in fuckin yonks, so he turns tae an auld boy whae's on the wey oot, — Jack, goan take this hame wi ye n ah'll git it oaf ye the morn.

— Nae bother, son, the auld gadge sais, poakitin the blade and shufflin oot ay the pub.

— All solved, Begbie smiles. — Calls fir a wee peeve. He turns tae the bar. — Les, nips ay Grouse aw roond, then, hen! Yin fir yersel n aw, princess!

As Lesley nods and starts firin up the shorts, Tommy's shakin his heid. — Fuckin madness, he goes.

Nelly's hearin nane ay it, but. — Franco's fuckin right. It's between him n the burd, these cunts should have kept thair fuckin nebs oot, faimlay or nae faimlay. Consentin fuckin adults. Cunts start tae make it thair problem, we make it oor fuckin problem.

— Too fuckin right, Franco goes. — The wey things ur gaun these days, ye cannae fuckin well hud back. Cunts jist try n take the fuckin pish if ye dae but, eh?

Tommy sees thit thaire's nowt tae be gained in discussin it further. —
Cunt's face wis a treat gittin intae that taxi, right enough.

Franco slaps um oan the back as Lesley lines up the nips. Ah'm no
really wantin whisky, rum would suit me, bein mair ay seafarin man ay
the port, but the Generalissimo'll get humpty if ah refuse. — That wis
good thinkin but, Tam, he says, — gittin that fucker intae the taxi. Dinnae
want him bleedin up n doon the Walk, drawin polis eyes.

— That's what ah thoat: git the cunt oot the road.

— Anywey, Nelly goes, passin the nips around, — cheers.

We aw toast Franco n that awfay whisky burns like a poker as it goes
doon, but it leaves a nice wee glow. Ye kin feel it whin ye git outside.

N we head up tae Tommy Younger's en route tae Edinburgh, aw buzzed
up, n it's the same excitement that ah used tae feel when ah goat up fir
work oan a good mornin at the furniture deliveries, where ye wondered
if ye were gaunny dae a big run, maybe up tae Perth or even Inverness
or somewhere like that, or if it wis jist gaunny be local, and aw the laughs
ye'd huv wi the boys. Now thaire's nowt like that, nae work fir the
unskilled man like me. But this feels good, no chibbin boys likes, Tam's
right, Franco's oot ay order, but bein part ay a team, huvin somethin tae
talk aboot, a tale tae tell. Cause wi aw need that; wi aw need something
tae dae n a tale tae tell.

Freedom

They say that freedom never came free. My grant's soon tae be abolished and made intae a loan, then it's game over. Fuck accruin arrears ye'll never be able tae pey oaf. Might as well have a baw n chain fastened tae yir ankle aw yir puff. When the likes ay Joanne and Bisto get hitched, become teachers or local government officers, they'll spend the rest ay their lives rackin up shitloads ay debt; student loans, mortgages, car payments. Then they'll look back on it aw, n see they were fuckin conned.

Why should the future matter? Ah've got my ain place, a lassie wi her ain place, even if we kip ower at each other's aw the time. Sitting in the college library thegither, debating, discussing our assignments, sourcing texts for each other, until we go back to her book-filled wee room or mine. We cook for each other; she's got me into vegetarianism, which ah've been interested in for a while. Ah like meat, but unless ye kin afford really decent stuff it's just fuckin poison. Fuck eatin aw that processed shite they pit in pies and fast food.

Most importantly, we shag at least twice a day. It's proper sex, relaxed and unhurried, no done on the sly. The sublime luxury ay removin aw yir clathes and no rushin tae put them back oan again. It strikes me that although I've shagged eighteen girls, Fiona's the only yin that's really seen us naked for any length ay time. Even now ah still feel as if some cunt's gaunny intrude. Ah have tae keep telling masel: *take yir fuckin time.*

But afterwards, when ah'm in her airms, like now, ah feel like ah'm trapped in a vice. Ah want tae get up, tae go oot for a walk. — You're so restless, Mark, she says. — Why can't ya evah relax?

— Ah kind ay fancy a wee walk.

— But it's freezin outside.

— Still but. Might go tae the shops. Get some stuff fir a stir-fry.

— You go, she says dreamily, loosening her embrace, turning and fighting her way back intae sleep.

And ah'm intae my clathes and oot the door. How can ye explain tae somebody ye love that ye still need mair? How dae ye dae that? Love is supposed tae provide aw the answers, tae gie us everything. *All you need is love*. It's fuckin bullshit though: ah need something, but it isnae love.

The communal phone in the residences' corridor is inviting. There's usually a mad Greek burd on it aw the time, spraffin fir ooirs. But now it's free, so ah call Sick Boy at Monty Street. He was up in court the other day, giein evidence. He answers, aw chary, — Whae's this?

— Mark. Call us back, the pips ur gaunny go, and ah shout oot the number, then again, as the line goes deid.

Sure enough, the Greek lassie appears, ghostin doon the institutional white corridor. Pus as tense as a plate at her sister's weddin. — You are going to use the phone?

— Aye, somebody's just calling me back.

She tuts loudly, cheeky fuckin monopolisin hoor, but sits doon on one ay the row ay three seats n pulls oot a book.

A minute later the phone rings. — Awright, Rents. Nae fuckin change, ya tight cunt?

— Naw . . . they phones just eat it up. How did it go up the coort?

— As bad as it possibly could have. A fuckin nightmare. As soon as I walked in and saw the coupon oan that judge, I thought: this isnae gaunny play oot well. Me, big Chris Moncur and another guy called Alan Royce aw said roughly the same thing. But it was Dickson's word against a deid man's as tae what actually happened. They bought aw his bullshit; an argument, an exchange ay blows, Coke fell, smashed his heid and died. An ordinary assault conviction wi a poxy five hundred quid fine. Nae jail, no even gaunny lose his fuckin licence.

— You are fuckin jokin . . .

— Wish I was. Janey's in shock, and wee Maria was greeting and started shouting at them in the court, she had tae be taken oot by her auntie. All the time the judge sat thaire wi that stony, arrogant coupon. Then he went oan aboot drink being the root cause ay this tragic accident, about how landlords continually have hassle fae drunks, and how Coke was a known pissheid . . . The family are devastated, Mark. I'm telling ye, it was the most fucked-up day of my life . . .

Sick Boy goes on and on, and although ah never kent Coke well, ah mind that he was always a happy, singing drunk; an occasional string vest, but never violent or aggressive. — The game's rigged, ah tell him, lookin doon at the Greek bird, who gies us the evil eye ower the top ay her book.

By the time ah put the phone doon ah'm despondent, n head ootside and walk for a bit. The hammering rain has given way tae a pearly mist

145

that wreathes over the city. Ah prowl for ages, the cold slowly biting intae ma face, then get back up tae Fiona, who's awake n dressed, n ah tell her aboot Coke. She's talking about how we should get a campaign going, a campaign for justice, on behalf ay an unemployed alkie, against an ex-cop, Freemason and publican, and a High Court judge.

Ah'm listenin tae her gaun oan, indulgin her, aw the time thinkin: *That's no how it works.* Then it's time for her to go. Ah'm meant tae be going ower tae hers later oan the night. Pulling oan her long, brown coat, Fiona places her loving fingertips oan the back ay my neck. Her eyes so serene ye could get lost in them forever. — What time do yer wanna come owah?

As ah consider this simple question, it seems tae widen until it splits ma thoughts open. What time?

Notes on an Epidemic 3

In 1827, Thomas Smith, a graduate of Edinburgh University's renowned medical school, took over his brother William's pharmacy. They started manufacturing fine chemicals and medicines prepared from plant sources. Ten years later, they would turn to alkaloids, particularly morphine, which they began to extract from opium.

John Fletcher Macfarlan, an Edinburgh surgeon, had taken over an apothecary's shop in 1815, establishing a substantial trade in laudanum. Later he made morphine, for which demand rose due to the development of the hypodermic needle. This increased the drug's effectiveness by allowing its direct injection into the bloodstream. Macfarlan's trade subsequently flourished and he also made anaesthetics (ether and chloroform) as well as surgical dressings. In 1840 he opened a factory and by the 1900s J.F. Macfarlan & Co. had become one of the largest suppliers of alkaloids in the country.

Both businesses continued to develop through takeovers and acquisitions, and in 1960, they merged to form Macfarlan Smith Ltd. The company was taken over by the Glaxo group in 1963. It still employs over two hundred workers at its plant in Wheatfield Road, in the city's Gorgie district.

The heroin that flooded the streets of Edinburgh in the early 1980s was widely believed to have been sourced from opiate-based products manufactured at the plant, through breaches of security. When these security issues were resolved, the huge local demand for heroin was satiated by cheap Pakistani product, which by this time had flooded into the rest of the UK. Conspiracy theorists point out that this glut of heroin importation occurred shortly after the widespread rioting of 1981, in many poorer areas of Britain, which was given most notable media attention in Brixton and Toxteth.

It Never Rains . . .

Janey can't say she wisnae warned; you'd need tae have been on Mars no tae have noticed that the Tories were cracking down on benefit fraud. So the courts make an example ay her. After issuing the six-month sentence, the judge describes himself as 'only being moved to leniency' by her tragic circumstances. He isnae the same yin who'd let her husband's murderer off with the fine.

That panicked bovine-to-slaughterhouse expression as they cart her away! She's begging them, imploring those stone faces to exhibit some kind ay mercy. The do-gooding, legal-aid vegetarian they appointed tae defend her looks almost as traumatised as Janey, and is probably already thinking aboot a career in company law. Maria, by my side, is once again in disbelieving tears. — They cannae . . . they cannae . . . she dumbfoundedly repeats. Elaine, her auntie and Janey's sister-in-law, a thin, bloodless woman who looks like a kitchen knife, dabs at her eyes with a snot-rag. Thankfully Grant, as with Dickson's trial, is kept oot ay the court, ensconced doon in Nottingham with Janey's brother, Murray.

I never thought it would work out like this. I'm quivering myself, as ah escort a lifeless Maria and Elaine intae Deacon Brodie's Tavern on the Royal Mile. The pub is like an annexe ay the court a couple ay doors along, full ay criminals and the odd barrister, and mair than a few tourists wondering how they've stumbled intae this weirdness.

Ah've set up a wee *too risky* for myself and Elaine, wi a Coke for Maria, who, tae our surprise, quickly throws one ay the nips back.

— What are ye daein? You shouldae even be in here, ah tell her, looking aroond, scanning the joint, as Elaine says something insipid in her East Midlands accent.

Maria sits in the high-backed seat, smouldering wi rage. — Ah'm no gaun back tae Nottingham! Ah'm steyin here!

— Maria . . . loove . . . Poor Not-ink-goom, Elaine begs.

— Ah telt ye ah'm fuckin steyin! And she seizes the empty glass, her knuckles gaun white as she tries tae crush it in her hand.

— Let her stay here for a few days, at my mother's, I urge the bemused

Auntie Elaine, and then murmur, — then I'll talk her intae goin back down on the train. Once she's a wee bitty calmer.

You can see a spark ignite in the sister-in-law's lifeless, beady eyes. — If it's no trooble . . .

It isnae exactly like cold-calling tae flog double glazing on a Barratt estate. Ah don't think Maria has been a particularly endearing house guest. Any roads, it's time tae get the fuck ootay here. As we head down the Mound to Princes Street, Maria's a wreckage; spewing vitriol about Dickson through her tears, causing passers-by tae steal furtive glances at us. We accompany the insubstantial, anaemic Elaine back tae the bus station, and watch her gratefully climb on the National Express coach. Maria's standing there on the concourse as the bus pulls away, arms again folded across her breasts, looking at me as if tae say, 'What now?'

I'm no taking her tae my mother's place. Too much disruption wi their recent move. We jump in a taxi and head back tae her now parentless parental home. Of course, ah ken the best way tae get her tae dae something is tae simply suggest the opposite. — Ye huv tae go back tae Nottingham, Maria. It'll only be for a few months, till yir ma gets oot.

— Ah'm no gaun back! Ah need tae see muh ma! Ah'm gaun naewhaire till ah git that fuckin Dickson!

— Well, ah suggest we pick up some stuff fae your place, then head up tae my mother's.

— Ah'm steyin in ma ain hoose! Ah kin look eftir masel!

— You'll dae something stupid. Wi Dickson.

— Ah'm gaunny kill um! It's him that's done aw this tae us. Him!

The cabbie checks us out in the mirror, but ah keep my gaze riveted on him and the nosy-beaked cunt soon switches his miserable, budgerigar eyes back onto the poxy road, where they fucking well belong.

The cab trundles down to Cables Wynd House, and ah reluctantly pay the fare. Maria exits swiftly n ah have tae run tae catch up with her. For a few anxious seconds I fear she's bolted and ah'll be locked oot, but she's waiting in the stair for us wi a challenging pout. We climb up tae oor landing and she opens the door. — Leave Dickson tae me, ah gently urge, as we enter the cold flat.

She crumples onto the couch wi her heid in her hands, her bottom lip hanging doon. Her body trembles lightly and there's mair waterworks. Ah switch on the lecky fire n gingerly sit doon next tae her. — It's only natural that ye want revenge, ah totally understand that, ah say in an even, soft voice, — but Coke was ma mate, and Janey's ma friend, so *ah'm* gaunny see that Dickson peys, and ah dinnae want you involved!

149

She birls roond tae me, blinded by snotters, rendered as repulsive as that bird in *The Exorcist*, and rasps, — But ah *am* fuckin involved! Muh dad's deid! Muh ma's in the fuckin jail! And he's doon thaire, she points ootside the big window, — walkin the streets a free man, pullin fuckin pints ay beer like nowt's happened!

Suddenly she springs up and she's charging oot the door. Ah'm right eftir her. But she's absolutely demented as ah hastily pursue her doon the stairs. — Where ye gaun, Maria?!

— AH'M GAUNNY FUCKIN WELL TELL UM!

At the bottom ay the stair, she tears across the concourse, doon the side street and tae the boozer, wi me a step behind. — Fuck sake, Maria! Ah grab her thin shoodir.

But she shimmies oot ay ma grip, throws open the door and runs intae the middle ay the pub, me follayin behind. Every head turns tae stare at us. Dickson, tae my great surprise, has actually resumed his duties behind the bar. He's idly talking tae a crony and daein the crossword. He raises his heid in response tae the deafening silence that fills the room. But no for long. — MURDERER! Maria screams, pointing at him. — YOU MURDERED MA DAD, YA BASTARD! YOU MUR . . . She starts choking as the fit ay frustration drains her, and ah grab her in a lock under her airms, and ah'm pulling her oot the door, as ah hear Dickson's smug but weak reply: — It's no what the coorts said . . .

Ah've got her ootside but the air seems to revive her. — LIT US GO, she roars, face mangled wi fury and grief. Ah'm struggling like fuck as her slender frame's fortified by hysteria and rage, and ah really feel like slapping her like they do in the films, but then it subsides, and she's greeting and whimpering in my airms and ah'm leading her doon the street and across the car park and back up the stairs, thinking that *this* was how it was meant tae pan out.

And as ah get her back indoors, and oan the couch, it's almost like her sherriking ay Dickson wis a bad dream, because she's in my airms and ah'm stroking her hair, telling her it's gaunny be alright. Telling her that ah'll stey here with her as long as she wants and we're gaunny get this Dickson cunt thegither, her and me . . .

— Will we? she asks in demented hunger, hyperventilating. — Me n you?

— Count on it, princess. Count. On. It. That fucking bum put Coke in his grave and, for aw we ken, Janey in the jail, and ah focus my spiteful, vengeful face oan hers. — He. Is. Fucking. Well. Getting. It.

— We'll fuckin well kill that murderin bastard!

150

— You and me. Believe it!

— Ye mean it? she begs.

Ah look right intae her desolate eyes. — I swear oan ma mother and sisters' lives.

She nods slowly at me. I can feel her tense body unwind a notch.

— *But* . . . we have tae box clever. If we're careless, we end up like Janey. Do you understand?

A blank, sluggish bow of her head.

— Think aboot it, I stress. — If we just steam in thaire and slaughter him, we spend the rest ay oor lives in jail. We huv tae be free tae savour it, tae enjoy the fact that we're daein oor thing while that bastard is drooling in a wheelchair or fucking well buried in some shallow ditch!

Her breathing slows down. Ah'm hudin her hands in mine.

— We have tae think aboot this. And when we strike our hearts have tae be as cauld as ice. As cauld as that cunt's doon thaire, ah point outside, — or he wins. He's goat the polis and courts on his side. That means we wait, play it cool, and suss out his weak spots before we strike. Because if we git sloppy or emotional, he wins again. We *cannot* let him win again. Ye ken what I'm sayin here?

— Ma heid . . . it's a nightmare . . . ah dinnae ken what tae dae . . .

— Listen tae me. We'll get him, I stress, and she's nodding and settling down, her hand on her forehead.

Ah feel sufficiently mollified tae get oot ma works and start cooking up.

The spark ay the lighter causes Maria's neck tae whip round. — What are ye daein . . . ? Her eyes widen.

— Ah'm sorry, it's your house, ah should have asked. Ah'm fixing masel up a wee shot ay skag.

— What? What's that? Is that . . . is that heroin?

— Aye. Listen, this is between you and me. Ah'm no proud ay it, but ah've been daein it a wee bit. Ah'm gaunny kick it intae touch, but, well, ah just sort ay need it at the moment. Since your dad . . . ah feel my head shaking, as ah look at her red, torn face, — . . . ah just feel so down, so powerless . . .

Maria's face is as immobile as porcelain. Her eyes are locked onto the bubbling liquid dissolving in the spoon. — This is the only thing that takes away the pain . . . ah tell her. — Ah'm gaunny take a wee yin, just tae keep the heebie-jeebies at bay. After aw, ye dinnae want tae get a serious habit, but it *has* been a fucking stressful day.

So ah'm sucking up the solution through the cotton ball, then piercing

151

my flesh with the point ay the needle. As ah draw some blood back, filling the chamber, Maria's eyes are darkening, as if some inky fluid is thickening behind them too. My blood goes back in slowly, but ah feel no pressure ay my hand on the plunger, it's like ma veins are sucking it in fae the syringe . . .

YA FUCKAH . . . YA FUCKIN BEAUTY . . . AH AM IMMOR-TAL, INVINCIBLE . . .

— Ah want some . . . ah hear Maria utter, in a choking gasp ay need.

— No way . . . it's not good stuff, ah tell her, sweating back oantae the sofa, gurgling like a rapturous infant as the gear unravels through me like a nursery rhyme. Then there's that almost honey-like nausea at my core . . . Ah take tight inhalations, letting ma breathing slowly regulate.

— What are you daein it for then?

— Ah've been feeling bad . . . sometimes ye feel so bad . . . it's the only thing that helps . . .

So baaaad . . .

— But ah feel bad! What aboot me! she says, her face going pinched and for a vaguely troubling second ah can see *both* Janey *and* Coke in it. — You sais ye would help me!

Ah look sadly at her, taking her trembling hands in mine. — You're a beautiful young girl, and ah dinnae want ye takin drugs . . . God, she is a shattered angel, cast doon tae this dark and despicable hovel. — . . . Ah mean, ah'm meant tae be taking care ay ye . . . no making things worse for ye. Ah shake my heid and feel the blood moving slowly through it. — No way . . .

— They cannae git any worse! she bellows, then seems tae think ay her current predicament. — But . . . but . . . just a wee bit, like you sais, she begs again, — jist tae make things feel better . . .

I feel ma breath pulling fae my chest, the same tight, drawing resistance a syringe plunger makes when you pull it back, that lovely *sealed* tug . . . — Okay, but this is a one-off . . . this is fucked up . . . n it goes against ma better judgement . . . just a wee bit, mind, tae relax ye. Ah stroke the side ay her face gently. — Then we work oot how tae get Dickson . . .

— Thanks, Simon . . .

— Ye must feel that the whole world's comin tae an end, ah nod as ah line up a fair auld dunt for her. — This'll help ye, babe; this'll take the pain away.

Her face is weak and bewildered as ah wrap my leather tie roond her thin, white airm and tap her vein up. Nice wiring she's got n aw. This wee yin craves, needs, oblivion, and the only decent thing tae dae is tae oblige a damsel in distress . . .

Ah gie it tae her one way, watching her groan softly and melting back intae the couch. — That feels good . . . it's nice . . . it's barry . . .

Then ah lay her down, resting her head on the couch armrest, tae prepare her tae get it the other way. — But you're the woman ay the hoose now, and you've got tae be strong for Grant. We baith need tae keep everything thegither here. For your ma's sake and your dad's memory. We'll go and see her soon, ah tell her, sweeping that fringe ootay her eyes and back across her foreheid, — okay, darlin?

— Aye . . . she says, looking at me, eyes glazed like shiny silver coins.

— Is that better?

— Aye . . . it feels nice . . . ah never thought ah'd feel this good again . . .

— We'll get Dickson; he's ours. You and me, we'll make that bastard pay, I whisper. Ah'm kneeling on the floor alongside her outstretched magnificence. Ah slide a hand under her heid, raising it up and slipping a cushion under it. — But just you relax the now. You've had a tough time. Want me tae lie wi ye . . . n hold ye?

A slow affirmative nod. — You're right nice tae us . . . and her hand rises and caresses the side ay ma face. Ah bend in closer towards those big wasp-stung lips.

— Course I am. You're nice tae be nice tae. Now gie's a wee kiss.

She looks at me wi a sad smile and kisses me on the cheek.

— Naw, naw, naw, babe, that's nae good. A proper woman's kiss, like.

And those lips are on mine and that tongue is in my mouth, and for now it's aw her work. Ah close ma eyes, briefly thinking aboot poor Janey, making soft toys in Corton Vale for the next few months. As the judge said, an example has to made of individuals who would seek tae exploit those in genuine need through fraudulent practices. I think he quoted the Home Secretary verbatim. But it'll be an education for Janey, she'll be licking mair fannies than a GPO clerk will stamps. But right now ah'm mair concerned wi her daughter's tuition, cause it's getting better with these long, wet kisses. Yes it is; ah'm certainly feeling nae pain. Cause she's mine now. Ah break off and tell Maria's sad, sexy, junked eyes, — Ah'll never leave ye, no like the others. Everything's gaunny be okay now.

A mournful smile moulds her features. — Ye mean that, Simon?

— Aye, I tell her, and ah've never been more sincere about anything in my fucking life, — I most serpently do.

Same Again

There's me getting off the number 1 at the fit ay Easter Road ootside the Persevere pub when ah see Lizzie McIntosh running for the bus, tryin tae keep control ay her big art-college folder that's being pushed and pulled by the gales. She is beyond gorgeous; sexy black boots ower woollen tights, a short red, black and yellay hooped skirt, or it might be a dress, ye cannae tell under that big broon overcoat, scerf n gloves. Her long broon hair's one shade darker that the coat. — Hud on, mate, ah tell the driver, who's about to pull away. Ah stick ma sports bag in on the platform in case he tries tae shut the doors, n git a sour look back for ma trouble.

Worth it but, cause she looks even better when she comes closer; hardly any make-up, just a bit ay eyeliner and some cherry lippy. — Thanks . . . Tommy . . . she gasps as she steps past Fearless Tommy Gun oantae the bus stickin her money in the slot. — Ah'm late for this do . . . She smiles at us. Ya beauty!

Well, faint hert never won fit bird, so: — That's a drink you owe me, ah try it oan, you've goat tae, as ah watch the doors slap shut and the grumbling driver makes some comment before starting up the bus and pulling away.

It's cauld; it's still October but there was a frost on the groond this morning and the pitches might be frozen. Much worse, fae a fitba viewpoint, is this shitey wind. But Rents is doon for the weekend fae Aberdeen, and we're oot the night, then at Easter Road the morn for the derby. So ah nash up tae my sister Paula's, tae dump the bag and get some scran doon. Ah got invited for my tea but ah'm no sure about her husband, this moaning-faced cunt fae Coventry who seems totally depressed aw the time. We can aw get that wey, but ye cannae let them beat ye and grind ye doon. Pecker up at aw times.

That Lizzie but . . . phoar . . .

So ah bolts the nosh doon n leaves my bag thaire and heads for the Volley, thinkin that ah'll be the first yin in. Nae chance! Thaire's a bunch sittin in the corner, wi Begbie haudin court, and he seems well chuffed tae see me. — Tommy boy! The very cunt!

154

— Awright, chaps? Ah nod at Rents, whae's wearin a rid-n-black-hooped *Dennis the Menace* jersey, then Nelly, whae's goat another tattoo oan his coupon, an anchor oan the side ay his cheek! The daft cunt. — Fuckin jailbait! ah joke, pointin tae it, then gie a mair distrustin acknowledgement ay that Larry, a twisted wanker that ah dinnae huv much time fir, and Davie Mitchell, an auld fitba mate ay mine whae works wi Mark at Gillsland's.

We're catchin up ower a few beers, huvin a crack. — D'ye git tae any Aberdeen games up thaire, Mark?

— Naw . . . Rents says. It's like he's stoned on hash aw the time. Sits wi a big daft smile on his face. Used tae rip the pish oot ay stoners and love speed n aw. Typical student cunt! — Cannae be ersed, he goes, fiddling with this spec case.

— You've no goat glesses, huv ye? Let us see!

— Naw, he says, n pits them in the inside poakit ay his jean jaykit. Must be embarrassed, poor fucker. Joinin the specky *and* ginger club that Keezbo's in!

Lucky for him that Begbie's talkin tae Nelly n Larry aboot tattoos, n they huvnae picked up oan it, so ah decide tae gie the four-eyed cunt a brek. Mark's sound, but for a ginger cunt he can sometimes be a bit bigheided and vain.

Begbie's bendin his ear now. — How's that Geordie bird yir seein? Fiona? He turns tae the rest ay us, pointin oot Rents. — Still waters run fuckin deep, right enough! No fuckin shy, this cunt!

— Barry, man, she's totally splendid, Mark smiles fondly. — She's away tae Newcastle tae see her sister. It's her birthday . . . ah mean, like, her sister's birthday, ken?

— If her fuckin sister's anything like her, pit a fuckin word in for me, ya cunt, Franco says.

— Will do, Rents goes wi that easy, wasted smile, but ye kin see that nowt would be further fae his mind. He turns tae Davie. — How's the boys at Gillsland's?

— Awright. Les was askin eftir ye. Young Bobby n aw, the wee fuckin dingul. Ralphy's still as much ay a cunt as ever, but, Mitch laughs.

— That man . . . Renton mumbles, then sits up straight, — . . . that fucker *defines* cuntishness.

— Aye, says Begbie, in darker tones, n ye kin tell he's goat something oan his mind, — thaire's a loat ay thum aboot.

— What's up? this Larry wanker goes tae Franco. Ah once had a run-in wi that cunt back at Leithy. He wis bullyin wee Phillip Hogan. Fuckin liberty-taker. Ye never forget these things.

155

Franco's voice drops in that scary wey, when ye kin hear him even mair clearly than when it's at its normal pitch. — Jist been hearin a lot aboot this cunt fae Pilton; the slag's brother, he goes, — ye'd think he'd shut his mooth eftir the wey the other two brars came doon here n goat fuckin dealt wi.

— Aye, ah nod, pure thinkin aboot that poor cunt bleedin aw ower the taxi. That was fuckin excessive.

— Well, this dippit big brother cunt's been gaun oan aboot how he's gaunny dae this, n how he's gaunny dae that. Cunt seems tae huv some fuckin rep doon in Pilton, Franco scoffs.

— So? Seems aw mooth tae me, ah goes, n Nelly nods in agreement.

The thought cheers Begbie up. — Well, if ah'd been fuckin well killed by every cunt that sais 'you're deid' tae us, ah'd hud tae huv hud ninety-nine fuckin lives!

Ah'm aboot tae change the subject, then that Larry goes, aw snidey, — He's meant tae be yin ay they karate boys. George Kerr-schooled. Black belt, they tell us.

— Fuck that, Begbie sneers, — some cunt kicks yir fuckin baws in, karate's no gaunny dae nowt against that. Does it fuckin well gie ye baws ay steel, then? he asks Larry.

— Naw . . . he's weasellin ootay it, — but ah'm jist sayin –

— Well, dinnae jist fuckin say, Begbie cuts um oaf.

Ah dinnae like where this is headin. Supposed tae be a few quiet peeves, then the big game the morn. Thaire's ey a charged atmosphere at the weekend ay a derby game; it's like a full-moon thing. — Ah think ye made the point, Franco, ah goes, n ah makes this chibbin motion n gits a wee grin offay him. — It'll be aw bluster. These cunts'll no be keen tae come ahead in a hurry eftir that.

— Aye, the cunt's brother's like a fuckin pincushion now, Nelly laughs.

Ah'm lookin tae Begbie but his coupon's gone that staney wey again. Ah ken that look. — Aye, but ye cannae make the point enough wi some cunts, but. Ah'm still hearin garbage comin fae this big brother cunt's mooth. It's like the wey things ur fuckin well gaun these days, yuv goat tae fuckin well kill some cunt tae get taken fuckin seriously. He looks aroond the table n makes the declaration: — Wir gaun doon thaire tae huv a wee fuckin blether wi this Hong Kong Fuey cunt!

Ah feel masel swallyin hard wi nowt in ma throat. — When likes?

— Nae time like the fuckin present. Franco's boatum lip curls doon. — Pey a wee fuckin visit. Huv a wee fuckin word wi the cunt.

Ah look aroond at the boys. They're aw game. Even Mark, whae's just doon for the weekend, smiles and goes, — Why not?

— *You're* no comin, Franco goes.

Mark looks at him, aw biscuit-ersed. — How no?

— You've goat that fuckin college. Yir no fuckin aw that up. This isnae your business. You've goat yir mate thaire. He points tae Mitch.

Rents shakes his heid. — *We're* mates, Franco. So it is ma business, he goes, but he's distracted, lookin past Begbie tae the pub door. Every time it opens, his eyes are trained on it.

Begbie pulls Mark taewards him, airm roond his shoodirs. He's lookin right intae they wasted eyes. — Is it fuck. Your business is tae dae well at that fuckin college n git the fuck oot ay here. Yir fucked oan that wacky baccy anywey, ya cunt. Some fuckin use you'd be!

Ah looks at Mitch. He's one ay ma best mates but ah've hardly seem um lately. Ah say tae him and Mark, — Youse two wait here. Ah'll be back inside an ooir.

Mitch nods, and Mark looks roond like he's gaunny protest, then shrugs. As we down our drinks, he looks sort ay relieved and unhappy at the same time aboot huvin tae stey. Rents isnae a violent sort ay gadge but he has his moments. He chibbed Eck Wilson at the school and he smashed this boy ower the heid wi a boatil eftir that Hampden semi. These things really stood oot cause he's normally no like that. He says he only gets violent when he's really scared. Mitch is very handy in a swedge but he's a Tollcross boy and this isnae his fight.

Nelly and Franco are maniacs and this Larry cunt, he's just a bully. We get ootside n pile intae Nelly's van, me n him in the back. We're drivin doon tae Pilton n Begbie's aw excited, giein us the instructions fae the front passenger seat. — Youse stey in the van n dinnae come oot till ah shout! Mind, wait till ah fuckin gie yis a shout!

— Ye sure aboot this? ah goes, cause it's beyond real n ah dinnae feel very Fearless Tommy Gun tae be honest. Sometimes it's right enough though, it takes bein a bit scared tae get ye gaun.

— Like ah sais, Franco roars, — ah'll fuckin well shout if ah need backup!

Ah say nae mair, cause he's made his point. Aw the wey doon, though, ah'm starin at Franco's heid thinking aboot how many punches it would take before he went doon. The combo that would put him away; jab, jab, straight right, left hook, right uppercut, straight left, right hook, left hook. N that fuckin Larry . . . one good right hook would crack that thin gless-boned jaw . . .

Doon in the scheme we see these wee boys playin fitba oan this bit ay waste groond. Nelly's rollin the windae doon. — Whaire's it the Frenchards live, mate?

157

The wee guys look at each other, then one points ower tae some auld broon tenements at the end ay a street that are gittin done up, n painted white. — Ower thaire in the Rise. Number 12.

N ah ken the Rise; it's a scabby narrow steep hill ay a street wi a church at the toap n some mingin shoaps at the bottom. We stops outside the hoose in front ay a skip, nearly full. Franco's oot the van, pointing tae the right-hand flat oan the groond flair. — That's the yin, he says, aw focused.

Then he's scowlin around the street, n he goes tae the skip, rummages for a bit. His eyes widen when he clocks this railing that's hingin oafay a buckled wrought-iron fence; like a car's ran intae it n fucked it. He works it free n huds it in baith hands, waving it aboot like a club. Then he heads tae the hoose, leavin his cudgel against the hedge outside thair gate. Aye, thir oan the groond flair, ye kin see them watchin the telly in the front room, n ah cannae believe it when Franco picks up a brick fae the skip n jist fuckin launches it through the windae! Thaire's an almighty crash follayed by some screams. Ah looks at Nelly n wir ready tae grab the daft cunt n git the fuck oot ay here.

— AVON CALLIN! ANY CUNT HAME? Franco shouts intae the street. You'd think the whole world wid be oot, but bar a few twitchin curtains, there's nae sign ay life. Maist ay the hooses are empty, derelict or bein renovated.

Apart fae the Frenchard hoose, that is. This big cunt's first oot the door, n the wifie's at the windae pointin at Franco n shoutin, — That's him! YOU! YOU! YOU TRIED TAE KILL MA LADDIE!

— Ah plunged the cunt, Franco half laughs, half sneers. — If ah'd wanted tae kill um he'd be fuckin deid by now!

The big cunt is fuckin incensed and he charges doon the path tae the gate taewards Franco. Franco's waitin n just takes a step back, picks up the railin and fuckin tans the bastard's jaw wi it, aw in one sweet motion. The big cunt goes doon like a ton ay bricks, it's a real fuckin seekner, the way the boy faws, n Franco's bringin doon the spikey end first wi baith hands n aw his weight oan it, right intae the poor cunt's baws. Then he leathers the boy a couple ay nasty shots across the coupon. — KEEP THE FUCK AWAY FAE LEITH!

The boy isnae movin at aw, n thaire's blood spillin ower the pavement. Aw, man, ah'm seek. For some reason ah climb oot ay the van n stand alongside Franco, who jist gies me a sharp, crazed look fae the corner ay his eye, n then ah look doon at the boy. It's a bad yin. Heid pure burst open. Teeth lyin oan the pavement like dominoes scattered fae a pub table. Jesus fuck.

The wifie's screamin at the two other boys, — GIT UM! The lassie's standin beside her chewin her nails, but the auld yin's jumpin up n doon like a Bowtow fishwife that's discovered shite oan her doorstep. — AH SAIS FUCKIN GET UM!

— COME AHEAD! Begbie roars tae the other two brothers. This poor big cunt's still groanin oan the deck at his feet. The brothers are jist standin n shitein it, like thir in shock.

They arenae the only yins. — Fuck sake . . . Larry goes, leanin oot the windae, his eyes bulging like a stud greyhound's baws.

The ma's still screamin at her sons, — GIT UM, YA CRAPPIN BASTARDS!

Begbie glances at them wi a mockin expression. — They'll fuckin well dae nowt, n he looks doon at the big muscle-bound cunt, sprawled oan the deck, — n he'll fuckin well dae nowt! He laughs at the burd. — If it's a laddie, geez a shout, but if it's a lassie, it's no fuckin mine!

He flings the railin doon, turns away, noddin tae us, n wi climbs intae the van, him in front, me roond the back. Nelly starts up, and we drive past the scene. The mother's still shoutin at her laddies, as they try, wi the help ay the burd, tae git the poor boy up offay the pavement.

Franco looks back at me n Larry. — This is what happens when they fuck aboot wi the YLT, n wir drivin past this circle ay run-doon hooses wi crap shoaps, n he's pushin his heid oot the windae. — PILTON FUCKIN LICE-HEIDED SCRUFFS, KEEP THE FUCK OOT AY OOR BIT, YA FUCKIN TRAMPS!

We're worried aboot the polis, no that they cunts would grass anybody up, and ah doubt they'd bother interruptin a tea brek at Drylaw Station for rubbish like that, but some auld cunt might have put the call in.

Franco's buzzin like fuck though, sittin wi a big grin oan his coupon. — An awfay loat ay fuss aboot some fuckin slag gittin up the duff. Next time ah ride her it'll be up her erse, so thit thaire's nae fuckin room fir accusations.

— Romance isnae deid, eh, Franco? Nelly grins fae the front, taking the van ootay the scheme, oantae the West Granton Road.

— Mibbe no, but they fuckin Pilton tramps ur. Ah'm no fuckin well finished wi they cunts yit. In fact, his face twists in outrage, — no even fuckin well sterted yit!

Ah have tae admit that ah'm shitein it, and ma heartbeat doesnae get tae normal until we stash the van in the lock-up at Newhaven, which is sortay Nelly's, but Begbie n Matty baith seem tae huv keys fir it n aw, then start tae headin oaf oor separate weys. Ah'm retracing ma steps tae

159

the Walk, tae meet Mitch n Rents back in the boozer. When ah get back there Mitch is sittin on his tod and the Rent Boy isnae aroond. — Where's Mark?

Mitch just sortay shrugs. — He headed off wi this wee guy that came in, that boy Matty. Said he hud tae go a wee message wi um, n thit he'd be back, Davie explains, then asks, — Is he awright? He wis acting pretty weird, ah mean, even for Mark, and ah've worked wi the cunt for donks.

— Aye . . . ah laugh, — well, ah think so.

— Ye sure?

— Probably too much hash. N ah think the cunt's in love n aw; this lassie up at Ebirdeen. He'll be away for mair grass or speed if ah ken that cunt, ah goes. N ah have tae say that ah envy Rents, everything's workin oot good for him; a nice bird, a good education, and ye ken that when he graduates, he'll be off somewhere, he'll no stick aroond here. Ah admire that aboot him, cause ah'm too much ay a home bird. Ah'd like tae git away, though. It would be great.

— Right, Davie says, raising the gless n drainin it. He shakes the empty tumbler and ah get the picture.

— Same again?

— As always.

Cold

Union Street

Another day of stoic ambulation through the city, walking down Union Street skelped by licks of hard wind. Edinburgh could be bleak, but Aberdeen really took the pish. A life could be wasted waiting for the sky tae change fae grey tae blue. But ah'm spending mair time up here now, no gaun hame so much.

The last time ah went back, ah got skag-hammered wi Matty, Spud n Keezbo at Swanney's.

Dunno how ah got tae Johnny's gaff fae a drug soirée at the abode ay veteran junky Dennis Ross at Scabbeyhill, though ah vaguely recollect gaun through ma pockets for donks, tryin tae find some poppy as a taxi cunt mumped like fuck intae ma lug, but ah resurfaced intae the conscious world at Tollcross. Ah mind the sun comin up, soaking Johnny's front room in a wreckin light that relentlessly blasted all our mortal decay and foibles back at us. Ah goat up, then Matty, Spud and me met the rest ay the boys in the Roseburn Bar, early doors before the derby, then a bunch ay us went up Haymarket n hit some mair boozers. The two sets ay fans were giein each other aw the big threat shite gaun doon the road, but the polis line stayed firm between them. The game was a grunting, sweating goalless draw. Bein fucked, maist ay the fitba passed us by, but ah mind that Hibs nearly swiped a late winner; McBride skippin past a Jambo and slippin it tae Jukebox, who skinned some other maroon cunt and passed tae Steve Cowan whose right-foot drive just missed the target wi the keeper beaten. Cradle-snatching Sick Boy had been indulgin in the gear as well, but he wis still gaun absolutely crazy, wi that perr wee Maria lassie in tow. She's a bit young fir him, and looked lost adrift the tempestuous sea ay radges.

A lot ay mental stuff wi Begbie went on eftir the game. Him, Saybo and a few others hammered these bams at Fountainbridge. That cunt's Saughton-bound if he keeps that shite up, nowt surer. But the chaos ay Edinburgh reminded me ay how much ah'd grown tae like the ritual ay ma life in Aberdeen. It made us realise that ma free-spirit pretensions were bullshit. In reality ah saturated ma days wi routine, until it pissed us off tae the point that ah wis compelled tae subvert it wi a dramatic break. A skag binge helped. Here, though, ah had Fiona, ma studies and ma walks. And the reason the trips back home had lessened: ah'd hunted doon a source ay gear.

Ah walked loads; trekking roond the streets for ages, and in all weathers. It seemed tae be aimless but ah was invariably drawn doon past the railway station taewards the docks. Ah'd stop and watch the big boats, gaun tae Orkney, Shetland and fuck knows where else. The squawking gulls would circle overhead; sometimes, as ah passed along Regent Quay, it was like they were raucously laughing at me, like they kent what ah was up tae, even if ah didnae.

Those nautical pubs: the Crown and Anchor Bar, the Regent Bridge Tavern (a great wee howf) n the Cutter Wharf. The tackier Peep Peeps, which lies doon the side street, n where ah eywis winded up; sittin wi ma lager, but wantin something else. Waitin for it. Almost smellin it. Sittin in that one spot, kennin if ah waited long enough it would come tae us.

That was where ah saw him; this cunt sitting oan his tod by the jukebox, readin the *Financial Times*, a Pepsi in front ay him. Untouched. His long black-but-greyin greasy hair toppin thin, cadaverous flesh with a bluish translucent hue. A wispy, scraggy beard growin fae a mustard-heided cluster ay spots on his chin. His big yellay teeth seemed likely tae faw oot if the cunt sneezed. In other words, he stank ay junk. Ah didnae. Ah was a clean-cut student cunt wi a nice bird. Ah couldnae have, no wi ma bright eyes and clear skin and white teeth. Fiona even had me flossin. But yet, when he saw me, it was like he kent straight away. So did I. Ah sat beside him.

— Fit like? he asked.

There was nae point fannyin about. — No so good. Ah'm a wee bit sick.

— Rattlin?

Fuck knows what that meant but it sounded spot on, and in its acknowledgement, it was like ah'd permitted masel tae feel crap. Before the shiteyness was a vague feelin ay flu-like symptoms; heavy limbs, watery heidedness and shiftin aches. Now something urgent lurked behind aw this shabbiness.

— Ye need some medicine then, min?

— Aye.

Don shot us a dim, candlelit gaze, similar tae the yin ah'd noticed in they aulder skagheids doon the road. — You go outside, take a wee walk around the block, he told us in a tinny, nasal voice, — N ah'll see ya at the dock gates in ten meenits, and he settled back tae his *FT*.

Ah actually waited fir seventeen minutes before Don deigned tae emerge fae the bar and scuffled taewards us lookin as shan as ah felt. Ah couldnae be physically addicted, no just eftir a weekend binge, but ma mind and body were keenin in anticipation ay a fix. Ah fought hard tae conceal ma almost overwhelmin excitement and anxiety as we went back tae his scabby flat roond the corner and did the deal.

Don's pad could have been Swanney's, Dennis Ross's, Mikey Forrester's or even ours in Montgomery Street. The same posters badly tacked oan-tae ugly, head-debasing patterned wallpaper, put up by cunts now deid or so auld as tae be as good as. The overflowing rubbish bins, chaotic dish piles in a sink like an earthquaked Mediterranean town, and the ubiqui-tous heaps ay auld clothes on the flair: the kitemarks ay chronically unto-gether losers everywhere.

Don cooked for us both. Ah tapped at my right airm where the best vein on ma wrist obediently popped up, and ah banged up in thaire. It wis decent shit and the rush wis excellent. It coursed through ma body, and ah wis flowerin irresistibly under its impact like a spring blossom. Then something fruity and sour was risin fae my stomach. Ah retched, and Don shoved an auld *FT* under ma face but ah slid it away. The moment had passed and ah wis now invincible.

Although ah wis content tae kick back and enjoy the gear (amazing how it rendered listenable even mawkit shite like Don's Grateful Dead tape), he insisted on makin conversation, even after his ain shot. The cunt took a healthy lick, which barely seemed tae affect him. Ah wondered how much he wis usin. — So . . . yir an Edinburgh boy, eh? Plenty decent shit doon thaire.

— Aye . . . ah said. Ah felt like explainin that in Leith we regarded oorselves as separate fae Edinburgh, but melted and enjoyin the buzz, it now seemed a trivial concern.

— That's where it aw comes fae. He held a wee placky bag fill ay white powder crumbs up tae a bare light bulb. — That's where they make it all: beautiful downtown Gorgie. Ye ken Seeker?

Fuck knows what aw this Gorgie stuff was aboot, ah was a Leith boy, but *que sera*. — By rep only.

— Aye, he's bad, man. Ya wanna keep away fae thon loon.

Ah smiled at the sweet futility ay it aw. It was inevitable that this Seeker and me would become associates at the very least. The only surprise was that it hadnae already happened. So ah sat there as Don droned oan and the room filled wi darkness. Ah wisnae interested whatsoever in anything he wis sayin; cunt could've been on aboot the new puppy he'd gotten his

165

niece or the deid bodies under his floorboards, but ah wis enjoyin the soothin rhythmic comfort ay his voice.

When ah felt able tae move, ah left and got back tae ma room in the residences. Fiona had slid a note under the door.

M
Called round, no sexy luxuriant Leith laddie. Boo-hoo.
See you tomorrow at Renaissance class or come round tonight for some tea . . . and crumpet?
Love
F xxxx

The note trembled in my hand. Ah loved that girl, ah really did. There was a horrible spasm inside as ah realised, even there and then, that she'd soon become less important tae me than a radge ah'd just met and didnae even like that much. But that was only a fleetin whisper, drowned oot by the song-and-dance act ay the skag, which crooned: 'You're awright, everything's awright.'

But ah never went roond tae hers. Ah lay doon on my bed and stared at the Artex swirl ay the ceiling. Eftir driftin intae an anaemic, bruised sleep, ah awoke tae hunger's cramps in the meagre morning light. Ah realised that ah'd eaten nothing whatsoever yesterday. Ma clobber lay discarded oan the flair by the bed; somehow, ah'd stripped oaf in the night. There was a yellay bruise on the crook ay ma airm. Ah decided no tae go tae my Renaissance class that morning.

But ah went walkin instead. It was cauld. For about a minute the grey sky ferociously split and sunlight burst through, pouring ower the city, reflectin off the glitterin granite. The blood pounded in ma heid, makin me want tae be somewhere else. Then it was away and that heavy cloak ay grey was back oan us. That was my preference; ah like the way my mind slows doon walkin under that sky, till ah'm numbed and thoughtless, free fae the oppressive burden ay endless mundane choices.

Ah'd just substituted one tomb for another, further up the coast. But that was okay; Aberdeen suited us. Ah liked the city, and generally liked the people. They were pretty cool and easy-goin; no brash, self-mythologisin wankers like so many lowland Scots who rabbited on, believing that ye saw them as movers and shakers, but they were invariably bores. In preference tae the student social life, ah'd drink wi auld fellys who telt me tales ay trawler fishing and the docks. Fitba gadgies who blethered about games and rows past; they seldom felt the need tae big themselves up, it was all very matter-ay-fact. Ah was always the lone student in these places.

Yet this was all so close tae Marischal College, Aberdeen University's graph-paper printout of a building. Only occasionally would ah venture intae the students' union bar, wi Bisto n some others, or Fiona. But ah avoided it as much as ah could. One time ah was dragged in for Joanne's birthday drink. She was a bit pished, turnin tae us in the company, in a nasty, accusin wey, — What do you dae aw the time, Mark, where do ye *go*?

Somebody else said something aboot 'the mysterious Mark Renton' and ah could check Fiona lookin at me wi encouragin intent. Aw they eyes oan me as ah laughed and said something lame aboot likin tae walk. In reality, ah now spent loads ay ma free time hangin around those dock-side bars, waitin for Don.

It was Saturday morning when Fiona next came roond. She was nae mug, but although we were in a relationship, we baith had independent lives as well. Edinburgh was close enough for me tae tell her ah was gaun hame for the night on some pretext or another, usually tae keep an eye oan ma grieving family. But ah'd be on Don's couch, in a section ay Aberdeen where few students or lecturers ventured. This time, though, ma bearing seemed tae confirm the impression ma absence fae classes throughout the week had gied her, namely that something was wrong.

— Mark . . . where have yer been . . . are yer alright?

— Ah think ah've picked a bad dose ay the flu.

— You look terrible . . . I'm ganna go down and get yer some Lemsip, pet.

— Can you dae me a photocopy ay your Renaissance notes?

— Course I can. You should have told me you were suffering like this, ya dafty, she said, kissin ma sweaty brow and headin out. She returned about half an hour later, with the medicines. Then she left us, tae go tae where she worked on a Saturday. Ah waited for a bit, and anxious tae get away fae the room's stale, chemical smell, *ma* smell (couldn't she smell me? Ah could smell me!), ah follayed her oot n doon the road.

Fiona did volunteer work on Saturdays wi deprived kids; rowdy wee urchins, who loved her. Jug-eared budding psychos would go aw flushed when she greeted them; hard-eyed, gum-chewing wee lassies would suddenly sook for attention. A few weeks ago, while on ma wanderins, ah'd clocked her meetin a bunch ay them ootside the Lemon Tree. She looked happy; she was a straightpeg. She'd talked about us findin a flat together next year. Then graduation, nine-to-five jobs and another flat wi a mortgage. Then engagement. Then marriage. A bigger mortgage on a house. Children. Expenditure. Then the four Ds: disenchantment, divorce, disease and death. For aw her protestations tae the contrary, that's who she was. That's what she expected. But ah loved her and thus fought tae conceal the ugliness she brought out in me. Ah kent, standin in the street, watchin her patiently herd the catlike kids intae the theatre, that ah could never be like that. Could never have her: *really* have her, in the sense of giving masel tae her. Or perhaps ah wis just being a bam. There was mair than a degree ay acceptance for me in her world. My ma and dad's aspirations were decent. Ah fuckin hated that word. It made my skin crawl.

But they cared.

In the bookshop, ah took up a spyin position, listenin to them in the adjoinin cafeteria. There was a speckoid, gawky and enthusiastic, with Fi and the kids. — Oh, boys and gerls, can you put your paper and pens away and come with me just now?

She would eventually be wi somebody like him. Maybe a cooler version, whae got a ride once in a while, perhaps a bit mair ay an arrogant cunt, whae might eventually fuck her around; but in essence the same. Dress them in an anorak and stick Coke-boatil specs oan thair coupon or a rugger shirt and pump them up wi muscle; it makes nae real difference, a straightpeg is still a straightpeg.

Ah head hame. When Fiona comes back, ah'm sittin up waitin. Ah huvnae taken anything else besides two Lemsips. Her hair's wet wi the rain. She dries it wi a towel she produces fae her backpack. The kettle's on and ah make some hot chocolate.

Knowin the thing ah've got aboot wet hair, Fiona glances tae the bed, then realises that my level ay sickness precludes grabbin her and throwin her oantae it. — You're shiverin, pet. You should go and see the docktah . . .

— Can ah tell ye something?

As soon as her pupils expand and she says, — Of course, Mark, wharrisit? ah know that ah cannae tell her what ah want tae, but in order tae conceal that fact ah have tae disclose something equally profound and important.

— My wee brother, ah hear myself say, almost shocked at ma ain voice, like somebody else in the room has grassed us up, — I've never telt anybody this before . . .

She nods, wrappin her hair up in the towel, and pickin up the steamin mug. She looks like the jilted bird in yon Nescafé advert.

168

Ah clear my throat as she coils intae the lotus position in the chair.
— Wee Davie, ah sort of worked out, had this kind ay thing aboot Mary
Marquis, who reads the Scottish news on telly. Ye might have seen her,
she's got . . . I suppose you'd call them Italian looks; dark, with loads of
make-up, big attention tae the eyes, and bright rid lipstick.

— Ah think ah know the one yer mean, pet. In the evening?

— Aye, that's her. Well, ah sortay noticed that Wee Davie got agitated
when she read tae camera. His breathin became deeper. N ye couldnae
really miss what wis happenin in they tracksuit bottoms . . .

Fiona nods understandingly. There's a red mark on her jeans at the knee
ah huvnae seen before. Probably paint fae some workshop wi the kids.

— Ah used to have tae watch him around teatime on a Friday. When
the Scottish news came on, ah'd see Davie stare at the screen, his cock
visibly erect, n ah started tae think, he's fucking fifteen, the poor wee
bastard . . . ken what ah mean?

— Yes, Fiona sais, sadly but analytically. — Like he's got a sexuality n
na ootlet for it.

— Exactly, ah exhale, just so relieved that somebody fuckin well *under-
stands*. — So . . . ah decided that ah'd wank him off.

Fiona's eyes briefly hit the floor, then rise to meet mine. Her lips press
tightly together. She's no tellin me to carry on, but she isnae sayin stop.

Ah take a deep breath. — So ah did. It seemed tae comfort him.

— Oh Mark . . .

— Ah know, ah know . . . it's my brother and it's a sexual thing, so it
wasnae a sensible move. Ah can see that now. At the time, though, ah wis
just thinkin about alleviatin his distress, like when ah used tae beat his
back tae help drain the fluid off his chest cavity. So ah did it. The poor
wee bastard went crazy and blew off a load in what seemed like a split
second. Then he fell intae a contented doze. Ah'd never seen him so at
peace. Ah cleaned him up and he had the best kip ay his life. So ah
thought: nae harm done.

— What happened? She unravels herself and lowers the mug tae the
flair, her eyes never leavin mine.

— He grew tae expect it. Autistic kids are programmed tae routine.
Like clockwork. Meals the same time, bed the same time. It became his
sort ay Friday treat; if he hudnae had his other physical issues he'd have
been constantly daein it for himself, aw day n aw night. But then, the other
days when the news was on, he'd look at the screen, then at me and shout,
and ah emulate that horrible cry, — MAY-HAY! MAY-HAY . . . Of
course, ah couldnae help him out, wi everybody else bein in the hoose.

Fiona's expression is now one ay distaste. She sits stiff and cross-legged in the chair.

— They aw thought he was shoutin 'Marky' and found it touchin. Only he and ah knew he was shoutin 'Mary', ah explain, and Fiona's now so still, it unnerves me. — Do you think ah wis wrong?

— No . . . she says hesitantly, — course not, pet . . . it's just . . . it's just . . . could you not tell them about yor Davie?

— We don't have that sort ay relationship. It's my *parents*.

A pensive nod, as Fiona picks up the mug and cradles it in her hands.

— Well, ah kept on wankin him off, every Friday, tae the image ay Mary oan the box. It wisnae easy; things got mair difficult. She'd be readin in the studio and he'd be aboot tae blow, then they'd cut tae an outside broadcast and he'd crumble and start tae scream and sometimes go intae a coughin fit. It went oan like this. It goat soas that tae get him oaf ye really hud tae go for it. Well, one day, ah forgot aboot oor Billy gettin hame on leave fae Belfast. Didnae hear him sneak in, the wey he used tae dae tae surprise my ma. He came up behind us on the couch . . . just as Mary came back on screen . . .

Fiona's eyes widen. — So . . . so . . . he caught yer doin this ta yor Davie? Yor Billy?

— Worse. Wee Davie's knob exploded and he shot off a wad that flew up intae the air and Billy copped the lot ay it, like a party streamer, doon his face and the front ay his army uniform.

Fiona's hand goes tae her mooth. — Oh my God . . . oh Mark . . . what happened?

— He hauled me n Davie apart, dragged me off the couch and booted me in the side. Ah got up and even though ah got a couple ay licks in, ah took a bit ay a doing. Wee Davie was screamin. The neighbours heard the racket and Mrs McGoldrick banged oan the door, threatenin tae call the polis, which probably saved me fae a real paggerin. We baith calmed doon, but when my ma and dad came back, they kent we'd been fightin. So they quizzed us and we each telt our sides ay the story.

It's started rainin ootside. Ah kin hear it crackle on the windaepane.

— What did they say?

— They mair or less took his part. Called me a twisted, manky wee fucker. Ah'd no that long left the school; ah couldnae articulate what ah wis gittin at by daein that for him. Disabled people's right tae sexuality! Ah punch ma chest, as if she's questioned me, but she's keepin stumpf, noddin in some kind ay sympathy. But through her silence ah suddenly tipple how it aw looks. Ah ken that if she had a disabled sister, the last

170

thing on God's Earth Fi would contemplate daein would be giein the lassie a frig ower, say, David Hunter fi oot ay *Crossroads*. For the first time, ah huv tae acknowledge that ah might be, on some level, a sick cunt, or at least misguided. My voice drops in anguished plea, — He wis in torment, n ah wis only tryin tae gie the poor wee fucker some release. It's no as if ah goat any kicks fae it!

For a while Fiona gazes out of the fading light at me, almost blankly, but her face has the composure of someone perfectly at peace. — Can't you tell em that now? Yor mam n dad?

— Ah've tried it once or twice, but it's never been the right time. Besides, ah think thair minds are made up aboot us.

She blows out through tight lips. — Why don't ye write them a letter? Set it all down in black and white?

— Ah dunno, Fi . . . it would feel like ah wis makin more of it than there was . . . ah says, suddenly feelin sick n tired, slumpin back in the chair, then lurchin forward, wrappin ma airms roond masel.

— It obviously means something to them though, Mark. And to you, or you wouldn't be telling me.

— Ah know, ah say, lookin up at her in defeat. — Ah'll think aboot it. Thanks for listenin.

— Of course, love . . . Fiona smiles sadly, acknowledgin my sweatin and twitchin. — Ah'll get off then, pet, let you get some sleep, she coos, risin and touchin my sweaty forehead with her palm, then kissin it. Her airms aroond me feel heavy and constrictin and ah'm relieved when she goes.

As soon as a decent couple ay minutes have passed, ah'm doon tae the payphone, callin Sick Boy at Montgomery Street. Ah go on a rant, tellin him about Don, askin him what he was daein about gear. He sais tae me: — You've nae interest in anything but smack.

When protest seems pointless and futile, ah realise for the first time that this statement is basically true. It makes me think, you really need to stop this. Ah dinnae register anything else he sais, till the pips go.

You're going to have to stop this right now or you're going to fuck everything up.

So what ah did was ah got ootside and walked through the cauld, squally city, and doon Union Street.

Baltic Street

The taste of metal blood in her mouth signalled to Maria Anderson that she'd run out of chewing gum. Spitting onto the grey wet stone, she pulled a tendril of hair from behind her ear, twirled it into a short spiral on her finger, replaced it; repeated the action. They still hadn't got Dickson, but her sickness wouldn't compromise on the imperative of getting sorted out. After all this, her and Simon were going away together, London or somewhere like that. He had big plans.

Sick Boy watched her from a street doorway. Her compulsive behaviour reminded him of that dog the Rentons used to have, how it had to turn around three times in its basket before it settled. Things had gone to shit quickly, after promising so much. Sick Boy had experienced a bitter pang of disappointment on learning that he wasn't Maria's first lover. Some boy at school and an opportunistic Spanish waiter had struck gold first. He compensated by expanding her horizons, and a few of his own. She was at her best when starting to get needy; that brief phase before the total debilitation where you imagined you could fuck the growing sickness out of your system. Skagged up she was compliant enough, but getting her to assume the positions with any gusto was problematic.

The bustling of an engine, and a car bumping over drizzled cobblestoned roads, smeared with orange light from the street lamps. A Volvo pulling up alongside Maria; window winding down, and a small-looking man eyeing her up, then addressing the advancing Sick Boy, whose head moves like a falcon's shaking free from its training hood. — Does your friend need a ride?

— Aye, he says, looking into her vacant face and glassy, abandoned eyes. He converses with the man for a bit then urges her, — Go on, Maria, get in, the boy's sound. He's just gaunny take ye for a wee spin, back tae his, then drop ye back here. Ah'll see ye back at the flats.

Anxiety rocks her frame. — But can we no just take him back up the hoose?

— Ye dinnae want everybody, neighbours n that, kennin our business. That Mrs Dobson was nosin aboot the other day. His big eyes scan the street. — Goan! I'll see ye the night, honey.

— Ah dinnae want tae . . . she protests.

This'll be her third punter. Dessie Spencer from the boozer had gone back, and then Jimmy Caldwell. He hates to share her, but it's just sex-for-money and it means nothing. — You getting in? the suit in the car whines.

Sick Boy smells off-duty bacon but they have wallets as well and in any case he's too sick to care. In fact arrest and incarceration now seem less a potential handicap, more a genuine opportunity to get cleaned up. It's all going wrong. Everybody's on the gear, not Tommy, Begbie, Second Prize or Gav, but just about everybody else. Maria was keener than he thought; not just sexually, but a proper hound for the junk. Being with her had helped spiral his own habit out of control. She's stiff and fraught, reluctant to get into the suit's car. Sick Boy tries to push her forward. — Just go!

She literally digs her heels into the cobblestones. — But ah dinnae want tae, Simon . . .

— I can't wait around, the suit moans. — Are you coming or not? Fuck it! And he starts the car up and tears away.

Sick Boy slaps his head, watching a small plastic bag containing a precious white kidney bean and few crumbs' worth of heroin speeding from him. He turns to Maria and in frustration vocalises what the suit was thinking: — Fuckin unprofessional!

— Ah'm sorry, ah dinnae want tae dae this . . . she wails, suddenly rendered weak-kneed with sickness and angst, grabbing the lapel of his silver herringbone jacket, — ah jist want tae be wi you, Simon . . .

Sick Boy's shocked at his searing contempt for this girl, so recently an object of unbridled desire. How she seemed to take to the gear so easily. Coke's pish-heid addict's genes, he supposes, brushing off her grip and spitting out the *News at Ten* theme song. — Dih-dih-dih, di-di-dih-dih! We're sick. Ding! We need gear or we'll get sicker still. Ding! It costs money. Ding! Maria's lips curve outwards and she hunches away from him. He looks at her waiflike figure and feels a pang of conscience through his junk need; she isn't ready for walking the streets. — Okay, okay, baby, you go back tae the hoose. I'll get somebody along for a wee perty.

— Ye still love me? she whines.

— Course ah do. He takes her in his arms, gratified to feel his prick stiffen. He wants her, believes he loves her. If they were different, if *he* were different . . . — Just go back n wait for us.

Maria traipses off. Sick Boy watches her go. There's something about her walk, more cocky and assured the further she gets from him, that

173

almost gives him the suspicion that he might be being played. Did she really believe he was going to kill an ex-copper with her? The big problem with introducing her to guys was that she was sensing her power over them. She fair had fat Caldwell mesmerised the other night. A dopey prick like that could be made to do *anything* for sweet young minge. It might be hard to keep a hold of her.

He walks about for a bit, brain burning with stampeding notions. At the Foot of the Walk in Woolies, a sloppy home-made sign with glitter glued around its border proclaims that there are only twenty-one shopping days left till Christmas. Then he spies a dark blue hooded Wrangler top, shivering in the dingy drizzle under the canopy of the Kirkgate shopping centre; knows that Spud Murphy is inside it.

— Ye hudin? they ask each other at the same time.

— Nup, Spud says, as Sick Boy shakes his head.

— Saw ye wi that wee Maria chick earlier, Spud ventures, chalky face long and fretful, like that of an old priest under his cowl.

— Dinnae mention her tae me. Dozy wee hoor thinks she kin keep us gaun oan fiver blow jobs. Not a fuckin scooby. Thir aw eftir tight pussy, tight erse. She could clean up, but she needs tae learn. Too soft, that's ma fuckin problem.

Forget Maria, Spud is the real innocent, Sick Boy thinks, knowing his friend is probably putting his bilious rant down to junk-stress fantasising, swiftly reconfigurating it in his mind to something acceptable. He can almost *hear* Spud's internal mantra of puppies and kittens and fluffy bunny rabbits, drowning out his own loathsome spiel. For a split second he wishes he could be like him, till something quickly rises in him to crush the notion.

The friends walk for a bit, but the rain intensifies beyond annoyance level, compelling them to stop outside the carpet shop under the bridge in the Walk. — Thir takin this doon, Spud says, looking up, — the bridge. It's the auld line ootay Leith Central Station.

— So it's confirmed then: no fucking escape fae this rat-trap.

A sulk loosens Spud's face. Sick Boy knows he hates to hear people talk down Leith, and it's inexcusable if they're actual natives. But Spud is desperate, cold and skint, so he informs his friend, — Goat chucked ootay the hoose, eh.

— Too bad.

Spud's eyes drip with need, as large, luminous and haunted as the most pathetic Disney character. — Ah wis jist wonderin . . . could ah crash at yours? Jist for a few days, likesay man, till ah git back oan ma feet . . .

Sick Boy graciously hands him the keys, to Spud's visible shock. —

Course you can, mate, any time, ye ken that. You get up there and get that fire started and I'll be roond later. I have tae go up the South Side tae my ma's, he says as Spud's grubby fist cagily takes them, half expecting them to be cruelly pulled away.

— Cheers, catboy . . . you're one ay the best, he says, in a gasp of relief.

You have to back up your mates, Sick Boy thinks, not without a satisfying tickle of virtue, as he heads up the Walk, reappraising his own strategy. Now he'll tap up his mother and sisters, go to Johnny Swan's, get sorted, then head back down to the port, hitting a boozer to procure a punter for Maria. He glances back at the grateful Spud, shambling down towards Constitution Street, probably heading for St Mary's Star of the Sea to light a candle and pray for forgiveness for his friend, and to ask God for some skag. No doubt he'll spy a distracted Cathy Renton, Sick Boy thinks, trailing caramel fingers in the holy-water font.

Sick Boy has just enough small change for the bus up to the Bridges and his mother's house. But reaching her new home, as he walks in, he feels something perish inside him. His father sits there, in his old armchair, like he'd never left it; stolid, transfixed on the television cop show. And his mother, wearing a big, contented smile.

— Nice billet, eh? Davy Williamson grins at his son.

— Ye took him back in . . . Sick Boy gasps at his mother. — I can't believe it. He turns the full glare of a favoured only son's accusation on her. — You took him back in. Why? Why did you *do* that?

She can't speak. His father plays an invisible violin, a spoof tortured look on his face. — That's the wey it is. Dry yir eyes, boy.

— Son, me n yira faither . . . in halting protest his mother finds her tongue, before being gently hushed by her husband.

— Shh, shh, sweetheart, Davy Williamson's finger at his lips. Having silenced his wife, the father then turns to his son, addressing him in a steady tone. — Keep it oot. He taps his own beak, an impressive hook of broken blood vessels. — Keep that fuckin neb oot!

Sick Boy stands rigid, his fists balling up. — You fuckin –

In a grandiloquent, dismissive gesture, Davy Williamson slowly outstretches an arm and upturns a palm. — Ah dinnae git involved in your love life, so dinnae you be botherin yirsel wi mine, he smiles, cocking his head to the side, his face clownish. His mother looks bewildered, as an involuntary gasp explodes from Sick Boy's chest. *This cunt knows everything.* — Aye, ye didnae like that, did ye? his father confirms with a smile. — Well, mind, keep yir neb oot ay *ma* business!

175

— What's aw this aboot . . . ? his mother asks.

Davy Williamson, in mock-formal tones, declares, — Nothing at all, my darling, in control of them all, yet again. He fixes Sick Boy in a coothie grin. — Isn't that right, my bambino?

— Fuck off, Sick Boy shouts, but he's the one leaving, his departure soundtracked by his mama's pleas and his father's derisive laughter as he vanishes onto South Clerk Street.

Confusion reigns on his burning-necked march down the Bridges; he's still skint and unsure of whether to stop off at Montgomery Street and see Spud, or to carry on right down into Leith for Maria. That's the one. He'll go there and he'll take her to bed, and hold her and protect her and love her; the way he was meant to, the way he should have done all along. No trawling pubs for dirty tramps to take back to her; they'll lie in bed for days together, sweating the shit out of their system, holding each other, looking after each other, till the nightmare passes and they finally wake up into a new, golden era.

It's the only way tae move on . . .

Then a car horn sounds, as a ruined Datsun pulls up. It transits the corpulent figure of Jimmy Caldwell, who rolls down the window. — Some perty the other night but, eh? That wee bird ay yours. Ah wis tellin Clint here aw aboot it, he nods to a jagged-featured accomplice, riding shotgun, who flashes a lascivious smile. A lone gold tooth gleams like a mansion erected in the centre of a crumbling scheme.

—Youse up for another one right now? Sick Boy says, stooping, thought instantly short-circuited by need.

— Hop in the back, Caldwell flashes an affable smirk, — wuv goat the hireys. The lure ay the lira, eh, Si?

— Aye, says Sick Boy, in an absent-minded fug, as he swings inside the cramped space, feeling his aching bones protest against the hard leather seats. — *Le cose si fanno per soldi . . .*

Heavenly Dancer

Ah'm sittin in the hotel bar waitin oan Fiona. Thinkin aboot her heart-melting smile and that sexy, concentrated frown when she evaluates books and the comments made by lecturers. Whenever she comes into a room, ma spirits soar. What ah feel is delight, pure and simple. Our life is all passionate kisses and soft wells of laughter. Ah love watchin her in class; even though we're shaggin, it's still great tae just look at her.

We've been thegither almost four months. If you dinnae count the weird relationship ah have with Hazel, it's the longest ah've been wi a lassie. But ah still ken next tae fuck all; cause tonight it's over. Tonight, in this hotel bar, ah'm gaunny dump the best girlfriend I've ever had; the prettiest, brightest lassie ah've ever known. Okay, so thaire might no be that much competition, but it still holds true.

This is a wee bar in a wee hotel, ah suppose in a wee country, but Scotland's always felt big tae me, cause ah've really only seen my ain wee corner ay it. The gaff has a travelling salesman vibe. A shiny blue cairpit spread apologetically thin across the flair; built-in seats line the waws, wi distressed copper tables and stools positioned aroond them; above the fireplace a signed, framed picture ay Martin Buchan in an Aberdeen strip.

A barman is polishing wine glesses. The door's opening n ah see what looks like a female figure, briefly hesitating behind its ribbed glass. At first ah think it's Fiona, but it's an aulder woman. Probably about ages wi muh ma; forties, wearin a tight black skirt and a white blouse.

Fiona Conyers. The courage tae be cruel. Tae say goodbye. Thoughts in ma heid that cannae be shared. The pint ay lager untouched in front ay me. It isnae what ah want. What ah want's doon the docks at Don's. Or back in Edinburgh. At Johnny Swan's.

Where is she? Ah check the cloak oan the wall; fast, like aw pub clocks, surely. Maybe she's dumped us first. Hopefully. Problem solved.

Fiona willnae be oan the market for long. She's a looker; moreover she's a student wi a fanny, livin away fae hame. She'll find somebody whae's proper boyfriend material, as fuckin manky Joanne might say. *Mark was okay, but not exactly PBM.*

177

The woman at the bar is chatting tae this mannie . . . Naw, man. Ah've been in Sheepland too long. Ah see it now; she's a prozzy, a hooker, a dirty big hoor. Ya cunt ye, ah dinnae believe it! Ah love the wey she's hudin that fag, the manufactured smile, the deep throaty laugh, straight oot ay Hollywood film noir, where the women were hard-arsed, dirty rides with fast, trashy gobs.

Ah've decided that this woman is the coolest fucker in the world. A middle-aged Aberdeen prostitute in a hotel bar full ay travelling salesmen whae huv tae haggle wi thair employer for every sandwich oan thair expense account. *Do you accept Luncheon Vouchers?* Look at the boy. Like me n Fiona in years tae come. Fuck that, ah'll never be like that. Never, ever.

The prozzy laughs again, loud and proud. Ah love that big, fuck-you laughter in people. In lassies in particular. Fiona n me laughed a lot thegither. She still does. Laughs for two.

Eywis thaire for me. The funeral, Wee Davie n that.

The sex wi Fiona might no have been particularly adventurous, but it was the most emotionally intense ah'd had. She helped us git ower that slightly squeamish thing ah'd eywis hud aboot shaggin. Mind you, jist gittin oot the hoose did that, cause ah'd always associated sex wi spasticated lunacy. Ma n Dad bathin Wee Davie n jokin aboot his erection. My spazzy wee brother's cock had tae be grotesquely outsized, another cruel joke on us aw, something that he'd never get tae use, in spite ay ma assistance wi Mary, but bigger than anything me or Billy wir packin.

The shame. The embarrassment. The horror.

The postural drainage.

Doof.

Doof.

Doof.

Clear the lungs. Paint the Forth Road Bridge. Patch up the sinking boat.

It's done.

Dae it again.

No more. I'll never have tae hear that horrible thumping, wheezing, coughing and gasping again.

Ah never, ever brought a lassie back tae the hoose: only ma closest mates that knew the score. Sick Boy, surprisingly, would be pleasant tae Wee Davie, and effortlessly charmin tae ma folks. Tommy was decent, he'd engage wi the wee fucker, joke aroond and laugh. Keezbo tae. Matty looked embarrassed, but he put up wi Wee Davie drooling and snottering ower him. Spud would attribute Davie wi mystical powers believing he saw mair thin he could express. Begbie was honest; he'd just sit in the kitchen wi Billy, puffin tabs, blowin the smoke oot the windae, ignorin the wee cunt as he twitched and gurgled while my ma constantly beat his back tae stop the build-up ay fluid in his bronchial tubes.

How did I feel about him . . . ?

N ah'm sittin here in this hotel bar aware thit it's aw bullshit. Tracin a line fae Wee Davie tae aw this; the junk habit, the soon-tae-be-single status when Fiona walks through that door. Cause Sick Boy, Matty, Spud, they nivir hud a Wee Davie. Nivir needed yin tae git oan the gear. Ma big brar, Billy, he hud yin, but he's nivir even smoked a joint. Cunts that try and psychoanalyse the fucked-up miss the crucial point: sometimes ye jist dae it cause it's thaire n that's wey ye are. Ah watched my mother and father tear themselves apart and rip each other's family trees up at the roots, trying tae work oot where all Wee Davie's bad genes came fae. But in the end, they grew tae accept that it doesnae matter. It just *is*.

N here comes Fiona. A dark green hooded top. Tight black canvas trooders. Black gloves. Purple lipstick. Makin me feel like greetin wi her big, easy smile. — Sorry, Mark, me dad was on the phone — She stops abruptly. — Wharrisit, love? What's wrong?

— Sit doon.

Dinnae say it . . .

She does. Her face. Ah cannae dae this. Ah need tae dae this. Because somehow ah sense that it's the very last unselfish thing I'll ever be able tae dae. Ah can't stop. Now ah'm gaunny hurt her but it's for her ain good. Weed-like fear creeps through me. — I was thinking we should go our separate ways, Fi.

Fuck . . . did ah really say that?

— What? She tries tae laugh in my face. A bitter laugh, like it's a sick joke ah'm makin. — What're ya ahn aboot? What d'ya mean, Mark? What's wrong?

It is a joke. Laugh. Tell her it's a joke. Say, actually, I was wondering what you thought about us gittin a place together . . .

— You n me. Ah jist think we should split up. A pause. — Ah want tae split. For us tae stoap gaun oot thegither.

— But why . . . She actually touches her chest, touches her heart, and at that moment mine nearly breaks in unison. — There's somebody else. In Edinboro, that Hazel lass . . .

— Naw, thaire's naebody else. Honest. Ah jist think wi should baith move oan. Ah'm no wantin tied doon. See, ah'm thinkin ay packin it in, the uni n that.

179

Tell her you've been depressed. You don't know what you're saying. TELL HER . . .

Fiona's mouth hangs open. She looks dafter and more undignified than ah could ever have conceived. That's my fault. It's me. It's me that this is aw doon tae. This shite. — We wor merkin plans, Mark! We were ganna travel!

— Aye, but ah need tae git away oan ma ain, ah say, feelin masel settlin intae a rhythm ay cruel apathy. Finding the cuntishness ye need, tae go through wi something like this.

— But why? Summat's wrong wi yer, you've been really weird. You're always sick with the cold, you've had it ahl winter. Yor brootha –

Yes . . . yes . . . that's it. Tell her it's him. Tell her SOMETHING . . .

— It's nowt tae dae wi ma wee brar, ah say emphatically. Another pause. Confession time. — Ah've been usin heroin.

— Oh Mark . . . Ye can see her workin it aw oot. The scabs on the underside ay ma wrist n the crook ay ma airm. The constant sniffling. The fever. The lethargy. The mingingness. The paring back and avoidance of sex. The secrets. She's almost relieved. — Since when?

It feels like since always, though it isnae. — Last summer.

Something sparks in her eyes and she pounces, — It's yor Davie's illness . . . and him passing away. You're just depressed. You can stop! We can get through this, pet, her hand shooting across the table, grabbing mine. Hers warm, mine like a slab ay troot oan ice in a fish shoap.

She isnae getting the big picture. — But ah *dinnae want* tae stoap, ah shake ma heid, pullin ma hand away. — Ah'm sortay intae it, but, ah confess, — n ah cannae keep a relationship gaun. Ah need tae be oan ma ain.

Her eyes bulge out in horror. Her skin glows a pink flush. Ah've never seen her look like this; it's like an extreme version of when we're in bed and she's startin tae get there. Finally, she erupts. — You're dumpin me? *You're* dumpin *me?*

Ah glance ower her shoodir at the reaction ay the barman. He pointedly turns away in displeasure. A tight sneer ah'd never thought her capable ay disfigures Fiona's face. It husnae taken long fir some arrogance tae come tae the fore. But ah'm gled ay it. — It's just me, ah tell her, — thaire's naeboody else. It's jist the junk.

— You . . . you're packin *me* in, cause you wanna spend more time doin fuckin *heroin?*

Ah look at her. That's it, in a nutshell. Nae sense in denyin it. Ah'm fucked. — Aye.

— You're runnin away, cause you're a fuckin coward, she spits, loud enough for a few mair heids tae turn. — Go on then, ya crappin bastard, she says, standin up, — pack it in, pack me in, pack *us* in, pack in the uni! That's ahl ye are, that's ahl ye'll evah be. A COWAHD N AH FUCKIN WASTAH!

Then she's off, slammin the frosted-glass door behind her. She briefly turns, as if to try n look back in. Then she's gone. The hooker, her cunty-bawed John and the cocksucker barman look briefly roond as she vanishes. In her rage, ah see a different side tae this gentle, loving girl and, although it shocks me, ah'm glad it's there.

Ah thoat it went quite well.

Supply Side Economics

Russell Birch, dressed in a white lab coat, clipboard in his hand, strode past Michael Taylor, clad in his customary brown overalls, on his way into the plant's largest processing lab. The two men ignored each other, as was their custom. They'd both agreed that it was better if all factory workmates remained unaware they had any relationship.

As he punched the security code into the new lock system, Birch satisfyingly reflected that Taylor would now be unable to access this area. Opening the door and stepping into the blindingly white room, he recalled the time he'd caught his partner red-handed here, about to fill up a plastic bag. No, Taylor, as a storeman, shouldn't have been there at all, but as Russell Birch was stuffing his own bag into his trousers at the time, they'd gaped at each other in mutual guilt, for a few stupefying seconds. Then both men had looked shiftily around, before their eyes met again and made an instant pact. It was Taylor who had seized control of the situation and spoke first. — We need tae talk, he'd said. — Meet me in Dickens in Dalry Road after work.

The entire scenario would not have looked out of place on the stage of a West End farce. At the pub, as the pints had flown nervously back, they'd even joked about this, before coming to the arrangement that Birch would get Taylor the bags from processing, which he would then smuggle out of the plant in canteen meal containers.

The instruments on the console blinked and moved slowly to a dull hum under the fluorescent strip lights above. Sometimes the room seemed as stark and white as the synthetic powder it produced, in this, the newest and most lucrative part of the plant. But Russell most reverently regarded the precious white powder, running in a steady, abundant stream from the tube into the perspex cases on the automated but almost silent line. His eyes traced back to the big bowl of cloth filters, then the ammonium chloride tank, where the solution cooled, back to another set of filters and the giant hundred-gallon steel drum. Into this drum, every hour, went sixty gallons of boiling water, to which thirty kilos of raw opium was added. The impurities would rise to the top and be filtered out. Then the solution passed into a smaller adjoining tank, where slaked lime – calcium hydroxide – was added to convert the water-insoluble morphine into water-soluble calcium morphenate.

After some drying, dyeing and crushing, the end product comes pouring out, pristine white, into the plastic containers. And it was Russell's job to test the purity of each batch. So easy, then, for him to scoop a load of the merchandise into a plastic bag, and stuff it down his trousers.

Russell Birch felt the satisfying padding in his groin. He was keen to leave, take that trip to the toilets, ensuring it was all Taylor's responsibility and risk from there on in. But he dallied for a while, taking some samples and readings. It seemed beyond belief, what people did for this stuff. Then, as he turned to go, the door suddenly flew open. Donald Hutchinson, the head of security, stood before him, backed by two guards. Russell read the discomfit on his long, drawn face, but then witnessed the steel in the man's eyes.

— Donald . . . how goes . . . what's up . . . Russell Birch felt himself run down like a record player suddenly switched off at the mains.

— Hand over the stuff. Donald stretched a hand out.

— What? What are you on about, Donald?

— We can do this the hard way if you like, Russell. But I'd rather spare you that, Donald Hutchinson said, pointing over Russell Birch's shoulder, at a black camera mounted on the wall. It was looking right at them, a red dot blinking by the side of the lens.

Russell turned round and gasped into it. He felt unmasked, not just as a thief, but worse, as a fool. It was as plain as all the other mundane apparatus of the plant, and he hadn't even noticed its installation. Russell stood gaping and powerless, as he wondered what the men watching the monitor on the other side saw in his face. Humiliation, fear, self-loathing, but mostly, he assumed, defeat. He turned round and reached down the front of his trousers, pulling out the large flat bag of white powder. Then he handed it over and followed the uniformed men, knowing that whatever happened next, he was leaving the processing lab for the last time.

On the humiliating march down the corridor, flanked by his inscrutable escorts, he saw Michael Taylor again, pushing a trolley of metal food containers from the loading bay, making for the canteen. This time Taylor made eye contact. His expression seemed to beg mercy, but Russell Birch was certain that his partner was only looking back into an empty void.

A Mature Student

Ah was avoidin everybody and they reciprocated, even Bisto; he and Joanne were still going strong. Ah was like a Quasimodo figure, the smelly, shufflin hunchback expelled fae the ranks ay decent folks, and ah fuckin well *loved* it. Ah stopped callin home every Sunday. My mother's unabatin sobs and tears, from gentle to ragin, were too distressin tae behold. Billy had been arrested; charged wi assault oan a boy in a boozer. As ma auld girl telt us the story, ah envisioned him wi a trail ay his spazzy brother's spunk skited across his pus. Drip, shock, humiliation, accusation, pagger. — But *you're* okay, son, aren't ye? Ma would bleat. — Everything's okay wi *you*?

— Aye, course it is, ah'd say, tryin tae maintain an acceptable degree ay focus and concentration.

But the waws were closin in oan us, everything aroond me turnin tae shite. Sick Boy was on at me tae head tae London wi him, for us tae stay with my 'Ingloid mates' for a bit. It grew a mair tempting prospect every day. But even wi a growin junk habit ah was too restless no tae look for clues. Ah read wi a voracious desperation. Read everything but what ah was supposed tae read for ma classes. In lectures ah'd sit at the back half dozin and ask some swotty kid tae photocopy their notes. In seminar groups ah often took speed tae buck us up, manoeuvrin the discussions towards ma personal obsessions, wi long, ramblin druggie speeches as ah mentally groped aroond, tryin tae scratch at the phantom itch in ma brain. Phlegm sat in my chist cavity like Wee Davie's, tricklin down from a constant stream in my sinuses. Ma breathin was fucked. Ah even noticed the wey ma ain voice had changed; it was as if it was easier tae force the sound up through my nose, producing a tinny, whiny sound ah hated but couldnae stop emittin. One lecturer looked sadly at us n said, — Are you sure you should be here?

— Naw, ah told him, — but ah don't know where else tae go.

It was true. At least ah had *some sort of reason* to be here, even if ah'd ceased handin in work: ah knew ah'd never get close tae ma 70 per cent threshold ay acceptability now. Ah stopped checkin ma student pigeonhole.

People often seemed tae assume ah'd already left, appearin surprised when ah occasionally showed up. In a sense ah had; all they were seein wis the ghostly remnants.

The odd time ah went in the student union bars, ah mocked people and their daft projects, their bands, InterRail travel plans, sporting activities, just because ah knew ah could no longer join in. Ah grew tae hate Bob Marley's music; ah'd loved it as a punk in London, but loathed the way white middle-class students had shamelessly appropriated it. Headin home tae the residences one night, I saw some drunk and emotional public-school wankers singing about sitting in a government block in Trenchtown. They were singin about livin in a *scheme* in Kingston, Jamaica. Ah shot them a brutal look and they snapped intae a guilty sobriety. It was pathetic. Ah wis pathetic. People avoided me. Ah'd gone fae being regarded as a warm, witty, fun-loving sceptic, tae a cynical bore: cold and caustic. Yet the more ah alienated people, the stronger ah felt. Ah fed off rejection. There was nowt good or normal or straight that ah couldnae sneer at. Ah was a critic ay everything, one ay the worst kind, whose every ounce ay bile is generated by their ain sense ay failure and inadequacy, risin off them like steam fae a jakey's pish.

And ah started tae stink like a wino in classes. Before, ah'd always been a bit compulsive aboot personal hygiene, tidiness and order; now ah could feel a permanent swamp ay fire and scum aroond ma weddin tackle, erse and airmpits. It wis like ah wis gaunny combust. One time ah met Fiona in a corridor. We couldnae avoid eye contact wi each other. — You still here then, she said, like a challenge.

But ah could tell that she still cared, or maybe no, perhaps ah was just kiddin myself. Aw ah could say was, — Hi, eh, see ye . . . n move the fuck on.

After this incident ah more or less stopped gaun tae the uni. Basically, ma plan, such as it was, wis tae stay in ma residence. Ah'd bang junk with Don and, occasionally, genitals with Donna, ironically, the prostitute from the bar where ah'd ditched Fiona. Ah started visiting it regularly, working up the bottle tae approach her. She took us tae a functional flat with Van Gogh sunflower prints, which was obviously just used for clients. Ah spent maist of the time eatin her pussy rather than fuckin her. I wanted to develop some expertise in that. Tae ma embarrassment, she had tae tell us it was called cunnilingus. Sick Boy would never have made that mistake. Ah'd cairry on till dosh or libido was exhausted, or ah formally got kicked oot, whichever came first.

Ah still wandered through the city like a phantom. At all hours. Then one day Don was gone. Naebody in the dockside pubs had seen him. There were aw sorts ay theories as tae where the radge had fucked off tae, maist ay them based oan his ramblings; Copenhagen, New York, London, Hamburg, Peterheid. Ma money was on the latter. It was mair than possible that Don could've been lying deid in his flat, overdosed oan the couch, but ah couldnae be ersed tae check. Then ah saw Donna in the street, and a Down's syndrome wee lassie came running up intae her arms. Ah shuffled doon the road, and kent ah would never visit her again.

Aberdeen suddenly seemed to have an omnipresent silence about it; a post-apocalyptic hush and stillness, where you could sense the sky sealin you in, like glass round a snow-shaker toy. It was ower for us here and ah was sweatin and shiverin oan a bus back tae Edinburgh. One bag full ay filthy clathes, the other stuffed wi books. And ma very first port ay call was Tollcross and Johnny Swan's doss.

Ah'm there for aboot ten minutes when the door goes and it's Spud and Sick Boy, lookin as fucked as me, but delighted tae be in the hoose ay pain relief. We're literally drooling, eye-popping, neck-sinew-strained, skin-crawling monsters as Swanney takes his sweet time cooking. He's in exuberant form, offloading his fucked-up obsessions oantae us. — Ah've nowt against darkies as such, but thaire's way too many ower here now. Pakis tae. That sort ay unselective breedin dilutes the fortitude ay a race. The morals go tits up. If the Germans invaded now, we'd huv nae chance. Ye git us?

— Aye, ah'm sayin, but feelin as alienated fae the boys here as ah did the right-on students in Aberdeen. *Twat. Fuckin Nazi twat. But ah don't care. Gie's the gear.* — You cookin, or what?

It's like he disnae hear us. — Ah dinnae believe n sendin thum aw back; the birds kin stey, especially they westernised Asian birds . . . phoar . . . he smirks, showin his rotten teeth. Sick Boy turns away in disgust.

— Luckily maist ay them widnae come tae Scotland, too cauld fir the dark skin.

Shut the fuck up and cook cook cook cook . . .

— Ah dinnae think that's right, likesay, Spud says. — It's mair like cause thaire's nae jobs up here, ken? N computers dinnae really count, cause ah dinnae believe in computers, man.

But now, thank fuck, Swanney's giein the matter at hand some proper attention; the gear has been placed in the spoon wi the water, and the lighter's burnin away underneath it. — Jobs dinnae come intae it. It's a well-known fact that niggers jist come ower here tae sponge offay the state, but. It's like revenge fir aw they years ay slavery wi the British Empire

186

n that. Post-colonialism or some shite, that's the fuckin scientific term. Tell thum, Rents, he signals us tae suck the gear intae ma works, oh thank you, Swanney, thank God tae fuck, ah will goose-step aw the wey tae the pollin booth tae vote National Front if ye like . . . — Psychology. He taps his heid.

— Too right, ah tell him. It's mair *physiology* ah'm worried aboot right now, wi ma dodgy Danny McGrain's; ah've got this boy tapped up and ah'm worried that ah'll lose the cunt, he's as precarious as a hard-on after a bottle ay whisky. But ah pierce the skin, slide it in, then let go . . . — Got ye again, ah gasp in laughter, smilin at the others. — Too quick for youse cunts . . .

Escape tae oblivion, where they cannae get at me . . .

Then it's back tae the flat wi Sick Boy and Spud, whae's moved intae the room, so ah was on the couch. We're daein a bit mair gear, even though ah'm still buzzin oan the last shot. These boys certainly huvnae been hudin back in my absence. — You should've stuck wi the uni, Sick Boy coolly tells us as he cooks, then expertly tourniquets hissel wi a Leith Academy school tie, dark blue wi that badge wi the boat n 'Persevere' emblazoned on it. His veins triumphantly spring intae the light like an army advancing over a hill. — You were the only cunt oot ay the lot ay us that could have got an education.

— You could've. Ah heard you were a swotty wee cunt at primary.

— At *primary*, aye, he concedes.

— Ah watched yir academic career explode in hormones the day Elaine Erskine came intae school in second year, wearin that rid miniskirt.

— Less talk mair rock, man, Spud moans, impatient for his turn as he watches the Scottish news. Mary Marquis is readin, n ah think ay Wee Davie's monstrous cock in ma hand and his gurglin spazzy breathin.

— Aye, Sick Boy recalls, big broon eyes glazing, — when she got sent hame tae change, ah wis right doon the road eftir her. Telt Munro in Geography ah wis feelin totally fuckin Zorba n gaunny puke up. Caught up wi Elaine oan the Links, provided a shoulder tae cry on, while complimenting her on her spot-on fashion sense. Fit birds should wear nothing but miniskirts −

— C'moan, Si . . . bang it! Spud pleads.

— Those fucking lovely tits that squeezed every bit ay sense fae me, made us brainless sluts thegither, stupefied by each other's flesh. And me, constantly planning and scheming tae manoeuvre her away fae the older, cooler cunts who coveted her minge . . .

— Simon, c'moan, mate, please, ah'm pure sufferin a bit, Spud gasps.

— . . . within the week, ma cherry was exploding like the last firework above the fuckin Castle on Hogmanay.

— SI! C'MOAN!

— Patience, Danny boy, a wee bitty shadow before the sunshine, Sick Boy smiles, suckin up some gear and passin the spoon tae the grateful Spud, — Aye . . . aw ah'm sayin is it set us on a path, Rents, and it's no necessarily the one I'd have chosen, he muses, his teeth clampin ontae the tie as his lovely big veins bulge in his arm, mair options than you ken what tae dae wi. — No necessarily the one I'd have chosen . . . he repeats, piercing, sliding in the needle, drawing back blood intae the barrel ay the syringe, then slamming the potion towards base.

A cauld but bright morning, the groond thick wi snaw and the hooses weighed wi a dense filigree ay ice, as a cheery sun glints offay towers ay cloud. After a derisory bit ay kip, ah got up and dressed, steppin ower Spud, washed up oan the flair in the narrow hall, n wis back at Gillsland's, hollow and metallic, like an empty, discarded can ay shavin cream. They'd taken ower the unit next door, and Gillsland had completely swerved fae high-end shopfitting and custom joinery, tae building even mair house panels to desecrate central Scotland wi shitey boxes.

Les was still obsessed wi his Monday-morning shitein competitions, but now ah struggled tae produce a Malteser. — What's up wi you, Mark? Les asked me, aw hurt. — What kind ay diet you been oan up in Aberdeen?

The skag diet. Soon it'll be the diet ay choice for all our porky, suburban housewives.

But the work suited us. While the other boys moaned about becoming de-skilled, just robotically workin the compressed airguns, knockin nails intae frames and boltin aluminium ties onto them, wis fair game fir me. Ah could stand there, junk-sick and miserable, and batter off ten panels in an hour withoot exchangin a single word wi any cunt.

House Guests

Totally skint, man, n the bread trap ay Christmas n New Year looms. It's a awfay scene. Mind you, everybody's in the same boat. Begbie comes roond the gaff, n yuv nivir seen a rooster in such a foul mood, ken? — Spud, he goes, pushin past us intae the flat, lookin around fir Rents n Sick Boy. — Whaire the fuck ur they two cunts?

— Dinnae ken, man, every cat jist sortay comes n goes here, ken? ah tell um. Ah'm feelin a bit shitey, jist tryin tae tidy up a bit roond the gaff, ken? Sortay pill ma weight a bit, likesay.

The Beggar Boy isnae a happy camper but, n it's Cha Morrison fae Lochend that's gettin the blame. He's up in coort next month fir chib-bin Larry Wylie, and everybody except Franco is pretty chuffed, man. Two dodgy bamsticks oot ay circulation through the jail and hozzy gigs, likes, sortay a pure result aw roond, ken? For every cat except Francis James Begbie but, whae's takin Larry's chibbin as a personal attack oan him. Franny Jim husnae been too chuffed lately, so whin he comes tae us wi news ay a hoose thit wants screwed, ah'm wary, Christmas hireys or no.

Cause yet again it wis a pure case ay me n ma big mooth! Thing is, it's the same gaff ah mentioned tae him likesay yonks ago, huvin inside info fae the deliverance ay a sideboard thaire last year. Thoat it wid be in one ear n oot the other. But the Beggar Boy's a pure elephant gadgie; sort ay never forgets, ken? — No that hoose but, Franco! The polis'll pure go through the list ay aw the people that've been thaire ower the last year, n guess whae thi'll pit in the frame, man? The disgruntled ex-delivery gadgie that's been peyed oaf!

— Shite, Begbie shakes his noggin aw that dismissive wey, — this is the fuckin Lothian and Borders Polis. These doss cunts are fuckin useless for anything other thin fuckin parkin tickets. Aw water under the fuckin bridge now, ya cunt, trail way fuckin cauld, n he opens the curtains n looks oot acraos the street.

— But the boy's a barrister, Franco, Conrad Donaldson QC!

Ken whin somebody jist isnae hearin ye, but? That's pure Franco.

News he disnae want tae hear, that cat's pointy ears jist swivel roond n aw the bad sound jist flies intae space. — Any fuckin peeve in this doss?

— Eh, aye . . . The ears twist back intae position, n he goes tae the kitchen n helps hissel tae a boatil fae the fridge, one ay they Peroni's Sick Boy bought fae the posh offy. He opens up n takes a glug glug slug, screwin his coupon up, hudin it at airm's length n lookin at the label. — Fuckin Italian? Beer? Italians make fuckin wine. Sick Boy ay aw people should fuckin well ken that. Ah'll pit that cunt right! Fuckin Italian beer!

— But Conrad Donaldson QC, ah says again, notin Franco's still drinkin the Tally ale.

— Aye, but aw the mair fuckin reason, cause the cunt's a defender, Franco says, pointin the boatil at us. — Defends bams like Morrison, so the polis hate the cunt. They'll dae fuck all fir that bastard, he sais, readin the Peroni label again.

— But, Frank –

— Nae fuckin danger at aw! Lexo fae the casuals wis telling us thit this QC fucker . . . QC, what's that fuckin stand fir . . . queer cunt? He punches ma airm sair, n ah wish the cat wid stoap that, man; even though it's meant in affection, it's like still bullyin, ken, it's still likesay sayin 'ah'm the big hard gadgie n you're the wee sappy dude', likesay. — Aye, the queer cunt wis defendin um in that case, n he's gaun oan holidays for six weeks tae America. Ah've cased the hoose, big fuckin Ravvy Dykes pad. Nae cunt aboot, so wi go thaire the night. Endy fuckin story. He looks ootside again. — Ye must huv some fuckin clue whaire Rents n Sick Boy ur? Might huv fuckin well sais whaire they wir gaun! Fuckin Italian beer . . . Still, nae sense in cuttin oaf yir cock tae spite yir baws. He gulps it doon n opens up a second.

— Eh, ah think they might be away gittin moosetraps. We've goat mice, likesay.

Franco raises his furry brows n looks aroond the kitchen. — Ah thoat this fuckin hovel wis way too gantin fir any fuckin self-respectin moose!

Well, ah dinnae say nowt, cause ah hud a big argument wi Rents n Sick Boy aboot it, cause ah dinnae hud wi killin mice. Thaire hus tae be a humane wey ay deterrin thum, without hurtin thum, likesay. Ma idea wis tae git a cat, jist tae scare thum. One or two might huv goat killed, but the rest wid git the message n move oan. But Rents started gaun oan aboot being allergic.

Me n Franco decide tae head oot n track thum doon, so wi pads the hoof doon tae the Walk. We gits tae the Cenny n Tommy's thaire; soas Second Prize, blootered, wi pish marks oan his troosers but like thuv sortay dried in, ken? But thaire's nae sign ay Rents or Sick Boy.

— They must still be lookin for moosetraps, ah go.

— Aw aye, Tommy raises his brows, — is that what they fuckin call it now?

Begbie catches something n seems tae tipple. — Thi'll be hingin aboot wi Matty n that fuckin junky Swan! Another cunt oaf ma fuckin Christmas caird list.

— Didnae ken ye kept a list, likesay, Franco, ah goes, lookin ower at Second Prize, who's sortay mumblin tae himself, n kinday fawin asleep in the corner, eyelids crashin doon like shoap-windae shutters. Business pure closed fir the day, ken?

No fir Franco, but; the cat looks at us aw jungle-jungle stalky-stalky, low hackles n that. — Every cunt keeps a fuckin list. He taps his heid. — A Christmas caird list, n that cunt's fuckin well oaf it!

Wi that cat in this mood ye pure jist huv tae . . . what's the word? . . . acqui . . . acqui . . . . faw intae line. So wi head ower tae the snooker club, leavin Second Prize tae his forty winks. — Fuckin liability, that cunt, Franco goes. Crossin Duke Street, we hits the club bar n Begbie talks tae two shaven-heided wideos wi gold chains n sovie rings. Ah clocks Keezbo oan the green baize, playin a frame wi this wee gadge in a rid hooded toap whae looks a bit like a lassie but no a good-lookin yin, ken? Then ah sees Rents, Sick Boy n Matty ur sittin right at the back in the corner watchin thum. Matty comes ower, n says he has tae go, tae git back tae Shirley. Ye kin see Franco giein um the evil eye, like he's pittin a hex oan the gadge, ken?

— Did yis git the Agatha Christies, likesay? ah ask Sick Boy n Rents.

— Eh, right, Sick Boy goes, lookin tae Rents. Then he goes, — Ehm . . . this boy's gaunny sort it aw oot fir us. Humane likes. They pit doon they pellets n the moose doesn't feel a thing.

— Good man, ah couldnae handle yon springin trap comin doon oan a furry friend, no somethin warm-bloodied, ken?

— Shut the fuck up aboot fuckin moosetraps! Franco snaps, as he bounds ower wi a boatil ay Beck's in his hand, then starts tellin them aboot the joab.

Well, they dinnae take tons ay persuadin. These boys huv a different sortay White Christmas in mind. — Sounds good sport, Rents says. Though ye dinnae ken if he's genuinely agreein or it's just stallin tactics tae distract and manoeuvre the Generalissimo intae something else. Rents is one ay the few cats that Franco sometimes listens tae, that kens how tae play um a wee bit.

Sick Boy raises a single brow, like Connery walkin intae a casino. — This could be interesting. Gaff like that, bound tae be stacked wi valuables.

— Aye, well, it's no aw gaun intae your fuckin airms, ya cunt, Begbie says, n this makes Sick Boy pill doon his jersey sleeve ower his track marks, then turn away wi a hurt look, pure upset his cool's been ruffled.

Begbie gies him, then me and Rents that frosty 'aye, ah ken youse cunts' look. — This is fuckin serious. Nae cunt hud better fuck up. We need a big mob cause we're gaunny clean the fuckin lot ootay that doss n store it doon the lock-up. It isnae a fuckin junky playgroond, ya cunts. Pittin that fuckin garbage intae yir veins . . . thank fuck that wee cunt Matty's away . . .

— Ah'm rarin tae go, Rents says. Ah think the Rent Boy really does want tae dae this. Usually it's Mark that's screwin the nut, but now he seems the gadge instigatin aw the villainy. Came back wi his holdall stuffed wi books the other day. Fair play tae um, but, he eywis reads thum aw before he flogs thum. Still a studious sort ay gadge, even wi the skag. N ah suppose he's eywis liked housebrekin.

— Aye, bit it's fuckin serious, mind, Franco glares at him. Rents nods back. — Tommy kin drive, Begbie says, — ah kin drive n Sick Boy kin drive. Ah've goat a len ay a van fae Denny Ross, a len ay a van fae ma brar Joe, n a len ay a van fae yon smarmy cunt, him fae Madeira Street, what's it ye call the cunt, him wi the quiff? You n Keezbo wir in that shite band wi the cunt, Rents!

Keezbo suddenly looks ower fae his shot, a bit put-oot. He seems tae huv the wee lassie boy stitched up like John Croan's breakfast finest, but.

— HP, Rents says. — Hamish Proctor: the Heterosexual Poof.

— That's the cunt, goes Franco.

— No fucking way is that cunt heterosexual, Sick Boy sneers as Keezbo sinks a red–black–red–pink. Nice brek by the fat laddie. — It's the classic cover-up scenario. The birds he hings oot wi are either professional virgins or fuckin fag hags. That pansy's nae threat tae them. Him n Alison went doon tae Reading thegither, then ower tae France. Away a whole week n he never laid a *fuckin finger* oan her! She telt us so herself . . . eftir a gentle interrogation.

Rents smiles n turns tae Franco. — Did ye tell thum what the vans are fir? HP n Joe n Dennis n that?

— Did ah fuck. What they dinnae ken nae cunt kin fuckin well beat oot ay thum. N ivray cunt here hud better keep thair fuckin mooths shut, right? He looks at us one by one. That cat's ridic, cause half the snooker hall can likesay hear the radge, but naebody's drawin it tae his attention. It's hard no tae laugh but, man.

— Goes without sayin, Rents says, poker-faced.

— Aye, well, ah'm fuckin sayin it anywey, Franco goes, reprimandin Rents, but ye kin tell it's really aw aboot the skag. Cat jist disnae git it at aw, man. — You clean? he asks.

— As a fuckin whistle, Rents smiles, but he's goat that tight jaw, n Sick Boy looks a bit bloated wi water retention, n thir baith blinkin n twitchin a lot. *No way, Jose.*

Ah ken the junk gits a bad press, but ah think it's barry. It's easy tae criticise something fae the ootside, but yuv goat tae experience everythin in life, ken? Think ay how shitey things would huv been for every cat if Jim Morrison hudnae droaped acid. He widnae huv broken oan through tae the other side n aw they barry tunes wid be shiter as a result. The Salisbury Crag is dangerous but, so ah'm sortay no daein it again. Wee Goagsie wis gaun oan about how it was makin him sick. But it's good stuff; Begbie's mentalness, Sick Boy's scams, Tommy's moans and Keezbo's crap jokes, and maist ay aw, the auld girl bein aw grumpy aboot us gittin oot fae under her feet n findin a joab, it aw disnae go away on skag; it just disnae bother ye any mair.

We're offski but; ye kin pure tell Tommy isnae too chuffed, but he comes along. Wi pick up the different vans n head doon tae the industrial estate at Newhaven tae rendezvous. Then we drive up tae the posh gaff n park up the vans doon the side lane ay the hoose, n wi climb ower the back waw, which is easy fir every cunt bar Keezbo, whae's toilin.

— Hurry up, big yin, Rents goes, blawin intae his hands, even though it's no that cauld. Wi huv tae push Keezbo up, me n Tam gittin a grip ay that big heavy erse, before he sortay waddles ower n splats oantae the groond oan the other side. It's too radge how cats kin cairry aw that weight aroond, man. We tiptoe through the gairdin n force the door, which opens wi one ay Begbie's shoodir charges. Wir ready tae nash wi the alarm, but sure enough, it disnae work! Barry! Wir in!

We comes intae this huge kitchen wi a stane flair n a big island in the middle like one ay they yins ye see in Beverly Hills; likesay in the films n that, ken? Keezbo turns tae Rents n goes, — This'll be what we'll have, Mr Mark, when the band takes oaf, but in LA or Miami n wi a pool at the back.

— Sure, Rents scorns, — the only thing that's rock n roll aboot us is aw the gear we're takin.

— Disnae affect the rhythm section the same but, Mr Mark, we kin still dae oor joab, Keezbo explains, n he's gaun through the cupboards, then starts pittin some breid in the toaster. — Look at the jazz men, they jist sit back and groove. Especially oan the skins. Ah mean tae say, take Topper Headon fir example. He pills at his tight *Clash City Rockers* XXL T-shirt.

— They threw him oot fir skag, Keith, Rents shakes his heid at the big gadgie. Man, how kin he eat at a time like this?

— Aye, they didnae like him *takin* skag, Keezbo says, findin a jar ay Marmite, — but they reinstated him when they realised it didnae affect his *performance* oan the drums. He wis still a better skins man than Terry Chimes, but.

These cats will argue anything rock n roll aw day, man. Begbie looks disgusted at Keezbo, but pills oot some cigarettes and the radge is aboot tae light up, so ah goes, — Dinnae, Franco, yi'll set oaf the smoke alarms!

— Aye, yi'll have tae go ootside wi that, Mr Frank, Keezbo says.

Begbie isnae chuffed at aw. — It's fuckin freezin ootside!

— But, Franco –

— Ah need fuckin snout, right, and he looks at Keezbo n goes, — Ivray cunt else is daein what they fuckin well want! Some cunt's gaunny huv tae go up n shut that fuckin alarm oaf!

We look at each other, then aw the beady eyes settle oan me. That's ma story, man. Cursed as a tea leaf fae the off by they monkey-boy climbin talents. It started as a sprog, brekin in tae help auld girls that hud forgot thair keys n shut thirsels oot. Then came the time ma auld man telt us his mate wis locked oot the hoose, pointin up tae a tenement flat at the back ay Burlington Street. 'Climb up thaire, Danny, that windae, perr Freddy here's loast his keys, eh,' the auld boy goes, lookin at his mate standin wi a glum pus. So ah shimmies up the pipe n nips in the windae, goes through the hoose n opens the front door tae lit them in, before they've even climbed up the stairs. The Freddy boy bungs us a couple ay bob, n the auld man tells us tae git oaf hame. Ah waited oan the snide ootside but, duckin behind a motor; pure sketched thum takin the chorrie fae the hoose intae a van.

So thaire's what the sports commentator cats call 'a certain inevitability' aboot it aw, likesay. Ah admits defeat n looks ower tae this utility room, through an alcove. — Thaire's ledders in here, n ah goes through n brings oot they big aluminium steps, — that should dae it.

— Hurry up, ya cunt, Franco goes, — fuckin gaspin here!

So ah climbs up the steps headin for that red light that's blinkin away oan that white disc. Ah kin hear Keezbo n Rents still gaun at it, but this time thuv switched tae fitba: — Robertson should be a fixture in the Scotland side, Mr Mark, the stats speak fir themselves.

— But Jukebox is a goalscorer *and* a goalmaker. A scorer *and* a creator's ey gaunny bring mair benefit tae a team than a ten-a-penny penalty-box chunkoid.

Ah'm thinking that Rents is bein unfair tae Robbo, cause ah like the wee gadge. A Hibby originally, before his corruption by the dark side, n ah'm aboot tae say something but ah'm no that happy cause they ledders are wibbly-wobbly oan that uneven stane flair, but ma eager mitt's closin in oan the detector n ah'm jist aboot tae unscrew it when ah feel a twist, n the squeak ay ma soles separatin fae the metal n ah'm flyin through the air, n next thing ah ken is thit ah'm lyin oan the stane flair . . .

. . . jist likesay lyin thaire, lookin up at that blinkin rid light . . .

— Oh ya fucker, Spud . . . Ah hear the panic in Tommy's voice.

— Fuck sake! Danny! Are ye awright? Sick Boy's gaun.

— Dinnae move, Rents goes, — dinnae try n git up. Jist try n move yir taes. Then yir feet.

Ah do, n it's awright, so ah try tae sit up but thaire's a funny sick pain comin fae ma airm, man. — Aw ma airm, ah'm fucked . . .

— Useless cunt, Begbie goes, n he's steppin ootside n lightin up, — fuckin well freezin oot here!

Ah'm up oan ma feet but ma airm is way, way fucked, man, cannae move it, it jist hings thaire by ma side. Whin ah try liftin it, it's jist this sick, sick, sick feelin, risin up in ma guts. The boys take us through to the lounge n sit us doon oan the couch. — Stey thaire, Danny, dinnae move, Rents goes, — we'll get ye tae the hoaspital once wi git loaded up.

Keezbo's chompin away oan his toast n Marmite spread, n ma airm's gaun throb throb throb

Begbie comes in and sees Rents defacing the waw wi a Magic Marker, pittin up in big, black letters:

CHA MORRISON IS INNOCENT

— Donaldson isnae gonnae try that hard tae defend the cunt now, he grins.

Franco starts laughin his heid oaf, n shouts: — Tam! Keezbo! Look at what Rents's done! That'll teach the cunts! He punches Rents oan the airm. — See this rid-heided cunt, then slaps his back, — some fuckin patter!

Ah feel shite but ah want tae see what sort ay a haul wir due, so ah stick ma wrist inside ma jaykit, buttonin up the boatum tae make a sortay sling, ken, n help the boys case the gaff. We're intae every nook n cranny, n it looks barry, especially some jewellery in a boax oan the dresser ay the marital boudoir. Ah ken it's wrong, but wi this airm giein us gyp, it means ah might no have sae much claim oan the big loot, so ah stash a couple ay rings, bracelets, brooches n necklesses intae ma pocket for percy, before ah announce the haul tae the boys.

Suddenly Tommy comes lurchin oot one ay the bedrooms, n he's white as a sheet. — Thaire's a lassie in that bed, he goes in this panicky whisper, — In thaire.

— What . . . ? Franco's neck muscles tense up.

— Fuck sakes, Rents goes.

— But she's sortay asleep . . . ah mean it's like . . . it's like she's fuckin deid! Tam's eyes are like elephant pish-holes in the snaw. If elephants kent whit snaw wis, likesay. — Thaire's pills thaire . . . n voddy . . . this bird's fuckin well topped herself, man!

Ah'm pure shitein it now n aw. — Whoa man . . . we've goat tae git right oot ay here . . .

Sick Boy comes up the stairs, eyes aw bulging oot. — Deid? A lassie? Here?

Franco shakes his heid. — The wey ah fuckin see it, he goes, — is if the cunt's deid, then wi keep daein what wir fuckin daein. Obviously nae cunt kens or gies a fuck aboot it.

— Nae fuckin wey, Tommy says tae Begbie, — ah gie a fuck aboot it, ah'm ootay here!

— Hud oan, says Rents, and he's movin quietly intae the bedroom. We follay um. Right enough, thaire's a burd jist lyin in the bed, looks sortay foreign. Spooky as, man. N ah'm pure gutted, cause it's bad when a young cat does that, like that Eleanor Simpson woman's laddie. So sad, man: a posh kid wi loads tae look forward tae n aw. It's likesay the no-hopers like muggins here whae ye think should jist cash in the chips, ken? Mind you, kenin ma luck, ah'd jist dae it n then some wee sweetheart like Nicky Hanlon would be at the funeral sayin, 'Funny, ah wis jist aboot tae gie Danny a bell tae see if he wanted tae come ower fir his hole, n aw.' That wid pure be it, kennin ma luck but, eh?

Oan the table beside the lassie, thaire's a load ay tablets n a boatil ay voddy thit's been practically tanned. Ah grabs a few leftower pills, fir the shoodir pain, n necks thum wi the last shot ay voddy.

— Fuckin stupid cunt, Franco hisses, — yir saliva's aw ower the neck ay that boatil!

— If you're likesay aw keen oan forsensic science, man, how come ye never sais nowt whin Keezbo wis makin toast? ah asks, pure annoyed.

— CAUSE AH NIVIR KENT THAIRE WIS A FUCKIN DEID BOADY IN THE BED, YA DAFT CUNT! he shouts in ma face, then quietens tae a low sizzle. — You could be a fuckin accessory if she's fuckin potted!

Ah nods, cause thaire's nowt tae say except, — Right enough . . . good thinking, Franco.

— As well some cunt's fuckin well thinkin!

Rents bends ower her, shakes her shoodir. — Miss . . . wake up . . . you have tae wake up . . . The lassie's totally spangled, but. He takes her wrist n feels fir a beat. — She's goat a faint pulse, he goes, n pure slaps her chops. — YOU HAVE TO WAKE UP! He turns tae Tommy. — Help us git her oan her feet!

Tommy n Rents start tae pill the burd oot the bed; she's quite a nice-looking lassie or she wid be if she didnae look shite, but sortay heavy-built, n she's wearin a long nightdress but ye cannae see nowt through it, like-say. No thit ye wid look that hard in they circumstances, but.

— What the fuck's aw this St Andrew's Ambulance shite aboot? Begbie moans.

Tommy n Rents urnae hearin um, but; thuv goat the burd whae's groanin wi snotters comin oot ay her beak, and they're draggin her intae the toilet. — Keezbo, Rents says, — goan git some hoat water in a teapot, no boilin but, n wi loads ay salt in it. Goan!

— Right, Mr Mark . . .

They've goat the lassie sittin balanced oan the edge ay the bath. Rents hus his hand under her chin, liftin her heid up, lookin intae her eyes, but she's aw ower the place. — How much did ye take?

Then the burd's mumblin somethin in a sortay foreign language. — Sounds like Italian, Tommy goes, n turn tae Sick Boy. — What's she sayin?

— It isnae Italian.

— It sounds fuckin Italian!

Begbie goes tae Tommy, — Dinnae look at that cunt: kens nae fuckin Italian, that cunt!

— Aye ah do, but this is sortay like Spanish . . . Sick Boy goes taewards her.

Begbie stands in front ay him. Blockin his wey. — Keep the fuck away fae her.

— What? Ah'm just tryin tae help!

— Rents n Tam huv goat it sorted oot. The lassie disnae need *your* fuckin help. Ah've heard aboot the kind ay fuckin help you've been giein burds, he goes and Sick Boy disnae like it but says nowt. — Jist watch what yir fuckin well daein, the Beggar Boy advises. — Yir startin tae git a fuckin name.

— What dae ye mean? Sick Boy's chin juts oot.

— You fuckin ken.

Sick Boy silently shifts his weight.

— What's your name? Rents is shoutin at the lassie. — How many pills did ye take!

The burd's heid's shakin and floppin tae the side. Rents huds it again n looks intae her eyes. — WHAT'S. YOUR. NAME?

— Carmelita . . . she manages tae gasp.

Ma airm's really nippin, n ah'm distractin masel by reading this plaque oan the waw that hus a rhyme in it:

> Please remember, don't forget,
> Never leave the bathroom wet,
> Nor leave the soap still in the water,
> That's the thing you never ought'er . . .

We should pure huv that in oor hoose cause oors is like a bomb hus hit it eftir ma wee sister Erin's been in thaire. Cannae tell her nowt, but. The flat wi Rents n Sick Boy, well, that's pure beyond any principles ay hygiene, man. Thaire's a barry spider in oor bathroom called Boris. He keeps fawin intae the bath. Ah keep takin him oot n pittin him oan the windae ledge. But whenever ye come back, he's in the bath again, tryin tae climb oot, up the slope, then slidin back. Ye'd think the gadge might learn, ken?

Keezbo comes back wi a teapot. — This is fill ay hoat salty water.

— A fuckin teapot, right enough, Begbie scoffs, headin away.

— Right, Carmelita, fuck knows what you've been takin but it's comin up. Rents pulls her heid back n pinches her nostrils, while Keezbo puts the spout in her mooth n tips the pot. Tommy's still goat a grip oan her, balancin her oan the edge ay the bath.

She swallays a bit, then pure sortay chokes, as the water flies aw ower the place. Then suddenly she snaps forward n starts boakin up intae the bath; man, ye kin pure see aw they chalky, undigested pills in the mix, jist loads n loads ay thum. When she stops, Rents pits the pot tae her mooth again. — No . . . no . . . no . . . She's pushin it away.

— She's mibbe hud enough, Tommy says.

— We goat tae empty yir stomach ay everything. Rents is insistent, n he forces her tae drink mair. Sure enough, she retches again and it aw comes up, n then once mair, till it's completely clear. Tommy n Rents keep her thaire till everything's up n it's just dry boaks. The way they're hudin the chick's hair back, n ah ken it's totally no a nice thing tae say, but it's pure like a porno film ah once saw when this lassie wis giein two boys a blow job!

Me n Sick Boy head oot n tae whaire Begbie's waitin in the hallway. — So now the daft cunts've went n revived a fuckin witness that can finger us aw bein in a QC's hoose. Brilliant, Si snaps.

— Shut up, Franco goes. — Start gittin the fuckin stuff doonstairs.

— Like what? Sick Boy shrugs.

— Like they rugs oan the fuckin waws, fir starters. Any cunt thit pits a fuckin rug oan a fuckin waw is fuckin well beggin tae git it fuckin chorried!

Ah'm away back intae the bedrooms. Man, ma airm's killin us thanks tae Begbie, so the jewellery's totally ma speed.

— Keep that burd in thaire, Begbie shouts tae Tommy n Rents. — If she clocks ma coupon she'll git mair thin a few fuckin pills n some voddy doon her fuckin gullet!

They ken he's no jokin, so it's pure, likesay, 'we obey, oh master'.

In another bedroom, like a teenage lassie's, thaire's some nice wee pieces, n ah'm gittin thum in ma jayket poakit. But it's aw awkward wi one airm, and Sick Boy comes in. He's caught us as rid-handed as an East Belfast march, but he says nowt cause he's pure ragin. — Did you *hear that* fucking psychopath? Him, he goes in a low, hissy whisper, — passing judgements on other people? And Tommy, Mr Straight Cunt; so desperate tae join the ranks of the Perfect People.

— What d'ye mean, likesay?

— You ken them, Spud. The Perfect People. Never takin drugs, unless it's hash or alcohol, which doesn't count. Always saying the right things. Never stepping out of line. He's just *dying* tae be one ay them.

— He's only tryin tae help the lassie, but, Si.

— And that fucking smarmy little poof Hamish and his poxy van . . . who the fuck does he −

Well, thaire's nae reasonin wi the cat whin he's like this, so ah'm relieved when we hear Begbie's voice blastin up the stairwell: — SICK BOY! GET YIR FUCKIN ERSE DOON HERE! YOU N AW, SPUD!

— Fuck, Sick Boy snaps, but he's headin doon anyway, n ah'm right behind um.

So we're loadin up, me daein wee bits, n eftir a while Rents comes doon n helps. Ah've fair cleaned up wi the auld tomfoolery, but it's makin a jangle in ma poakits, so ah sneak back up tae the bog n relieve Tommy, whae's been watchin the lassie. She's sittin oan the lavvy seat, gittin her breath. — Eh, yir muscle's needed, Tam, ah point at ma airm.

— Right . . . Keep an eye oan her, Tommy goes. — When she's strong enough tae stand up, get her back intae the bedroom so she kin lie doon.

The lassie looks at us, n she's sobbin softly, pillin this gown somebody's brought for her roond herself, sippin a gless ay water. Thaire's something aboot her face, round, kind, n wi big, dark eyes; she'll no grass us up. Ye kin pure tell. Wi gits chattin n she tells us that she felt depressed bein here, away fae her family.

Eftir a bit ah helps her stand wi ma good airm, n takes her back tae her room n tells her tae lie doon, then ah goes n lits the boys ken the score. We decide that Tam's gaunny leave separate wi her n me, n git us a cab up the hoaspital. The story'll be she'll be thaire when the doss goat turned ower, n it'll pure be oan the hozzy records. When she comes back, she'll sortay discover the burglary n call the polis. The lassie's totally game for this: ye kin tell thaire's no much love loast wi the employers.

— She *sais* she'll no grass us up, but whae kens what the sow's gaunny be fuckin sayin tae other people up thaire, in fuckin Spanish? Franco goes.

— She's just properly seen me n Tommy n Spud, we're really the only yins at risk, Rents says. — We just fuckin well saved her life, so ah'm happy tae take a punt thit she'll keep stumpf.

— Awight, but it's your fuckin sentence, Begbie snorts but thankfully seems tae agree, n they git back tae loadin up the vans.

Eftir a bit, me, Tam n this Carmelita lassie, wearin jeans, trainers, a jumper n a big black coat, step oot intae the evening. It's dark under the orange street lamps n it's goat tons caulder. We're walkin slowly up tae the main road, whaire Tam flags doon a cab.

— Hurt ma airm . . . eh, arm, ah explains tae the Carmelita burd.

— Ye awright? Tommy asks her.

Carmelita nods aw sortay ashamed, letting her hair faw ower her face, as Tommy opens the cab door. Me n her gits in. — You two be okay? Tam asks.

— Aye, sound, Tommy.

So it's me n Carmelita sittin up in the A&E. It's fill ay the usual bams, maistly catnipped-up felines whae've hit the food bowl at the same time, hud a wee spat n clawed each other crazy. — Ye must miss bein hame, in Spain likesay, ah sais tae her. — Be barry in Spain.

— Yes. This winter was so cold, much colder than Seville.

The lassie's quite sound; aye, it's sad tae think ay a young burd tryin tae dae that tae herself. It just goes tae show that naebody really kens what's gaun oan in somebody else's heid. It's pure answers oan a postcaird time, ken? — Dae ye no like workin here?

She's lookin straight ahead, then she turns tae us. — My mother is ill back home, my boyfriend . . . he is killed in a motorcycle accident. The family here do not treat me in a good way. I got so drunk and I feel so very, very down . . . thankfully you and your friends were sent by God to find me.

— Eh, aye, right, ah goes. It wis mair like wi wir sent by Begbie oan the chorrie, or, in the case ay Rents n Sick Boy, sent by skag tae find her. Ah suppose the gaffer in the sky works in mysterious weys but, n we could've likesay pure been His agents. Him as that Bernard Lee gadge n us as Bond n Carmelita as the exotic foreign spy that pure gits saved. *Sent by skag tae save her.* The way this airm's nippin, ah widnae mind a wee shot ay the Salisbury right now, ken?

Whoa, man, a wide-eyed honey ay a nurse wi blonde hair pinned back n a sexy fringe comes ower tae us. There's a kitten ah widnae mind sharing a basket wi. — Carmelita Montez?

Carmelita looks at us wi big tearful eyes, n goes tae shake hands. Ah awkwardly take her hand in ma good yin. — Thank you, Dahnee . . . she sobs, as the ultra-fit nurse leads her away tae a treatment room.

Nice lassie, n she isnae gaunny grass us up, ah jist ken that. Ah ken it's wrong tae hud oot oan the boys wi the coos and bulls, but they've plenty other loot tae divvy, ken? Thing is, ah'm jist wantin sorted oot up here cause ah'm feelin bad, bad, bad, man. Ken? Ye sortay wonder if the cats'll gie ye morphine fir a burst airm. If no, ah'm pure hightailin it doon tae Johnny Swan's, wi aw these rings, neckies n bracelets in ma poakit.

The Hoochie Connection

Alexander is barry in bed. Makes love like he wants *you* tae enjoy it, no like he's just there tae dae *his* business, like some laddies I could mention. It freaks us but, when he starts telling me that I'm beautiful, n that he wants tae see more ay me. He's my boss, we see each other every day, I tell him. Not what I mean, he goes.

Beautiful. What Dad often said: when I first saw your mother at the Alhambra, not the pub, the dance hall, he'd always add, I'd never seen anything so beautiful.

I ken I'm no bad and I can make masel look dead smart, but when a guy tells you that you're beautiful, what's aw that aboot? Freaks ye oot, n that's pittin it mildly.

I want to explain tae him that it's a nice diversion, but that's all it is. Trouble is, he *is* my boss. I swear tae God, I excel in making things difficult for masel. He steyed round at mine the other weekend. It wisnae a good idea. He'd left this bag in the bathroom, wi his shaving gear in it; a razor, stick and brush. I keep meaning tae bring it in for him, but somehow I cannae. Dunno why. Maybe cause it would be tacky taking it intae the office. It's no cause ay him, anyway! Aye, he's just a diversion.

Anyway, after this evening's session, I head up the Hoochie to meet Hamish. He's mad intae poetry and he likes ma stuff. I ken it sounds wanky, but we meet up, drink coffee, get a bit stoned and read each other's shit. Hamish and I never fuck; I don't know if he's queer, shy with lassies or just sees me as a mate, cause he's a strange guy, hard tae read, but I like him. 'I hate it when friends fight and I hate it when friends fuck,' he once said, though it was like a sort ay rehearsed speech. I used tae ask him if he was gay, but he maintained he wisnae interested in sex wi other men. He's no really ma type but I'd probably bonk him; he has a certain charisma, and that goes a long way. A couple ay years back, him and me went tae Reading for the festival, then oantae Paris for a few days. It was weird tae sleep in a bed wi a guy withoot shagging him, even though I once woke up with his hand on my tit.

That makes me think of my mother, sitting at home, titless, both breasts

202

removed by the surgeon's scalpel. Androgynous and skeletal; I swear tae God she looks like Bowie on the cover ay *David Live*. I should be spending time wi her but I can hardly look at her. Now I know that I'll do anything: cock, drugs, poems, films, or just work, tae avoid thinking about her.

Back to Paris back to Paris back to Paris . . .

. . . I met a French guy at a disco, whae I got aw horny wi, which seemed tae upset Hamish, but no enough to make him try and ride me. He's a skinny wee bitch of a laddie (as Simon once described him), with his small girly eyes, which tear up when he reads his poetry, and he goes a sortay pinky orgasmy colour. The sort of guy who'd be sought-after in prison, n that's pittin it mildly.

I got dead pissed off when Mark Renton and Keith Yule joined Hamish's band, because they started hanging about the Hoochie and I suppose I'd kind ay looked on that as *my* scene, and didnae want loads ay Leith keelies mucking about there, lowering the tone. (Cept Simon, that is!) People fae Leith look doon oan every other part ay Edinburgh; they think that if you arenae born a Leither, then you're nowt. I might have been brought up in Leith, but I was actually born in Marchmont, which makes me total Edinburgh. Another thing is I sortay went oot wi Mark's brother Billy, for a bit, though I was still at school then. But I swear tae God I never let him shag me though everybody thinks I did, or *assumes* I did. But that's Leith and laddies, and, I suppose, lassies tae, for ye.

Any roads, I get up the Hoochie, that wee space above Clouds where ye always hear the best sounds, and meet interesting people, and the first faces I see are Mark (boo!), shuffling around in that crafty way of his, then Simon (yum!), hair swept back, but who's at the bar talking tae that Esther bitch, an arrogant cow who thinks she shites roses.

Please don't be fucking her please don't be fucking her . . .

I swear tae God I never get that jealous ay who Simon shags, cause we go our ain weys and dinnae make demands on each other, even though I've always sortay fancied him fae way back at Leithy. Well, maybe sometimes, cause there's some hoors ye jist cannae fuckin well stick and that Esther falls intae that category. I see that Hamish's wi Mark, they're gaun up tae two lassies I vaguely ken. Ah think one ay them's this bird that was meant tae have gied Colin Dugan a gam, but ah could be mistaken. Whatever, the poor cows've nae chance ay getting a length in that company!

As I move ower tae them, I kin hear Hamish seamlessly fib, — Wendy, Lynsey, meet my very good friend, Mark. A highly talented bassist.

Highly talented my arse: he sacked Mark fae *two* fuckin bands cause ay his lack ay competence on that instrument!

Mark, aw hoody-eyed n snottery-beaked, goes, — How's your music gaun these days, H?

— Don't do it any more, Mark. Hamish shakes his head, aw full ay pomp, as one ay the lassies, blonde bob, cool made-up eyes, looks devoured by this affay news. — All I do now is write poetry. Music is a crass, vulgar and commercial art form. It's spiritually bankrupt.

The blonde (Lynsey, I think) bats her eyes in rough grief, while Wendy-the-possible-blow-job-specialist stays neutral. Hamish sees me standing beside him and kisses me on the cheek. — Hey . . . Alison. How goes?

— No bad, I smile.

Mark's slavering away tae the lassies, the usual sortay bullshit he comes oot wi. — Myself and some friends in London are involved in this industrial art-rock project, he speed-lies, droppin me a wee wink. — It's sort of Einstürzende Neubauten meets the early Meteors, 'In Heaven' rather than 'Wreckin Crew', but with a four-four disco beat and big ska influence, and featuring a Marianne Faithfullesque vocalist. Think of a Kraftwerk who had loads ay sex in their teens and hung around Scottish and Newcastle brewers' chain pubs listening tae Labi Siffre and Ken Boothe on the jukebox and dreaming ay well-paid jobs in the Volkswagen factory in Hanover.

— Sounds cool! this blonde-maybe-Lynsey lassie goes. — What are you called?

— Fortification.

Cue for a slightly wrong-footed Hamish tae deftly change the subject back tae his 'Baudelaire-, Rimbaud- and Verlaine-influenced' poems, and for one ay the lassies tae say something aboot *Marquee Moon*. And for me tae elbay Mark, tae git his attention. — Fort chancer, lowerin the tone!

He looks me up n doon. Even though Mark's wasted, he fixes me in an appreciative stare I haven't seen from him before. — Wow, Ali. You're lookin very gorgeous.

No the compliment I expect fae him, but it fair puts Hamish on his taes, as his heid swivels taewards us. — And you're looking very . . . Mark.

He laughs at that, and gestures me to move aside, as Hamish havers oantae the girls aboot some gig he n Mark once played at the Triangle Club in Pilton. — How's it gaun?

— Fine. You?

— No bad. The bouncers widnae lit Spud in though, jist cause he hud a sling oan his airm.

— Poor Danny!

— Aye, he hud tae head hame. But ah saw Kelly in here earlier. Wi Des.

— Right.

He lowers his voice and leans intae me. Mark's a laddie who's taller than he first seems. — Anything gaun oan?

— By that do you mean what I think ye mean?

— Aye, ah think so.

— Naw, I called Johnny earlier, but he wisnae in or wisnae picking up.

— Aye, me n aw, he goes. Then there's a silence, and he asks, — How's things wi yir ma?

— Shite, pittin it mildly, I goes, no wanting tae talk aboot it, but it's good ay him tae ask.

— Right . . . sorry tae hear it. Ehm, if ye hear anything fae Johnny or Matty or that, gies a shout, he requests.

— Thanks, right, you n aw, I says.

Hamish breaks off fae Wendy and Lynsey n hands me this slim book ay poems. — Life-changing, he says emphatically, as Mark rolls his eyes.

— Right . . . ta . . . I goes, but ma attention's oan Simon, who's still chatting tae that horrible Esther at the bar. Lynsey's asking Hamish aboot the book, and he starts going on aboot Charles Simic's work. — Can you believe that at one time he couldn't speak a word of English?

I turn tae Mark. — At one time nane ay us could speak a word ay English, n he grins back, as I nod ower tae Esther. — Do you think she's good-looking? That platinum-blonde Simon's chattin tae?

Mark looks across, almost drooling. — Marianne? Aye, as fit as a butcher's dug.

— That's no Marianne, it's Esther.

— Aye? They look jist the same.

— Believe it: totally interchangeable. Lit's go n say hello, I suggest, slippin Hamish's thin book ay poems intae my bag. As soon as Simon meets my eye, he's right ower and we throw our airms roond each other and his head's buried in my neck. — Hey, gorgeous, he whispers, — don't say a thing, just let me hold you.

I do, but cannae resist cracking an over-the-shoulder smile at Esther who's been lumbered wi manky Mark! Ha! I swear tae God she looks a broken woman as Simon and me snog, and ah hear Mark rabbiting tae her, first aboot the Minds' *New Gold Dream* album, then his fictitious industrial rock-n-roll project, adding some new components as he goes. As Simon's tongue and scent fills ma heid, ah hear Esther's fractured voice moan how it must be hard tae get aw they different elements tae work thegither. Simon and me come up for air, and watch the show. Mark's agreeing wi her: — This is essentially the main challenge we face, but also what makes the assignment so intrinsically rewarding . . .

When she asks what it's called he tells her, but under the jaw-clicking roll ay the amphetamine, he's wasted and mumbly and it comes oot something like 'Fornication' and Esther thinks he's being fuckin wide, and looks tae us in appeal! Mark just shrugs and ditches her as this cute Asian lassie, but wi a total schemie accent, comes ower n announces, — Ah'm speeding oot ay ma nut!

— Me n aw, Mark eagerly goes, as Esther realises that even *he's* KB'd her!

She goes to say something tae Simon, but he cuts in, — To be continued, and tugs on my wrist and we head intae a corner for a cosy wee chat! I look back at Esther: *take that, ya fuckin trampy posh bitch! Let's just keep the best Leith lengths in fuckin Leith!*

The music's a lot louder than usual for the Hooch, and the speaker's close tae our seat, so Simon n me have tae sort ay shout intae each other's lugs. As I tug the back ay my belt tae ensure my arse-crack's covered, I ask him about Spud no gittin in, just cause ay his airm bein in a sling.

— I'm with the door staff on that one, he sniffs. — An unpardonable lapse in style. The fact he looked like a jakey probably didn't help.

Then we start talking aboot that wee Maria Anderson, cause my brother and his pals hang about with her and her mates fae the school. People's been saying that Simon and her are *gaun oot* thegither. I can't quite believe that cause she's just a wee lassie, and why would he when he's got loads ay girlfriends?

He pins me wi his big sad stare, telling me he's walked intae a nightmare. — It's a mess, he moans over Prince urging the revellers tae go crazy. — I'm her neighbour, and with her dad deid and her ma in the jail, I felt kinday responsible cause she'll no go tae her uncle's doon in Nottingham. He draws in a deep breath and looks tae the ceiling. — The problem is that she's formed a big attachment tae me, and worse, tae the skag. Ah'm trying tae keep her away fae it, but it's aw she wants.

— But what's aw this got tae dae wi you? It's no fair that you're lumbered like this!

— It's my ain fault. I stupidly . . . aw shite, he groans, — we ended up in bed . . . ah slept wi her. I was trying to comfort her and she was aw that needy, desperate wey and one thing led tae another. It was a *big* mistake.

— Fuckin hell, Simon, I tell him, trying tae tick him off without sounding jealous, cause I am a wee bit. Still, ye cannae blame the lassie for bein oot ay control wi everything that's happened tae her.

— She was *way* too young and distressed, and I can see now that ah was weak and stupid, and took advantage ay somebody in a bad situation. Now she thinks we're gaun out thegither. Ah'm gaunny see her mum in prison wi her next week, hopefully tae convince her tae go back doon tae her uncle's and get hersel sorted oot. This mess . . . it's just taken ower my life! I only wanted tae dae the right thing, but it's backfired big time. He draws in some breath, staring oot vacantly across the dance floor. — The thing is, even now, I'm worried sick about her being alone in that flat; you dunno what a young lassie in her state's gaunny dae. She's already had a dash at the boy that killed her faither, that Dickson fae the Grapes. I worry that she's jist gaunny end up like her ma or her dad: in jail or six fit under. She's been hanging aroond wi some sleazy creeps; I'm tryin tae keep her away fae them, but I cannae be around her every single minute ay the day, it's sick . . . twisted . . . he shakes his heid, — and I cannae keep sleeping wi her and bringing her fuckin skag, but it's aw that calms her doon . . . She should be sitting fuckin O grades, he gasps miserably, then looks intae my eyes. — God, here I am going on about *my* stuff, when your mother . . . he grabs my hand and squeezes it.

I feel myself tearing up. — Sorry, Simon, I . . . and I cannae speak, as music and people swirl roond us. Eventually I hear myself think out loud: — Why is life such a fucking mess?

— Search me, he says, gripping my hand tighter, his own eyes misting up. Then he looks around in distaste as the Style Council's 'You're the Best Thing' comes on.

— Dae ye no like this tune?

— I like it *too* much – it's far too good for the poseurs and pricks in this dreary howf, he spits. — I hate that these people are actually *allowed* tae listen to music like this.

— Ah ken what ye mean, I nod, bewildered; lookin ower at Esther, I sortay git the gist. She's makin her escape fae the rabid bluster ay Mark and that wee Asian lassie, whae I remember is called Nadia.

— Listen, I've a suggestion. Why don't we go round to Swanney's, get a wee something, then head back tae yours or mine and have a little of what we fancy and just hang out and talk? We've both got a lot ay shite gaun oan and this crowd in here are startin tae dae my nut in. Mark's going a bit crazy wi the skag n the Lou Reed; I'm no saying I'm an angel, but he's got so fucking myopic . . .

We watch Mark rantin away wi that mental wee Nadia, baith ay them aw ower the place on the speed.

— Now there's a marriage made in powder, Simon smirks, then says, — I'd rather get sorted before he shows up at Johnny's, or we'll never get rid ay the fucker.

I don't take any persuading at all. A coffee and poetry night wi Hamish will have tae wait. And Alexander had left a message sayin he wanted tae hook up, but now that's off tonight's agenda n aw. — Sound. Let's go.

We walk outside into a chilly night. Something unnameable turns behind my eyes. Simon's hand feels warm and his hot breath is like the whisper ay angels in ma ear.

Johnny's stair door's open; somebody's blootered in the lock and the security intercom – a spaghetti of wires spews oot a black hole where the aluminium grille box used to be. We can hear him on the first-floor landing, arguing with this guy, who shouts back in a voice I sortay recognise: — You've nae fuckin idea, mate!

Simon pulls me back into the shadows at the bottom of the steps.

— Yir *mate's* been huckled, Michael, we hear Johnny's low heckle, — *you've* no, you're still in the game. Find another fuckin wey tae git it oot!

— Ah telt ye: that cunt'll grass us right up. Watch this fuckin space, the boy half whispers, turns away, then we can hear him comin doon the steps. He stops, cranes his neck and shouts back up the stairs: — It's game ower, and he twists roond and nearly walks intae us, pushin past us wi a nasty look on his face, but daein a quick double take when he sees me. Johnny's followed him doon the stairs tae the first bend. He looks a bit surprised tae see us, then shouts a stagey cheerio tae the boy, who doesnae answer back. Thing is, ah ken where I've seen that guy before: in this pub in Dalry Road wi Alexander's brother.

— Fuckin business, Johnny shrugs at us, but he's aw tense and bothered. — It's gettin like Waverley Station up this fuckin gaff. How we've no been busted by the polis, ah dinnae ken.

— This is Edinburgh, Simon laughs. — The cops in this city aren't particularly big on law enforcement.

We go up tae the flat and make the deal. Johnny wants tae dae some wi us right now, but we're anxious tae get away. Then the door bangs and it's Matty. Johnny cheerlessly lets him in and heads back through the front room. Matty follows him like an anxious lap dog. — Ali. Si.

— Matteo, says Simon. — How goes? Lookin a wee bit peely-wally there, my old chum.

— No bad, he says, n he does look terrible, his eyes are rid n it's like the side ay his face is streaked wi dirt. He barely acknowledges us as he glares at Johnny. — Cunt, ah need sorted oot, Mikey Forrester tae.

— Let's see the colour ay yir dough then chavy, Johnny says coldly.

Simon gies me a 'fuck this' nod and we're off. As we depart Johnny and Matty start arguing and it seems tae get mair heated as we head doon the stairs, where we run right intae Mark, charging up towards us wi demented octopus eyes as we hear Johnny's door slamming shut. I wonder which side ay it Matty's oan. — Marco . . . Simon says, raising a brow, pointing at his ghastly green fleece. — What the well-dressed man about town *isn't* wearing . . . No luck with the girlies, I take it?

— Whaire are youse gaun?

— A party. For two. As in *you* ain't invited, Simon emphatically says. Then he nods upstairs, adding, — If you want sorted oot, I'd get in there sharpish. Young Matteo's just arrived wi a horse-choker ay a wad, dropping Forrester's name like it was premium acid. I think he wants tae sort oot the whole ay Muirhoose.

Mark needs nae mair encouragement, pushing past us and storming up the stairs. We hear him hammering on Johnny's door, stifling our laughter as we exit into the street.

We walk for a bit, step by step across the black pavements in the incessant rain. We're soaked through by the time we get a cab doon tae my place at Pilrig. I put on the fire and go to the bathroom tae get some towels. Alexander's shaving bag is still sitting there on the cistern. I put it in the linen press, in case Simon sees it. Heading back into the front room, a towel wrapped round my heid, I hand him another and switch on the answerphone messages.

— *It's Dad, princess. Just tae let ye know that Mum had a good night last night. Very peaceful. She was a wee bit agitated and confused cause ay the stuff they're giving her . . .*

Sweet Simon tightly grabs my hand.

— *. . . but she sends her love and she's looking forward tae seeing ye. Bye then, darlin . . . love you.*

Simon intensifies his grip and kisses the side of my face.

— *Hi . . . it's me . . .*

Alexander.

— *. . . I was wondering if you're around . . . Obviously not. Not to worry. Anyway, see you Monday.*

Simon lets go my hand. An eyebrow raises, accompanied wi a wry smile, but he says nothing. Kelly's up next, sounding squeaky and excitable.

— Whaire did you get tae? Saw Mark at the Hooch. Had a bit ay a fawoot wi Des. Too radge! Call us when ye git this message!

Simon looks at me, but we both know there's no way I'm calling Kelly or anybody else right now. — She's still with Des, then?

— Aye, but guess what? She telt us she kind ay fancies Mark!

— Hmm, says Simon, — the words frying pan and fire spring immediately tae mind.

I'm noddin in agreement as I go tae the fridge n pour some neat voddy ower they rocks ay ice, so cauld they make a sound like bones cracking. I look at the white powder in the placky bag Johnny's gied us.

— You desperate? Simon asks.

— I'm okay, I tell him sharply. I like a bit ay skag now and then, but it's no like I'm some fuckin junky like Johnny, Mark or Matty.

— I think it would be great tae go tae bed first, he says. — Make love.

I'm *right* into that. We go through tae the bedroom, and I'm taking my damp clathes off, struggling with this top, it's stuck tae me wi the wet. Then it's gone and I'm watching Simon slowly undress, carefully folding each garment, and thinking how, apart fae him, the best sex I've had is with Alexander, who's aboot thirty-four or something. Older guys are better cause they really ken their way aroond a lassie's body, but it took me ages to get him tae ride me. He let me suck him off, but it was like he kinday thought a blow job didnae constitute infidelity. Then he went doon on me, which was good, but I thought, 'Fuck sakes, it's Nora aw ower again,' but the first time we shagged it was barry (as first times go). Then he sortay ruined it by talking about his separated wife eftir, and I telt him straight, if we're daein this again, I didnae want tae hear any ay that shite. I don't know if it's because he's no been with many women, or not for a long time, but it's like he thinks I expect him tae fucking well mairry me! He's giein his mind a wee treat, n that's pittin it mildly. A barry lay, though. But Simon fucks like an aulder guy, like he's got aw the time in the world, and he gets ye in a fair auld lather before he pits it up ye. He switches fae making love tae fucking and back again, so you're eywis oan yir toes. Ye spend a night wi him, ye git yir money's worth. And ye don't think ay anything else for a while, and that's what I need: no tae be thinking ay anything else.

We start snogging; dirty, wet kisses, and I feel something red and inviolate gather force within me. He whispers in my ear, — Ever had a guy make love tae you in your arse? I really fancy daein it that way.

I feel myself being pulled right oot ay the horny zone cause that doesnae appeal tae me at all. In fact that's pittin it mildly: the idea of Simon's big, fat cock up ma bahookay makes me feel queasy, but then that dildo that Nora left behind pops inspiringly intae my mind. — You can fuck me up the arse if I can dae it tae you first!

— What . . . Don't be . . . how can you . . . ?

I leap offay the bed, go over tae the wardrobe and pull the dildo doon fae the top shelf, strapping it on like Nora did, positioning the base on ma pubic bone.

Simon's black pupils expand and gleam. — Where in the name ay fuck did you get that?

— Never you mind! I want tae fuck you up the arse first, I tell him. I swivel my hips, watching my big placky plonker move fae side tae side.

He raises a doubtful brow. — Aye, that'll be right. You're no putting *that* up ma erse!

— It's only the same size as your cock, I tell him, though I think the dildo's a bit bigger. But this flattery seems tae appease him, and his mouth twitches, and I see a germ ay contemplation spark in his eyes. So I'm imploring him: — C'mon, it'll be fun. You can dae me after.

— Eh . . . I dunno about this . . .

— C'mon, Simon, it'll be an experience. You'll enjoy it much mair than ah will.

— Aw aye, he says, — how d'ye reckon that?

— Cause you've got a prostate gland tae stimulate and I dinnae. The male prostate gland's a sensitive zone. My pal Rachael's a nurse; she telt us aw aboot it. You've much mair going on up there than I have. Look at homo guys; they get off on receiving as well as giving, you know.

He thinks about this. — Gen up?

— Aye, I contend, as I start to slather the Vaseline onatae the dildo. — I willnae hurt ye.

He grinds his jaw, scoffing as if that prospect was impossible, — Awright, I'm game, let's dae it. I'll try anything once . . . obviously no wi a guy but!

— You'll love it.

— Aye, right, he says doubtfully.

So he's on the bed, crouching, legs apart, and his protruding bum is like a girl's except that it's a bit more muscly and hairy in the arse-crack. No that I've experienced lassies' arse-cracks, but mair hairy than I can *imagine* them as being. I line up the end ay the dildo and push it in. His arsehole seems to give way a bit tae allow the bell-end entry, and then tighten around the top part ay the shaft.

— Oh . . . fuckin hell . . .

211

— You okay?

— Course I am, he snaps.

I push in a little more. Then pull out a bit, then back in . . .

— Oh . . . aw . . . that's well nippy . . .

I push against him and he lets himself sink slowly doon oantae the mattress, and I'm oan top ay him, pushing in, and pulling out, fucking him slowly, more of the dildo vanishing up his arse as his body tenses and relaxes, then tenses again. He groans away, grippin the bedspread tightly wi baith hands, but he's no the only yin intae this. — Fuckin good this, eh; me fuckin you up the erse like the wee Bannanay flats bitch ye are, I spit, enjoying it, turned on like fuck, dripping, working my clit with my fingers, the other hand clamped oantae his shoodir.

With my fingers and the dildo base rubbin against me, I'm bringing myself off while fucking him, *a boy*, and I swear tae God this feels so good, to be able tae totally control the pace, tae penetrate . . .

We're at it, we're at it, we're at it . . .

— EUUHHHGGGGGG! Simon suddenly convulses, stiffens up, and then collapses into relaxation. Soft groans bubble from him, like they're half trapped in his throat.

I'm pulling away at my clit, rubbing it, N I'M ABOOT TAE FUCKIN EXPLODE! – YA FAHKIN BEAUTY . . . WHOA . . . whoa . . . whoa . . . ohhh . . . EEEGGGH . . .

I faw oan toap ay Simon. We're like a heap ay Alexander's felled trees, ready tae be incinerated. I stay prone on him for a bit, feeling the knobbly bone and muscle of his back on ma squashed tits n belly. Then I push myself up, no so much pulling the dildo oot ay his bum, as watching him eject it, as if it was a shit, as he lies sprawled on the sheets. I clip off the device and hold it up tae the light. It glistens with the Vaseline, but there's nae trace of shite on it. — You okay? Did ye enjoy that?

— It was . . . sort of medical . . . he half mumbles intae the sheets.

I throw the dildo onto the floor and pull him over on his back. He rolls compliantly for me, and his eyes stay half shut. Then I spy sticky patches ay cum on the bed sheets and oan his stomach and chest. — You shot yir load!

— Did I . . . ? His eyes snap open and he sits up aw agitated. — I didnae realise . . . He turns from the mess tae me, his eyes bulging. — Listen, Ali, ye willnae say nowt aboot this, will ye?

— Of course no, I dinnae kiss n tell, this is between us!

— Right . . . right . . . he says, and we pull back the covers and get intae bed. — It was a bit intense, but that was cause it was with you, he

212

says, pulling me close tae him. I love the way he smells; some boys are mingers but Simon has this sweet pine-like smell, like how I imagine an expensive cologne.

— It was intense for me n aw, cause it wis you, I tell him. — I couldnae stop touching myself . . . I grab his cock and it's stiffening in my hand, prising my fingers outwards. — Fuck me, I whisper in his ear, — fuck me really hard in my cunt and tell me you love me . . .

Simon's face takes on a dumb, cruel twist and he looks at me like he's going to remember our pact, but instead he's on me and slowly pushing inside my fanny and every fibre ay me aches for more as he rides us really good in that way of his, first slowly, then hard, and he says 'I love you' which I ken he doesnae mean, and then stuff in Italian, and I'm swimming through mists as I'm orgasming time and time again, and I'm so demented that it's actually a fucking relief when he finally blows and screams, — *Avanti*!

As we hud each other in a sweaty grasp, he thankfully seems tae have forgotten all about ma arsehole, but only cause I suspect he's thinking ay his ain, or mibbe the gear.

Skaggirl

Towards the Trossachs, pillows of snow, like fallen clouds, cling snugly to high hills and the roofs of good homes. Some windows are already ablaze with Christmas tree lights. From her cell inside the women's prison, Janey Anderson looks out at the big flakes tumbling from the sky, wishing she could see more. Snow had never been an enemy. But what sort of a Christmas could this be?

Janey grows animated as she leaves her cell and walks down the corridor in a line of women, led by a solitary uniformed one, who opens a series of locked doors. Eventually, they reach the visiting room, where each prisoner sits at one of the desks, lined in neat rows. After a few minutes, the visitors start to file in, and there's Maria, walking towards her, acknowledging her with a strained smile.

Janey Anderson's limited experience has already shown her how the women's prison can be as much a haven as a place of incarceration. Maria looks menaced and in need of protection. Dark circles smear under her eyes like bruises. Her hair seems matted in some parts, lank and greasy in others, and two angry spots flare on her chin. It wasn't her child, more a Bizarro version; some refugee from that parallel world in the DC Comics her brother Murray used to collect. Maria remains standing, so Janey instinctively rises and reaches out to her. — Sweetheart . . .

A heavy-knit screw with short-cropped hair, who'd seemed to take a dislike to her, perhaps on account of their similar ages, pounces to warn Janey about touching. Bullneck craning round, she barks, — Enough! Ah'll no tell ye again!

And crumbling back into her seat, Janey can't believe her eyes when she sees *him*, standing behind Maria, with a sense of prerogative that revolts her to the core. Now Coke's gone, she's locked up in here, and this usurper has his arm around the fragile shoulders of her daughter, her Maria, who was meant to be safe at Murray and Elaine's in Nottingham! The letter he had sent her! — What're *you* daein here? She looks at her former neighbour, the friend of her deceased husband, and briefly, shamefully, her lover.

— You'll be in here a few months, Janey, he says, pulling up a chair, his glance at Maria *giving her permission* to do the same. — Somebody has tae keep an eye on Maria, he sniffs, in put-upon tones.

— Ah ken what you mean by keepin an eye! Janey gasps incredulously. — She's jist a young lassie!

Simon, Sick Boy, she'd heard his nickname was, lowers himself onto the hard seat, grimacing in discomfort then adjusting his weight. He looks around the rows of visitors in their chairs in what Janey feels is nervous distaste, but this sensation soon diminishes as she watches him fill the room with his presence, as he sits up straight and stretches out. In the event it's Maria who protests, — Ah'm nearly sixteen but, Ma.

A bolt of shame skewers Janey. Simon had been a wee boy when Coke and her moved next door to the Williamsons all those years ago. As a young mum, she'd openly flirted with his father. One time, at New Year . . .

Oh my God . . .

Then she slept with the son. And now he has her daughter, her wee lassie. — Look at ye but, look at the state ay ye! Ye should be back in Nottingham wi oor Murray n Elaine!

Maria suddenly focuses in loathing, the look on her daughter's face chilling Janey. — Ah'm gaun naewhaire till ah git him! That Dickson! It's him that's ruined everything! It wis probably him that grassed ye up aboot ma dad's money!

— She has a point, Janey, Simon Williamson agrees.

— You shut the fuck up, Janey snaps. Bulldyke Screw briefly stirs from her Ken Follett novel, looks out with pale blue eyes, deeply set into bulbous pink flesh. Janey lowers her voice and sits forward, scowling at him. — You . . . wi ma wee lassie! What kind ay a person are you?!

— I'm trying to take care of Maria, Sick Boy bites back, outrage in his big eyes. — You want her tae be on her ain, while you're hanging out in this cosy little sorority? Cause she's told you and me that she ain't going back tae Nottingham, despite me telling her till I'm blue in the face that it's the best place for her. So fine. I'll just leave her, and he throws his hands in the air Italian-style, prompting Bulldyke Screw to lower Follett to her meaty thigh in warning.

— Dinnae, Simon . . . Maria pleads.

— I couldnae walk away now, babe, don't you worry. He shakes his head, putting his arm around Maria and kissing her on the side of her face, all the time never taking his accusing eyes from Janey. — You need *somebody* to be here for ye!

Deflated, Janey can only bleat across the table, — But . . . but she's just a bairn . . .

— She's almost sixteen. I'm just twenty-one, Simon Williamson declares pompously, though he seems to sink slightly in realisation that Janey knows he'd recently celebrated his twenty-second. — I know how it looks, and I'm by no means proud of the fact that we've embarked on a relationship, but it's happened. So deal with it, he commands, sitting forward towards her, then wincing on the hard seat.

Janey feels her essence crumble further under his unwavering gaze. She lowers her head, before whipping it up and looking into her daughter's confused, tired eyes. The dread thought settles: *the eyes of an old woman.*

— I'm not a cradle-snatcher, Janey. Sick Boy keeps the cold stare trained on her. — As I think you know, ah prefer more mature women as a rule, and she feels herself drowning in her abashed silence.

The target of Janey's silent wrath slowly shifts: in uncompromising clarity she sees again that Coke's drinking had inflicted this misery on them all. Destroyed him, incarcerated her, sent her son to England, to relatives he barely knew, and delivered her daughter into the arms of this shady neighbour. Every glass his stupid, befuddled eyes had looked into and raised to those big, rubbery lips, had inched them all closer to this horrible destiny. Her feelings for her late husband, once shrouded in all sorts of ambivalence, crystalise into a searing hate.

Then Sick Boy gives her daughter another squeeze, this time on Maria's thigh, evidence to Janey of a proprietary intimacy. — As awkward as this is, I *love* this lassie, and I'm going to do the right thing by her while you're in here, he declares.

Janey glares at him again, then whiplashes to her daughter. — But look at ye! Ye look terrible!

Through her blouse, Maria claws at the skin on her arms. — We've picked up the flu —

— There's been a few sleepless nights, aye, Sick Boy cuts in. — But we're okay, aren't we, babe?

— Aye. Honest, Ma, Maria contends.

Though far from convinced, Janey sees no gain in stoking her daughter's alienation, or scuppering what gallingly seems to be her sole source of protection. And then there was Bulldyke Screw. Her nemesis had lowered Follett's *Eye of the Needle* and was now slowly waddling down the lines of tables, lowering the volume like a hi-fi slide control, before settling at the doors, folding her meaty arms over a suitcase-like protrusion of bosom and gut.

The final phase of the excruciating visit is a stilted dance around banalities, as Janey aches for phone access to speak to her Nottingham-based brother, as much as Sick Boy and Maria do for gear. All parties are relieved when visiting hours are over.

— We need tae get busy-busy, chop-chop, Sick Boy tells Maria, as they prowl through the prison gates and the drizzle towards Stirling town centre, to the railway station and onto a Waverley-bound train.

A bus takes them to the foot of Easter Road, where they cut across the Links, shivering against a strong wind, which whips stinging layers of rain into them. Despite their discomfort, Maria looks around in a wonderment that stuns him, as if this sodden, manky walk is evoking the end of the school year, bringing with it the memory of a girlhood's innocent summers; tumbling onto grass, head throbbing with the heat, the dazed, empty streets of breezeless afternoons, the gossip of radios from passing cars, the rich smell of diesel, the melancholy intoxication of her father, the husky voice of her mum, carrying over the balcony through a powdery dusk that would fall so slowly that you felt cheated by the light's departure. All that gone with the onset of breasts and hips, which heralded newer, more dangerous games and the deployment of disdainful sneers and aloof postures, those paltry defences against the unremitting attentions of feral boys. He regrets his role in her recent string of tragedies, but shrugs it off by rationalising that if it wasn't him, then some other, less caring predator would be keen to take up the assignment.

È la via del mondo.

Sabotaged by an emotion between euphoria and panic, Sick Boy fingers the pocket of his jeans. It wasn't a dream! Those tenner notes he'd gotten from Marianne the other day were still there, sharp to his touch. She had opened the door, wide-eyed, and he'd stepped right into her, silencing her with a kiss. As she responded, his eyes picked out the boudoir, where her bag sat on the bed. He'd eased her onto it and slid his hand up her skirt, his fingers caressing her thighs, working inside her panties. He'd almost cheered out loud on discovering she was wet, gasping as his forefinger pressed against her angry clit. As he'd pushed her lips apart, his other arm, round the back of her neck, was reaching towards her bag. His hand had meandered into it, fingers deftly tracing the brass lips of her purse, moving north till he found that tight knot. Slowly pulling the sleek lips apart, he'd picked his fingers inside: it was fresh with crisp banknotes. He picked a couple from her tight, folded stack, mindful to keep slowly working her other lips with his right hand, his mouth on hers, pinning

217

her to the bed. The two hands working two sets of lips, the right easing off, stopping her climax until the left had clipped the brass edges back together and exited from the bag, tugging, so slowly, the zip home. Then he pulled his arm back from behind her neck, and increasing the pressure on her vaginal lips he'd looked in her eyes, and declared harshly, — After this we *will* fuck, and waited for her to scream out, — Oh Simon, oh my Godddd . . . knowing he'd have to make good that promise when all he was thinking about was the notes he was slipping into his back pocket, and how he'd spend them.

Now, rubbing those notes, there is no question as to how they would be disbursed. Maria sees the two tenners in the pornographic rub between his finger and thumb, catches his eye, and he's about to explain, when a voice booms in his ear, — These'll do nicely, and he turns to see the burly, slick-haired figure of Young Baxter has stepped out of the bus shelter right in front of him.

What the fuck! — Graham . . .

— I'll take those, Young Baxter says, extending a leather gloved hand. — And I'll have the rest by the end of the month, or you'll find all your shit in the street and the locks changed.

— Right . . . Sick Boy swallows hard, looks into Young Baxter's glacial eyes, then hands over the notes, his lips trembling. — I haven't seen your dad around, I heard he wasn't well . . . that's why I'm a little behind with the rent. A bit of a communication breakdown between me and the flat-mate —

— I couldnae give a toss about your bullshit, Young Baxter snaps, — You might be able to mess the old man around, but you'll no dae the same wi me.

— I never —

— No rent, no flat, Young Baxter shakes a chunky head, — and I'll be right in there, taking everything you've got and flogging it and then if that's no enough tae reimburse me, I'll be taking you tae a small claims court.

Sick Boy stands speechless in abject misery, as Baxter gets into his car and drives off.

— Who wis that? Maria asks. — What did ye gie um money fir?

— My fucking landlord's son . . . he's been stalking me! Jesus fuck!

— We've still goat money for gear but, Simon? Eh?

She reminds him of a crazed bird in a nest, frantically yearning for a feed. — Aye, we'll get it. Stay calm, he says, though he himself feels anything but.

When they get back to the Andersons' home, Sick Boy drinks some cold tap water, but a skull-splitting headache sets in. Thinking of Young Baxter with rancour, he delves into his small notebook and immediately sees the name: Marianne Carr. Guiltily moving on past the 'C's, he hears Maria in the toilet, wonders why can't she be more like Marianne, with a job and money. Hunting for two is tiresome. He calls Johnny Swan but is dismissed outright. — Nae hireys, nae skag. Ah cannae dae tick, buddy, specially no whin thaire's a drought oan.

Then it was back to 'C', but this time Matty Connell. Matty seems to be back in with Shirley, but Sick Boy gets the same forlorn tale. — No go, mate. The boy let us doon, eh, Matty says, — cunt, somebody got busted, a contact ay Swanney's.

To Sick Boy's pained ears his voice drips with wily bullshit. — I see, he replies, — catch ye later, and puts the phone down without waiting for a response.

So there had been some kind of a bust, and there was a shortage. But Swanney would have a personal stash to ride out the rough times. With a habit like his, he had to. Sick Boy calls him again.

— Sorry, mate, Swanney says, and Sick Boy can *see* his grin down the line, as if he's sitting in the chair opposite, — when ah said ah cannae help ye, ah meant ah cannae help ye. Ah hate repeatin masel. Squawk. Ah hate repeatin masel. Squawk . . . and he hears Raymie's hyena-like laughter, high-pitched and derisive, resonate in the background.

— Listen, Sick Boy's voice drops, — ah've goat a wee bird back here in Leith, tidy as fuck n gantin oan it, but ah'm too skaggy-bawed tae ride her. She's horned up tae fuck: wants tae perty big time.

He hears Maria slamming the bathroom door shut, heading into her bedroom.

— Aw aye? Johnny's voice is cynical, and he responds in the parodied *Crown Court* tones now ubiquitous within their company: — I put it to you that this is nothing more than a tissue of lies, carefully constructed in order for you to get sorted out with free skag!

But Sick Boy can feel the hook's tug, though he knows he'll have to play the game. — Objection, Your Honour! I would humbly request that this hearing be adjourned for one hour, then reconvened at Tollcross, where Exhibit One can be presented to the court.

A silence. Then, — I would sincerely hope that for your sake, Mr Williamson, the said exhibit is up to scratch. This court takes a very dim view indeed of its time being wasted.

— Gen up, Johnny. She's a very naughty wee raver. Sick Boy's voice drops as he hears Maria going through the cupboards, rummaging, cursing. — You're welcome tae a poke at that hot wee pussy. Fir a wee fix, likes.

The line goes quiet once again, for two horrible beats within which Sick Boy dies a thousand deaths. — Aye? Fit, is she?

— Johnny, this is a *ballissimo* wee angel. Pure as the driven snaw, till ah broke the seal myself, like, he lies. — Been teachin her some moves n aw, he expands, now enjoying his spiel, countering his own crushing need by trying to set up a greater one in his opponent. He reverts back to *Crown Court*-speak, this time casting himself in aggressive prosecution tones: — I put it you that you will be every bit as bewitched by this young vixen as I myself was, then adds, — She just wants tae perty.

— Well, we aw want that. So come on down, Johnny says expansively, before snapping like a sprung trap, — Just youse two, mind!

— Nae worries, telt her aw aboot ye, she's keen tae meet up. Sick Boy fights back a gasp, watching Maria appear, ghostlike, in the doorway. He speaks to her, but into the phone: — We'll see ye awright, eh, Maria?

The only response, though, is from Johnny. — Right then, see yis.

— See ye in an hour tops. Sick Boy rests the phone on its cradle. — Game on!

Maria greets this news with an ulcerated smile. Sick Boy heads into the bedroom to see that she's taken everything from her drawers and wardrobe and dumped them on the floor. She follows in behind him. — Ah've goat nowt tae wear!

He manages to find an orange-and-white top in the laundry basket that isn't too soiled, and coaxes her to change into it.

Soon they're outside again, shivering at a bus shelter in Junction Street. They board the bus which wheels up Lothian Road. An amber-coloured sky hangs behind blue-grey ropes of smoky cloud. — No long now, Sick Boy says into the window, feet tapping on the floor of the bus, watching girls through the muck-streaked glass, imagining them naked, relieved to feel a twinge in his trousers. Resolves he'll never let junk master *his* libido.

The bus wheels up Lothian Road and by the time it reaches Tollcross, Sick Boy is shattered. Maria is worse, shaking so much he's moved to reach down and place his hands on her knees. Stepping off the vehicle, he affects nonchalance. — Mind, Maria, be cool. Flirty. Sexy. Dinnae think aboot gear n say nowt till Johnny mentions it. Did you, ehm . . . take the pill this morning?

220

— Course ah did!

— Ah'll only be in the next room, so dinnae worry. Johnny's nice, he says faithlessly, as they mount the stairs of the tenement dwelling.

Maria starts chattering, biting on her nails, but as they approach the black door, Sick Boy raises his palm to silence her. He tries to look into the letter box before he knocks, but it won't yield to the push of his fingers. He bangs on the door and whoever opens it shouts, — Come in, and heads right back into the flat, and they follow. Sick Boy looks back, seeing that a piece of plywood has been nailed over the letter box.

In the living room, along with a couch and chair, a coffee table with a broken vase, an empty birdcage on an old sideboard, an advent calender with each day already opened and all the chocolates removed, and what appears to be a bloodstain on the battered floorboards, Maria registers two men and looks anxiously at Sick Boy, before he introduces them. — Maria, my good friend Mr Raymond Airlie, and our host, Mr Johnny Swan. This is Maria, and he steers her forward, both hands on her shoulders.

— Any gear? Maria begs.

Fuck, thinks Sick Boy.

From the armchair by the empty fireplace, Johnny laughs loudly. — Aw in good time, honeychile. The rules ay the house are: you be nice tae the White Swan, n the White Swan is nice tae you. Ah'm sure Simon here's telt ye the drill.

Maria moves over and immediately disconcerts him by sitting on his knee. Her hand reaches up and strokes his rough chin. — Let's go tae the bedroom.

— That's much, much better, Swanney says in a low growl, then motions her to rise, winking at Sick Boy who cringes as they step out together.

— The flowers of romance, Raymie says disdainfully, but Sick Boy notes, glory, glory, that he's cooking up.

— You're a prince, Raymie.

— Prince Buster Hymen, he laughs, nodding to the door, then singing, — *This may not be downtown Lee-heeth, but we promised you a fix . . .*

Twenty minutes later, Sick Boy emerges from his daze to hear shouting. It's Maria. — Jist cook up! she shrieks, following Johnny into the front room. Her top is on inside out, thick braided orange seams running down her arms.

— The impatience ay youth. Let the White Swan have his wee post-coital moment, Johnny protests, clad in a red silk kimono, with golden dragons emblazoned on it. He turns to Sick Boy. — These moves ye taught her . . . that the best ye kin dae?

— Just gie the lassie her shot, Sick Boy responds with a mimimal shrug.

— Awright, Johnny says, briefly shamed, then starts preparing the shot in cold deliberation.

He insists on fixing for her, seemingly enjoying this penetration even more. As Maria gasps in gratitude, falling into his arms, he covetously strokes the girl's tousled hair with a tenderness that disturbs Sick Boy.

So he's over to them, thanking Johnny; begging, hustling and pleading for a 'wee something' to take away with him. Johnny stonewalling in response, delivering a smug lecture on the basic laws of supply and demand, but eventually succumbing and dangling a bag in front of a grasping, grateful Sick Boy.

A smile on his face masks the violence of his yank, as he pulls Maria to her feet. Despite Johnny's mild, skagged protests, the wasted duo depart, heading off on the bus back down to Leith, Sick Boy with his arm around his girl. — Ah'm really, really sorry you hud tae dae that, babe.

— It doesnae bother us, cause it's for you, she says, then corrects herself, — for us, you n me. It feels barry now. You're right good tae me, Simon, she says, although he knows she knows that he isn't, but is hoping to somehow shame him into becoming the version of himself she wants him to be, — dinnae ever leave us . . .

— No danger, babe, you're stuck wi me. We'll get back doon tae yours. I ken a couple ay boys who want tae perty, it'll be a laugh.

In the bus window, Sick Boy surveys Maria's reflection, surprised at how young she looks; pallid, wonderstruck. He turns away, anxiously surveying the other passengers. Back in Leith they eagerly head up the stairs of Cables Wynd House, where Maria immediately retreats to the bedroom to lie down.

Sick Boy heads out again, returning an hour later with Chris Moncur from the Grapes of Wrath pub. Chris is six foot two and solid muscle, the first in his family for at least three generations not to work in the now practically defunct docks. Sick Boy wonders if he's built in proportion. — Go easy oan her, he says in sudden anxiety.

Chris nods in acquiescence, but is offended. *If she cannae take a good panelling, what the fuck was she daein in this game?*

He emerges twenty minutes later and squares Sick Boy up. Neither man can bear to meet the other's eyes as the notes change hands. Then Chris says, quite sadly, thumbing back towards the bedroom, — Ah think she's pished the bed. Ah'd git her showered oaf n change the sheets if ah wis you. No gaunny dae much business thaire.

Shortly after this, Maria comes out. — Ah feel sair, Simon.

He'd been fixing up; it was as if she could smell the cooking skag, and they both take another shot. Maria lies back on the couch and whispers in broken contentment, — Ah feel better, Simon . . . sorry aboot the sheets . . . ah feel barry now, but . . .

— No worries. He slowly but cheerfully rises, getting the old bedclothes, bundling them up and dragging them into the washing machine. He looks outside as a round moon blazes magnesium in the mauve sky, above tenement windows frosted with stark yellow light. Heading back to the bedroom, he curses as his wasted limbs struggle to turn the mattress over. He finds some fresh sheets and makes the bed up as best he can.

When Maria sees his handiwork, she's right back under the covers. She wants to doze, and him to join her. He slides in and feels a jolt of fear.

— Was he big?

She nods.

— Bigger than me?

— That fix . . . it was barry . . .

— Aye, but how would you compare us, like, size-wise?

— You're bigger, Maria says, as Sick Boy senses with both gratitude and regret that she's learning the game, — but he isnae as gentle as you. He didnae make us come like you do.

Is the correct answer, he concludes, in bleak admiration.

He's quickly up and dressed in anticipation, slotting a cassette of Pink Floyd's *Meddle* into his Walkman. It's a little slower than usual, as the batteries are starting to go. The next guest is punctual, and Sick Boy lets him in with a blank look, securing payment up front, watching him go into the room where Maria dozes in the bed. The client pulls back the duvet and admires her nakedness. Then he looks pointedly at Sick Boy who steps back from the door, but keeps it ajar so he can look through the crack, where the man undresses in a few swift movements. *Thank fuck his dick is small.* Sick Boy feels a relief, as, in a sudden violent leap and series of thrusts, he's on her and inside her.

Maria becomes aware that the mass is heavier than the cloak of sleep and drugs. Sick Boy can't see her face but she almost says his name, — Si . . . before realising that the weight, the dimensions, the scent, the feel are all wrong. Her body freezes and she opens her eyes into a nightmare.

— Ah'm sorry about yir daddy, darlin, he says with a slack grin, as he thrusts inside her.

— Naw . . . leave us . . . LEAVE US! Maria screams, trying to push him away with her thin, wasted arms, as Sick Boy cringes outside, looking away, turning up Floyd's epic track 'Echoes' on his dodgy Walkman.

— Nivir mind though, ah'm your daddy now, sweetheart, Dickson says, as the batteries die and the guitar riff fades. Sick Boy visualises him putting his hand over Maria's mouth, simultaneously twisting her head round so she has to look into his eyes.

It's Sick Boy's chance, and he runs through to the coat cupboard, and drags the claw hammer from Coke's toolbox. He watches the white flabby arse of the beast going up and down, these black flannels round his ankles. The ex-cop's skull is waiting to be smashed to pulp by his heroic intervention, as his beautiful princess twists her head away to scream loud enough to shake the Bannanay flats, then is smothered by the landlord's hand again.

I could do the cunt now . . . it would be rape . . .

But his grip weakens and he lets the hammer fall to the floor as he stands rocking himself slowly, watching the grim proceedings through the door crack.

Dickson seems to take an age, before finally spazzing up and bucking then flopping to a grateful rest on top of the trapped girl. He removes his hand and Maria's disbelieving whimper rises to a blood-curdling bellow: — No . . . no . . . no . . . Simon . . . SI-MIN! SI-MI-HI-HIN . . .

Watching Dickson roll off the girl, Sick Boy notes him hesitate for a second, then pulling on his clothes and springing out the room. — You're some fuck-up, he says admiringly at the door, and slapping his host's shoulder, sees himself out.

Maria's crying softly into the pillow, and Sick Boy's on her, hammer in his hand, smothering her like a blanket, as if she were on fire, and holding her as she's bucking and twisting under his grip, all snotters, tears, screams and deep, deep burns. — YOU LET HIM RAPE US . . . FUCK OFF . . . KEEP AWAY FAE ME . . . AH WANT MUH MA . . . AH WANT MUH DA-HAH-HAD . . .

— AH HUD THE HAMMER! AH WIS GAUNNY DAE HIM! BUT NO HERE, AH MADE A MISTAKE!

— YE LET HIM RAPE ME –

— SOAS WE COULD GIT HIM! THEN AH REALISED THAT WE CANNAE DAE HIM HERE! WE'D GO DOON!

— AH WANT MY MA . . . HUH-HA . . . Maria convulses, and Sick Boy knows he just has to hold her till her rage is spent and sickness creeps into her junk-deprived cells and they scream for another shot.

And he does. The banshee howls fade into the background as his mind wanders off to scams and schemes and Maria feels warm and soft again, like somebody else is making the noise.

224

Then she sleeps. It's only when the phone goes off that Sick Boy feels moved to leave her. It won't stop.

He picks it up, and it's Uncle Murray, from a motorway Little Chef. He's spoken to Janey and he's on his way to get Maria, and Sick Boy had better fucking well be gone by the time he gets there. Despite repeating to the increasingly irate uncle 'You've got the wrong end of the stick here, Murray' and 'That's not my style, Murray' and 'We all need to sit down and talk this through, Murray', when the phone is slammed down Sick Boy suddenly thinks it may not be such a bad idea to vacate the premises. He leaves the dozy girl and heads out and up to Junction Street, then onto the Walk. He thinks he'll go straight up the thoroughfare to Montgomery Street, where Spud and Renton will be waiting, or even press on to the Hoochie Coochie Club at Tollcross, where there will be girls who are much less high-maintenance.

Notes on an Epidemic 4

The Needle Exchange in Bread Street, Tollcross, was shut down in the early 1980s by the police, after increasing concern about this facility had been mooted in the local press.

It meant that members of Edinburgh's growing intravenous drug-using community no longer had easy recourse to clean injecting equipment. Consequently, people started to share syringes and needles, unaware of the threat of HIV transmission (then publicised almost exclusively as a gay man's disease) from direct blood-to-blood contact.

Users began to get sick in hitherto unheard-of numbers, and soon some sections of the media were describing Edinburgh as 'the Aids capital of Europe'.

The Light Hurt His Eyes

Stepping into the dusky room, his hand had instinctively reached for the light switch, before abruptly stopping. Tracing the hulking silhouette of his former brother-in-law and business associate sat in the chair, he remembered that the light hurt his eyes.

Following his exit interview at personnel, where they'd alternately humiliated and terrorised him, Russell Birch had spent most of the afternoon trying to get drunk. He'd hopped around several west Edinburgh bars, slowly fuelling his rage against the man who'd brought this nightmare down on him, who was silently ensconced in the wicker-basket chair, so still his bulk produced not even the faintest creak. Russell thought he'd been successful in his mission, but suddenly felt way too sober.

The awareness that he now faced a different ignominy, even starker and less compromising than this morning's ordeal in that shabby office, gripped Russell and he found himself internally cursing his stupid fucking slut of a sister who had actually *married* this animal, in that tawdry biker ceremony in Perthshire. He burned at the memory of that wedding, with its procession of muscled-and-tattooed leather-clad freaks. But Kristen wasn't that stupid, she soon extricated herself from the relationship. Russell hadn't been able to do the same.

He'd come to accuse, but now recognised the inherent lunacy in such a course of action. His lot was to explain. And that was what he was trying to do, in a thin, whining reed of a voice that even offended his own ears. — They pulled me into the office, they'd caught on me on these new cameras they've installed everywhere. Told me tae clear my desk, Russell shuddered, thinking briefly of the glacial expression on Marjory Crooks, the personnel manager. He knew the woman, they'd been *colleagues*. Eight years of service down the drain, and for nothing, save a couple of grand in a bank account.

Yet he found himself parroting Ms Crooks, almost verbatim, to the shadowy hulk in the chair. — They said the only reason they'd decided against criminal prosecution was due to my outstanding previous service and the adverse publicity the company would receive.

Po-faced security guards (he knew those men!) had been waiting to escort Russell on the short walk from office to street. As they prepared to embark on this humiliating hike, one of the directors had asked him, — Is there anybody else involved?

— Michael Taylor, he'd immediately said, anxious to cooperate, to try and ingratiate himself. That was his weakness; too hungry to be accepted.

— He's a driver-stroke-storeman. Crooks had turned to the director, who had nodded twice, once in slow understanding, the second time to the sanction the security guards to continue ushering Russell Birch outside, onto the cold street.

He'd given them something, given them Michael, and received nothing in return. And now Michael would want some payback. He recalled the time his now former associate had threatened him. Russell had remained cool, countering by stating that that he could easily have this conversation with his brother-in-law. Michael had gone silent, keen to keep it between them. That had been the time his tree-shagging yuppie brother had walked into Dickens in Dalry Road, of all places, with that young shag he'd then brought to their mother's birthday party. Alexander had made a fool of himself that evening, but he'd gone home with that drunk, slutty, youthful piece of minge. But then Alexander always seemed to land on his feet. The injustice of it all torched Russell inside out.

And now he had this brooding force sitting opposite him. To think he'd got involved as a personal favour, to help him out. He was in pain, he'd said, since the crash; Russell had to help him. Then, as soon as he did, the former brother-in-law was putting the squeeze on him for more. He cut him in, of course, but Russell had been the one taking all the risks. Bags of it, stuffed inside his underpants, him waddling duck-like to the toilets like he'd had a non-industrial accident.

Now it had all come home to roost, as his mother was fond of saying. Now he was unemployed, and unlikely to get references for any job in this specialist field. The four-year BSc (Hons) in Industrial Chemistry at Strathclyde University was now a worthless piece of paper in a frame.

And as he told his former brother-in-law the story, restating the dangers of the security review he'd previously warned him about, with the new monitoring systems, a disembodied voice ripped out of the darkness, silencing him: — So what you're saying is that yuv fucked things up, fucked things *right up* fir every cunt.

— But ah lost my job trying tae help you!

More silence. Russell could make out the man in the chair now. He

228

was wearing sunglasses. His pain must be bad today; the weather had gotten colder. — You know what ye dae now?

— What?

— Ye shut the fuck up.

— But I tried tae help you . . . he pleaded. — Craig . . .

The dark shape rose from the chair. He'd forgotten the gargantuan mass of his former brother-in-law. About six five, as if hewn from marble. He recalled a film he'd recently seen, featuring a bodybuilder turned actor; it was like the Terminator coming out of the mist. — I don't think you get it. He shook his head at Russell, like a disappointed parent.

All Russell Birch could do was play out the craven, infantile role he'd been cast in. His arms extended, his head turned to the side, his shivering mouth pleading, — Craiiig . . .

One sharp blow to the stomach squeezed all the air out of his body. The pain was overwhelming; it couldn't be fought down or thought away or negotiated. He doubled over, keeping a weak hand out in pathetic appeal. The immobilisation of his body didn't surprise him, he'd no experience of violence in any form, but what got him was how feeble he was: his pulse urgent, like the keen heartbeat of a small, trapped animal.

The former brother-in-law looked down at him. — One thing has fuckin well happened. One thing only. You've cost me money, through yir fuckin stupidity.

He'd worked out an unsatisfying contingency plan for this moment. That the plant would eventually uncover their scam had been apparent to him for some time. But while this change in strategy would keep him in the game, it meant a decided demotion. Now he was no longer The Man. All the people he'd been supplying the quality stuff to, through in Glasgow, down in England, with their fucking useless Paki brown shite, stuff the junkies here wouldn't look at or even know what the fuck it was, now *he* worked for *them*. And who was left working for him? Only the worthless wretch at his feet, the clown whose bitch of a sister he'd been poking a while back. He had a debt to pay off, and he needed reminding of this. — Ye still work for me. Ye fuckin drive. Anywhere ah say. London. Liverpool. Manchester. Hull. Ye pick up stuff. Ye bring it back. Goat that?

Russell Birch looked up at his former brother-in-law, into those impenetrable dark glasses. All he could say was, — Okay, Craig –

— If you ever fucking call me that again, I'll tear yir stupid heid oaf. Ma name's Seeker. Say it!

And it was. How could he have been so stupid? It was Seeker. Always

229

Seeker. — Sorry . . . sorry, Seeker, he coughed, feeling like his stomach had been torn open.

— Right, now git the fuck ootay ma sight.

Russell Birch groped for the door handle in the swimming twilight. Fear was working through his pain and he was out of there. Out, out, out.

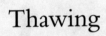

Thawing

Seventh Floor

I don't mind Mark dossing here, he's a decent geezer, but I ain't sure about the fella he's brought with him. Swans around like he owns the place, and that's when he's here, which thankfully ain't that often. Fack knows what he gets up ta.

It all makes things a little tense first thing in the mornings, specially as I ain't been sleeping too soundly of late. The one big problem with this flat is that we're next to the rubbish chute. Bottles and all sorts go crashing past me head inside that wall, hurtling down that farking chute into the big garbage bin, and at all hours.

This morning ain't no exception to the uptight vibe; I get up to find that other cunt, Sick Boy by name and Sick Boy by nature, sitting at the window with a plate of toast. — Good morning, Nicksy, he snaps, then, surveying the manor, with that bleedin look on his boat, — Hackney: not exactly a great part of town, is it? he says, like he was expecting farking Buck House or something.

— You're welcome ta find another, I tell the cunt.

And he just turns ta me, cocky as ya like, — Rest assured, I'm working on it.

Cheeky fucker. And I heard he's ruffled a few feathers down the local n all. I ain't got much time for blokes who think they're better than anyone else, like they're the only ones full of big ideas and dodgy scams. And it ain't like he's had me up stayin at his Jockland shithole, so a little bit of respect is called for.

And it ain't so bad on this estate. There's a lot worse tower blocks round here than Beatrice Webb House. Even up on the seventh floor we get a decent view; right across Queensbridge Road and over to London Fields. And the lifts usually work; well, they did yesterday. The gaff ain't brilliant, but I've dossed in worse. I inherited a gigantic American-style fridge-freezer which takes up half the kitchen, not that there's ever anything in it. I got my own room, and there's mattresses in the spare bedroom for the lads to crash on.

At least this Sick Boy cunt actually gets up. Ain't having a go at Mark, but he does a lot of farking kipping; he's just surfaced now, squinting and rubbing sleep from his eyes, and it's nearly one o'clock. He picks up a video box from on top of the telly and goes, — Ah prefer Chuck Norris tae Van Damme.

Sick Boy looks at the cunt like he's farking tapped. — I'm sure you would, Renton. I'm absolutely certain *you* would, he says, now sitting in the kitchen at the table, writing on a series of cards, in a very neat, deliberate hand. He's got his back turned, so we can't cop a butcher's. Not that we give a toss what the cunt's up ta. Mark flops back on the couch and picks up the Orwell novel he's been reading: *A Clergyman's Daughter.* It was the first proper book I read at school, after the dyslexia got diagnosed and I started ta get help. Didn't matter that it was about five times the size of everybody else's text and I got the farking piss ripped outta me for being a div, I just loved it. Orwell was the bollocks. Way I see it, the cunt ain't ever been equalled.

— Apparently there's still a bit of a drought up the road, skag-wise, Sick Boy says, absent-mindedly. — I called Matty the other day. He was rattling like a panda in a Chinese takeaway.

Matty: now there's a top geezer. Wish it was him Rents brought down. Would've been like the old days back in Shepherd's Bush. Good times, they was. Rents briefly turns to eyeball Sick Boy's hawklike profile, then goes back to the book.

So I've been treading water: putting up with Scotch geezers, but thinking of Marsha upstairs.

I catch the bleedin awful pong coming from the kitchen. The flat smells like a farking bear pit, and that's probably an insult to the ursine race, who seem quite a tidy bunch when all's said and done. Mark puked in there, chasing too much brown, the cunt, and he ain't cleaned it up, and him and Sick Boy are arguing about it. — I'll sort it, he says, but without looking like he's in any big hurry ta do it. Fucking well turned his nose up at the brown first n all, he did, said it couldn't be proper skag; went on about how it was white back home. Can't get enough now though, the cunt.

I've had it here; I leave my filthy Jock guests and exit into a cold, crisp, fresh day, filling my lungs with air and instantly feeling better. Heading towards the market, I scans Marsha's sister, Yvette, a big fat gel, who looks nothing like her, outside the overland station on Kingsland Road. — Alright?

— Yeah, sound.

— How's Marsha?

— She's restin, innit. Ain't been well. Yvette shifts her weight onto one leg and a heavy tit almost seems ready to spill out from her blouse like a slinky.

— Sorry to hear that . . .

Yvette's got that Jamaican-London thing going on. — She naht told you, has she? she says, as she makes the reparations to her top, pullin her coat tight.

— Told me wot?

— Nothing . . . it's nothing. Just women's problems.

— She ain't talkin ta me. I need ta see her. I just wanna know what I done wrong, that's all.

Yvette shakes her head. — Leave it, Nicksy. If she don wanna know ya, she don wanna know ya. Ya won't change her, she says, then gives a little chuckle to herself and repeats, — Nah, mon, ya won't change her.

I shrugs and leaves the fat gel, thinkin that it ain't as if I'm out for changin anybody, I'm a no-questions-asked sort of geezer normally. After all, I'm still a young man, and she's a very young gel. Seventeen. Older in some ways, but younger in others. With a two-year-old son, little Leon. Lovely little kid.

I ain't met the little chap's old man, and maybe he's back on the scene; I dunno if he's got any claims on her. All she would say when I broached the subject was, — Nah, it's all cool, man.

Cause I know the lie of the land; I certainly ain't enough of a farking div to step on some big spade's territory. The white man's long moved out to the Shires; bar a few pockets like Bermondsey (and them Millwall cunts don't count), inner London's pretty much ruled by the spade and the yuppie. It sometimes feels as if the likes of us are just farking guests in our own city. You gotta behave yourself, and besides, wars over skirt: you can forget it.

But I really thought that me and her had something. Then I thought about how a lot of people, black and white, don't like the idea of a white geezer and a black bird getting it on. One day it won't matter a fuck; we'll all be coffee-coloured with a tint of yellow. Till then we got a load of grief ta get through.

Bad Circulation

Thank God that wee Maria lassie is safely back at her Uncle Murray's in Nottingham. I found her a couple ay weeks ago, a total mess, begging up the Bridges, when I was heading back fae work, so I brought her wi me tae Johnny's. But she freaked when we got tae the stair; said she'd been here before, and was too feart tae go in. So I went up and sorted her oot something, then got her uncle's number and phoned him. I took her hame wi me – I was shitein it that she'd rob us in the night when I left her on that couch – and the next day we went up tae St Andrew's Square bus station. I bought her a Nottingham ticket and stuck her on that National Express coach n didnae leave until it pulled away. I called her Uncle Murray the next day, tae make sure she got there, and he telt me he was looking tae line up treatment for her. Murray was really tearing intae Simon, blaming him for Maria being on junk, but I didnae want tae get intae that with him. Sometimes families jist project their shit onto other people. Fair play tae her Uncle Murray but, he sent me up a cheque for the ticket.

The last thing I wanted was tae go oot the night after work. Alexander wis aw funny the day, probably because I've no been seeing him, outside the office, as much as he wants. Sometime I catch him watchin me, lookin out from his wee room aw sad-eyed and hopeful, like a dug wi a leash in its mooth. Ah like him but it's too much right now, and that's pittin it mildly. Toon's cauld and mingin: thaire's been a thaw, n the melting snow and ice has left the city like a giant ashtray ay fag ends, grit and dug shit. I even thought I'd gie it a miss going up tae see Mum the night, but Dad's left a message on the answerphone, telling me to come up tae the hospital right away, saying he'd telt Mhairi and Calum tae get there n aw. I didnae like his tone. I get changed quick, all jumpy with nerves and head oot.

When I get tae the ward my mum looks like she's sinking intae her bed. Wi her bandages she's like her ain mummified remains, like she should be in an Egyptian tomb. I'm about tae speak when it hits me in stark horror: this *isnae* my ma. I realise I'm in the wrong room, and I numbly trot one down, where my mother looks almost exactly the same as the

236

poor cow next door. It's as if she's leaking intae the mattress, like a deflating balloon. My dad's by her side, his thin shoulders shaking, like he's fighting tae control his breathing. He's pale and his pencil moustache has been almost shaved off on one side, like he's made a real mess of trimming it. I nod to him, and bend over Mum. Her eyes, dead and glassy, like my old teddy bear's, stare vacantly up the ceiling. What's left of her is pumped so full of morphine I doubt she even registers me as I bend tae kiss her papery cheek, smelling her fetid breath. She's rotting away from the inside.

The ward sister comes in and puts her hand on Dad's shoulder. — She's going now, Derrick, she says softly.

He locks his hands roond my mother's scraggy claw, and he's pleading, — No . . . no . . . Susan . . . no . . . no little Susie . . . no ma little Susie . . . it wisnae supposed tae be like this . . .

I'm minding how he used tae sometimes sing that song, 'Wake Up Little Susie, tae her, usually when he brought her breakfast in bed oan a Sunday. I'm doon beside her, saying tae her, — I love you, Mum, over and over again, tae this sack ay skin, bone and tumour, wrapped in bandages across the chest the surgeon's made flat; hoping and praying for a God I've never really thought much about tae suddenly enter those wounds.

My dad rests his heid on her stomach, and I run my fingers through his still thick, spiky black hair, but wi some silver strands in it that look like ghosts, walking among the living. — It's okay, Daddy, I say stupidly, — it's okay. I realise I huvnae called him that since I was about ten.

Somewhere in all this, Mum convulses mildly, then stops breathing. I didn't see her last breath, and I'm glad. We wait there in silence for a bit, my dad making groaning noises, like a small, wounded animal, me feeling guilt at the awful swathes of relief that cascade over me. It wasn't Mum any more, she could barely recognise us on the drugs they were giving her. Now she's gone and nothing can hurt her. But no tae see her again, ever, that's just way too much tae get ma heid roond.

I'm twenty-one years old and I've just watched my mother die.

My wee brother, Calum, and wee sister, Mhairi, come in, both of them destroyed. They've got that condemning stare, like they think I've stolen something, as Dad rises, himself looking like a man pulling his body oot ay a grave, and hugs both me and Mhairi. After he goes over to Calum and tries tae dae the same to him, but Cal pushes him away and looks tae the bed. — Is that it then, he asks, — is that Ma away?

— She's at peace now, she didnae suffer . . . she didnae suffer . . . my dad keeps repeating.

My brother is shaking his heid, as if to say, 'She had cancer for four years, a double mastectomy and loads of chemotherapy, of course she fuckin well suffered.'

I'm gripping the cold metal bars at the foot ay the bed. Looking at the oxygen outlet in the wall. The plastic jug on the locker. The two stupid Christmas cards on the shelf by the windae. Focusing on anything but that corpse. I'm thinking about my mum's morphine stash that I took fae the hoose and is in the bedside table back at mine. For a rainy day. Fucked if they're getting that back, the hospitals; they owe us that, at least.

I take Mhairi ootside for a fag. — We shouldnae be daein this, I tell her, — no after Ma.

— It'll happen tae us anyway, Mhairi says, silent tears ruining her eye make-up, faced scrunched in misery. — Tits cut oaf n dyin like that, like a freak! What's the point?

— You dunno that'll happen tae you!

— It gits handed doon!

— Ye dinnae ken that! C'mere you, ya dough heid, n ah wrap my arms aroond her. — We've got tae look eftir these boys in thaire, you n me, right? That's what Mum would want. Ye ken how fuckin useless they are. Seen Dad's tache? Christ almighty! She laughs in a painful explosion, then screws her face up n greets again. Ah kin smell the Coco Chanel on her, that stuff that went missin before ah moved oot, the fuckin wee thief, but it's no exactly the time tae say anything.

Cal and Dad come oot, but I want tae leave them now, tae go n see Alexander or mibbe go tae Johnny's and get sorted oot. Some hash or even a wee bit ay skag; anything tae take the edge off aw this crap. We stand ootside for ages, chattin aboot Ma, then I flag doon a cab and get them intae it, but I'm no getting in masel. Dad winds doon the windae. — Ye no comin back wi us the night? he plaintively asks.

He's in such pain that I nearly change ma mind, but naw, it isnae gaunny happen. — No, I'm gaunny go hame tae bed n come roond early the morn's mornin, tae try n take care ay aw the paperwork n stuff. Register the death n that.

Alexander or Johnny . . . cock or skag . . .

My dad's arms are stretching oot the cab, his hands are locked on mine. — Yir a good girl, Alison . . . he says, and starts tae sob. I've never seen him greet before. Mhairi comforts him and Calum turns away intae the windae tae be somewhere else.

— Goodnight . . . I hear masel weakly say as his hand slides, wet n fishlike, oot ay mine, and the cab moves off. I watch it rolling away, n suddenly want it tae stop.

Instead I turn n walk down towards Tollcross.

Cock or skag . . .

When I get up tae Johnny's I sees Matty, filthy and feral, lurkin outside the building. I come up behind him. — What's up?

He vernear sheds a skin, the wee snake that he is. — Eh . . . Ali . . . eh . . . nowt . . . just gaun up tae see Johnny.

— Moan then, I tell him, pointing tae the wrecked intercom n the open stair door, — nae need tae hing aboot!

— Right, he goes, aw cagey, and we go up the stairs. Then Matty makes us stand in front ay the eye spyhole, as he rings the bell. — Cunt, they'll no let us in, he says, in a low whisper.

— Well, I'm no your Trojan Hoarse, I tell um, really annoyed, as Raymie opens the door. He's wearin a T-shirt wi *I Was Born Under a Wandering Star* oan it, but put on in that crappy home-made lettering, blue rounded plastic script against white.

— Paint your wagon . . . he says, — come on in, then sees Matty. — Naughty, Matthew, naughty, naughty, naughty, he says in the voice ay that wifie that trains the dugs oan telly.

— Gie a white boy a brek, Raymie.

Raymie shrugs and lets us in. I go tae the front room and Johnny's sittin wi this guy I've seen before. It's Alexander's brother's pal, the guy me n Simon caught arguin wi Johnny in the stair. He's straight-lookin, dressed in ordinary clathes this time, n wi a shorter haircut. His face contorts when he sees me, as Johnny rises fae his chair. — The lovely Ms Lozinska! Always a pleasure, dar—

He stops deid as Matty shuffles in behind me.

— What the fuck are *you* daein here? Ye wir fuckin well telt!

Matty just sort ay looks aw sheepish and shrugs, but his presence, or probably mine, has made the guy in the chair jumpy. — What's gaun oan here, Johnny?

Johnny's inclined tae reassure him. — They're sound . . . he says, turning tae smile at me, — although it would have been nice if Ali had brought some of her *female* pals along . . .

— So they can get leered and pawed at by you, I sortay half joke, but I dinnae feel like laughin, I'm mair chokin . . .

OH MY GOD . . .

— Hi! The White Swan's always a gentleman, and he stops, cause he can see the tears that I suddenly feel rolling doon my cheeks. — Hi! Ali! What's up, darlin?

I tell them everything; where I've just been, and Johnny is just really *nice*.

— Fuckin hell, Alison, ah'm so sorry. He shakes his heid. — It's a horrible disease. Ma faither hud it. It was heartbreakin: he battled every inch ay the way. Ah was pleading wi him at the end, just let go, but naw. It was terrible. Just the fuckin worst, he says, hugging me, then ruffling ma hair like I was a bairn. He moves intae the kitchen and sticks the kettle oan, wi Matty n me following him.

— Eh, ah wis just wonderin aboot gettin sorted oot, Johnny, Matty says.

— Her ma's just fuckin died, ya dozy wee cunt, he shouts, pointing at me. — Have a bit ay fuckin respect!

— Right, eh, sorry, Ali, Matty says, and he gies my hand an awkward squeeze. It's amazing tae think that we actually slept thegither a couple ay years back.

The other guy, Alexander's brother's pal, has got up and comes through, whispering something tae Johnny, who nods. Then he sais, — That's me away then, but soas the rest ay us can hear.

— Righto, my bonnie lad, Johnny responds in forced cheer.

As the guy makes tae leave, Matty takes a step taewards him and says, — Sorry, mate, ah didnae catch yir name.

— N ah didnae gie ye it, the guy curtly responds, then he turns tae me. — Ah'm sorry for your loss, hen, but you can tell yir boyfriend that his brother's a grassin little cunt and he's fuckin well gittin it!

— Hi, c'mon, buddy, her ma's just passed away, Johnny snaps, but he's lookin at me aw quizzically.

— Ah dinnae like the company yir keeping, Johnny, ah dinnae like it one bit, the guy goes, n he walks oot really pissed off. Johnny is as well, and follows him. I can hear them exchanging urgent whispers oan the landing. I run ootside n shout at the boy: — I dinnae ken anything aboot his brother or your fuckin deals, aw I'm daein is shagging a guy who's got a degree in botany and a high-up council job! Right?!

The boy looks at me, n goes, — Sorry, hen, mibbe it's nowt tae dae wi you . . . sorry.

Johnny nods, n I go, — Well then, n head back inside.

They've heard the fuss, n Matty tries tae look nonchalant.

Johnny comes storming back into the kitchen. — Sorry aboot that, doll, he sais, then glares at Matty, totally livid, his hands ballin intae fists. — You are really fuckin pushin it the night!

240

Matty goes cowed n his eyes water, his voice droppin tae a high-pitched pathetic whisper. It's that wee-laddie defence he uses, I've seen it before, n it gits borin awfay quick. — Cunt, how?

— Aw this 'ah didnae catch yir name' shite. Ah ken what you're aw aboot, Matty; just keep yir fuckin neb oot ay ma business. Right?!

— Right, Matty shrugs, now a surly adolescent like our Calum, makin oot he doesnae ken what Johnny's talking aboot.

And Johnny's on aboot the time Simon brought that wee Maria roond here. I really hope he didnae mess that lassie aboot like Johnny's hintin, n like Murray sais, but no Simon, I ken he'd really be tryin tae help her. I kinday wish he was here. I wonder if he's thinking aboot me right now?

Northern Soul Classics

Lucinda's lustrous hair lifts in the breeze as we surface from Piccadilly Circus tube station into the chaos of the West End. Yes! This is the *real* London: Soho, that square mile of fun and debauchery. It's a parky early evening but they're all out and about on that grid ay narrow streets; advertising execs, record-company types, shop girls, ponces, hustlers and hoors, chancers and tourists. There's a cheery Christmas vibe in the air, as drunken office parties lurch along in transit between restaurants and bars. The *ride-alert* button going off so much it's practically on constant pulse. I watch in jealous awe as some short-arsed media-type scumbag nonentity struts intae a private club, no doubt tae be indulged and cock-sucked by a fawning hostess.

I want what you have and I will *get it.*

Aye, this is London proper, no some fucking baboon-stuffed south Leith version full ay scum and lowlife going nowhere but fae their ghetto scheme tae bookie, pub, prison or hozzie ward. And my ticket to this urban paradise island could well be Lucinda. We're walking arm in arm, sleazed up fae a day's solid cunt-fucking at her place back in Notting Hill. Spunk and fanny juice everywhere, mind games and physical gymnastics, my cock going off like an AK-47 in the hands ay an epileptic. The carnage started when ah began my routine ay murmuring Italian phrases in her ear. The lassies back up the road love that, but she started begging me tae speak in my *Scottish* voice. Well, ah'd always suspected posh birds were as dirty as fuck, and that certainly confirmed it tae me.

Lucinda has the arrogance that wealth brings; ironic, then, that she was just one of the recipients ay the cards I randomly issued. Oh, that wonderful device! Ah wrote out another batch ay fifty last weekend:

> *Beautiful woman, I didn't believe in love at first sight until today. Please call me. Simon X* 01 254 5831

Fifty handcrafted scraps of intrigue; through previous experience, they should net me around five or six sure-fire calls. Who can resist the prospect ay love and romance? All that's needed are the cards and a certain equanimity, the designated word on this 'E' day.

They would never work in parochial Edinburgh or, indeed, any other population centre in the UK bar this yin. They are made for an alienated, spacious, disconnected, no-comeback metropolis. A fortnight ago, ah handed my first batch oot around Knightsbridge (striking gold with Cinders), where the best consumers are. Last week ah steamed selected targets in Kensington, St John's Wood, Notting Hill, Primrose Hill, Canonbury and, striking out for the big time, Mayfair. The problem here is that ye get a lot ay good-looking chickies on *salary*, when I crave *trust fund*. Another curse is Nicksy's phone number and its embarrassing 254 code, but only the clued-up relate those digits to the poisonous E8 postal district.

The one-in-ten rule generally works and it's self-selecting. When ah told Rents about it, he started waffling on about statistics: correlation and regression, the bell curve. All ah was interested in was the *bell-end curve* in my troosers. This system is a magnet for either lovestruck idiots with truly unreal expectations ay life, or the most curious and daring. And that generally means a shag is about the worst you're gaunny dae fae the arrangement.

Lucinda has been my best hit so far; not exactly a blue-blood Ingloid, but with St Martin's College of Art and Roedean Girls' School on her CV, plus a smart Notting Hill pad, she'll do nicely till the opportunity to upgrade presents itself.

Across the street, a swarthy-looking chap emerges fae a sleaze shop door wi this washed-out, bottle-blonde bird. This fucker evidently kens how tae deal wi damage. *Watch and learn, Simon.* Yes, I fucked up wi that wee gold mine back hame; got greedy, weak wi the skag, emotionally involved and overstepped the mark, even if Dickson did put in a good offer. No very nice, but ah went tae see Father Greg and it's just another sin ah've cheerfully repented. With the gift of faith, we move on.

I want tae follow this Arab-looking cunt and his tattered squeeze, and ah'm almost replicating his movements, my arm roond posh Lucinda's waist, guiding her intae the Blue Posts. — We've had the sex, perhaps some alcohol now, I whisper like a stereotype bad boy, with clandestine grin, and her fruity smile tells me she's onside. Ah'm one step behind my man, and as he orders up and manoeuvres this powerless sow intae a seat, so too do I deposit Lucinda in the one next tae them, under a nest of tinsel and glitter balls.

Ah like the wey this boy moves; steely eye contact maintained, he has this chicky in his tractor beam and he's no gaunny let go. Nae need for the iron fist, it's aw velvet glove. S-T-Y-L-E, it sticks out a M-I-L-E. Ah'm sold that this boy is the real deal when ah hear him saying, — Of course I care for you, baby, but you is trying to use reverse psychology on me and it just ain't on.

— I ain't, Andreas . . . I ain't . . . she pleads, shaking her head. She's a looker in a trashy, deranged way. Ah cannae make out whether it's jakey shakes or junky twitches but the brain is incorrectly wired tae the skin and the motor functions are a tad askew. — I just wanna know you care . . . she pleads.

— Ah brush back Lucinda's hair and whisper in her ear. — I'll wonder if one day that you'll say that you care . . .

— I care, this Andreas the Arab sincerely says tae his dopey consort. You can tell that the first wideo that's banged her on her 'estate', as the Ingloids ludicrously call their schemes, has left cock prints and fist prints all over her, like target signs for subsequent hustlers. You grow to realise, just through talking tae them for a few minutes: maist predators are pretty fucking thick. So for the system tae work, the prey hus tae be *really* fucking dim, desperate and needy beyond belief.

— Just please say you'll love me madly, I'll gladly be there, and I plant a little kiss on her cheek, as she grins at me. Ah have to listen attentively tae her slavering oan about her job and the dull office politics that so enthrals those involved, but bores the fucking shit oot ay every cunt else. Over her shoulder, as his train-wreck bird goes to the toilet, ah tip the swarthy Andreas a wee wink. He looks glacially at me for two dreadful Begbiesque seconds, when I think ah've called it wrong, as he takes in and processes a mental picture. Then a warm smile, like the sun coming up, splits his face. Tae Lucinda's slight annoyance, we strike up a friendly conversation across her bows. The boy isnae an Arab, he comes fae Athens.

Lucinda chips in tae say that she visited his home town once, muttering something aboot the Acropolis. Andreas smiles tightly, flinty white-hot eyes full ay mischief, as they run a subtle check over her curves.

— The Edinburgh of the South, ah grin, as Train Wreck comes back doon and smiles at Lucinda, then looks a little harshly at my good self. — Hi, I'm Simon, ah nod at her.

— And should I care – this narky mare whinnies, but Andreas is already waving her intae silence.

— Like a puppet on a string . . . pup, pup, pup, I murmur to Lucinda, as Grecian 2000 Andreas talks over Train Wreck, with a fleeting, disdainful apologetic look, as she sits like a wayward schoolgirl who's been ticked off by the teacher she's got a devastating crush on. — You think? He asks, — Edinburgh and Athens? There is a connection?

— Defo. Twinned cities, ah'm led tae believe.

Andreas seems tae gie this some thought and scratches at a five o'clock shadow. — I must go there sometime; but only to visit. I love London. Where can you go after London?

I turn to Lucinda and give her a smile; happy but grateful, with added sincerity. — I must say, I raise an eyebrow, — it hasn't been bad to me so far. You know what they say: love is just like a merry-go-round, with all the fun of a fair . . .

— This is what they say in Scotland? Andreas sinks back and purrs and we're already cookin at the same nice soft beat, like a jazz rhythm section, like Keezbo and Rents try tae, but never can. — If you have already met such a beautiful lady so soon, then I would say that you are navigating our town very well!

— *C'è di che essere contenti*, I playfully concede.

— Ah . . . that is Italian? Andreas asks.

— Ooh . . . Italian . . . Train Wreck Chickloid tries to battle back into the conversation, but she's so much the lowest rank here that I'm comfortable ignoring her.

— Yes. My mother's side, I tell Andreas.

Our Med playboy patter sets off a blush in Lucinda, and a flirtatious but polite round of chatter. Ah watch the posh bird in profile, elevated by our attentions, just glowing, singularly unaware that she's merely another random stat in a game ah've devised. I feel urbane, sophisticated, and most of all *miles away from fucking Edinburgh*, where there's always some heidbanger fae Leith who staggers intae a sophisticated city-centre wine bar for a late drink tae catch me canoodling wi some out-of-town lovely and blows my cover, usually with the blood-curdling cry ay 'SICK BOY, YA CUNT, WHAT UR YOU FUCKIN WELL DAEIN HERE?!'

So we spend most ay the evening getting pleasantly mellow wi Andreas and Hailey (Train Wreck's real or stripper name), then head back on the Victoria Line tae his family's hotel at Finsbury Park. It's right on the edge of the actual parkland which gives the district its name, and caters for frayed-suited salesmen, Andreas discreetly telling me he sets them up with the services that gentlemen away fae hame so often crave. Hailey, meantime, embarks on a whingeing, nasal monologue of breadline disasters, encompassing the usual litany ay social security cheques stopped, housing evictions suffered and children placed intae care. Fortunately, the recipient ay most ay this guff is Lucinda, whom Hailey painfully announces is her new best friend.

We adjourn to one of the rooms, and I'm impressed when Andreas produces some of that London brown. Lucinda looks at me, tense but excited. — I haven't . . . are you going to . . .

— We've done the sex and the alcohol, I whisper in her ear, as Andreas cooks up and Hailey gapes at him in desperate concentration, willing every drop of that brown shit tae dissolve in the spoon, — so opiates are the next thing.

— Wow . . . you think so?

— We're being very, very naughty, I tell her as I roll up my sleeve, — but sometimes it's nice to be naughty, provided, of course, that we maintain perspective and a sense of equanimity, and we're grinning together and ah know that even though she's a skag virgin, ah'd huv tae cut off her limbs with a chainsaw tae stop her now. Sometimes, as Renton says, *it's just your time.*

Ah know it's a weakness, as ah've been clean since we hit London, apart fae the odd chase and some speed, but we bang up. Christ, I swear ah can *feel* the needle bend and curl hook-shaped inside Lucinda's airm, getting ready tae tug her into an extended nightmare that'll cost Daddy money and precious time to buy her out of. Like a true debutante, she collapses on the bed as soon as it hits her. She isnae exactly Zorba but some gutty slaver trickles oot fae the corner ay her mooth. As she makes nae attempt tae move, I fucking shite it for a few seconds, urgently ascertaining, — You okay, babe?

— Mmmm . . . she's blissfully murmuring, grabbing my hand and stroking the back ay ma wrist. Just as well it's this poncy brown shite: some of that white gear ay Swanney's would have sent her sailing north of Iceland or south ay the Falklands.

Andreas smiles and prepares tae vacate the room, pulling a bombed Hailey tae her feet. — Rest, my friends, he smiles, — or if you prefer, play.

— Nice tae meetcha . . . Hailey says wretchedly as they vanish, and I help Lucinda oot ay her clothes and get her into bed. I'm enjoying the warmth of her soft body against me and the comforting duvet, and we're talking shite, drifting in and out ay semi-sleep as she sticks her hand inside my pants and secures it round my prick. Even skagged, her body moves with that horny, hearty masculinity ah've noticed in rich chicks. My knob stiffens and we fuck slowly, and when she comes it's like a large extended yawn, though possibly that's all it was.

In the morning, breakfast is on Andreas, coffee and stale-ish croissants. We're aw feeling a bit rough and rattling slightly, but joking about the previous day, all except that trollop Hailey, who silently chain-smokes. Her trembling hand jackhammers china cup to saucer tae the extent ye almost feel she's doing it deliberately. A flaying glance fae Andreas and she steels herself tae sort it oot.

Enter a sweaty, obese cunt in a badly fitting suit, nodding as he picks up a croissant and helps himself tae orange juice and coffee. Andreas rises tae greet him and they share a whispered joke. That Greek cunt is just like a fucking Bond villain, or at least one ay the dodgy sidekicks who liaise wi him in foreign parts, which pretty much makes me *The Man*.

— Oh gosh, Lucinda suddenly says, checking her watch, — I must fly.

And so she departs to head back to Notting Hill and get changed for work. Those lazy posh Ingloids: it strikes me that anybody turning up at that time in a *real* job back in Scotland would soon be staring at their P45. Andreas and myself plan tae hook up later on — there's a club he wants tae take us tae. After extending my gratitude for the hospitality, I get outside and stroll doon tae Finsbury Park tube station. One stop south takes me tae Highbury & Islington, but instead of alighting to board the shitey overland train east to Dalston Junction, I decide to make use of my all-zones Capital Card and cruise the tube network for a bit.

From Green Park, my westbound train on the Piccadilly Line, in what's usually prime minge-stalking territory, offers a distinct lack of rides. I get off at Knightsbridge and run into the next carriage. Instant ride alert, a serene beauty engrossed in the sort of novel Renton might read. I sit down beside her. — I was in the next carriage. I saw you through the glass. I just had time to scribble this note.

I hand it to her as ah grip the rail and yank myself upright. She takes it with a wary, confused expression on her face. Ah catch her looking aroond tae see whae else has witnessed this exchange. Then I'm on the platform, the doors are shut, and now that she has the power, I strike *the look*; sincere and imploring, but with a self-deprecating shrug and honest twist of the brows that hopefully says 'I tried'. And as the train pulls away, I'm sure ah can see warmth radiate from her face, though it could be my imagination.

That'll do for me. Time to go 'home'. What a fuckin joke this shithole is, east of Islington; the London Borough of South Leith. No even a poxy fuckin tube!

I get back tae the Holy Street gulag ay Beatrice Webb House, and step intae the minging lift, which, thank fuck, is working. The only other occupant is this dark-skinned young maiden, who looks cowpable, and I'm getting the eye big time. Perhaps a baboon, but an exceptionally young one, which usually means the offspring is dumped on grandma. Sets up the horn at the *base* ay the baws, always a good sign. Ah've only ever been wi one black bird before, a student fae NYU as she put it, me no knowing or caring what the fuck that was, but spending an agreeable week baw-deep in her at last year's festival.

This yin fixes me in a loin-grinding gaze ay steel. — You live with Brian, doncha?

— A temporary measure, I assure her. Ah realise now that this wee chicky wis the yin that scorned Nicksy at that Northern Soul night at Twat's Palace when we first arrived in fair Londinium. The evening ah ended up banging that Shauna bird, daein loads of amyl nitrate wi her soas ah could get it up her erse. — So, any festive frolics planned?

— We got a big New Year's party comin up, innit.

— Any space for a lonely neighbour?

— Yeah . . . come on up any time ya fancy, for a chat, like. Numbah 14-5. I'm Marsha.

— Lovin your style, babes, ah say, taking her hand and kissing the back of it, eliciting a toothy giggle as ah step oot oantae floor seven. Another solid prospect, though a bit close tae home, wi aw the advantages and drawbacks that entails.

Sometimes I feel I should have a leg amputated or something. Just tae gie them some sort of a sporting chance . . .

Dirty Dicks

Ma fist pulverises that beepin bastard ay a clock intae silence. Sick
Boy's lyin next tae us oan the mattress, beanie hat on, in a deep
slumber; never even heard the alarm. If ah'd been rimmin the fucker aw
night thaire couldnae be a worse taste in ma mooth. Ah gits up n the
flat's like a fuckin fridge, n ah pull on a jumper and some tracky bottoms
and socks. Ah looks oot east ower London Fields; the weak sun is comin
up and ye can just aboot make oot the lido. Wish it wis summer, this is
beyond shan. It's Christmas the day eftir the morn, though ah'm steyin
doon here, savin masel for New Year. Ah go ben the kitchen tae turn oan
the heating and water.

Thinkin aboot the interview this affie, ah'm surprised tae see Nicksy
sittin up at the table in the retreating dark, chasin some broon. He's goat
a foil ay speed split open n aw n he's boiled the kettle and made coffee.
— Have we no got that interview this affie?

— Yeah . . . plenty time, couldn't kip, he explains and he offers the
pipe, and dabs at the Lou Reed.

Ah look at the cocoa-brown powder dustin the burnt foil and it seems
cuntish tae refuse. Ah take the lighter tae the base ay the aluminium, batterin it wi flame. Ah pit the jaggy pipe tae ma cracked lips n suck, feeling
ma lungs glaze wi smoke and metallic particles as ma heid lightens and
the tension leaves my body.

> *Either up your nose or through your vein,*
> *With nothin to gain except killing your brain*

Sweet home Leith Alhambra . . . Ah slump back against the wall. Ah feel
like gaun straight back tae the feather n flip. Instead ah take a dab at the
salty speed. Then another. Eftir aboot ten minutes it's gied me a lift, but
ah feel like a skagged doll, being shaken by a manic puppeteer. Ma nails
pick at the Formica on the edge ay the table. — So this boy's . . . got us
sorted oot . . . oan the ferries, then?

— Tony's got us the interview, Nicksy says. — We gotta keep it together

249

ta get yer actual job. We get in, we can start bringing gear back through. They got a different customs arrangements for staff, and he got lads there that's all on the firm.

— Sounds pretty sweet, ah concede.

— But we gotta keep it together or the whole thing'll go tits up.

— Easier said than done, ah nod tae the foil, n take another poisonous dab. — Yuk . . . coffee time.

— Yeah, it takes a lotta gumption ta keep it together now. Nicksy's speeding, stabbing the air. — We're all under the farking cosh. The thing is ta keep moving. Keep off their farking lists or you're screwed. Everything is temporary. Don't expect a job for life. A house for life. A bird for life.

— Sayin that tae Sick Boy the other day. Rippin off the state is a noble act in these circumstances. It's fuckin obvious if ye have even half a brain cell. Ah focus on Nicksy. — Ah mean, we're only gaun for this job this affie cause ay the chorrie prospects, right?

A loud, throaty laugh bubbles fae him. — I enjoy ripping orf the farking state as much as the next geezer, but you Jocks are something else; you see it as a sort of birthright.

Cheeky cunt, him; ah've gotten intae mair giro and housing benefit fiddles doon here than ah ever did up the road. It's easier wi the different boroughs so close tae each other. But ah'm no complainin, ah'm grateful tae git hooked up wi Tony's syndicate.

The phone goes and ah answer it, even though ah ken it'll be some lassie for Sick Boy. The notepad is full ay girls' names, aw looking for 'Simon'. — Hello?

— Awright? That you, Rent Boy?

Fuck.

Begbie.

— Aye . . . Franco! Muh man, ah manage. He starts gabbin excitedly, tellin us that he's moved in wi June.

— . . . so ah goes tae her, under the mistletoe at her ma's, ye fuckin game? N she goes, 'Ah certainly am,' ken aw that daft soft wey wi a big fuckin smile oan hur coupon? Daft cunt only thought ah wanted a fuckin *kiss* under the fuckin mistletoe. Aye, that'll be fuckin right.

Kiss me underneath the mistletoe, do, do, do . . . Franco n me at primary, singing that song wi aw the other wee laddies n lassies. The wee lassies lookin coy, the wee laddies gittin beamers. Wonder if he minds ay that? What's your name, what's your nation . . .

— So it shuts its fuckin eyes n puckers its lips aw that fuckin daft wey, n ah gits a hud ay its heid n ah'm sayin, 'It's a fuckin gam ah'm eftir, ya daft fucker,' n ah'm loosenin ma belt, gaun, 'C'moan, nae cunt's in yit! Git thum roond it!' . . . You still thaire?

— Aye . . .

We also sang that song aboot the Titanic *sinking: 'It was sad when the great ship went down . . . husbands and wives, little children lost their lives, it was sa-had when the gray-hate ship went down.'*

A Scottish education . . . wonder if he minds ay that?

— Cause tae me that's part ay the fuckin excitement n aw that, ken? Well, she's no too fuckin chuffed, bit she kens the Hampden Roar, so ah've pushed it doon oan its knees, n this is in the front room ay her ma's hoose, under the fuckin mistletoe. So wir gaun fir it, nice n steady, n ah've goat it by the hair now, twisted roond ma hand so as tae control the fuckin pace, n ah'm fuckin batterin it in thaire, gittin right fuckin intae it, ken that wey whin yir eyes ur aw screwed up n yir mooth's fuckin puckered?

— Eh . . . right . . .

— Well, ah sortay sees this cunt through these half-shut eyes, n tipples it's her fuckin auld man! The cunt's only fuckin well went n walked in. She's goat her back tae um, she cannae see um comin, eh. Turns oot he'd just been in the gairdin, in that fuckin shed probably huvin a fuckin wank, the mingin auld cunt, n he goes, 'What the hell's gaun oan here?'

— Aye?

— Fuckin right, ya cunt. So ah jist turns roond n sais tae the fucker, 'What does it fuckin well look like, ye durty cunt? Git the fuck ootay here,' n the cunt jist fucks right off, fuckin mumblin away a load ay shite as he goes. Could feel hur panickin, she's gaggin n tryin tae pill away, but ah keeps a tight fuckin grip, she's gaun naewhaire till ah shoots ma duff, n she fuckin well kens it n aw. N ah does that thing in the porno, ken whin ye pill oot n shoot aw ower the burd's coupon? Well, she's shitein it, eyes aw big, till she gits a fuckin wad shot right in hur pus! Ya cunt, ye'd huv thoat thaire wis two fuckin barrels in this pipe intead ay jist yin. Face like a painter's radio, ya cunt!

— What did she say aboot her faither?

— Ah'm gittin tae that, ya fuckin impatient fuckin rid-heided cunt, Franco snaps, making me super-glad ay that sweet four hundred miles.
— So she's wipin the spunk offay her face, gaun aw fuckin panicky, 'Whae wis that, wis that ma dad?'

'Fuckin durty pervert sneakin up oan cunts like that,' ah goes.

So she goes aw that fuckin ice-cauld, frigid, huffy wey, but fuck her, ye need a wee bit ay fuckin romance at Christmas. So she goes ootside n ah hears thum shoutin at each other n she comes back in, sayin she's been kicked oot the fuckin hoose. So ah says, 'Right, wir gaun roond tae muh ma's.' 'Thanks, Frank . . .' she goes n starts packin, aw fuckin grateful now, ken? Well, ah wisnae gaunny leave hur thaire wi that fuckin pervy auld cunt, wis ah?

— Right . . .

— So she's goat some stuff thegither, n this big fuckin poker-ersed donkey-faced faither cunt comes back through n starts oan at her again. 'You're a disgrace,' he goes, fuckin standin thaire shakin his daft heid like a fuckin mongol. 'You're the fuckin disgrace, mate,' ah telt the cunt, 'sneakin up oan cunts like a filthy auld pervert!' 'What . . . ?' he goes, looks at us, then turns tae hur, n sais, 'You two deserve each other. You're out of control, June Chisholm, what a little slut you've become –' 'But, Dad –' she's fuckin whingin. 'Just go,' the cunt sais, 'the baith ay yis, just get oot ay ma hoose!' So ah just says tae hur, 'C'moan,' n gits her ootside. Then ah goes back in n squares up tae this cunt. 'If she's a fuckin slut then that's aw doon tae you: you fuckin well brought the cunt up,' ah tells um. 'N dinnae shout the fuckin odds at me, cunty baws, or yi'll git yir fuckin mooth burst, right? Ye might be *her* fuckin faither, bit yir no *ma* fuckin faither!' So the cunt fuckin well shites it! Dirty, wide auld cunt. 'Aye, ye'd better fuckin well no say nowt either,' ah goes. Cheeky cunt him but, eh?

— Too right, should've burst the cheeky fucker's mooth, ah supportively suggest, just tae encourage the radge tae resort tae mayhem now thit ah'm miles away n dinnae huv tae deal wi the consequences!

London, I love you!

— That's exactly whit ah fuckin well telt Tommy, he says in tight, proud affirmation. — But ah jist fuckin leaves it, eh, cause ah'm no wantin tae git involved in thair daft fuckin faimlay business, but that cunt better watch hissel. So anywey, it's moanin n greetin, so ah gits it hame, then it suddenly fuckin well cheers up n starts gaun oan aboot us gittin a place thegither. Ah thoat, she's no fuckin kippin wi me, no in a single bed, she kin stey oan the fuckin couch. Ah goat it tae come through fir a fuckin ride then sent it right back oantae the settee eftir ah'd cowped it. Fuck that, ya cunt, ah need ma fuckin beauty sleep! Hud the horn later oan, so ah wakes hur up n brings it back through fir another fuckin session. But in the mornin it's aw fuckin faces; her, muh ma n oor Elspeth, lookin at ye like fuckin sugary porridge.

— Ye git grief, aye?

— Aye, the usual shite, bit ah'm thinkin, time ah hud a place ay ma

252

ain anywey, n she's no a bad ride, n thaire's nae sense in cuttin oaf yir cock tae spite yir baws, that's whit ah eywis sais. You fuckin listenin?

— Aye. Nae sense cuttin off yir cock, no jist tae spite yir baws, ah repeat back doon the line. He *does* eywis say that.

— Too fuckin right. So ah phones Monny, n wir movin intae that fuckin place in Buchanan Street next week. Hope the cunt kin fuckin well cook as good as it rides! Telt her tae watch muh ma; for the cookin likes, no the fuckin ridin! Aye, so that's me sorted oot wi ma ain pad, n a fuckin ride every night. Now ah've jist goat tae git it tae shut its fuckin mooth n ivraything's fuckin barry, ya cunt.

— Sound . . .

— Right, ah've goat tae nash. Cannae sit here bletherin wi you aw day, ya daft cunt! Runnin up ma fuckin phone bill, ya muppet!

— Sorry tae keep ye, Frank.

— So ye fuckin well should be. Ah'm a man ay business now, ya cunt. So when ye back up?

— New Year . . .

— Barry. That'll be a classic. See ye, buddy.

— See ye, Franco, mate.

Eftir that psychic shafting ah need another dunt ay yon gear. Sick Boy comes in, rubbing sleep fae his eyes. — You drug perverts getting loaded *now*? What aboot the interview for the boats?

The state ay that cunt. *Methinks the laddie doth protest too much.* Nicksy and me look at each other wi wasted grins. — Medicinal . . . ah hud tae talk tae Begbie on the phone, eh? Ah push the pipe at Sick Boy.

He waves it away. — Just because he's a socially retarded psychopath doesn't mean that youse arenae fuckin irresponsible cunts, he goes, taking a dab at the speed. Then his eyes soften. — Forgoat tae tell ye, Alison's ma died the other week. Think the funeral wis yesterday.

— Fuck . . . that's fucked, man. Wish ye'd have sais, Simon. Ah'd've went up fir it!

Begbie nivir even sais nowt. Cunt.

— Aye, right. He looks doubtfully at us, wi the pipe in ma hand. Mibbe it wis a bit optimistic. — If anybody should have been there, it should have been me. Her and I are close, he says gravely.

— She went tae ma wee brar's funeral n aw, ah sais. Aw this shite: the wey life can jist go fae a constellation ay possibilities tae a scabby dirt track lined wi potholes.

— Yes. She went tae support you n Billy. She'll understand though, London n that, n we'll see her the week eftir next at New Year, he says.

He looks tae Nicksy, who's staring meaningfully at the waw, lost in skag contemplation, — We should get Nicksy up there, it'll dae him good, he observes, turning pointedly back tae me. — Listen, Marco, I need a teensy-weensy favour. I've some fences tae mend wi Lucinda . . . said I'd meet her at noon in Dirty Dick's pub opposite Liverpool Street Station.

He spills the details, n ah'm no too happy, but he's a mate, so ah huv tae back him up.

It takes an age tae git washed, dressed and doon tae Hackney Downs Station, but we git a train right intae Liverpool Street and cross ower tae the boozer. Dirty Dick's is packed wi lunchtime City workers, and even in what's supposed tae be interview wear, we still look chronically miscast, no that we gie a fuck. Me n Sick Boy have made an effort wi our Leith Provi Co-op funeral suits, but Nicksy's sporting purple hair teased intae a Mohawk, a pink-and-white-hooped fluffy jersey, thankfully covering up *The Queen Gives A Good Blow Job* T-shirt, n while his black Sta-Press are acceptable enough, the red nine-inch lace-up Doc Martens sortay catch the eye. Funny how he's shed the soul boy look n got back into being an unreconstructed punk. As he finds a stool up at the bar, Sick Boy spies the Lucinda lassie in a seat at a corner table, and pulls me ower. He briefly introduces us, then they spark up an animated conversation, during which his chest swells out, like a mating pigeon's, as she crumbles. — You're obviously upset, he disdainfully concedes as he drums on the big wooden table. — It's no good us talking when you're in this state. I mean, it's like you're hearing me but you're *not* hearing me, if you catch my drift.

This perr lassie wi her fair Anglo-Saxon skin sits on her hands, her jaw locked tight. Seething tae the point ay implosion in that frightfully decent, repressed English middle-class way. Ah feel uncomfortable being stuck here and want tae go.

— It's wasting your time and it's wasting my time, Sick Boy, features stiff, expands in his gruff and formal manner, before offhandedly turning tae me. — Get them in, Rents.

Ah'm happy tae leave them n join Nicksy at the bar. Ah ain't in a big hurry ordering up the drinks either. But Nicksy looks fuckin shite; like the weight ay five ay the stinkiest London Boroughs is sittin oan his thin shooders. Wi the garish dye through his cartoon punk Mohawk, he looks just like that wankstain on the postcairds they sell at Piccadilly Circus. It reminds us ay that Les Dawson quote aboot punks: 'All blue hair and safety pins: just like the mother-in-law.' But Nicksy's telt us the tourists still flock tae git snapped wi him doon the West End, n it's good for a beer or a quid, even an occasional ride.

Despite aw his scamming he's totally brassic aw the time. London's an expensive habit, and pretty much a pointless yin unless ye huv dosh; if ye live in somewhere like Dalston or Stokie or Tottenham or the East End, it's mair like steyin in Middlesbrough or Nottingham. The economics ay the postcode prison make the West End good life just as inaccessible. Not one cunt in our local boozer, bar us, ever drinks in the West End.

Ah get him a pint ay lager, which he sips the top ay and turns tae the telly above the bar, no meeting ma eye. This Marsha lassie's really fucked him up. Ah've never seen a boy so down eftir a bird's elbayed him. She must be some ride. He looks ower tae Sick Boy n this Lucinda lassie. — He's some cunt, ain't he? With the gels. Now he's got a Sloaney bird in tow!

One thing London does offer, even in its marginal areas, is hope for the aspirational predator. — Don't ah jist fuckin know it, ah acknowledge. Then ah survey Nicksy's attire again; a wee bit full-on for our purposes. — Ye might have toned doon the look. It's meant tae be a fuckin interview!

— It's what I am, innit? he shrugs, as Sick Boy gestures us ower. Ah deliver his pint and Lucinda's gin. He glances tae me, ready tae make his move, but he's still addressing her. — If I may say so, Lucinda, I'm pretty disappointed. I told you the God's honest truth, and you obviously don't believe a word I've said. Fine. If that's the level of trust we're operating on, then I just don't see the point in all of this.

Lucinda sits bolt upright in her seat and glares at him. Her eyes are red. — But you're forgetting that I *saw* you with her. Don't you fucking well understand that? I *saw you* both in the bed with my *own eyes*!

Letting oot a sharp exhalation ay breath, Sick Boy goes, — I've explained this until I'm blue in the face. The lassie was Mark's girlfriend, Penelope. He looks at me.

Lucinda does the same, and ye can see her thinking: this skinny, ginger-heided Scottish schemie jist isnae the sort that shags birds called Penelope. A weight seems tae faw through us, n ah briefly toy wi the idea that it might be conscience before it quickly dissolves as the buzz ay deceit hits me. — I was paralytic drunk, Sick Boy's eyes widen, — and I got into this bed. I didn't have a fucking clue she was in there until you came in and started shouting the fucking odds.

— But come *on*! You must have known!

Sick Boy shakes his heid slowly. — Mark's accepted this as the truth, cause he knows me. And he trusts me. He knows that I'd never do anything like that with his girlfriend. He's my best buddy, right since first year at school, he gasps, tears welling in his eyes. — Mark! Tell her!

255

Lucinda's stiff gaze is trained on me. She's a nice girl. She doesnae deserve one lying Leither in her life, never mind two. Her big orbs are wide and pleading and ah think she really does want tae be convinced. So ah gie them what they baith need. — I was annoyed, Lucinda. In fact I was fucking livid. I mean tae say, you know how it looked. Her face makes the slightest flicker ay acknowledgement, as ah turn tae Sick Boy. — If that cunt had've been shagging ma Penny, well, ah'd've fuckin well glassed the bastard!

— Fuck off, Mark, hear him! He turns tae Lucinda, then tae me. — It's like *you* dinnae believe me either!

— Ah'm no saying that, Simon, ah'm just saying how it looks!

Lucinda nods in affirmation, then turns tae him. — Well, how else *would* it look, Simon? Try seeing it from other people's point of view, and she looks again to me, her big eyes hungry for alliance.

— Exactly my fucking point, ah chip in.

Sick Boy lets out some air. In the painful silence that follows ah kin hear, Williamson: one–nil, in my heid. Ah feel that if ah look at him, ah'll burst oot laughin. But ah do, n somehow keep it together as he nods sadly. — I see how it is, he says accusingly, his face full ay hurt.

Ah had nae option but tae suck it doon n go through wi the spiel. — I'm sorry, mate, I do believe ye. It's jist that Penny n me, well, we've no been gettin on so well lately, and ah suppose ah wis just as para as fuck.

Slapping his heid, Sick Boy briefly turns away in disgust, before facing me again. — Yes, you certainly were, he scolds, face fraught with bitterness. He's sprinted to the moral high ground and it would take an atrocity for him tae relinquish this position. — A little word of advice, Mark: don't take amphetamines and stay up all night if you cannae handle the consequences, the cheeky bastard reprimands. Then he looks at a softening Lucinda with a deeply nuanced expression. — And I think I might just be due an apology for those histrionics. He folds his airms and turns away fae her.

— Okay, okay . . . Simon . . . I'm . . . I'm sorry . . . but surely you can see how it looked . . . Lucinda tries tae put her airm roond him.

A huffy brush-off, before he regally sits up, as if addressing the pub's occupants, and some red-faced suits do briefly look round as he sings, — One little word which might not mean anything down here in the metropolis, but still has some currency back up the road: trust. Lucinda goes to speak but he raises his hand tae silence her as he spells it oot: — T-R-U-S-T.

After playing hard tae get for a bit, he allows her to embrace him, and then they're necking deeply and wetly. Ma cue tae retire tae the bar, wondering what this Penelope was like. Anybody else, ah'd have said she must've been a looker tae risk alienating a bird like Lucinda, but this is Sick Boy. He really is a total cunt as far as girls go.

But now it's time for business. We're biddin tae enter the dual worlds ay modern employment: a legit job on the ferries and drug scamming through a contact ay Nicksy's. Ah look at ma watch, signal tae the others, and we drink up and cross the road tae Liverpool Street Station. Sick Boy has one last snog wi Lucinda on the platform, before he follows Nicksy and me oantae the Harwich train.

— Unbelievable, he sais, shaking his heid in a strange mixture ay disgust n sadness as a million possibilities seem tae spin through his brain. — Thirsty work, though. He drums the table. — Is there a buffet car oan this fuckin train? Tell ye what, this cunt had better be oan the level, Nicksy, cause ah kin get hooked up wi Andreas in Finsbury Park any fucking time.

This constant Andreas stuff is really gettin oan my fuckin tits, but if I say anything, he'll put it down tae jealousy. He really is such a total fuckin prick.

But Nicksy remains silent, sitting crumpled against the windae. — You awright? ah ask the cunt, wondering if he's sick eftir that wee bit we chased this morning. My throat and lungs still huv that bad taint ay the foil.

— Yeah, he sais, — the thing is, Mark –

— Ship ahoy. The carriage door flew open and a scraggy gadgie wi bad skin stands before us. Must be aroond thirty-plus. Nicksy intros him wearily as Paul Marriott, an auld junky acquaintance ay his and Tony's, whae's been a seasonal oan the Sealink boats fir yonks. Marriott has a gammy leg and lurches up tae us, fawin intae the vacant seat beside Sick Boy. — Alroight, chaps? he enquires, in the tones ay that cat cunt, the purple fucker, thit wis Roobarb the green dug's mate. Nicksy had explained that he wis basically the fall guy for the real gangsters further up the line, the sacrificial lamb that wid dae the serious jail time if it aw went erse ower tit. Tae be fair, he seems under few illusions aboot his status; his heavy habit means that he's naewhaire near as risk-averse as a man intending tae transport a fair auld amount of class As should be. That said, he doesnae want tae go tae jail if he can help it, and he looks us ower with a keen eye. It's obvious that need is something he can scent a mile away in others. He frowns at Nicksy's punk gear. — That quiff'll need flattened down before we go in to see Benson.

Nicksy says something under his breath aboot it no bein a quiff. Marriott doesnae hear or chooses no tae respond, looking mair approvingly at Sick Boy, who has his hair scraped back and tied in a ponytail. Poor Nicksy looks sweaty and strung-out, displaying aw the composure ay a spider trying tae get oot a bathtub.

— So what's the story with this Benson character? Sick Boy asks, wi his usual taking-over air ay authority.

Marriott looks warily at the cunt. He seems tae suss right away that Sick Boy will either be an incredible asset tae him or a total cuckoo in the nest: there'll be nae middle groond. — He's the man you need to get past at the interview to get a start. Remember, he's looking for cheap, seasonal labour, Marriott sais in his camp, skaggy whine. — His big catchphrase is 'willing cooperation'. That's what he wants in a start.

— Don't we all, Sick Boy grins.

Ignoring him, Marriott carries on. — The ferries were union shops for years but Maggie's mob fucked them over with new contracts after this privatisation lark and the split from BR. So no bullshit about industrial militancy, workers' rights, n all that 'it ain't my job' shit. What Benson wants is flexibility. He wants you to say you'll work anywhere – kitchens, cabins, car decks – and you'll do anything – cleaning up the puke, unblocking the shithouses. That you'll do double shifts if he needs you to, and you'll do it with a farking big smile on your face.

It suits me fine. Ah kin keep ma tongue in ma cheek n dae three-bags-full, if the rewards wir thaire.

— What aboot the gear? Sick Boy enquires.

— You sort out the employment first, then we worry about that later, he snaps, and looks accusingly round at Nicksy, who turns miserably back intae the windae.

The train snakes right intae the port at Harwich International Station at Parkeston Quay. We disembark and go practically fae the platform intae a warren ay prefabricated office buildings, merging with other anxious bodies, being ushered intae a sterile room. Although ah'm starting tae feel badger's-erse rough, ah check oot the crowd. There's about a dozen of us, and we look like the dregs, apart fae this cute lassie with crazy hair. We've a form tae fill in, then we get our individual interview wi Benson. He comes ower as hostile, a snowman wi hot coals for haemorrhoids. He's flanked by a fat, middle-aged, personnel officer wifie.

Ah realise that ah've nae chance ay getting the job, so ah'm only half-heartedly responding tae their bullshit questions, when Benson says, — Well, as you've done a bit of short-order cooking, we'll probably start you off in the kitchens. Just general portering duties, then see how things progress.

Ah'm totally fuckin astonished! There's about six million cunts on the dole, and they've not only gied us the job, but there's already the implicit offer ay a promotion! Ah briefly feel good aboot masel, until ah get oot n realise that every single fucker that trawled thair scabby erses along tae the interview has been signed up. It seems this fiasco wis merely a screening process tae weed oot any total bams previously sacked and daft enough tae reapply under a different name. Fuck knows how Marriott continually slithers through the net. Ah'm asking masel: what kind ay a fuckin job is this? The other punters were beyond real. No bein wide, but some ay they cunts looked as if they couldnae huv filled in the fuckin form on thair ain.

We're asked tae stall while aw the individual interviews are finished. It's only aboot half an hour but it seems an eternity. At one stage ah jist want tae tear through they plasterboard waws. Then Benson comes in tae address us, his lamps still scanning us all, lookin fir a wee exposure ay damaged soul. It's like the Rolodex in his heid tumbles in rhythm: junkies, dealers n poofs . . . junkies, dealers n poofs . . . Me n Nicksy are trying tae queen it up a bit, like we're an item, a genuine homosexual couple rather than frivolous fun-boys whose indiscriminate brown bombing might reduce the rust tub tae a hive ay infection.

We suspected that even here junkies were no-go, jist completely fucking *persona non grata*. Poor Nicksy: kent how he felt, ah wanted tae go n get sorted soon. A horrible fuckin itch was comin on.

Focusing on the windae behind Benson, ah could see *The Freedom of Choice* docked in the quay, a roll-on, roll-off, or 'roro vessel', as Benson refers tae it. His real mission, however, is tae gie us the party line: — It goes without saying that anyone found under the influence of, or in possession of, controlled drugs, will not only receive instant dismissal, but also be liable to prosecution.

Ah admire the affronted expression on Sick Boy. He's flogged it tae Benson as the genuine article, squeezing oot some back-pedalling penance.

— Not that I'm casting aspersions on you ladies and gentlemen. It's just that Amsterdam is not far from the Hook of Holland and . . . well, where people go when they're off duty is their own concern, as long as it does not affect either the safety or the quality of service provided on this vessel . . .

He waffles on n ah'm tryin tae tune oot the rest ay his shite by focusing oan the erse ay that wee lassie wi the big sortay Robert Plant hair.

259

Sick Boy's eyes, predictably, are nailed tae the same spot, while Nicksy looks gaga, staring off intae space. Ah hear Benson saying, — Congratulations. You are now officially part of the Sealink family. I shall see you all early next year!

So we were in work. Three, four or six million unemployed, nae cunt kent cause the calculation methods changed wi the frequency ay keks, and the most motley crew yuv ever seen, a combo ay junkies, poofs and fuck knows what else, are engaged in gainful employment for the start ay the spring season at Sealink. Can't wait to convey tae Mater and Pater the uplifting news that the ginger middle offspring has finally made good!

We take the train back tae London in a celebratory mood, crackin open some cans, as Marriott fills us in on the scam, aw businesslike and Mr Swinging Big Baws. We're tae go tae the Dam, buy shit fae this gadge there, n take it back oan the boat. — That geezer on the desk, the one I pointed out, Marriott explains, though ah noticed fuck all, — Frankie, he's the man. He drinks up in the Globe pub in Dovercourt. When we start I'll take you lads in there to buy him the odd beer, so he gets to know yer faces. Just keep that fucker sweet and you'll go through on the nod every time. He leaks me the rota details, cause it's farking crucial to know which of those Customs and Excise cunts are on duty, particularly if a bastard called Ron Curtis is doing the supervisory round. Nobody can get to that cunt. If he rumbles anything we just go ta ground and suck up the pain, even if we're as sick as hounds.

Ah'm finding it hard tae listen tae the cunt, so are the others. This speed is the business; I've done two fat lines up the hooter, and every time that steel wheel sparks on the points, the jolt goes right through the train n up ma spine.

Yee-hah! Roll along covered wagon, roll along . . .

The festive vibe intensifies tenfold when a group ay pished lassies in Santa hats get oan at Shenfield. This blonde bird produces some Christmas crackers, and Sick Boy's right in there, pullin one wi her, then pittin the purple crêpe party hat oan. — I know the Christmas cracker I'd like to pull, he teases lecherously, and as her mates cheer, he ducks in and whispers something in her ear. She jokingly punches his airm, but within a minute they're snogging each other's faces off.

Ah'm well sparked up n fill ay mischief, so ah cannae resist pillin oot ma lighter n settin Sick Boy's hat ablaze.

One lassie puts her hand tae her mooth as the flames shoot up, spreadin instantly tae his hair wi a cracklin, burnin sound. The blonde lassie he's snoggin wi pushes him away n screams.

260

— What the fuck — he shouts, feverishly pattin at his heid, as burnt bits ay the hat flake off n flutter ower the carriage.

— *Fi-uh . . . deh-reh-reh . . . ah take it you'll burn . . .* ah sings.

— WHAT YE FUCKIN WELL DAEIN?! PSYCHO CUNT! FUCKIN STUPID BASTARD! FUCK! He lunges ower n punches us in the baws. — THAT WAS FUCKIN DANGEROUS, YA DAFT CUNT!

Ah folds like a razor bein snapped shut, laughin through ma sick pain. — Bastard . . . Crazy World ay Arthur Broo-ooh-oohn . . . ah protests.

— You'll fuckin well pey tae git ma hair cut n styled! Stupid fuckin . . . Sick Boy mumps, preening himself in the reflection ay the gless windae, but he's soon back tae the lassie, waving a dismissive back hand at me. — Keep over there. Fucking child.

– I farking despair, Marriott mumbles under his breath. Then one ay the Shenfield lassies, eyes wide and deranged, opens her gob and shouts, — I EHM THE GOD ORF 'ELL FI-AH AND I BRING YOU . . .

Nicksy n me take up her cue tae burst intae song: — *FI-UH . . . DEH-REH-REH, I take it you'll burn . . .*

Sick Boy's still glancin daggers at me but the blonde bird's gittin the maist ay his attention. Ah'm chattin tae the singin lassie. She's pished, but as cool as fuck. — Owzit them two get ta ave all the fun then, eh?

— They're amateurs, ah tell her. — Ah'm gaunny snog your face off!

— Whatcha waitin on then?

Ah wisnae waitin, n no bothered at aw aboot ma cracked lips n snottery beak, ma tongue's right doon her throat. Ah see, though, that Sick Boy's one step ahead, as per usual; the cunt's up and leadin the blonde piece through tae the bogs. When we come up for air, Marriott's hacked off aboot being ignored, but Nicksy's tellin him we got plenty ay time tae iron oot the details. The cunt kens it n aw; he's just showboating. We start up another chorus ay 'Fire', but argue aboot the words in the verses, as our tins scud oan the tables n the peeves fly back. So we prepare tae hit the West End wi the Shenfield lassies, n Christmas has jist fuckin well started, big time!

Hogmanay

Ah turn fae the pish-yellay pages ay ma paperback novel, then deek oot the bus windae at the shimmering half-moon behind the pylons, cutting clean shadows oantae the concrete motorway sidings. It's the dregs ay December and cauld enough tae freeze the dribbles in yir piss-tube, but the heating's finally kicked in oan the bus and there's sweat and condensation rivulets running doon the windae where ma heid's been resting.

Nicksy n me are ignoring each other under the tepid glaze ay our personal overheid lights as the farts, growls, snores n cackles ay the jakeys oan the rancid coach erupt out ay the semi-darkness at us like the noises ay wild animals in a forest. It's a cool silence between us though; we've kent each other long enough no tae fill the void jist fir the sake ay it. We baith like oor ain space, especially whin wir a wee bit fucked.

Sick Boy wis pretty keen for us tae take Nicksy up tae ours, tellin me how he keeps gaun oan aboot seein Matty, arguin it's the least we kin dae after him puttin us up. He explained that he'd decided tae stey in London for New Year to go tae parties with Andreas and Lucinda as 'the histrionics' ay Edinburgh didnae appeal. He tells me he's still nipped at Begbie's 'aspersions' towards him, and isn't inclined to hang out wi him till he gets at least some kind ay apology. Ah telt him no tae hud his breath waitin oan that yin. Ah'm happy tae leave him tae it: fuck being in England at Hogmanay.

As soon as the bus rolls intae St Andrew's Square we head straight doon tae Montgomery Street, pickin up a cairry-oot on the wey. We're an ooir late wi aw the traffic tryin tae git intae Edinburgh, cunts comin hame for the New Year, n it's the back ay ten by the time we gits tae the Monty Street pad, which Spud and Keezbo have sort ay inherited. A perty's in fill swing and we join in wi gusto. It's a barry atmosphere, except thit Matty's barely speakin a word tae Nicksy, whae's aw ower him, but that wee cunt's actin like he's some stranger, instead ay the boy who took us under his wing n showed us London during the height ay punk. Ah'm hacked off wi that wanker. At least Franco's pally. — So you're fae London,

262

mate? he asks Nicksy, — Ah shagged a bird fae London once, in Benidorm. Mind ay that, Nelly? Benidorm? They two London birds?

Nelly looks a bit scoobied but nods in agreement.

The instruments are oot, n we start fuckin aboot. It develops intae a wee jam, Nicksy strummin Matty's acoustic guitar wi a competence its owner cannae match, as Franco sings about drinkin wine and feelin pretty damn good about it, in a strong, clear voice, rich in evocation.

Me n Keezbo pluck and pound, tryin tae keep in time wi each other, n gie Franco n Nicksy some backin. Franco's voice is something tae hear, it's like wi it bein Hogmanay, he's absorbed just the right amount ay alcohol n good vibes and they intersect at this wonderous vector as he briefly becomes something else, this force ay grace and soul.

Ah'm looking roond at aw the candlelit faces; Nicksy, Keezbo, Tommy, Spud (wi his sling now off), Alison, Kelly, Franco, June, Matty, Shirley, Nelly, n some frazzled burd wi long, raven hair that Nelly's wi but husnae bothered tae intro. The social skills ay a stormtrooper, that cunt. We've got a big roaring coal fire blazing away; the council can stick their smokeless zone pish up their erses, and everybody is visibly moved by Franco's singing. We join him in the chorus and we're aw the gither as one, sharin that broken dream . . .

Begbie's that wrapped up wi the performance, he almost whispers, through his half-closed eyes, about the time people go tae thir kip . . .

Poor auld Spud, the sentimental cunt, he's tearin up as Franco croons deeply. Matty's still mumpy, despite Shirley smilin and shakin his shoodir, and ah'm watchin Kelly and Alison lookin at June, whae's gapin up at Franco like he's a rock-n-roll star, and the night he sortay is. Aye, Franco has the flair and Nicksy's strummin wi tight concentration. Keezbo's keepin a soft beat n ah'm lulled intae a low-key, simple rhythm on the Shergold fretless, wishin ah hud the Fender, cause it's hard tae see the locatin dots in this meagre candlelight, as Begbie fills his lungs wi air fir the big climax, that final refrain in the song, which really is pure him.

We wind up tae cheers, which Franco just aboot takes. Ah gie him a subtle wink, which ah can tell the cunt loves best for the understated appreciation it conveys. Ma puny pinkie is numb and dead fae tryin tae hud those octaves.

Spud's eyes are red and wet. — Franco, man . . . that wis likesay . . . amazing, he goes, but his comments make everybody look tae the singer.

— Aye, Begbie goes, but ye kin tell Spud's annoyed him by makin that fuss, — ye cannae beat Rod Stewart at fuckin New Year, and he fills Spud's glass wi whisky, tae divert everybody's attention.

Poor Spud's too pished tae pick up the vibe but, n he's still gaun on:

— Naw bit that wis amazing, see if ah could sing like you, Franco —

— Shut the fuck up, Begbie says wi soft menace. Nicksy looks ower tae me wi a fraught, raised brow.

— But ah'm jist sayin — Spud pleads.

— Ah sais tae fuckin well shut it! Right!

Spud falls silent, as does the rest ay the room. We all instantly understand how Begbie sees that this wee fragment ay beauty in his soul has been exposed, and how even through his ain ego and the flattery received, he looks on it as a potential weakness, something that might one day compromise him.

— It's jist fuckin singin, right.

Nicksy puts Matty's acoustic in its zipper bag. Ah makes a show ay lookin at the clock on the mantelpiece and goes, — Right, we'd better git a bend oan if we're gaunny git tae Sully's perty for the bells!

We're aw relieved tae huv a change ay scene. We get oot oantae the street, intae the cauld, still air. The toon is locked in ice; like a paperweight ay trees, waws and snaw. Everybody else is headin up the Walk tae the city and the Tron for the bells. We're gaun doonhill though, soles slidin n cracklin oan the icy pavement, Leith-bound. Kelly and Alison have locked airms oan either side ay us, jist for safety oan the treacherous path, but it feels good anyway. Kelly's heid whips roond lemur-like, her gaze taking a quick snapshot ay me before turning tae Ali. Inside me, ah feel the pulse ay the magnesium scar left by her smile. — Ah'm really sorry aboot your ma, ah whisper intae Ali's ear, — n aboot no bein up for the funeral. Ah didnae hear till it wis aw ower.

— It's okay. Tae be honest, it's a relief, cause she wis suffering that much at the end. Ah ken it sounds horrible, but ah wis willing her: just let go.

— Well, ah'm really sorry ye lost her, and that ye had tae go through aw that.

— Isn't Mark sweet, says Kelly, looking at me, exciting another tweak in the pit of my stomach, before turning tae Ali.

— He has his moments, Ali acerbically concedes, but gies ma airm a tight squeeze. A big smile ignites Kelly's face n for a second ah think she's game for some ginger baws, but it's a ridic notion; she goes oot wi that Des Feeney gadge, this boy who's some sort ay relative ay Spud's.

In your rents, Dream Boy.

The girls look ethereally beautiful in half-profile as they talk tae each other across me, the sodium lamps twinkling in Kelly's mischievous and

Ali's forlorn eyes. Enobled by ma status as consort, a wasted grace settles in my soul through the whisky's warm glow. It's a raw night, but wi nae wind, as ah look back tae see that Nicksy's bonded wi Spud n Tommy in wild-eyed laughter, while Franco, June and Keezbo are up ahead. — He's fuckin well tapped, n that's pittin it mildly, Ali whispers, noddin in Begbie's direction. — Danny wis only tryin tae compliment him!

Ah'm gaunny say something but decide no tae as Begbie suddenly stops dead, violently hauling June intae a doorway. We walk past them, and hear her saying, — Dinnae Frank, in a loud, scared laugh, — no here . . .

The manky fucker's gaunny knee-tremble her oan the spot.

— He's a total starry-eyed moonlight serenader, ah offer, once we're safely past them. Alison rolls her eyes in disdain and Kelly tilts her head tae the side, smilin in that cute, sexy way ay hers. She's such a good-looking girl, her face covered in freckles, with short browny-blonde spiky hair, exuding the quirky new confidence ay somebody who's grown intae her skin nicely. That's what the auld boy sometimes says, n ah never got it till now. She's asking us aboot Aberdeen, telling us she's started daein this access course for Edinburgh University. Ah tell her ah've taken a year off n thit ah'm thinking ay gaun tae Glesgey or doon south.

The rest have stopped tae let us catch up, but there's nae sign ay Franco, whae's probably banging June wi extreme prejudice in that scabby stair.

We carry on taewards Easter Road as Sully's gaff's at that end ay Iona Street. The derby game's oan the morn, so we're well set. — These cunts have no beaten us on New Year's Day since 1966, Matty, brandishing a bottle ay whisky, declares, lookin challengingly at Keezbo.

— That record's gaunny go the morn, Keezbo says.

— Beat it, ya mongol, is it fuck, Matty spits, then snipes under his breath, — fuckin fat cunt.

That's a bit nippy and uncalled for, but Keezbo lets it slide. Shirley pouts n looks at the pavement. Matty's eywis oan Keezbo's case. One ay these days the big felly's gaunny turn roond n lamp that stroppy wee fucker. N ah fir one will shed nae tears when it happens.

We see Begbie and June emergin fae the stair. They head taewards us, Franco wi a dirty smile oan his chops, June lookin awkward n coy as they come up the road. We wait for them in silence. Franco has picked up the vibe. Despite bein willy-nilly aboot causing aggro, he kin git awfay sensitive when some other fucker creates an atmosphere. Maybe Sick Boy's called it right wi the festive plans eftir aw. — What's up wi every cunt?

Matty breaks the silence, and points at Keezbo. — Cunt, jist telling this fat Jambo fucker that his team's pish!

— Ah'm no arguing wi ye aboot fitba before the bells, Matty, Keezbo goes.

— Aye, Franco asks Matty, — what ye oan fuckin Keezbo's case fir, ya fuckin radge?

— Cause he's a fat Herts cunt.

Franco's airm whips oot n smacks Matty roond the heid. It's quite a sair yin, but also a fuckin humiliation cause ay it bein in front ay Shirley. — Shut yir fuckin mooth! Wir aw fuckin mates the day, fitba or nae fuckin fitba! He looks tae Keezbo wi a predatory grin. — If ah see this fat ginger cunt the morn, ah knock his fuckin teeth doon his throat, He turns to Matty. — But the night wir best fuckin mates, right?

In the absence ay any argument tae the contrary, we swing roond tae Iona Street n climb the stairs in a close jist doon fae the Iona Bar. Ah cannae wait tae get intae the warm. Sully greets us aw; a big, gruff genial host wi craggy features and slick-backed rockabilly haircut that ah ey think belongs oan an aulder dude. Ah hit the kitchen and see Lesley, Anne-Marie Combe, a skinny, short-haired brunette, who inevitably works as a hairdresser n whom ah felt up in the Goods Yard years ago whin wi wir fill ay voddy, and Stu Hogan, a chunky blond gadge wi a penchant for practical jokes, whae pours us a nip ay whisky. Ah much prefer voddy, but somebody says something aboot it bein New Year, n everybody's gittin yin. Ah'm no touching skag right now, or even speed. Gittin masel thegither a bit. Stu's askin us aboot London, telling me that Stevie Hutchison's been doon thaire, n gies me a number fae a tatty auld address book. That's good news; Stevie's a sound cunt, decent singer n aw, or at least he wis whin we wir in Shaved Nun thegither. Like anybody wi talent, he outgrew us. — He's in Forest Hill, Stu tells us, — is that near you?

— Aye, quite near, ah goes. It isnae really but. Well, it is and it isnae, in that London sortay wey. — Is he still seein that dozy fucker?

— Sandra? Stu goes.

— Aye, that's her, Chip Sandra, they used tae call her. Liked eatin thum n wearin thum oan her shoodir.

— Naw . . . they split up before he went doon tae London.

— Good, she's a fuckin sour-faced hoor. Ah fuckin cannae stick her. Did ah tell ye the story ay – ah goes, then ah hesitate as Stu's face has gone aw serious.

— Actually, *ah'm* seein Sandra now, he cuts in. — She's jist oan her wey roond here. In fact, before ye start making any mair snidey comments aboot people, ah'd better lit ye ken that we jist goat engaged the other week.

Fuck . . .

— Oh . . . ah mean . . . ah dinnae really ken Sand—

Stu's face lights up as laughter erupts fae somewhere deep in the cunt's chist. — Goat ye, he grins, slappin ma shoodir n headin off.

— Bastard! Ah'll fuckin remember that yin, Hogan!

Fuckin nailed tae the waw big time thaire, but whae cares, the perty's in fill swing. Tommy's toppin up a half-pint gless wi a big dash ay whisky.
— Whaire's Second Prize?

— Fuck knows, no seen him. He'll be lyin in a gutter somewhaire.

Tommy grins in acknowledgement n tops up ma gless, but ah'm no fuckin well enjoying this drink. It burns ma guts. Lesley notices me wince, n as Tam looks eftir Nicksy, she sidles up tae us. — Any skag?

— Naw.

— Want a hit?

— Aye, ah say. Ah've been tryin tae avoid the Scottish skag n the bangin up, cause it's fuckin lethal shit, n ye kin really feel it gittin a hud ay ye. The broon's easier: doesnae seem tae cunt ye up sae much. But fuck it, ah'm sortay oan hoaliday . . . oan hoaliday at hame . . .

We troop off through tae a bedroom and sit cross-legged oan this big, tartan duvet-covered brass bed, as Lesley starts cookin. It shocks me, as ah thoat she jist chased, but she's goat a fill set ay works n she's highly competent. She lights up a candle, stickin it in a baccy tin, and switches off the main light. We fix up wi oor separate equipment, me gaun first. Ma vein sucks the shit in so greedily, it's like ah barely need tae put any pressure oan the plunger.

Ohhh . . . YA FUCK –

Ya fucker . . . aw man . . . oooh . . . nice, nice, nice . . .

Ah forgot the power ay this shite. Lesley never prepped up that much but ah collapse back oantae the Royal Stuart . . .

— Ah found this the other day in ma jeans poakit, she explains, pushin her blonde hair behind her ears n tappin patiently before fixin, as ah lie back melted. — Forgot aw aboot it fae weeks back. Ah took it up the Bendix, n vernear put it through the wash, jist as well ah didnae, cause thaire's a drought oan . . . What ye giggling at?

. . . aw ya fuckin beauty . . .

Ah try tae tell her the Bendix joke, but ah kin barely speak, n in any case, she's banged up hersel and a few seconds later she's in the same state.

Mother of Bendix, wash house gods, ah give youse thanks for king heroin; thank you for that whiter than white wash . . .

The candlelight goes oot n we're baith spangled oan the bed, then

267

hugging each other, wi emotion, but sortay chastely. Lesley's wearing a blue slidey-material top, which feels like silk but isnae. Then we're sort ay crashed out, me restin my heid oan her stomach, her top rolled up, listenin tae the sounds her guts make. — Bubbles n sizzles, bubbles n sizzles, ah goes.

— Ah'm wasted . . .

— Me n aw. It's cauld . . . Ah kick oaf ma trainers n pill oaf ma jeans n git under the tartan duvet. She does the same, scrambling alongside me, kissin us coolly on the lips. Then she puts her index finger inside ma jumper n traces it ower ma ribcage. — You're that thin, Mark.

— Ah've kind ay lost a bit ay weight. Fast metabolism, ah suppose, and ah props masel up on ma elbaws tae look at her.

Lesley smiles grimly at me through the semi-dark. There's light pouring in fae under the door, and through the curtains fae the street lamp ootside. — Skag metabolism, mair like. You're a pretty weird guy, she goes, still outlining ma ribs.

— How? ah ask, interested tae ken if she means cool weird or geeky, spazzy weird. No that ah'm bothered either wey, cause ah'm feelin fuckin barry.

— Well, maist guys, ye kin tell if they fancy ye. Lesley's pupils seem slitty n catlike in this meagre light. — But ah dinnae ken wi you . . .

— Course ah do, ah tell her, — everybody fancies you. You're a beautiful girl, ah go, pushing her hair behind her ear, the wey she did when she prepared the gear. She is. Kind ay.

— Aye, right, she says doubtfully, but she's sort ay flattered. So her hand suddenly reaches doon tae ma groin, inside ma pants, and grabs some playdough. — So how come we're in bed thegither n yir no hard?

— Ah'm just too wasted. Takes ages tae git it up eftir ah bang this shit . . . chasin a bit ay broon, nae worries, root like a Californian Ridwood, but see bangin this stuff . . .

Lesley isnae really ma type, wi her big bust, but of course ah'd still ride her if ah wisnae fucked up. We baith take oor tops off, then hug and kiss for a bit, but she's as wasted as me, n we mumble shite for a while, then faw intae something like sleep, wi her still cuppin ma soft genitals.

Ah'm aware ay a passage ay time and then a rat-arsed Alison and Kelly barging intae the room, follayed by Spud, bringin in a ragged, morning light. — Whoops, somebody says, and they quickly close the door. They half open it again tae shout in, — Happy New Year!

Ah try n mumble something back. Lesley and me are baith stripped

268

doon tae oor underpants, the duvet having slid oaf us as the heating kicked up in the night. Ah pull it back across those heavy, solid lily-white breasts.

— Fuck sakes . . . she goes, waking up as the others, giggling like daft wee bairns, shut the door.

— Mmmm . . . ah kind ay agree, sick n wi a tinny taste in ma mooth.

— What time is it? Lesley sits up, wi the duvet in front ay her tits. She yawns and turns tae me.

— Fuck knows . . . ah moan, but it sounds like the party's rambling on. Ah can hear 'Cum On Feel the Noize' by Slade, n ah'm guessin that Begbie's still monopolising the turntable. As we heave ourselves slowly intae consciousness, Lesley and me are baith pretty embarrassed, wi the works oan the bedside table, but also aboot the general situ. We crashed right through the bells and never even shagged. The door goes again, a soft series ay raps. It doesnae open but ah hear Spud behind it: — Fitba, catboy, fitba. Pub. The derby. The Cabbage.

— Geez a minute. Take Nicksy doon the Clan wi ye and ah'll see yis in thaire in a bit.

Lesley and me can hear the flat emptyin. You ride somebody when you're fucked up and horny, then in the morning they often look as rough as fuck. She's the reverse, she's gorgeous n ah'm sortay seein it for the first time. Ah've goat a belter ah a hard-on n she looks as sexy and sleazy as fuck, but the moment's passed n she's up and getting dressed, leavin me nae option but tae follow suit.

— Right, see ye later, she says.

You fuckin bam, Renton, you fuckin bammy simple dingul.

— No comin doon the pub for one?

— Naw. Gaun tae my ma's at Clerie for a New Year perty.

We get oot intae the cauld, headin oor separate weys. Ah soon sort ay wish ah'd gaun tae Clerie wi her, even if ah wisnae invited. The pub is chaotic, wi everybody singin Hibs songs. A middle-aged gadge in thick glesses has stripped off and is dancing oan the stage the go-gos use. He has PADDY STANTON wi two eyes tattooed in Indian ink oan his buttocks and ELVIS oan his cock, which an auld wifie tries tae conceal wi her knitting as he gyrates.

— That's his ma, somebody explains.

Nicksy's fair enjoyin hissel, looks like the change ay scene hus done him good. Ah'm strugglin wi the drink, but. It makes us seek; Queen Skag's quite a jealous bitch, she doesnae seem tae like other drugs tryin

269

tae muscle intae her meat, particularly Princess Peeve. Ali n Kelly look like they're in deep conspiracy, Nicksy's tellin Tommy n Spud a tale aboot Sick Boy, n ah'm forced intae the pain seat beside Begbie, whae slams his trademark elbay intae ma ribs. — Nice one wi Lesley, ya dirty, lucky cunt! You're no fuckin shy! Ah'd cowp it in a fuckin minute! Fill hoose for the rid-heided cunt, ah take it?

— Naw, just a wee kiss n cuddle, ah goes. — New Year pleasantries, n ah look ower at Tommy, who looks rough as fuck. He shakes his heid in self-loathing.

— Aye, that'll be right, ya fuckin clarty rid-heided bastard! Ye wir up her aw night, ya spawny cunt, he declares, daein that one-handed switch fae nip tae fag n back that strangely impresses. — Fuckin hud ma eye oan that yin fir ages! No shy, this cunt, he announces tae the table.

The rest join in, no believin ma honourable protestations. The best thing ah could've done wis tae tell every cunt that ah wis bangin Lesley aw weys, that she couldnae get enough. Then they'd think, 'Aye, right.' By simply telling the truth, they now believe ah've done her in every orifice. It must be shite bein a bird. Ah go up tae the jukey and pit oan 'Lido Shuffle' by Boz Scaggs, thinking ay 'Baws Skagged', ma new nickname for masel that will be kept tae masel.

When ah git back tae the seat Kelly's sortay listenin tae Nicksy n Ali gaun oan aw seriously aboot relationship problems, him still slaverin aboot that Marsha bird fae upstairs at oor Dalston gaff, n her gaun oan aboot some mairried gadge she's seein fae her work. Suddenly she looks keenly at Nicksy and asks, — What's Simon daein fir New Year?

— Dunno, Nicksy shrugs.

— Ah love Simon!

— Yeah, Nicksy says warily, — he's a top geezer.

Franco's shuffled closer tae me and lowers his voice in confidant mode. — Listen the now, mate, cause you're the only cunt ah kin fuckin well trust roond here . . .

— Right . . .

— Fat Tyrone, ye ken him?

— By rep jist, ah goes. Ye heard aw sorts ay stories aboot Fat Tyrone, aka Davie Power. He either ran the toon wi an iron fist, or was a blobby shitebag and a cowardly grass, dependin on whae wis telling the tale. It never interested me, aw that gangster stuff.

— Ah'm daein a wee bit work fir the cunt.

— Right.

— But ah'm no sure aboot it.

— What's it yir daein?

— Helpin um git his fruit machines installed. It doesnae go through the books, so it's fuckin barry. Money fir nowt n aw. Me, Nelly n this big cunt, Skuzzy, jist go roond tae the pubs n gie thum a copy ay the fruit machine catalogue. Maistly the cunts git the message n they ken tae take the one thit Power's gaunny pit in, he says, looking at Nelly who's fuckin well equipped for that joab, as he's constantly up at the fruit machine, ignorin his burd, as he bangs in the change, his pus a picture ay concentration.

— Right, well, if yir no sure, leave it alaine.

— Aye, he goes, — but Nelly's daein stuff for um n aw, n ah dinnae want that fucker swannin aroond like he's the cunt wi the tadger the size ay the fuckin Scott Monument. Nae point cuttin oaf your cock tae spite yir baws, ken what ah mean?

It made sense now; if Nelly was daein work for a top gangster, no way could Begbie leave that oaf his CV. These cunts professed tae be great mates, but they'd been in competition wi each other ivir since school.

— There is that, ah suppose, ah goes, tryin tae sound as if it ah gied a fuck, and just aboot pullin it off.

— At first ah just fuckin well thoat, Nelly goat a wee taster n he wis fuckin well puntin a bit action his buddy's wey. Now ah see it fuckin different but. It's like he's sayin he disnae fuckin well rate us, ah'll fuck it aw up, that's how he's fuckin well giein us it, soas ah'll faw flat oan ma fuckin face, Franco glares at me. The bam's buildin up a head ay steam here.

Aw ah kin dae is nod. Suddenly, Tommy springs up, face crinkled like a Chinese lantern, n we aw look roond startled, as he puts his hand tae his mooth. Puke's sprayin oot between his fingers as he runs frantically tae the toilet, tae big cheers fae the table.

Except Franco.

Ah couldnae gie a fuck aboot these cunts n thair business, nor their covert war wi each other, but ah dinnae want it kickin off here. — Naw, ah think Nelly's bein sound, Franco. The wey ah see it is that he rates ye, n it reflects better on him wi Power if Nelly intros him tae a gadge that kin obviously handle things.

Franco thinks aboot this for a bit. Looks ower tae Nelly, then back tae me. Seems tae agree. — Aye, mibbe ah'm bein a wee bit hard oan the cunt. Sound cunt Nelly, eywis wis, he says as Nelly looks ower tae us. — Awright, Nelly, ya cunt! Git thum in then! Lager n whisky fir me, lager n voddy for this dirty ginger-heided fucker! N the boys here n the lassies n aw! C'moan, Tam, ya fuckin lightweight, he roars at Tommy, whae

271

returns fae the bog lookin like a ghost. He creases his face up in pain as somebody hands him a drink.

Nelly gies a strangely fetching wee salute and leaves the fruit machine tae shout up a round. We join in a chorus ay 'We Are Hibernian FC' which blasts oot fae another table, then doss back the drinks and head off tae the game.

Notes on an Epidemic 5

They called him Andy. Most people said he was American due to his accent, even though he held a British passport. He was a largely circumspect individual, but nobody bothered much about that. Strangers appeared, came and went, were free to be silent or tell tall stories as they saw fit, to try out new identities before vanishing like ghosts. If you had gear or money, few searching questions were asked.

One persistent version of his tale was that Andy's parents emigrated to Canada from Scotland when he was four years old. As he grew into his youth, he became estranged from his family and drifted over to America, then joined the Marine Corps, in order to obtain US citizenship. Saw active service in Vietnam. Perhaps came back with undiagnosed post-traumatic stress, or maybe just couldn't settle into life outside the disciplined structures of the military. Drifted through several American towns till he ended up in the Tenderloin District of San Francisco. Became a political activist in the Vietnam Veterans movement. Fell foul of the authorities. They saw his UK passport, and discounting his American service record, sent him back to a home he scarcely remembered.

Whether its genesis was in Vietnam, or the Tenderloin, came through sharing needles, blood transfusions or unprotected sex, a sickness settled on Andy. Back in Edinburgh he fell in with a loosely federated group of desperados who adopted him. They had access to the medicine he needed. There was Swanney from Tollcross, Mikey from Muirhouse, the old hippy Dennis Ross. Shifty Alan Venters from Sighthill, a little thief from Leith called Matty, and a sinister biker named Seeker. They were just some of the prominent members of a diffuse, often fractious community, which grew exponentially with every closing factory, warehouse, office and shop. It was in this scene, where, unknown to himself or anyone else, through sharing those big hospital syringes in Edinburgh's shooting galleries, Andy became the Johnny Appleseed of Aids.

The Art of Conversation

Ah sais tae fuckin June earlier, ah goes: thank fuck that's January nearly ower. A shite fuckin month. Baw cauld n every cunt steyin in aw the time, Renton sneakin away back doon tae fuckin London wi that wee cunt he hud up here. Wisnae a bad wee fucker, but every cunt should stey whaire they fuckin well come fae, that's what ah eywis fuckin well say. At least Rents came back; Sick Boy nivir even fuckin showed up at aw.

That Cha Morrison cunt fae Lochend's inside eftir daein Larry ower. Still runnin oaf at the fuckin mooth, n aw, or so they fuckin well tell us. *How come Begbie nivir does time? Makes ye wonder if the cunt's a fuckin grass.* Fuckin innuendo. Ah'll gie that cunt a fuckin grass awright. That cunt dies: spreadin fuckin innuendo. Cunt's nipped cause it's me the likes ay Davie Power wants to git fuckin involved in the world ay business. No a schemie tramp like that fuckin fandan. But that Hong Kong Fuey, the Pilton cunt that goat his jaw tanned when he goat wide eftir ah bairned his slag ay a sister, he's the cunt ah really feel fuckin lit doon by. No a peep oot ay that cunt, but ah suppose he must've goat seek using fuckin straws tae eat his dinner. Still, it'll be company fir her fuckin bairn whin it comes; that's what ah fuckin well sais tae fuckin Nelly the other day: her fuckin bairn'll be oan fuckin solids before that cunt!

Thaire's nae conversation oot ay fuckin June, good fir pokin jist, yon. Now thit she's huvin a bairn, she's chuffed tae jist sit in the hoose watchin the box wi her fags n Babychams. So ah'm gled tae git oot n sign oan the fuckin dole then head up toon n dae some graft. Gav Temperley's sound, he kens no tae bother us by sendin us tae fuckin interviews, cause ah telt the cunt oan the quiet that ah've been daein a bit ay work fir Fat Tyrone Power.

So ah gies them ma autograph, then gits in the motor wi Nelly n shoots up tae George Street, tae the office. Goes up tae see Fat Power n he's in thaire wi big Skuzzy. Ah'm lookin at this big fuckin map ay Edinburgh oan the waw, n it's goat aw they coloured plastic tag things pinned intae it, showin whaire Power's fruit machines are sited. Aw the pins are green, except a couple ay white yins. Power points tae yin wi a chubby finger like a fuckin sausage in a butcher's windae. — This poxy little boozer. A very lippy auld chap just took it ower. Doesnae want a fruit machine in the shop. Your mission, gentlemen, should you choose tae accept it, the cunt laughs at his ain *Mission: Impossible* joke, but ah keep ma face straight cause ah'm no here tae laugh at any cunt's jokes and if that cunt's goat a fuckin problem wi that, it's too fuckin bad fir him, – is to convince him of the considerable benefits that would accrue should he choose to reconsider his position.

Nelly's huvin a wee lassie's giggle n even Skuzzy's goat a grin oan his fuckin coupon. Fucked if ah'm playin sidekick tae a two-bob villain but; if the cunt wants his fuckin equity caird he kin git up oanstage at the King's fir the Christmas fuckin panto. So me n Nelly leave Skuzzy n the fat fucker n head off tae the boozer, tae see this auld cunt.

We're comin up tae the bar n ah'm realisin that this place is ringin a few fuckin warnin bells. Somethin isnae fuckin right here.

— Lit us handle this, ah tells Nelly, — You stall here.

The cunt looks like he's aboot tae say something, then shrugs as ah nashes ootay the motor n intae the bar.

Ya cunt, ah'm no wrong aboot this boozer. Sixth fuckin sense. Ah believe thit some cunts've goat it; ah've fuckin well goat it n it's stood me in good fuckin stead. Ah ken this shop awright, but ah'm even mair surprised when ah see the auld cunt thit's workin here. It's Uncle Dickie, Dickie Ellis, well, he's really a mate ay ma Uncle Gus, whae wis my ma's brar, but he wis like an uncle tae me n aw, n the cunt's delighted tae fuckin well see us. — Frankie boy! Long time no see, son. How goes it? How's yir mother?

— No bad, Dickie, she's okay . . . ah goes. — When did ye take ower this place?

The bar's a mahogany-panelled shop, stocked wi aw they different whiskies. It's goat a clean lino flair n it's smellin ay polish. Auld n tidy, a bit like Dickie, wi the sortay white hair but thin enough tae see the spammy bits oan the scalp, n a neat, trimmed beard n mowser, n they thin, gold-rimmed specs. His coupon fair creases up like an auld accordion.

— Goat the licence aboot three months ago.

Ah'm lookin around, casin the doss. — No goat a telly fir the hoarse racin, then?

— Nae telly, nae jukebox n nae fruit machines, he goes, — people come here tae drink n tae talk, Frank. That's how a pub should be!

— Right, ah goes. Aye, they git aw they commie student cunts in here, and aw the auld fuckers. Aw talkin politics. Like Dickie. Ah'm thinking ah cannae dae nowt tae this auld fucker, but at the same time, ah cannae fuckin disappoint Power. If ah dae that it jist means thit ah git nae fuckin wages n that cunt Nelly or Skuzzy comes in n deals wi auld Dickie. N then Power gits some cunt like Cha Morrison tae dae ma fuckin joab! Ah kin hear that jailbait cunt's stirrin voice in muh heid right now: *Begbie wisnae up tae it, too sentimental . . .*

A fuckin lose–lose situ.

Somethin seems tae tipple wi auld Dickie, cause he goes, — Power's thugs huv been oan aboot us takin thair fuckin fruit machines. He puffs hissel up. What the auld cunt disnae ken is that he's no seen thugs yit. — But ah telt them tae git fucked. What're they gaunny dae tae me? Batter us? Big deal. Ah'm no feart ay Power, ah kent the cunt whin he hud nae erse in his troosers, he goes wi a big smile.

Power's no the only cunt he kent back in the day. — You kent ma Uncle Gus well, eh, Dickie?

The auld boy's eyes go aw moist. — Frank, me n Gus, we wir like brothers. Ah kent the whole family on yir mother's side, the McGilvarys. Good people. The auld cunt grips ma sleeve. — Gus n me, God rest his soul, we wirnae *like* brothers, we *wir* brothers. Yir ma, Val; her and ma Maisie wir best friends for years!

Ah'm starin at him, and he lets go the grip n looks worried.

— Look, ah goes, — cause you n me go back, ah'm no gaunny bullshit ye. Ah'm workin fir Power, ah tells um. — He sent us doon here tae pit the bite oan ye.

Ah watch the auld cunt's face fuckin faw doon like it's gaunny smack the fuckin lino. — Aw . . . he says.

— But the wey ah see it, you n Gus wir like brothers. That makes you like ma uncle. Mind ah ey used tae call ye Uncle Dickie?

— Ah mind fine well, Frank.

— Cause ye *wir* like an uncle tae me. N nowt's changed. Mind ye used tae take us tae the pictures?

His worn auld face lights up. — Aye. The Seturday-morning matinees. You n Joe. The State, the Salon. How is Joe, by the way?

— Wir no talkin right now, ah tell um.

— Aw . . . sorry tae hear that.

— Well, it's doon tae that cunt, ah goes, then ah changes the subject cause ah dinnae want tae talk aboot ma fuckin brar. — Aye, n ye took us tae Easter Road n aw.

— Aye . . . we were thaire that night when Jimmy O'Rourke scored that second half hat-trick against Sportin Lisbon, mind ay that?

276

— Aye . . . ah goes, mindin ay it well, barry fuckin game n aw, — Jimmy O'Rourke . . . that wis a gadgie that fuckin well played for the jersey, could dae wi some cunts like that nowadays!

Cunt took us tae Hampden n up tae Dens Park n aw. The good thing aboot Gus n Dickie wis that when they took ye tae an away game n went tae the boozer, they lit ye stey *in* the motor wi crisps n Coke. No like the auld man whae locked up that scabby fuckin van n telt us tae play ootside the pub, usually in some fuckin Weedgie slum. Make a fuckin man ay ye, the cunt goes. A wonder we wirnae kidnapped by fuckin nonces. Nae bairn ay mine's gaunny be fuckin well treated like that.

But the auld cunt Dickie jist fuckin well smiles aw sad like he's gaunny burst intae tears n shrugs, — Any blood ay Gussie's wis eywis gaunny be faimlay tae me, Frank.

— Aye. N as ah say, you wir like ma uncle, n nowt's fuckin changed, ah goes. Cause ah mind that's what happened; the auld cunt basically took ower eftir poor Gus fell offay that fuckin bridge. So ah knocks back the nip. — N that's the story Power's gittin.

Dickie shakes his heid. — Listen, Frankie, son, ah'll take the machine. Oot ay respect for your position, that auld white heid nods aw sad. — Ah dinnae want ye fawin oot wi Power if yir workin fir him.

— Nup, ah goes. — Yir no takin any fuckin machine ye dinnae fuckin well want, ah dinnae care what Power or any cunt sais. If the cunt wants tae make a drama oot ay it, ah'll tell um tae fuckin well git oan the stage.

— Dinnae be daft! I'll take it, Frank, n the auld cunt's fuckin beggin us. — Ah'll take the machine. It isnae really a big deal.

— Nup, ah'll fuckin well sort it, ah goes, headin oot. — See ye later.

So ah gits ootside intae the car n Nelly goes, — Is that it sorted?

— It will be, ah says. — Take us back up tae Power's office.

Nelly shrugs n lights a fag, without fuckin crashin thum, which is bad fuckin manners, n drives oaf. We gits back up the toon, n ah bails oot n heads tae the office. That cunt steys in the motor, wi the fuckin mumpy face oan um.

Ah'm back in Power's office, lookin at the young receptionist bird that wisnae here before, n ah kin feel ma hert gaun boom-boom-boom. But then ah'm thinkin, what's he gaunny dae? He'll huv tae fuckin well kill us tae fuckin well stoap us. Ah dinnae fuckin well care if it's Power or Skuzzy or any cunt; they've goat tae fuckin well realise that. But ah'll stey cool. Eftir aw, the cunt's been awright tae me.

Whin ah goes through Skuzzy isnae thaire n Power's leanin back in the big chair. — Frank, take a pew. How did it go?

— Listen, Davie, ah goes, sittin doon in the seat oan the other side ay the desk, — mind whin ah started like, you sais any time ah needed a favour?

— Aye . . . ah mind, Frank, Power goes, suddenly lookin cagey. Cunts like him dinnae like it whin ye answer a question wi another fuckin question.

— It's Dickie Ellis; ah never kent it wis him that had the boozer. He's a sortay relative ay mines. Ma uncle. Ah ken you've been good tae us . . .

— You've been good tae me, Frank. Power stubs oot a cigar. — Ah like the wey ye handle things.

— . . . but ah dinnae want the auld cunt tae git any hassle. So ah'd appreciate it, as a favour tae me, likes, if ye could lit the fruit machine pass here. Any other cunt ah dinnae gie a fuck aboot, but no auld Dickie.

Power sinks even further back in that big fuckin padded chair, then suddenly moves forward, pittin his elbays oan the desk n restin that big shaved heid oan his fists. He looks us right in the eye. — Ah see.

Ah huds the gaze, starin straight back at the cunt. — Ah'm askin ye this as a favour between you n me. Nae fuckin strings. If you say naw, ye cannae dae it, ah'm right back doon thaire n that fruit machine goes in. No matter what it fuckin well takes, ah goes, makin sure the cunt gits what the fuck ah'm oan aboot.

Power picks up a pen and drums it oan the desk. He never breks the stare. — You're loyal, Frank, n ah like that. Ah can understand that this has put ye in a difficult position. Tell me, though, now the cunt's tappin his front teeth wi the pen, then pointin at us wi it, — why dae ye think ah sent ye doon thaire?

— Tae git the fuckin machine pit in, ah goes.

Power shakes his heid. — Ah dinnae gie a fuck aboot the machine. Ye dinnae run a business by strong-armin n threatenin every cunt. Maist times they see sense, n if they dinnae, we move on and respect thair decision; *if* they huv enough fuckin savvy tae stey discreet. He raises his brows tae make sure ah'm gittin his fuckin drift. Then he goes, — But auld Dickie's got a fuckin mooth oan him, Frank. Ah'm perfectly happy for him no tae have any ay our machines in his pub, but his gob is such that he sees that beneficence as a weakness. In short, the auld cunt thinks that me, he points tae hissel wi the pen, — and, by extension, you, n now the cunt's pointin the pen at me, — are a pair ay fuckin fannies.

Ah feel masel tense up. Ah'm thinkin aboot that auld cunt doon the boozer. Cunt's been playin us fir a fuckin mug!

Fat Tyrone Power kin see that ah'm no fuckin happy. — What I suggest, Franco, is that you go back doon there and have a wee conversation wi yir Uncle Dickie. He gets tae keep the machine oot ay the boozer, ma favour tae you, Power smiles like a big fuckin fat cat thit's jist stuffed a budgie doon its fuckin throat, — but make sure he kens that this is solely down tae his connection wi you, ma respect for you as a colleague, and, the cunt grins even mair, — ma general sunny disposition.

— Right . . . cheers, ah sais, n ah gits up n turns tae go.

But then the cunt sais, — One good turn deserves another. *Ah* need a wee favour.

— Nae worries. Ah sink back intae the seat.

— This fuckin smack, it's aw ower the toon. Every cunt's intae it.

— Tell us aboot it. Fuckin daft cunts, ah goes.

— Too right, a mug's game for sure; but thaire's money in it, big money. The place is flooded wi it, n some cunt that isnae me is laughin aw the wey tae the bank. Ah'd love tae ken whae's puntin it and whaire thir gittin it fae. If ye could keep yir eyes n ears open, ah'd be obliged.

— Right, ah goes, — ah'll dae that, n ah'm thinkin ay Rents n Sick Boy n Spud n Matty n aw they daft cunts that've goat intae that fuckin shite. Ah kin see what it's daein tae they fuckers, especially that rid-heided cunt Renton, n if ah find oot whaire it's comin fae, ah'll no be pittin it Power's wey, ah'll be dumpin it in the fuckin Forth n droonin the cunts fuckin well puntin it!

So ah heads right back doon tae the motor. Nelly's reading the *Record* n eatin a bacon roll. Cunt nivir even sais eh wis gittin a fuckin roll. We'd aw like tae fuckin well sit thaire readin the paper n eatin fuckin bacon rolls! Wide cunt. So ah tells um thit wir gaun back tae the boozer. Cunt looks aw snidey n goes, — Power tell ye it's goat tae go in?

— Power telt us fuckin nowt, ah tells the cunt, n that shuts his fuckin pus.

Nelly does that slow noddin ay the heid he ey does whin the cunt's impressed but disnae want tae say. He takes a bite ootay his roll. The cunt kens thit that means thit it's me thit's Power's main fuckin man in Leith, no him, even though that means fuckin nowt tae me. Whin wi gits back doon tae the pub, ah tell um tae keep the fuckin motor runnin.

Ah goes inside n takes Dickie through the back tae the office. — It's aw sorted, nae fruit machine's gaun in here.

— Thanks, son, but ye shouldnae huv went tae any trouble, he whines, n he's gaun oan aboot muh uncle n muh ma n grandma, right until ma heid stoatin intae his fuckin coupon shuts the auld cunt right up. The specs fly offay his face n hit the flair, n ah've goat ma hands roond that

scrawny auld throat n ah'm throttlin him ower the desk. — Ahh . . . ah
. . . Frank . . . ah'll take it . . . ah'll take the fruit mach—

— AH DINNAE WANT YE TAE TAKE THE FUCKIN
MACHINE! Then ah lits ma voice go doon tae a whisper: — Ah telt
ye: that's aw fuckin well sorted oot!

— Heeeuughhh . . . Francis . . . heeeuughh . . . it's . . . dinnae . . .

— But if you fuckin well mooth oaf aboot Power again, ah haul the
auld cunt doon oantae the deck n boot um in the ribs, — that fuckin
fruit machine is the least ay yir fuckin worries! Right?!

— Ri-right . . . the auld cunt gasps.

Ah boots the fucker again, n he lits oot this big groan n starts pukin
up. Thaire's nae real buzz fae daein an auld cunt, but ah hate the bastard
fir pittin us in this fuckin position, so he takes a fair auld leatherin.

Eftir a bit, ah realises it's jist ma auld Uncle Dickie, the gadge that took
us up tae the Salon fir the pictures and Easter Road fir the fitba, when
ma auld man never gied a fuck n couldnae be ersed leavin the fuckin
boozer. So ah helps um up n finds the specs, pits thum oan um, gits him
oot intae the bar. — Ah'm sorry, Frank . . . sorry tae pit ye in this position . . . he wheezes.

Ah kin smell the fuckin whiff n realise thit the auld cunt's pissed hissel. Like a fuckin jakey! Mingin auld bastard! A big dark wet stain, right
acroas the auld cunt's baws n thighs. The lassie oan the bar looks like she's
gaunny fuckin well shite hersel. — Ye awright, Mr Ellis?

— Aye . . . it's okay, Sonia . . . take charge the now . . .

— Does he fuckin look awright? ah snaps at the dozy fuckin hoor.
— He's hud a bad faw. Ah'm takin him up tae the hoaspital.

So ah gits the moanin auld cunt intae the bogs, n tells um tae clean
up best he fuckin well kin before gittin um oot the side door n intae the
back ay the motor. Nelly looks at him. — Auld Dickie goat a fright n
pished hissel, ah goes. Nelly says nowt, but ye kin tell wi the look he gies
Dickie he's no that fuckin well impressed wi him either. Too right. Fuckin
disappointment tae me, that auld cunt.

Skin and Bone

At the kitchen table, Cathy Renton silently gaped into space, smoking her cigarette, occasionally pretending to read the *Radio Times*. Her husband Davie could hear his own breath, heavy with fatigue and stress, over the bubbling pot of stovies on the hob. Time seemed to hesitate, as frail and weary as either of them; Davie found the burden of his wife's silence even more heartbreaking in its insidious, levelling way than her sobs and tortured soliloquies. Standing in the doorway, letting his fingers pick at the paint on the frame, he considered just how much they had all interacted through Wee Davie. Now he was gone, and Billy, idle and unsettled in civilian life since his army discharge, was in bother with the police. As for Mark, well, he didn't even want to think about what he was up to down in London.

His middle son had become a stranger to him. As a kid it had seemed that Mark, studious, obliging and with a cogent serenity, was the one who embodied the pre-eminent qualities of both he and Cathy. But a contrary, wilful streak was always apparent. While lacking Billy's upfront aggression, a colder aspect was often visible in Mark. He was odd with Wee Davie, seeming repelled and fascinated by him in equal measures. With adolescence's onslaught his secretive nature had acquired an underhanded, calculating feel. Davie Renton optimistically believed that we all hit a point in life where we strived to become the best possible versions of ourselves. Neither of his remaining sons had gotten to that junction yet. He hoped that by the time they did, they hadn't ventured too far down the wrong track to get back. It wasn't that he didn't understand the respective angers of Billy and Mark. The problem was he understood them only too well. It was Cathy's love, he thought, watching the blue smoke rising from the tip of her cigarette, that had been his own get-out-of-jail-free card.

Dismayed to see a pile of filthy dishes soaking in the sink's cold, stagnant water, Davie moved over, busying himself on them, his Brillo pad rasping against the stubborn waste encrusted onto china and aluminium. Then he felt something he hadn't for a long time: his wife's arms as they wrapped themselves around his expanding waist. — Sorry, she breathed softly into his shoulder. — Ah'll sort maself oot.

— It takes time, Cathy. I know that, he said, his finger tracing a vein on the back of her hand, which he pressed as if to urge her to continue talking.

— It's just . . . she hesitated, — wi Billy getting intae bother n Mark bein away in London . . .

Davie turned round, breaking her grip, but only to take Cathy in his own arms. He stared into her big, haunted eyes. The light from the window revealed some new lines in her face, and some of the older ones cutting a little deeper. He pulled her head into his chest, not just to comfort her, but because this sudden confrontation with her mortality was too much for him to endure. — What's wrong, love?

— When ah wis doon at the church, the other day, lighting a candle for Wee Davie . . .

David Renton senior forced himself not to roll his eyes or unleash an exasperated breath, his habitual responses when he learned that his wife had been at St Mary's.

Cathy raised her head, digging her sharp chin into his collarbone. Her body felt so slight against him. — Ah saw the laddie Murphy thaire, she coughed, wriggling free from his embrace, moving over to the ashtray on the table and crushing out the last of her cigarette. She briefly hesitated, and then promptly lit another, with a semi-apologetic shrug. —Ye should've seen the mess ay um, Davie, he looked terrible; skin and bone. He's been taking that heroin – Colleen telt me when ah saw her in the Canasta. She flung him oot, Davie, he wis stealin fae her. Her rent money, her club money wi the Provi . . .

— That's terrible, Davie said sadly, thinking of his own mother alone, in that house in Cardonald, then Mark, on a couch in some dismal squat' in a far-off city which briefly flared with menace in his imagination, before he converted that vision into a swish flat full of swinging metropolitan professionals. — It just makes me gled that Mark's in London wi Simon, away fae that waster!

— But . . . but . . . Cathy's face creased into a self-caricature that unnerved him. — . . . Colleen said thit Mark wis the same wey!

— No way! He's no *that* stupid!

Cathy's eyes and mouth stretched, pulling the skin on her face taut. — It sort ay explains a lot, Davie.

Davie Renton couldn't bear to hear this. It just couldn't be true. — No, he shook his head in grave finality, — no oor Mark. Colleen's just

282

upset at whit's happened tae Spud, she wahnts tae make oor Mark a scapegoat!

The lid grumbled, farted and rattled against the pot, and Cathy was over to the cooker, reducing the heat and giving the stovies a stir. — That wis what ah thoat, Davie, but still . . . ah mean, ye ken how secretive he is. She looked at him. — It took him ages tae tell us aboot packin in the university . . . n then thaire was that girl he was seein . . .

Davie gripped the windowsill. Leaned forward, felt the pressure in his tense shoulders as he looked wistfully outside. — You know, he spoke to his ghostly reflection, — ah used tae think that if he brought shame on this hoose it would be through getting a lassie pregnant or something, ah never thoat it wid be drugs.

— Ah know, ah know . . . sometimes he jist seems awfay weird . . . sometimes . . . Cathy pushed out some smoke from her lungs, — . . . ah mean that thing wi Wee Davie . . . that wis twisted. Ah ken it's an awfay thing tae say aboot yir ain flesh n blood, n ah love him tae bits, ah wis that proud when he went tae the university . . . but . . .

Davie rested his forehead against the cool glass pane. He recalled his last conversation with Mark, his tones high and distressed, telling his son they were planning to shut the door on the working classes in education. How it was the last chance for people like him to get a degree without being in hock to the banks for the rest of their lives.

Mark had just kept repeating 'aye . . . aye . . . aye . . .' as he crudely stuffed clothes into his holdall, then came out with his usual nonsense about starting a band in London, just like the last time he went down there. — That punk rock shite's tae blame, it's that rubbish that turned his heid, Davie Renton mused, turning from the window, recounting the proposition he'd put to his son, — Tear everything doon; aye, fair enough, but what are ye gaunny pit in its place?

— Drugs, Cathy cried, — that's aw thir pittin in its place!

Davie shook his head, — Ah cannae see it but, Cath. He's in London wi Simon. Thir baith gaunny be startin oan the boats soon. They'll no let junkies on a boat, Cath. Dae ye want somebody whae's hallucinatin on heroin, shootin up that LSD or whatever they call it, talkin tae pink elephants aw day when thir tryin tae sail a boat? No way. This is the *sea*. Thi'll no tolerate that sort ay thing at *sea*, Cathy. They have tests for that sort ay thing. Naw, it's just that daft bloody hash. It makes him dopey. Wi his bloody brains n aw.

— Ye think so?

— Aye, course ah do. He's no *that* stupid!

— Cause ah couldnae take it, Davie, Cathy gasped, stabbing out one fag and lighting another. — No eftir Wee Davie. No wi oor Billy up in coort!

— Simon's doon thaire, he'll steer him awright, n thaire's Stephen Hutchison fae that band n aw, he's a nice laddie, they widnae git mixed up in anything –

The phone's shrill ring from the lobby halted Davie. Cathy ran to pick it up. It was her sister. They would talk for ages, Davie considered, comparing misfortunes. Feeling redundant, he left the house to walk down by the docks.

The port, swathed in an omnipresent drizzle, had become a home from home, reminding Davie of his native Govan. He recalled how he'd come east to be with Cathy, moving all those years ago from tenement to tenement and shipyard to shipyard, getting work at Henry Robb's. The old yard was now deserted; it had shut down a couple of years ago, bringing to an end over six hundred years of shipbuilding in Leith. He was one of the very last men to be paid off.

Wandering around old Leith's complex maze of streets, kicking through the thaw's debris, Davie marvelled at the disparate buildings constructed by the merchants who'd brought the wealth into Edinburgh city, when it owed its good fortune to maritime trade. Great stone contructions with gilded domes and pillared, pseudo-Athenian temples proliferated. They were once churches or railway terminals like the Citadel Station Davie trudged past, but now temporarily designated shops or community centres, covered in tawdry, incongruous fluorescent-coloured posters advertising bargains or activities. Many were in disrepair, succumbing to vandalism and neglect, now augmented by rashes of public housing; cheerless sixties utilitarian designs. Consequently, there was nowhere else in the world that looked quite like Leith. But the place was a ghost town. Davie looked down a set of old railtracks leading into the defunct docks, recalling the swarms of men toing and froing from the shipyards, docks and factories. Now, a pregnant girl rocking a pram on a street corner argued with a flat-topped youth in a shell suit. A lonely baker's shop in a rash of TO LET retail outlets had one window smashed in and boarded up. A woman in brown overalls and stiff lacquered hair looked warily out at him as if he were responsible. A stray black dog sniffed at some discarded wrappers, displacing two seagulls, who screeched in protest as they glided above him. Where had all the people gone? he wondered. Indoors or hiding, or down in England.

As the urban gravity of central Scotland seemed to inevitably dictate,

Davie Renton found himself in a pub. It wasn't one that he frequented. A vague, distressing odour lingered about the place, detectable through a fug of cigarette smoke. However, it was a tidy shop in other ways, the bar and tables gleaming with polish. The barmaid was a pretty young girl, whose bashful and awkward demeanour suggested her that looks were a recent acquisition she'd yet to fully grow into. He felt for her, working in a pub like this, and forced up a cheery front as he ordered a pint of Special and a whisky, surprising himself by his actions, as he seldom drank with gusto these days. It was a young man's game, best done when you were free from nagging thoughts of your own mortality. But he finished it quickly, and requested the same again, staying at the comforting bar. It was good. Davie felt warm and numb. It was slipping down easily.

As the barmaid refurnished him with drinks, he saw his oldest son, Billy, in the corner with his mates, Lenny, Granty and Peasbo. He nodded and they gestured him over, but he waved them away, content to let them do their own thing, as he picked up a discarded copy of the *Evening News*, which lay on the bar. The young men emanated power and confidence, but unemployment had shrunk their horizons to their locality, while making them angry and restless. The devil did indeed make work for idle hands, as his Wee Free grandmother from Lewis had been fond of saying.

A man had emerged from the office to take up pole position behind the bar. From the corner of his eye, Davie realised he was staring at him. He looked up and saw the ex-copper who ran the pub. — Miners, eh? he smiled mirthlessly at Davie, pointing at the NUM badge on his lapel, the one he'd been given at Orgreave. — Maggie got those lazy bastards sorted right oot!

His words stung Davie Renton at the core of his soul. He felt another version of himself, long discarded fifty miles back on the M8 motorway, rising to the surface of his skin. His features stiffened and grew coarser. He witnessed a hint of trepidation on Dickson's face, which combusted into anger when Davie coldly mentioned an incident where a policeman had been hacked to death in a London riot. — Heard one ay your boys lost the heid doon south.

Dickson stood hyperventilating on the spot for two seconds. — Ah'll show ye losin the heid, ya Weedgie bastard, he snapped. — Get the fuck oot ay here!

— Dinnae worry, Davie smiled stiffly, – this place stinks ay scabby bacon, and he stared evenly at Dickson, before slowly finishing his drink, then turning and walking outside, leaving the landlord seething.

As he headed back towards the deserted shipyard, distress gnawed at

Davie Renton, now almost in tears when he thought of the decapitated policeman, his family and widow. How, in a moment of rage, he'd shamefully used this man's horrific death at the hands of a demented, hateful mob as a way of hitting back at that creep in the pub. What had happened to this country? He thought of his father's generation, where men of all classes had stood together against the greatest tyranny known to the human race. (Though one class, as always, had borne disproportionate casualties.) The *esprit de corps* engendered by two world wars and an expansive empire now seemed a long way away. We were slowly, but irrevocably, coming apart.

When the boys in the corner had seen Davie come into the pub, Lenny had run a narcissistic hand through his crop of sandy hair. He'd turned a crimson, high-blood-pressure face to Billy. — Yir auld man no comin ower?

— Naw, ah think he's jist in tae git oot the hoose, Billy had said, a bit miffed, as he loved his dad's companionship in a pub. The old man was never an imposition; far from it, he was the life and soul, always with a good tale to tell, but never hogging the floor, a great listener and full of banter. It distressed him to think his dad might assume that he bored the younger men. — The auld girl's been crackin up since Wee Davie died, n oor Mark fuckin oaf tae London husnae helped.

— How's he gittin oan doon thaire? Peasbo, angular-faced and flinty-eyed, had enquired, casting a shifty glance to the door as a cloth-capped pensioner entered and creaked his way slowly to the bar.

— Fuck knows.

— Saw his mate Begbie in the Tam O'Shanter the other day, gaun oan about some cunts fae Drylaw that did his Uncle Dickie, Lenny smiled slyly, fixing Billy in his gaze, — Jambos seemingly, he half jokingly accused. — Spat on Joe Baker's picture, so Dickie got stroppy n pilled them up. The boys gied him a real leatherin. Broad daylight n aw.

Though sensing his buttons were being pushed, Billy reacted anyway. — Ah'll check that oot next week at the Merchy Herts Club before the game. See if ah kin git some names fir Franco. Ah hate youse Hibby bastards, he only partly jested in retort, — but it's no right daein that tae an auld man, especially faimlay . . .

Lenny nodded in approval, locking his hands together and cracking his knuckles, displaying sinewy, cord-like muscles in his long arms. — Well, Franco Begbie isnae the kind ay cunt anybody wants tae git oan the wrong side ay.

They'd acknowledged this point and sipped at their drinks. Billy had looked across to his dad again, thought about trying one more time to entice the stubborn auld cunt over for a peeve. He couldn't get Davie's eye though, engrossed as he was in the paper. Then the next time Billy Renton saw his father, he was exiting from the bar. Distracted and angry, he hadn't even acknowledged them as he'd went. There had been some sort of exchange with Dickson, the landlord, which Billy had half witnessed, putting it down to pub banter. *Maybe no,* he thought, as he watched the still swinging pub doors.

Billy turned his gaze back to the bar. He knew Dickson from the Lodge. He'd always been okay with him, but he was a funny cunt and a known liberty-taker. Springing up from his seat, Billy hastily headed across the floor, towards the counter. Noting his swift movements, his friends looked to each other in confirmation that the weather had gotten stormier.

— What was up wi the boy there, Dicko? Billy asked, nodding back to the door.

— Jist some fuckin mingin jakey. Dirty commie Weegie bastard. Telt him tae fuck off oot ay here.

— Right, Billy nodded thoughtfully, then headed for the toilet. He took a long piss, looking at his face in the mirror above the latrine. He'd had a big row with Sharon over money last night. She didn't want him back in the army, but there was fuck all for him here. She wanted a hoose. A ring. A bairn. Billy himself was as keen to move on to the next phase of his life as she was. He was tiring of things as they stood; drinking, talking shite, punching radges, watching his jeans size go from a 32 to a 34 and tightening still. A house and a kid would be good. But that took money. She didn't seem to get that. Unless you wanted to live like a fuckin tramp on the state with no self-respect, it all took *money.* And when you had no money, everybody, *every single cunt,* seemed to be takin the fuckin pish. Sharon, Mark, the mouthy twat at the Elm and now this fuckin ex-bizzy prick at the bar.

Billy finished, zipped up, washed his hands and returned to the bar. He flashed an insurance man's smile at the landlord. — Hi, Dicko, you'll never guess what, that auld jakey ye flung oot, he's gone roond the back n he's sittin on one ay the beer barrels, rat-arsed. Ah think he's done a pish oot there.

Dickson sprung to alertness. — Is he now? he waxed in anticipation. — Ah'll show that cunt! Doesnae ken ah've got him just where ah fuckin well want him! And he hurried towards the side exit to the yard, followed by Billy.

287

In the small, paved quadrangle, Dickson glared around in confusion. Looked behind the stacked empty barrels. The place was otherwise deserted. His eyes registered that the back brown door to the side street was bolted from the inside. Where was that auld cunt? He turned round to face Billy Renton. — Where is that mingin bastard?

— He's away, Billy said quietly, — but his son's here.

— Aw . . . Dickson's mouth fell open. — . . . Ah didnae ken it wis your dad, Billy, it was a mistake –

— Fuckin right it wis, Billy Renton noted as he booted Dickson full force in the balls, watching the publican turn red and gasp, holding his testicles and collapsing to his knees on the cold stone floor. Billy's second kick knocked Dickson's two front teeth clean out, and loosened a few more.

Lenny and Peasbo had followed Billy out and, quickly surveying the situation, weighed in with a couple of hefty boots each on the prone figure, to show solidarity with their friend. Big Chris Moncur came out to investigate and looked on, lips twisting in a grin. Alec Knox, an old drunkard who'd experienced Dickson's manhandling on several occasions, took cold revenge with two vicious kicks to the head of the insentient landlord's spreadeagled body.

Peasbo strode back through to the bar, nodded at Granty, and brushing the barely protesting barmaid aside, opened the cash register, snaffling notes and pound coins, while Lenny, following behind, grabbed a bottle of whisky from the gantry and hurled it through a mounted television screen. Three old boys playing dominoes close by shuddered as they looked up briefly to the source of the impact, then went back to their hand, as Granty shot them a fire-starting glare. The group of assailants quickly departed, with instructions to staff and regulars of what to tell the police. The consensus was that three Jambos from Drylaw perpetuated the damage to the landlord and his property.

The Chute

The brighter mornings don't make this place look any better, and it's whiffy as a wrestler's jockstrap. Every cunt just throws the rubbish in the corner; there's a poxy little plastic bucket under that pile of crap somewhere, and it's been a bleedin war of attrition ta see who's gonna crack first and tidy up. And all those farking beer bottles.

The phone rings. I pick it up.

— Is Simon there? Another posh bird's voice.

— Not at the moment. Can I take a message?

— Can you tell him that Emily Johnson from South Ken tube station was trying to get in touch? And she gives me a number, which I scribbles down on the notepad beside the rest.

I goes ta the kitchen and I can't stand it any longer. I get a couple of bin liners and start filling them up.

— Did you get your Hackney giro, Nicksy? Rents asks, the farking div, wandering around in his underpants and T-shirt with his skinny legs, like a milk-bottle ginger Jock Biafran.

— Nah, it ain't farking well come yet, I tell him as I'm heading out with the rubbish to the chute, cause those fuckers won't shift their arses from neither couch nor mattress. All these cunts been doing is farking gear; stupid fuckers seem ta think smoking skag don't count, and we gotta start work on Monday. I'm putting myself on the farking line here, with that Marriott geezer. If they fack it up . . .

— Who was oan the blower?

— Some other posh tart for Sick Boy, need ya ask, I tell him, stepping outside. It's still a bit nippy, but spring's definitely in the air.

All of a sudden I hears this high-pitched whine, and when I get to the stairwell I see these little herberts have got this puppy, a tiny black thing, and they're putting it in the farking rubbish chute! A cute little black Lab n all! — Oi! You little fackers!

I run to them but this farking scumbag drops it and it yelps as they shut the door on it and when I yank it open it's disappeared, like a rabbit in a magician's hat. You can hear a descending squeal, all the fark-

ing way down. — You cunt! I turn on the little bastard, absolutely farking livid.

— My mum says I gotta get rid of it, innit, says this urchin.

— Take it back ta the farking pet shop, you dozy little troll!

— It's shut, innit. My mum said if I came back with it here she'd kill
me!

— Farking wally . . . I jump in the lift with the bags, and I ain't gonna
put nuffink down there on top of that little puppy. I get down ta the
rubbish room. It's locked and there ain't no collection till Monday. Could
it have survived the fall? But the rubbish would be mostly soft garbage.
I gotta check. I drop the bin liners outside the door. It's cold out here. I
can't think. I go back into the stair. Fack! I see *her* coming out the lift.
Alone. Blue jacket. Fag in hand. Marsha.

She looks like shit. Her eyes are all puffy n swollen. — Marsha, stop.
Wait.

— What *you* want? she says, turning away from me as if I'm farking
nuffink.

I stand looking at her. — I wanna talk ta ya. About . . . the baby.

She swivels back round and looks me in the eye. — There ain't no
baby, is there? Not no more, and she pulls her yellow T-shirt tight to her.

— Wot you talking about? Wot happened?

With a big farking sneer, she goes, — Got rid of it, didn't I?

— You wot?

— Mi mam was sayin dere's too many babies havin babies roun here.

— A bit farking late, wasn't it?

— A'll ya need ta knows is it's gan.

— How? What d'ya mean?

— I ain't fucking talking ta you bout nuffink, she suddenly explodes
in a loud squeal. — Get the fuck outta my face!

— But we gotta talk abaht this . . . we was –

— What's ta farking talk abaht? she says, but in estate London. — I
was seein ya, now I ain't. I was havin a baby, now I farking well ain't.

— You was put up to this by somebody! That was my farking kid n
all, didn't I have no farking say in the matter?

— Nope, you fucking well didn't, she shouts, a look of raw fucking
hatred on her face.

My farking kid n all . . .

I feel the pulse racing through me body, as I watch her turnin away
and walkin off through the stair door with a strut, her tight little arse
moving slowly in those jeans, doing the catwalk model thing, like she's

just taking the farking piss. — Please come back, babe, I hear myself say, following her outside.

I dunno if she can hear me, but she don't look round and she don't stop moving off, down the path between Fabian and Ruskin houses.

Then I hears this breathing noise and look down ta find this big Alsatian sniffing around me bollocks. A thickset skinhead looks over at me. — Hatchet! Leave it!

The dog turns away and bounds towards him, and I think again about the little puppy trapped in the rubbish. I hurry back up ta the flat where Mark and Sick Boy are sitting on the couch, smoking gear off the foil. Jesus Christ, at this time of farking day. — Celebrations . . . working men, Mark says, all farking ripped. — A wee celebration, Nicksy.

I didn't want no farking kid, she did the right thing. I just wanted to help, that's all. To be kept in the bleedin picture . . .

Sick Boy's talking to himself, in that rambling, junked-up way. — That Lucinda, it's like the worse ye treat her the mair she wants ye; total daddy complex. Could pimp her oot easy. Like some ay they wee hairies around here, eh, Nicksy . . . only this yin would be quids in . . . quids in, ya cunt . . .

Rents puts the foil pipe down on the coffee table. Then he starts waffling n all. — Ah hud tae gie Begbie career advice oan fuckin criminality at New Year. Me! That's ma problem; ah'm too fuckin poncy tae be a proper Leith gadgie n too fuckin schemie tae be an arty student type. My whole life is betwixt and between . . . He slumps back into the couch.

I stand in front of them. — Listen, I cut in, — I need you two ta stand guard on a couple ay floors. Floor fifteen and floor fourteen. Don't let any cunt put rubbish down the chute.

Of course, Mark starts farking protesting. — But *Crown Court's* on in a minute.

— Fark *Crown Court*! There's a puppy trapped in the rubbish downstairs! Fucking useless junky cunts!

As I tear out I can hear Mark saying, — Speed psychosis. Classic symptoms.

Cheeky cunt; it's these Jock fuckers, doing my farking head in! I get downstairs again, sharpish. The caretakers ain't been here for a long time cause of council cutbacks, but there's a big black woman I talk ta on the stairs who tells me that a Mrs Morton on the second floor has got keys for the waste room. — It wan ah dem chunky T-shaped tings.

I gotta hurry or the dog, and this is assuming the poor little cunt has survived the fall, will get buried under more rubbish, or crushed by empty

bottles. I get ta the second floor and at Flat 2/1 there's the name –
MORTON – on the door. I gives it a bang and before long a stocky
barrel of a old gel comes out.

— Mrs Morton?

— Yeah . . .

— I need the keys ta the waste room. Some kids've only gone and put
a puppy down the chute. It's trapped in there.

— Can't help ya, Mrs Morton says, — you'll ave ta see the council.

— But it's Saturday!

— They work Saturdays. Well, some of em does.

I argue the toss, but the old gel ain't budging. At least she lets me in ta
use the phone. I get through ta the council cunts and my blood's soon
boiling, cause when I'm trying to convey the farking seriousness of the
situation, they put me onto the Cleansing Department who put me onta
Housing who transfer me onta Environmental Health, who put me in touch
with the central office, who tell me to see the local area office, who then
say that it really should all go through the farking RSPCA! And all the
time this Mrs Morton's glowering at me, then at the clock on her wall.

I'm sweating like a rapist thinking about that poor little dog and I
phone me mate Davo who works for the council; thank fuck he's on OT
today. — Don't care how ya do it, mate, but I need ya ta get us the key
ta the bins room at Beatrice Webb House on my estate at Holy Street.
Like yesterday.

Fair play to Davo, he don't even ask no questions. — I'll try. Hang fire
der and I'll get back to yer on dat number. Warrisit?

I cough out the number and I'm standing in this old gel's draughty
hallway trying to reason with her, as she wants to throw me out. — I
didn't say ya could give out me number, she moans, — I don't like givin
out me number, not ta strangers.

— It ain't strangers, it's the council.

— They're bloody strangers round ere!

— You ain't wrong, I tell her, and she starts droning on about how
badly she's been treated by them over the years, which is fair enough, but
all I'm thinking about is Marsha and that poor little pooch.

Fifteen minutes later the phone rings and it's Davo, God bless that nasal
Scouse whine, and blow me if he ain't sorted it all out. — The key's on
its way round to yer in a minicab. You'll have ta pay the friggin driver,
but its only come from the Neighbourhood Housing Office so it'll just
be two quid. I need it back in me hand by five o' clock today.

— I owe ya big time, mate.

— Too friggin right.

As I put the blower down, I leave the old gel, putting some change by her phone, and I get ta the bottom of the flats. It's got really bollock cold again, and I button up me overcoat. I ain't waiting too long before a Turkish geezer pulls up in a cab, flashing the key, a big farking solid thing which I stick in me pocket sharpish and square him up.

I open up the big heavy black wooden door, and holy fucking hell, the place smells. There's a switch and I click it on and a sick, yellow overhead light floods the room. I look ahead to the big aluminium bucket on wheels. It's about seven foot high. How the fark am I gonna get up there?

Then I see there's loads of crap discarded furniture piled up along the walls. I lock the door behind me so I don't get no herberts snooping round and disturbing me. The farking ming is overpowering and I'm gagging for a bit, before I start ta get used ta it, after a fashion. I pull over an old sideboard, jump on it, and look into the bin. It's almost full to the top with shit. There's loads of fucking flies, huge bastards, buzzing around me and battering off me face, like I was one of them kiddies in Africa. But I can't see no dog. — Here, boy . . . here, boy.

I can't hear nuffink. I climb in and my feet sink down into the compressed shit. My guts go into spasm, I'm shaking with nausea; it's like a farking fever. I put my hand up against the top of the chute's shaft to steady mesel and it's covered in some kind of farking putrid excrement. I retch again, then try and wipe off as much as I farking can. This is farking horrible; there's everything here; nappies, household garbage, jam rags, used condoms, bottles, fag ends and spud peelings everywhere. Everything except the farking puppy.

Suddenly there's a big smashing sound coming from above and I have to duck back against the side of the bin as a load of bottles come whizzing and crashing down. Cunts could've farking killed me! Probably came from the top floors I told them useless farking Scotch cunts to farking well guard! The stench is vile; it burns my nostrils and all this grit's flying inta me eyes, blinding me.

A farking pit bull in a suit of armour couldn't have survived this. Poor little fucker'll be smashed and buried under all this crap. I breathe in and the old dirt and fag ash swirling around in the backdraught from the chute gets in my lungs and I cough and puke up. I can only see out of one watery eye. This is making me farking ill, and I'm about to give up when I suddenly hears this faint whimpering. I dig a bit more, then pull back some wet newspaper and it's the little dog, lying in crushed eggshells, old tea bags and potato peelings. Its big eyes look up at me. But it's got something in its mouth.

I feel my stomach contents rising again and I slam the brakes on cause it's got hold of this farking floppy doll thing. It's about twelve inches long with a big head and skinny rubbery limbs. It's like a space alien covered in tomato sauce and dirt and all sorts of gunge. Its leg's in the dog's mouth. I don't like the farking look of this. My blood goes all cold and I can hear it pound it me head. The way this thing's leg hangs in the pup's jaws . . . its eyes are shut, but the blue lids are sorta bulging out. It's got black, matted hair. There's a wound on the side of its head, a big hole in the flesh with shit seeping out. This ain't no farking doll. It looks like –

It's got me in its mouth –

By the leg –

My little face –

Her little face –

I can't move. I just sit there in the rubbish, looking at the puppy and this bloody red, coffee-coloured and blue thing it's chewing on. The dog lets it go and comes to me. I pick him up, tucking him under me chin. He feels warm and makes little soft whines and I can see the hot breath coming out his tiny nostrils in the cold air.

I'm still looking at the thing lying in the rubbish. Its eyes shut, like it's at peace, sleeping.

I don't farking well . . .

It ain't a baby. I ain't that fucking daft. You'd have ta be one sick cunt ta call this thing a kid; it's way, way short of that. But that ain't ta say that some respect ain't bleedin well called for. It don't feel right leaving it here like rubbish, like a dirty farking filthy slag would.

Oh my God, what has she farking well done?

I dunno what to do, but I gotta get out, as another parcel of shit comes crashing down from above and thumps against me back. The puppy's licking me hand and I tuck it under me arm and climb out. I leave the room, locking the door behind me.

I'm stinking of rubbish as I walk for ages with the dog under me coat. The sun goes down and it's freezin as I find myself heading up by the canal. The dog's stopped whining now, it must've been cold. It feels like he's fallen asleep. All I can think about is that thing back in the chute. First why, then how and after that when. Dates. Times. The Neighbourhood Housing Office ain't far, n I drop the key off at the reception. The girl on the desk stares at me like I'm a cunt, like she's about ta dig me out, but she don't. I suppose I ain't looking too clever; I'm farking stinking, covered in all sortsa shit, wearing this old coat with a puppy peeking out of it. I'm right outta there; I go back ta the canal.

What can I farking do . . . what was she farking thinking about . . . ? It was too far gone, it's against the farking law, surely . . .

I keep walking along the bank, under the bridges, and it's starting ta get dark. The puppy starts crying, in long pathetic whines that get louder. I leaves the canal, stopping off at a Spar for some dog food. I've come the full circle back down ta the flat, and head up in the lift. I get in and put the puppy on the floor and head into the kitchen to spoon out some grub for the little cunt . . .

— Did your giro no come yet, Nicksy, cause, cairds oan the table time, ah need a sub, mate . . . Renton goes, then clocks the dog, sniffin around on the floor. — We've got a dug! That's barry, he says, big, dark circles under his eyes, then he tells me, — You are mingin, by the way.

— God, aye, Nicksy, ye really are, Sick Boy agrees.

I can't farking very well dispute that. The dog's licking Rents's hand, and they play with him half-heartedly. — Let's call him Giro . . . Renton says. As I put the pup's food down in a soup bowl, I see that they're smoking some more gear.

— Ah like the pipe, Rents says. — Ah've goat shite viens. That's how ah cannae gie blood, it takes them ages tae find it.

— A total waste ay gear, Sick Boy argues. — Maist ay the stuff just burns intae the air. But ah kin take or leave skag. Ah'm jist daein this cause it's oor first day at work oan Monday.

— Can't you cunts do farking nuffink? Eh?

— Geez a fuckin brek. Sick Boy points to the kitchen. — They beer bottles that huv been lyin around for months have gone, he points all proud at himself, — cause guess whae's jist eftir throwin thum away!

— You wot?

The cunt could've farking killed me!

I'm standing with me fists balling up in rage but they don't even notice. I take off me coat. I hit the foil pipe, taking that shit back inta me lungs and me head and suddenly everything's better. I ain't even bothered that cunt Sick Boy's on the blower ta farking Scotland now, running up the bill. — Of course I'm eating enough now, Mama, eating enough for two. No, naebody's pregnant. No bambinos. He puts his hand over the phone. — Jesus Cunty Baws Christ! Italian mothers!

I go through ta the room, carrying me coat. I'm sitting with me head in me hands trying ta bleedin think. I can't hear for that racket they got on. It's the Pogues album. I go through and ask them ta turn it down.

— It's *Red Roses for Me* but, Nicksy, ah pit it oan for this track, 'Sea Shanty', cause we're gaunny be seafarin men! Mark says, going through me Northern Soul singles for the upteenth time. — These really do rule, Nicksy.

I have a little smile ta mesel as Mark passes the pipe again; I'm up for a good blast this time. Me lungs and then me head fill up with the shit. I sit back in the chair, enjoying the heavy-limbed, light-headed feeling.

— I couldn't give a monkey's. What's it all about? Music. Waste a time, just lulls ya inta believing that things are less shit than they are. Fucking aspirin against leukaemia, I tell him.

— Barry but, he goes, he ain't listening. Not that I give a monkey's now.

Cause no cunt listens ta any cunt else round here. And what's this farking 'barry' all about? How come ya never see Jocks on TV saying that? I'm thinking as the gear flows through me, calming me right down. The puppy's pissing in the corner and I'm laughing. Mark's shaking his head and going, — This is the good stuff though, Nicksy.

— You can have them, mate, I tell him. I mean it n all. What good they gonna do me?

— Dinnae say that, or they'll be in the shops doon Berwick Street before ye can say skag, Mark laughs, then he seems to take fright realising what he's just said. — I'm no that bad, his voice dips, — keep an eye on Sick Boy but, he whispers, as his mate puts the phone down.

Sick Boy waves away the foil pipe. — I'm off tae make myself look pretty. He does an imitation of this nutty mate of theirs back home, a seriously mad Jock I met at New Year, thrustin out his pelvis. — Fuckin ridin duties the night. Cunt better no be shy!

Poor old Frankie boy's ears must be burning all the way up in Jockland, cause they don't half rip the piss outta him. Not the sort of geezer you'd do that ta his face, though.

— That'll take some time, Rents says, — no the ridin, that'll be ower in seconds, the makin yersel look pretty bit.

Sick Boy flashes a tired V-sign in response as he heads out.

— Is it awright tae gie a mate back in Edinburgh a wee tinkle? Ah'll gie ye the money likes, Renton pleads with a dopey smile, holding a clenched fist ta the side of his face.

— Go ahead, you daft cunt, I tell him, cause I ain't giving a toss now.

— I will then, he smiles with his yellow teeth, — Just as soon as I get another hit ay that pipe . . . this broon . . . dead mellow likes, he says, beckoning the dog over to him, — Giro . . . c'mere the now, pal . . .

barry name for a dug . . . Fuck sake, said ah'd meet Stevie doon the West End later n ah'm Donald Ducked . . . cunt's a straightpeg n aw . . . bound tae ken . . . but jist one wee hit tae git us sorted . . .

And I realise I want another n all, in fact I feel like a starving Russian peasant in a well-stocked French patisserie, cause we got ta start farking *work* on Monday morning.

Waters of Leith

The light came back. It always came back. Lizzie remembered him from school, the football player. He had always seemed like a nice guy, and he was good-looking. But she had been an aspiring artist, continuing her education past the mandatory sixteen, and moving in different circles. From an early age, an invisible membrane of aspiration had been crystallising between them.

Just back at the College of Art, New Year resolutions still intact, Lizzie McIntosh had had been dealt a crippling blow. Taking her portfolio to her tutor's room, she had heard Cliff Hammond in conversation with another male lecturer. About to knock on the half-open door, she had frozen at the mention of her name and had stood listening to them tearing up her life. — . . . stunning-looking girl, but with absolutely no talent whatsoever. I'm afraid people have indulged her, by leading her to believe that she has technical skill and something to offer, when, quite frankly, there's nothing . . . Hammond had said, in those tones of tired disdain she'd heard him deploy on others, without ever believing she'd hear them used about her.

Suddenly, the glass floor Lizzie had built was cracking under her feet and she had felt herself falling. Blood pounding in her head, but a numbness pervading her limbs and face, she'd yanked her hair back into a ponytail, holding it with her fist. Then she'd turned, wondering if she'd find the strength to get down the corridor. She'd left her portfolio against the wall outside his office and walked back down the stairs and out of the college building. It was cold, but Lizzie had been only vaguely aware of this as she'd sat down on a bench in the Meadows, looking at the mud on the shiny leather of her boots. As she'd lifted her head, Lizzie had regarded the weak glow of the moon, waiting impatiently to displace the fading late-afternoon orange sunlight, which shone in spokes through a darkening sky. Could she consider herself an artist now? All that vanity and fanciful indulgence!

She'd barely taken in the football game finishing a few yards away from her. But he'd noticed her, lost in herself, and prayed her distraction would last till the ref blew his whistle and he could quickly ready himself and emerge from the changing room. Tommy Lawrence had sensed that this was his chance, and the fates had been with him; a perfunctory shower, quickly knocking back drinks invitations, and shooting across the park to her lonely figure. Then he was standing over her, his face earnest and handsome under a wet mop of crayon-brown hair.

Lizzie hadn't argued when he had said she looked upset. They had gone for a coffee, and he'd listened. He had noted there was no ire in her tone; she had told her story with a detached grace, or perhaps it had been the shock. Tommy had instinctively known he had to enable Lizzie to find her anger and arrogance again. — It's just his view, one person, he'd told her. — He sounds a right slimy creep. I'll bet he fancies you.

An understanding had started to dawn. This was Cliff Hammond. On more than one occasion, he'd asked her to come for a drink, or a coffee. He had a reputation. It all made sense. She'd rebuffed this egotistical fop, this wrinkly old predator, and now he was striking back in his pathetic, bitter way.

— Well, he's no exactly impartial, is he? He's a sleazebag, Tommy had declared. — You cannae let a wanker like that put ye off!

— No way, Lizzie had said, — no fuckin chance, suddenly realising that this boy had reaffirmed and restored her.

— We should go and get your folder.

— Aye, too fucking right. Lizzie had risen. It all seemed important again. Thanks to Tommy Lawrence from Leith.

The folder had been right where she'd left it the corridor. She had picked it up, just as Cliff Hammond had emerged from his office. — Oh . . . Liz . . . there you are. Didn't we have an appointment over an hour ago?

— Yes. I was there. But I heard you talking to Bob Smurfit.

— Oh . . . Realising Lizzie had an escort, Hammond's face had taken on a paler hue.

Then Tommy had stepped uncomfortably close to him, and Hammond had tensed up, involuntarily taking a backward step. — Aye, we heard a lot ay stuff fae you, Tommy had accused, eyes narrowing.

— I . . . I think . . . there's been a . . . mi . . . Cliff Hammond had stammered, the word 'misunderstanding' caught hopelessly in his throat.

— It's rude tae talk about people behind their back. Especially when it's shite. Do you want tae repeat what ye were sayin?

For a man who stressed art's visceral power, who loved the clutch of young painters currently emerging from Glasgow, Cliff Hammond was devastated to be confronted by his own weakness in the face of righteous indignation. Had Lizzie been alone, he'd have tried to explain, to work something out, but now he felt small and puny beside this tall, fit-looking youth, whose bearing and accent suggested harsh places Hammond had previously just seen as peripheral names on the city map, the terminus on the front of the maroon buses, or settings for a seedy newspaper story; places he would never be inclined to go to. One side of his face had broken into a twitching spasm.

It was that uncontrollable reflex that had saved Hammond from physical violence. Tommy's contempt for Lizzie's tormentor's cowardice had quickly turned into self-loathing at his own bullying. Both men had stood paralysed, before Lizzie had said, — Let's go, Tommy, pulling his sleeve, and they'd left the college for a nearby bar.

So Tommy had come into her life two weeks ago and they'd been inseparable. But any speed Tommy Lawrence had was confined to the football field. So last night, Lizzie had taken matters into her own hands, suggesting they went out drinking, then dragged him to her place and bed. It had been so good to get that out of the way.

Now the late-morning light is shining through the curtains, spreading across them. Lizzie looks at Tommy asleep, his smile a glaze of contentment. Like the books on her shelves and prints on her walls, he promises some sort of paradise. Yet the things she'd heard about him had not been unambiguously good; she knew some of the people he associated with, mainly by reputation. Goodness was not the first quality that came to mind when she thought of them. It might have been the post-coital situation, but could anyone look bad in sleep? Even evil bastards like Frank Begbie probably attained an angelic innocence when they were out for the count. Not that she'd ever want to find *that* out. It's hard to imagine that Tommy, being such a nice guy, was friendly with a nutcase like Begbie. Lizzie can't see why he would associate with people like that.

A pigeon coos noisily from the window ledge and Tommy's eyes spring open. He gratefully fills them with Lizzie, sitting up next to him reading *Slaughterhouse-Five*. She wears reading glasses; he's never seen her in them before. Her curly brunette hair is pinned back. She has a T-shirt on, and he wonders how long she's been awake and if she's somehow put her blue knickers back on. — Hiya.

— Hiya. Lizzie looks down at him with a smile.

He pushes himself up on his elbows, to better take in the airy, scented room.

— Ye want some breakfast? Lizzie asks.

— Aye . . . he hesitates. — Ehm . . . what d'ye fancy?

— I think I've got some eggs in the fridge. Scrambled egg and toast?

— Great.

Then a sudden loud, truculent bang on the door. — Who the fuck can that be? Lizzie angrily wonders aloud, but instantly rises and pulls on a dressing gown. Looks back at Tommy, to catch him looking at her. She is wearing her blue knickers but the sight of her still makes his lips sting.

— Leave it, he pleads.

She considers this. Then that knock again, insistent like a polisman's. — It sounds important.

Lizzie momentarily wonders if her flatmate Gwen will get it, before recalling that she's away for the weekend. That's why she brought Tommy back. She finds her cat-face slippers and goes through to the hallway, as the pounding on the door starts again, matching the rhythm of last night's red wine in her head. — Alright! Ah'm coming!

She opens the door and is astonished to see Francis Begbie standing before her.

— Tommy here?

Lizzie is briefly rendered speechless. She brought Tommy back and now this nutcase knows where she lives!

— Sorry tae disturb ye. Begbie cracks a facsimile of a smile, evidently not sorry at all.

— Wait here, she says, turning away.

Begbie keeps his foot in the door so it won't spring shut on him. Lizzie can feel his eyes tracking her as she moves down the hallway. She gets into the bedroom, where Tommy is getting dressed. He thinks he heard Franco's voice; *surely not.* But Lizzie's scowl, it tells him, *surely yes.* — It's for you.

As Tommy departs, Lizzie seethes, rethinking everything.

— Fuckin result, Tommy boy! Franco bellows as Tommy moves down the hallway. It totally disarms his anger, and Tommy has to fight back the urge to smile.

— What you daein here?

— Thoat ye'd fuckin well be here, ya cunt! Ma cousin Avril steys in this stair: nowt thit fuckin well goes oan in Leith gits past Franco, mind ay that, ya cunt. Fill hoose fuckin last night then, Tommy, eh? Oafay wee teeny drawers n aw! That'll seeken Sick Boy's fuckin pus, ya cunt!

Tommy smiles, glancing back down the hallway. The cold stings his bare arms in his T-shirt. Begbie, though clad in an Adidas tee and thin jacket, doesn't appear at all uncomfortable. — What d'ye want, Franco?

— What the fuck d'ye think? What wis ah fuckin well sayin aw this week, ya daft cunt? Heid too fill ay aw this fanny nonsense, that's your fuckin trouble! Ebirdeen! The day. Easter Road. The YLT: show they wee casual cunts how it's done. You, me, Saybo, Nelly, Dexy, Sully, Lenny, Ricky Monaghan, Dode Sutherland, Jim Sutherland, Chancy McLean n loads ay other cunts. Larry's oot ay hoaspital! Some fuckin mob! The auld school ur back oan the rampage! Cannae git a fuckin hud ay Spud but he's jist like Renton n Sick Boy doon in London: nae fuckin loss. Fuckin liabilities whin it comes tae the fuckin swedge, they cunts.

Tommy stands agog, listening in disbelief to Franco's spiel.

— Aye, wir aw doon the Cenny right now. Even Second Prize! No drinkin n aw. Meant tae be oaf the peeve; like that's gaunny fuckin last! Hates a bevvy, that cunt. That'll be a laugh, him n that fuckin Ebirdeen cunt that looks like Bobby Charlton, rollin around in the fuckin gutter thegither! Mind ay him, the cunt thit's baldy as fuck at twenty-two?

— Scargill, Tommy says, remembering this plump guy with a frizzy comb-over, leading an Aberdeen ambush in King Street from the Pittodrie Bar. — Ah'll see yis doon thaire later, he says with as much enthusiasm as he can muster.

— Be sure ye fuckin well dae. Franco looks on in accusation. — Thuv brought doon a big fuckin mob, n it's aw hands oan the fuckin deck. Thir no fuckin swaggerin aroond Leith, fuckin well surein thair no. A bunch ay fuckin sheepshaggers wi thair diddy European Cup Winners' Cup, comin doon here, drinkin in oor pubs, chattin up oor . . . Franco hesitates, looks at Tommy.

Tommy can't resist it. — Sheep?

Franco just shuts down for a few seconds. He goes still and silent and the oxygen seems to leave the stair. Then a thin smile dances on his lips. He laughs loudly, allowing Tommy to expel the air he hasn't realised he's been holding on to. — Good yin, ya cunt! Right, mind, jist be thaire, Begbie says, turning abruptly and bouncing down the stairs. He looks back up at Tommy from the stairbend and says in a low, even growl, — Mind, dinnae keep us waitin.

Tommy shuts the door and tries to gather himself. Lizzie's quick appearance with her hands on her hips, and that expression on her face that says, *well?* It shunts him from despondency to desperation. — Franco . . . ah forgot ah'd arranged tae go tae the game with the boys.

— Ah dinnae like fuckin psychopaths comin tae ma door in the morning, Tommy.

— Franco's awright . . . he says half-heartedly. — His cousin steys doonstairs. Avril.

302

— Aye. I know who she is. Three kids and aw wi different faithers . . . she begins in disapproval but his wretched, cartoonish expression of repentance under that chestnut wedge of hair softens her. — We've nae milk.

— I'll go doon for some, he volunteers.

Tommy sticks on his jumper before venturing outside. There is a skip in his step as he emerges from Lizzie's stair. But one thought ignites inside him: *me and Lizzie.* Even Franco can't dampen that. It *is* a result.

The street is slowly coming to life, as bleary party heads who've stayed up all night merge with those making a fresh assault on the weekend. As he passes a phone box, Tommy feels a surge of inspiration, as Franco's words, sly and crass but also thoroughly vindicating, ricochet inside his lit-up skull. *Fill hoose fuckin last night then, Tommy, eh? Oafay wee teeny drawers n aw! That'll seeken Sick Boy's fuckin pus, ya cunt!*

He double-backs to make a call to London. A faraway voice answers, as he drops in the coins. — Hello, hello, it's good to be back . . .

It's Renton. He sounds wasted. — Mark.

— Tommy . . . yir nivir gaunny believe it, ah wis jist gaunny phone ye . . . what did ah jist say tae you, Nicksy?

A cockney voice, which Tommy recognises; *the wee guy we met at Blackpool, the boy that was up at New Year. Nicksy.* — Olroight, Tommy mate? Come dahn ere n take these cunts back up ta Jockoland . . . we gotta bitta farking graft lined up tamorra and them fuckahs ain't able . . .

— Naw, mate, you're stuck wi them now. We dinnae want these bams back up here!

— Another flaming cross ta bear . . . Alright, geezer, see ya . . .

— Cheers, gadge . . .

And then Rents is back on. — How goes bonnie Scotland, Tam?

— The usual. Begbie's oan the fuckin warpath again.

— Aye . . . the boy just needs a wee bit ay love . . .

— Wantin tae go battlin at the fitba wi Aberdeen. It's bad enough wi Lochend n that, now he's wantin us tae fight wi cunts ah dinnae even ken! What's it tae me if these Aberdeen boys batter some gadgie fae Granton or somewhere? Begbie's aw fired up by aw this casuals shite. He's six or seven years aulder than these wee cunts. It's pathetic.

— Ye ken the Generalissimo. Any excuse for aggro. It's his thing . . . Renton collapses into a strange laughter Tommy hasn't heard from him before. — Heuh . . . heuh . . .

— What was that?

— Sick Boy's sayin that he needs tae git rode.

— Makes nae difference. That Samantha Frenchard tramp fae Pilton's hud his bairn and now he's goat that June Chisholm up the stick.

— Aye, but they'd need tae a bit fuckin doolally lettin Franco ride them in the first place. So what aboot youse then? Any serious girl action? Or is it aw still drugs?

A pause. Then Renton says: — Ah ha! Guess whae's shaggin and phonin up jist tae rub it in oor faces!

— Well, aye, ah met somebody the weekend before last. And it's aw goin pri-tay fuckin sweet if ah say so masel.

— Aboot time you got yir Nat King. Anybody we ken?

— Lizzie, Lizzie McIntosh.

— No way!

— Aye way. We're proper gaun oot.

— Jammy cunt! Snobby ultra-shag Lizzie fae ower the Links –

— Whaat . . . he hears Sick Boy saying, — *Tommy's* riding Lizzie Mac?

— Aye, it's mental, Rents goes, then says into the phone, — Ah used tae wank aboot her . . . Did ah tell ye aboot the time ah once caught Begbie wanking ower her at the school sports – no wanking *ower* her physically, or like *ower* her in porn, wanking *aboot* her –

— Ah sais *we're gaun oot*, Mark! Tommy protests, remembering how Rents and Sick Boy together are often a devastatingly cruel combination. While professing to get on each other's nerves, they constantly egg each other on like malevolent twins fixated on the woe of others.

There follows another uncomfortable hiatus on the line, which Renton eventually ends. — Aye . . . eh, sorry, Tam, we should be mair, eh, mature . . . nice yin. Result. Nae riding gaun oan wi me, but Sick Boy . . . well, Sick Boy's Sick Boy, eh?

— Ingloid fanny-fest! Sick Boy shouts defiantly into the phone.

— We've goat a dug but, Renton continues. — Nicksy wanted tae call it Clyde, eftir Clyde Best, cause he's a black Lab, but me n Sick Boy started callin him Giro n that's what he answers tae –

The pips start to rattle. — Right. See ye later, Mark.

— Right . . . Tell Swanney . . . Rents starts to ramble and Tommy enjoys the sensation of the line going dead before he lowers the phone to its cradle.

In the shop Tommy buys some milk and a newspaper. His inclination is the *Record*, but he thinks the *Scotsman* might impress Lizzie more. He picks it up and is about to hand it over to the shop assistant, then decides to swap it for the *Herald* on last-minute considerations of sexism. He doesn't know whether Lizzie is a feminist of some sort, but this early in the gig, it pays to tick every box.

Lizzie versus Begbie. Could anything be less of a contest? At twenty-two he's too old to be fighting boys from Aberdeen, or Lochend for that matter. It's nonsense. You grow out of that shite. That Kevin McKinlay boy from Lochend's sound. He met him recently, playing football. They crossed swords before and on seeing him in the changing rooms at the Gyle, Tommy was geared up for a confrontation or at least a hateful stare and a snub. But the McKinlay boy just nodded and smiled at him, as if to say: *Water under the bridge. Silly boys' stuff. All over now.*

It's different with bams. There's never any water under the bridge. There are no bridges. One day they'll be MALT: Middle Aged Leith Team, and still fighting the old battles of their youth. Not him. Now, for the first time, he's seeing that there really is a way out of this, and it's all so simple. You don't have to run away. You just meet somebody special and step sideways into a parallel universe. Tommy has never been in love before. He'd wanted to with previous girls but he hadn't felt it. Now it's squeezing at every part of him; beautiful, silly, obsessive and taking up all his time and thoughts. He's hungry to get back to Lizzie, with a desperation that completely unnerves him.

Alison, laying down a tray of toast and tea on the glass coffee table, now saw her family home as a hotchpotch of furniture from different eras. In the small front room a seventies teak fireplace jostled for space with a Victorian mahogany chest of drawers, a contemporary oak-framed suite, while the blobs of a sixties lava lamp grew fat before launching themselves north. Her father, Derrick, had never been able to give up on an old piece of furniture, simply shuffling it around the house. Now his mind seemed as full of unconnected clutter as she watched him attempt to interrogate her brother, Calum. — You think ah dunno what yir up tae? Think ah wis born yesterday?

Calum's disdainful look seemed to say: *If ye were born yesterday that would make ye a greetin-faced bairn. So, aye, it sortay fits.*

— Eh? Answer us!

Calum remained mute, having barely spoken two words to anyone since their mother's death. Alison knew this wasn't good. Nonetheless, she sympathised with her brother, hating it when their father was like this. She'd always considered him a clever man, but grief and anger had rendered him stupid. Had he any idea what a spaz he looked with that retarded tache, crouched hung-over in front of the lecky bar fire, that tartan dressing gown hanging over his thin shoulders?

Derrick couldn't hold back another dose of cliché. — It's just that ah dinnae want ye tae make the same mistakes ah did.

— It's only natural, Cal, Alison supportively intervened. — Dad widnae be human if he didnae care . . . right, Dad?

Derrick Lozinska chose to ignore his oldest daughter, remaining focused on his son. Calum's eyes were on the soundless TV where Daffy Duck silently scammed a bemused Porky Pig. — Ye ken fine well what that crowd are. Trouble. Big trouble. Ah ken. Ah seen yis, mind!

This couldn't be contested. Their father regularly bored Alison by recounting his unfortunate witnessing of the Baby Crew in action. That ambush at the Crawford Bridge at Bothwell Street; mob on mob, then in pursuit of an escaping group of Rangers fans. Calum had been to the fore, with a piece of broken stone cladding in his hand. When she'd asked her brother for his version of the events, he hadn't denied it, just retorted that Derrick and his dingul mate shouldn't have been there, as nobody went that way but away fans and boys looking for an off.

Calum hit the handset, changed the channel. Alison looked at the screen. *That auld bag wi aw the make-up oan her coupon's reading the lunchtime news. Funny, she usually does the evenings.*

— A brick in his hand! Ready tae fling it intae a crowd! Derrick appealed to Alison again. She dutifully shook her head, though the image of her brother holding a brick in the street inexplicably amused her.

As Calum looked at his father, Alison could almost *see* his derisive, silent thoughts: *A piece ay stane claddin, ya radge, no a fuckin brick!*

Derrick shuddered, shaking his tired head. — Borstal, that's where he's headed.

— They call it approved school now. Polmont, Calum informed him.

— Dinnae get smart! Disnae matter what they flamin well call it, you're joinin nae casuals, no at this game or any other!

— Ah'm no joinin nowt! Tryin tae listen tae the news . . .

Calum's attention was focused on a shot of a place Alison recognised. It was the Grapes of Wrath pub, down near the Bannanay flats, where Simon came from. She heard Mary Marquis in voiceover, — . . . spearheading a new campaign to prevent local publicans becoming the victims of violence.

Then there was a shot of this old guy, the pub landlord, sitting all spazzy in a wheelchair, drooling out the side of his mouth, talking like a wheezing dummy about how some thugs had done him over and wrecked the boozer. Alison remembered that one: it was rumoured to be three guys from Drylaw, but they were never found.

They cut to this stern-faced polisman, Robert Toal, of Lothian and Borders Polis. — This is just one of the disturbing cases that have recently come to light, where an upstanding member of the community was brutally assaulted and robbed on his own premises, in broad daylight. In this case, the victim's injuries have left him disabled and unable to continue working in the licensing trade. It's sad that people who provide a community service are no longer safe in their own hostelries. Unfortunately, cash-based businesses are extremely vulnerable to this kind of attack.

They cut back to the quashed and downcast Dickson, wretchedly declaring, — All I wanted was to do was ma job ay work . . .

Cut to an exterior shot of the Water of Leith, the sun glinting off the river offering a sedate ambience, before the camera rose slowly to a bleak, disused factory on its banks, evoking an air of ruined menace, and finally, back to Mary in the studio. — A sad tale indeed, she sympathetically declared. — But now over to the sports desk, as we've a full Scottish football fixture card this afternoon. Tom?

— Indeed we do, Mary, said a svelte-looking youngish guy in a suit, — and it's John Blackley's Hibernian who have the unenviable task of trying to derail the all-conquering Aberdeen bandwagon of Alex Ferguson. But if the Hibs boss is nervous at the prospect, he's doing a good job of concealing it . . .

And they cut to Sloop, trademark ginger hair greying slightly at the temples. Alison remembered how he'd come to the school one time, to present some prizes on sports day. She was glad of the Hibs feature; it allowed father and son to continue their temporary truce.

Alison didn't really get the casual thing. Spending money on decent clothes, then rolling around in gutters brawling, it seemed perverse and self-defeating to her. Her dad, after initially approving on the grounds of smartness of dress, soon grew hostile. He confessed that whenever he saw Calum's eyes peeking girlishly out from behind that daft fringe, it just enraged him. Made him want to take a pair of scissors to that hair. There was an *insolence* about it, he argued.

Nonetheless, Calum and Mhairi were going through some kind of hell. They were young, angry and scared. I'm not doing much better, Alison thought, picking up a magazine.

As the feature on Hibs finished, Alison saw Derrick draw in a creaky breath and steel himself, knowing he was going to start on her brother again. — You're gaun tae nae fitba, n that's that. Ah dinnae want ye joinin up wi they . . . he spat the word out, — casuals.

— Ah'm jist gaun tae the fitba wi ma mates!

— Aye, like ye did wi that rock in yir hand? No way. You're still fifteen, no long fifteen, and livin under this roof. God, if your mother was here – Derrick stalled, instantly wishing he could take the words back.

— Well, she's no! Calum sprang to his feet and headed out the door, upstairs to his room.

Derrick weakly crowed his son's name, letting it dissolve into a sigh. He turned to Alison with a perplexed shrug. — Ah dunno what tae dae wi them, Alison, ah really don't.

— They'll be okay. It takes time.

— Thank God you're fine, Derrick said. You were always a mature, sensible lassie, he noted, with a swell of pride.

You don't fucking know me, she thought, as she heard herself register a faint protest. — Dad . . .

— Always was the bright one. Aye, you took charge. Stepped up tae the mark. No Calum and Mhairi but; they're finding it tough. Ah really worry, Derrick shook his head, — that that laddie's gaun oaf the rails.

— Isn't he no just daein the same things you did at that age? They've got new clothes, new slang, different music, but that's aw superficial. They've probably got the odd psycho that's destined tae go down, but for each ay them you'll have a dozen ordinary laddies who'll go through it, n come oot the other side with nowt worse than a few good stories tae tell.

Derrick smiled appreciatively at his daughter. — You've got a point. He appeared to acknowledge her wisdom, then shook his head. — But it's nonsense; he has tae be telt. Ah hate tae say it, but he's no strong like you or me. There's something ay the victim aboot him, he contended.

All Alison could do was look at her father, sat there in his dressing gown.

— Ah mean, Derrick said, discomfited and pulling his garment closer to him, — it makes him easy prey fir the less scrupulous types; the yins that ken that when aw the ugly stuff goes doon, it really is every man for themselves.

— You're just being paranoid.

— Naw, cause ah ken who's gaunny be the one in five hundred tae git huckled in the rammy n dae the serious jail time or trip n faw n git trampled intae a vegetable. That boy needs put right!

Alison wondered how her father was going to do that, sitting in his threadbare slippers and dressing gown. Why didn't he just shower and dress like he used to, instead of slouching around like this every morning?

The front door opened and Mhairi came in. Alison took her sister into the kitchen, anxious to make alliance, to discuss what was to be done about the men in their family. For cover, she turned on the kitchen table radio.

As Duran Duran performed 'The Reflex', and Alison talked of the discord between their father and brother, she could see that she was losing Mhairi's attention. Then her sister put her hand to her mouth, and Alison turned, to watch Calum scuttling down the drainpipe outside the kitchen window, dreeping the last of the distance into the backgreen.

— Calum, she shouted, moving to the back door, to see his figure recede, ducking behind the washing that hung on the lines.

— What's happened? Derrick shouted, emerging into the doorway.

— Cal's went n sneaked oot n bolted, eh, Mhairi said, a smile on her face.

— What . . . ? Ah bloody telt him! Derrick ran to the door, then, realising he was in his dressing gown, halted abruptly.

— I'll find him, Alison said, her tone more condemnatory than she wanted, and grabbed her bag and headed outside. She looked around the undifferentiated backgreens. There was nothing but washing, hanging on lines.

Calum must have climbed the garden wall, onto the overgrown path by the side of the block of dwellings. It was a bit early for him to have headed up to Easter Road, so she was betting he'd be around the Foot of the Walk.

She saw him up ahead in the street talking to Lizzie and Tommy Lawrence. When she got closer, he made no attempt to move.

— Hi, Ali, Lizzie said, and Tommy echoed.

— Hiya.

— Youse gaun tae the game? Calum asked the couple, ignoring his sister. Lizzie looked at him, then Alison, as if Calum was mentally retarded.

— Naw. It'll be mad up thaire the day. Fill ay bams, Tommy said dismissively. — Keep away fae that place the day, pal.

— That's what Dad said. Alison looked at Calum.

— Ah'm no gaun back in, he told her.

— Dae what ye like. Ah'm no yir jailer, Alison said, hoping this altered tack would compel him to move towards reason. She looked at Tommy and Lizzie, and nodded to the cafe across the street. — Want tae get a coffee?

— Sound, Tommy said. Alison didn't know if Calum would follow, but he did. They went into the Up the Junction cafe. It was busy, but one table was free and they squared around it.

Alison was asking Lizzie about her course, while Lizzie enquired about her work. All the time, she was trying to listen into Tommy and Calum's conversation, to ascertain what her brother's plans were. Was he really involved with that hooligan mob?

— Aberdeen are some team right enough, Tommy said. — Leighton, McKimmie, Miller, McLeish, Simpson, Cooper, Strachan, Archibald, McGhee, Weir, it's unbelievable what they've achieved under Alex Ferguson.

— Aye, Calum agreed, looking sheepishly at Lizzie, and it was clear to Alison that he had a debilitating crush on her, — it's crap that they're so much better than Hibs.

— But ye cannae hate them in the same way ye do Rangers and Celtic, Tommy argued, — cause they've done it by fair means, no by pandering tae thickos wi aw that sectarian shite.

— Aye, Calum agreed, and his voice went high for an embarrassing moment, before he coughed violently at the frog in his throat, — they've sorted oot the Old Firm and conquered Europe, and there's Hibs and Herts yo-yoing between the divisions!

— Is that aw youse kin talk aboot, Alison shook her head at Lizzie, — fitba?

— There's other reasons tae go tae the game, no jist the fitba, Calum said.

Alison went to say something, bit her tongue.

— At least things are picking up oan the terraces, he grinned, and he seemed young again, a cheeky wee boy.

Tommy nodded in agreement. — Relegation's good for a mob's soul. Man U, Chelsea, West Ham, Spurs, aw they firms got forged through adversity; defending yourself fae local yokels huvin a dash. It did Herts good; Keezbo's telt us aboot the crazy trips tae places like Dumfries. Ye hud police helicopters circling above Palmerston Park, the lot.

— Aye, the drop wis good in helpin tae build up the Hibs casual mob.

Alison knew Tommy was indulging her brother. He was too sensible to be associated with them, or even his old YLT mates. You could tell he was scenting a new future with Lizzie. She was up talking to the lassie behind the counter, who Alison recognised as having gone to Leith Academy. Tommy got up, and headed for the toilet. Alison took her chance. She looked at Calum imploringly. — Come hame. We'll git a video. You, me n Mhairi. Huv a laugh n a blether.

— There's nowt tae laugh aboot, n aw the bletherin in the world's no gaunny change that, Calum said, sitting back in the chair.

As he flexed his thin, but wiry body, Alison realised that he'd grown physically more powerful than her. *My wee brother could batter me now*, she permitted. When had that happened? — Dad disnae want ye –

— He'll dae nowt, n you'll dae nowt either, Calum challenged, in a tight sneer, rising and shaking his head, a sour smile on his lips.

Tommy returned from the toilet, spoke a few words with the departing boy. Alison watched Calum nip outside and hurry up the street, as if Tommy Lawrence had just passed her brother a baton.

Lizzie rejoined them at the table. — Is he okay?

— He's been a bit mental, pittin it mildly, since my ma went, Alison conceded.

— He'll be awright, Tommy said hopefully, — Calum's sound.

— Aye, Alison exhaled. — So what youse up tae?

— Going tae see *Indiana Jones and the Temple of Doom*, Lizzie said.

— She chose it. Tommy was quick to make the point. Alison reckoned that was because more than one person had mentioned he looked a bit like Harrison Ford. She envied the couple, sitting in a warm picture house together, their love incubating in the silent hothouse dark. The odd smile and kiss, the squeeze of the hand, then intertwining as Harrison cracked the whip on-screen. She thought of calling Alexander, and then wished that Simon was here. She wanted to ask Tommy if he'd heard from him, but something stopped her. Her relationship with Simon was non-exclusive and more than a little clandestine. It suddenly seemed cheap goods compared to what Tommy and Lizzie had. His hand was resting on hers. The way they looked at each other . . .

Disinclined to play gooseberry any longer, Alison left them and walked down to the river, settling onto a bench. The sun was starting to fall over the disused warehouses in front of her, as the odd person and dog ambled by on the walkway. Her poetry book was in her bag and she took it out and looked through its contents.

The book now seemed pointless. Real life wasn't reducible to the written word, and even spoken words, our interactions with others, just seemed like distracting drama. She lowered the book, and let her gaze fall across the still, black river. *This* was real life, when we were alone in thought, lost in memory.

She had barely noticed him coming towards her. When she did, he at first cut a tentative figure, growing more gallus as he slumped onto the bench a little bit apart from her. — Good book, aye?

Alison was too distracted to immediately get up and walk away. Instead she looked up. He was young; much younger than her even, just a laddie. He had a cheeky face, with busy eyes observing her from under the ubiquitous fringe. — So-so.

— You're Calum's big sister, eh?

— Aye. Ye ken ma brar, like?

— Aye. Really sorry tae hear aboot yir ma, likes.

— Thanks.

— It's shite, eh? My ma died two years ago. Ah stey at ma auntie's now.

— Sorry . . . she said, then acknowledged, — Yir right. It is shite. She was going to add that was putting it mildly, but Kelly had half jokingly pulled her up for saying that a lot. She realised he was chewing, and he noticed her noticing, and offered her some gum, which she accepted. Moved to reciprocate in some way, she gave him a cigarette.

— Was meant tae be gaun tae Easter Road, but ah couldnae be bothered. Fancied a wee walk instead, he explained, bending in to accept her light. — What's your name?

— Alison.

He extended his hand and she felt herself reaching out to take it. — Bobby, he nodded, then rose and awkwardly blew out some smoke. — You're a barry lassie, Alison, he said quite ruefully. — Wish ah hud a sister like you, and he gave a small wave and went off down the walkway. He held the cigarette strangely, like he wasn't a smoker. She watched him go, all the time wondering how this daft, sweet wee boy had left her on a riverside bench with her heart in fragments.

It had grown cold down by the water but she sat there for ages, until jakeys and perverts started hassling her for cash and sex. One really old, frail man, going past painstakingly slowly on a Zimmer frame, asked grimly, — Whaes fanny dae ye need tae lick tae git a gam in these parts?

It was time to go.

Crossing from Constitution Street, Alison came round the corner onto the Foot of the Walk. She saw him straight away, sat down on the bench under Queen Victoria's statue, still and silent. *It's like he's waiting till closing time tae smash the first lippy cunt he sets eyes on.* — Frank. How's it goin?

He looked at her as she joined him on the bench, his eyes narrowing into sharp focus. She could smell the drink off him, but his movements and thoughts seemed premeditated, everything deliberately executed; he was holding onto a form of sobriety through the exercise of his will. It took him a couple of seconds to respond. — Awright. Sorry tae hear aboot yir ma n that.

312

— Ta. Alison stretched her legs out, staring at the fur trim at the top of her boots. She looked up the Walk. The rim of a full moon shimmered over them, opening up the layers in the dense, smoky sky, casting curious shadows. Queen Victoria towered above, partly concealing them from the street lamp. — Where ye been?

— Dockers' Club. Some ay the boys ur still in thaire. Frank Begbie cast a brief glance towards Constitution Street. — Jist came oot cause a couple ay cunts wir gittin oan ma fuckin nerves. A bunch ay us went doon eftir the fitba n got stuck intae the peeve. Ah wanted tae go up the toon, but they wir jist sittin thaire. Playin at bein two-bob gangsters, acting like an auld-fashioned pagger wi some wide cunts wis fuckin beneath them. Especially Nelly wi his fuckin Davie Power this n Davie Power that bullshit!

Alison could see them all, sitting round a table in the club; the stylised movements and slick gab. No wonder Tommy wasn't into that any more. No wonder Simon and Mark had left for London. Under the amber glow of the street lamp, she thought of Calum again: saw what her gangly, dopey young brother might become. She wanted to ask Franco about the game, whether there was any trouble.

— Nearly smashed a fuckin tumbler intae that cunt's face, Francis Begbie snarled — jist went ootside tae git some air n clear ma fuckin heid but, eh. Aye, it's aw changed now. Nivir fuckin well see Rents or Sick Boy, eh, no. Dinnae ken whaire Spud is. Every cunt's oan that smack. Tommy never even fuckin showed up fir the fitba.

As Franco spat out his bitter litany of grievances, the air seemed to gather mass, like a barometric dip before the descent of a thunderstorm. Alison felt herself wincing inside.

— It wis London that fuckin ruined the likes ay Rents n Sick Boy; they cunts doon thaire, Begbie declared. — They wir fine till they went doon thaire; nae airs n graces. That wee cunt they broat up, he wis awright, ah'm no sayin nowt against him, but it wis London that fucked wi thair heids.

It was unmitigated nonsense, but Alison didn't feel like arguing. Nutters. How did they keep it going? Sustain the energy levels required to fuel all that rage and indignation? Didn't they ever just get *tired*?

— Ye git a laugh wi Rents n Sick Boy n that. Nelly n Saybo n they cunts dinnae git ma sense ay humour, Begbie said sadly. Then he looked pointedly at her. — June loast the bairn.

— Aw . . . I'm really sorry, Franco. Poor June . . . ah didnae even ken shi wis . . . how long . . . is she okay?

— Aye, course she is. Franco looked at Alison as if she was crazy, then explained, — It's the bairn that's no okay, *she's* fuckin fine. He lit up a cigarette, then as an afterthought, offered her one. She hesitated for a second, then took it and leaned into him to accept a light. Franco took a drag, filled his lungs with smoke and sat back. — Aw she hud tae dae wis keep the fuckin thing up thaire, n she couldnae even dae that! Fuckin useless. Tae me that's murder, or as fuckin good as; murder by peeve, murder by snout! Ah telt her that, n she sterted fuckin greetin, showin us aw this rid-brown stuff in her fuckin pants. Ah jist took thum n rubbed thum in her fuckin pus. Telt her it was her fault: telt her she wis a fuckin murderer!

Alison stared at him in disbelief.

— Aye, ah caught her puffin oan a fag the other week. Whae's tae say it wisnae that thit made it fuckin well fire oot before its time?

Alison felt a gasp of incredulity tear from her. — It doesnae work that way, Frank. It's a terrible thing for a lassie. Naebody kens why it happens.

— Ah ken! Ah ken awright; it happens cause ay snout! It happens cause ay peeve, he moaned, his brown and yellow fingers pointing with the fag in them up the Walk. He suddenly shook his head with implausible vigour, reminding her of a dog emerging from the sea. — Maybe it's the best fuckin thing thit could've happened, cause if she's that bad now, what kind ay mother would she have fuckin well been whin the bairn wis born? Eh?

— It's no her fault, Frank. She'll be in bits. Ye should go hame n comfort her.

— Ah'm nae good at aw that shite, he shook his head.

— Just go tae her, Frank, she'll appreciate it.

For a second, Alison almost entertained the notion that the blurred reflection of the burning sodium light was a tear in Franco's eye, but it was probably her own. Then he said in cold certainty, — Nup. It's doon tae her. She's goat mates n sisters for aw that shite.

Alison stood up. She'd grown to believe that suffering only led to more suffering. There was just comfort, it was the only thing we could offer each other. Yet her hand, hovering in stasis over Franco's dense shoulder, couldn't quite bring itself to land. She saw they were fated to their separate pains, and was relieved by the discernment. — Right, Frank, take care ay yirsel, ah'll see ye.

— Aye, see ye.

And she marched up the Walk, now too numbed to feel the cold's burn. She could see the sparkle and hear the occasional crunch of the spring frost under her feet as she looked for the night bus that would take her to Tollcross and Johnny Swan's place. Closer still was Pilrig, and her dead mother's morphine. She'd quickly, instinctively, expropriated it, telling her dad it was going back to the hospital, and her friend Rachael, who was a nurse, would know what to do with it. To his befuddled, grateful mind, it had just been another practical task she'd completed, like registering the death, booking the crematorium, the Dockers' Club for the do, arranging the catering, putting the notice of the death and funeral in the *Evening News*, taking her mother's old clothes round to the charity shop.

The Walk was filling up with singing, wolf-whistling drunks spilling out of the pubs. Then, from some distance behind her, she heard glass shattering and shouting followed by a terrible stillness in the air, which was dramatically breached by screams more animal than human. Alison kept walking, knowing who would be responsible. Yet she was afflicted every step of her journey home by Begbie's pained, malevolent spirit. In her own psychosis of loss, his was the devil's voice, permeating all the other sounds; the grinding of cars down the street, the shivering of the bare trees in the wind, the guffaws of drunk girls, the shouts of men weaving in and out of the public houses. Her brain was blackened with remorse, gummed up like damp, dirty amphetamine powder in a wrap. She thought of June's pain, the death's head of her mother, then the women at the poetry group, those lassies who seemed like they'd graduated from a finishing school on some far-off planet. Making love to Simon, to Alexander, then that guy she'd met the other night at the Bandwagon, Andy? No, Adam. For a second she sensed that if she just closed her eyes, something like a pattern, a semblance of order, might insinuate itself, but she was too scared to try.

From out of the darkness, a wailing police car, followed by its bigger sibling of an ambulance van, tore past her at speed.

Ocean

Sea Dogs

1. Customs and Excise

Sick Boy, rucksack on his back, considers his friend Renton really is *a skinny junky cunt*; that even Spud or Matty might now appear sprucer. Walking quickly through the brightly lit customs area, every fibre in Sick Boy's being screams: *he is not with me.* The air hangs heavy with old sweat, augmented rather than buried by the tang of cheap, noxious deodorants. The thickset official, tattooed spiderweb straddling the bridge of one hand, pulls on a cigarette, feigning disinterest, but Sick Boy can tell that he's clocked them. He'll have to pass through this gate every day, and, if Marriott has his way, sometimes with a sizeable packet of class-A drugs sweating in his underpants.

Nicksy, carrying a large imitation-leather travel bag, mirrors Sick Boy's decline. He's conversing with Marriott but focused mordantly on a trickle of spittle coming out of his gob, which slops down the older man's chin. Nicksy is transfixed by the horror of his private dilemma; if he suffers this for just *one more second* then he feels death will surely follow but, if he breaks off, he'll never work in this town, sordid as it is, again.

In the event, Renton, with two plastic carrier bags, is the only one detained and searched. He wears a goofy, nervy smile as the grim-faced customs men tip some faded T-shirts and underwear onto a table for inspection. Meantime, his personal stash burns his toes at the bottom of his trainers. He took a fortuitous late decision to leave his spec-case works at home, and gives thanks with an awkward nod as he's waved on. Nicksy's way up ahead, not looking back.

They move outside the customs area, a set of glass doors transiting them to the dock where they're lashed by a viciously bitter wind. Bloated, slate-coloured clouds suck the light out of the sky as they head onto the gangway to board the large white ship, renamed *The Freedom of Choice*, following privatisation, from its former designation, *The Arms Across the Sea*.

Though imposing enough from the outside, the interior of the vessel seems a charmless warren of green-and-white-painted steel decks, cabins and stairways. Manoeuvring through several sets of hostile swinging doors, they descend a nightmarish staircase, proceeding deeper and deeper down towards their billets.

Renton inspects the narrow coffin of the cabin he's to share with Nicksy (ensuring that his cockney friend is in the bottom bunk as he's detected a bit of the bed-wetter about his persona), and craves getting his head down. But they're swiftly whisked back up those stairs to a deck – sweating, lungs punching for air and calves burning – for a potentially torturous induction. Here they get issued with reasonably smart blue holdalls, bearing the Sealink logo. Each bag contains a red waistcoat and silk tie or scarf and either two shirts or blouses, depending on the gender of the 'operative'. (In the post-privatised, non-union epoch, they are all referred to in this way rather than 'stewards'. Operatives are paid less.) The supervisor, a thin, short, bespectacled man of around thirty, sporting a neat Beatle cut and resplendent in his own cream shirt, is telling the dozen-strong group of new recruits how it's their responsibility to make sure that the issued attire gets washed, and that they're wearing a *clean* top at all times. — This is of paramount importance, the overseer they've instantly dubbed Cream Shirt lisps, focusing on Sick Boy, who stands at the rear of the assembly with Renton and Nicksy, — do I make myself clear?

— Affirmative, Sick Boy barks, causing the assembled inductees to whirl round, before adding, — Can't run a ship if we're not shipshape.

Cream Shirt looks at him as if he's taking the piss, then thinks he might not be, and lets it slide, escorting them on a tour around the vessel. Renton and Sick Boy simultaneously recognise the wild-haired girl from back at the interview. — The only half-decent bird on offer, Sick Boy says to Renton in disdain. — I got a smile fae those chunky Pauline Quirke barrow girls, he nods towards two women moving in coy, close proximity to them, — but sorry, girls, you're destined for a life of kitchen sweat, as opposed to the bedroom variety!

Renton looks over cursorily, thinking that one isn't too bad, before his eyes flick back to their original position. — You gettin the baboon vibe?

— Don't be so immature and sexist. Just cause a chick's had a kid doesn't mean thir written off, Sick Boy scoffs.

Renton chooses to ignore him. — That wee honeybunch, he licks his lips, again acknowledging the girl with the big hair, his eyes pulling around in a guileful way that Sick Boy almost appreciates, — she's gorgeous, he whispers, as they ascend another narrow set of stairs.

— She's acceptable, Renton, no gorgeous. Sick Boy sucks more air into his chest, hoping some of it will reach his legs.

— Get tae fuck. Check that Robert Plant hair, Renton says, as the inductees struggle onto the next deck, fanning out in assembly. He sees Nicksy, scratching at one really red ear, but can't locate Marriott anywhere.

— You are a highly disturbed young man, Mr Renton. You would say Robert Plant; I'd prefer to think Farrah Fawcett-Majors, Sick Boy tells him, as Cream Shirt, grasping a clipboard, glances their way. He's started his spiel and, in face of the competition from the back, raises his voice a decibel, picking them out as potential troublemakers. — So when the alarm rings, we all have to be fully pursuant with our evacuation duties.

— Aye, but great hair, Renton nudges Sick Boy, — however ye look at it. Besides, fuck Farrah Fawcett-Majors: Kate Jackson's the sexiest Angel. That husky voice . . .

Sick Boy looks to Cream Shirt, still blowing compressed hot air through those tight, pursed, cock-sucking lips that would undoubtedly make him a hit in fagland, now whingeing on about what to do if the boat sinks. *Fuck aw that baws, if such an event occurs ye run tae the nearest lifeboat elbowing every cunt in your path ootay the fucking road.* He edges closer to Renton. — We're talking about a woman here, Rents. A *sexy* woman. We can debate Fawcett-Majors versus Jackson, or Plant versus Page, but the analogy you used in this context was disturbingly homosexual. Are you getting curious being on this boat, Rent Boy? he asks, as Cream Shirt stiffens, and once again picks up his volume. — . . . to know exactly where each evacuation station is situated . . .

— Fuck off, your cock would be the last yin ah'd suck, Renton says, and the Girl With the Big Hair hears this, placing her hand over her mouth to stifle a giggle.

— The last, perhaps, but I notice that you still fall short of ruling it out. Kind ay makes my point for me, wouldn't ye say?

— Ah deployed a fuckin figure ay speech, ya cunt, Renton whispers. — Ah'm happy tae rule it oot, one hundred per cent.

The Girl With the Big Hair again looks round, this time checking them out, forcing Cream Shirt once more to raise his voice. — . . . under the 1974 Health and Safety at Work Act . . .

— Delighted tae hear it, Sick Boy says to Renton.

— Dinnae sound sae hurt then.

— Oh God, Sick Boy retorts in bitter sarcasm, — see it fae my point of view. I've always wanted tae gaze doon on your badly dyed heid wi the ginger roots while your rotten teeth grate on ma baws. That's been a fantasy ay mine since ah was knee-high tae a grasshopper. Now it'll never be. Boo-hoo. Woe is me!

His indignant tones soar further on this tirade, attracting the laughter

321

of more inductees, and Cream Shirt has had enough of the distraction. — Perhaps . . . he looks at Sick Boy with what the recipient worryingly sees as bend-over-and-spread-em eyes, then back to his list, — Simon . . . might share his little joke with us? Seeing as it's obviously more important than our health and safety on this ship!

— No joke, ehm . . . Martin, the self-styled Scots-Italian Renaissance man suddenly recalls how the overseer had introduced himself, — I was just saying to my friend that, as a son of a seafaring community, whose family have taken to the ocean for generations through whaling, the trawlers and the mercantile fleet, just how great it feels to be given this opportunity by Sealink.

Cream Shirt's expression indicates that he again suspects he's being messed with. However, Sick Boy remains poker-faced to the extent that the supervisor is actually moved. — Thanks, Simon . . . it might not be the best job in the world, he declares, with emotion, — but it's not the worst. But this part of the induction is particularly important so I would urge everybody to give it their full attention.

— Of course, Martin, I let my excitement get the better of me, he smiles sweetly, — please accept my humble apologies.

Cream Shirt flashes a brief dinner-invitation grin that makes Sick Boy's guts flip, before he drinks in Renton's whispered admiration. — Vintage Sick Boy, especially the term 'mercantile fleet' instead ay merchant navy. I'll jot that yin doon!

Nicksy has sidled up to Renton, going on about the meaning of life. — Wot's it all abaht, Mark? Eh?

A good question, Renton thinks, as Cream Shirt drones on. – . . . the legislation was framed largely as an enabling act. It aims to place the responsibility for health and safety at work on every individual employee. Therefore, we are all, in some sense, health and safety officers, with the responsibility to . . .

We all have tae take responsibility, he recalled his dad saying, concerning Wee Davie. A thump of death's uncompromising beat in Renton's chest: the knowledge that he'd never see, or hear his brother again. He swallows a ball in his throat that isn't there: you really were a long time deid, as the old saying went.

Thinking of Wee Davie makes him consider Giro the dog. He's started barking in the night; a sharp, oddly rhythmic sound, suggesting Wee Davie's cough. It's taken over from that noise as the source of something beyond torment for Renton, more like a peculiar attestation. Now he's the only one who'll rise in the darkness to scoop food into the pup's bowl. One night he realised Giro had been at the wraps of speed on the coffee table. — It's no good you living with us, pal, he'd said sadly, lamenting that he was getting too fond of this animal. Renton admired the way that Giro could just get up; no need to wash, brush teeth, dress, he was just instantly ready to go out to the park. And he loved the attention the dog got him from girls in London Fields. *Ain't ee luverly!*

That dug will get me a ride, almost in spite ay masel.

But Nicksy is bugging him. — What the fark are we doin here, Mark? I mean . . . really?

What the fuck does that cunt ken aboot the meanin ay life? Renton thinks, as Marriott's now in his sights, standing motionless, hands clasped together in front of him.

— . . . so the first thing we need, Cream Shirt is saying, desperate to engage with a dozen pairs of eyes, — are two volunteers to be our designated health and safety officers . . . on the basis that a volunteer is worth two pressed men – or women, of course . . . he scans the blank faces, — . . . so please raise your hands if you're interested . . .

All hands resolutely stay down and most heads bow to regard the green-painted metal floor of the deck. — C'mon, Cream Shirt begs, aghast, — it's health and safety! It affects us all!

Still no takers: just a series of shifty sideways glances. With a bitter head-shaking sulk, Cream Shirt consults his clipboard, then scrutinises them again.

Renton now accepts he has the heebie-jeebies. He needs a little something.

Fortunately, Cream Shirt has arbitrarily designated a young man with constantly blinking eyes and lunar acne scars, and one of Sick Boy's meaty-thighed, flirtatious barrow girls to the health and safety roles, mercifully ending the talk. A second supervisor minces alongside Cream Shirt and simpers in a high, fey sound, — Now if you'll kindly adjourn to your cabins to get changed into your uniforms, we'll assemble in twenty minutes in the canteen, where you'll be designated to your workstations.

They head off, Renton stalling for a second or two, hoping to chat to the Girl With the Big Hair, but her attention is taken by the other supervisor, whom he's dubbed Beige Blouse, so he heads down to the staff quarters in the bowels of the ship. When he reaches the cabin Nicksy's already there, the Sealink bag at his feet, changing into his uniform. — Okay, bud?

— Farking not really, mate, and he pulls the cream shirt over his thin frame and buttons it up, adjusting the elastic on the bow tie for comfort, then the waistcoat, which is too big and hangs limply. — See ya up in the canteen.

— Righto . . . Renton elects to tough it out. He leaves the skag, the stash crushed into the toes of his trainers, and instead he takes some speed from a wrap in his jeans watch pocket. It's the only way to get through this shift. Once the buzz kicks in, he heads up to the canteen to meet the others. He feels terrible, as if he's papering over the cracks, the speed in some ways making the junk withdrawal pains keener, but the frenzied energy mentally distracting him.

Amphetamine pushiness gives him a wild swagger through several sets of swing doors into the staff area of the refectory. Fortune does indeed favour the brave, as it becomes clear that the roster's designations have given Cream Shirt the impression that he's in Beige Blouse's team, while Beige Blouse seems to believe the opposite. Disinclined to disabuse either of them, or their rota, of this notion, Renton opts to stay non-assigned, deciding that he'll walk the ship like a ghost.

A line has formed for the food. Renton's not hungry but the lentil soup on offer looks edible and he feels that he should try to eat *something*. He rips the pish out of the chef, proud and military-stiff in his big hat and whites. — Awright, cookie boy? he barks, playing to the gallery, toxic speed energy notched up further by the gushing screams of queens, the appreciative chuckle of wideos, and a delectable smile from the Girl With the Big Hair.

Chef stands impassively: thick, black-rimmed glasses and red liver spots on his neck, a smouldering volcano in starched white linen. Renton suddenly feels, even through his drug arrogance, that this insolence just might be a mistake. This is confirmed when a veteran English homosexual cabin steward lisps, — Don't fuck Chef out, mate, he's a real bastard.

It's a phrase Renton has never heard before; don't fuck Chef out.

Nicksy's gone and he can't see Sick Boy, and the cute Fawcett-Plant lassie is chatting to one of the barrow girls, so Renton decides to forgo the soup and commence his wanderings, to get out of range of Chef's cold, dangerous gaze. As he leaves, he hears him bellow at a kitchen hand, — Who is that cheeky little Scotch cunt?

As he climbs a staircase, Nicksy feels the weight of his breath in his lungs. At the top he looks outside the portholed swing doors to the sea. They are on the decks, the staff, waiting for the vehicles and foot passengers to embark. He spies Marriott leaning on the rail, smoking a cigarette, the burning eyes in his wrecked, cadaverous figure forever trained on them.

Following the line of vision, Sick Boy is revealed chatting to that bird with the big blonde hair all over the place. Studying her small tits, tight curvy figure and all that hair flying in the wind, Nicksy's thinking: tasty, but without a semblance of prurient lust.

— Got any hash? Sick Boy asks her.

— Yeah, a bit, she says, vainly trying to restrain her swishing locks, as the first cars roll over the ramp and eager foot passengers trudge up the bridge hoping in futility that the bar is already open.

Sick Boy overhears Cream Shirt saying to a languid sidekick, — It's this bit that always gets me, as he grandly sweeps his arms, watching the passengers pile forward, — this is what makes me realise why I'm here.

Sick Boy stares at the passengers and decides that he already hates every last one of them. Then a chat of 'Man-chis-tihr na, na, na . . .' comes up as a gang of sallow, strutting youths around his age emerge onto the deck. He turns to the girl with the hair. — In that case, I'll need to swing by your cabin later. I can't sleep without a smoke.

— Okay, she says, her head whipping briefly to acknowledge the singing. — I'm Charlene.

— Simon, Sick Boy curtly nods.

Cream Shirt squeaks out instructions to the welcoming cabin staff, as the travelling British public stream onto the vessel. Nicksy sidles off, heading up another flight of metal steps onto the upper deck. After a spell, a farty-sounding siren blares, followed a little later by a rumble and shake as the ship's engine starts up. The boat leaves the harbour slowly, picking up speed and being pursued by excited gulls as it reaches open water. Then he's aware of footsteps behind him, followed by a shout: — Nicksy you cahnt!

He turns to see the floppy fringe of Billy Gilbert, an old West Ham mate, wearing a brown-and-cream Adidas top. He's prominent in a squad of boys, who march along the deck towards him. They all share a coiled, alert look, like greyhounds in traps waiting for the doors to fly open and the mechanical bunny to bolt down the rail. Billy gives Nicksy's uniform the once-over. — Nice threads, mate. High fashion is wot you might call it.

Cackles all round, as Nicksy sees another Ilford friend, Paul Smart, and a few more mob faces of his acquaintance. He doesn't know what's going on. — Fuck's all this about?

— Gor blimey, you're narky, Nicks. Ain't they treatin you right on the *Titanic* here?

He sucks in some air and forces a smile. — Yeah, sorry, Bill, it ain't so bad; a relatively honest crust.

— You off ta the game later?

— Thought I might, Nicksy lies. Although he'd read a piece in the *Standard* about it, he'd somehow thought the first leg of the forthcoming UEFA Cup tie was at Upton Park. — If I get finished in time after this bleedin shift.

— Great, see ya in the Bulldog then, Billy says, then rubbernecking, as if in anticipation of an ambush, — Heard there's a load of Man U on this fucking boat.

— Ain't heard nuffink. You planning on chasing them back to Surrey, then?

— Might just do that, Billy laughs.

A pasty-faced kid with a fringe, wearing a green Sergio Tacchini top, comes running towards them with urgency and squeaks, — There's a load of Man U in the farking bar downstairs!

And the mob are off, stalking down the steps, surging past the ascending Sick Boy, Cream Shirt and some other members of staff, as Nicksy sharpishly heads in the other direction.

— That looks like trouble, Cream Shirt says. — Simon, could you and your friends . . . he looks at the sheet, — Mark and Brian, come with me? Where are they?

Sick Boy realises that both Rents and Nicksy, like Cream Shirt's health and safety officer designates, have vanished. — I'm not exactly sure.

— The first sailing of the season and the place is crawling with hooligans, Cream Shirt hisses in distaste. — Let's keep an eye on them and make sure they settle down.

— Eh, okay . . . Sick Boy says reluctantly. Cream Shirt has evidently taken some sort of a shine to him. He's as yet unsure as how to work this in his favour, but highly intrigued at the prospect of being able to do so.

On deck Nicksy runs into a meaty-armed woman in a sleeveless quilted jacket. She seems in distress and tells him she's lost her daughter. — Come with me, love, we'll find her, he says, and he leads her away.

2. Reasonable Duties

I admit that ah'm a wee bitty too fond ay the Salisbury Crag for my ain good, but something's flipped in Renton's ginger dome. He's an embarrassment, with his continually streaming beak, and that metallic nasal voice he seems tae have adopted; he'd suck the pish ootay a jakey's crotch if he thought there was a buzz in it for him. He's hiding; it's so obvious tae see. From what? What else but his fears? His biggest fear? That the spazzy gene, which produced the fucked *fratello*, is apparent in him. Well realised, Rent Boy. Realised.

I wasn't feeling too bad at first; ah'd sorted myself out wi a ride for the shifts. I miss Lucinda, and ah cannae abide sleeping withoot a bed-warmer. That Charlene seems like a feisty wee banger, a no-questions-asked-or-demands-made fuck-artist. We're chewing the shit, watching the passengers, who really are the dregs ay this planet, tramping onto the boat like cattle. Happily, though, there are one or two filthy-looking lassies in the mix. Then we're off. Basically, we cabin staff, or 'operatives', are simply a presence designed tae monitor the 'customers', as the passengers are now redesignated.

Then ah was aware that ah wis starting tae get edgy, wondering where that cunt Renton was. He'll have found a darkened, enclosed space tae entomb himself in, ay that I've nae doots. The words *holding out* are resonating in ma brain, when ah'm torn away fae Charlene and compelled tae follow Cream Shirt in his pursuit ay a mob of London lads who rush past us towards the bar. Ah hear the fractious singing that has been coming from that direction suddenly stopped by a shattering sound ay what can only be breaking glass. Then there's shouting and Cream Shirt runs through the bar doors waving his arms in the air, as passengers panic and stampede outside.

Ah follow him in, through the retreating travellers. A rammy has kicked off on the other side ay the bar area. I think it's West Ham versus Manchester United, but I know not and care less. Violence is an occasionally useful tool, but the recreational stuff is the vice ay losers like Begbie, whom I heard got a year for wounding some Lochend prick. This is all getting a little heavy though; a few clowns ineffectively windmill on the peripheries, and still more indulge in hollow gesticulation, but the main brawl's like a tornado, with about a dozen bodies at the centre of it, having a proper toe-to-toe. Passengers panic, charging outside, kids and women scream, and straight fuckers indulge in pained protest about 'animals'. Crème de la Shirt shakes my shoulder, pleading, — We have to stop them! They're wrecking the place!

— I think I might just opt to pass on that one, Martin, and leave it to security, I inform him, as a glass shatters against the bar behind us. — Or the police? You know, people who get paid decent money tae risk life and limb in such situations?

— It says in your job description 'any other reasonable duties as determined appropriate by management'.

— Right! ah trumpet, turning sharply away from the ruckus. — Is there a shop steward on this poxy fucking rust bucket?

327

Creambo briefly looks at me with a betrayed pout, but fair play, he's certainly going for the Queen's Industry Award, as he marches right intae the heart ay the Reg Varney. Ah cautiously follow, and all hell's breaking loose as the last absenting passengers, stag lads who were on the verge ay steaming in but have now decided it's too rich for their blood, pile past us tae get away fae the fracas. More glass smashes and beseeching, gullet-wrenched invitations to join the row fill the air. Ah should get the fuck ootay here, but this ah huv tae see, cause Cream Shirt is lisping, pouting and farting his wey right intae the middle ay the swedge, screaming, — STOP! STOP IT!

To my astonishment, some ay the football lads briefly pause, each too embarrassed tae be seen tae be the yin banjoing this midget, Cuban-heeled fag. They are obviously all actual, or aspiring, top boys, quickly realising that any hands-on involvement in a skirmish wi a short-arse nancy can only diminish their standing. Eventually a young ragamuffin foot soldier in a rather smart top steps up and panels Creambo with a sweet right hook, knocking him on his arse and bursting his nose open. The northern mob take this as their cue to withdraw, shouting threats as they inch towards the exit. Everything has just miraculously stopped.

— You want some n all, you cahnt? the kid asks me.

With that ugly crack ay fist against bone still resonating in my ear, ah can dae without pursuing that particular option, thank you kindly. Ah gesture towards some older lads, who thankfully tell the impatient young Jedi tae calm doon, pointing him in the way ay the retreating northern-ers. The few remaining passengers sit paralysed with fear, but the West Ham boys, with the possible exception of young Skywalker, seem too disciplined a mob tae have any interest in bullying civilians.

— I'm sorry we interrupted you chaps from your business, ah say appreciatively, but they're away in pursuit of the northerners. Ah help Cream Shirt tae his feet and out ay the bar, taking care tae avoid that doubtlessly infected claret shooshing fae his smashed nose aw ower the sacred company garment that gies him his nickname.

— It'sth not on . . . he protests, holding a hand tae his shattered beak as ah escort him through double doors, — they're wrecking the boat . . .

— Worry ye not, shipmate, ah urge, sliding ma hand inside his jacket and removing a wallet which ah slip deftly intae ma trooser pocket. That yin will be put doon tae the melee. — These boys will punch themselves out soon. Let's get you doon tae sick bay.

Ah take the stricken brown-hatter downstairs and deposit him in the medical room, where a fat Hattie Jacques-type nurse is bandaging a nutter's head wound. His two mates stand around sheepishly, smirking at each other as the wounded lad moans in a Manc accent, — Didn't coom ere t'fight West Ham, — came over ere t'ave it wi Anderlecht . . .

— Wait here, Martin, I'll see if I can try and calm things down, and ah leave Creambo, planning on heading straight back tae ma cabin tae crash. Ah'm no getting peyed enough tae try and separate bams hell-bent on smashing each other up. Ah could *never* be paid enough.

En route, ah stroll along the deck, counting oot the loot; forty-two quid, a bank card, n a picture ay a ludicrously bright-eyed gay nephew wi a blond cooslick spiralling heavenwards, like the ice cream on a Mr Whippy cone. Ah pocket the cash and chuck the rest into the cruel sea. It's a great feeling tae know that ah've executed the perfect crime. The wallet will never, ever be found and probably every West Ham and Man U lad will be given the full cavity search by the Dutch polis at the Hook, when the avenging queen phones this yin in.

Getting back doon intae the cabin, ah chase some brown and slump intae a contented semi-doze. Ah mind ay some cunt knocking at the door, but no way was ah answering for a single soul. Ah know that Renton's holding out on me for the simple reason that if ah've kept some percy back then he'll undoubtedly have followed suit.

Rising at my leisure, determined tae track doon ole Ginger Baws, ah was surprised tae note that the ship was already berthed in the Hook and the cars had started rolling off. Upstairs the bar had been wrecked; a couple of donkeys and a chunky barrow girl are sweeping the floor as Beige Blouse snaps pictures ay the damage, presumably for insurance purposes. I see a squad ay Dutch polis at the pier, but it seems like they can't be bothered tae make a single arrest, as the cockney mob pile off, chanting, 'We are the bastards in claret n blue.' A shocked queeny staffer tells me that one lad was taken tae hospital wi his throat cut; the sea air must have got some bam carried away.

Yar, me hearties!

Ah head back up tae the office where ah see Cream Shirt wi a heavy bandage taped across his neb, talking on the radio, no doubt tae polis or port security. He puts the receiver down, and looks like he's about to chastise me for vanishing.

— How are you? I get in first, full ay bogus concern.

— I'm fine . . . thanks for your help there . . . but where have you been?

— Looking for Mark and trying tae calm down some of our more irate passengers. An elderly lady was very distressed by the violence. I thought it prudent to sit with her for a bit.

— Yes . . . good thinking . . . God, there will be hell to pay when Mr Benson hears of this. He cringes at the thought. — I'll see you down in the bar.

— Righto, I say wi a crisp salute. Outside the doors, on the glass-strewn deck, an open-mouthed flycatcher pushes a brush along with the gusto of a crippled sloth on Mogadon. Fuck me, there are so many community-care types working on this boat that somebody even vaguely normal immediately becomes indispensable whether they like it or no.

So ah go back doon tae the wrecked boozer, and there's Nicksy, without his bow tie and his waistcoat open, sat at the bar sipping a Scotch. The barman, who introduces himself as Wesley from Norwich, isnae giein a flying fuck, he's happy to be in one piece, so I help myself to a malt ah dinnae intend tae drink and faux-toast Nicksy. — Slàinte.

There's nae sign ay wee Charlene, and where is that cunt Renton?

3. Car Deck

Ah love this idea ay huvin what the fitba pundits call a 'rovin commission': sortay no being stuck in any one role. So ah'm taking it on masel tae walk roond the vessel, chattin tae people as ah go, making sure that everything is shipshape. Schopenhauer said that a man can only be himself so long as he's on his Jack Jones, while Nietzsche reckoned all truly great thoughts are conceived by walking. Ah could see masel as a ship's captain ay the people; huvin a wee stroll aroond checking cunts oot, perhaps inviting a pretty lady or two tae join us at the captain's table, while ah entertained them wi racy tales ay nautical life in the port ay Leith.

Ah'm a seafarin man: it's in ma blood. Ah'm thinkin that Sick Boy wid just love tae be in ma shoes right now, though he's probably workin some scam ay his ain.

Raised voices comin fae above signal aggro, which means work, so ah head doon, away fae the action, descendin the metal staircase tae the bowels. Doon below us, there's tons and tons ay parked motors n lorries. A gadgie in a boiler suit shouts fae the landin above that ah shouldnae be doon here. Story ay ma life. Always somewhere ah shouldnae be. Like Planet Earth. — Aye. Right. Catch ye later, ah wave, carryin on ma merry wey.

A metal clang comes fae above, soundin like the crashin ay a giant cymbal. Ah feel the engines below me pumpin up the ship, drivin it on across the North Sea. Ah hit the bottom, tae the rows ay vehicles. Ah'm well blissed out; it's good gear, this broon. So ah'm sittin doon between some cars. Time passes, or it doesnae. Whae cares? Ah start tae idly key a smart estate motor then ah think, fuck it, the class war can wait, the class As cannae. Eftir a bit ah'm roused by the sound ay footsteps and chatterin as people descend and get intae their motors. Risin, ah haul masel up the metal steps back onto the decks and ah go intae the bar, which is totally trashed. — Have ah missed anything exciting? ah smirk at Sick Boy and Nicksy.

The Cream Shirt gadge is here, giein orders tae the staff whae ur tryin tae clean up. One ay the barrow girls is daein her Mrs Mop routine on a trail ay thick droaps ay spilled Roy Hudd. Cream Shirt's taken a healthy lick across the snout. He clocks me and goes, — Where have you been? Then he inches closer, showin me his burst neb. — Have you been drinking?

— Ah felt really sick, ah say, aw torpid and heavy-eyed, — ah think it's the flu. Had tae lie doon for a bit. Drank tons ay that Night Nurse. Tell us that stuff doesnae knock ye oot, ah say, lookin tae Sick Boy for backup.

He steps in wi a reluctant, — If you have a wee lassie's constitution, then aye.

It just aboot throws Creambo off the scent. — If you were sick you should have come to see me or your supervisor.

— That's the problem, ah concede, — ah dinnae seem tae be oan anybody's list but, eh . . . wisnae sure whaire tae go tae, eh, no . . . ah tell the cunt, sliding intae the slack-jawed schemie defence ay contrived ignorance, a tried and tested method for exasperating authority figures.

— Julian! Cream Shirt calls over Beige Blouse and as sure as *Songs of Praise* comin oan the telly when you're brutally hung-over, the cunts cannae reconcile ma name oan their poxy lists. — Right, well then, we'll have you in the kitchen, working with Chef, the Cream-Shirt-lifting arse bandito pouts in petty triumph.

Aw-aw . . . hate comes tae toon . . .

Not good news. But I'll sort that later, as now we have time off and ah want tae hit ma scratcher. Sick Boy's hearin nane ay it but, he's got his Amsterdam party heid oan. — We're half an hour away from the most fun place on Planet Earth, and you're going to lie in a box in the sweaty bowels of a docked ship, feeling sick and indulging in half-hearted, feeble attempts at masturbation? Fine. Be my guest. Lightweight!

331

Ah feel pit oan the spot, cause there's a few gazes oan me, and that wee Fawcett-Plant's one ay them, a twinkle in her eye and a crease on her lips.

— Okay, ah hear myself concede. — Ah need some speed but.

One–nil, Williamson.

Nicksy's reluctant but Sick Boy's leadin the charge wi gusto. Ah learn that the Fawcett-Plant lassie's called Charlene, and she sleekitly says, — I'm up for it.

Ah realise that the spawny bastard's probably went n pulled her. Ah suppose it wis inevitable.

— C'mon, you party-pooping cunts, Sick Boy says, — we'll get some speed and suss out the situ.

— I dunno, Nicksy goes, — Marriott might want us to, you know . . . He looks towards Charlene.

She takes the hint and says, — Right, I'm gonna get changed. See you in fifteen minutes?

— Sound, Sick Boy says to her, then snaps at Nicksy, — Fuck Marriott. I'm no that sure about this deal, Nicksy, ah want tae check it oot first.

— Goat tae agree, ah'm noddin. — This is our first night off. Ah'm no hanging aboot wi that junky fag and listenin tae his gangster bullshit. Cunt'll jist huv tae cool his fuckin jets fir a bit.

Ah thoat Nicksy might be miffed, cause he set aw this up, but he doesnae seem tae gie a fuck. — Okay, he shrugs. — I gotta say that he's getting right on my farking tits, he looks around the bar, — in yer farking face all the time.

So we get changed, then we're off the boat and oantae the choo-choo tae the Dam. It's me, Sick Boy, Nicksy and the lovely Charlene, who's all made up, and wearing what looks like really expensive threads. It's like she's some yuppie gaun tae a presentation or something, but she's goat her Sealink holdall wi her. As she goes tae the lavvy, Sick Boy whispers tae us, — What's gaun on there? She fuckin DS or what?

— Naw . . . dinnae be daft, ah goes.

He raises his eyes, then a slow look ay concentration creeps ower his coupon. — Anyway, listen, ma thinking is that we're daein this erse about face. We should be punting Swanney's white Edinburgh skag tae these trolls doon here.

Nicksy looks witheringly at him.

— Sorry, mate, nae offence, but ye ken what ah mean, Sick Boy smiles.

Charlene returns with some coffees, which is very thoughtful, as it helps get the speed doon. I crash a wrap, and we aw take a big dunt, except her, she's content wi a wee dab.

We get oaf at Central Station. Like maist ay the tourists offay oor boat, we're heading left, straight for the red-light district. It's wild watching the lassies in the windaes and every cunt openly dealing gear in the streets aroond the Newmarket. We go tae a bar and me n Sick Boy order lemonade, Charlene and Nicksy settling for a beer that comes in a wee gless. We're gabbing away, especially me and Nicksy, who's recountin loads ay tales aboot us in that auld squat at Shepherd's Bush wi Matty. Charlene seems tae be distracted eftir a while and she heads off.

— She must be an agency hooker, off tae pit in a shift on her back at some hotel, Sick Boy says, but he's lost interest and quickly departs on 'a spying mission' wi instructions tae meet us at Central Station in a couple ay hours. He's probably arranged something wi Charlene, the sneaky cunt. They dinnae huv tae be aw cloak-n-dagger aboot it. As if we care.

Nicksy's drinking heavily, those empty beers lining up like sodjirs, and slavering shite. He seems a bit freaked oot. He talks about that Marsha lassie again, then his ma and dad, and how he's ey fightin wi them, but how much he really loves them. That boy is one ay the best cunts ye could hope tae meet. It was excellent ay um tae pit baith me and Sick Boy up, when he barely kens Sick Boy n aw. Ah'll make it up tae him one day.

But ah get restless and decide to pad the hoof fae a bit and leave him with his peeve. So ah'm ootside wanderin aroond the cobbled streets, watchin the drunks watchin the lassies in the windaes, thinkin how mental this place is. Ah'm headin doon this canal and end up in this big square they call the Leidseplein. Then ah check the time and realise ah should be gettin back. This wasted-lookin gadgie, whaes accent ah cannae place, starts gabbin tae us in the street. He sells us some speed. Ah take a dab and it's surprisingly good. In fact, it's fuckin rocket fuel and ah feel less slumpy and start tae enjoy the skag mair. Amsterdam fuckin rules! One day ah'm gaunny live here. The boy tells us he's a Serbian, then says that if ah go up this narrow street ay shops, it'll be quicker tae get back tae Central Station.

Even though it's late and dark, aw the shoaps ur still open. Britain is a fuckin graveyard compared tae Europe. Headin up the street, ah run intae Charlene, who's comin oot a lassies' boutique. First ah clock the Sealink bag she's carrying, then that hair. — Hiya, ah goes, and she looks aw wild-eyed and jumpy. — Where's Sick Boy?

— Fuck knows, I ain't seen him. He's your mate, she says, chewing and looking busily aroond. She might have hud mair speed.

— Sorry, eh, ah thought you were . . . eh . . .

— With him? Do us a favour! He might really fancy himself, but not everybody does!

It's impossible tae convey just what sweet, sweet music these words are tae ma ears. — Shopping? ah ask her.

— Something like that.

We go for a coffee in a side-street cafe and she's askin us aboot Nicksy, who ah realise ah've loast, n Sick Boy: whae kens what the fuck he's up tae. Ah decide no tae tell her about his rendezvous plans and we chat for ages, then jump back oan a later train. Ah'm wrecked but buzzing on the speed, as the train hurtles through the darkness. Judging by what ah saw comin oot here, we arenae missing much, the Dutch countryside is flat and shite. Ah've a terrible urge tae run ma fingers through that mad hair ay Charlene's. Lassies' hair totally rules; ah fancy that ah might train as a hairdresser, just a lassies' hairdresser mind. Sick Boy did that eftir leavin school, his first n last legit job. His boss jist aboot tolerated his fingers in the female apprentices, then the customers, but he drew a fuckin line at the till.

Charlene, sweepin a hand through that mop, says, — I've got a cabin ta myself. They didn't put anybody in with me. Come back for a smoke?

— Okay.

— When I say smoke, I mean shag, obviously, she smiles tightly.

— Sound, ah say, likin this burd's style, but realisin that's another reason why ah take drugs. If ah wisnae oot ma face ah'd huv goat a pure beamer at such a remark. Now, ah'm right in that zone. Ah'm sortay wonderin if ah should pit ma airm roon her or kiss her or something. Ah dinnae bother, in case ah picked her up wrong, or she wis takin the pish, n ah keep spraffin.

We get back oantae the boat. It's pretty quiet and thankfully we dinnae see Sick Boy or any cunt, as we get tae her cabin and she immediately slips oaf her jaykit. — C'mon then, she says, and she's unbuttonin her blouse. Fuckin hell, she's no kiddin! Ah git ootay ma gear, worryin that ah smell because ah huvnae washed much ower the last few days and my breath is probably minging. Ah'm naked and ah must look like a flick knife, cause ah've a dirty hard-on, which seems tae be takin aw the blood fae ma emaciated frame. Ah feel like it's gaunny brek off and slither away, a parasite leavin the host it's sucked dry, ma body crumbling like a pillar ay ash.

Charlene disrobes methodically, hanging up her smart jaykit and skirt. She removes her blouse but keeps her bra and pants on; they're a brilliant lilac see-thru, and you can see the nipples on her small breasts and make oot the bush, even though it looks natural blonde. She has a very small frame and she steps ower tae me and shimmies past my cock like Jimmy Johnstone, and embraces us. — You're really thin, she whispers, her airms round ma neck and her small, almost oriental eyes, looking up at us.

Ah realise that she must get the hair thing aw the time, so ah start feeling her erse, easin us back oantae the bed. Ah slip her panties off, exposin a silky golden bush, as she says, — Doncha wanna snog first?

My breath might be a big turn-off but fuck it, Charlene's hair's spread ower the manky pillay and we're kissing and she doesnae seem tae mind it, so ah say those magic words that kind ay work, even if they excite me mair than any lassie, — I want tae eat your pussy . . .

— I really don't think so, she says, tensing up.

— How no?

— We're not *lovers*. It's just a shag. C'mon, Mark, fuck me!

— Later, ah mumble, movin doon and oantae her, tongue across her stomach, intae her navel and oantae what is a very fine, thin bush. — Mark . . . she protests, but ah'm on her clit and feel it stiffen under ma tongue. Her hands ur pushing at ma heid, but then she's exhaling n gaun, — Oh fuck . . . do what you fucking well like . . . and ah can feel her beginnin tae loosen up and then suddenly tense again, but this time in a barry wey, and now ah couldnae get ma heid away if ah tried, as she comes ower n ower again.

She eventually pushes us away, then gasps, — I'm on the pill . . . c'mon, give it to me . . .

— Nae worries, like, ah goes, n ah push inside her we fuck for a bit and she comes again; she's oan the circuit eftir they clitoral orgasms. It reminds us ay . . .

Fuck . . . how long does this go oan?

Ah realise that the drugs, which can sometimes make it difficult tae get it up, have made blawing ma muck impossible. Ah pull out and she's oan top, then ah'm giein it tae her from behind, then she's on top again, and it's best cause ah'm lovin the spread ay that big hair, n ah feel ah rampant tickle rising through the numbness in me n ah finally shoot ma load. It actually hurts ma cock, but it's such a fuckin relief.

We collapse in a sweaty heap oan that single bed in the metal box ay the room. It's barry that we're baith that thin. Imagine the likes ay say,

Keezbo n Big Mel fi Gillsand's or one ay the barrow girls tryin tae shack up here. Nae fuckin chance! Must be a vicious circle for the cunts: hard tae git yir hole, so git depressed, eat too much, git fatter, harder tae git yir hole, git mair depressed . . .

— That was fantastic . . . fucking brilliant . . . she says, and that's the sweetest symphony tae my ears cause ah've never had a lassie say that tae us before, well, jist once, and ah almost expect there tae be somebody else in the cabin she's talking tae. — Where did ya learn ta give head like that?

Ah couldnae bring masel tae say an Ebirdeen hoor. — Oh, you know . . . jist got an aptitude for it . . .

— You certainly have, she purrs in appreciation, and the ego's swellin up nicely, but ah'm sair as fuck in ma pish-tube. It burns like some cunt's shot a laser beam up it, and ah'm way too buzzed tae sleep so ah ask her, — What did ye dae before ye worked here?

— Stole, she smiles, rubbing my earring as if she's aboot tae thieve that. — Still do, and she points at the Sealink bag on the table.

Of course, the clothes; she's a total pro tea leaf. Ah almost want tae tell her aboot the scam wi Marriott. But naw, ah leave it, and ah faw intae a weird, druggie kip in her airms, aware that the morning shift is gaunny come up soon and fuck us both.

Sure enough, the cauld morning brings in an atmosphere ay mistrust, poisonous hatred and paranoia. No wi me n Charlene, that's barry, although she raises her knees intae ma chest tae effectively banish us tae ma ain cabin in the early hours. Ah climb ower Nicksy tae the top bunk n doze fir aboot forty minutes till the alarm pulverises me awake.

Naw, the bad vibes are roond the breakfast table in the canteen. Apparently, Marriott wis knockin oan ma door aw night n mornin. He's no amused, his mawkit pus tripping him up. He lowers a tray containin a bowl ay cereal and a coffee oantae the table, then comes behind us and bends ower tae gie us an earfil. — I needed you cahnts around last night, he says in viper-like sibilation tae me, Sick Boy and Nicksy. — What would've happened if I had farking merchandise?

We look at each other, but say nothing.

— Keep on the farking case, he threatens, slidin intae a seat.

— Well, Sick Boy says, — a pleasant 'good morning' to you too!

Ah'm startin tae feel pit-oan n stalked-oot n aw. Like we've been rail-roaded intae this. Ah've been daein some calculations: amount taken through, time served if huckled and remuneration offered, n it aw jist disnae add up. This cunt seems tae think that he owns us. Well, he disnae fuckin own me.

— It ain't meant ter be pleasant, Marriott says, and ah can see resent-ment burn in Sick Boy as the wasted auld skagbag looks searchingly at him tae make sure he can hud up his end. — Am I making myself clear, Simon?

— It's this man you should be worried aboot. Sick Boy points at me, miffed that ah copped off wi Charlene, no doubt. — *Mancanza di disciplina*.

— What's he on about? Marriott asks Nicksy.

— Fuck knows.

This cunt thinks we're junkies like him. Dinnae think so somehow; there's a big difference between a wee habit where ye smoke it and occasionally bang up, and being a total career drug addict, the soul-dead puppet ay some prick whae disnae gie a fuck aboot ye.

Marriott starts slavering on again, in that maundering self-obsessed smackheid wey. — As soon as you're marked, you get the fuck back into town and start hustling for your fix, cause if you're seen trying it on when Curtis is on shift, if he don't get you, we farking well will, he says, bug-eyed, lookin and soundin about as intimidatin as Larry Grayson in a tutu. — Don't give him any reasonable cause ta search yer or he'll have you buck naked with his gloved hands up your arse pulling yer dinner through your intestines with half the Essex con-stabulary in attendance.

Ah catch Sick Boy rollin his eyes in a mock-theatrical gesture that indicates the idea isnae withoot appeal. Marriott reacts tae the chucklin conspiracy and goes genuinely dark; he's no messin around tae try n get an effect any mair. — Then it gets really messy, cause the chaps find out and you're welded into a leaky oil drum and lost at sea.

If he was bullshitting or exaggerating aw ay us now feel disinclined tae call his bluff. Ah feel ma gaze shift tae ma lap, then tae Nicksy.

Marriott gets up, he's hardly touched his cereal, but he rests ower the table, his knuckles white. — Keep in control or you ain't gonna get any farking change outta me, he snorts and heads off.

Sick Boy's shaking his head. — Who is that prick? What have you got us intae here, Nicksy?

— Well, you shouldn't have signed up for it, Nicksy moans.

— I've signed up for sweet fuck all. The cunt outlined a proposition. It sounded good. Now it doesnae. End of. Ma buddy Andreas can get tons ay broon. If we're haulin it through the customs for fuckin sweeties . . .

Sick Boy lowers his voice, as it seems it's now Cream Shirt's turn to hover. Presumably the boat is ready to fill up again and we should be preparing tae set sail on the high seas for merry England. He clears his throat, ubiquitous clipboard in hand, points to his watch, then pirouettes on his Cuban heels and heads off.

— Fuck, Sick Boy scorns, — cannae fuckin breathe on this boat without being accosted by faggots. The official economy, the underground economy, it makes nae odds; every cunt wants tae ram it up yir erse, he declares. — Aw well, better git moving. Another filthy morning beckons. Action stations!

Nash Stoorie Bomb

Grim stuff this wet and dreary morning, man, gaun tae see Franco in the nick, likesay. Ah'd arranged wi June, his ma n his brar Joe a time tae go in when naebody else wis thaire, ken. It's a twelve-month stretch, but he'll be oot in six. Aye, a couple ay Lochend boys were oan the peeve eftir the fitba, n Franco's logic wis seein as Cha Morrison chibbed Larry, he hud tae slash two Lochend laddies. But the boy he goat wisnae really a mate ay Morrison's n it turns oot that he's Saybo's cousin. So it's caused a bit ay a split in the ranks, wi Saybo no gaun in tae visit the Beggar Boy in HMP Saughton. Aye, Ali saw um earlier that night, sais he wis defo oan the warpath.

So we visitors ur aw cauld n wet, as we pit oor stuff intae wee boaxes, oor keys n watches n that, no thit ah've goat a watch, likesay, but ye ken whit ah mean. They gie ye a wee token fir it, then we go through tae sit at they tables n chairs, wi the screws supervisin. Whin Begbie appears, ah huv tae say he looks in barry nick. Even mair filled oot through pumpin prison steel. The only thing he seems really gutted aboot is that Cha Morrison's in Perth, he was really lookin forward tae lockin claws wi that cat. As he says hissel, that wis the only reason he wanted tae dae jail time. He asks us aboot Leith n that, then sortay jist starts giein us a right hard time for bein intae the gear.

Jist as ah'm kinday thinkin ay it bein a mistake tae come, it's likesay he jist sortay gits tired ay it aw. — Listen, thanks fir comin . . . he goes, — it's jist that it's shite seein people visitin. Nowt fuckin happens in here, n ye end up no fuckin wantin tae hear aboot what's gaun oan ootside.

— Right, man . . . ah nods, cause ye kin see the cat's point, ah nivir liked people comin tae see me whin ah wis in Doc Guthrie's, ken?

— So dinnae waste yir fuckin time visitin. Yi'll no git any conversation oot ay me, he looks round tae whaire the guards are standin, — n it's no exactly like wi kin git oot fir a fuckin peeve. Any news, go n see muh ma, n she kin fuckin well bring it in tae us.

Ah must huv looked a wee bit pit oot, n, well, sort ay underappreciated,

man, cause he looks at whaire the plaster oan ma airm used tae be n goes,
— Dinnae fuckin well pit that greetin-faced look oan, like um fuckin tellin
ye oaf; ah'm no fuckin tellin ye oaf! It's good ay ye tae come, right. Ah'm
jist sayin: dinnae fuckin well waste yir time comin in n expectin a fuckin
conversation oot ay me.

— Right . . . sound. Eh . . . Hibs did awright oan Setirday.

— Ah ken how fuckin Hibs did, Spud. Thuv goat fuckin papers n telly
in here, ya daft cunt, the cat shakes his heid.

Ah sortay try another approach. — Did ye see that programme the
other night aboot the apes ay Gibraltar? That wis barry, man. Ah'd nivir
thought aboot apes before, well, ah'd thoat ay thum, likesay, but no *really*
thoat aboot thum, if ye ken whit ah mean. But this really made ye think,
ken? Thaire wis this one ape —

He pure raises his hand tae silence us, like he's a Roman emperor or
something. — Nivir saw it, he sais, endin the conversation. Then he goes,
— How's the airm?

— Barry, man, brand new, like it nivir happened.

— Telt ye it wis gaunny be awright! Fuckin fuss tae make aboot a
broken airm! Ya cunt, ah thoat ye wir fuckin deid the wey ye wir kirrayin
oan!

— Right, eh, sorry, man, ah goes, then ah tells him that Rents and
Sick Boy send thair best fae London, which is kinday a lie cause they jist
take the pish when his name gits mentioned, but jist as a sortay mates
thing, likesay. No thit the Beggar Boy wid likesay appreciate that but. The
thing is, though, underneath it aw, ah think he really is gled tae see us.
It's jist the gadge's wey, ken?

But seein a caged man isnae very good fir the soul, likesay, so ah'm
delighted tae git oot they prison gates n back intae the real world. No
thit it's much better oot here. If thaire's nowt tae dae in the nick, it's
sortay the same ootside, withoot the waws. But at least in the chokey the
three square meals ur provided, ken? Boredom, man. It's like a wee tap
inside ye, drippin oot acid intae yir gut. Eatin away at aw yir organs. In
bed at night it's the worst. Ah try an stretch ma limbs out, but before ah
sortay ken it ah'm aw cramped again, ma fists balled, talkin a load ay
weird, scared stuff tae masel. Cannae be good fir a cat, man.

N ootside its aw nash, stoorie and bomb wi some cats, likesay, ken?
Could never dae wi hurryin aboot masel, even though ah wis ey a dead
fast runner at school. Bit bein twenty-one n huvin the key tae the door
but, you've jist goat tae sit back n mellow oot, likesay. Too much chargin
aboot: it's killin us aw, man. The rat race n that. Stressed if yuv goat a

340

joab, stressed if ye huvnae. Everybody oot fir themselves, at each other's throat n daein each other doon. Nae solidarity nae mair, ken? The work is ower, it's aw gaun, n thaire's nae particular place tae go.

Ma mooth's been feelin awfay dry the day, but ah pit that doon tae that weird broon skag ah got at Johnny's last night. Thought the cat wis extractin the urine when he brought it oot, cause it looked mair like cocoa powder thin Salisbury Crag, ken? Ah wis aboot tae start singing: 'Cup hands, here comes Cadbury's!' But he sais it was aw he could git. Ah lifts ma shirtsleeve n deeks at this scratchy sore oan ma airm. Ah poke it n some yellay pus oozes oot. Ah jist rolls that sleeve doon sharpish; aw, man, ah cannae even look at that . . .

As ah gits oaf the bus back at Leith, the last gadgie ah expect tae see in a tracky, poundin the windswept boulevards ay the fair port, is Second Prize. — Hey, Rab, man, ah goes as the cat comes hoppin intae view oan Bonnington Road.

— Spud . . . he goes, n he stoaps but keeps runnin oan the spot as he sortay raps oot what he's up tae between breaths, n ah git that he's oaf the peeve n goat a new burd called Carol, whae's a mate ay Alison's, n he's gittin fit again and talkin tae a boy at Falkirk aboot a trial, but he might phone the auld boss at Dunfy. Then he's off, bouncin oan they Nike soles taewards Junction Strasse.

Well, it's fabby tae see a boy oan the up. Lean n fit, no intoxicated, indulgin in hot sex wi a fräulein, wi the chance ay earnin a crust or two fae the beautiful game. When ye think aboot it, the cat's goat the lot, man, but ah suppose that aw that means nowt if it's aw badness n despair percolatin inside ay thon furry dome. Ah'm as jealous as, but, man, pure turnin as green as Jimmy O'Rourke in a cabbage patch.

But ah've goat a wee bitty business masel this affie, so ah'm turnin doon the Newhaven Road, Bowtow-bound. Whin ah gits tae the lock-up Matty's awready thaire. Ah've goat tae say right fae the off that Matty's one ay the few boys ah jist cannae git oan wi. It's ey purely biz wi us, ken? N ah ken thit ah wis only asked tae help oot cause ay Rents n Sick Boy bein in London, Tommy no wantin involved, another cat loved up at the moment, n Franco now residin courtesy ay Her Majesty.

Used tae think aw the hostile vibe wis cause ay Matty bein fae the Fort n me bein fae the Kirkgate, which isnae oan the other side ay the world, but naw, cause Keezbo's fae the Fort n Matty's even worse wi him. But ah still do sortay think it's that. They've goat a different mentality thaire fae every other cat in Leith; likesay me comin fae the Kirkgate or Sick Boy fae the Bannanay flats. These boys but, thair jist awfay, well, *Fort* in thair mentality, if ye git ma drift. So ah tries tae discuss this wi Matty. Ah goes, — Youse Fort cats huv goat tae huv a defensive mentality cause yir in this scheme thit's called the Fort, thit looks like a Fort, n yis are actually wawed in, like yir bein kept apart fae the rest ay Leith. See, likesay me or Sick Boy, we're schemies, we've goat that Edina Cooncil rent book n aw, but we're sortay expansive, cause we're no wawed in like youse cats. We've goat the open sea ahead. Bound tae breed a different mentality, Matty, but. Ken?

The likesay Rents or Sick Boy or Keezbo would pure git intae discussin this point, but Matty jist goes, — Cunt, ah'm gittin the keys tae this flat in Wester Hailes. She wants it, bit ah'm no that bothered, eh, no.

N that's it, man. That's the level ay conversation. It makes us think thit Matty wid nivir make it in the world ay rock n roll; ah mean, even if he wis likesay better oan the guitar. Ah mean, imagine that cat in the studio wi Frank Zappa n the Mothers ay Invention, thir gittin up tae aw thair high jinks n he jist turns roon n goes, 'Ah've goat the keys tae this flat in Wester Hailes.' Ah mean, how ur they cats gaunny respond tae that, likesay? 'Barry, gadgie, lit's dae some acid.' Ah mean, yuv goat tae sortay pill yir weight in the social situ, ken?

So wir jist loadin n unloadin different boaxes ay delinquent durables fae the van tae the lock-up, n it's no hoat at aw but ah'm still pure sweatin. N ah'm telling Matty aboot Swanney's weird broon, but he's jist sayin, 'Aye, it's true, thaire's nae white aroond.' Then ah starts talkin aboot visitin Franco, n it turns oot thit Matty's been tae see um n aw. N it's a wee bit ay chat at last! He's gaun oan aboot how Franco wis oan at him aboot the likes ay Swanney n this other gadge Seeker n Davie Power but ah realise ah cannae really hear what he's sayin cause everything's went aw distorted and blurred. Ah feel dizzy n ah huv tae sit doon oan the concrete n ah'm thinkin, wis that gear ah did yesterday right dodgy or what . . . ? Ah look at the pus-filled scab oan my airm whaire ah shot it up, but it wis wi ma ain works n Keezbo did some n aw . . .

— Cunt, what's up wi you? Ah hear Matty's voice, as ah look up intae the weak sunlight. — C'moan, ya mongol, wuv goat tae git this sorted oot!

Ah'm no right here. Something's wrong. Ah'm fucked. Ah feel seek n likesay everything aroond us is aw dark n looks miles away . . . — Ah huv tae go tae the hoaspital, Matty, ah'm gaunny die, likesay . . .

— Cunt, what's wrong wi ye?

— Ah'm away, man, n ah stagger tae ma feet n it's like bad dream n

Matty's sayin how's he meant tae unload aw they boaxes oan his tod, but ah'm right staggerin like a wino up oantae the Ferry Road. Ah puke up n faw ower, hudin oantae the railins n this wifie n her bairn are askin us if ah'm awright, n ah pill masel up n walk a bit doon the road . . . then . . .

The High Seas

The first week at Sealink wis certainly eventful enough; a riot, a bit ay gear, n some barry sex. You *cannae* fucking well say fairer than that. Oan toap ay it aw, Marriott's planned the first walk-through for the night. There's nae chance ay us lasting the month here.

This is the weirdest place ah've ever worked; even Gillsland's, wi Les's Monday-morning shiteing competitions, cannae compete. Staff-wise, *The Freedom of Choice* is like the *Marie Celeste*. We're experts at avoiding work; no just the seasonals, but the established staff tae. They've aw been issued new contracts ay employment, which meants longer hours fir far less pay, so motivation is non-existent. Therefore any passengers with enquiries cannae find us. Oan occasions when we ur visible, we strut aroond the ship wi a phoney expression ay purpose oan oor faces, eywis in flight fae real graft. Cream Shirt's lispy voice seems tae be chasing ghosts; a name prefixed by an anxious 'Where's . . . ?' Of course, nae cunt hus a fuckin scooby.

Being assigned tae the kitchen was meant tae be punishment, but it's turned oot a fuckin boon; much better than stewarding duties. For one thing, thaire's less risk ay confronting fitba mobs or drunk stag parties. Ah've nae inclination tae deal wi that kind ay shite. And, bein honest, ah cannae gie a fuck aboot Marriott's smugglin gig either. If ah kin walk through the customs between shifts wi a couple ay grams ay percy and hud the job doon, then ah'm daein fine. But takin ten gs ay uncut broon through customs in ma strides, jist soas some fat cunt can buy sovies, drive a BMW n sit in a villa oan the Costa del Sol? Fuck that for a game ay sodjirs. There's millions ay mugs in Thatcher's army linin up fir that job. Sick Boy n me talked aboot it, n he's in agreement. The only small matter is how tae brek the news tae Marriott. But ah dinnae gie a fuck; ah've goat other things oan ma mind.

Clang, bang, bang goes the ship, frothing through the North Sea, flocks ay squawkin gulls trailing behind feedin oan its excrement. Bang, bang, bang go me and Charlene, her grabbing a hud ay us and pulling us downstairs, riding us hard oan the bunk, her hair flying, or me sucking

344

and licking her enchanting tufted fanny till she either squeaks wi delight or ah asphyxiate. Her small doll's mooth around my cock, crazy eyes burning as it bangs oan the back ay her throat. Wir competitive orally; baith want tae bring the other oaf the quickest. Ah usually win, through making myself think ay Ralphy Gillsland's vaginal coupon at the crucial moment, in order tae stave off the muck-spurt. My sex-drive still isnae what it should be, but at least smokin the broon disnae seem tae decimate it completely, no like bangin up the white. Youthful libido versus chronic heroin addiction is perhaps the ultimate battle between irresistible force and immovable object. But there's only gaunny be one winner, so ah've goat tae keep the skag in check. In some weys there's a pay-off though; instead ay gittin too excited and jist wantin tae git ma cock up thaire, it makes us mair relaxed n intae foreplay. Never realised ye could dae so much wi yir fingers, and as fir this fuckin tongue, ah'm like that boy oot ay Kiss or the fat gadgie fae Bad Manners whae looks like Keezbo . . .

On deck it's perma-party time as drunk customers sway blindly intae the intense junky-n-uptight-faggot staff. Sick Boy's antagonism towards me and Charlene for us getting it oan quickly dissipated when he realised that the nice girls really do love a sailor, n that having yir ain berth oan a boat fill ay drunk hen-night parties is a terrific asset. He's the only male whae has his ain cabin, due tae some scam he worked oot. He'd said tae Cream Shirt, — I have unusual sleeping habits, Martin, which might prove embarrassing if someone was put in with me. I'd be very much obligated if you could spare me and any other party that awkwardness, by allocating me a private cabin if possible.

The short-arsed buftie had looked sympathetically at him and said, — Leave it with me, I'll see what I can do.

But up till now skagwise, we'd only taken a bit ay percy through the customs. Ah wis shitein masel, even when ah saw the boy Frankie, who we'd drank wi up the Globe pub. He was sound. But there was once ah was ready tae go through n he wisnae there, it was jist some other gadge. Ah bottled it n walked back, away fae the ship, before ah saw Frankie comin towards us. — Just went for a shit, he smiled cheerfully, takin ower fae the other boy, and lettin us through oan the nod.

A bigger problem for me initially was Chef. Well, no him really, he turned oot tae be an okay gadge when ye got tae ken him. It was the work and specifically the fuckin heat. Naebody who husnae worked in an industrial kitchen can have any concept ay just how constant and draining it is. Ah goat oan wi the graft but, largely thanks tae bein wi Charlene. She described us as 'friends who fuck'. She went oot her way tae let me ken that she hud a felly who'd got pit away n that ah wis basically jist a subsitute ride.

So ah huv tae keep ma infatuation in check, n it isnae easy. Tae me she's ma English female equivalent; a Kentish dockyard princess fae Chatham. N thaire's the boy in the chokey tae consider. Charlene doesnae want tae talk aboot him, which suits me, but she sais he's in fir thieving rather thin violence, which comes as some relief. But whatever anybody's in fir, thir no gaunny take too kindly tae some cunt cowpin thair lemon curd. Ye cannae say it's overly romantic but, shaggin oan a narray bed, but at least she's as restless as me, and eftir we've done the biz, we go up oan the deck, no many clathes oan, jist enough tae be decent if any cunt sees us, n watch the rough, sickly dawn rise ower the port. Frozen flurries ay rain lash low breeze-block harbour and shipping buildings and whistle roond the vessel's structures above and behind us. Big puddles swell oan the uneven stanes ay the dock. Solitary figures struggle against the wind, tying heavy ropes oantae bollards or simply walking between buildings wi clipboards. Charlene's big hair's whipped by the gales, and we stand in T-shirts n tracky bottoms, playin a game whaire we git so unbearably cauld, one ay us'll shout SURRENDER and we'll beat an urgent retreat, crab-walkin doon the loads ay narray stairs tae the mingin bowels ay the ship n that festering nest, before snuggling up and riding again.

So on Amsterdam shore leave eftir our shifts, we're sittin in the Grass-hopper, me n Sick Boy, while Charlene is playin pool wi they two chain-smokin Scouse lassies wi throaty laughs, passengers whae came ower oan the boat. Nicksy comes in, lookin like a frightened schoolboy, wi an itchy, bug-eyed Marriott, whae clocks the girls and isnae happy. He nods tae the door.

Ah look at Sick Boy. We apologise tae the lassies n follay Nicksy and Marriott ootside, tae a busy ootdoor cafe across the square, n take some seats. A waitress comes n we order coffee.

— It's on tonight, Marriott says. — We take through ten gs each.

Ah'm aboot tae say, no way, but Sick Boy gets in first. — Sorry, ship-mate. Nice offer, but on this particular occasion I'm forced tae decline.

— What? You . . . you farking what? You're having a laugh . . . I've got the farking shit here, he nods to the Sealink bag at his feet, then zips it open, pulling it apart to expose five packets.

— As I've said, I'd love to help you out, but *on this particular occasion*, I'm forced tae decline.

— You farking . . . what am I meant to do with this farking shit? His constipated owl eyes take a crotchety scour at a couple ay backpackers sitting doon at the next table. One has a Canada flag wi the maple leaf stickin fae it. In Scotland we've been exporting every straight cunt tae Canada fir generations. Result? They're boring fuckers, and we're a drug-addled underclass.

— Not my problem, Sick Boy says snootily.

Marriott turns tae me in blind panic. — You ain't gonna let me down n all, are ya?

— Now ye mention it: aye, ah tell him, as his chin nearly hits the cobblestones. The cunt looks like he's deciding whether tae slap ma chops or burst intae tears. — Sorry, pal, nowt personal likes, ah lies, — but you've been railroading us intae this scene. Ah've been daein the sums in ma heid: grams, jail time, pay-off. It just disnae add up.

— There won't be any farking jail time, he squeals in frustration, — I told ya about the customs geezers! It's watertight!

— Then there should be absolutely no problem at all for you in finding suitably enlightened parties all too keen tae grasp this unique business opportunity yir presenting, ah goes, now really enjoyin masel, as ah clock Sick Boy's widening smile.

Marriott starts hyperventilating and turns tae Nicksy. — You told me they was staunch, you cunt –

Nicksy goes fuckin radge. — Who the fark are you callin a cunt! He springs up and bends over Marriott, who skulks back in his chair. — I got farking well more to think about than you and your shitty farking drug deals, you scrawny farking two-bob wankah!

The Canadian backpackers, both white-faced, wholesome speckoids, turn roond in their seats, lookin oan anxiously. Nicksy boots the Sealink bag and it tips ower oan its side n one packet ay gear slides oot oantae the cobblestones. Ah have tae say that ah've never seen ten grams ay skag before in ma puff, and although it's only the size ay a wee packet ay sweeties rather than the standard copin bag ay half a g, which is aboot two big gairden peas' worth, ah just want tae fuckin well grab it! Marriott's first though: he makes a gurgling sound n dives doon, scooping the packet intae the holdall and zipping it up in one manic motion.

We nod tae each other and get up, headin back ower tae the Grasshopper. — You ain't heard the last of this, Marriott shouts, as the waitress comes ower with four milky coffees. We look back and laugh as the twitching imbecile tries to fish the guilders out ay his pocket tae pey her.

— You fucking well telt that choob where tae go, mate. Sick Boy raises Nicksy's arm in the air, victorious-boxer-style, as we cross the square. — ICF!

— Got a feeling I'll be needing all the contacts I've got ta get us outta this farking mess, he says ruefully, — but he was takin the farking piss, wasn't he?

— Aye, ah agree, — but he's a fuckin gobshite. He's gaunny dae nowt.

— It ain't him I'm worried about. Nicksy shakes his heid, then looks pointedly at me. — Ya don't think that was *his* gear, do ya?

— Right . . . ah suddenly tipple, feelin a bit ay a prick, n git a sinkin sensation in ma gut.

— Gentlemen, I think our little stint at Sealink might be coming tae an end, Sick Boy declares, as he throws open the doors and we move back intae the Grasshopper. As Nicksy and I nod in agreement, he adds rakishly, — But right now there are ladies to be entertained, and entertain them we must!

Desertion

At breakfast the following morning, Marriott greeted his deserting ex-comrades with an expression of loathing only a man compelled to make a solitary run through customs with fifty grams of heroin could hope to muster. Despite his success, he'd lost what felt like several pounds in sweat his gaunt frame could ill-afford. He resolved that he'd sort this problem out himself rather than call his boss; that would only incur Gal's displeasure, and he'd still end up having to fix things. But a dark resentment flooded him. Once he'd found new recruits, he'd call in some favours and those arseholes would pay dearly.

Marriott's brooding silence informed Renton, Sick Boy and Nicksy that vengeance was certainly on his mind. So, on returning to Hackney, they decided it was unwise to go back to Sealink. That Charlene had also opted to pack in the high seas made it an easy decision for Renton. Despite the fact he knew little about her, other than that she thieved for a living, came from Chatham and 'usually' lived in Kennington (he'd somewhat hopefully mixed it up with Kensington till she put him right), he liked her and wanted to learn more. They spent the next night together in Beatrice Webb House, Renton elated that Sick Boy had absented himself, presumably to Lucinda's or Andreas's, where he more often than not seemed to stay. On the mattress in the spare room, she tells him, after some morning love has warmed up their bodies, — I'm glad you ain't goin back on that poxy boat either. I know what you were up ta . . . with that Marriott geezer n all that. Everybody talked about it.

— What? Renton is aghast, now even more relieved they had literally jumped ship. It wasn't that they were discreet, he glumly realises; the stark truth is that nobody even cares. But that'll change: the company'll see to that. This is, after all, the epoch of the scab and the grass.

— Leave that shit, Charlene advises, head propped up on her elbow. Her tight features pinched together in the thin morning sun that spills through the wicker blinds give Renton the first impression that, despite her stub nose and elfin frame, she's perhaps older than him. — You'll do

349

serious time if ya get yer collar felt for that. Blimey, I know something well dodgy when I see it. Benson had a security firm come in last week, ya know.

— But that was just tae review the procedures for dealing wi bother. Cause ay the riot wi the fitba boys n that.

Charlene narrows her eyes further. — You seriously think that's all it was, you wally?

He doesn't. Renton knows what's happening at the company. But he's led her to believe that it was this, along with Marriott's rancour, which has sealed the deal for him. Doesn't want to tell her that there's no way he's going back to Sealink if she isn't. But what *is* she planning to do, in the long term? He certainly knows her immediate concerns, as they once again head into the West End.

Suited up, Charlene's blonde mane is tied into a low ponytail, save for two tendrils hanging loose over each ear, curled into spirals and blasted stiff with hairspray. He's dressed, at her promptings, in his solitary dark blue Leith Provi weddings and funerals suit. As he sits waiting in Carnaby Street, she steals him some black leather shoes and a light blue silk shirt with matching tie, a gesture that makes him almost cry in appreciation. Renton's blown away by her professionalism, her Sealink bag lined with tinfoil to avoid setting off security alarms. Ducking down a side lane he replaces his old trainers and T-shirt, and steps back blinking into the light and shoppers. — Now you're ready, she says, straightening the tie like it was his first day at school. They get to John Lewis's in Oxford Street and fill up on goods, Renton swiping a Fred Perry for percy. In the toilets, he chases a bit of brown he'd recently procured, along with some good base speed, as he inspects his haul. He sits there for ages with the small window open trying to disperse various fumes. Finally emerging, loose-limbed and slack-featured, paranoid that Charlene has done a runner or got huckled, his expression lifts as his eyes meet her mischievous smile. They link arms and swagger out of the store, buzzing with their success.

They snog and grope all the way to Highbury & Islington, Renton sucking mucus down the back of his throat to avoid slathering it in Charlene's face. The flat of his palm sits pushed against her stomach, secured by her skirt waistband, content to slide no further. Her hand grapples his thigh, her wrist rubbing against his drug semi-erection. While he's making dizzy plans for the future, Charlene is being browbeaten by the nagging recollection that she loves somebody else and is supposed to be preparing to dump her Scottish consort. By the time they've left the Victoria Line for

350

the overland to Dalston Kingsland, her guilt induces a coldness and distance, but Renton is both too skagged up and emotionally inexperienced to really notice or care that much about her mood swings. They get to Beatrice Webb House, and when the lift works they unleash simultaneous sighs of victory, disconcerted at how completely they've fallen into a joint rhythm.

Inside the flat, Nicksy's sitting in the armchair, pretending to watch repeats of *Crown Court*, while contemplating grim options. How it was way too far gone to have been done legally. They said they scraped them out when it was at the right time, but had to get the forceps up there and pull the lot out in a oner, or in broken bits, when it was more advanced. How it, IT, deserved at least more than the chute.

He gives Renton and Charlene a perfunctory greeting as they bounce in and crash on the couch, but their attention is on each other and the telly.
— *Crown Court* . . . barry . . . Renton says as Nicksy looks to the kitchen.
— Mark . . . I really need to talk to ya . . . Charlene says, sitting forward stiffly, but Renton lunges at her, silencing her with a deep kiss. They start a tickling fight, laughing hysterically, and then they're necking again. Nicksy registers that his Scottish friend and the Bird With the Big Hair have adopted that arrogant 'look-at-us-we've-just-invented-sex' demeanour of people who're fucking after a long hiatus. Their Bonnie and Clyde routine gnaws at his own celibacy and he thinks again of Marsha, seven floors of systems-built concrete above him, and the abortive fruits of their love, rotting on some council tip.

Charlene suddenly slaps Renton quite forcibly, pointing at him, demanding, — I'm being serious, but he's still clowning, snapping at her fingers like the puppy, who lies on the floor at their feet.

Nicksy doesn't like a mousy type of girl, but thinks that Charlene's way too full of herself. The way she always runs her hands through that hair, observing the geezers for their reaction; it sets her up as a poseur in his book. He also feels that she's nowhere near as good-looking as she thinks, although he has to admit that barnet is something else.

Renton and Charlene whisper a terse exchange and relocate to the spare room and its mattress. Nicksy decides to check out Dalston market. A mate of his back in Ilford has a pile of contraband Walkmans, and he knows a no-questions-asked West Indian fence.

Outside, it's not a stimulating day. It's already rained and filthy, saturated clouds threaten to dump more. Gobbing into the gutter, to try and spit out self-hate's sour taste, Nicksy ponders the next move in his chaotic life. Like the Sealink job, the tenancy in Beatrice Webb House has possibly

351

run its course. Perhaps he'll take Giro with the Northern Soul singles to his mum's in Ilford. She likes dogs and he'll be happy there, with the back garden. He'll check with her first: wouldn't want him joining the post-Christmas canine holocaust at Gants Hill roundabout.

Back upstairs in the flat at Beatrice Webb House, Charlene and Rents play with Giro in the front room. They pass her leather purse back and forward, the pup trying to grasp it in his slavery jaws. On the seventh snap he gets a tight grip, as Renton holds resolutely onto the other end.

— Give us it ere! Blimey, you're gonna pull yer teeth out, Giro, Charlene says, looking at the dog, then to Renton, unhappy that they'd once again made love, and she still hadn't said what she'd wanted to. *Well, that was the last time.*

— Naw, ye cannae let go, he says.

His words carry a phantom weight and she feels a tenderness grip her. Fights it down. — You wot?

— Ye cannae let go, he keeps a grip on the purse as Giro emits low growls through his nostrils, — or the dug gits badly trained. It thinks it's the dominant one in the pack.

— It ain't got much bleedin competition in this flat, has it?

Renton looks at her and is about to say, 'Fuck me, I think I'm in love with you,' although he isn't quite sure that he means it, and if he does, whether it would be a good strategic move at this point. So he hesitates. Then Charlene turns to him and says, — We gotta stop all this.

— What? Renton asks, experiencing an instant subsidence from somewhere deep within. His fingers go limp on the purse and Giro tugs it free, trotting off victoriously with his prize.

Charlene's eyes are hard and focused. — You know what I'm on about.

— Fine by me, Renton says, in utter devastation. Then he starts to rant in anguish, — But . . . but it's barry . . . the chorrin thegither. N the shaggin n that. You said so yirsel . . .

— Yeah, it is, she concedes, — but I told you all along, it ain't as if we're going out together.

— Never said we were. He hears the child in his voice, and in flashback envisions himself as a small boy, wielding a stick around inside the walls of the Fort. Then, on the promenade at Blackpool, tearful face pushed into the bosom of a stranger.

— You're a nice bloke, but I told ya, there's somebody else.

— So you've got this felly. Renton's stung by his own bitter tone and by the fact that he wants to say: 'I'll bet he's got a bigger cock than me,' but checks himself and instead remarks, — He'll be a handsome chappie, I take it.

— I think so. You'd like him. He ain't that different ta you.

— Sure, Renton says dismissively. — How?

— Well, he's a bit too fond of drugs, for one thing. And he likes Northern Soul and punk. Look . . . I told ya from the off that there was someone else. It was never gonna be a permanent arrangement.

— Sound by me, he says unconvincingly, then shakes his head ruefully and speaks, almost to himself: — Funny, aw ah wanted was a lassie where it wis like we sortay wirnae really like gaun oot thegither, we were just, like, mates. Like you sais, mates that fuck. Like Sick Boy has wi a couple ay birds back hame; nae complications or nowt. And ah'd goat that wi you . . .

— Yeah, well, problem solved, innit.

— Naw, cause it's like ah want mair now, and he thinks of his previous encounters in the past year or so; Fiona, then that sound lassie from Manchester, Roberta her name was, and some others he doesn't want to remember.

— Sounds ta me like you dunno what ya want.

Renton feels his shoulders flex in a shrug. — Ah jist like getting fucked up n chorrin n hingin aboot n shaggin. It rules.

— Don't look at me like that, then!

— Like what?

— Like an orphaned baby seal caught on the ice that's about to have its brains clubbed out!

The stiff smile on Renton's mouth reluctantly crawls into his eyes. — Ah didnae realise . . . sorry. It's just that you're a cool lassie . . . he shakes his head fondly, — that foil in the bag thing ruled.

Charlene looks at him, then eases back onto the couch and thinks of Charlie, in the Scrubs. His two front teeth knocked out, giving him that simpleton smile she perversely loved. The two of them: childhood boyfriend and girlfriend from the Medway Towns. Rochester and Chatham. Yes, she loves Charlie. Mark is better in bed, but that won't last, not with all that heroin he smokes. But she likes him. — You're the first geezer wot didn't go on about my fucking hair all the time; it gets on me nerves, she says unconvincingly.

Renton's shoulders inch upwards in a disparaging thrust. — It's really brilliant but ah sometimes think it would be better short. Accentuate those beautiful eyes, he drawls, feeling a muffled, queasy throb from somewhere deep inside him, making him think of skag again.

Charlene smiles at Renton, wondering if he's taking the piss. But he seems quite upset. She loves Charlie, but knows prison hasn't done him any good, and she suspects that she's yet to see the full extent of the damage. She's pragmatic enough to keep her options open. It's good to know Mark cares. She gets up, scribbles a name, 'Millie', and a number down on the notepad by the phone, tearing of the slip of paper. Renton rises too; he feels the moment calls for it. She crushes the paper into his jeans pocket. — It ain't mine, it's a friend's in Brixton. She'll know how to get in touch with me if ya ever wanna hook up. Leave your number with her and she'll pass it on ta me, and I'll get back ta ya.

Renton is in front of her and making no move to stand aside. Charlene thinks for a second he's blocking her way, but she hasn't tagged him as the sort to make a scene. In fact, as she puts her arms around him, she's disconcerted at how distant and accepting of the situation he now is, how easy, after a brief flush of need, this has suddenly all become for him. A rush of regret swells in her. — You're a lovely bloke, she says, tightening her grip.

But he's squirming like an unruly toddler in the arms of an indulgent auntie. — Right . . . you're barry . . . eh, ah'll see ye, Charlene, he says robotically.

Leave me leave me leave me . . . skag skag skag . . .

Charlene breaks off and stands back, holding his hands, taking him in. Marvelling at the angles of his thin frame, his yellow-toothed smile. — Ya will phone me, won'tcha? It was good . . . in bed n all that . . . she says.

— Aye, ah telt ye, Renton says, every nerve in his body screaming GO as to his massive relief Charlene walks out, the Sealink bag slung across her shoulder on the extended strap, thus obscuring his last view of the tight arse he'd come to regard as his altar. Even though its image was well burnt into his brain, a farewell glance would have been appreciated.

Chucked the student, given the elbow by the shoplifter.

I will survive, wey-hey.

As soon as he hears the lift doors outside, Renton rushes to his stash in the grumbling, tutting fridge. The heroin is cooling with some rotting lettuce and celery in a drawer. With his spec case, he heads back to the couch, arching over the coffee table littered with wastrel detritus, and starts to cook up. He's piqued as the sound of the door going snaps in his ears, worrying that Charlene has returned. However, it's only Nicksy, who looks down at Renton in disdain, then heads to the kitchen where he instantly chops out two big lines of speed on the shaky-legged table and declares, in punk-style, that England's shit. — It's all gone to pieces, mate.

Renton is burning the heroin, lighter flame lapping round the spoon.

He's a bit worried at its lack of purity, but it *seems* to be dissolving into a bubbling elixir. — Scotland n aw, he says empathetically, looking to Nicksy. It was true; the post-war optimism was most certainly over. The welfare state, full employment, the Butler Education Act were all gone or compromised to the point of being rendered meaningless. It now really was everyone for themselves. We were no longer all in this together. But it wasn't all bad, he considered; at least we're getting a wider choice of drugs now.

Nicksy springs to his feet, standing in the doorway of the kitchen and the front room. He points at the spoon and its contents, nerves jangling, bottom puppet-jaw in spasm, lank hair plastered to his skull. — Give it a rest, Mark. You said you was through banging up that shit.

Renton looks up, face a picture of surly, recalcitrant entitlement. — Geez a fuckin brek, Nicksy. Ah've just been chucked, eh.

— Oh . . . right. Sorry ta hear it, Nicksy says, stepping back into the kitchen. Doesn't know why. Pirouettes on the tiled floor and hops back into the front room. — Have to be dynamic, he muses to himself.

— You've been thaire, buddy, Renton observes, clamping the flex from the table lamp round his thin biceps, then gripping the cord in his teeth. — No very nice, is it? he whines, disconcerted that his voice sounds the very same. *Fuck. Ah really do speak through ma beak now.*

— Nah. It ain't.

— Aye, Charlene's fucked off. She's goat this boyfriend. He's just gittin back oot the jail. Renton taps up a vein in his wrist.

— Well, that ain't gonna help.

— It isnae aboot helping, it's aboot *being*. If being Scottish is about one thing, it's aboot gittin fucked up, Renton explains, working the needle slowly into his flesh. — Tae us intoxication isnae just a huge laugh, or even a basic human right. It's a way ay life, a political philosophy. Rabbie Burns said it: whisky and freedom gang thegither. Whatever happens in the future tae the economy, whatever fucking government's in power, rest assured we'll *still* be pissin it up and shootin shit intae ourselves, he announces, pulsing with glorious anticipation as he sucks his dark blood back into the barrel, then lets his ravenous veins drink the concoction.

Home, boy . . .

Whoa . . . ya fuckin beauty . . .

Renton topples back onto the sagging couch and its pinging coils that hold up his shifting weight like pall-bearers, and laughs in a fathomless yawn, — Smokin shit . . . it just isnae cost-effective . . .

Nicksy has no time for the television or his friend's junky observations.

355

He can't settle, the speed has kicked in and he's vibrating in the armchair. Catching a sharp whiff from his own trainers, he leaps to a standing position. Looks up at the dull cream ceiling.

Marsha.

He charges out the door as if the flat was on fire.

Junk Dilemmas No. 1

Nicksy didnae half tear oot the door. Cunt's way too uptight these days. Whatever happened tae the cheeky wee cockney sparrer, the ducker and diver whae let nothing get under his skin?

Probably that Marsha bird upstairs. Women. What a fuckin minefield. The student you hump and dump. The shoplifter steals your heart and –

SHARP THROB . . .

Fuck sake . . .

SHARP FUCKIN THROB . . .

Whoops . . . ah'm on ma feet n through tae the bog. A long pish which seems tae last months. The dug's up, balancing against the bowl wi his front paws, watchin ma pish stream. He pits his nose tae it, gits a splash fi the jet, yelps and dances off, lookin up at me like ah'm a cunt. — Giro . . . sorry, compadre . . .

Ah'm bored wi this pish . . . end . . . end . . . end . . .

END . . .

END . . .

BANG BANG DOOF DOOF –

A knock on the door. Shake it oot. Pit it back. Move. Open the front door.

It's this wee black lassie, that Marsha bird, n she's screamin a loaday shite at me. Aboot Nicksy, oan a ledge . . . rantin about dead bairns . . .

Fuckin nut job . . . but then the polis . . . my God, it's the fuckin polis . . . a blobby WPC n a jug-eared copper, n thir tellin us baith tae git doonstairs in the lift . . .

The lift goes doon n she's still screamin aboot Nicksy bein sick and twisted and what does he fuckin well want fae her n ah'm thinkin . . .

FUCK ME . . .

Thi'll no lit us back in fir the gear . . .

IT'S MA FUCKIN GEAR!

Towers of London

Lucinda is my ticket to the good life. It's time tae stop fannying about and strike; get the ring on her finger, myself moved intae her Notting Hill pad on a permanent basis, then her right up the duff as an insurance policy. At which point her posh Ingloid old boy will have tae come round and acknowledge that Young Williamson is *not* going away. Then it's all about sitting tight for a few years before stepping intae the family fortune. In ma pocket is the key that spells commitment with a capital K, the ring ah bought fae that semi-decent jeweller's in Oxford Street.

She's defo the sort ay girl you could take home to Mama, and ah might do just that, as Rents and I are feeling the pull ay Caledonia. The giro syndicate means one fortnightly National Express coach trip south tae sign on, and Nicksy is talking about leaving the flat and heading back tae his ma's for a bit. Ah also want tae check in on poor Spud. He's meant tae be in a bad way.

And Lucinda wants to slum it. It astonishes me that so many ay her friends have that thing going on. Tae the untrained eye, they perhaps look, act, smell and even talk poor, but somewhere along the yellow brick road, stuffed in a hidey-hole up ahead of them, a big stack ay unearned loot awaits. A pile that changes everything. A heap of dosh that says tae me: *fuck off, you empty fake*, whenever they drone on in their artificial cockney whines. She's trying this shit on now, wi irony at the moment, but we both know that if ah gie her any encouragement at all, it'll be shamelessly adopted as a stylistic device. She's telling me that ah sound like Sean Connery, while displaying a worrying curiosity about Leith and the Bannanay flats. But if she wants scheme, ah can certainly dae scheme, and I have tae admit that the prospect ay pumping her on a mattress saturated wi the spunk stains and fanny juices of a hundred transients in a Hackney tower block does have a certain trash aesthetic. Then, in that post-coital moment, I shall bring out the ring, and we'll head north tae meet Mama. There are faces (tae say nothing of fannies) ah miss back hame, and most of all, ah want tae make sure that the scumbag whose rancid cock dribbled me intae existence is not messing my mother about.

We get off the tacky North London Line at Dalston Kingsland, which has the one advantage that it's effectively free, and head down tae the Holy Street Estate. Lucinda, for all her swagger, tightens her grip on my arm, confirming she's just that wee bitty too soft for this terrain. *Fear not, fair damsel, Simon's here.*

That thieving wee Charlene Fawcett-Majors-Plant chicky that Rents has been canoodling with is coming across the road. Our heads mutually swivel away; we pretend no tae notice each other. Ah've better goods on my airm than *that* wee hing-oot, thank you very much, although Lucinda's daein ma crust in, slavering on about how it's so 'real' around here. If ah wanted 'real' ah'd've steyed in Leith, but ah let her cling tae her rich bird's delusions. But she's caught Charlene and me pointedly ignoring each other: more suspicion-framing than any gushing acknowledgement.

— Who was that girl?

— Oh, just this hostile bint Mark's been shagging.

— What about that Penny? she says darkly.

— Exactly, I snap. — He has the morals of a sewer rat, that one. I think –

What in the name of fuck . . .

— What's going on? Lucinda's grip tightens on mine again, as a crowd has gathered below Beatrice Webb House. Following the line ay vision ah can see that someone is standing on a ledge ay the tower block, having climbed right oot the fucking windae! It looks like one arm is fastened inside, securing them to this world. And fuck me, it's *Nicksy*. — Fuck sakes! That's my flatmate! Nicksy!

— Simon, that's terrible . . . what's he doing . . .?

I have to admit that ma first instinct is a fervent hope that he jumps; simply in order tae place myself as a central player in the drama of a short and tragic life. Ah think ay that record collection divvied up between Rents and myself. A stake for a wee bit ay brown, exported back up the road. Cunts wouldnae ken what it was. Then ah realise that it's no our place he's hanging ootay, it's right near the top. It's that dippit wee pump-up-the-breek's gaff!

Then ah spy her in the crowd, the doolally Marsha, surrounded by a group ay hungry-eyed black yute and some aulder Caribbean bloaters whae wirnae at the back ay the queue when the rice n peas wis daein its rounds. She clocks me and comes ower, eyes blazing and demented. — He came into my farking flat and started farking shouting! Then he climbed right aht the farking windah, innit!

— He's a nut job, ah tell her.

Marsha looks at me in acknowledgement that ah couldnae gie a fuck, so she shouldnae really bother pretending tae, or at least no that much. Lucinda and her, two London ladies of different social standing, the posh and the impoverished, regard each other in mutual wariness and intimidation. Marsha turns back tae me and says, — You oughta be looking after him! He's your flatmate!

— Que sera, sera, ah observe as the wee radge bird's loony lamps blaze fae me back up tae the fourteenth floor. We've nothing more tae say tae each other.

Ah spy the ginger heid of the Rent Boy and approach his edgy, quivering back, though when he clocks us his sly eyes still briefly dance across Lucinda's chest. — The polis telt us tae get ootside, he whinges. — They willnae let anybody in the stair. They've sent some cunt up tae talk tae um! Gear on the coffee table n ivraythin!

He now has ma full attention; ah slap ma heid in exasperation. — If he does anything stupid . . .

— Fuckin polis could turn the fuckin gaff ower, Renton snaps through clenched yellow teeth.

Lucinda pulls on my hand. — It's okay, Simon, she reassures me, — the Metropolitan Police know what they're doing. They receive proper training for these situations.

Receive proper training. Brixton. Broadwater Farm. Stoke Newington. David Martin. Blair Peach. Colin Roach. — Aye, they're well up wi the game.

He's still on that narrow ledge, hanging onto the frame. How the fuck did he git oot there? There's a safety catch so you have to unscrew it tae open the windae past the point where somebody could step out. There's a polis cordon at the entrance tae the flats; naebody can get in. One old munter is moaning that she has to get through cause her cat needs fed. It falls on deef polis lugs. What the fuck is that dipstick daein, aw this hassle ower a ten-a-penny wee spunk-bucket? Marsha was jumping around on the spot, now she's weeping and being comforted by her sister. The wee bird's a decent enough ride, but so damaged as tae be completely unfixable. He musht be able to shee that, Sean, surely? *Love ish blind tho, Shimon.* This shavyor complex, Sean, why do sho many people have it? *Shearch me, buddy.*

It's hard to discern whether Nicksy wants tae jump or has decided it's no such a good idea, and is too frozen up wi fear tae get back inside. Ah catch Rents muttering something that sounds like, — Fuckin attention-seeking cunt, and I couldnae agree more with the sentiment. Then he spoils it by adding, — If any cunt should be daein that it's me, and he turns his chalky, spotty, druggie face tae us. — Charlene's jist chucked us!

— Sorry to hear it, I say, twitching a bit, as you can see Lucinda's wheels turning as if she's thinking, *I thought he was in a relationship with that Penny* . . . The fucking ginger tramp has only been shagging her for a couple ay weeks; hardly Romeo and Juliet, ah would have thought. — I think he's trapped himself. I squeeze 'Cinder's' hand, pointing up at floor fourteen, tae divert her dangerous train of thought. Her eyes widen and her mouth forms a fraught, trembling oval.

I'm thinking that a straight-line fall would see Nicksy smashing onto concrete paving stones, while pushing off in a dedicated hari-kari jump might mean him hitting the gress. Either way, he's fucked. More ay a nasty clean-up job on the concrete, one would imagine. That's if the body splits open. At that thought, I feel shivers running up the backs ay my legs and intae my hands as my ringpiece starts to go intae a spasm. Ah suddenly want him no tae jump, tae be saved, and want it wi every fuckin fibre ay ma being. That cunt took me in. The boy is fucking sound. I feel the tight plastic box in my pocket, containing that diamond-studded band of gold, and ah just want to get Lucinda up the stairs and fuck her beautifully, then, when she's in a demented trance, pop the question and slip the fucking thing onto her finger. Game, set and match, Williamson, and this selfish cunt Nicksy's ruining everything!

Cinders shall go to the ball!

Then you can see this copper appear at the windae. He's talking to Nicksy, who looks really scared. Ah wish ah had binos, but it's clear some negotiating is taking place. The cop is still, I can't make out his features, but his movements are economical. The circus goes on for what seems like an age, though it's probably just a few minutes tops, before Nicksy glances doon and shuffles along the ledge. The cop takes his airm, smiling reassuringly at him, helping him climb back intae the flat, one leg first, then the other.

As he vanishes inside a big cheer goes up followed by a polite round ay applause, like clapping at a cricket match. Despite the fact that there is now nothing gaun oan, two retards in polis uniform – a jug-eared gawkoid and a blonde, overweight, low-self-esteem minger – refuse tae take the cordon doon. — We need to wait for clearance, the fat bint says, hudin a scratchy walkie-talkie tae her lug.

Eventually, the thickoid Old Bill decide that there's nae mair bodies waiting tae climb oot windaes in the flats, and we're very graciously allowed back intae our homes.

Thank you for that, flatfoot.

The lift is broken again, so it's a gruelling seven-flight climb. At least

361

it shows a sweating Lucinda how the other half live, while Renton mumbles and snivels away about life's injustices, the yins supposedly pertaining to him inevitably taking prime spot. I recognise a laughing sneer coming from the stairs up ahead of us, and it's that Marsha. She looks doon at us, her hands on her hips. — So this is your posh gelfriend then? That why you don come up an fuck me no more, boy?

Ah see both Lucinda and Renton rubbernecking tae me and feel the blood draining ootay my face. Lucinda turns and storms down the stairs, and ah'm in hot pursuit. — Cinders! Wait!

She stops and pivots roond tae face me. — Leave me alone! Just fuck off!

— Every other night he's up here, innit. Ah look up and see Marsha leaning over the balustrade, cackling like a Caribbean voodoo witch, a mass of huge white teeth in a wizened face.

— She's crazy, Cinders! She's Nicksy's bird!

— He gotta big black mole on one of his white balls, she shrieks in laughter, her sister joining in.

— Which baw? Renton wastedly asks, and in a way that the doss cunt is *actually trying tae be fucking helpful*. I clutch my forehead in anguish, digging forefinger and thumb intae ma pulsing temples.

— Just leave me! Fucking leave me! Lucinda shouts, then lowers her voice. — To think . . . you're such a liar and a creep . . . I actually feel sorry for you, she laughs, a horsy, throaty accompaniment tae the shrill sound ay cockney-Jamaican ridicule coming fae above, reverberating around the stairwell.

— Fuck! I slap my head again as the raucous clucks above recede, Marsha and her sister bolting up the stairs.

— Gittin ditched is shite . . . we've aw been ditched now . . . Renton gormlessly observes, — Go eftir her!

— Not a fucking chance. It's all ruined now: my life is effectively over, I tell him, pushing past him and mounting the stairs. Then I hear a snakelike — Fuck! And then he's tearing past me, bounding demonically up the steps. When ah get intae the flat, Renton is manically clearing up the skag and attendant paraphernalia from the coffee table. — HELP AYS YA FUCKIN DINGUL! There's nothing to do but comply and we're just in time as the door bangs. They've taken Nicksy back down; he's in the company of the cop, and this woman who wears a disapproving scowl. Renton puts the kettle on and makes some tea. The woman nervously holds a chipped and stained West Ham mug as her and the cop settle Nicksy down on the couch. I'm destroyed, and badly need tae lay doon and consider my ever-shrinking options. Ah go tae the windae tae see Lucinda striding with purpose across the green towards Kingsland Road and the overland station, which will take her west and to real life.

My life is over. Wrecked.

— Fuck sakes, you awright? Rents stands behind me.

— I'll live, I tell him.

— Ah meant Nicksy. He points tae the wreckage on the settee.

— Yeah . . . Nicksy groans, looking up like a half-drowned sewer rat.

The cop puts his hand on the pathetic vegetable's shoulder. — Brian has to come with us for a chat, then he can go home later. He looks tae the hostile lassie, who ah assume is a fucking social worker. Far be it fae me tae simplistically vilify an entire occupation, but all social workers are fucking cunts. — Nothing sinister, he says, catching Rents's belligerent expression, — he just needs somebody ta talk to.

Cinders . . .

I sort of loved her.

— He can talk tae us, Rents says defensively, — we're his mates.

I'm thinking, *speak for yourself, Rent Boy.* Collecting lame ducks (or at least ones without vaginas) is not my style.

Oh, Cinders, come back . . . I even paid for that fucking ring!

The cop looks at us with a tired smile and a shake ay his heid. Nicksy shrugs in sheepish apology, as if in acknowledgement that he's been a right twat, which he most certainly has. I've changed my mind again. If you're gaunny dae something like that, at least have the backbone tae go through wi it instead ay crapping out and looking like a dickless clown. Look at poor Spud, fighting for his life on a fucking ventilator, when this spineless Ingloid poof doesnae even have the baws tae throw his away. Look at me, jilted by my almost-fiancée, but still in the game. Still fighting.

Renton follows the wretch down in the lift. I tag along: just cause ah cannae think ay anything else tae dae. *Perhaps Cinders will have turned back.*

At the bottom ay Beatrice Webb House, Nicksy gets in a car wi the social worker woman, who drives him off, doubtless for a hearty mind-hump somewhere. The copper who talked him in turns tae another polisman, then looks up at the council grey ay the tower against the pale blue sky, and notes, — It's a long way down.

What brilliant fucking powers ay observation! We're privileged tae have a Met high-flyer on the case! Nonetheless, ah find masel looking up, thinking ay ways ah can get revenge on that wee black nympho hoor. If fuckin Nicksy had've been giein her a proper length, she wouldnae have needed tae have played away wi me, and ah'd be planning a society wedding now!

Renton seems fascinated by the rescue copper, a tall, thin, shaven-headed mutation wi olive skin. He has these kind ay laughing eyes, which dinnae match up wi his cruel slash ay a mooth. — How did you get him to come in?

The cop looks at him in mild contempt, then seems tae soften a wee bitty. — Just listened a bit. Talked and listened.

— What's up wi him?

— You're his mates, the pig shrugs, — maybe he'll tell you himself, in his own time.

Renton seems a trifle chagrined by this. He shuffles uncomfortably, then focuses on the polisman. — But what did ye say tae get him tae come back inside?

The cop smiles earnestly. – I just told him that no matter how bad it all seemed right now, it's just part and parcel of being young. That it gets easier. That he has to remember this and not throw it all away. That life is a gift.

My life with Lucinda. Wrecked. My big chance. Blown. All thanks to Nicksy!

Renton appears tae consider this for a bit. He's daein the junky pose wi his airms wrapped around himself even though it isnae cauld. Skaggy fucker will draw mair polis heat than Nicksy, rattling away like that in public, and in front ay a copper. — Does it? Get easier, I mean, he asks urgently.

The cop shakes his heid. — Does it fuck; it gets bleedin worse. All that happens is that the expectations you have of life fall. You just get used to all the shit.

Renton looks as perturbed as ah feel, and we gaze at each other and realise that the cop isnae fucking joking. Ah think about poor Spud. Renton looks starkly at Bacon boy. — What if ye don't get used to it, what if ye *can't* get used to it?

The copper looks back up tae the flats, shrugs his shoulders and curls his bottom lip doon. — Well, that window's still gonna be there.

Wound Botulism

Tam sortay ambles intae the ward, sees us n comes right ower. He's goat a worried look oan his coupon, but ah want tae shout, ah kin breathe, man, ah kin pure breathe! How barry is that?! Aye, ah want tae tell um they sais thit ah'm gaunny be awright, but ah cannae say nowt, likesay, cannae answer him back wi this tube in my throat. Aw ah kin dae is breathe. N Tam's goat the picture, squeezin ma hand. So he starts gabbin, tellin us he's been away fir a week, up north, likesay hillwalkin wi that Lizzie, n he came as soon as he could. Ah'm sortay thinkin, ah'd certainly be comin quick wi her n aw, even though ah ken that's no what he means n it's good ay him tae git here. Now he's lookin at us aw sad n gaun, — Aw, Danny, ya daft cunt. What are we gaunny dae wi ye?

Ah'm pointin tae the tube, but then the duty nurse, Angie, comes in. Tommy asks her the Hampden Roar.

Ah kin hear Angie giein him the details, like she's hud tae dae wi everybody thit's come in tae see us. — He staggered into the A&E with double vision, slurred speech, drooping eyelids, and eye-muscle weakness.

Tommy's noddin, then lookin at us as if tae say aye? And what's new, exactly?

— The diagnosis has turned out to be wound botulism, Angie tells um.

— What's that?

Angie shakes her heid. Brand new, Angie, even if she is a Jambo fae Sighthill! Or mibbe a Jambette if that's what ye call lassie Jambos. But naw, that might be sexist. — Something very nasty, she tells Tommy. — But thankfully the doctors made a quick diagnosis, so we were able to offer appropriate treatment, including putting Danny on this ventilator and giving him botulinum antitoxin. We're expecting him to make a full recovery.

— Was it ska . . . heroin that did this? Tommy's askin the same question that my ma did the other week when ah wis wakin up. They aw jist talk aroond us n it pure gits oan ma nerves; jist cause ah've goat this tube doon ma throat disnae mean that ah cannae hear, likesay. Ken?

Angie doesnae answer him direct, but, she jist pits oan a cross but kind face, like the best teachers at the school used tae dae, n says, — He's been a right daftie, haven't ye, Danny?

Thaire's no a loat ah could say tae that, even if ah didnae huv a tube in my throat, likesay.

— You dae what they say, n shape up when ye git ootside, Tommy says, his piercin broon eyes lookin right intae us, n he squeezes ma hand again.

Ah try tae say 'sound' but ah kin feel ma throat muscles contrictin aroond this sortay unyielding pipe n ah convulse a bit, so ah jist squash his hand back n nod. So Tommy starts bletherin away aboot what he's been up tae, ken in the Highlands n that? Ah dinnae want tae pish on the pageant ay a man in love wi a barry-lookin bird, but it's pure 'me n Lizzie this' n 'me n Lizzie that'. Ah suppose it's his life, but the thing is, other cats' rooftop trysts are right borin, especially if you're no gittin any Ian McLagan in yirsel, likesay. Eventually he gies ma hand a real bonecrusher ay a squeeze n says, — See ye behind the goals.

Then he's away, but that Paki doaktir boy, Mr Nehru, comes in, the yin that saved us by aw accounts, n he's goat this lassie wi um. She's in a sortay suit n glesses, but she disnae look like a social worker. She's goat barry shiny black hair, sortay collar-length.

— Danny . . . Danny boy . . . we're going to have you off this thing tomorrow! That is good, yes! Mr Nehru goes.

Ah gie the cat the thumbs up, cause this gadge is totally cool n pure saved ma life, man. Ah dig the sing-song voice he hus, n the wey his heid moves side tae side when he talks. Aye, man, when a gadgie is that enthused, it sortay gits us aw carried away masel, likesay. Ken? That's what ah need, man, a motivator by ma side each n every day. Tae coach us n encourage us, likesay. Somebody tae tell us ah'm awright, n ah done good. Somebody like Mr Nehru.

Mr Nehru turns tae this lassie, she's goat they really cool rid-framed glesses wi a slight tint, and she's really thin, likesay daddy-long-legs thin, and he says tae her, — Danny had contracted wound botulism. It's a potentially fatal illness that occurs when spores of the bacterium *Clostridium botulinum* contaminate a wound then germinate, and produce botulinum nerve toxin. He's a very lucky chap, aren't you, Danny boy?! He sings tae me n ah wink back. He tells the thin, specky bird that they're seeing a higher incidence ay wound botulism, n it's aw aboot injectin heroin intae skin or muscle.

— Why should this be? the bird asks, in a posh voice.

— The reasons for the increase remain unclear, but may involve con-

366

tamination of specific batches of heroin as well as changes in injection practices.

— Very disturbing . . . Can I talk to him?

— Sure! He can hear you fine. I'll leave you two alone to get acquainted.

The lassie gies Mr Nehru a strained smile, but when she sits doon next tae us, her eyes light up n it's like she's really excited. Ah'm pure thinking, 'what's gaun oan here?', but ah cannae say nowt!

— Danny . . . I understand you've had a terrible time, with your illness and your heroin-dependency issues. But I'm here to help you, to help you put it all behind you.

Ah cannae say nowt, but the sun's up behind the lassie n throwin a big glow ower her, framin her in this luxurious blindin light, n mibbe it's like they prayers huv been answered, man, cause she's likesay goat this Virgin Mary-style purity, ken?

— I want to help you, to work with you in this new, innovative unit that we've set up. There will be other people like you, in this state-of-the-art facility, and we'll be working with a guy called Tom Curzon, who is one of the best in the business. He's probably the UK-wide expert on client-centred drug rehabilitation. Will you work with us, and let us help you to get better?

Ah'm noddin and sayin aye aye aye in ma heid, n ah gie her the thumbs up.

— That's really, really terrific news, she smiles. — As soon as you feel stronger, I'm going to arrange to get you transferred out of here, and into the rehab project, she says, and the lassie seems really enthusiastic aboot it. — I'm Amelia McKerchar, and I'm here to help you, Danny, n she shakes ma sweaty hand.

N ah feel like ah've been pure saved, man, saved by an angel ay mercy! The only wey is up for me now!

Drought

Junk Dilemmas No. 2

That cunt must be a baw hair away fae flatlining, the wey he's been batter-ing the shit intae hissel. Ah stagger ower fae whaire ah'd crashed oot, oan the cauld, manky, broken lino tiles ay the kitchen, n pit ma heid tae his chest: a thin, watery heartbeat. — Matty, wake up.

Ah was soon wishin ah hudnae bothered cause the cunt revives n it's aw tor-ment and despair. First him and then Alison, whae ah didnae even notice wis lyin oan the couch. They just whine oan aboot how sick they feel, and how it's aw fucked up and how they want offay this. Then that wee Maria emerges tremblin fae the bedroom whaire her n Sick Boy crashed, greetin aboot her ma and dad. Sick Boy's behind her, also shiverin like a new kitten, one eye blinkin in a spasm, sayin, — Shut the fuck up! What a crowd ay deadbeats! Am ah the only cunt here that kens how tae perty?

Ah head oot tae the toilet n dae a pish, too scared tae look in the bathroom mirror. When ah finish, that wee Jenny lassie, Maria's mate, comes oot ay the bedroom. Wi her big, watery eyes, she looks terrified, and aboot ten years auld, as she tentatively approaches me. — They says that they wir gaunny git some mair ay that stuff, *she whimpers, rubbin a red mark in the crook ay her airm. An injury ay commerce? Culture? An industrial accident.* — Maria spiked us, jist thaire, *she goes.* — Ah dinnae want any mair though, ah want tae go hame now. *She looks at me, like ah'm some sort ay jailer, n she's beggin tae be set free.* — What d'ye think ah should dae?

— Go hame, *ah say, shakin ma heid urgently, then lookin back tae the door ay the front room,* — dinnae even go back in thaire tae say cheerio. Yi'll jist git involved, *n ah throw the door open, showin her the stair.* — Ah'll tell them thit ye felt sick n hud tae go hame. Just go, *ah urge her, n ah kin hear the high, hysterical voices comin fae the front room and ah want this lassie tae git the fuck oot right now.* — Go hame! Hurry . . .

N she heads oot, noddin at us in fearful gratitude. Ah shuts the door behind her n goes back doon the cauld, fusty hall n ben the front room.

Sick Boy, whae's slumped doon on a beanbag against the waw, is makin him-self heard above the clamour. — I'm oot oan the hunt. *His big eyes scan us aw.* — Whae's up fir it?

371

They aw jist sit there, shiverin and wailin. It's like some anguish-laden Palestinian mass funeral tae commemorate the latest rock-throwing martyrs. Maria says somethin aboot wishin she wis deid, and Ali's oaf the couch, comfortin her.
— *Ye cannae say that, Maria, yir jist a young lassie . . .*

— *But it's like ah'm deid awready . . . this is like hell,* she blubbers, *her face scrunched up and utterly wretched.*

— *Mair fuckin melodrama,* Sick Boy says, *lookin at me, pullin hissel tae his feet, wi the help ay the radiator.* — *Whae's comin oot?*

— *Ah'm up for it . . . ah tell um, n wir right oot intae the hall.*

He gapes at us wi big sad eyes, and pits his hand gently oan ma shoodir. — *Thanks, Mark,* he whispers. — *Git the fuck away fae these manky birds. Gone are the days when ye could keep them quiet by filling them wi spunk, it's aw just skag, skag, skag now.*

— *Aye . . . ah goes.* — *Goat tae keep gaun, but, eh?*

He nods tightly, n we're shufflin taewards the front door. — *We should never huv came back up tae this place,* he moans, *shakin his heid,* — *ah could've got us sorted wi Andreas . . . the giro-drop wi Tony . . . we were in clover down thaire, man, in fucking clover . . .*

Maria's shoutin, — *Whaire's Jenny? If she's fuckin well sneaked away she's gittin her cunt battered in!*

Ah kin hear Ali sayin somethin tae calm her doon, as Sick Boy n me quickly slip oot the front door, like thieves escapin the scene ay the crime. Matty's voice screeches eftir us in terror: — *Shout us if ye score!*

We dinnae stop, dinnae look back. When we emerge fae the stair intae the street, somebody's shoutin fae the windae, but we're no turnin roond tae see whae it is.

Notes on an Epidemic 6

Gordon Ferrier, 18, Edinburgh North, motorcycle messenger and amateur boxer, intravenous drug use.

Robert MacIntosh, 21, Edinburgh North, window cleaner, intravenous drug use.

Julie Mathieson, 22, Edinburgh North, drama student, mother of one, intravenous drug use.

Philip Miles, 38, Edinburgh North, unemployed chef, father of three, intravenous drug use.

Gordon Murieston, 23, Edinburgh North, unemployed welder, intravenous drug use.

Brian Nicolson, 31, West Lothian, unemployed civil engineer, intravenous drug use.

George Park, 27, Edinburgh South, unemployed labourer, father of one, intravenous drug use.

Christopher Thomson, 22, Edinburgh North, unemployed baker, intravenous drug use.

A Safe Port

My hands are eywis cauld now. Like the circulation's gone. They didnae used tae be like that. Even oan a warm day ah'm rubbin them, cuppin them, blawin intae them. Ma chist is tight; there's thick phlegm permanently gummin up ma respiratory system.

Doof doof doof . . .

But ah've done this tae masel. Naebody else has fucked me; neither God nor Thatcher. Ah've done it; destroyed the sovereign state ay Mark Renton before those cunts could get anywhere near it wi their wrecking ball.

It's weird bein back in the parental home. It's so quiet eftir Wee Davie's death. Even when he was in the hoaspital he was still a big presence; my ma and dad ran aroond preparing endlessly for visits, gettin stuff tae take intae him, constantly jabberin on aboot his condition tae relatives and neighbours. Now the energy levels in the hoose have tumbled and the sense ay purpose gone; they wir baith already in their kip when ah got doon, late Friday night. Billy was still up.

Ah'd only come doon tae pick up some LPs tae flog, but hud ended up sittin watchin the boxing wi Billy, then just crashin in my auld bed. Ma body's metabolisin the gear quicker. Ah used tae go fir days between fixes. Now it's about four fuckin hours. Ah've grown mair lethargic and lazy, basically tae conserve energy and no burn off the skag. Ah'm irritable. Bored. Inattentive. Above all, listless. Gettin oaf a couch (for anything other than skag) takes monumental effort.

Keezbo and me went oan the methadone programme, followed by Sick Boy. It takes the edge offay withdrawal, but it's shite, and we're still heebie-jeebied n eywis lookin for gear. Ah tell the lassie at the clinic that, and she says that we jist need some 'tinkering' before aw the symptoms ay withdrawal sickness are sorted oot. Too fuckin right!

Maist days, when ah'm no huntin junk, ah'm reading Joyce's *Ulysses*, which ah wis surprised and delighted to find at McDonald Road Library. Ah'd never really got it before, it wis just tedious waffle tae me, but now ah'm loast in it, trippin oan the words and the images they conjure up like ah'm oan acid. Ah wish ah'd brought it doon tae my ma's wi us.

Oan the methadone programme ye huv tae report daily at the Leith Hoaspital clinic. The hozzy's scheduled for closure next year, but we huv tae go thaire for assessment and my bog-cleaner-tastin syrup. It feels a bit like the dole, but wi mair ay a sense ay belongin. Ye meet a lot ay skag-heids thaire. Some seem ashamed, skulkin in aw furtively, others dinnae gie a fuck and are swift tae ask if yir hudin. Some ur bams, pure and simple. If it wisnae skag it would've been something else. Most urnae, thir just ordinary boys who've drugged themselves intae nothingness tae avoid the shame ay daein nothing. Boredom has driven them crazy, drug crazy. By and large they keep aw this inside, maintaining the mask ay composure, through fierce, mocking talk and gallows humour. They cannae afford tae care, and ken if they front apathy for long enough, it'll soon embrace them. And they're correct.

The methadone's shite. Thaire's nae buzz oaf ay it, but they tell us tae persist, cause wi the 'fine tuning' ay ma script, it'll take away ma discomfort, and be way better than the alternative. Sometimes at the clinic, they look at ye like yir a lab rat and talk in these hushed and reverential tones. They took blood tests; no just for HIV, the boy wis at pains tae stress. At least they're daein something though. They've finally sussed thaire's shite happening oot here.

Thaire's certainly nowt much happenin in muh ma's hoose. It struck me that when ma auld girl and auld man arenae aroond, Billy and me stoap competing, forget that we hate each other, and actually git oan reasonably well. We watched this black American boxer overwhelm the latest hapless white hope.

Then Billy said something like, — Cannae fuckin stick civvy street.

— Reckon ye'll join up again?

— Mibbe.

Ah resisted the urge tae discuss it further. Billy and me are miles apart oan such issues, and although ah think he's a complete fuckin tool, it's his life, n it's no fir me tae tell him how tae live it. But he talked on for a bit; about the officers bein wankers and shitein it oan the foot patrol, but huvin yir mates behind ye and feelin like ye really belong somewhere. He's up in coort next week for batterin this cunt in a boozer, so his heid's aw ower the place.

Billy's moved intae Davie's auld room, the good yin that overlooks the river. The allocation ay the prime bedroom tae somebody whae would have been as happy in a cellar or an attic, caused a bit ay united resentment wi me n Billy when we moved doon here fae the Fort a few years back. Wisnae shy aboot stakin his claim following Wee Davie's demise, the cunt; but fair dos, it's no like ah'm plannin tae be back. Now his auld side ay the room looks bare. He's taken his framed picture ay Donald Ford in the Ajax-like seventies Jambo strip, and the calligraphy scroll that he did in art (his one visible accomplishment fae eleven years ay state education), which has the complete lyrics ay 'Hearts, Glorious Hearts' inscribed in maroon ink. The plastic King Billy oan the horse that sat oan the windae ledge, lookin oot over the Hibernian-infested tenements wi disapproval, has also thankfully gone.

The masking tape that he pit doon yonks ago is still oan the flair, running acroas the cairpit. Ah pull it up and see a thick darker line contrastin wi the light, sun-bleached blue. He called that the invisible Berlin Waw, dividin him fae ma Stanton-prominent '72 League Cup poster, a '73 Hibs team photae wi the two cups displayed, n a picture ay Alan Gordon in shooting pose. There's a recent yin ay Jukebox. Ah've got a great photae ay the church in St Stephen's Street where Tommy sprayed IGGY IS GOD oan the side ay the building, and a montage ay teen punk and soul boy pictures, each haircut mair embarrassing than the last. Ah should move ma bed nearer the windae, cause Billy willnae be back in here.

He's actually gone and *bought a double bed* for Wee Davie's auld room, soas he kin bang Sharon in comfort when she steys ower. A Jambo shagging pad. How the fuck can the pervert get it up wi my ma n faither lying next door? Has he nae fuckin self-respect? Ah'd never take a burd back here, tae my *ma's hoose*.

So ah rise late on Saturday morning; it's the back ay eleven. Ah'm no hungry, but my ma and dad, surprised tae see me, insist ah stey for my Setirday mince. It's sort ay a tradition that she makes mince early, usually noon, so that we could go tae Easter Road or Tynecastle, or sometimes through tae Ibrox in my dad's case. Even though the fitba doesnae loom so large in our lives these days, the noon mince custom has perversely carried on. The white tablecloth comes oot, then the casserole dish wi the mince bubblin away in it, a big onion floatin in the middle. Then the mashed tatties, follayed by the peas. But in the silence and stiffness ay muh ma's movements, there's a distinct edge tae the proceedings: they seem tae have tippled that something's up wi me. The auld girl's wild-eyed at the table and she's run oot ay fags. She asks Billy, but he shrugs in the negative. Ah mind ay him sayin something aboot cuttin doon or tryin tae gie up. — Ah'll need tae go doon for cigarettes, she says.

— You don't need cigarettes just now, Catherine, the auld boy says tae her like she's a child. He seldom uses her formal name, and ah can tell something's afoot as they're lookin awkwardly at each other and stealin glances at us. Ah'm pushin the mince roond ma plate. Ah've eaten a bit ay the mashed tatties, but this mince seems too salty, stinging my dry and cracked lips, and the peas are like shrivelled wee green ball bearings, through having been left in the oven too long. The auld girl cannae cook for shit, but even if she wis Delia Smith ah couldnae eat fuck all, and ah'm shiverin and blinkin in that light pourin in fae the big windae.

Fuck sake, ah was only doon tae pick up some LPs!

Oot the corner ay my eye ah watch the auld girl rise, ransacking drawers in the sideboard, turning ower the cushions in the settee and chairs, in case a stray smoke has fallen behind yin. She's creepin us oot, ah want tae say tae her, 'Please, sit the fuck doon n eat,' when ma auld man turns oan me and says in steely-eyed accusation, — Ah wahnt tae ask you somethin. Somethin serious. Are you wan ay thaim?

This time he means junky, rather than poof.

— Tell us it's no true, son, tell us! Ma pleads, standin behind the chair she'd vacated. She's hudin oantae the back ay it, white-knuckled, as if braced for impact.

For some reason, ah cannae even be ersed lyin. — Ah'm oan the methadone programme but, ah tell them, — ah'm getting off the junk.

— Fuckin idiot, Billy sneers.

— Well, that's it now then, Dad coldly states. Then he stares at us wi a beseeching, — Eh?

Aw ah kin dae is shrug.

— Yir a junky, ma faither's eyes narrow, — a dirty, filthy, lyin junky. A drug addict. That's what ye are, is it no?

Ah look up at him. — Once you label me you negate me.

— What?!

— Jist something Kierkegaard sais.

— Whae the fuck's that? Billy goes.

— Søren Kierkegaard, Danish philosopher.

My auld man's fist smashes oan the table. — Well, ye kin cut that crap oot fir a start! Cause that's aw gone now, aw yir studies, aw yir chances! A bloody philosopher's no gaunny help ye now! This isnae jist one ay yir daft fads, Mark! It's no something ye kin jist play aroond wi till ye git bored! This is serious! This is yir life yir flingin away here!

— Oh Mark . . . muh ma starts sobbing, — ah dinnae believe it. Oor Mark . . . the university . . . wi wir that proud, weren't wi, Davie? Wi wir that proud!

— That stuff kills ye, ah've read aw aboot it, muh dad declares. — Like messin aboot wi a loaded gun! You'll end up in the hoaspital like that Murphy laddie; nearly bloody deid, bi Christ!

Ma starts greetin; gaspin, haltin, breathless sobs. Ah want tae comfort her, tae tell her it'll be okay, but ah cannae move. Ah feel fuckin paralysed in this chair.

— Fuckin mug, Billy jibes, — it's a radge's game, that shite.

Normal service between us is evidently resumed, so ah openly regard the muppet in sheer fuckin contempt. — As opposed tae the mature, sensible and socially cohesive practice ay rammin the nut oan total strangers in public places?

Billy looks angry for a beat, but he lets it go as a lenient smile creeps across his coupon.

— We've discussed that! my dad shouts. — We've discussed this yin n *his* bloody stupidity aw week! He thumbs dismissively at Billy without lookin at him. — It's *you* we need tae talk aboot now, son!

— Look, ah say tae them, spreadin my palms, — it's no big deal. Ah've been pertyin a bit too much, and got masel ah wee habit. Ah ken ah've goat a bit ay a problem but ah'm sortin it oot. Ah'm at the clinic, oan the methadone programme, weanin masel offay the heroin.

— Aye, but it's no that easy! muh ma suddenly squeals. — Ah've heard aw aboot it, Mark! That Aids!

— You've goat tae inject it tae git Aids, ah shake ma heid slowly, — n ah wis jist smokin it. But that's me finished. It's a mug's game, like Billy says, but as ah mooth ma agreement, radge that ah am, ah cannae stoap ma eyes gaun tae ma airm.

Ma auld man's follayed thum and, lightning quick, he grabs it n rolls up ma sleeve, exposin scabby, pus-leaking tracks. — Aye? What's that then!

Ah reflexively pill the withered limb away. — Ah very, very rarely inject and ah never share needles, ah plead. — Look . . . ah ken it's goat oot ay hand but ah'm tryin tae sort it oot.

— Aw aye? muh ma screeches, lookin at ma airm in horror. — Well, yir no tryin very hard, ur ye!

— Well, ah'm daein ma best.

— Mutilatin hissel, Davie!

— At least he admits he's goat a problem, Cathy, ma dad reassures, — at least that's wan thing, he seems tae concede. Then he turns they blazin, hungry eyes ay his oan me. — Wis it London that did this?

Ah cannae help but laugh out loud at that yin. I've mair access tae gear up here than ah ever hud doon thaire.

— Ye might well laugh, he says in lament, then, — Simon's no like that, is he? Stevie, wee Hutchy, he's no like that?

— Nup, ah tell him, for some reason, no wantin tae drop Sick Boy in it. — They nivir touch it, eh. It's jist me.

— Aye, the bloody mug, muh ma says bitterly.

— But why, son? Dad implores. — Why?

Ah kin never think ay what tae say tae that question. — It's a good buzz.

His eyes bulge oot like some cunt's belted the back ay his heid wi a basebaw bat. — Christ, jumpin oaf a cliff's probably a good buzz, till ye hit the boatum! Wise up, for God's sake!

— Ah feel like ah'm livin a nightmare, Ma groans, — that's aw it is: a bloody nightmare!

There follows a gratifying silence, ye can hear the soft ticking ay that posh clock wi the swinging pendulum, the one the old boy got fae his crooked mate, Jimmy Garrett, at Ingliston Market. Then it goes off. It's slow, sending oot a dozen leaden strikes even though it's way past twelve, measuring oot our lives in heartbeats . . . doom . . . doom . . . doom . . .

Ah tries tae get a bit ay mince doon, but ma swallowin mechanism is fucked. Ah can feel it runnin doon ma gullet but the muscles urnae workin. It's like it's just buildin up in ma oesophagus n ah'm drownin wi every small mouthful, until ah feel sudden relief as it finally hits ma tight, tennis-ball gut. My mother, whae's been scrutinisin me, seems tae think ay something, then rises wi a sudden, demented urgency that upsets every cunt in the room, and bounds ower tae the sideboard, pickin up an envelope, which she hands us. — This came for ye, she accuses.

It has a Glasgow postmark. Ah'm scoobied as tae what it is or whae it could be fae. Suddenly, ah'm aware ay the six fervent eyes oan us which say it would be bad form tae pocket it for later. So ah open it up. It's an invitation.

Mr and Mrs Ronald Dunsmuir
humbly request the attendance of

Mark Renton
....

at the wedding of their daughter
Joanne April to Mr Paul Richard Bisset
at
St Columba Church of Scotland,
Duchal Road, Kilmacolm, Renfrewshire, PA13 4 AU
on
Saturday, 4th May 1985, 1p.m.
and afterwards at
Bowfield Hotel and Country Club,
Bowfield Road, Howwood, near Glasgow Airport, Renfrewshire, PA9 1DB

RSVP: 115 Crookston Terrace, Paisley, PA1 3PF

— What is it? muh ma asks.

— Nowt, just a weddin invite. My auld mate Bisto fae the uni, ah tell her, surprised that they're gettin married and astonished that they've invited me. Joanne must be up the stick; it's the only wey that would happen as they baith have another year tae go at Aberdeen eftir this. The last time ah saw Joanne was on Union Street. Ah was like a jakey, skulkin doon taewards Don's. She wis wi another lassie; widnae look at us, but jerked her sweatshirt hood tight tae her face n stepped across the road.

Ma starts lookin oaf intae the distance, shakin her heid as a teary lens amasses ower her eyes. Then she glowers at me in anguish. — That could have been you . . . wi that lovely Fiona lassie, she sniffs. — Or even wee Hazel. She turns tae my auld man, whae nods tae her and gies her hand a squeeze.

— Aye, a narrow escape, ah say.

— Dinnae start, Mark! Just dinnae bloody well start! You know fine well what yir mother means, my dad shouts.

What ah know fine well is that ah've hung aboot here long enough, and now the junk thing's oot in the open, ah'm disclined tae listen tae any mair ay their tedious where-did-we-go-wrong disquisitions. Basically, whaire they went wrong wis indulgin thair ain selfish whims in bringin mair lives intae a fucked-up place. Ah didnae ask tae live n ah'm no feart tae die. Aw that'll happen is that it'll be like before ah wis alive; it could-nae have been that great, but it wisnae that shite either, or ah'd have minded aboot it. Ah was just here tae get ma fuckin records. Billy looks at us, kenin *fine well* what ah'm daein, but sais nowt.

Ah stoap oaf in the bathroom tae swipe the auld girl's Vallies, n head up the Walk, strugglin wi the weight ay they albums packed in the auld Sealink holdall. Thankfully, ah run intae Matty and Sick Boy at the Kirkgate. They look as shite as ah feel, n neither is too enthusiastic when ah ask them tae take a shot n cairry the bag. Matty takes a shift though, but ye could tell it wis basically jist tae sketch what wis inside. That's when it aw kicked in wi me: Bowie, Iggy, Lou, they wir aw gaunny go.

— Cunt, that'll be a sad loss, Matty slyly articulates ma thoughts.

— I'll tape them, ah sais defensively.

— Cunt, kin see you sittin thaire daein that, right enough, he goes. Sick Boy's quiet, stooping forward as he walks, his airms folded acroas his chest.

Fucked if ah'm arguin wi this cunt. — Ah'll get Hazel tae tape them then, she's goat a capacity for boredom.

Matty shrugs and we git up tae the shoap. Sick Boy hings ootside smokin, while ah stick the records oan the counter. The boy goes through them wi the sort ay face ah ken; ah've used it tons ay times masel at work. — Bowie ah kin always shift, he says, — but naebody's bothered aboot Iggy and the Stooges or Lou and the Velvets. Too seventies.

FUCKIN CUNT.

So ah get a rip-off price for them, Matty pretendin tae look through the records n tapes oan display but mentally countin oot every note n coin the boy pits in ma hand. When we get ootside we see Olly Curran comin up the Walk, the straight-backed National Front closet-buftie fucker. — Awright, Olly?

— Yesss . . . he sais in that sleekit snake-like wey ay his, lookin doon his beak, first at me, then Sick Boy, then Matty. Ye can tell he thinks we're the scum ay the earth: a big disgrace tae the white master race. — You're a Connell, he says tae Matty in mild accusation.

Matty, fag in hand, turns his earring like he's tryin tae tune in his brain. – So?

— You dinnae stay at the Fort now, Olly shakes his heid.

— Nup, Wester Hailes, eh.

Olly dispenses a security-guard look, one too thick and crass even for a polisman, then thaire's a silence. So ah goes, — Ye got a fair auld military starch in that collar, Olly.

He smiles, his devious eyes fill ay imbecile's hate, then looks aw self-congratulatory n goes, — Well, some of us like tae keep up standards.

— Aye, well, it's certainly looking pristine. Heard yir missus takes the dhobi up the Bendix.

— Yesss, he whistles softly, wary but smug, — she certainly does.

Sick Boy nods and says, — Ah kent a bird whae wis mad on that. Ye couldnae stick anything in the washing machine. Eywis hud tae go up the Bendix.

— Aye . . . sometimes it can be a pest, Olly muses, — because she's got a perfectly good washing machine.

— But if she's used tae takin it up the Bendix . . . Sick Boy sniggers.

Ah'm fuckin well strugglin tae keep a straight face, n Matty's open-cavern mooth n squashed-grape eyes indicate the cunt's aware some wind-up's gaun oan but he's scoobied as tae what it's aw aboot.

— Aye, Olly declares, — her mother wis just the same.

— She surely must use the washing machine sometimes but, Sick Boy contends.

— Very rarely.

— I'll bet you like tae stick a load in there but, eh? Sick Boy goes.

— Oh, ah do try sometimes, but it's Bendix, Bendix, Bendix aw the way wi her.

— Do ye ever take a load up thaire yirsel? ah ask him.

— In my younger single days, aye. But ah wis a sailor then, and neatness was expect– what . . . what . . . Olly's gaun, as we cannae contain oorsels any mair, – what yis laughin at? Youse ur bloody well on something! Ah ken youse! Ah ken yir game!

— What game is that then? ah goes back.

He looks at ma wrist, pus seeping fae rusted mounds ay crust, on white, goosefleshed skin.

— Industrial accidents, ah wink, but he turns in disgust and strides up the Walk.

— Right up the Bendix! Sick Boy shouts. It hurts tae laugh. My sides sting wi it. But ah realise that the joke is oan me, oan us, as the pain sets in and we look at each other, blinded by snotter, feelin like lepers in our ain place. Passers-by ur starin at us in horror and loathing: ye kin feel their contempt. — Lit's git the fuck ootay here, Sick Boy sais.

Pain. Psychic pain.

N thaire's mair ay that tae come when we git up tae Tollcross. Matty opts tae wait ootside. — Cunt, ah'm no welcome, eh, he says. Inside, the tomatay plants in the windae look as rotten and shabby as Johnny, whae sits thaire wi lines ay speed. Ah make the big mistake ay giein him the cash ah owe him. He snaffles it, then refuses tae sub us anything else.

— Jist a wee bag, mate.

— Sorry, chavboax, it's business, buddy boy.

— But ah jist gie'd ye some dosh, ye ken ah'm good fir it.

— Nae hireys, nae gear. Thaire's no a lot gaun aroond so what thir is goes tae the boys wi the poppy upfront. Ah'd git the dosh n ah'd move sharpish if ah wis youse.

— C'mon, Johnny, we're mates . . .

— Nae mates in this game, chavvy, we're aw acquaintances now, he goes. — The White Swan's just a cog in a wheel these days, compadre. He fills his lungs wi sulphate. — Ah'm a branch manager ay Virgin rather than the owner ay Bruce's Record Shoap. If ye ken what ah mean.

He's right. There's nae white now, n the broon's hit toon big time. Swanney's puntin it for somebody else, so he's way doon the peckin order. So we wir back tae square one. Matty starts moanin when we hit the bottom ay the stair. — Nowt? Cunt, what dae ye mean, nowt?! The cunt accuses us ay hudin oot oan him n the argument carries oan doon the road. – Fuckin mongol, he goes.

— Ah wish ye'd stoap this mongol shite, Matty.

— Jist cause yir brother wis one, he says, the taboo words sizzling oot ay the mingin wee fucker's tight campfire mooth.

— Naw, Down's syndrome was just about the only medical condition the spazzy wee cunt never had, ah tell him, shaming him and myself at the same time.

— Telt ye wuv nae fuckin gear, Sick Boy narks at him. — N stoap aw this *hudin oot* shite. Tell us how you can possibly *hud oot* oan a moochin cunt whae's nivir pit his hand in his poakit in the first fuckin place!

Matty shuts up at that, n we walk on in silence. We get tae the Fit ay the Walk, fucked and shivering, tae hear a blood-coagulatin screech: — SI-MIHN!

Two antsy jailbait chicks are ootside the Central, beckonin us ower. It's the last place we want tae be right now but they willnae take naw fir an answer. It's that Maria Anderson lassie and her wee pal, Jenny. It turns oot Jenny's Shirley's cousin, so Matty doesnae look too chuffed. Ah'm no either. Ah tell her tae bolt, n she nods like she's gaun tae, but keeps hingin aboot, no in any hurry tae nash. They willnae git served in the Cenny, so we go tae the Dolphin Lounge. We're sittin in a corner, aw drinkin Pepsi cause it's fill ay sugar, n Nelly comes in fae the Crown Bar next door, n gits a pint n joins us. He starts spraffin shite about Begbie and Saybo, but ah'm no interested as ah'm tryin tae tune oot aw the conversations roond us n think ay whae ah kin hound fir skag. He's droning in ma ear though, and he asks, — Dae ye think thit ah made the wrong move?

Ah huvnae been listenin tae him, n ah've no got the faintest idea what he's oan aboot, so ah say, — You made the decision, Neil, ah shrug, catchin that Jenny's eye, n ah git an apologetic glare which quickly steels intae defiance. Fuck her, daft wee hairy; thir fawin like dominoes now n ah'm naebody's social worker, least ay aw ma ain.

Nelly gies us his tortoise-lipped expression. — So?

Another two young girls come in tae join Sick Boy's harem. — Sealink, one lassie goes, pointing tae the now empty holdall at ma feet, pronouncing it *Sealunk*, in proper Leith style. Normally ah'd be sniffing at some ay the crumbs ay Sicko's rich man's table, but no way right now. Bowie, Iggy and Lou, aw gone. Fuck sakes, ah'm hurtin inside. — Look around the world, baby, it cannot be denied, ah assert tae Nelly.

— Too fuckin right it cannae! the cunt goes, thinkin thit ah gie a fuck aboot his dramas. Ah think it was the Boy Søren who said, one can advise comfortably fae a safe port, and total unconcern is the safest of all.

Sick Boy's main girl is wee Maria, the death-masked beauty ay the Bannanay flats. A looker, but a proper wee skag hound. There's whispers that Sick Boy goat her hooked; but in thair stampede tae discern the sinner, people usually miss the point wi aw this 'which evil bastard got ma son or daughter oan drugs?' bullshit. Once the shit's oot there, people are gaunny try it. It's as futile and pointless as tryin tae blame some other kid at school cause their bairn caught a cauld. Forget transmission, it's *transition* that's the issue. Basically, it's aw self-loathing because they never saw when thair bairn became somebody else.

Sick Boy *is* a cunt though, and he certainly didnae help. — Sweet sixteen, ain't that peachy keen, he grins, the caress of his Judas palms forcing her weirded smile, — n school aw kicked intae touch, eh. That's us aw legalled up now, eh, babe? A union blessed by the state! He's wearing a pork-pie rude-boy hat, which he's somehow picked up, probably off one ay the girls, which ye can see is annoying the fuck oot ay Nelly.

Nelly clocks me looking at the hat. Flashes us a smile that says 'that is fucked'. Then he goes in a low voice, — See Goagsie's got the cowie. Cunt was caught sneakin intae that clinic.

— It wid jist be fir his methy script, but. Wir aw gaun thaire now.

— Nah, the cunt broke doon in the boozer whin he goat fuckin pilled up aboot it. Greetin like a wee fuckin lassie, Nelly snorts.

Ah'm lookin tae Sick Boy, who's aw ower Maria but at the same time flirting wi Jenny. — A wee honey, this lassie. See, if ma hert wisnae devoted tae you, Maria, he half threatens tae her discomfit and Jenny's giggles.

Matty gies us a tense nod. — Cunt, lit's fuckin split, ah'm seek tae fuck, he sais oot the side ay his dribbling mooth.

Ah turns tae Sick Boy. — Ye comin?

— No . . . Ricky Monaghan has a connection. Ah'm gaunny stall here and see if he shows.

— Cunt, Monny'll no huv nowt, Matty spits in contempt.

— Take yir choice, red or black, spin the fucking wheel. *I'm* steyin here, n his arm tightens roond Maria, who looks aggressively at us.

Ah nod tae Matty. It seems important tae keep movin, and we elect tae leave them tae it.

So Matty n me's in the street, exposed in that cruel light wi aw they straightpegs millin roond, cunts whae mean ye nowt but herm n hassle, n ah'm tremblin like a Cadbury's Flake gaun intae an anorexic model's mooth.

— Listen, Mark, sorry aboot that . . . sayin that aboot Davie, likes. It wis oot ay order.

— Forget it, ah goes.

— Cunt, it's jist thit ah'm aw strung oot n that.

— Forget it, ah repeat, too edgy tae get intae any shite wi the cunt right now.

We shuftie intae the shoap tae procure snout for Matty. Mrs Rylance is behind the counter; magnesium shock ay hair eruptin fae her big ruddy face. She sees ma eyes gaun tae the yellay collection tin. — Animals cannae tell ye when thaire's something wrong, son. Tae be honest, ah prefer them tae humans. Or some humans, she fixes us in a pitying gaze. — How's ma Danny boy daein? Lovely laddie.

— Seems tae be better, but eh, ah state gruffly, badly wantin tae split, lookin at Matty slowly prospectin in his pockets for change, hating being a slave tae the petty and pointless addictions ay others. — He's away oan this project now.

— Project . . . the auld bat parrots mindlessly as she gingerly fishes the coins fae Matty's soiled paw like they were jewels fae a blocked toi-let bowl.

A group ay young kids come in and her hawk eyes narrow on them from behind those lenses. Ah see Matty's face freeze as ah pawkle the yellay collection tin oan the counter, swiftly stickin it intae ma holdall. Charlene taught us that yin; eywis huv a chorrin bag. Theft is as much aboot opportunism as planning. Executing the deed, ah'm lookin aw the time fae the steel-wool heid ay Mrs Rylance, as she chastises the bairns, tae Matty, his shifty eyes scannin roond.

We head ootside and as the door shuts behind us Mrs Rylance's howls tear oot, — MA COLLEKSHUN! MA CATS' COLLEKSHUN! WHAE'S TOOK MA CATS' COLLEKSHUN?! But it's directed tae the perr kids as we steal doon the road. We're gaun right back up tae Swanney's once we open this fucker. We catch our puff in Queen Char-lotte Street, shakin the placky collection boax. Thaire's a fair weight in it. It's fill ay they new pound coins.

We suddenly realise that we're right acroas the street fae Leith Polis Station, so we get the fuck ootay the road n take a 16 back up tae Tollcross. Johnny's no in but thankfully Raymie's hame. — Come and buy my toys, he sighs in a Bowie-Tony-Newley-era voice, before shutting one eye and looking at Matty. — Weren't you *sine die'd*, Matty me boy? Perhaps youse might want tae conclude this business before the White Swan returns?

— Aye . . .

So we start fartin aroond wi a knife but we cannae get this cunt ay a tin open! Matty stabs it and the blade skites oaf that reinforced placky, back intae his other hand that's hudin the boax secure, spurting rid blood onto the yellaw boax n the fag-burned wooden flair. —YA BASTARD! he screams, sucking up his ain blood like a vampire. Ah take ower, but it's totally fuckin useless. We can see it's fill ay ten-bob bits n pound coins but we cannae even prise any oot, wi these inverted teeth blockin us.

Fuckin hell's bastardcunts!

Raymie gets a hammer oot and batters it, but the thing just isnae yielding. — I serenade, they decorate, he says, laying down the tool. His remarks, apropos of nothing, once humorous, now grate like fuck. Ah pick up the hammer and huv a go at the fucker but this evil unyielding resin, this synthetic, carcinogenic, non-biodegradable pishy fuckin polymer will barely fuckin scratch. Even a hacksaw widnae dae it; this needs a fuckin grinder oan it. Raymie's getting impatient. — Gentlemen, you should leave this humble abode before Johnny returns. Business ain't booming on the supply side, chickadees, and there will be fuck all happening in the Salisbury Crag department till you get this open.

Raymie's a strange yin, but he's daein us a favour. Johnny's goat funny wi dough and mair volatile wi aw the speed and downers he takes. If he thinks he's bein fucked ower he'll hud oot.

Matty and me look tae each other and decide tae split n see if Sick Boy's contact, Monny, has somehow emerged. We head back doon tae the port, but then elect tae bodyswerve the Fit ay the Walk n the Kirkgate for Keezbo's at the Fort. He lives on the D floor ay Fort House, two doors along fae whaire ah grew up. — Ah'm gaun up tae see Keith, Matty, you stey doon here.

— What fir?

Ah open up the holdall, takin oot n shakin the collection tin close tae his lug. The side ay his face seems tae seize up like he's huvin a stroke. — Cause ah'm gaunny droap this fuckin thing doon tae ye. You let it hit the deck n split open, n then fling the dosh intae the bag. Okay?

Matty's blinkin like some cunt's flung pepper in his eyes. — But . . . cunt, it might go aw ower the place n –

FUCK WIS THAT?

Wi baith hears this yabberin sound echo fae above. It rolls around in ma heid. Raw panic crackles ower the back ay ma neck. Ah'm fucked awright, it's this cunty methadone . . . Ah tug Matty's jaykit sleeve. — Keezbo n me'll be right doon tae help ye, wi dinnae fuckin well huv time tae discuss it!

Matty sucks back some snotter n nods, lookin roond n shiverin. Ah droap the bag at his feet. Ah'm right in the stair n boundin up tae the D flair. Oan the balcony ah sees Keezbo's mother n faither; Moira, wi her signature frizzy broon hair n horn-rimmed glesses, n Jimmy, still a chunky wee barrel ay a gadge in white shirt n black trews, standin ootside thair flat. As ah stride taewards thum, the shouts git louder; thaire comin fae *inside* Keezbo's. Jimmy n Moira look tae each other in panic n they step back intae the flat n try n shut the door oan us. — What's up? Is that Keith shoutin?

—Yir no welcome here, nane ay yis, Moira goes, pittin her weight oan the door, but ah've goat a shoodir n hip in, n ah'm no budgin. The tin's in ma hand, oan the inside, n ah'm worried she'll snatch it so ah push intae the flat. The birds are oot ay the aviary, flappin aroond ma fuckin face! — Dinnae lit they burds oot! Moira screams, now pillin us in n shuttin the door behind us.

It's a mental scene: a few budgies and a zebra finch flutter aroond Moira; one's oan her shoodir n another lands oan the back ay her hand. She's wearin an angora cardigan, but wi nowt else oan underneath, nae blouse, jist a bra, n the cardy isnae buttoned up right cause ah kin see a faded rid scar gaun doon intae her padding, n ah'm sure ah saw something move doon thaire, like her tits. She pills her cardy thegither n fastens a couple ay buttons, n wi baith look away, mortified. Jimmy's standin sheepishly in front ay the staircase, wi his mooth turned doon. The birds cheep aroond us, urgent and demanding. — C'mon, Moira . . . Jimmy, ah appeal, ah jist want tae see Keith . . .

Then ah hears this scream: — MARK! GIT THE FAHKIN POLIS!!

The bird leaves Moira's hand as Jimmy looks tae the kitchen n roars, — SHUT IT!

— Jimmy, what's the fuckin Hampden . . .

Fuck sake, ah'm strugglin tae take aw this in, but ah can see that they've constructed a wire fence, like a giant cage, tae divide the stairs fae the rest ay the hoose. There's newspaper aw ower the stair cairpit wi bird shit layerin it. It's like they've made the entire doonstairs ay the hoose – the living room, bedrooms n lavvy – intae a giant aviary, wi thaim just huvin the upstairs hall n kitchen! Moira looks poisonously at me, wi Keezbo shoutin for help, as she opens the cage tae the stairs, guiding the flocking birds through. They follay her like rats wi the pied piper, then she deftly moves oot the wey n shuts them inside, turnin tae me.

— Go, she sais, openin the front door.

Keezbo's still shoutin, but it's like it's comin fae *ootside* the hoose. It hus tae be the auld balcony aviary at the back ay the kitchen! — MARK! HELP US! THUV LOAKED US OOT HERE!

— What the fuck? Ur you oot oan the balcony, Keezbo?

Then his sister Pauline appears, standing on the stairs, inside the cage, as yellay n green n blue n white budgerigars flock, chirpin aw aroond her. — They locked him oot oan the balcony. She turns tae them. — Ye cannae keep him oot thaire, Ma, n she starts sobbing.

Moira's still hudin the front door open, shoutin, — GIT OOT! and that nosy Margaret Curran cunt pokes her neb in, the hatchet-faced cow a picture ay misery. — Wi cannae stand it, Moira, we're gaunny huv tae phone the polis if the noise doesnae stoap. It's been aw day now! N they birds . . . ah nivir minded the aviary oan the balcony but no in the hoose! It's insanitary! How much longer?

— As long as it takes, it's ma laddie's life!

They start oan at each other, but ah cut in and ask Moira, — What huv youse fuckin done tae Keith?

— They've locked him oot oan the balcony, Pauline blubbers, her anguished face pushed against the mesh ay the cage, surrounded by fluttering birds.

Ah push past Jimmy and Moira intae the kitchen. The wire n dimpled glass that divides the room fae both the aviary and the walk-out section ay the balcony has been removed and boarded ower. Keezbo's ootside, batterin oan it and screamin, — HELP US, MARK . . . FUCKIN HELP US!

— He's no comin in here till that poison's oot ay his system, Moira says.

Ah whip roond, right intae her face. — Are you fuckin mental?! He's in withdrawal, ah say, thinking aboot Nicksy. — He'll jump oaf or try n climb doon! Let us see um!

Ah turns back n ah'm fighting tae get the big bolts oan the door open. Jimmy isnae stoaping us but Moira's white scraggy fingers wrap roond ma wrist. — No . . . no . . . wir pittin um through that wild turkey –

— Yir killin him, he needs proper fuckin rehab! HE'S SEEK ENOUGH TAE JUMP! ah scream intae her face, and she suddenly relents, loosenin her grip.

That mawkit-pussed hoor Curran's goat intae the hoose. Ah hear her moanin away at us fae the hall. — You left here! You're no welcome back! Away tae yir ain bit doon the river, tae the hoose *we* should've goat!

— We're no thaire any mair . . . moved oot, ah tell her n watch her stupid bovine coupon hing slack in uncomprehending shock, as ah work one bolt open. Ah kin hear Keezbo groan oan the other side. — They gave us a better place doon by the Shore, ah lie tae Curran, as ah work on another bolt. — Aw the windaes face oantae the river . . . n thaire's a private balcony that fair catches the sun . . . lovely spot . . .

She's choking in fury. — Balcony . . . river . . . how the . . . how the bloody hell . . . how the hell did youse . . . ? she stammers, then a glint snaps intae her eye. — Your auld place . . . it'll be empty now then, eh?

Ah click back another bolt. Fae the corner ay ma eye, ah notice that one budgie's still attached tae Moira's angora cardigan just oan the ootside ay her placky tits. Jesus fuck . . .

That angora cardy's worked its wey open again n thaire's some baby birds in her tits, ye kin see thair wee heids poking up, mooths open, demandin tae be fed. *What the fuck* . . . Ah look at her, n she gies us a hard, tight-moothed stare, that says, 'So?'

389

Ah turn back tae the last bolt . . . ah cannae watch this . . .

— Your hoose! Margaret Curran insists, — that'll be it empty then!

— Naw . . . a Paki family moved in last week. Ah work the bolt loose as Jimmy says something tae Moira aboot makin herself decent.

— How did they . . . how in the name ay Christ did they . . . ? Curran's freakin oot n gittin ready tae visit the Housing Association. The bolt snaps back n the door flies open.

Keezbo stands in his long coat, lookin like a big pink sausage wrapped in black puddin. — They tried tae fuckin kill us! Youse! He points at Jimmy and Moira, — YOUSE!

The big budgie on Moira's jumper flies up as she looks at Keezbo in horror, pillin the cardigan tae her tae conceal the nest ay birds in her tits. She realises that he's ripped doon the mesh they pit ower the balcony. — DINNAE LIT CHEEKY BOY OOT! THE WILD BIRDS'LL KILL UM!

— FUCK YIR BUDGIES! YOUSE TRIED TAE KILL US!

— WE'RE THE BUCKIN YINS TRYIN TAE BUCKIN WELL SAVE YE! Moira roars back in his face, n ah realise she's no goat her teeth in, n she turns tae Jimmy: — TELL UM, JIMMY!

— Ah wis cauld, Keezbo moans in desolation, — cauld n hungry!

— Hungry fir buckin drugs, drugs, drugs! Moira squeals, — TELL UM, JIMMY! BE A BUCKIN MAN, BI CHRIST, N TELL YIR LADDIE WHAIRE HE'S GAUN WRONG!

— Moira . . . c'mon . . .

— Ah've goat poppy, Keith. Ah shakes the boax. — We'll open it up n git sorted oot!

— Ah ken how tae open these yins, Mr Mark, he goes, his eyes huge and luminous, as Moira scowls at Jimmy n slams the balcony door shut, enticing Cheeky Boy back tae her false bosom.

— Now everybody hus tae calm doon . . . Moira — Jimmy pleads.

— CALM BUCKIN DOON! AH'LL GIE YE CALMIN BUCKIN WELL DOON, JIMMY YULE! IT'S YOUR BLOODY LADDIE!

— Nae time, ah goes tae Keezbo, lookin ower the balcony tae see Matty standin aroond oan the concrete forecourt. — MATTY! But it's windy up here n oor voices get carried away as we shout. — MAH-TAY!

Eventually the daft cunt looks up wi a scoobied coupon.

— What's gaun oan here? Jimmy demands, stepping oot ontae the balcony as Moira's blusterin aboot where she went wrong. Then she suddenly threatens, — Ah'm gittin the buckin polis oantae the baith ay yis! See how yis like that!

— That's right, Moira! Margaret Curran shouts.

— You . . . well, if you . . . if you fuckin bring thaim intae it, Keezbo stammers, — ah'll tell the RSPCA aboot you keeping birds in yir tits! That's no right in the heid!

— Thir no in ma tits! Ah've nae tits! And now ah've nae buckin son, bi Christ!

As they rage on, ah shakes the tin, as Matty gies a daft wee salute. Ah drops it n watches it fall, hittin the deck wi an explosive crack as it splatters open n the coins strew in a glittering shower across the forecourt. Fuck, ah didnae think they'd scatter like that! Matty's thaire, but a crowd ay young kids are appearin fae fuckin naewhaire n they're rummagin wi Matty for oor fuckin poppy! — FUCK OFF! FUCK OFF, YA WEE CUNTS . . . DINNAE LIT THUM . . . FUCK!

Keezbo n me are right oot through the kitchen, past his ma, dad, Pauline n fusty-fud Curran, oot the front door, along the balcony, n wir bombin doon the stairs as fast as we can.

— DINNAE LIT CHEEKY BOY OOT! Moira shouts.

We gits oot n doon the stairs n thaire's Matty pathetically shoutin at these thievin wee bastards, — Gie's it back . . .

We're pickin up the fuckin coins n the wee cunts are leggin it, but then Mrs Rylance comes roond the corner and sees the yellay shards ay the shattered collection box n she's pointin n screamin, — IT'S MA MONEY . . . IT'S THE CATS' MONEY!

Mrs Curran's gittin in oan the act, screamin doon fae the balcony, — THIEVES! THIEVES! THE RENTONS N THE CONNELLS . . . . DURTY THIEVIN GYPSY BASTARDS! THEY GIT EVERY-THING THIT ISNAE MEANT FIR THUM!

We're scramblin fir the dosh but Jesus fuck, thaire's a cop car pullin up, n two polis git oot, so we're offski, oor poakits laden wi change. We kin hear them radioing fir help, and we head doon Madeira Street, nashin ower Ferry Road, doon Largo Place, n the steps taewards the river, coins swingin n jinglin. One copper's goat back intae the motor, but one stocky cunt's fuckin well flyin eftir us as we hit the Water ay Leith walkway. But fuck him, ah even looks back, like *he's* gaunny catch us doon here, his wee pish-hole-in-the-snaw eyes set in a white, bulbous face, growin rid-dir by the second, as he stores air in his cheeks, the fat hamster-faced cunt so comical ah kin feel ma sides spazzin up jist thinkin aboot it. They send this overfed Gumley-raised suburban jackass oot tae chase three Leith schemies? Boys whae wir *specifically fuckin bred* tae run fae the polis? Lab-dicks dinnae huv a fuckin scooby!

391

Sure enough, when ah look back again, he's stoaped, gaspin, bent ower hudin his knees, as we pass under the Junction Street Bridge. Then he stands like an incompetent fitba player, blawin hard, shaking his fat noggin in disbelief, as if a ref will blaw the whistle and we'll suddenly stop n take a disgruntled walk intae a meatwagon as a rid caird gits raised skywards. No dice, fat boy! This tree-lined riverbank loves us, this rash ay warehouses, cobbled streets and tenemented dwellings adores its sons and hates auld flatfoot who's brought nowt but grief doon here since the year dot. Even Keezbo's takin the pish oot ay him, breathin quite smoothly, though his face is crimson n the sweat's whippin offay him. Matty's away ahead, then lookin back, stoapin, n littin us faw intae line. — Cunt, he says breathlessly, — wee cunts were right in thaire . . . it wis they wee Maxwells fae Thomas Fraser's . . . shouldnae even be at the Fort . . .

Ah'm thinkin ah could nip up the steps at West Bowling Green Street n duck intae the parental home, but ye never shite oan yir ain doorstep, so we keep tearin doon taewards the Forth, passin the ducks swimmin by the derelict factories and the new apartments. We see the Bannanay flats towerin behind the new constructions across the water, as we slow doon tae catch our wind n try tae look casual. Keezbo's breathin hard, hands oan his hips, Matty's heid's swivellin roond like an owl's. Ah realise we've left the Sealink bag, but that's fuck all.

There's a slip road that cuts oantae a street leadin tae the courtyard ay this new yuppie scheme n we could cut through it, but the homesteaders are unlikely tae be shy at pickin up the blower if they see natives hingin aboot their property. So we press oan, at a brisk march. Oan the bridge at Sandport Place, we dinnae even see them tae oor right, lurkin oan the slip road ay Coalhill, waiting for us, no in a meatwagon, but in two squad motors.

FUCK . . .

Thaire's nae runnin left in any ay us now. We run oan junk and we've burned the dregs ay that ootay oor systems.

They handcuff me n Matty thegither, and Keezbo on his ain, wi his hands in front, n wir taken tae a holdin cell up the High Street. Funny, but although ah'm bein plunged intae what promises tae be the worst sickness ah've ever known, ah'm relieved in a wey, just cause it's aw ower. Now ah'm anticipatin the next big challenge: gettin detoxed. Ah'm thinkin, they'll help us, surely tae fuck, they'll no leave us like this, cause ah'm rattlin n that methadone is fuck all use.

Keezbo's really fucked. He's nearly greetin, as he keeps gaun up tae the

Judas Hole n bangin oan the door. — Ah goat oaf the balcony, he moans, — now ah'm stuck in here!

Dae yir fuckin nut in, that fat cunt.

Matty's sittin oan a bench, heid focused oan the flair in front ay him. Two polis come in wi cups ay tea, n he looks up n takes the words oot ma mooth: — We really need the hoaspital, mate, he says tae one copper. — We're aw really seek, like.

The polisman keeps his face set in a neutral expression. He's a fairly lardy cunt but with keen eyes, a porker who's just demolished his trough's contents but eagerly awaits its new load ay swill. — I wis thinking that ah might check youse intae the North British Hotel for a couple ay weeks. Till yis ur feelin a wee bit better like. Or maybe youse might prefer the Caledonian?

Like the daft cunt he is, Matty turns tae me n Keezbo n goes, — Dunno, what dae youse think?

— Ah think you need tae learn tae spot a wind-up, Matty, ah goes.

— Aw . . . right . . .

The cops are laughin thair heids oaf at his miserable torn-up coupon. Keezbo's sittin doon oan the bench and is turned away intae the waw, n while ah feel like ah'm betrayin Matty, ah cannae help, even through ma pain, joinin in the joke.

Junk Dilemmas No. 3

The copper stares at us in utter contempt. Nae wonder; aw he sees in front
ay um is this mingin cunt, twitchin n spazzin oan this hard seat in the
interview room. — Ah'm oan the programme, ah tell um. — Check if ye like.
Ah'm aw seek cause they nivir gied us enough methadone. They said they hud
tae fine-tune ma dosage. Check wi the lassie at the clinic if ye dinnae believe us.

— Boo-fucking-hoo, he sais, a mean expression oan his face. — Why am I
not tearing up on your behalf, my sweet, sweet friend?

This cunt has cold black eyes set in a white face. If he didnae huv a dark
pudding-basin haircut and his neb wis bigger, he'd be like one ay Moira and
Jimmy's budgies. The other polisman, a louche, slightly effeminate-looking blond
boy, is playing the benign role. — Just tell us who gives you that stuff, Mark.
Come on, pal, give us some names. You're a good lad, far too sensible tae get mixed
up in aw this nonsense. He shakes his heid and then looks up at me, lip curled
doon thoughtfully. — Aberdeen University, no less.

— But if ye check yi'll find that ah'm oan the programme . . . at the clinic
likes.

— Bet these student birds bang like fuck! In they halls ay residence. It'll be
shaggin aw the time in thaire, eh, pal? the Pudding-Basin-Heided Cunt goes.

— Just one name, Mark. C'mon, pal, begs Captain Sensible.

— Ah telt ye, ah say, as sincerely as ah kin, — ah see this boy up at the
bookies, ah jist ken him as Olly. Dinnae even know if that's his right name. Gen
up. The staff at the clinic'll confirm —

— Ah suppose prison's like the halls ay residence, apart fae one thing, Pudding
Basin goes, — no much chance ay a ride thaire. At least, he laughs, — no the
sort ay ride ye'd want, anywey!

— Just gie the clinic a quick phone, ah beg.

— If ah hear the word 'clinic' come out ay your mooth again, son . . .

They keep this shite gaun fir a bit, till a legal-aid lawyer, whae's been appointed
for us, thankfully comes in tae end the torment. The polis leave n the lawyer gadge
gies us the news ah want tae hear. It's a stark choice: basically either jail (at least
remand until it goes tae court) or rehab, in a new project, which ah huv tae sign
up tae for forty-five days, or ah'm charged wi the original offence. — It's not the

easy option. It means being drug-free, he explains, — even your methadone will be stopped.

— Fuck . . . ah gasp. — Ah'm no sure tae definitely get a prison sentence, am ah? No jist fir thievin a poxy collection tin?

— Nothing's certain at all these days. It doesn't look good though, does it? These were monies collected by an elderly shopkeeper for an animal-welfare charity.

— Ye pit it like that . . . Ah feel ma shoodirs hunch up in acknowledgement.

The boy takes his specs off. Rubs at the indentations they've left oan the side ay his beak. — On the one hand the government are encouraging the authorities to come down hard on drug use, on the other they're acknowledging the growing problem of heroin addiction in the community. So there is the strong chance of a custodial sentence if you don't cooperate with this rehab programme. Your parents are outside, and have been informed of the situation. What do you want to do?

Decisions, decisions.

— Ah'll sign up.

St Monans (Peer Education)

Ah'm no chuffed aboot the rehab situ but it looked like it wis either that or the jail, n ah wisnae up fir a gamble. Fuck knows what happened tae Matty, but Keezbo went for a similar deal. He moved intae the Monty Street pad wi us, markin time oan the methadone programme, but there was gear oan the streets and we still liked getting fucked up thegither. It wis a barry laugh when ah took him doon tae the clinic fir the first time n they gied him the blood test for the cowie, that Aids, eh. The lassie, askin questions aboot transmission, goes tae um, — Are you sexually active?

— Usually, aye, Keezbo goes, no gittin her at aw, — but sometimes ah jist like tae lie back, wi a bird oan toap, daein aw the work. Goat tae mix it up, but, eh?

— What I mean is, do you have a current sexual partner?

— How, Keezbo goes wi a big smile, — ye pittin yirsel in the frame then?

That wis the only fun part. Normally it wis loads ay questions. Ah hud a couple ay interviews wi this heid-fucking dwarf-like guy called Dr Forbes, and one fae this big-boned Englishwoman whae wis a clinical psychologist. Ah telt them what ah thoat they wanted tae hear, jist tae git thum oaf ma case. Keezbo said he wis the same.

Back in the gaff, we'd tried tae jam fir a bit, but his drums n ma amp, then the Fender went intae Boston's second-hand shoap oan the Walk, in exchange fir gear. Kept the Shergold fretless, but.

Some cunts thought it was okay, but ah wisnae gittin intae the methadone, n ah wis feelin sick a lot. When ah wisnae too fucked tae go oot, the toon just seemed deid. Sick Boy had vanished, his ma said he'd went tae his auntie's in Italy. Swanney had gone tae ground, n Spud wis meant tae huv been transferred fae the hoaspital intae rehab. Begbie wis in jail, Tommy n Second Prize wir in love, Lesley wis rumoured tae be up the stick, n Ali, whae's seein this straightpeg aulder dude, never answered her phone.

But the biggest mystery wis Matty; nae cunt had heard anything aboot him. He'd taken the prison option and hud been oan remand, but the rumour wis thit he'd got oaf wi a suspended sentence, which wis fuckin lenient, cause they were meant tae have searched his hoose. If so, they'd have found aw the snidey goods. Ah wondered what he'd telt the polis, sweatin away under they lights, junk sick. As fir everybody else, aw the staples ay Leith – mates, burds, Hibs – jist seemed tae huv nae real appeal. Aw ah cared aboot wis skag.

Eftir we went for oor swallay doon the clinic at the auld Leith Hoaspital, they gied Keezbo a letter n he wis oaf the next day intae rehab. Ah must've looked left oot, cause the nurse, a barry lassie called Rachael, whae wis a mate ay Ali's, informed us, — You'll be next, Mark. Just try tae hang in there.

So ah mainly sat in the flat, readin, n thinkin aboot Matty. How he isnae a grass. You're either made that wey or yir no. You're either a scab or a grass or you urnae. N he isnae. So it wis a bit ay a surprise when he crept roond the flat one night, a somewhat chastened look oan the cunt's normally sleekit pus. He asked us whaire Keezbo wis n ah telt him.

— Fuck that, he goes, — ah'm no detoxin. Ah'm no daein cauld turkey.

— But they gie ye stuff tae help.

— Baws! They take ye oaf the methadone! Fuck thair sleepin pills or paracetamol or whatever shite they gie ye! However they fuckin try n dress it up, it's still cauld turkey! Cunt, nae fuckin wey, Matty contends. — Cunt, ye should've taken the sentence. Ah jist goat four days in thaire, oan the methadone, then ah wis oot oan a six-month suspended. Cunt, ye could've done four days' remand – better than a week ay cauld turkey n five weeks gittin yir heid fuckin nipped in thair shitey rehab centre!

Ah hate tae admit it, but the cunt hus us crappin ma keks. The methadone's far fae perfect, but bein withoot it, n wi nae access tae the Salisbury Crag, wis a fuckin grim prospect. But while ah shat it offay rehab, ah still wisnae prepared tae take a punt oan any jail time, even jist a few days' remand.

Matty didnae stick aroond. Ah telt um ah hud nae gear, but ah wis totally hudin oot oan the wee cunt. He fucked off eftir a bit, wi the usual 'phone us' shite.

A couple ay days eftir they took Keezbo, muh ma n dad showed up at the flat. They'd found oot ah wis here oan ma ain, so they telt us they were takin me hame till ah got ma place oan the rehab project. Ah wisnae chuffed, but they insisted that ah might OD or something if ah wis left alaine. By this time the methadone wis kickin in, and wi it a weary, heavy-limbed passivity, so ah allowed masel tae be led. Nowt much happened at my folks' hoose, ah mainly kipped, read and watched the box. Ah mind Nicksy phoned, sayin that Giro the dug had settled at his ma's, but he wis bored n thinkin ay movin intae a place wi Tony. Ah kent how he felt. As it was, ah wis only hame fir a few days, reading James Joyce in ma room, when muh dad came in, tellin us tae pack ma stuff up. When

397

he telt me that ah'd 'got a place' in rehab, it wis like him boastin tae other people that ah'd 'got a place' at the uni a couple ay years back. He couldnae keep the excitement ootay his voice.

The downside wis that when ah went roond tae the clinic, they'd been informed aboot what wis happenin, n ma methadone wis cut back in prep fir the detox. So ah packed some clathes and books. Ah found some council-headed notepaper Norrie Moyes had gied us yonks ago that ah'd forgotten aboot; we wir plannin a revenge scam on the Currans but it came tae nowt. Ah slipped them in a folder and stuck it in the bag.

It pishes doon oan the drive tae the middle ay fuckin naewhaire in Fife. Ah sit in the back as ma faither drives in silence, Ma gabbin nervously in between chain-smokes. When we git thaire, gaun through some poxy village wi a few hooses, a church and a pub, and park in front ay this one-storey white buildin, ah'm hurtin bad, cramped and stiff, feelin the reduction in the methadone awready. Ah cannae even climb oot the back seat ay the car when the old boy exits, openin ma door. As cauld air flies in, a sweat-inducing pulse ay terror rises in me. — Ah dinnae want tae dae this!

As ah hear muh ma say something aboot a fresh start, ma faither goes, — Well, it's oot ay your hands now, pal, n he grabs ma airm, n starts yankin us oot the motor.

Ah grip the back ay the seat. — What gies youse the right tae force us tae go here?

My ma looks at me, twistin roond wi her big doolally eyes, n she wrenches ma hand fae the seat. — We care, son, that's what gies us the right . . . Lit go! N muh dad gies us another tug n ah fly oot the motor, stumblin, wi him helpin tae keep me oan ma feet, hudin us up by the jaykit like a rag doll. — C'mon, son, shape up, he says wi gentle, encouragin firmness.

As ah stand upright oan ma shaky legs, ah realise ma itchy eyes are gushin oot tears n ah wipe thum oan ma sleeve wi aw these snotters. Ma gets oot the car, shakes her head, musing, — Ah dinnae ken why this has happened tae us . . .

— Mibbe it's God, ah venture, as ah feel ma dad's grip loosen on me, — giein ye another test, likes.

She looks at me and springs ower, shouting at ma dad, — Did ye hear um, Davie? He's evil! She points at me. — Listen tae yirsel, ya ungrateful wee –

— It's the drug talkin, Cathy, the withdrawal, Dad sais wi grim authority, starin at me wi squinty eyes. Now that the auld girl is kickin oaf, he kin play good cop. The auld boy has a temper but is loath tae lose it. The auld girl is generally easy-going, so ma tactic hus been tae get her tae play the bad fucker, which often strangely disarms the auld boy's anger. But now ah'm puppy-seek n runnin oot ay time. Ma throat tickles and ma eyeballs feel like they need tae be scratched oot. Ah sneeze twice, seismic convulsions that shake ma body, n ma auld man looks at us in concern.

Ah glances aroond, but thaire's naewhaire aboot here tae dae a runner tae. — C'mon, Dad commands, an impatient edge in his voice. We walk doon the gravel path tae the front door ay the white buildin, n step inside. The place hus that omnipresent vibe ay state control: magnolia waws, broon cairpit tiles, harsh overhead strip lighting.

We're met by the centre director, a skinny woman wi dark curly hair which is tied back, rid-framed glesses n fine, delicate features. She ignores me, electin instead tae shake hands wi ma parents. A big, wholesome cunt wi a blond fringe smiles at me. — I'm Len. He picks up ma holdall, — I'll take this tae yir room.

The auld man swivels his heid roond, takes it aw in. — Seems a no bad billet though, son. He gies ma hand a squeeze. There's mist in his eyes. — Fight through it, pal, he whispers. — We believe in ye.

The skinny-specky bird is blabbering oan tae ma mother, whae's looking warily back at her. — The essence of St Monans is a collaborative venture between two health boards and three social work departments. It comprises detox followed by the client-centred individual therapy and group-counselling sessions.

— Aye . . . that's nice . . .

— The group is crucial to our philosophy. It's seen as the way to combat the peer structures on the outside that support the substance-dependent client's behaviour.

— Aye . . . cosy, Ma sais, lookin at the curtains, rubbin the material between her thumb n forefinger.

— Well, ye'll get nae bother fae him, my dad goes, turnin tae me. — You'll take yir chance here. Right?

— Right, ah say, lookin at this timetable thing displayed on the waw behind him. It says WAKE UP 7.00 A.M. Fuck that.

I'll take ma first chance tae git the fuck oot.

— Anything tae get ye oaf they streets, away fae they losers n bams like that Spud laddie. N thon Matty. Nae ambition, that crowd. He shakes his heid.

— Removal from the environment which supports the drug-taking behaviour is one of the key elements of our programme. We provide a disciplined and structured framework, and give the substance-dependent client the chance to take stock, so sayeth Skinny-Specky.

— They'll drag ye doon tae thair level, son. Ah've seen it, my ma warns, glaring hauntingly at me.

— That's ma mates. Ah've goat the right tae hing aboot wi whae ah want, ah say, hearin a door slam somewhere in the distance, follayed by a raised voice makin a threat.

— Thir junkies, she scowls.

— So? Thir no hermin anybody, ah goes, catchin Skinny-Specky's pained look; her recognition that she's walked intae a family feud, but still wi the sense ay prerogative that it's takin place in *her* centre. Naebody else seems tae hear the consternation comin fae a far-off room, the stormin footsteps doon a corridor.

Could be big fun n games in here, right enough.

— No *hermin anybody*? ma faither groans miserably. — Ye wir caught red-handed, son, leavin that shop wi that tin! An auld woman, son. A pensioner, tryin tae make a livin and dae her bit for sick animals. Ye must see how messed up that is, surely, son, and he looks tae an intense but neutral Skinny-Specky fir support, then turns back tae me. — Ye must see how that makes ye *look*?

Some auld minger that's gaunny be fuckin deid soon anywey . . . grassin auld cunt . . .

— Ye were better oaf hingin aboot wi Tommy n Francis n Robert, son, Ma urges. — The fitba n aw that. Ye eywis liked the fitba!

A sudden bolt ay panic, n ah want tae jist hunker doon cause ay the dizzy chill that assails us. Instead, ah turns tae ma new hostess. — If ah feel really bad, will ah still git ma methadone here?

Skinny-Specky's glance is measured and unfazed. It's like she's seein us fir the first time. She slowly shakes her heid. — This project is about being drug-free. You'll come off the methadone maintenance here. You'll be part of a group, a *society*, here at St Monans, one that works, rests and plays together, and make no mistake, it *will* be tough, she says, lookin tae ma parents. — Now, Mr and Mrs Renton, if you don't mind, we really should get Mark settled in.

Fuck sakes!

My ma gies me a bonecrushing hug. Ma faither, noting my obvious discomfort, settles fir a wear nod. He hus tae pull her away as she's sobbin her fuckin eyes oot. — But he's ma bairn, Davie, he'll eywis be ma bairn . . .

— C'moan now, Cathy.

— Ah'll get masel sorted oot here, Ma, you'll see. Ah try n crack a smile.

Just fuckin go! Now!

Ah want tae lie doon. Ah dinnae want tae be part ay Skinny-Specky's daft wee group, her fuckin society. But nonetheless, as ma parents shuffle ootside, ah'm awready daydreamin aboot fawin in love wi her; me n Skinny-Specky oan a Caribbean island wi an endless supply ay gear, procured fae her employers in the NHS. She's like one ay they sexy librarian birds thit wid be shaggable as fuck when the hair comes doon n the bins come oaf.

So Len escorts us tae ma room. For aw his scrubbed, affable demeanour, he's a big cunt, like a benign bouncer, n ah widnae fancy tryin tae git past him. He flips on the fluorescent light, which blinks like a night-club strobe, then stabilises, searing the room in a sick glow, with accompanying insect drone. Ah lie oot oan the bed, takin in the gaff. It's a mundane hybrid ay the residences at Aberdeen and the cabin on *The Freedom of Choice*. There's the same wee built-in desk-and-shelves unit with chair as at the uni, and a similarly designed wardrobe and chest ay drawers. But Len-the-Fringe tells me no tae git too comfortable. Thaire's an induction session in the meeting room, seemingly aw soas little old me can meet the others. Ah'm wonderin if either Spud or Keezbo'll be in here, or if they got sent somewhere different. — How many's here?

— We currently have nine clients.

But first he issues me wi a timetable, the same one as ah saw on the waw at the reception area. — Just want to quickly take you through this . . .

Lothian Health Board/Lothian Region Department of Social Work
St Monans Substance-Dependency Group
Daily Timetable

7.00 A.M.	WAKE UP
8.30 A.M.	BREAKFAST
9.30 A.M.	MEDICINES
10.00 A.M.	MEDITATION
11.30 A.M.	PROCESS REVIEW GROUP
1.00 P.M.	LUNCH
2.30 P.M.	INDIVIDUAL COUNSELLING
4.00 P.M.	GROUP WORK – ISSUES ON DRUG DEPENDENCY
6.00 P.M.	DINNER
7.30 P.M.	RECREATION/FITNESS
8.30 P.M.	SUPPER
11.00 P.M.	LIGHTS OUT

— Wake up at seven in the morning? That's goat tae be a joke!

— Aye, it's a tough one at first, Len acknowledges, — but people soon get used tae it. It's all about getting some order back intae those chaotic lifestyles. We assemble for breakfast, which everyone must attend, even if they're in detox, after which you're issued with any relevant medicines you need.

— Seven in the mornin's ridic, ah moan. The last time ah wis up that early wis Gillsland's. — N meditation? What's aw that? Ah'm no sayin prayers or chantin or nowt like that!

Len laughs and shakes his heid. — It's no about religion, we dinnae follow the NA/AA model. We don't demand that you to submit tae God or a higher power, though if you do feel so inclined it wouldnae be discouraged. It's proven very effective and popular with substance-dependent clients in the past.

The only higher power ah'd ever submit tae would be Paddy Stanton or Iggy Pop.

— What's aw this substance-dependence stuff?

— We prefer that tae the term *addict.*

— Fine, ah shrug.

Len's thick finger taps at the sheet, redirecting ma attention back tae the timetable. — The process review group gives us the opportunity to look at how we're functioning as members of this community, and flag up any issues we have relating to that. As you might imagine, they can get lively. After lunch we have our individual sessions, where you'll be working with Tom or Amelia. Then we do a group session to look at the issues of substance dependency. After dinner, it's free time, and we have a television, a pool table and also some fitness and musical equipment. It's not a great deal, basically just some hand weights and a guitar, but we're hoping to get more stuff soon. There's an optional light supper, usually just a hot chocolate or Horlicks and biscuit. We put out the lights in all common areas and switch off the telly at eleven o'clock. During the forty-five-day programme, you aren't allowed any phone calls, unless on compassionate grounds and by prior agreement with a senior member of staff. You *are* allowed letters, but any incoming mail will be opened and vetted before being issued to you. No drugs, including alcohol, are permitted on the premises. We make a reluctant exception for nicotine and caffeine, he grins. — You aren't allowed off the facility during the period of your treatment, unless on a project outing and under staff supervision.

— This is like the fuckin jail!

Len shakes his heid dismissively. – The jail they just lock you up, then

402

throw you out. We want you to get better, He stands up. – Right, we have a little induction meeting, all for you, but first let me show ye aroond.

He gives me a tour ay 'the facility', as they call it. He explains that we're by the village of St Monans, in the East Neuk of Fife, close tae Anstruther, a small, picturesque former fishing town, now given ower tae tourism. But as we'll never get oot tae see the place, it could be fuckin miles away. The village and this project are named after St Monans, a saint that nae cunt kens a thing aboot. The Patron Saint of Fuck All, and thus perfect for this place. The centre is a U-shaped building wi a walled gairden tae the back. It has ten bedrooms, a kitchen, dining room and a recreation room wi a pool table n telly. Off the recky room is a small conservatory, leading tae a patio n the gairden, which is hemmed in by big trees.

— And this is the meeting room, Len says, opening a door, but as ah step inside, the first thing ah hear is: — RENTON, YA CUNT, then aw this laughter follayed by a round ay applause. Ah cannae fuckin believe it. Thir aw fuckin here!

— Fuck sakes! Youse cunts, ah hear masel squeal in delight. It's like walkin intae a surprise birthday perty!

— Goat the fill set now, boys, Johnny Swan, wearin a fuckin *collar n tie*, laughs.

There's Keezbo, half zonked oot, elbaw on the chair airmrest, wi his big heid propped oan a doughy fist, and Spud, whae's sittin shiverin, airms wrapped roond hissel, in that classic junky pose. — Catboy, he sais.

And Sick Boy's slumped in a corner seat. Ah nods n sits doon beside um. — Nice place yir auntie's goat.

He pills a tired smile. — Hud tae be done.

Spud asks Len aboot getting something for his cramps as Sick Boy and Swanney intro us tae a boy fae Niddrie called Greg Castle, whae inevitably gits called Roy. Thare's a jumpy-lookin wee cunt, Ted fae Bathgate, n a Weedgie boy wi black eyes n a long, broken and bent nose thit gits kent as Skreel. He jist goat in yesterday n he's rattlin like fuck. Thaire's jist one lassie, a curly-mopped bird called Molly, who looks at me wi naked hostility through pinched features. The track marks on the underside ay her thin, white wrists are angry enough, but dwarfed by surgically proficient crimson lacerations ay varied depth. Maist scary, though, is this big biker called Seeker, whae ah've never met but ken by rep. His glassy eyes briefly stare intae me wi X-ray potency, before he turns away, as if he's seen everything and is now bored.

Swanney gies me a stealthy wink n discreetly pills oot a wee razor

403

blade. Ah clock him nick the inside ay his mooth, catchin the blood in his hands, looking tae Len, whae's shitein it. — Ma stitch is burst . . .

— The nurse isn't in . . .

— Ah'll chum um tae git cleaned up, ah quickly volunteer.

— Right . . .

Ah catch Sick Boy, Keezbo and Spud lookin daggers at us as Swanney n me nash ootside doon the hall tae the bogs. He's goat works doon his boot n he quickly cooks up. — Last ay the summer wine, buddy. Enjoy it, cause wir in fir a rough ride . . .

He pills oaf his tie n tourniquets ma airm. We're dabbin away at a wrap ay speed n it faws oot ma hand as he slams me up and the heroin goes tae ma brain, killin aw the world's pain.

Fuckin barry, ya cunt . . .

Ah sit blissed oot oan the crapper as Swanney fixes, tellin me that he wis hudin, n this is the last. He retrieves the speed wrap n we finish it, even though it's the last thing ah want. — Take it, he commands, as he struggles tae fix his tie. — If they kin tell yir wasted it's game ower. He rolls his eyes. — But it's awright here, a great network ay contacts.

— Ta, Johnny, ah gasp, — sound ay ye, man.

— Nae bother, he goes.

When we get back Len-the-Fringe and Skinny-Specky have launched intae this spiel, but nae cunt's listenin, thir aw slumped back intae thair chairs, n we join thum. It's gaunny be awright in here. These are ma people: the St Monans crew.

The Cusp

To Alison, time had become a fractured series of base biological impulses.

Bill and Carole, the other co-workers in her team, knew all about the relationship but were discreet, even supportive, in a quietly protective way. But like Alexander, they noticed the state Alison was coming to work in, when she came in at all. This couldn't go on. Now here she was again, ghosting in at ten thirty. Alexander made a show of getting her straight into his office, eyes blazing, a gallows set to his mouth. — Look, it might not mean anything to you, he began, — but we're on the cusp of an epidemic in this city. I can't show you favouritism above the others. C'mon, Ali, he entreated suddenly, the lowered voice of the lover supplanting that of the boss, — you're taking the piss here!

— Sorry . . . it's just . . . she blinked at the silver light spearing in between the blinds of the big window behind him, — they buses are mental . . .

— I really think we should consider getting you transferred, maybe back to the RCP. It's my fault, I shouldn't have got involved . . .

An other-worldly glint sparked in Alison's eye. Her mouth twisted in sulky defiance. — If it's your fault, how is it me that's gettin transferred?

Alexander starkly saw her as a young lassie, and for the first time, experienced a fleetingly snobbish sense of her as common: as a *schemie*. And it shamed him, thinking that way. He could say nothing in response. It wasn't fair; he knew that. Yes, he could cite his status and crucial role in fighting this plague, but he didn't think that was what she'd want to hear. It was time to be honest, as callously forthright as she had been with him, when she'd told him she was seeing other people. — Tanya and me . . . we've decided to make another go of it, for the kids' sake.

Alison felt herself burn at this news. She didn't know why; she'd neither wanted nor had any sense of her and Alexander ever being a long-term thing. Perhaps it was just the shock of rejection, or maybe being with him had bestowed more than she'd realised. — Good for you, she responded, with as much grace as she could muster. His doleful stare told her she'd not done too badly. — I'm pleased, and I'm no just saying that, Alison declared, even though, on at least one level, it was a lie. — Kids need both parents, she continued, mustering conviction. — I never wanted tae *marry ye*, Alexander, it was just shagging. Get a grip.

That slightly mocking, somewhat arcane expression of hers, struck at his core. He loved her, and felt so downcast at the irreparable nature of it all. — I really don't know if it's appropriate that we continue working together –

— Oh fuck off, yir really starting tae creep me oot now, and that's pittin it mildly, she scoffed at him, her laugh hollow and bitter. — I've had shit going on, you've had shit going on, we shouldnae have ended up in bed, but we did. It's over, and I've nae fuckin interest in broadcasting it tae the world.

— Right . . . he said falteringly, feeling small, wee-boy weak.

His passivity jolted something inside her. Alison thought about her mother, dying, yet unable to rage against it. The lines from that classic Dylan Thomas poem resonated in her. She had gaped at that withering body, so ruined and decayed it was practically a corpse long before her last heartbeat. It was accompanied by the realisation that she herself was moving forward in life, at the same time as her expectations and ideals were being profoundly shaken. What was it, all this council stuff, this nonsense about fucking trees? It was a pile of meaningless shite, for pompous little cretins to get self-absorbed over. — But ken what? Ah'm gaunny make it easy for ye, she said, in a sudden low growl. — Ah resign. Fae the council. Ah've had it here!

— Don't be silly, you can't lose your job, Alison, I won't let you do that, Alexander said, sensing his words falling hopelessly into the widening chasm between them.

— Fuck all tae dae wi you, she said, and walked out of his office, through the open plan, not looking at Bill and Carole, slamming the door shut. Heading down the oak-panelled corridors and across the marble-floored hallway, through the heavy revolving doors, she reached the pillared square outside the City Chambers. Tore up the Royal Mile, the opposite direction of home, feeling better than she'd done in ages, all the time knowing it wouldn't last.

He was weak, she thought with contempt. She'd also been weak, but she'd been that way with an essentially feeble man. Perhaps that was a blessing. You couldn't know.

Ye couldnae know anything.

The city was beautiful. It was perfect. Yes, the schemes were horrible and there was nothing in them, but in the centre you had everything. Alison walked on, allowing herself to be awestruck at how amazing her home town was. The light, pouring over the castle, turning the streets of the Old Town silver. It was the most beautiful place in the world. Nothing could compare. The trees were beautiful too. You couldn't let them take away the trees.

Alison passed under some scaffolding as four drunk, arm-in-arm girls waltzed by, singing as if on a hen night, though it was still morning. She turned, enviously, to watch them sashay up the road, desperate to know the story of their mysterious joy. It inspired her to keep her faith in impulse, propelling her into a functional bar in the shadow of the castle. It was early, and still devoid of custom. A heavyset, sulky girl, with judging eyes, dispensed her a glass of white wine. She sat down on a seat under the window, picking up a discarded *Scotsman*. The thought amused her: *I grabbed hold of a tatty old Scotsman in a grotty bar. Again.*

She rubbed the long stem of the glass between her thumb and forefinger, regarding the urine-coloured liquid nestled inside it. Then one sip of the sour vinegary substance almost made her puke. The second one was better, and the third seemed to satisfactorily reset her taste buds. She browsed the paper, arrested by an editorial:

The Scottish Office and Edinburgh District Council are to be commended for their timeous action in tackling the most serious epidemic to face Scotland's capital. The rampant assault on our treescape, and thus our history and heritage, posed by the terrible Dutch elm threat concerns us all. The disease has taken its toll, but the casualties would have been so much higher had not the current strategy of felling and burning infected trees been so swiftly and decisively enacted.

Alison felt her eyes go down the newspaper to the readers' letters. There was something from a general practitioner in one of Edinburgh's big schemes. It warned that random testing had uncovered an inordinately high instance of infection by the Aids virus. She studied a sore track mark on her thin wrist.

A notion gnawed at her consciousness; trees rotting away on one side of West Granton Road, and people, inside the varicose-vein flats, so called because of their patched-up cladding, similarly decomposing. All that death. All that plague. Where did it come from? What did it mean?

What's gaunny happen?

She left the bar, pondering this on the way home. A strong wind had started up, swirling through nooks and crannies, seeming to shake the city like it was a film set. Strange that a place built around a castle rock could seem so rickety, but that rock was now covered in scaffolding, as they tried to treat it and prevent it from crumbling. Cutting down Lothian Road, she walked to the east end through Princes Street Gardens. Heading down Leith Street, then Leith Walk and reaching her Pilrig flat, she hung up her jacket. Then she looked at herself in the bathroom mirror. Thought about her mum, how she loved to meet her for a coffee, to show her a top or shoes she'd bought, to gossip about neighbours or relatives, or talk about what they'd watched on the telly. Soaping and rinsing her hands, she recalled that she'd put the towels in the wash basket. She went to the press to get some fresh ones. Then it caught her eye, stuffed forlornly at the back of the cupboard; the shaving bag Alexander had left. She, unzipped it open and regarded the contents of brush, razor and block of shave stick. Picking up the brush, she held it against her chin, to see what she would look like with a goatee. Then she put it back in the bag and pulled out the bone-handled razor. Opened the blade. How light and lethal it felt in her hand. Alison rolled her sleeve up over her biceps and cut across the vein and artery. Warm blood splashed onto the tiled floor.

Mum . . .

It felt good, like the pain in her was leaking out with the blood, like a terrible pressure was being removed. It was soothing. She slid down the wall.

Mum . . .

But as she sat there, things quickly changed; there was too much blood. First she was gripped by a creeping nausea, then a desperate fear rose up inside her. Her thoughts faded, and she felt she was going to black out.

Dad Mhairi Calum . . .

Tearing the towel from the rail, she wrapped it tightly around the wound, applying as much pressure as she could manage. She pushed herself up, staggered into the front room, lurching towards the phone. Her pulse battered in her skull as she dialled 999, and grunted for an ambulance. — I made a mistake, she heard herself gasp over and over again. — Please get here soon.

And that's putting it mildly . . .

The towel was already saturated in the blood. Crawling on her knees, she forced herself to the front door and opened it. Sat waiting by the door, feeling her eyes grow heavy.

. . . mildly . . .

Emerging into some kind of consciousness in the hospital, she was assailed by a procession of solemn faces who explained that they'd got to her in time, told how her how close it had been, and stressed the luck she'd enjoyed on this occasion. — Please don't tell my dad, she repeatedly begged, when they'd sternly asked about contact details and a next of kin.

— We need to inform somebody, a short, middle-aged nurse explained.

All she could think to do was give them Alexander's number.

They stitched her up and gave her a pint and a half of blood. Alexander came round later, and took her home to the Pilrig flat the next day. He brought her Chinese food and spent the night on her couch. She was asleep in the morning when he checked on her before he went to work. As he left, he looked at the picture in his wallet of his two children. He and Tanya, they had to be there for them. But he came by to check on Alison that evening, telling her he'd signed her off on two weeks' leave, informing her with a grim smile that he'd ignored her resignation request. — I didn't get a formal letter.

They'd sat up, her on the couch, him in the armchair, and started talking about their own bereavement experiences. Alexander was conscious that his had been more limited than hers. — Tanya's father died three years ago. Massive coronary. She's been really angry since; principally, it seems, with me. But what can I do? I didn't kill him. It's not *my* fault.

— It's no hers either.

Alexander thought about this. — No, it isn't, he conceded, — and neither is it your fault that your mum died. So you shouldn't be punishing yourself as if it was.

It was then she looked at him, in mounting anxiety, letting him see her cry for the first time ever. It didn't make him feel the way he'd envisaged it would; big, manly and protective. Her face was horribly distorted, and he shared her wretched pain, and powerlessness at being unable to make it go away. — I never wanted to die, Alison said, looking really scared, then tightly shutting her eyes, as if confronting the possibility. — No for one second . . . The doctor telt us if the arterial cut had been a millimetre deeper, I'd probably have bled tae death in a few minutes. I just wanted tae take the pressure off . . .

— You can't get rid of the pressure. Nobody can. It's horrible, but all we can do is try and learn to carry its burden.

She glanced miserably at him when he said that. She was thankful he'd been there for her, but was relieved when he was getting ready to go. Hoping he wouldn't come back. He seemed to understand. — I really wish you well, Alison, he said to her.

When he left, she was content to lie on the couch in the dark, still able to smell his aftershave in the room, to feel the soft burn on the back of her hand where he'd gently touched her. Then Alison fell into a bruising sleep, ignoring the calls racking up on her answer machine. At some point she rose, eventually pulling herself through to the bedroom, and slipping under the duvet. She slumbered in some kind of peace till midday, rising and feeling stronger. Then she heated up a tin of soup, ate, put on a long-sleeved cardigan and headed down Leith Walk to visit her father.

The Rehab Diaries

Day 1

Stoned like a slug after Johnny's hit. I knew it would be my last for a while and it started to leave my system almost as soon as I'd gained an awareness of how good I was feeling. Within a few hours I was writhing in discomfort. Lay most of the day on the wee bed, trying to catch my breath, sweating like a backshift hooker, as the vigour boiled out of my blood.

The narrow windows, which you can't open, are surrounded by big, forbidding trees that overhang the walled back garden, shutting out most of the light. The building seems airless; the only sound the disturbing moans of some poor fucker from an adjacent room. I'm evidently not the only cunt in detox.

As the leaden dusk takes hold, bats dance outside in a small illuminated patch the trees can't get at. I go from bed to window to bed, pacing like a madman but too scared to leave this room.

Day 2

FUCK THEM ALL.

Day 5

They've left this big, ring-bound, loose-leaf diary on the desk, but I've been too fucked to write anything the last couple of days. There have been times when I've really wanted to die, the pain and misery of withdrawal so fucking intense and incessant. They've given me some painkillers, which are probably useless placebo shite. You sense they want you to experience the torment of it all.

If I'd had the means and the energy to dispatch m yself yesterday, I'd have been seriously tempted. For the last few days I've been feeling like I could drown in my own sweat. My fucking bones . . . it's as if I'm inside a car that's being crushed in a breaker's yard. It's just so fucking relentless.

And I think about Nicksy and Keezbo, and how I'd have jumped in their circumstances if I was feeling like this. Why the fuck put up with it?

I NEED A FUCKING FIX.

I need it bad.

I only leave my room for the toilet, or for breakfast, the one time detoxers are required to join the others. I take my tea with five sugars, and Coco Pops and milk, scranning it back as quick as I can. It's about all I can eat here; I usually have the same for lunch and dinner, which I always take in my room.

Last night, or the night before, I got up for a piss. There's a couple of thin-glowing night lights in the corridor, at skirting level, and I very near shat myself as this uplit, sweating beast came lumbering towards me. Some part of my brain told me to just keep walking, and the monster looked briefly at me, mumbling something as we passed each other. I said, 'Awright?' and carried on. When I came out of the bogs the thing had thankfully gone. I don't know if this was a dream or hallucination.

Day 6

Woken from a jaggy, nightmare-stuffed sleep by an aggressive storm of birdsong. I force myself to rise. Can barely look in the mirror. I've been way too uncomfortable to try and shave and I've grown a thin, scraggy ginger beard which looks redder and thicker than it is, cause of the spots on my face. The yellowheads are repulsive enough, but it's two big boil-like fuckers on my cheek and forehead that cause the distress. They throb under the surface of my skin like a Peter Hook bassline, hurting my face every time I try to move it. But my eyes provide the real shock; they seem pushed right back into my skull sockets, a deathly, defeated look to them.

The 'monster' the other night was that big biker gadgie, Seeker. Cunt doesn't look any better in the daylight.

Sick Boy's been chatting up that hostile Molly lassie. 'Love's the most dangerous drug of all,' he solemnly declared, eyes full of seriousness. Of course, she's falling for this garbage, nodding away. I was too fucked to enjoy his shite and Spud was rabbiting in my ear, about how detox isn't so bad. 'Ah jist keep thinkin thit it's barry somebody cares but, Mark.'

As I left the table I heard some smirking cunt, probably Swanney or Sick

Boy, referring to me as Catweazle, after the crazed jakey on telly. With my straggly hair and beard and stooping gait, I sense that's _exactly_ how I look. I'm happy and relieved to get back to my room.

Get assessed again by that Dr Forbes, who came in from the community drug clinic. He basically asked the same shite questions as before. Couldn't stop looking at his head; it's too big for his body, the Gerry Anderson puppet look.

More Coco Pops for dinner, before retiring to my suite. Happy days. Len comes in and talks for a wee bit, mainly about music. We have a half-hearted Beefheart discussion on the merits of _Clear Spot_ (me — a barry record) versus _Trout Mask Replica_ (him — a shite album). He tells me again aboot the guitar in the recky room.

Day 8

At breakfast I had a wee bit of porridge. With salt. Skinny-Specky made some comment about salt in porridge (she took sugar in hers) and we playfully derided her English habits. She insisted that she was Scottish, but Ted and Skreel told her that posh Scots were, to all intents and purposes, the same as the English. I mentioned that there were actually working-class people in England, and social class supplanted nationality as the parameters of our discussion. (Fuck sake — check the student cunt here!)

The Tom gadgie listened intently, as did Seeker, and a new, dark-heided, pointy-jawed, blue-eyed lassie who was introduced by Skinny-Specky as 'Audrey, from Glenrothes', as if she was a contestant on the _Generation Game_.

NOICE TA SEE YA, TA SEE YA, NOICE!

Audrey has replaced Greg 'Roy' Castle, who was the first dropout of the rehab programme. Apparently, he couldn't handle it and opted instead for residency courtesy of Her Majesty at Saughton. Audrey gave us a fretful nod, then sat in silence biting her nails. I felt for her, just shakily emerging from the detox cocoon of her room, the only lassie but one in the group. She looked even worse than I felt, rattling like a bairn's toy.

'I'm sure you'll be very happy here, Audrey,' Swanney said, sarcasm trickling from his tongue, then added, 'You don't have to be addicted to hard drugs to stay here, but it helps!'

413

Day 9

I take in another dull, fearsome morning. Outside, the white of the daisies on the dewy lawn, and crocuses, yellow, white and purple, spreading like a wave along the bottom of the stone wall. It's not so bad.

I'm sitting here, writing this shite and wondering why – probably because there's fuck all else to do. The folders we've been issued have two sections; a diary, with one page for each of this forty-five-day programme, and appendices where there's what they refer to as a 'journal'. Skinny-Specky explained that this is for 'developing any themes from the diaries that we may want to explore further'. Apparently the diaries are for our eyes only, and we can put anything into them. The journals we can elect to read out in the forthcoming group sessions. But nobody is going to write a fucking thing (at least not anything important); there are no locks on the doors here and nothing is secure. The fuckers that run this facility haven't got a clue as to what the cunts in here are like. Keep a private diary when Sick Boy and Swanney are lurking about? Aye, right!

All I can think of is: why the fuck are we here? How the fuck did I get here?

Day 12

WHAT THE FUCK DO THESE CUNTS WANT FROM US?

Day 13

'Honesty,' skinny-Specky says, when I raise the issue at breakfast. A runny egg and toasty sodjirs. 'You'll understand more when you join the process review group.'

Well, that's me telt. I must have flashed a soor pus as she adds, 'That's what the diaries and journals are all about.'

But when I get back to my room, I immediately start scribbling. If every other fucker's writing nothing (as seems to be the consensus) then I'm going to get everything down.

Skinny-Specky pops round and tells me she'd like me to join the meditation group. I agree, just basically to spend more time in her presence. We're sitting cross-legged on the flair, as she puts a tape on and takes position in front of us. I'm ogling her small breasts through her tight, elasticated black top, awed by the way she stretches out, catlike, arching her back before getting into position. She gives us breathing exercises, and instructions to tense and then relax various muscle groups in our bodies. We should shut our eyes, but I'm watching her, then I see that Johnny has his lamps trained in the same direction. He gives me a collusive sex–fiend wink, so I close my eyes and breeeeaaaattthhhhheeee . . .

After the session, I chat to her for a bit. She's telling me that by learning to relax our muscles, we can therefore subsequently reduce agitation levels. I don't trust any theory that inverts cause and effect, and show little enthusiasm for what she's saying, but when I get to my room, I try the exercises again.

Keezbo has left us. Spud tells me after lunch, as I'm sitting reading Joyce, looking out the window. The Fat Fort Felly was due to finish detox, but they've taken him to the hospital, due to supposed 'medication complications', whatever the fuck that means. They say he'll be rejoining us soon. Fat Jambo cunt's probably already sitting in the Village Inn with a cold pint of lager now that he's chemical-free.

'Is that a barry book, Mark?' Spud asks, looking like he's formulating something in one of the more intriguing chambers of that labyrinth inside his skull.

'Aye.'

Then he's off, and I'm back at the desk. What to write about? Our feelings, says Skinny-Specky. How do I feel? Well, I feel horny as fuck. I can tell that I'm detoxing, not just because I'm by turn depressed and miserable, then anxious and excitable, but because the only respite is my increasing carnal obsessions. I think about Lesley in the bed at Sully's at New Year, wishing I'd licked her oot, had rode my cock between her heavy tits or even got a gam off of her. It now seems like an opportunity missed and I feel foolish and weak, eaten up with self-reproach – another chance blown. YOU CUNT YOU CUNT YOU CUNT YOU CUNT YOU CUNT.

Later in the afternoon I masturbated about Joanne Dunsmuir.

Other than Joyce and jerking I keep quiet, detoxing, doing my time.

Day 14

Reading all this back, I realise that by repeating the dialogues I've heard, it's reading more like a novel or series of stories than a diary. And that suits me. I couldn't ever be arsed writing a conventional diary.

Attended my first process review group. It was fucking mental! People got wired right into each other, no punches pulled; a stand-up shouting match between Johnny Swan and that Molly lassie, forcing intervention from Tom and Skinny-Specky. Too much for me in this state, and I opted to lunch in the privacy of my room, some bland steamed fish which I shouldn't eat as I'm a veggie.

This evening I shakily joined them all in the recky room. The pool table has its yellow striped ball missing. I suspect Johnny Swan, who ran an appreciative hand over my fresh-cropped skull, had maliciously slung it ower the garden wall, as he's the only one who doesn't play. Sick Boy and Swanney were deep in conspiracy, talking aboot Alison. Sick Boy was going, 'Lozinska the great feminist. How does sucking cock for heroin advance the cause ay women's liberation? Please explain. It was all because I was fucking somebody else as well as her; aw the spiteful bitch wis daein was trying tae keep us away fae the tightest pussy I've ever had. Clamps ye like a vice.'

'Quality fanny,' Johnny conceded.

Fuck knows who they were talking about, but she must be something special for them to agree. However, I noticed Spud listening in, then cringing and turning away, wilting like a hamster in a microwave.

I headed back to my room, planning to have another chug about Joanne Dunsmuir.

<u>Joanne Dunsmuir.</u>

What's the fascination? She isn't even particularly good-looking and certainly doesn't have an agreeable personality, but I wank much more about her than I do about anybody else.

I'm scene-setting and fluffing up nicely. In my mind's eye Joanne's lying on her stomach and I'm pulling up her brown-and-black-checked skirt and hauling down her shiny black panties to expose a tight, curvy pair of buttocks.

That was as far as I got, as there was a knock and Spud burst in. He was in some distress, failing to notice that my hands were <u>inside</u> my tracky bottoms. He sat on the small basket chair fretting, sucking in his bottom lip. 'People are sayin things . . . this place is a pure nightmare . . . ah feel shite, Mark, pure shite, n people are talkin rubbish.'

I told him not to worry, that it was only Sick Boy and Swanney trying to show off. That it was all bullshit.

'But how does he huv tae say they things aboot Alison? Alison's a barry lassie!'

'Because he's a fucked-up arsehole, gadgie. We all are. But hopefully we're getting better. Forget aw the sexist crap, it's just them aw posturing tae each other. Aw these radges might talk like rapists among themselves, but they'll aw grow intae hen-pecked husbands who'll worry like fuck aboot their daughters. It's just a pose.'

He looked at me in melancholy accusation, like a bairn who's been told that Santa Claus doesnae exist. He kept glancing fae me tae the flair n back, as if building up to say something, then he let fly. 'You n Matty . . . ~~you~~ youse stole that Cat Protection League money! ~~Off of~~ Offay Mrs Rylance! ~~Out of the shop~~ Ootay the shoap!'

FUCK THAT.

~~'We certainly did. That's how we got here, for some poxy cash. When you think of the bother we had opening it.~~ 'We certainly did. That's how I wound up here, for a few fuckin bob in a gantin plastic collection boax. The bother we had openin it . . . that's what landed us in the fuckin cells! Some troll makin an example ay druggies! A poxy collection tin!'

'Well, ye shouldnae huv done that, Mark,' Spud bleated, 'no tae auld Mrs Rylance, no tae the cats . . .' Cause it's no likesay stealin oot ay shoaps, it's a charity tin likesay, an auld woman, whae's daein her best fir abandoned animals. Animal charity, likesay.'

'Point taken, buddy, point taken,' I waved a hand in emphasis. 'When ah strike it rich, ah'll write the CPL and Lothian Cat Rescue a big cheque.'

'A cheque . . .' he parroted blankly, the notion seeming to calm him down, though our feline pals will be the last cunts ~~to see any dosh I ever come into~~ TAE SEE ANY DOSH AH EVER COME INTAE. (~~That~~ is more like how I sound in my ~~head~~ heid. Sometimes. Mair like. Sometimes. Why try tae sound different? Why the fuck be the same as every other cunt? Ah mean, whae's fuckin interest does it serve?)

417

So ah tells Spud, 'See, ma idea is tae get clean, then get the habit manageable. Never go ower, say, two or threeish grams a week. Make that a hard n fast rule. Stey at the point where ye git the buzz, but if thaire's a drought, the withdrawal's fuckin mild n ye can ride it oot oan painkillers n Vallies, till it's biz as usual. It's science, Danny. Or maths. Everything has an optimum point. Ah jist goat far too reckless and went past mine.'

'That new lassie that's came in, that Audrey; she seems a nice lassie, ken? Pure sat next tae me at breakfast,' he went in that shy primary school qwally way he sometimes goes when manto flutter oantae the scene. 'She doesnae say much, ken, so ah just looks at her n goes, "Ye dinnae need tae say nowt, but if ye need tae talk, likesay in private, ah'm here, ken." She jist nods.'

'That was very thoughtful, Spud. Fire in there, mate. Ah'd certainly ride her. In a fuckin minute.'

'Naw, it wisnae like that,' he bashfully protested, 'she's a nice lassie, n ah wis jist tryin tae be helpful, ken?'

'Still, you'll be oot soon, Spud, free tae impress the fair maidens ay the Port wi yir near-death and rehab tales.'

'Naw, ah dinnae want tae go back tae Leith. Thaire's nowt tae dae.' He shook his head. 'Ah'm pure no ready, man . . .'

Then he put his ~~head~~ heid in his hands and I felt masel turn tae stone as he ~~started to cry~~ started tae greet. Proper greeting, high, snivelling, wee bairnish whines. 'Ah've messed things up that much . . . wi muh ma . . .'

I put ma airm roond him; it felt like hugging a workie's pneumatic drill. 'Whoah, c'moan, Danny, take it easy, mate . . .'

He stared up at us, face red, beak all snottery. '. . . if ah could jist git a joab, Mark . . . n a girlfriend . . . somebody tae care aboot . . .'

Then Sick Boy pushed the door open. He rolled his eyes camply, as Spud rubbed at his own red, bloodshot lamps. 'Am I interrupting anything?'

Spud sprang to his feet. 'You kin stoap slaggin oaf Alison! You keep yir mooth shut aboot her, right! How you're like wi lassies . . . IT'S WRONG, KEN! IT'S JIST PURE WRONG!'

'Daniel . . .' Sick Boy went, palms upturned, '. . . what's wrong?'

'YOU! PEOPLE LIKE YOU!'

They squared up, shouting at each other, faces inches apart. 'You need tae git fucking laid!' Sick Boy sneers.

'N you need tae treat people wi respect!'

'Spare me the tired axioms.'

'Dinnae think ye can get oot ay it by usin big words,' Spud screamed, his face florid and eyes watering. 'Ah sais you need tae treat people wi respect!'

'Aye, n it's done you loads ay fucking good!'

'YOU'RE IN REHAB N AW, SON!'

'AT LEAST I NEED MAIR THAN ONE HAND TAE COUNT THE NUMBER AY RIDES AH'VE HUD!'

'YOU'RE GAUNNY GIT YIR BIG MOOTH SHUT ONE AY THESE DAYS!'

'N YOU'RE GAUNNY DAE IT, LIKE?'

The palaver rippled through the centre's wafer-thin walls and Len and Skinny-Specky burst in trying tae calm things doon. I was fucked if I was getting in between them: let them swedge away. Although a gentle soul, Spud can row when he has just cause and I'd wager he could take Sick Boy. It would've been damn fine sport tae see them exchange blows.

'This is not the way we deal with conflict, by shouting and making threats. Is it, Simon? Is it, Danny?' Skinny-Specky ticked rhetorically, in her school-marm style.

'He started it!' Spud squealed.

'Like fuck ah did! I came in here tae see Mark and you started shoutin the odds!'

'Cause you wir . . .' Spud hesitated, '. . . cause your wir sayin things aboot other people!'

'You really do need tae git fuckin laid!'

As Spud turned away and exited, I ventured, 'I think we all do, that's a general axiom,' stealing the latest word Sick Boy's obviously found in his trusty dictionary, lamely hoping that Skinny-Specky might get flirty, or at least humorous with me, but she pointedly ignored the comment. Poor Spud was seething but he'll be apologising to Sick Boy for the next ten years, once the Catholic guilt kicks in. If you're gaunny be saying sorry anyway, you should at least panel the cunt and make it worthwhile: an error of judgement on his part. Len followed after him, while Skinny-Specky looked at Sick Boy n me as if we were going to _disclose_.

We stood staring back at her. 'It's a domestic dispute, Amelia,' I smiled, 'a sort ay Leith thing.'

'Well, keep it in Leith,' she snapped.

419

'Not that easy when half of Leith's in here,' Sick Boy observed, as Skinny-Specky looked piqued, then followed Len out.

Sick Boy looked down the corridor towards the departing Skinny-Specky. 'Amelia, Amelia, let me fuckin feel ya,' he said tae naebody, raising his brows and patting his crotch. 'I reckon she'd go . . . if conditions were favourable'.

Day 15

The racket-making birds are black, white and blue magpies, nesting freely in the tree outside my window. I've been here now just over two weeks, which seems like two years.

My senses are almost overwhelming. These smells from the past: the thick, rich aroma of Ma's chocolate cake, the sharp ammoniac tang of Wee Davie's piss that watered your eyes as you sat in front of the telly.

Sick Boy cracks me up, the way the cunt constantly changes his clathes. He dresses smartly in the evenings, as if he's going to a nightclub, and he totally mings ay aftershave. During the day he wears tracksuit bottoms and T-shirts. We're both at the washing machine a lot, because of the sweat. Saw Molly around there after breakfast, loading up some underwear. I dinnae like her but the sight compelled me to go back tae my room and batter one off. The carpet looks like Murrayfield ice rink wi aw the dried spunk.

Molly is in the meditation group, as is Sick Boy, who chips incessantly at her defences. 'Ah'm finished wi guys after Brandon', I hear her announce. He responds with; 'You don't have the right to say that. You have a heart and a soul, and an emotional life. You're a beautiful girl, with so much to give. Some day the right guy'll come along,' he proclaims, holding that deep gaze of probity. It forces her fingers to her hair, whispering, 'Ye really think so?'

'I know so,' he pompously declares.

It's the process review group that reminds me of why I take drugs. We're meant tae be looking at how we interact with each other here in the centre, but it generally descends intae shouting matches and name-calling, inevitably 'resolved' by insincere hugs instigated by Tom or Amelia. Nonetheless, it aw feels a bit like the Cenny, the Vine or the Volley at closing time. The positive feedback we're encouraged to gie each other seems tae be little more than wishful thinking or damning wi faint praise. For instance, the best thing Molly can find tae say aboot Johnny in one ay their stagey reconciliations is that she likes his navy-blue-and-white-hooped jersey. Their main bone of contention is Johnny's dealing, which he gets a fair bit of stick for. He eventually rises, announcing, 'Fuck this. Ah'm no takin this shite. Ah'm gaun.'

'I want to go means I want to use,' Tom entreats his departing figure. 'Don't do this, Johnny. Don't run. Stay with us.'

'Aye, right,' he says, walking out and slamming the door behind him.

'When we start taking ourselves away, using isolating behaviour, that's when we risk relapse,' Tom explains. The meeting ends in confusion and disarray. Tom thinks we've 'made progress', describing it as 'healthy' that such conflicts are coming out into the open.

To borrow the immortal words ay the White Swan: aye, right.

We'd been allowed tae make our own tapes up, to play in the recky room. Swanney, who we find sitting there on his tod following his exit stage left, has brought in a C45 featuring 'Heroin' by the Velvets, Clapton's 'Cocaine', Floyd's 'Comfortably Numb', the Stones' 'Sister Morphine', Neil Young's 'The Needle and the Damage Done' and some other belters. Side Two has 'Suicide is Painless' (the theme from _MASH_), Terry Jacks's 'Seasons in the Sun', Bobbie Gentry's 'Ode to Billie Joe', Bobby Goldsboro's 'Honey', and the Doors' 'The End', among others. Skinny-Specky instantly confiscates it on the grounds of 'inappropriateness'.

I now spend most mornings out on the back patio. In a corner there's a rack of hand barbells at different weights. The big biker, Seeker, is the only cunt using them, so I join him. It's ~~cold~~ cauld, but after a while ~~you don't~~ ye dinnae notice because ye work up a fair old sweat.

Roast chicken for lunch. I eat it.

Wank and read for most of the afternoon. I'm just getting ready to go to my kip when Swanney, eyes wide like he's wired, bursts into my room and sits on my bed ranting at me. I learn that Raymie's in Liverpool (or is it Newcastle?) and Alison's 'gone straight and sold out'.

'Polis came in and turned ower the flat. Lucky there was a drought on and aw they could huckle the White Swan fir was some percy and a wee bit ay speed. They offered us this shitey deal. It's a smoking gun, Rent Boy,' he says. 'Ah cannae be clean. Ah hate it. Ah git too worked up aboot aw the shite ay the day withoot ma skag. Ah just _need_ it!'

'Ah ken what ye mean.'

'But some cunt defo spilled the Coco Steins. That polis raid, it hud aw the hallmarks ay a textbook grassin-up job, ah'm sure ay it. But who? ah thoat. Well, I ain't in the biz ay naming names, it isnae they wey ay the White Swan, he prefers tae just gracefully cruise doon that river ay love n enlightenment; but who is the _only cunt_ who's been nicked lately n no goat sent tae the chokey or pit through here?'

I instantly ken who he means, but elect tae play dumb.

'That snidey wee cunt Connell, that's who. Ah ken Matty's your mate, Mark, auld Fort loyalties n that, but he's eywis hoverin aroond askin aw sorts ay questions, like wantin tae ken where ah git ma gear fae, n aw that shite.'

I think of an old picture ay me and Matty, standing outside the walls ay the Fort in Hibs strips. We'd be about eight. 'He's a tea leaf. He just wanted in on your action, Johnny. He wouldnae gie info tae the polis.'

I'm genuine. Like most people, I thought it was weird that Matty just got a suspended sentence and a few poxy days on remand, rather than proper jail or detox, but I cannae see him as a grass.

Day 16

I've had my first individual counselling session with Tom Curzon, the 'superstar of rehab', according to Skinny-Specky. She's defo got the hots for him.

Tom seemed tae expect me to dae all the talking. No way: I clammed right up. It must have been like trying tae get a drink out ay an Aberdonian coconut. It was quite a tough session: jockeying for position in a covert battle of wills.

Day 17

Woken up by the chattering birds again. Go for a stroll in the garden, even though it's pishing doon. A disturbing sight under a bush at the back wall: a *waddling crow jabs its beak through the breast of a dead pigeon repeatedly, till it locates a coil of gut, then twists out a slimy stretch and starts to devour it. This scene transfixes me, and I wonder if the pigeon was still alive, dying, but yet to perish, when the crow punched its first few holes into its chest.*

I think about this during breakfast, and feel queasy and distracted.

Keezbo returns, but he's deep in his room, he never leaves it. I refuse to chap on his door, it's better to give the chubby cunt some space, it's obviously what he needs. Ted fae Bathgate tells me he heard that Begbie battered some cunt in Saughton, but it apparently wisnae Cha Morrison.

One gadge I've warmed to is the Weedgie boy, Skreel. He got done for trying to bump a taxi. He'd been living in various homeless hostels here and through in Glesgey, and still has yellow-black bruised eyes from swedges. On arriving here, his long hair was shorn off as it was infested with lice – we telt him we'd have expected nothing less from a Weedgie. He has more abscesses on his hands, feet, arms and legs than I've ever seen, and he wears them like badges of honour. He's a bit gimpy from a bad fall, and the fact that he has practically no usable veins left in his limbs and had started injecting in his arteries. He boasted that last year he was on 750 mg of heroin per day, which I don't doubt. His teeth are rotten and give him constant gyp; he blames that on the barbiturates, which he loves as much as the skag. You have to respect Skreel, he's proper. I'll say one thing for the Weedgies: they don't go in for half measures.

'Ah'll be deid soon, big man,' he cheerfully informs me over a lunch of almost inedible cheese salad for me, and pie, chips and beans for everybody else. (Skreel is, at six foot, an inch taller than me.) 'Ah jist wahnt tae stey aff ma face till it happens, know whit ah mean?'

Day 18

Wake up to a gold sun, shimmering in a blue sky. On the patio, I marvel at its heat on my bare arms, listening to the excited magpies nesting in the sycamore tree, sounding like 1950s football rattles. I have an urge to get beyond those big, dark-stoned walls and that dense foliage; that light-bladed horizon.

Getting more into the weights. Seeker and I generally do a few sets together every morning and afternoon, following breakfast and lunch.

I like the discipline of it, pushing upwards, the rushing of the blood in my body and head, feeling the ebb and flow of eternal, mysterious forces inside me. Seeker does much bigger weights than me, and has really started tae bulk up, he has that kind of physique, but I notice wee clusters of muscle coming up on my arms and shoulders. It would be cool to have that sleek, feline, Iggy Pop look; muscular and defined but still slim and lithe. Seeker shows me how to be systematic about it: sets, reps and all that stuff. Before, I would have just lifted them till I got tired or bored. This interaction is a big deal, as Seeker isn't a man of conversation, in fact his comfort with silence is probably his only redeeming feature. He wears shades indoors.

A spiky session with Tom; he asks my about my discussions with cunty baws Dr Forbes, fae the clinic. 'Are you depressed, Mark?'

'I'm in _rehab for heroin addiction_,' I tell him. Then add, only half jokingly, 'In _Fife_.'

'But before. Your brother died last year. Did you mourn him?'

I want to ask him, 'Why in the name of suffering fuck would I mourn the loss of constant humiliation and embarrassment? If _you_ were a gangly, sensitive, yet highly egotistical kid growing up in Leith, would you not be pleased that a source of your torment had been removed?' Instead I say, 'Obviously. It was a sad loss.'

Day 19

I spoke too soon! Seeker speaks! He tells me he was in a bad bike smash a few years back. They put a steel plate in his nut and a pin in his leg. The pain was bearable in the summer. In the winter, though, only gear could sort it oot, and he ended up hooked. I also learned that he wears the shades on account ay being light-sensitive since his accident. Fair fucks tae the cunt; the overhead strip lights in here are harsh as, and I usually have a thumping headache just bubbling under migraine level by the time I turn in. We discover we're baith early risers, so agree to do a larger set of weights before breakfast.

Now I know how Tom feels with the rest of us. Like I've made a _breakthrough._

Day 22

This diary bullshit is getting as addictive as the skag. But it's also as dangerous; that personal shite you're somehow compelled tae put intae it. I had to rip oot the diary page yesterday, and a couple ay pages in the journal section, screwing them up and flinging them in the waste-paper basket. Suppose some cunt had read it? They say it's confidential, but what's that in here?

Len's clocked me daein the weights with Seeker, so I'm deemed ready for the group sessions on addiction issues – SORRY! – substance-dependency issues.

While the process review group looks at our general behaviour, this one focuses purely on the issue of our drug addiction and matters directly pertaining to it. We sat in a semicircle, the bones in my skinny erse pressing on the curved and slidy, one-piece laminate chipwood chair. The only other items were a flip chart and some pens. Tom sat with his long fingers locked together, clasped roond his knee, also uncomfortable, the traction and strain in his gangly frame belying the nonchalant air he tries tae exhibit. He wore slip-on shoes, the cunt unaware this means about 80 per cent of the room automatically think he's an irredeemable wanker.

I was dreading it as there had been plenty of shouting in the process review group that morning; that Ted is quite an aggressive wee bastard, and he and Sick Boy and Swanney were having a fair go at each other. They only stopped when Seeker suddenly said, 'Turn the fuckin volume doon. This is daein ma heid in.' And they did, cause everybody's feart ay Seeker.

Tom introduced me, even though I kent every cunt. 'I'd like to welcome Mark to the group. Mark, can you tell us what you want from these sessions?'

'Just tae stay clean and get myself sorted out, and help others do the same,' I heard a squeaky Boys' Brigade voice wobble from somewhere between my mouth and nose. Swanney sniggered and Sick Boy puckered his lips.

That kicked things off, though; everybody started chipping in, but the group consisted of rambling discussions that went nowhere.

Afterwards I decided to go and see Keezbo, who'd bolted straight back to his room.

When I walked in he was sitting on his bed, looking through a photo album. At least the old pictures helped me get some conversation oot ay the cunt. There was a lot of us as kids in the Fort. I'm one of the tallest and my hair seemed so much more pure ginger then.

One picture seized ma attention, simply because I hadn't seen it before. A bunch ay us as wee laddies are standing on the waste ground, outside the Fort. It was a team photo in the Wolves strips we had all agreed that we were going to get for Christmas. We'd be about nine.

Anyway, I warmed tae Wolves as they'd totally pumped Hearts in the Texaco Cup at Tynecastle, even after letting the muppets win the first leg at Molineux! In this photo there's me, Keezbo, Tommy, Second Prize, Franco Begbie and Deek Low stood along the back, and, sat crouching in front ay us, Gav Temperley, 'English' George Stavely (who moved back to Darlington), Johnny Crooks, Gary McVie (who died in a joyriding accident some years back), half-caste Alan 'Chocolateface' Duke (the product of some West Indian se(a)men that had drifted into the port) and Matty Connell.

'I've never seen that picture before,' ah telt Keezbo. It struck me that in those old photaes, Matty was already fading away, a ghostly smudge, or, as in this yin, sneaking off; face bisected by the white edge ay the Instamatic's prints, only one furtive eye visible.

'Ye must huv,' Keezbo said, looking at me properly for the first time. 'Ken whae took it?'

'Nup. Your dad?'

'Nup: your dad.'

'How's it you've goat it but?'

'Ah goat it done fae the negatives. Your ma gied my ma the negatives cause it hud that New Year perty at oor bit oan it.' He flipped forward, showing me some pictures ay my folks and his, wi some other friends and neighbours, getting rat-arsed. That fascist cunt Olly Curran was there, looking as sly as ever but with black hair instead ay silver. But it's another snap that cuts through me. My heart misses a beat as Wee Davie's magnificent, mindless smile, on that accordion-like body, filled the frame ay the glossy Kodak print. My dad's looking at him with a mixture of love and sadness. It's a snap I always found compelling and repulsive in equal measure. I wanted tae say something tae Keezbo, but it came out as: 'Funny how I've no seen that picture before.'

Dinner was haggis, neeps and tatties. I tried no tae eat the haggis, but it was either that or a fried egg, which would have been utterly shan wi mashed tatties n neeps, so I went for it.

In this affie's individual counselling Tom asked me about the diary. 'Have you been keeping up with it?'

'Aye. Every day.'

'Good. What about the journal?'

That section at the back. Mine is mostly full of wank stuff (literally), but Tom looked so serious and keen that I decided to lie. 'They read more novelistically, or like essays. I suppose I'm experimenting, working on a few things.'

'What sort of things?'

'An essay I couldn't finish at the uni,' I started bullshitting, warming to my theme, 'I mean, I handed it in, but I didn't feel that I'd really _finished_ it. It was on F. Scott Fitzgerald. Do you know his work?'

'I confess that I haven't read him. Not even _The Great Gatsby_.' He made a passable imitation of regret.

'I prefer _Tender Is the Night_, though', and as I spoke, I got a raw jolt in my chest that could only be described as tender, as an image of Fiona, on the Bosphorus ferry, under a lambent soak of light, sweeping her hair out of her face, flickered in my brain. Even wasted she looked so poised and dignified. I loved her I loved her I loved her I wanted to melt into her bones. Her absence now felt like I'd been eaten from the inside. I couldn't work out how I had got from her and the halls of residence at Aberdeen to here with Tom. In my mind's eye a quick procession ay faces flashed by – Joanne, Bisto, Don, Donna, Charlene – and I felt myself swallowing hard as a dark memory swooped down like a stricken plane. Whatever the pencil says is erasable, unlike oor dirty, spraffing mooths, smoking our lives wi billowing toxic fumes, coal-black and indissoluble. Ootside, a sudden angry squall ay rain thrashed at the windae, as if begging entry. As I looked tae it, Tom glared impatiently at me, urging me to continue.

'That was the novel I was writing about,' I embellished the lie, in order tae divert his attention fae my anxiety. 'Just being in here made me realise that I'd completely missed the point of that book, perhaps a wee bit like F. Scott himself.'

'How so?'

427

And as I was sitting there, making all this up, it came to me in a raging epiphany: a rerun ay something that first dawned on me while tripping on that boat back in Istanbul, the shit I ought to have written. 'Fitzgerald thought that he was writing about his wife's mental illness. He was actually writing about his own descent into alcoholic oblivion. The second part of the book is just a rich guy jaking out on the peeve.'

HOW COULD I HAVE MISSED SUCH A BASIC, OBVIOUS POINT?

'Interesting,' said Tom, looking searchingly at me. 'But might his wife's mental illness not have been one of the reasons for his excessive drinking?'

I could see where the cunt was going with this. For mentally ill wife, read handicapped deceased brother. I thought, fuck that. Smokescreen time. 'There's a thesis that F. Scott was sort of bullied by Hemingway, a more dynamic figure, whose approval he sought. But it's still wrong. It's a bit like suggesting that E. M. Forster's decline was precipitated by the critical attentions for the less inhibited D. H. Lawrence. But it was Fitzgerald's alcoholism and Forster's fear of the consequences of expressing his sexuality – he was a closet buftie boy' – (Tom looked puzzled) – 'homosexual – that did that. But that's no tae say that Hemingway and auld D. H. werenae above being bad bastards who could smell a weakness in their more fragile peers. After all, literary rivalries are like any other.'

'I'll check out those books with great interest. I did read Lady Chatterley at university –'

'Sons and Lovers is better.'

'I'll read it,' Tom declared, and getting intae the spirit ay things, handed me a copy ay Carl Rogers's On Becoming a Person. Ah'll get tae it when I'm done with James Joyce.

Later Sick Boy came tae my room, and I told him about my session. 'They think everything is about sex.' He waved his hand disparagingly. 'It is, but not in the way they imagine. Never got on with that Tom cunt, that's why I asked to be transferred tae Amelia. At my first session he told me he wanted candour. So I told him that I wanted tae fuck just about every woman I met. Not only that, but I wanted to make them fucking well beg for it. He said I was exploitative and sexually dysfunctional. I told him, "No, mate, it's called male sexuality. The rest is just denial." He didnae like that! He didn't like reality intruding in

428

his _Guardian_ reader's carefully constructed world of poncy middle-class bullshit.'

'Good for you . . .' I yawned, tired and wanting him to leave, so that I could get some kip in. '. . . surprised Amelia took ye on, eftir that.'

'Yes . . . either I'm a challenge tae her or she fancies me. It can only be one of the two. Both situations can be worked in my favour.'

I raised my eyes doubtfully, but he wasnae joking.

'Listen, speaking of sexual matters . . .' His voice dropped cagily. 'I want your view on something. I heard a wee tale aboot this gadge . . . a boy who let himself get fucked up the arse by a bird . . .'

'What the fuck are ye oan aboot? A bird fucked a boy up the erse? Was this so-called bird really a tranny or something?'

'Naw . . . it was a genuine lassie. They went back tae hers thegither, and she strapped oan a big dildo, and rode him up the erse wi it —'

'Wow . . .' I felt my sphincter involuntarily snapping shut.

'— and he enjoyed it . . . or so she said.'

'Sounds dubious tae me!'

'Aye . . .' he said, then seemed tae reconsider, '. . . well, the boy claimed that he wisnae interested in having a guy's cock up there, it was only a lassie he'd let dae that tae him.'

'Right . . .'

'So is the boy straight or gay?'

'Dae ah ken this gadgie?'

He rubbed his lips tightly together. 'Yes. Don't say anything . . .' he paused, as if he was rearranging the furniture in a room in his heid, '. . . but Alison telt us aboot it.'

'Wait . . . Ali was the lassie that rode this boy wi a dildo?'

'Aye . . . she said the only way this guy would go to bed wi her was if she did that tae him. Ye can surely guess whae we're talking aboot here!'

The face ay ma former bandmate, pinched and sweaty, as when he strutted that stage ay the Triangle Club in Pilton, jumped right intae my consciousness. 'Hamish? HP?'

Sick Boy smiled darkly. 'Heterosexual Poof by name and, it seems, by nature. Alison was adamant that he never did this with men. Personally,' he shook his head, 'ah hae ma doots. What do you think: hopelessly queer, or straight and just experimenting?'

'He didnae ride Alison eftir she'd tanned his erse in?'

429

Sick Boy hesitated for a second, 'No . . .' then he said more emphatically, 'no, there's no way he rode her.'

'If he had rode her eftir, ah'd have said experimenting. The fact that he didnae, ah'd say mair screaming poof than heterosexual.'

'My view entirely!' Sick Boy said in triumph, seeming tae seize on this as an important point. 'It's no the fact he experimented wi her thrusting the dildo up his chorus n verse that makes him a raving queen – Hamish, likes – but that he never shagged her eftir! Ran away fae her gash like it wis a black hole in space, the fuckin nancy! And this came straight fae the horse's mouth. Obviously, as I don't kiss and tell, I'm trusting your discretion with this information.'

'That's a given,' I lied.

An interesting enough tale, for sure, but then he wouldnae leave for ages. He talked about girls, his family, Hibs, Leith, Begbie and girls again, '. . . one of the drawbacks in having such a huge cock is that you can sometimes hurt them . . .' basically anything tae keep me awake. I fell asleep and when I awoke some hours later, the light still on, I expected him to still be sitting there on my bed, gabbing shite, but he was gone.

Journal Entry: Alan Duke

I always felt bad about the way that I treated Alan 'Chocolateface' Duke, back when we were wee laddies. Back then, Matty's dad, Drew, affectionately called me 'Ginger Nut'. The other kids in the Fort embraced it, but often in a derogatory manner. One time we were on the steps outside Leith Library and I was taking some stick, so I turned on Dukey and said: 'Beat it, Chocolateface.' This instantly caused howls of laughter and transferred the abuse from me to him.

I witnessed him suffer growing up. He became a scapegoat. Matty, a malnourished gypo scruffbag in hand-me-downs, Begbie, wi an alco jailbird father, Keezbo, wi his bloater issues, his budgie-loving ma wi the aviary in the hoose, and aye, me, wi the spazzy brother, could aw round on Dukey when the heat fell oan us. Later on, people like the Currans would spread more overt and hateful abuse his way.

While any cunt could have started the 'Chocolateface' ball rolling, I was the culprit. Always felt pretty crap about that.

Day 23

Ah've goat post! It's a mixed tape from Hazel. (Bands include Psychedelic Furs, Magazine, Siouxsie, Gang of Four — Hazel always had a decent taste in music.) They issue it a day late after they've checked it tae ensure that nae drugs are secreted. If they kent Hazel they wouldnae bother; the only drug we ever shared was voddy. It's nice to get post. Of course, the cunt who seems tae get loads, and all ~~from girls~~ fae lassies, is Sick Boy.

Back in my room, as Bowie sings about always crashing in the same car, I read the note:

> *Dear Mark,*
> *I hope the rehab is going well, and that you find the strength to stick with it. I saw your mum in Junction Street the other day. She said she was off to the church to light a candle and pray for you. I know you'll just laugh at that, but it shows she really cares about you so much, all your family do. As do I.*
>
> *I'm still at Binns and I'm planning a trip with Geraldine Clunie and Morag Henderson to Majorca. Geri works with me and you'll mind of Morag from school.*
>
> *Saw Roxy Music at the Playhouse! Honestly, Mark, what a gig! A few faces there in Mathers pub in Broughton Street afterwards, Kev Stewart, Gwen Davidson, Laura McEwan, Carl Ewart, all asking for you, and all, like me, saying that they miss seeing you around. Can we PLEASE have our old Mark back?*
>
> *Take care.*
> *Love*
> *Hazel xxxx*

As I read it I feel something shrink in the hollow of my chest. I screw the note up into a ball and chuck it in the empty bin (the cleaner's evidently taken my discarded diary entry and soiled Kleenexes away) then instantly retrieve it, flattening it out and sticking it in my back pocket.

The old Mark? <u>Who the fuck is that?</u>

I compose myself and head for some meditation with Spud and Seeker. Then, after a break and coffee, where Seeker talks aboot the bikes he's owned, Skinny-Specky tells us the process review session's about to begin, and we troop like weary zombies intae the meeting room. It's saccharine-

431

positive with a creepy touchy-feely vibe to it; lots of hugs and phoney veneration. But this only displaces the aggro to the afternoon addiction-issues group.

Tom's eyes are a wee bit too busy. His red-and-black lumberjack shirt is covered down the front with crumbs from one of the sugary shortbread biscuits that go down a storm in these sessions. 'I'd like to introduce Audrey, who is joining us for the first time in the group. Hi, Audrey.'

'Enjoy de re-hab-il-i-tay-shan,' Swanney drawls in a ersatz Jamaican accent. Now I know where Matty gets this irritating trait. He professes to hate Johnny but he wants to be him.

Molly, who Audrey sat next tae, has taken a fancy tae Tom, and, it seems, a dislike to everybody else, apart fae Sick Boy. 'Well,' she says grandly, 'ah came in here tae get masel sorted oot and ah'm prepared tae keep an open mind n gie Tom the chance tae dae his job. N ah'm sure Audrey is n aw.'

All eyes on the silent, nail-biting Audrey, with the big, haunted blue eyes.

'Thanks . . . Molly,' Tom says, as the room resonates with crashing sighs and the odd snigger. Tom's lookin right at me, as if encouraging me to speak, but, sorry, shipmate, ah've set sails tae Port Silence. Seeker stretches his legs out, throws his arms behind his heid, issuing an enormous yawn, then sweeps his biker's locks back. He looks like a lion that's just eaten a pit bull.

I can't stop stealing glances at Audrey. She looks a bit of a mess, but everybody does ~~after~~ eftir detox. She's already been nicknamed 'Tawdry Odd' by Sick Boy, on the basis that her name's Audrey Todd. No wonder she stays deep in her room maist ay the time. She's wearing faded blue jeans and ye kin tell that her legs would be barry as fuck if you got a proper deek ay them. Tom looks around at the others, then back to me. '. . . Mark?'

The intrusion grates, more so because he's caught me letching. How uncool a situ is that? It's time tae quickly deflect: 'You cannae fix me, mate. It's no gaunny happen.'

'Ah'd fix ye,' Swanney speaks up, 'if ah hud gear, like.'

He gets a few gallows laughs.

'I didn't say I could fix you.' Tom shakes his head. 'Only _you_ can do that.'

I nod, accepting the obvious truth in what he says. 'So, that begs the question, why are you here?'

I can hear Molly tutting in response tae my enquiry.

'I'm here to help,' Tom says.

'So, wait,' I find myself saying, 'ye cannae fix me, but ye can help me tae help masel. Enable. Facilitate. Is that the deal?'

'That's it.'

'Now why would you want to do that?'

'I see. You're questioning my motivation?'

'No,' I smile, 'just clarifying.'

That's one of the weapons in Tom's interpersonal arsenal. He'll probe away till you take exception, then go, 'I'm just clarifying.' He doesnae like this being used against him. His nostrils flare as he slowly expels breath. 'Mark, we have these circular discussions all the time, and we get nowhere. Let's keep this stuff out of the group and leave it for the individual sessions, as we agreed.'

'As *you* agreed.'

'Whatever, let's just keep it out of the group.'

Molly interjects at this point. 'Huh! That'll be the day. Cause it's eywis goat tae be aboot Mark, that's the problem!'

I'm happy enough tae joust with the dippit wee slag. 'Wow. Junky indulges in self-centred behaviour! Hud the front page!'

'At least some ay us try. You just want tae show oaf tae your mates,' and she looks around the semicircle in scorn. Audrey has another chomp on those nails.

Molly's actually spot on. I thought her schooling stopped at bicycle-shed blow jobs but evidently I was wrong; she has some insight. The only real point of these sessions for me is to have a laugh with the boys. It won't do me any good to let Tom know that, but, so I find myself saying as earnestly as I can, 'Look, ah'm just findin it hard tae get tae grips wi aw this,' I glance around, 'and I'm tryin tae work out where everybody stands, that's aw.'

Fair play tae Tom, but; he raises his eyebrows in mild exasperation, and he just looks round the circle. 'What I want to talk about today are triggers. What are the triggers that make you want to use?'

'A day wi a "y" in it,' Spud says, and this remark fairly triggers smirks all round. Tom ignores Spud (although he's deadly serious), cause that's not what the boy's after. He needs something to work with.

'Steppin ootside the front door,' Keezbo says, again deadpan. I'm a wee

433

bit worried aboot the big yin. He's completely lost his sense ay fun, which is a huge deal fir him.

This time, though, Tom acknowledges the intervention. 'Thanks . . . Keith.'

'Hanging aroond wi these cunts,' Sick Boy says, looking at me, Spud and Swanney.

'Well, now we're getting somewhere,' Tom contends, sitting up and forward in his chair. 'Keith has said outside. Where we live. The environment. Simon has mentioned particular relationships, friendships. Peer pressure that reinforces this inappropriate and self-destructive behaviour.'

I cannae help but emit a volley ay derisive laughter at that yin. 'Well, this is a fucking barry idea, get every cunt banged up in a residential unit thegither!'

'Rents is right,' Skreel goes. 'Ah've met some sound peepul in here, dinnae git me wrang,' he looks around ensuring no offence had indeed been taken, 'but thaire's no wahn ay thum gaunny help us git aff the gear.'

Tom stays cool though. Perhaps it wasn't bullshit from Skinny-Specky when she described him as 'one of the best in his field'. 'There are obvious limiting factors on any service provision. But – and I'm just throwing this out there – might peer groups not also be used to reinforce _positive_ behaviour?'

'These being abstention? Sobriety?' I dive in. As if any cunt here wanted to be sober.

'But you _want_ to get clean?'

There follows a long, deathly silence, as we look at each other, _The Big Lie_ hanging in the space between us. On all our lips. The Big Lie that made this rehab game possible; that sustained the whole stupid, ludicrous cult. What to say? Swanney seems tae tipple the stakes are high, so he pitches in tae deflect. He has a smile on his coupon but is deadly serious at the same time. 'I've fucked ower that many people, if ah stey clean the guilt and remorse'll fuckin kill us. It just isnae worth it.'

'He's got a point,' I say, again jumping in too quickly and hating myself for it. But I mean what I say, because I know Johnny does too. How many stones of regret would he need to carry in his gut over his life? You either have to learn to be better and cope wi what ye've done, or just learn no tae care.

'Well . . . yes . . .' Tom says, 'but remember that this unit is experimental. If it doesn't deliver, it _will_ be shut down.'

Sick Boy gets Tom in his sights, perhaps a wee bit miffed that I've

434

been making the running in the sneering cynic stakes. 'So, we must all pull together for the sake of the unit! That's absolutely top hole!'

It takes a lot tae faze Tom though. 'You know the alternative . . . Simon. Everybody here is
either on an actual or *de facto* suspended sentence.'

That always concentrates our minds. As fucked as this gig is, it's a total doss compared tae even the pansiest nick. One thing ah ken, even fae the odd drunken night in the cells, I just isnae cut oot for the chokey. I vowed then and I vow now: *I WILL NEVER BE INCARCERATED FOR JUNK.* Any bullshit rehab I'm offered by the system, I'll sign right on the dotted line before I spend one fucking minute behind bars.

Tom turns to Skreel. 'Martin –'

'Cry me Skreel.'

'Sorry, Skreel. What would you like to get out of this group?'

'Ah jist wahnt tae stoap usin, tae git well again,' he lies.

Tom nods slowly, maintaining the gaze for a second, before turning to Johnny.

Swanney's just a total cunt, God bless him. He really kens how to wind everybody up. 'Of course it's difficult,' he shrugs, 'because we aw ken how barry, how fuckin *brilliant*, a fix ay skag kin be, especially when yir sick,' and his tongue darts across his lips, a grin moulding his face, making him look like a lizard who's plucked a juicy fly oot ay the air. Skreel starts twitching and Molly's pallid coupon sets more firmly. Audrey gies her nails a brek and starts chewing oan the ends ay her hair, while Spud's sittin wi his heid in his hands, emitting soft groans, as Johnny carries on, '. . . just that beautiful, rapturous release as it flows through yir veins intae yir brain, and the incredible euphoria as the world's problems, aw the *crap*, just dissolve intae dust aw aroond ye. Pain aw gone. For just one wee hit, *one wee hit* . . .' he muses pornographically as Molly, Audrey, Spud, Ted and Skreel squirm in their chairs.

'That's enough, please, Johnny,' says Tom.

'Jist sayin, like,' he flashes a manufactured smile, 'it's no aw bad, cause if it wis, naebody wid dae it.'

'Or make money oot ay it,' Molly spits, wanting tae fight an auld battle.

Tom waves her down, 'I'm hearing you, Molly, but I want to focus for now on the losses. I'd like you to think about what you've *lost* through being on heroin.' He rises, and goes over to the flip chart, picking up a pen.

435

'Poppy,' Sick Boy shouts.

Tom turns with a puzzled look. 'Is that your girlfriend?'

'Best one I've ever had,' Sick Boy grins, as everybody laughs. Poor Tom stands as stiff and still as a vibrator withoot the Duracell.

'Eh, dosh,' Spud says helpfully.

His attempt to spare the blushes is welcome, though Tom's neck takes on a mair florid hue than usual, as he writes 'MONEY' in even block capitals.

'Mates,' says Ted.

Tom's black marker pen spells out 'FRIENDS'.

'Ah dinnae ken aboot anybody else,' Keezbo says, looking sadly at Sick Boy, 'but what you said aboot girlfriends, Mr Simon —' he looks tae Audrey and Molly, 'or boyfriends, no bein sexist aboot it — but the shaggin desire goes.'

Cue a few nervous giggles around the room.

'No necessarily,' Swanney cuts in. 'Best sex ah ever had was oan skag, at the start, like.'

'Aye, at the start,' Sick Boy sneers. 'Probably the only time you hud a ride that ye didnae pey for.'

Swanney flicks him the V-sign. 'Wisnae that when ye were seek n bangin at ma door, eh?'

Sick Boy squirms in the chair and falls silent. It all goes quiet. It's like everybody feels something stirring inside their pants, those cocks that ain't been used in a while, screaming for action. Or, in Molly's and Audrey's cases, fannies that huvnae been used much, or mair likely, hav been used tons, but huvnae _felt_ that much.

So we talk away for a bit, the usual shite. We tire easily however, and our gathering yawns signal a stop for a coffee break: the most oily, tarry elixir imaginable, so caffeine-laden it hits you like base speed. This is accompanied by some sugary shortbread and, most of all, the fags. Practically every cunt in here is a serious nicotine addict, even Tom. I'm treated with suspicion, as I hate tabs.

Break times are the best, though. Everybody ends up telling everyone else at least the potted version of his or her personal stories. Except Audrey, and I admire her circumspection in this company. Sick Boy and Maria Anderson had been in a naughty wee scene and when her ma got out of jail, she took Maria right back tae her brother's in Nottingham. Sick Boy plays at being outraged. 'They accused me ay being her pimp,' he snorts tae Seeker. 'Anti-drug hysteria gives some people very, very lurid imaginations.'

'It's the best wey tae keep a wee bitch under control, but,' Seeker says, and this really is one disturbing cunt, 'get them oan the gear. Then it's yir ain wee personal harem. Ye jist reel them in oan the invisible line,' he simulates fishing, 'then when yir finished, fling them back.'

Sick Boy acts disdainful, though you can tell he enjoys Seeker's misogynist spiels. Molly's freaked by it and Tom chivalrously attempts tae distract her by pulling her intae conversation. She's having nane ay it, but, and she turns tae Seeker and says: 'You're the lowest ay the low!'

'Aye? High n mighty talk fir a hoor,' he smiles, then goads, 'That wid be how it wis wi you n yir felly, but.'

'You ken nowt aboot us!'

Seeker looks impassively at her. 'Ah ken thit _you_ wir the yin oan yir back gittin yir wee pussy pummelled by aw sizes n colours ay tadger n he wis the yin oan first dibs whin the Salisbury Crag came oot.'

'Brandon wis sick! What else could we dae!'

'He's done a good joab on you but, that boy,' Seeker observes appreciatively. 'Still goat ye whaire he wants ye.'

Molly pushes both her fists into her chest, as if trying to pull out a goring spear. She erupts in tears, turns on her heels and exits, heading for her room. 'This isn't helpful,' Tom says to Seeker, and makes tae go after her, before being stopped by Sick Boy, who's seen his chance. 'It's okay,' he coos at Tom, 'I'll talk tae her.'

The rest ay us finish our coffees and get back tae the group work. After a few minutes, Sick Boy and Molly rejoin us. I'm disappointed in him, I really thought he'd have been right intae her keks. We have a discussion on how heroin made us feel and the term 'anaesthetic' comes up. Tom immediately seizes oan this. 'If heroin is an anaesthetic, what are we anaesthetising ourselves from?'

When did _you_ and _us_ become _we_, Mistah Big White Motahvay-tah Man?

So the cunt splits us intae two groups and issues us marker pens and flip-chart paper, telling us tae brainstorm or free-associate oor responses. Group One consists ay Spud, Audrey, Molly, Ted and Keezbo. Group Two are the more troublesome little princes: me, Seeker, Sick Boy, Swanney and Skreel.

The groups come back wi their offerings, which are Blu-tacked up onto the wall.

GROUP ONE	GROUP TWO
SOCITEY	HUMANS
LIFE'S TRIALS AND	LIARS
TRIVILATIONS	AMBITION
OTHER PEOPLES HASSLES	MONEY
ANIMALS BEING EXTINCT	CARS
(MAN'S GREED)	COMPUTERS
RED BILLS	PHONES
SIGNING ON AND	TELEVISIONS
DOLE HASSLES	DENTISTS
POLITICIANS	TIME
BOREDOM	SPACE
FOOTBALL TEAM LOSING	MUSIC
ENGLISH COMMANTATORS	SEX
THE BIAS NEWS MEDIA	HISTORY
GIRLFRIENDS/BOYFRIENDS	JAMBOS
FAMILY HASSLES	RUGBY
	BEARDS
	SLIP-ON SHOES
	REHABILITATION

Tom scrutinises the lists, fanny-stroking that chin with a troubled expression. 'Anybody from Group One like to volunteer to take us through their thoughts on these issues . . . ?'

Spud's appointed spokesperson and stands up and starts waffling on about animals. 'Seeing thum suffer makes me pure depressed, man. Ah cannae help it likes. See, the thought ay animals bein made extinct jist cause ay man's greed –'

A few laughs go up but Spud's urged tae continue. Everything seems tae end in 'hassle'. 'So ah suppose,' he summarises, 'hassle in general, likesay.'

When it comes tae our group, nobody's prepared tae get up and present the list. We maintain radio silence. Tom asks us one by one, but is uniformly blanked. Eventually, Spud, trying tae help, points tae our group's efforts and goes, 'Ah agree wi computers, they kin be pure hassle; likesay when the dole send ye oan one ay they courses.'

A long, rambling discussion on the dole and training schemes starts up, and goes on and on.

The clock on the wall needs a battery, having stopped at four thirty.
Suddenly, a visibly weary Tom calls a halt to proceedings, and we're slithering oot
ay there intae the next mundane box on oor timetable.

Result.

Sick Boy immediately vanishes with Molly. I should never have doubted
the spawny cunt.

*'I put my arms around him yes and drew him down to me so he could
feel my breasts all perfume yes and his heart was going like mad and yes I
said yes I will Yes.'*

Back in my room, I play Iggy Pop and James Williamson's *Kill City* on
my crap tape deck with the headphones. I'm obsessed particularly with the
song 'Johanna', reminding me of Joanne Dunsmuir.

I almost pull off the end of my knob masturbating about her.

I defile the toilets with a

logo, simply in order to start a graffiti debate.

Day 25

It's still gloomy this morning, but at least the rain's eased off. As usual,
Seeker's the only other person up, and we go through our routine in
silence.

The rest of the morning I write, write, write. All the time loving the way the
sharp, smooth tip of this pen pulls my hand across the page. I've come to believe
that everything you write, no matter how shite and trivial, has some sort of
meaning. Writing that journal entry yesterday has made me remember that the
Christmas we got the Wolves strips was the one just before Hibs beat Hearts
7–0 at Tynecastle.

We'd gone downstairs tae get that team picture: only one, because it was
freezing cauld. After New Year it had been Billy who got sent round to
Boots in the Kirkgate tae get the spool ay festive snaps developed. But I

439

never eyeballed that Wolves team photae. I mind ay Begbie asking us tae let him see it and giein me a Chinese wristburn at school when I telt him it hudnae turned oot. He thought I was hudin oot on him.

That cunt Billy must have destroyed it oot ay spite for my constant derby massacre teasings.

Mystery solved. Fuckin prick.

But the muppet forgot about the negatives, which my mother passed oantae Moira Yule. So mair than a decade later, I see the picture in Keezbo's photae album.

Glory to the Hibees. A Steve Cowan winner from a Jukebox Dury pass at Fir Park.

Every place has a top dog and Seeker is the main man here, which you can tell Swanney's no too happy aboot. It seems obvious that both have had competing access tae heroin fae the same source, and they're very cool with each other.

While the rest ay us hit the recky room Saturday eftirnoon tae watch the football scores come in, Sick Boy was absent, riding Molly, then returning tae big it up tae Seeker about our ruinous experience on the boats in Essex, though he fell short of mentioning Marriott or even Nicksy by name. You could tell both Seeker and Swanney were interested though. Skreel started on aboot Glasgow and boys he kens in Possil. Ted, although fae Bathgate, spent a bit ay time in Dundee, and he reckons there's a scene up there. I mentioned Don up in Aberdeen, which seemed to impress Seeker. 'Some boy, him.'

'How's he daein?'

'Fuck knows.' A visor ay cauld suddenly shut down over his pus.

For tea, liver that smells of pish and onions seals my single-minded retreat back into vegetarianism. To be fair, there are quite a few core carnivores turning their noses up at it and looking enviously at my scarcely more edible egg flan, dry as an auld nun's chuff.

Despite the acuteness of my senses sometimes overwhelming me, I'm still happy to be off the methadone: it was like having a giant condom stretched all over your skin. My jitters have subsided, but I'm still feeling up and down. One minute life seems pointless, the next I'm full of optimism and thinking about the future. Keezbo's being a wet blanket about band plans; it's usually all he wants to talk about. I wanted to blether about music and my song 'Cigarettes R Us', but Keezbo went, 'Shhh, Mr Mark, _Only Fools n Hoarses!_' So I headed back to my room and read more _Ulysses_.

After a bit Seeker tapped at my door and sat doon in the wee chair, his big frame filling the room up. I put the book doon and he picked it up. 'Ever read that _Hell's Angels_?'

'Hunter S. Thompson? Aye, love it.'

'The cunt's a bullshitter. Made maist ay that up. Ah ken a couple ay boys fae Oakland.'

'Aye?'

'Aye,' Seeker went, then emphatically stated that he's giein up smack; it's dealing only for him fae here oan in. 'Otherwise, it's true what they say: ye just get high oan yir ain supply. The drug's shite anyway. First time is best. Yir jist chasin that high eftir.'

Strange how I could absolutely agree with everything he was saying, while all the time thinking that there's very little I wouldnae dae for some skag right now. Something is crawling under my skin, biochemical information sluicing around my body. The sheer physicality of it; it's like what boxers call 'muscle memory'.

Seeker stared at the cover of _Ulysses_ wi a scary intensity, like he wis trying to will the contents of the book ~~into his head~~ intae his heid. Then he looked up, pushed his hair back and went, 'Ah think that _Fools and Hoarses_ shite's finished now.'

I recollect that I did a huge, championship-winning shite after breakfast this morning. Things are really starting tae work as they should. I still feel edgy, but kind ay barry as well. Euphoric is pushing it, but definitely _anticipatory_. I feel that good I feel like gaun oot and getting totally fucked up!

Therein lies the problem!

Day 26

Our isolation and the constant rain outside make me speculate that the world has drowned and we're the sole survivors. _The future of the human race is safe in our hands!_ The grim, hesitant sounds of Bowie's masterpiece 'Low' mingle with the din of the crashing downpour outside.

441

We said goodbye to Spud. At breakfast we presented him with this pony letter in which we told him why we'd miss him. It was another exercise devised by the Rehab Kingpin Tom, where you had tae finish the sentence oan the caird:

I'll miss Danny because . . .

I had put doon:

. . . he's my best mate.

Spud read it and looked at us all, choking up, but particularly focused on Audrey and Molly. Molly was tearing a coupon out of some magazine, while Audrey bit into the knuckle of her right thumb. He kept glancing fae one tae the other. As we exchanged hugs, he held an alarmed Audrey, then Molly, for a painfully long time, and even gave Skinny-Specky the same treatment. He looked tearful and confused as he was taken oot, turning back tae gaze at the lassies with a poignant expression. In the corner Sick Boy stood, jaw clenched tight, but I knew that look, could tell that the fucker had pulled some sort ay stunt!

A taxi had arrived and Spud's ma, Colleen, came and took him away. I couldnae help wilting inside under her judging stare as I waved him goodbye fae the doorstep. As the taxi ground doon the gravel path, wi Spud still looking back in sad confusion, Sick Boy pulled me intae his room. He was bent over, face contorted, barely able tae speak through his laughter. 'Did you . . . did ye see his face? Did you actually see him . . . oh my God . . . did ye see him . . . checkin oot the lassies? These big, sad, puppy-dog eyes? Huding them in that desperate embrace?' He exploded in a loud guffaw. I slowly started tae understand.

'I wrote in his card: "I'll miss Danny because . . . he's the sweetest boy I've ever met, and I think I've fallen in love with him." I kent he'd think that it was one of the lassies! Result! Did you actually see the dippit fucker's pus?'

I couldnae help but join in the laughter. Poor Spud. 'You bad bastard . . . the poor cunt'll be gaun mental . . .'

'Positive affirmation though, that's what the group's aboot,' he roared.

'Yes, but based on honesty.'

442

'Just lubricating they social wheels a wee bitty.'

So we went intae the recky room sniggering like daft wee bairns, Tom commenting about how he was glad tae see us in such high spirits.

At the process review meeting, we discussed the journals, Tom urging us tae share their contents in the group. Of course, not one cunt except me has written a fucking thing, or if they had, they were keeping stumpf. So was I. I started tae entertain the perverse but plausible notion that every bastard secretly has a junky War and Peace sitting in their rooms.

Another disappointment for Tom (what a fucked-up trade he's in!), and the meeting ended after the usual shoulder-shrugging, nail-biting, crap jokes and virtuous platitudes.

Sick Boy and me had a wee idea, so I asked Tom if we could use the electric typewriter in the office. 'Ah'm ready tae start on the writin, but ma handwritin's that bad, ah need tae use the typewriter.'

'Of course!' he said, nipples doubtlessly rock hard at the prospect of a juicy wee self-disclosure feast. 'Feel free. I'll see that you aren't disturbed!'

Feel free.

Poor Tom, the journal and diary will never come to light, but I'd led the cunt to believe that some sort of breakthrough was imminent. The fact is that, encouraged by Sick Boy, I'd decided tae get my ain back on the Currans, my old neighbours fae the Fort, for causing that scene at Wee Davie's funeral and generally casting aspersions on the clan Renton. I got out the sheets ay Council Housing Department notepaper procured fae Norrie Moyes. I got Sick Boy tae help me compose the letter, his trusty Collins dictionary on his lap.

City of Edinburgh District Council
Housing Department
Waterloo Place, Edinburgh
Tel: 031 225 2468
Director: J. M. Gibson

Mr and Mrs Oliver Curran
D 104 Fort House

Leith
Edinburgh EH6 4HR

25 March 1985

Dear Mr and Mrs Curran,

THE NEIGHBOURHOOD UNITED TENANCY SCHEME

As you may well be aware, the central government policy of promoting the sale of council housing has led to a decline in Edinburgh District Council's levels of housing stock, most markedly in the higher amenity properties. This obviously has an adverse impact upon our ability to discharge our housing obligations to all our citizens in need.

In response to this and in keeping with our commitment to equal opportunities and fostering a multicultural Edinburgh, the council has developed an innovative progamme known as the Neighbourhood United Tenancy Scheme (N.U.T.S.). This scheme seeks to integrate homeless families into current housing provision (with special points for ethnic minority families) and follows a needs-based and city-wide inventory of our existing housing stock.

It has come to our attention that your daughter has recently married and moved out of your three-bedroom apartment tenancy at the above address.

Please note that as of Monday, 15 April 1985, this room will now be allocated to Mr and Mrs Ranjeet Patel.

The kitchen and living-room facilities will initially continue to be solely for your personal use as cooking and refrigeration equipment is to be installed in the room allocated to the new family. Please note, however, that this is subject to review. You will, of course, be expected to share toileting facilities with Mr and Mrs Patel, their children and elderly parents.

In order to facilitate a smooth and effective transition to N.U.T.S., the council are, in partnership with the Lothian Education Department, running classes at a centre near you, on basic Bengali language and culture, which, under the conditions of your tenancy agreement, you are expected to attend. This comes under the banner of Cultural Unification for New Tenants Scheme. You will be notified of the dates and venue of these classes shortly.

You have three working days to appeal against this ruling. To do so, please contact Mr Matthew Higgins at the above number on extension 2065, quoting reference: D104 FORT/CURRAN/CUNTS.

Thanking you in advance for your cooperation regarding this matter and I look forward to working with yourselves and other tenants in the area to ensure the success of this exciting and innovative project.

Yours sincerely

J.M. Gibson

J.M. Gibson
Director of Housing

The contact guy, Higgins, was a supervisor in another section. Norrie hates him, so we were doing him a favour as well. We finished and were laughing our heids off. Attracted by our vociferous frivolity, Skinny-Specky and Tom came in, the latter asking, 'What's going on?'

'Just doing the journals, like you says.'

'I didn't realise it would all be quite so amusing . . .'

'It has its lighter elements,' Sick Boy said, arching a Roger Moore eyebrow at Skinny-Specky Amelia.

'Good, we could use some appropriate levity at the group meeting,' Tom said urbanely, and Skinny-Specky shot him one of those admiring groupie I'll-gam-ye-right-now looks.

Day 27

My puckish diversions with Sick Boy unfortunately meant that I now had to knuckle down and knock out something for Tom. So last night I stayed up writing, looking out into the moonlight filtering through the thin trees into the walled garden. The old stone wall tells you that an ancient house was probably sited here, most likely a grand villa, before being torn down to put up this fucking ugly, utilitarian construction.

But with this pen and blank notepad, just looking outside, I've never felt so focused or alive. I came close when I was writing essays at the uni, but this is different. Instead ay building facts tae develop, challenge, then ultimately sustain a hypothesis, writing freestyle subjective stuff in ma journal makes me feel I'm getting closer tae some sort of veracity. By writing, you can use your own experience but detach it from yourself. You nail certain truths. You make up others. The incidents you invent clarify and explain as much as, sometimes more than, the ones that actually occurred.

Then I'm back to Ulysses. *If I get through this shite, it's all down to Jimmy J; it's great tae lock intae his Dublin. I'll go ower thaire and check it oot one day.*

When I eventually fell into a sleep Sick Boy woke me up – cunt never seems to kip – only to tell me that he's been kicked off the one-on-ones with Skinny-Specky and now has to work with Tom again. That he ain't too happy is an understatement. 'She said that I was behaving inappropriately. Of course, she's just scared her ice-maiden front will slip. Just because I telt her straight: "I need to be honest, Amelia. We have a problem. I've developed strong feelings towards you." Of course, she immediately goes, "This is inappropriate." Fuck me, she's like a Dalek. IN-A-PROP-REE-ATE . . . IN-A-PROP-REE-ATE –'

'Fuck sake, Williamson, ah'm cream crackered here. Ah've just goat oaf intae nodland. Can this no wait till the morn?'

I might as well have been talking tae masel.

'So I sais tae her, "You can't tell me to express my feelings, then start hiding behind roles whenever I do. It can't be me *putting up barriers, then* you *setting boundaries when it suits your purposes; that just reeks of hypocrisy. It's fundamentally dishonest." Well, you could tell that goat it right fuckin up her.'*

In spite ay ma exhaustion, I wis getting interested. 'What did she say?'

'Oh, the usual pish: went on about how she was here tae help enable my rehabilitation, and it was me who was being dishonest and manipulative – ye ken how they try and twist things. Said I should explore why I can't relate to a woman in any way other than a sexual one.'

I tried to keep a straight face. 'What did you say?'

'I told her: who mentioned sex? That I wisnae trying tae cynically seduce her and was frankly offended at the inference. I agreed it would be completely inappropriate for us to have anything other than a client/practitioner relationship in here; that would undermine both my recovery and her position at this facility, and I respected her too much to do that. That I was only mentioning those feelings to try and get some transparency into what could be a tricky situation. That put her right on the back foot.'

'Brilliant. You're a sick cunt, but a fucking genius. What did she say? How did she respond?'

You could see him bridling back some indignation, deciding to simply take the praise. 'She was flustered, so I steamed in. "I'd really like to see you outside, once this is all over," I told her. "I appreciate that you may have a partner, perhaps even be in a committed relationship . . ." she kept her pus straight, but I read it like she wisnae getting a length, ". . . I'm talking about as a friend, to have a coffee and a chat. That's all I can ask at this stage."

'So she looks at me that inscrutable way and says, "You're a very young man, Simon . . ."'

'"And you're a young woman," I hit back.

'At that point I sensed she was fighting back a girly blush, but she said, trying to be that urbane way, "I think I'm considerably older than you imagine."

'"Funny . . . I put us at around the same age," I told her. "Obviously, with your qualifications, you must be maybe one or two years older than me . . . but this is all irrelevant."

'"Yes," the frosty hoor went right on the counter-attack, "it certainly is. What _is_ relevant is that our working relationship has been compromised. I'll arrange for you to go back to Tom for your one-on-one counselling."

'Fuckin hell, I could feel myself panicking big time as I tried to talk her roond, "I just don't relate to him like I do you." Ken what she sais?'

'Nup. What?'

'"It's _how_ you're relating that's the issue." And she wouldnae discuss it further.'

Once again, he sat up most of the night talking in an even monologue, almost all of it self-justifying bullshit. After a while, I couldnae pick oot a word he wis saying, but the weird thing was that I didnae want him tae go now, as his voice wis oddly relaxing, and it wis helping me drift off. But the fucker snapped his fingers in my face a couple of times so I telt the cunt tae get tae fuck. But as soon as he left, I was wide awake again.

Day 28

How long does it have tae fuckin rain ootside? It seems tae have been pishin doon with nae respite since I got here. How long can you feast

447

your eyes on the scrawny limbs of the trees, watching birds drop out of the sky? Looking out at the shadowy overhang, reproaching yourself for living badly?

Depressed as fuck. Feeling like Neil Armstrong, walking around in a heavy spacesuit, a layer of ay steamed-up glass between masel and the rest of ay the universe. I'd be happier on the moon. Armstrong, Aldrin – and the third poor bastard that no cunt kens, him who went all that way and never got tae step outside the command module – you wonder why they bothered coming back.

Day 30

Breakfast: Porridge, toast, tea.

Meditation: A shaky, ill-constructed, frustrating wank in my room.

Process group: Molly being passive-aggressive to Audrey, making her deliberately uncomfortable by trying to force her into opening up. 'It makes me sad when ye jist sit thaire sayin nuthin, Audrey, cause ah feel you've a lot tae offer the group n we're no seein that right now. It also makes me feel isolated as ah'm the only lassie speakin up in the group.'

Auds sits chomping intae the skin around her nails. No comment.

Tom nodding slowly, then regarding Audrey, 'Audrey, how does that make you feel?'

Audrey turning to him, and saying, in an even voice, 'Ah'll talk when I want tae talk, no when it suits other people.' Then she looks at Molly wi steel in her eyes. Molly's as shocked as the rest ay us, visibly backing doon, shrinking intae her chair. So barry to witness!

AUDREY RULES!

Substance dependency group session: Molly Bloom, after her psychic mauling from Auds, has come back out punching at the patriarchy. It's old adversaries Seeker and Swanney that she has in her sights. 'How can they be part ay this group if they're dealers? If they make thair money by supporting people's addiction, sorry,' she looks at Tom, 'substance dependency? Ah cannae see it. Ah jist dinnae git it.'

They sit back impassively enjoying her anger. But I'm a tad miffed at her constant criticism of oor muckers on the supply side. Where would we be without them? There's a scary thought! Skag, skag, skag, how we loved it; that pure, white shite we'd cop for wi such enthusiasm doon at Johnny's. He called it China White, but this shit had never seen the Orient n it wis an open secret it came fae a lot closer tae hame. For me it was love at first bang, marriage at first chase. Aye, ah love ma skag. Life should be like it is when you're skagged up. 'Maybe the point is that we all support addiction in our own ways,' I venture, suddenly scared ay how much I sound like Tom.

The man himself speculates, 'Is that not the nature of the disease?'

'It's *not* a disease.'

'Okay, condition,' he does that inverted-commas-wi-the fingers thing, 'if that makes people feel more comfortable.' He looks around the shoulder-jolting sea of call-it-what-the-fuck-ye-like faces. 'We don't operate on a strictly medical model of addic— substance dependency,' Tom concedes, and I can't help a triumphant swagger in the chair as the ooohs go round the stadium at this faux pas.

Great pro that he is, Brian, I think the lad Curzon will be as upset as anyone by that enforced error.

Individual counselling: Felt crap and said nothing 'of significance'. Then Tom asked me about my relationships. I felt too uncomfortable talking about my family, or Fiona or Hazel, so I mostly rabbited on about Charlene, describing her as 'the love of my life'. He seemed only mildly perturbed when I told him she was a professional shoplifter.

'What did you love about her?'

'Her hair. It was amazing, a real force ay nature. She had a barry erse n aw.'

'What aspects of her personality appealed to you?'

'I liked her professionalism. How she could spot a store detective easily. They were generally male, thirty-five to forty-five and, in body-language terms, looked like amateur shoplifters. In between pretending to scrutinise goods, they glanced at shoppers; judging clothing, then searching faces and watching hands. Simply dressing well took you off the radar of around 80 per cent of them. All eyes would be on the shell suits or the scheme labels. An Adidas crest on a

449

garment always set off alerts. Charlene's chorrie bag usually had a badminton racket sticking ootay it, tae convey a sporty and thus wholesome image. She wore great make-up when she went out to thieve; it shot her right up the social ladder fae Thames Estuary estate tae Young Conservative. Wisnae much impressed by ma clobber, though. "You look like a junky shoplifter, Mark," she'd tell me.'

I watched the muscles in Tom's visage slowly slacken and droop.

Journal Entry: Insight into my condition

I accept that I'm somehow, and for some obscure, pervasive reason, doing this stuff with heroin to myself. I'm not going along with all that powerless loser shite that it's a <u>disease</u>.

<u>IS IT FUCK A DISEASE</u>.

<u>I've done this to myself</u>. I could be anticipating graduating from university, or perhaps getting engaged tae a beautiful girl. Aye, I could go on about addiction as an ailment, absorb myself in the medical model, but now that I've detoxed, I'm officially no longer physically addicted to heroin. Yet at present I crave it more than ever; the whole social thing; copping, cooking, banging up and hanging out with other fucked-up ghosts. Shuffling around at night like a vampire, heading for grubby flats in run-down parts of the city, tae talk shite with other deranged, unstable losers. How can I sanely prefer that sort of activity to being with – <u>making love to</u> – a sweet girl, going to a film, or a gig, or having a few beers and heading to the ~~football~~ FITBA FITBA FUCKIN FITBA with my mates? But I do. The psychological dependency is stronger than ever. It's wrecking my life, but I <u>need</u> it.

<u>I'm no ready tae stop</u>.

But if I say that in all honesty tae Tom and Amelia, the game's fuckin over.

Day 31

Swanney leaves; his time here is up. Most people are relieved, cause he's been a bit ay a cunt tae them. I think it's a defence mechanism with him. Something scares him: it's buried deep, but you can sense it. He's usually

*fine wi me, like when I first kent him at the ~~football~~ fitba. As he comes
to my room to say farewell, he talks about getting some poppy thegither
and gaun oaf tae Thailand. He starts slaverin about oriental girls, stuff
about their fanny slits running east–west rather than north–south, and I
find myself tuning it out. It's hard tae listen tae anybody else's libidinous
fantasies when your own are so raw and vivid.*

<u>I would fuckin kill for a ride right now.</u>

Journal Entry: On housebreaking

*I have to be honest and admit it: I love housebreaking! And the main
motivations are not even monetary gain or class-war politics (although I've
only ever screwed, or intend to screw, big, posh homes). No, it's primarily
about being interested in how other people live. I generally treated the places
I broke into with respect, encouraging accomplices to do the same. In one
house, judging by the pictures on the walls and the fridge, the holidaying
family seemed really nice, so I wrote them a note apologising for any hassle
and trauma caused by the break-in. I stressed that it wasn't personal and we
needed the money, told them how we gained access and even offered some
basic tips on home security.*

*The behaviour in my last house, the QC's place, where I wrote the stuff
on his wall about Cha (basically to placate Begbie, who I felt was getting
dangerously radge), was pretty much out of character.*

*I knew it wasn't the case, but I always regarded myself as more of a guest
than a thief.*

Day 32

*Missing Spud and Swanney (I'm probably the only one with regard to the
latter). Keezbo very depressed. Talks the same shite over and over. He always
seems like he wants to tell me something profound, so I sit him down, all
ears, and then it's back tae the same old about being imprisoned by Moira
and Jimmy oan the balcony at the Fort. I love the man, but he's starting tae
fracture my tits and I find myself avoiding him as much as I can.*

Now I'm empathising with Tom and Skinny-Specky; they must feel like that all the time. But fuck them, they're gittin fuckin peyed fir it.

Journal Entry: Concerning my ma and her ma

My ma was taking me to the dentist. I was about ten. It was a hot day so we stopped in Princes Street Gairdins for some tea for her n juice for me. A group of tourists asked us directions in broken English, and she started spraffin away in perfect French, engaging them in an extended conversation.

Afterwards, when they left, she looked guilty. Embarrassed that she'd done this in front ay me. I kept asking her how she kent so much French; I wouldnae let it go. She eventually confessed tae us that she'd got a scholarship tae James Gillespie's Girls' School, but her cunt of a ma, auld Granny Fitzpatrick, wouldnae let her go. Said it was 'too far' fae Penicuik, being 'two buses' away. The worst part wis I mind ay Ma sayin, 'Ah suppose it wis for the best.'

Even then I thought: <u>wis it fuck for the best</u>.

Day 33

After brekkie, two newcomers tae the unit. A wee gadgie, his gait hobbled tae a slow shuffle, and wi a pronounced tendency tae drool, and an astonishingly fat lassie, even bigger than Keezbo. There's no fuckin way she could've been a smackheid, surely. But the politics ay the situation hold little interest fir me, as I'm anticipating getting the fuck oot myself, and am determined to tough it oot.

Yet I find myself oddly resenting them, this duo who look so alone, so scared. It's pathetic and wrong tae feel this way, but tae me the cunts are strangers, intruding on our wee scene.

Day 34

Some fucker's always upset some cunt the previous day, so breakfast is generally where the nervous reparations are made. The porridge is good this morning, thick rather than watery or lumpy.

Molly getting humped regularly by Sick Boy has upset Seeker, who – as alpha male – obviously feels that he should have first dibs on any ganting-on-it minge. Too bad for him that, in human society, dominance is always a wee bit more complex than in the animal world. The hardest cunt might no always be the biggest fanny merchant; in fact, they very rarely are. Sometimes they might be behind the handsome gadgie or the gabby, cocky fucker, or even the sportsman, comedian or intellectual in the riding queue. No wonder they can get so uptight.

Seeker and I are still doing the weights. It's been this ritual, much more so than the group or individual sessions with Tom, that's kept me going through this nasty and debilitating bout of depression. The other day, when I tried tae tell him I wisnae up tae it, the cunt just wisnae hearing us. 'C'moan. Yir daein it.' I know enough about psychopaths through Begbie to sense when they have their non-negotiating heids on, so I got up and struggled through my sets. And yes, by forcing myself intae it, feeling the burn, getting the blood circulating, my mood started to swing north.

So I've been saved by the biggest drug dealer in the city!

Him standing over me, mother hen watchful behind those cold, dark lenses, ready tae catch the weights in his huge hands when I work tae the point ay failure. Ironically, through this activity, thicker veins are coming up oan my airms, forcing themselves tae the surface ay ma skin. I wonder if this is the real motivation?

I found a skipping-rope in a drawer the other week, and I started doing boxer's three minutes skipping, one minute rest, working up to six rounds after the weights, and I'm still at my push-ups and squat thrusts. I reciprocate and get Seeker intae the rope, despite his initial cynicism. It looks strange, him skipping on the back patio, stripped to the waist, hair tied back, mirror-lens shades still on.

Started writing mair stuff in the journal. Trying tae think ay how I got intae this mess. All that came out was being with my auld man in Orgreave.

Day 35

Feeling fucking brilliant again! That rope rules. Can't shut the fuck up in the one-on-one session with Tom. Although I ken I'll probably feel different tomorrow, I've decided right now that he's an excellent gadge. He's actually read

Tender Is the Night, and it's great tae have somebody here who you can talk tae about books, films and politics. A long discussion on Scorsese and De Niro, him insisting that their best collaboration was *Taxi Driver,* me holding out for *Raging Bull.* '*Taxi Driver* was Schrader's film,' I insist, 'he was the genius behind it.'

I sit outside in the garden after dinner, when everybody else goes straight tae the telly. The evening shadows the overhanging trees, as sparrows flutter down to feed off our discarded crumbs. I can hardly hear the rambling, squabbling junky voices above the booming tones of the television newsreader.

Journal Entry: Stabbing Eric 'Eck' Wilson at school

It was second year at school, in the Tecky Drawing class, and the teacher was out somewhere. Two blows to the back of my head, with accompanying slack-jawed laughter. Not the first time this had happened, and I knew instantly who the perpetrator was. I turned round, instinctively pulling out the flick knife.

SLAM! One in the hand of Eck Wilson. Horror! His coupon was a sight to behold. SLAM! The chest. SLAM! The gut. The nastiest, most contrived strike, really wanting tae hurt the paralysed Eck wi that yin.

They weren't bad wounds, but they drew blood and Eck went into shock. As did I. Among those who witnessed this was Fort joyrider Gary McVie (RIP) whae took the blade offay us. 'Gie's that, Mark,' he said, pocketing it. He shouted at everybody tae sit doon and shut the fuck up, and they did, bar a couple ay sooky cunts whae clucked away as the teacher, Mr Bruce, came back. I worried that Bruce would see the blood, then the polis would come, and I'd be taken off to the chokey. But the bell went and Eck walked out, slightly doubled over. He never grassed, and after rabidly threatening to kill me outside, he left and went somewhere tae get his wounds treated.

I saw him a couple ay days later in Geography. I was chivless and terrified, a knot of fear in my guts. I envisioned a physical fight and I was confident that Eck would kick my cunt in. But he didn't: he sat beside me and started tae sook up, offering me sweeties – sherbet lemons, as I recall – saying 'we've always been mates . . .' which was, of course, nonsense.

454

I sat in silence, enjoying and drawing power from the desperate eager-to-please fear in his eyes, and the taste of the sweetie, wedged against the roof ay my mooth, as it slowly dissolved in a burst ay sherbet.

Day 36

Sick Boy leaves, packing up his belongings, including the infamous tattered Collins dictionary. A tool for enlightenment in most hands, but deadlier than a loaded revolver in his. His sister Carlotta picks him up in her Datsun. She looks so sexy . . . I'll have forty wanks aboot her the night! Too fuckin right! He was a bit perturbed at my heavy flirting. At one stage my palms are running up and down her bare arms, and I'm catching the scent of her black glossy hair. Trying tae get as much sense data as possible for later. She was giggling, and Sick Boy broke off a clinch with a heartbroken Molly tae gie us a half-playful, half-vicious kick on the shin.

'Look after my man here,' I tell Carlotta, locking him a matey embrace, enjoying his uncomfortable, helpless wriggling in my now stronger arms.

I only became pals with the cunt in the first place, soas I could go roond for him and ogle his sisters, and his ma, before she got fat. You only got in the hoose if his hostile prick ay a faither was oot. If he came tae the door, he'd go, 'So you're the laddie fae the Fort then, eh?' aw snobby, like the Bannanay flats were fuckin Barnton or something! He'd make ye wait oot ootside till Sick Boy wis ready, where ye'd invariably git hassled by local radges whae kent ye wir fae the other side ay Junction Street.

'Behave,' Sick Boy says, eyes pilled in narray focus, 'and I'll see ye in a few weeks.'

'I'll be oot next week,' I remind him.

'I'm gaun tae Italy for a spell: but for real this time. Dae me good to get out ay this savage Pictish swamp,' he says, looking round disdainfully over the trees tae the smoky-grey sky, before turning tae an anxious Molly.

'Phone me as soon as ye git back!' She wraps her thin arms around him.

I can see his face over her shoulder. He winks at me and widens his eyes before whispering in her ear, 'You just try stopping us, babes. You just try stopping us.' Then he breks oaf abruptly and heads tae the car.

We watch them leave. Molly runs inside. Tom puts a light hand oan ma shoulder. 'You've lost Danny, Johnny and now Simon. But cheer up, you'll be finished next.'

Back in the recky room Molly looks devastated, but Keezbo's consoling her, which keeps the fat Jambo cunt oot ma road.

I go back tae my room and read.

I get disturbed by Skinny-Specky, who tells me that I have a session with Molly. I'm wondering what the fuck she's on about, and she tipples and says, 'Sorry, the other Molly.'

The other Molly is a straight-backed, horsey Englishwoman called Molly Greaves, who is a visiting clinical psychologist. She couldn't be more different from our own beloved Moll if she tried. I first met her at the clinic, where I answered her probing, insistent questions in a dazed compliance. Now I'm far more testy and resistant to her violating edge, and it doesn't go well.

At night I sit on the back porch with the guitar, strumming under the inky-black sky, but a string breaks and there's no replacement, so the party's over.

Day 38

Tom's getting under my prickly skin. I'm due tae be discharged next week, but as well as scheduling me for another fruitless session with the clinical psychologist, in our one-to-ones he's changed his softly-softly tactics. Today, he looked me in the eye and said in frosty detachment, 'Don't lie to yourself, Mark.'

'What?' I was wrong-footed, and I thought, once again, about The Big Lie. If he wis gaunny pill us up oan it.

'Work with me.'

'What d'ye mean?'

'You're an intelligent guy. But you're not _that_ intelligent. For as well read and educated as you are, you can't solve the mystery of why you're doing this to yourself.'

'Ye think so?' I challenged him, while aw the time ah kent that the cunt was spot on.

'You don't know why you're a junky and that bugs the shit out of you. It offends your intellectual vanity and your sense of yourself.'

It was like being punched in the guts. Because it was true. I was perplexed, but more than that, a bit shaken, as much by his U-turn towards this more confrontational approach, as by what he said.

CUNT.

I could hardly hear my own words over the blood bubbling in my brain and I started to rant. It went something like this: 'Ah cannae value this type of world. It's no good for me, this shithole we created and cannae make better. That's what offends me. Ah'm choosin no tae engage, tae drop out, if you want tae use that shitey hippy term!'

And that's making it sound more articulate than it was.

'That's not normal talk for a young guy,' Tom responded. 'You're simply depressed. What's making you depressed, Mark?'

Couldnae think ay anything to say. 'The world.'

'It's _not_ the world,' he shook his head emphatically. 'Yes, it's bad, but people like yourself should be trying to make it better. Besides, you're smart enough to get by and thrive in any sort of society. What is it?'

'Skag's a good buzz,' I telt him. Anything tae burst the bubble, tae avoid confronting The Big Lie. 'Ah eywis liked a good buzz.'

'So you're at an age where you discover that the world is fucked up and it can't be easily fixed. So deal with it. Grow the fuck up.' There was a new iron in his eyes. 'Get on with your life. So what?'

'So this.' I rolled up my sleeve and show him the scar tissue ay my healed track marks.

The Big Lie.

We were all playin a fuckin game: the rehab game. We had tae collude wi the staff in the myth that we wanted tae stop using heroin. Few, if any ay us, really gied a flying fuck though. What we wanted was to clean up, soas we _could get back tae using at a reduced dosage._ But we didnae want tae stop, fuck that! We wanted a clean slate so we could use without things getting out ay hand. Success in this game was based on our ability tae deceive the staff, and their ability tae con themselves, by buying intae the myth that we actually wanted tae embrace this bullshit ay a drug-free life.

TO DO WHAT?

Only Seeker wanted something else: tae find a place in Tenerife so that the crippling winter cauld wouldnae get at the metal in his body.

Scribbled ~~more~~ mair aboot that Yorkshire trip wi Dad. The writing's *my refuge; my life here would be intolerable without it. For experimental purposes I tried tae frame it in the form ay a story, writing as events actually affected me.*

Journal Entry: Concerning Orgreave

Even the plank-stiffness of this old, unyielding settee can't arrest my body's slink into deliverance. It reminds me of the university residences in Aberdeen; lying in the dark, basking in exalted freedom from the fear that coalesced in my chest, like the thick phlegm did in his. Because whatever I hear outside, cars scrunching down the narrow, council-house streets, sometimes sweeping their headlights across this fusty old room, drunks challenging or serenading the world, or the rending shrieks of cats taking their torturous pleasures, I know I won't hear that noise.

No coughing.

No screaming.

Day 39

High drama, as Skreel was discovered tae have gone AWOL late last night. He comes back wasted early this morning, shuffling in wi a dopey smile on his face, and some blood tricklin fae his big, bust nose, responding tae aw interrogations wi an offhand shrug. It seems he managed tae score smack in Kirkcaldy. The way I see it, the cunt deserves a medal for initiative. He's only around for half an hour, presumably as some sort ay negative example tae us all, before the polis arrive and he's carted off tae jail.

We have an emergency process group meeting tae discuss, predictably, 'our feelings' about the incident. Emotions are running high and Ted, who had become close tae Skreel, gets intae a shouting match with Len, Tom and Amelia, storming out the room, calling them 'grassin cunts'. Molly shrilly parrots on about Skreel 'letting everybody doon'. Well, the cunt certainly let me fuckin doon, no telling us that he was daein a runner and had a connection locally. I'd have been right ower that fuckin waw behind him. Being contrary by nature, I say absolutely fuck all, except a philosophical, 'He's gone. Can't really see the point of inquests and recrimination. Let's just get oan wi it.'

458

The fat lassie — Gina, her name is — she's fresh out of detox but still rattling like fuck, is constantly whining, 'Ah cannae handle aw this . . .' as she rocks away, sitting on her hands, meaty airms tight by her side. The wee felly wi her is called Lachlan, or Lachy, he tells us timidly. Lackey of the state, I'll think of him, as he's in the care of a state agency.

Molly and ~~Skinny-Specky~~ Amelia are now big buddies, Ms Bloom having almost turned intae a clone; posture and gestures shamelessly thieved fae her posher sister. She starts gabbin oan in the recky room that evening aboot 'destructive relationships that enable negative behaviour' and how she would 'never get involved with guys like Brandon or even Simon again . . . he jist tries tae trick ye wi words'.

How soon they forget! Aye, I fair had a wee smirk at that yin, knowing full well that if Sick Boy walked in that door her keks would be roond her ankles in seconds.

'Great thit yuv learned yir lesson,' Seeker says, and flashes me a grim, collusive smile, while Keezbo picks and chews at the dry skin aroond his heavily bleeding nails.

'Aye, ah huv!' she says belligerently, then looks at us in disdain before storming off.

Day 40

Today in the junky transfer market: <u>OUT</u>: Seeker, <u>IN</u>: old smelly Leith hippy Dennis Ross and a rodent-faced radgeworks fae Sighthill who goes by the name ay Alan Venters.

I'll certainly miss Seeker (again, it's a club of one I'm in), basically cause I know it'll be harder to motivate myself tae exercise every morning and afternoon.

Day 41

It's a lovely morning, and I'm up early to do the weights and the rope. To my surprise, Audrey comes through, tapping on the patio doors. I think of her as Bowie's little girl with grey eyes, say something, say something . . . as she joins me in her customary silence, doing some weights and

459

skipping. But afterwards, we sit and chat in the garden. Audrey doesnae say, but it's clear she didnae care fir Seeker. Perhaps understandable. After a bit we go in for breakfast, as the others rise in a cacophony of groans and yawns.

On the menu: scrambled eggs and surprisingly good vegetarian sausages, with tons ay broon HP Sauce. The downside: that Venters gadge sitting on his tod, shaking, but giving out a malevolent vibe. Audrey and Molly are both visibly creeped out by him. That cunt is trouble. Not my problem, though.

Having cracked Joyce, I've finally moved on to Carl Rogers. More interesting than I thought: I want to finish it before I go, for Tom's sake.

Day 42

It pishes heavily half an hour at a time, before the rain seems tae vanish back up intae a silvery sky ay nippy, ragged-ersed clouds.

Audrey has replaced Seeker as my fitness partner. After a session we sit and chat about music and life. She tells me she worked as a nurse with terminally ill people but got seriously depressed and started raiding the morphine in the controlled-drugs cupboard.

So she's become a friend, which instantly knocks her off my J. Arturoing jukebox. Ye cannae wank aboot mates, even ones with tits and fannies: it just disnae work for me.

Molly and Ted leave us. Their time here is up. Ted comes up to me and goes, 'Ah didnae like you at first cause ah thoat ye wir aw snidey n superior, eywis sneakin away oan yir ain n no mixin. Then ah realised that ye jist wanted a bit ay peace n tae git through it yir ain wey.' I give him a surprisingly heartfelt hug. I'm even more shocked when Molly embraces me and kisses me on the cheek, and says, 'I'll miss arguing wi you, ya radge.' I return the kiss and wish her well. Ted and Molly are the two I like least from the original crew, but I'll miss them, as I'm singularly unimpressed by the new intake. Thank fuck I'm offski on Thursday. Can't wait.

I sit up alternating between reading Rogers and writing mair aboot Orgreave.

Day 43

Keezbo graduates with honours fae our drug users/substance abusers project, but doesnae seem too excited about it all. 'Chin up, buddy,' I tell him, 'the Fort Rhythm Section'll be back in action soon. Toughest skiers.'

'Toughest skiers . . .' he sadly responds.

What's up wi that fat Jambo cunt? The fuckin coupon on him! He's breaking my heart! Before he walks out he hugs me, and it's like being mauled by a fat, shaved, sweating bear. 'Ah'll miss ye,' he says, as if we'll never see each other again! Then the fat cunt hands us this envelope. When he's gone I open it up; inside is the team photae ay us aw in the Wolves strips.

Day 44

Brian Clough spent forty-four days at Leeds United. I'd rather have been him than me. No a great deal ay time tae turn roond a club. No a great deal ay time tae turn roond a life.

I mind of that superb John Cooper Clarke number, 'Beasley Street' and the lyrics: 'Hot beneath the collar, an inspector calls . . .' Well, fucked if we dinnae have three ay them today, fae the NHS, Social Work Department and Scottish Office respectively. The Daily Express ran a piece on Skreel's 'escape' and did a feature on the 'junky five-star hotel', with a helpful editorial saying that the place should be shut doon. Len tells me that a sleazy paedophile-type with a press pass was hanging around outside, harassing the staff for quotes.

It's amazing how seedy scumbags (the press) can write shite, and demented retards (the public) suddenly go up in arms and then opportunistic slime (the politicians) jump right on the bandwagon. Such is British life. So now there is to be a 'comprehensive review of the facility'.

It actually brings us all together. We feel like celebs and are very complimentary about the unit. As the veteran, I do most of the talking, though Audrey's now saying her piece and Dennis Ross as the oldest, most mature and articulate member of the new breed is making a sterling contribution. (In the gairdin ay eunuchs, even the gadgie wi the two-inch cock cannae help but swagger.) We're stressing tae the po-faced bureaucrats that it's no easy ride. This is no piece of cake.

Tom, Amelia and Len and the other staff are obviously edgy. The unit might shut down. I refuse tae attend the 'emergency house meeting' as I'm hame the morn, preferring instead to watch the news. There's a big heroin bust and the polis and politicians are lining up tae suck each other's knobs and lick each other's fannies, trumpeting on that they're winning the 'war against drugs'.

Aye, right. Of course ye are. Clueless cunts.

Day 45

And the next contestant in the Rehab Game is: none other than my old pal Mikey Forrester! Again, he'll be creaking and sweating in his room for the next week, keeping out of everybody's road and feart ay his ain shadow.

I caught the anxiety and confusion in his eyes and regarded his skeletal frame. It couldnae happen tae a nicer cunt, I thought.

Then, as he saw me, his eyes lit up, and he shuffled ower tae us and went, 'Mark . . . awright, mate?' He looked roond aw shifty and worried. 'What's the story here?'

I realised that I looked just like him, only a few weeks back, and was just as scared. So I took him tae ma room, where he sat shivering, skin pitted like plucked chicken, and gied the cunt ma honest view ay the situ. Apparently, the nondy fucker tried to brek intae a chemist's at Liberton. 'Ah hud seen that Christiane F oan video, ken?'

The fuckin bam slavered on, and I tried tae listen, but kept anticipating Mater n Pater's arrival in the motor tae take me away fae aw this. Sure enough, Len came in and Mikey let oot a groan, as I handed him the psychic-rehab baton, and the doss cunt was led oaf tae his room and the long days ay detox that stretched ahead.

But I was oot ay here, packing up the last ay ma shite. The final item ah put in my bag wis ma diary and journal. He's been a good friend, but I doubt ah'll be seeing him again. Life can only be understood backwards, but it must be lived forwards.

I say goodbye tae Audrey, who still has a week to go, and tell her that her strategy ay saying fuck all and keeping her heid doon is exactly the right yin. A kiss, cuddle and exchange ay numbers, and I'm roond tae the office tae get discharged.

Postscript – Day 45 (afternoon)

It's true what they say: never, ever eavesdrop, cause ye might hear somethin aboot yirsel ye dinnae want tae. Ah'd packed up, was waitin for muh ma n dad, and ah thought ah'd take Carl Rogers back tae Tom. The door ay his office was ajar and ah heard Amelia's voice, n Sick Boy's name being mentioned. Well, it wisnae exactly his *name*, but ah kent for a cert whae she wis talking aboot. — . . . very manipulative. I think he almost believes his own propaganda.

Ah closed in, doomed tae pain like a moth aroond a flame. Ah heard her suddenly change track. — . . . but that's Simon. Then we've got Mark, leaving today.

Ah froze.

— I'm not too concerned about him in the long term, Tom's soft, reedy voice. — If he makes it to twenty-six, twenty-seven, his sense of mortality will kick in, he'll shed all this existential angst and he'll be fine. If he can just keep from OD'ing or contracting HIV till then, he'll simply grow out of heroin addiction. He's too intelligent and resourceful; eventually he'll get bored with pretending to be a loser.

So ah walked in on them, rappin the door as ah went. — Mark . . . Skinny-Specky blushed tamely. Tom's pupils visibly dilated. Baith ay them looked as embarrassed as fuck. Was it being caught talking about us, or using the 'A' word, or perhaps that unprofessional and pejorative designation, 'loser'? Whatever, ah savoured the moment, thrusting *On Becoming a Person* oantae Tom. — Interesting read. You should have a look at it sometime.

And ah turned on ma heels n headed tae the recky room, where ah said cursory goodbyes tae the other cunts, whom ah couldnae be daein wi; only Audrey was important and ah'd said a proper *adieu* tae her. Tom steyed in the office, evidently too embarrassed tae pill one ay his farewell caird stunts.

Ah take my stuff ootside tae wait for muh ma n dad. Vanilla-milkshake clouds splatter ower the light blue sky, as a big oak tree blots oot the sun.

The pebbles behind me crack under somebody's steps, and ah see Tom movin stealthily taewards us, a hurt and confused expression oan

463

his coupon. He evidently wants tae kiss n make up. — Mark. Look, I'm sorry . . .

He kin git tae fuck and take aw his smarmy platitudes and insincere hugs and stick them right up his manipulative, duplicitous rectum. — You dinnae understand the rage inside. You never will, ah tell him, thinking aboot Orgreave, then, for some reason, Begbie. — Ah hurt myself, disable myself, so ah cannae hurt anybody else that doesnae deserve it. And that's cause ah cannae get at people like you, cause you've got the law on your side. Ah feel the bile rise up inside me. — If ah really could fuck your world right up, ah wouldnae be wastin ma time screwin up ma ain life!

Just then, a familiar motor crunches intae the driveway, Ma and Dad's big excited faces negating a large portion ay what ah'd just said. The pain ah've caused them makes a mockery ay ma conceit and vanity: the idea that thaire's any intrinsic nobility in ma actions. But fuck that. Ah turn ma back oan Tom n the centre, and walk taewards the motor.

— Good luck, Mark, Tom says, — I mean that.

Ah'm angry at masel, but livid at that cunt. Fuckin lying, smarmy, cowardly bureaucrat. — You are *way* oot ay touch wi what ye mean. If ye ever meant fuck all in the first place, ah tell him, as muh dad emerges fae the car. — If ye want tae dae something useful, keep yir eye oan that cunt Venters in thaire. Ah swipe the air dismissively. My old man scowls, but they're delighted tae see me, and me them, as ah climb intae the back ay the car.

— Ma laddie, ma laddie, ma laddie . . . muh ma says, pushing intae the back seat after us, huggin me, firin a volley ay questions at us, while my dad talks tae Tom and signs some stuff. Ah'm fuckin scoobied as tae what the documentation is. Release forms?

After a bit, Dad comes back ower tae the motor and climbs intae the driver's seat. — What wis that aboot? You and Mr Curzon?

— Nowt. Just a daft wee argument. It kin sometimes git a wee bit intense in thaire.

— Funny, that wis exactly what he said, muh dad smiles, shakin his heid, as something sinks in ma chest.

— Oh son, son, son, muh ma says, tears streamin down her face, on top ay a great big smile. It takes years off her, and ah realise ah huvnae seen it for so long, — ye look that well! Doesn't he, Davie?

— He does that, the old boy says, pivoting round and squeezing my bulkier shoulder, contemplating me like a farmer does a prize bull at the Royal Highland Show.

— Thank God this bloody nightmare's ower!

For a couple ay missed heartbeats ah worry that the wheezing motor isnae gaunny start, but Dad wrenches it intae life, n we gratefully pull away fae the centre. Some people have gathered oan the steps, but ah dinnae look back. Ma keeps my hand in her lap in between sparking up, still prisoner tae the cigarette. We're heading back across the bridge tae Edinburgh, when a familiar song comes oan the radio talking so temptingly about riding that white line highway.

They dinnae notice, they're busy chattin aboot how it's a lovely day, n we can aw start lookin forward again. But my mind and body, pristine pillars ay the temple ay abstinence for six weeks, thrash in unison like a drum machine towards that first bag ay skag. Just thinkin aboot it causes a frozen sweat ay excitement tae gush fae ma pores. Ah cannae fuckin wait. But ah resolve that ah'll try, for their sakes. The auld boy's really pushing the motor for some reason, and the auld dear n me cowp intae each other as the tyres screech on every bend.

June 1969, in Blackpool. The moon still made ay green cheese but soon tae be wrapped up and labelled by Yank astronauts, before being dumped in cold storage. A stroll doon the Golden Mile. The distance between Granda Renton's stiff, overwrought breaths and the last time we walked the prom so much more than just one year. Remembering when we once looked at his medals in that tin. Him wryly observing, 'They only want tae pin this metal oantae yir chest tae cover the scars fae the metal thuv pit inside it.' I minded thinking at the time: no, no, Granda, it was the Germans *who did that. The British* gave *you the medals!*

Now ah realise that the poor old cunt had it sussed.

We head through the city, bound for the port of Leith. It's no that late; shopkeepers on the Walk are lowerin their iron grilles with a vengeance. When we get tae the hoose, ah sense that somethin is up. Suddenly, the front room lights click on and a sea of puses: Hazel, Tommy, Lizzie, Second Prize (lookin fit and with a cute blonde lassie in tow), Billy, Sharon, Gav Temperley, Mrs McGoldrick fae next door, Billy's mates Lenny and Granty, aw wearin grins n toastin us wi glesses ay champagne; aw bar Second Prize, whae's goat an orange juice. In the kitchen above the table, full ay cakes, sandwiches and the mini sausage rolls ye get at weddings and funerals, a home-made banner ay green lettering against a white background proclaims:

WELL DONE MARK, AND WELCOME HOME!

No quite the graduation ceremony they had in mind for us, but still. My old man hands us a gless ay champagne. – Get that doon ye. But go easy, mind.

465

Go easy.

Lookin doon at the swirlin, sickly orange glare comin fae the plastic logs in the fireplace, ah sip ma drink, feelin it windin doon ma throat, intae ma stomach, liver, kidneys, goin through ma bloodstream, then lightin ma brain up. The bubbles fizz in my heid, as Hazel rubs ma airm in appreciation, her mooth liftin at the corners. — Are those muscles?

— Kind ay, ah concede, gettin another drink, in sure-fire knowledge it'll only render mair acute rather than satiate a need ah can feel creepin up on us. Ah'm headin right back tae her when Tommy intercepts, locking me in a matey embrace. — Leave that shite alaine, Mark, he breathlessly urges.

— Too right, Tam: ah've learned ma lesson. That isnae *exactly* a lie, cause ah have learned *a* lesson. Just no the yin they hud in mind. — How's Spud?

— Dinnae ask. As bad as ever. Imagine pittin yersel through aw that rehab shite for nowt.

— Aw, right, ah say aw hangdog, but inside ah'm elated. *Go on, the laddie Murphy!* — And Matty?

— As bad as Spud, but in *Wester Hailes.*

Ah take Tommy's point. So it's about as bad as it can get for oor Mr Connell. Ah note Hazel's talking tae Second Prize and his bird, so ah grab ma holdall and head tae ma auld bedroom, puttin my diary at the bottom ay a cupboard full ay books and other auld shite.

When ah go back ben the front room, muh ma is arguin wi Billy, wavin some caird she wants him tae sign. — No way, he shakes his heid, — ah wouldnae sign anything fir they Currans. You no remember how they carried oan at Wee Davie's funeral?

— But they've been neighbours, son . . . She looks imploringly tae me. — You'll sign perr Olly's git-well caird, won't ye, pal?

— Didnae ken he wis . . . what's up wi um?

— Aw, ye willnae huv heard . . . he hud a massive heart attack, Ma says sadly. — Claims he goat this nasty letter fae the council. Aye, he wis that enraged he jist flung it straight in the fire. Then he went up thaire and started shoutin the odds, aboot coloured people n that, ye ken how they could git . . .

— Bams, says Billy.

— . . . n he goat himself awfay worked up, cause the council denied aw knowledge ay any letter. But he wis ragin, n he tried tae git at the clerk behind the screens, so they called the polis. Well, he left eftir that, but he collapsed ootside in Waterloo Place, so they took him right intae the Royal.

Ah feel this chill spreadin over me, n the colour drainin fae my face. Ma thrusts the caird and pen intae my hands. Billy looks at me. — You're no gaunny sign that, ur ye? You hated that bastard!

— Ye huv tae live n let live. It's only a caird, n ah widnae wish that oan anybody, ah tell um. Then ah deek the caird, which has a cartoon ay a downcast-looking boy in a hoaspital bed, thermometer in his gob, wi the caption: SORRY TO HEAR YOU'RE ILL. Ah open it up n the same gadgie's now full ay zest, gless ay champers in his hand, winking at a sexy nurse, whae pats her hair. The message reads: HERE'S TO GET-TING BACK TO YOUR OLD SELF SOON!

So ah lay the caird doon oan the sideboard and scribble: *All the best, Olly. Mark.*

— That's ma boy, Ma smiles indulgently, then whispers intae my ear, — that's the *real* you, son. That's the goodness ay ye comin oot, before aw they daft drugs made ye aw funny n nasty, n she kisses *the real me* oan the cheek.

Ah winks at her n turns tae Billy. — Mind that Wolves team that beat Herts in the Texaco Cup final? Youse won one–nil doon thaire but goat gubbed three–one at Tyney? How many players kin ye name fae that team?

— Fuck . . . he says, his brow furrowing, — ah kin hardly name any Herts players! Let me see, there wis Derek Dougan, obviously, Frank Munro . . . was it Billy Hibbitt? . . . Kenny Hibbitt . . . talkin aboot Currans . . . that was the boy who scored twice, Scottish guy n aw . . . Hugh Curran! N whae else? Billy turns tae ma faither, whae's chatting tae Tommy and Lizzie. — Dad, he shouts him ower, — that Wolves team that beat Herts, the Texaco Cup . . .

— Some team, muh dad says, wipin his beak wi a paper towel. — Mind, youse aw got Wolves strips that Christmas? Ah hud tae send away for your yin?

— Aye. Fort Wanderers. You took that team photae at Christmas. It never came oot, ah state, lookin pointedly at Billy. — Shame that, eh? Nivir mind, but; ah kin still see it ma mind's eye. Left tae right, back row; me, Keezbo, ah glance over tae the boys wi their birds: Tommy, Rab, then back tae Billy, — Franco and Deek Low n aw. In the front, crouchin in front ay us, again, left tae right; Gav, English George, Johnny Crooks, Gary McVie, mind ay poor Gazbo? Chocolateface Dukey and Matty wearin a goalie's jersey.

Billy looks a bit disconcerted, as muh Dad cheerfully says, — Well, at least aw that bloody rubbish ye were takin husnae destroyed yir memory!

No, it has not. Because one thing ah mind ay clearly is a certain address in Albert Street, and the seven digits ay a phone number gied tae us by Seeker. Ah move across tae Hazel n pit my airm around her slender waist. She smiles at me, immaculate in that yellay dress wi they pop socks, and smellin wonderful, lookin like a fifties suburban American girl of the cinema. Ah git a stirrin in my breeks. Ah think aboot whether ah should take her up tae the flat in Monty Street n have crap sex wi her, or track doon Johnny, Spud, Matty, Keezbo and co, or go and see ma good buddy and personal trainer, Seeker.

Avanti

When I tell you that the best part of the place is the railway station, you begin to get some idea of what I'm talking about. Of course, I'd never let them know back in Leith that my mother's home town is a shithole, far removed from those Tuscan landscapes swathed in breathtaking light, where ah led the gaping simpletons tae believe the Mazzolas originated from. In possibly the most visually stunning country on God's earth, this toon is a thorn among roses. Even in Italy's shabbiest region other shitheaps in the locale look down on it. Ah can even see why my mother's family left for *Scotland*.

It never seemed so bad when ah was a kid. The fact that a large section ay it was still buried under a landslide since the 1960s didnae escape me, but then ah only saw a place of mystique, the child's imagined underground city, rather than the reality of a festering den of municipal complacency and corruption. While hardly artist-inspiring, the auld family farmhouse had seemed romantic, instead of a draughty rural slum, and even the huge car breaker's yard full ay rusty Fiats that still dominates the dusty hamlet was a playground to us, not an eerie blot on the landscape. And I didn't notice that the ground around the settlement was barren and its citizens unsavoury and depressed-looking enough no tae seem oot ay place on Gorgie Road.

The only parts I think of affectionately are this cafe bar in the station, where ah sit drinking fantastic Italian coffee, and the old barn where cousin Antonio thoughtfully left a pile ay knock-off hassocks fae the church before he married and went to Napoli tae become a minor civil servant. In the family tradition, it was there that I finally had my way with Massima. Before ah was allowed to break the seal, I endured two weeks of frustrating kisses and gropes and the Catholic girl blow jobs I knew from back home (thank fuck ah went tae a non-denominational school, one thing ah do owe that cunt of a faither), followed by plenty of pleading, cajoling, threatening and, finally, the desperate mentions of love and marriage. And Massima is almost twenty years old! My cousin Carla pointedly warned me, after practically throwing us together in that

Italian apprentice matriarch way: she has a boyfriend. So we've been sneaking around like fugitives, fae the station tae the barn.

But persevere is my middle name, and right now ah'm enjoying my coffee, not at all miffed that Massima's train, coming fae another village two stops down the line, is delayed by almost thirty minutes. Where is the Duce when you need him most? No matter; I can't think of anywhere better tae wait than this wee bar with its glass door, watching the fat old men playing cards at the next table. Sipping my coffee, comforted by the gleaming, hissing espresso machine, which evokes the old steam engines of yesterday. Thinking about how, for the poor bastards in this town, things dinnae seem tae have changed that much since then: it's still a lifetime ay commitment for one fuckin ride! It's a 'C' day, and the word is:

CONTRETEMPS, noun, pl same, an unexpected and unfortunate occurrence, *a minor dispute or disagreement.

The coffee's kick pushes against the drowsy effect ay the eftirnoon sun, cascading in through the window. The cashier closes the register with a ping. A fat ginger cat that reminds us ay Keezbo sprawls across a sunlit patch on the tiled floor, looking up indolently as it forces customers to either walk round or step over it.

Outside, through the half-clear, half-frosted windae, two young gadges, who were at the pinball machine earlier on, playfully jostle each other. One wears a Juve T-shirt, the team Antonio supports. A lot ay them seem tae around here, though that's probably changed wi Napoli's signing ay Maradona. Those poor wee fuckers; I predict loads ay pent-up sexual frustration ahead, *fratellos*. It's weird the way those wee chappies hud hands here, like lassies ay that age back hame sometimes dae. And it goes right on through their teens! Imagine heading up the Walk, hudin hands with Renton, Spud, Tommy or Franco! Franco would probably enjoy it though, and I entertain the notion ay him in a cabin boy's outfit, pulling the train up in toff class back on *The Freedom of Choice*. Thinking of home, my thoughts drift tae Mark and rehab, and ah pull oot the folded pages fae ma wallet. It's the ones ah liberated from the waste-paper basket in his room, the diary and journal entries. It was all he deserved, and payment for his rudeness in dropping off when I was endeavouring to discuss key concepts. Such carelessness eywis invites a tax; you have to be on your guard in the modern world or ye get punished.

470

Day 21

Pulled out of a dream about Fiona, in the waking hours of the morning. I'm feeling her up against a wall, but she's slipping through my hands as she assumes hideously demonic shapes. Even though she's a monster, it still seems important to fuck her before I wake up . . . but in her ectoplasmic form it's like trying to nail a jellyfish to a wall . . . I'm awake, wilting cock in hand, in a noisy twilight of birdsong.

After breakfast (porridge, toast and tea), it's the now familiar ritual of weights on the patio with Seeker. When I get back to my room I'm buzzed but tired, normally optimum conditions for reading, but I can't settle or concentrate. I'm beset by a terrible sensation of dread and loss, so strong it makes me shudder. Then I feel my breath catching. The room seems to swirl, and I'm aware that I'm having some kind of panic or anxiety attack and have to lie down, trying to get my breathing under control, until it subsides. It quickly passes and everything is as it was, except that I'm really shat up.

In my session with Tom, I get irritated at fuck all. He sees through it and asks what's bugging me. I tell him that I'm feeling bad because I was a total cunt to somebody I loved, but I can't talk about it. He suggests that I write it down in my journal. I almost have a fit again, this time in a burst of sardonic laughter, and the session ends.

I'm restless; I feel something eating at my insides. My breath catches again, even though my respiratory system is better than ever. With the weights and exercise, air's been flooding into it like smack from a needle. Not now. I try and fight through it, recalling Kierkegaard saying 'anxiety is the dizziness of freedom'. But maybe ah'm no meant tae be free.

I spend hours inside my own heid, thoughts bubbling with such velocity and force that I can envision my skull splitting open. Tom's right: it seems my only option. The words need expelling before they burst out of their own accord. I go to the pages of the journal and I write.

Journal Entry: Betraying Fiona by
fucking Joanne Dunsmuir

I was the one who instigated it; in the Talisman Bar at Waverley Station. Joanne and I had been drinking with Bisto and Fiona on the train up from London. It was like we couldn't end it, couldn't end this amazing adventure we'd just been on. We got off at Waverley, leaving Bisto Aberdeen-bound. They departed with a chaste kiss, in stark comparison to the intensity of Fiona and I's separation at Newcastle.

We went to the station bar and had another few drinks. Joanne got distressed, saying she didn't want anybody to know that her and Bisto were going out. The conversation developed that ferocity and profundity that can often signal trouble between genders. On some crazy impulse, I asked her for a kiss, and then we were snogging. We were both rampant.

'What d'ye want tae dae?' she asked, eyes fierce with purpose.

I whispered in her ear, 'I really think we should fuck . . .' I was almost creaming myself with excitement.

We left the bar and started walking wi our gear, her a backpack, me a scabby holdall, out the rear exit of the station, up the hill, to the entrance tae Calton Hill Park, where the bufties went at night. But it wisnae night, it was still late afternoon and daylight.

I'd just just left Fiona, a girl I'd fallen in love with. But this would just be sex. Fiona and I had never made any declarations, not negotiated terms as to what our life would be like. We never said we wouldn't see other people. We weren't pathetic and bourgeois. (I cringe as I write that word; only a student wanker uses it, but that's how I felt.)

So Joanne and I climbed up the steps in silence, the round ornate pillars of the Dugald Stewart Monument towering above on our left. A youngish cunt in an auld gadge's bunnet passed us as we saw the big, phallic Nelson Monument loom ahead; it reminded me why we were ascending this hill. I felt sick and giddy, but we kept walking, carrying our awkward luggage, matching each other's stride. I watched Joanne's red Doc Martens, her black tights, figure-hugging short skirt, jean jacket, her hair swishing to the side, sharp features in profile, backpack like it was trying to mount her. It was all unreal and dreamlike, and I almost considered running away, like a kid. But although there was something really cold and detached about it, I'd never been so fucking horny in my life. The snarls of the city traffic below us started to fade. The next symbol of how I felt, the Portuguese cannon, stood accusingly as we came up to the Nelson Monument.

Did that cunt really need another yin, here? It stands right on top of where people are keeping a round-the-clock vigil for democracy, at the site of the Scottish Parliament. And yes, they even had the words inscribed on a plaque outside:

ENGLAND EXPECTS EVERY MAN TO DO THEIR DUTY.

We stopped to look at it, both of us flabbergasted as to how blatantly and effortlessly fucked up Scotland could be. Joanne spat with venom, 'Ah fuckin hate that! It's like we're nuthin! Here, in our own country! They get everything!'

I was swamped by an anger at everything; me, her, the world. The shagging moment seemed to have long passed. Then Joanne looked at me and kissed me harshly on the lips. I was instantly aroused again and we started necking. Joanne kissed well. 'C'moan,' I said tersely. For some reason, I thought she'd turn and walk away, but she was alongside me as we headed to the back of the park, looking over Salisbury Crags.

On the right, we saw the thick bracken, and knew it was the spot. There was a clearing in the clustered growth of ferns, trees and bushes. An oasis made for outdoor shagging. We threw our bags down and sat on the grass like a picnicking couple. In an oddly demure gesture, Joanne even smoothed out her skirt. She had a thin scar above her eye that I'd never noticed. I pulled her to me and kissed her. I licked it, the scar, and slobbered over her face like a dog. She kissed me, biting my top lip. My hand went tit-bound up her T-shirt, which she yanked off and unclipped her bra, letting me caress and fondle her small, firm breasts as she unbuttoned my jeans and pulled my prick out of my trousers, urgently saying, 'We should fuck now . . . we should dae it now . . .' Then she stopped, tae quickly unlace her Docs, as I pulled off my trainers.

I asked her if she'd ever had a boy eat her pussy and she said, 'Naw, you gaunny dae it, well?' and I told her, 'Aye; aye, ah fuckin am . . .' n I was yanking off her tights and panties in a oner, and was down on her sweet velvet tuft. My tongue parted her vulva and twisted to the spot. I was unprepared for the ferocity of her reaction, she immediately let out a series of gasps, then started growling, 'Ah'm gaunny suck that fuckin cock . . . ah'm gaunny suck it till it bleeds . . .' and she bucked and inched roond on her back, digging her elbows into the grass, until I felt her tongue licking my dangling baws then her mooth tightening round my cock. We're both at it, and I let my eyes roam around the bushes tae try and distract myself from the intense pressure building up inside me. Suddenly, she pushed my hips up and pulled my cock out of her mouth, but dug her nails into my buttocks. I realised she was coming in violent, rapid spasms, so I turned round and started fucking her slowly, then hard, and she came repeatedly. Arthur's Seat and Salisbury Crags surged above us and we weren't giving a toss about the odd passer-by or jogger on the path below the sheltered bank. We trusted the sycamores and ferns to obscure us as we fucked out the Edinburgh skyline. We were trying no tae make noise, but she was gasping like an epileptic, to the extent I even had tae ask her if she was okay, but she flushed crimson and exploded again in reply. 'Aw for fuck sake . . .' she said, almost hating her final climax, but compelled to carry on and squeeze out the last drops of her rapture. I felt exalted, locked in the moment; I'd never had a bird so rampant that I've fucked so senseless before. But I'd still no come, so I pulled oot and turned her floppy, spent body over, parting her soft arse-cheeks, spitting on the tight hole and working my finger in to the first knuckle, then the second. She stayed silent as her sphincter gripped my digit, but was still pretty relaxed which was wild, as whenever I've put or tried to put my finger up a lassie's erse or them mines, there's always been a real tensing up. I told her what I was going to do, and I started pushing my cock into her arsehole. It took a long time to get it in, but it slowly went. I bit at her ear and her neck, spitting out mouthfuls of hair, while she was screaming, 'Finish it! Finish it!' like a boxing coach, and despite no being able to get a good fuck-motion going cause of the tightness, I was demented with lust and blew a load up her bum.

My crumbling cock slipped out and we lay side by side like train-wreck victims, before a thick veil of panic and abhorrence descended on us. I was immobilised by it; Joanne rose first. At this point all I'm thinking about is Fiona, then Bisto, who was probably no long off the Aberdeen train. I'm eaten up with fear and self-loathing, facing the repercussions of what I've just done. Joanne sat with her knees up to her chest for a bit, then pulled on her bra, pants and top. Then her tights went on and she was lacing up her Docs. In a daze, I was resolving I'd pack in uni, and never go back, thinking of skag, skag, skag; I needed it now more than ever. I started to recover my clothes and get dressed. Joanne barely looked at me, she just stood up and said, 'Ah'm gaunny go,' and she walked away without a glance back. And I sank even further into the mess of my own soul, when I realised that it *wasn't shame on her part; it dawned on me that she wanted nothing from me that she hadn't already had.*

FIONA. . .

I tried to get a grip.

FIONA. . .

I'd cut out my heart and tear it into chunks like a loaf of bread, and feed them to the ducks, just to be with her again.

KILLING MYSELF AS I WRITE THIS SHITE.

It was just sex. Fiona and I had never made any declarations, any arrangements as to what kind of life we'd have.

So why did I feel so fucking low?

Why did I feel like I'd done something terrible, wrecked something utterly precious, for nothing at all?

And haunted by Joanne's harsh stare, her desolate, twisted mouth, I lurched down the hill to Leith and a death in the family.

You think you know somebody. Loyal Mark Renton, who stuck by his wee school girlfriend, that sulky Hazel hoor, who can crush a party vibe wi the downturn ay one petted lip. Then he bored every cunt stupid about how much he loved that Fiona ride. All those tiresome, non-sexist male pretensions, and it turns oot he's a predatory grotbag like the rest ay us. The thing is, such a minor little *contretemps* is commonplace for most chappies, but he'll agonise over it for years like the wimp he is. And not even one mention of me, the cunt! His sexual guru! He'd never have had the confidence tae nail anything if it hudnae been for hinging aboot wi me! That time with slutty Tina Haig, in the park, ah practically had tae take his cock ootay his troosers and physically push it up her fanny for him! Like cleaning a toilet bowl with a ginger bog-brush. Ah'm almost sad; almost, because the choo-choo's pulling up at the platform.

Ah fight an impulse tae get up tae greet Massima, though ah can see her emerging from the train, stepping oantae the platform with such grace, looking aroond, catching my eye and waving a tight, concerned smile that signals something's up. I hope the Catholic guilt hasnae kicked in tae the extent ah'm gaunny have tae work for ma hole. The seal's been burst so the deed's done. So let's just fuckin well party and repent them aw at once; last ah heard the sin supermarket didnae have an express checkout for fewer items! Massima's eyes are almost freakishly huge, her hair as black as ink, with big crescent brows to match. Ah seem tae go mair for bold features and left-field beauty now. Conventionally pretty blonde lassies like Marianne and Esther are like bland dolls, their faces purely defined by the cosmetics they fuss ower for hours. When they annoyingly take their make-up off *before* going to bed, it feels like fucking a ghost.

Massima appears through the swing doors wearing a short, dark blue gingham cloth dress, like a Ben Sherman ah had yonks ago; with her bare pins, it sets up enough horn to make any self-respecting hippo develop rhinoceros tendencies. — Simon, she greets me in that gargly, almost mechanistic burr that a lot ay Italian lassies have, but there's something no quite right here. Her posture is stiff as she sits down, and there's defo misgivings in those eyes. — I have been so frightened . . . she confesses, then says something in Italian, which ah dinnae get. She gleans from my expression that ah'm scoobied, so she reverts back tae her pidgin English. — I am . . . behind in my time.

Contretemps! Cosmic forces again!

— You mean late? Ah swallow hard. — Your period is *late*?

— Si . . . She looks into my eyes with her glassy lamps.

The key is not to crumble. Keep the heid. You've heard this one before, you'll probably hear it again . . . you have legs, and there are trains. You will never be the sort who passively accepts cards that are unfairly dealt to him . . .

So ah take her hands in mine, and say, — Don't jump to conclusions, babes. Let's get a wee test done . . . a test, so that we know one way or the other. Whatever happens, we'll get through this little *contretemps* together. C'mon, ah look around, — let's get ootay here.

And we leave the bar and the station, taking the rocky road out of town towards the auld farm, making plans as we go. By the time we get to the barn at the back of the farmhouse, where scabby goats graze on the feeble grass, I've reassured her. So much so that the front straps ay that dress slip easily fae her thin shoodirs, and ah push aside the dark curtain ay her tumbling locks to expose that exquisite neck, which was made tae be kissed, vampire-like.

— You will show me Edinburgh, Simon, she gasps under my love bite.

Ah whisper intae her ear as ah work my hands round her back tae skilfully unhook her white bra, marvelling at just how brown those paps are, — You just try stopping me, babes, you just try stopping me, ah tell her, but you know what? Ah'm not thinking of church, bambinos and watching her bloat and develop kitchen expertise and settle for the Saturday-morning pumping that will allow me to flirt with the town lovelies; no no no, she is mistaking Simone for someone else. My overt concerns might be the almost unfeasibly magnificent curve ay her waist as it cuts intae her hip, but pulsing away in the background is an image ay me on that local train tae Napoli, then heading on to Turin, Paris, London and Edinburgh. — Alone, my darling, always alone, ah murmur in a deep croak, as ah slide my hands down her waist and intae her underpants. — If there is life inside you, Catholic Princess, head north where some cold-blooded Nazi abortionist will scrape it out, or pay the price of living in a papist backwater . . . She gasps something back, and thank fuck she doesnae ken what ah'm on about, because eftir this ah'm fucking right off hame; a tough sell tae the Holy Papa, this yin, but these are my mountains, and this is my glen. Hail, Caledonia!

Chasing Brown

Ah'm sortay keepin ma heid doon cause ah'm still feelin Shakin Stevens eftir rehab n that bout in the hoaspital. Ah wis sweatin bad the other night n pure hit the panic button: jist cause ay bein feart that ah've goat that cowie thir aw gittin. At one stage ah couldnae git ma breath; it wis like ah'd forgotten *how* tae breathe. Ah ken ah likesay took the test n they sais ah wis fine, but somethin's no right. They used tae say that it wis just poofs that goat it, no that ah'm sayin poofs deserve it like, but it worries us thit ye kin git it jist fir bangin up wi the Jeremy Beadles n that. So ah wis up maist ay the night, tryin tae git ma breath, listenin tae they cats ootside at the back, fightin n huvin sex. Total relief when the mornin light came in; it meant ah could finally git tae sleep.

Everybody's gittin intae skag nowadays. It used tae be jist a few hip aulder cats like Denny Ross n Sambuca Agnes, then it was the wannabe cool dudes likesay Rents, Sick Boy n moi, whae mibbe goat too enmeshed in the 'fuck youse' rock n roll culture, likesay, ken? Tryin too much tae shock the establishment n that, man. As if they cats ivir gied a toss what schemies did, as long as it nivir bothered thaime. Now it's hit fair Edina's peripheral concrete bastions (as Sick Boy calls thum) wi a vengeance n aw they boys whae'd huv been oan Tennent's lager n laughin at us six months ago ur aw huntin it doon, basically cause thuv goat nowt else tae dae. Johnny Swan's rakin it in, but he's pure para that the polis'll be chappin oan his door soon wi aw they radges floatin aboot.

So ah'm steyin in loads. At least things are likesay better wi muh ma, so that's one good thing. She's ey oan at us tae move back in, but ah kind ay like it up here in Monty Strasse. It's cool tae huv yir ain pad for a bit, the sortay sophisticated man-aboot-toon gig, ken? Rents is still in rehab, but due oot any time, n Sick Boy's back in the mother country. Or the mother's mother country, mair like. This pad's good wi two, but mibbe too much wi three, n jist pure decadence fir one, so ah'll probably relocate back hame whin they cats re-emerge through yon flap. Right now it's pure peachy sittin here, watchin this Stallone movie, but ah cannae sortay git intae the film. Too much violence, man, which is

478

ey a total bummer *pour moi*. Cats like Begbie in the jail, they dae bad stuff in real life, n aw they actors like Stallone jist kid oan thir daein it n git peyed the big dosh. Jist fir pretendin tae be radges like the likes ay Franco or Nelly! So that means thit thaire's nae incentive for a gadge like Franco tae be better, no if every rich Hollywood cat wants tae play at bein thum, likesay.

It's true but, eh?

So ah takes it oot n pits in *The Wizard ay Oz*. Ah ken ah might be a bit too auld n that ah'm no a buftie, but ah could easy watch this movie aw day n ivray day, ken? Then ah gits this totally daft idea that it might be bad luck tae watch the film, cause ay aw the bufties gittin the cowie, n they ey watch *The Wizard ay Oz*. But naw, man, that's jist plain daft; ye cannae be too much ay a superstitious radge. N it's great tae watch it oan ma ain, in peace, n withoot likesay gittin slagged off. Ken?

Ah've goat ma mug ay tea, it's actually a soup bowl ay tea (it's goat a handle like, ah'm no that uncultured!) wi *Souper Hibernian* oan it, and half a pack ay McVitie's chocolate digestive bickies. Pure heaven! Went a bit too crazy oan the dunkin but, n totally broke oaf a bicky which sank tae the bottom ay the sea. Never mind, ah'll reclaim the wreckage once ah've drained that ocean ay hoat, sweet tea. Ah'm totally in the zone, thinkin aboot they wee Munchkin gadges, how the Hollywood studio treated them like second-class citizens, a wee bit like us dole-moles under Thatcher, likesay, when ah hears the key in the loak n somebody comin in the door.

Aw, man . . .

It hus tae be Rents, it cannae be Baxter the landlord, cause Gav Temperley telt us that the perr auld boy was found potted heid in his flat at London Road. Mind you, Sick Boy telt us tae keep a beady oot fir his son, whae's meant tae be a sharp-taloned mouser, but ah've heard neither heid nor hair, ken? But aw, man, that wis such a sin, an auld boy wi aw they hooses n clients that he's landlord fir, dyin oan his ain, n no bein found fir donks. Just call the perr auld cat *Eleanor Baxter* . . . aw the lonely people, right enough.

So ah gits up tae investigate, n ah sees Sick Boy in the hall, n he's goat his bags n hus an *Evening News* under his airm. — Spud.

— Sic— Simon, awright, man?

— Danny boy . . . lost weight, he says, then goes, — Everything hunky-dory?

— Aye, course it is, ah snaps, cause that's what cats huv started sayin when thir really askin ye aboot Aids. Like the cowie, the David Bowie, ken? — What ye daein back? Thoat ye wir in Italia, likesay?

El Sickerino's goat that slightly sheepish look n he goes, — Ehm . . .
village politics. Ye cannae behave thaire like ye do ower here, Danny, he
pats his baws, — ye goat tae watch where ye stick this; the Holy Papa
runs a tighter ship than this slovenly heathen dive. Thaire wis a bit ay heat
and I thought it might be prudent tae exit stage left. He throws the *News*
doon oan the table. — Check this, Claudia Rosenberg is on at the Venue
tonight. I'm on the blag for tickets for us. He pushes past us intae the
front room. — Where's that phone? He sees what's playin oan the vid.
— Phoar, Judy Garland looks well fuckin bangable in that gingham skirt
. . . sorry, mate, did ah disturb ye huvin a crafty wee chug tae yirsel?

— Naw . . . jist watchin the film, likesay . . . ah goes, as Sick Boy
picks up the phone n starts diallin a number.

— Hello . . . can I speak tae Conor? . . . Just tell him it's Simon David
Williamson, he'll ken . . . Sick Boy pits his hand ower the receiver. —
Fuckin wankstain. 'Can ah ask whae's calling . . .' He rolls his eyes. —
Hello! Con! . . . Barry! . . . Not bad, mate, not bad at all. And you? . . .
Excellento! Listen, mucker, time is of the essence, so rudely, *unforgivably*,
I'm cutting tae the chase. What's the chances ay a couple ay buckshee
tickets tae see a certain Dutch chanteuse tonight? . . . Sound as sterling!
You, my man, are a fuckin genius!

N that's him blagged it. Ah'm no really that chuffed, cause ah amnae
diggin crowds these days, it's a pure claustrophobia situ, likesay, ken? But
El Sickerino seems that happy, n it's pure shitey tae bring a cat doon when
they're that keen, ken? Besides it *is* Claudia, the Dutch singer, n she is a
total legend!

Sick Boy goes ower tae one ay his bags and unzips, pillin oot a boatil
ay rid vino, — Git a couple ay glesses washed Danny, it's Chianti time!
A result for the Leith laddies, cause we're gettin backstage tae the eftir-
show perty n aw! C'mon, compadre, jildy!

So ah goes through tae the kitchen but it's likesay thaire's jist one gless
left. He kin huv that yin. Ah wash oot the *Souper Hibernian* bowl wi the
gungy bicky for masel. We kick back wi a couple ay scoops n watch a
bit ay *The Wizard ay Oz*. Then we hoofs it up tae the gig, stoapin en
route at Joe Pearce's for a beer. Ah'm feelin barry, n ah'm no even bothered aboot the crowd when we gits intae the Venue. The great thing aboot
Sick Boy is the wey he takes ower, the dude has that sense ay . . . no sae
much authority as mair *right*, it's bein the Italian bambino n growin up
wi Mama and these sisters that spoiled the gadge, that's whit Rents sais,
n he's spot on, cause it sortay sticks oot a mile. Sound gadge though, Sick
Boy. Can be a bit warlock-wicked aroond the chicks, but it seems tae

work fir him. Ah often wonder if ah treated lassies worse whether they'd like me mair, but ah kin never bring masel tae dae it.

It's mobbed in here, n the thing is tae git past they annoyin pillars. Sick Boy's pushing through the crowd like he owns the place but, n ah'm pure in his slipstream. Thaire's one or two tuts and blank looks, but he's wearin that big disarming smile, n we soon hit the front. No long eftir, a four-piece band – guitar, bass, drum n keyboards – come oantae the stage n go intae this instrumental. This cool chick standin beside us is gaun: — CLAUDIA! CLAUDIA! WE LOVE YOU! and, sure enough, *The Woman* comes oan, dressed in gothic black, tae big cheers.

Ah ken it's no right tae say it, but ah'm sortay disappointed, cause ah ey think ay Claudia Rosenberg as lookin like that curly-mopped, willowy, supermodel catgirl oan the cover ay *Street Sirens*, but ah suppose that that wis donks ago, ken? This vintage kinday looks like somebody's ma. Well, ah suppose she is somebody's ma, but ken, like a middle-aged Leith wifie up at the bingo. She's aw bloated and haggard, n she chain-smokes oan the stage. The lassie beside me screams oot again, — WE LOVE YOU, CLAUDIA! n Claudia hears this, n gies the crowd a frosty, sour look n launches intae 'They Never Stay'. Her voice is as barry and doomy as ever but, n the band's duck's-chuff tight, so we're aw gaun radio rental.

Sick Boy cannae help bein a bad cat though, n he goes tae us, — Look at that ol' Nazi turkeyneck. Tae think she was such a honey back in the day!

— She's knockin oan but, man, n she's no a Nazi, she's a four-by-two, ah shouts.

— She's Dutch, and they're just maritime Germans, he scoffs. — Fuck North Europe, South Europe rules, he bellows, and smiles at the cute catgirl beside me.

— But she's nae spring chicken, so ye cannae expect her tae look the same as she did in the glory days, ah persist.

— That's skag-scrag, that, he points tae the stage, — it's no normal ageing. We got off the merry-go-round at the right time, Danny boy.

— Too right, ah goes. Didnae want tae say mair, cause it's no like ah huv goat oaf it, as such. Jist tryin no tae git a *proper* habit again, likesay. Ah heard that skag wis meant tae keep ye lookin younger, but ah cannae be ersed debatin it wi Sick Boy, cause ah'm well intae this gig. Ah really like that song 'My Soul Has Died Again'. It's aboot feelin shite, n ah kin sortay relate tae that. She goes through the best ay her back catalogue and thaire's a barry encore wi 'A Child to Bury' and a totally sublime version ay 'The Nightwatchman's Cold Touch'.

Eftir, Sick Boy says, — Let's get backstage. How jealous will Renton be?

Ah'm thinkin: aye, a bad yin for the Rent Boy tae miss, likesay.

Backstage it's pretty radge, wi maist people gittin turned back by the bouncers, but Sick Boy catches a gadge's eye, n we're straight through intae this room wi tons ay booze n food. There's a couple ay sweet-lookin lassies n Sick Boy's right ower tae them. Ah pure wish thit ah hud his confidence roond the chicks; disnae happen but, man, just does not happen. Eftir a bit, the band come in, and start chattin n sittin doon, n ah suddenly realise that Claudia's sittin right next tae me! She's goat a plastic gless ay spirit in her hand.

Ah want tae say, 'Barry gig,' but ah go pure shy n jist smile aw nervous, likesay. Then she speaks tae us, pure sais, — So vot do zay call you? in that harsh, sing-songy voice. Her breath really stinks ay fags. Ah mean, everybody's does likesay, well, no Rents, cause he doesnae smoke, or Tommy, cause he hardly does, but normal people likes. Her breath is as smoky as a certain Mr Robinson, but.

— Eh . . . Danny . . .

— I like yoooo . . . she says, grinning, and ye kin see that her teeth are in a bad wey, man, aw yellaw, n some ay thum broken. A bit like mine, ah suppose. — Vot do you do for a living, Dah-nee?

— Ah'm sortay on the dole, likesay unemployed.

Her elbay goes right intae ma side; man, she's as radge as Begbie! — I know vot ze dole is. You are vun of Maggie's millions, yes?

— That's pure it, man. Cast oan the scrapheap by Thatcherism, likesay.

She looks aroond n bends in close tae ma ear. — I think I should take you back vis me to my hotel room, where we can drink proper brandy. She huds the plastic beaker up intae the light n screws up her face. — Real brandy. Vood you like that, Dah-nee?

— Eh, aye . . . barry! ah goes. — Ah'll, eh, jist tell ma mate thit we're headin oaf.

She pills this soor pus n looks ower tae Sick Boy, whae's in his element wi they two birds, him n the guitarist boy fae the band. Ah see her sortay snort, n it's barry that she's no as impressed by him n she is by me, but! So ah goes ower tae him n pills um aside. — Eh, ah bit ay a result, catboy. Claudia wants us tae go back wi her. Ah'm no really sure what tae dae, but.

He looks ower tae her, she's talking tae this lassie, then back tae me. — She's a fuckin auld boiler but you've goat tae get in there! Jist think ay the brownie points! How jealous will Renton be! Fuck sake, Iggy's been there! Lennon n aw. And Jagger. And Jim Morrison. You could have *your cock* in the same place as Iggy's has been!

Ah nivir thought aboot it like that, but it wid be a bit ay a feather n the auld cap, likesay. — Too right, catboy. Ye pit it that wey, it's no an opportunity tae be sneezed at, eh.

— Fuckin sure, Sick Boy says, then his expression goes aw tight n he droaps his voice. — Speaking of brownie points, a wee word ay advice: ram it right up her fuckin choc box!

— Eh?

— Fuck her up the erse. Squidgy or hard centres, get them crammed right back up that fuckin shit tube.

That's no very respectful, so ah sais, — Eh . . . ah'm no really intae that sort ay talk, likesay . . .

Sick Boy's big lamps are burnin. He's taken something, probably coke, likes. That guitarist boy was defo dishin stuff oot. — Listen tae me. He pills ma sleeve. — Her sweaty auld pie'll be like the fuckin Grand Canyon. Iggy Pop wrote that song 'Rich Bitch' offay *Metallic KO* aboot her. Mind when he sings about the lassie's cunt being so big you could drive through it in a truck? Well, that was reputedly aboot her. And that was Iggy, who's hung like a donkey, and this wis back in the seventies, before she'd hud a score ay orphaned bairns, a prolapsed womb and a hysterectomy. Unless yir packin the Eiffel Tower in they troosers, you willnae even touch the fuckin sides. So grease up that pole and gie her it tight up the chestnut stash, he sortay commands, stickin a packet in ma jaykit pocket.

— What . . . ah've goat spunk bags, ah tell um. Wi Aids n that, man, it likesay makes sense tae cairry thum. Nivir ken whae ye might meet, eh.

— Lube. Slather that pole, bend her legs back in the missionary, aim low, n it'll go up there like a treat. Just persevere. She'll love it. European lassies dig that sort ay action. In Italy we use it tae avoid the bambinos and keep sweet wi the Holy Papa in Rome. You're Irish, you should ken aw they moves! Pin the starfish wi that auld shillelagh ay yours n yi'll no ken whether she's talkin double Dutch, or speakin in tongues, ya cunt!

— Right . . .

So ah heads back ower tae Claudia, whae's rising fae the chair, her heid tossed back in the air, n she leaves the room. Ah follow her, n as a go, ah look back tae see Sick Boy giein me the thumbs up, and the guitarist gadge makin a throat-cuttin gesture. Ah turns away. This wee gadgie's wi Claudia, and ah'm a bit worried thit he might be in the threesome, ye ken how liberal the Dutch kin be, aw permissive n that, but ah realise thit he's jist the driver. We go ootside n he climbs intae the front ay the car, n her n me are in the back. The cute lassie that was next tae me is waitin ootside, n shouts at Claudia, — WE LOVE YOU!

Ah pure widnae huv minded takin her along wi us, but Claudia just says, — Fuck off, you moron, as we pull away. We're bound for the Caley Hotel. Man, ah'm as nervous as fuck now, so ah starts totally gabbin tons, tellin her aboot the gig n sayin that ah loved the new version ay 'The Nightwatchman,' wi Darren Foster's guitar work, n she jist pits a hand ower ma mooth n goes, — Shhh. I do not like it when you are for talking so much.

So ah says nowt, but we're soon at the Caley, n the doorman opens the car n we git oot and intae the hotel. We baith look like jakeys but the staff cats ur bein ultra sooky cause ay it bein her. Ah could pure tell ah would never huv goat sae far acroas this luxurious lobby on ma ain. Big gless chandeliers n pillars n velvet n a thick rug under yir feet . . . wi walk under a big alcove tae the lift . . . aw, man . . .

So we gits intae the lift n up tae the room. It's a cracker n aw; ye could likesay fit two Kirkgate flats intae one ay they gaffs. Thaire's a bathroom that's ginormous, n she flops oantae the big four-poster kip, n pats the space beside her. Ah'm shitein it, cause ah eywis ah'm wi lassies, n ah widnae say this tae the boys, cause ah've jist done it wi three lassies before. Steyin cool's the art, man, but once that adrenalin sets in, that tight, jittery tension, it'll be pure no go, man, cause ah feel the nerves knittin inside us. Pure shy wi chicks ah fancy, that's ma downfall, ken? N ah dinnae fancy Claudia much tae be honest, cause she's gittin oot ay her tight jeans, n she's goat big flabby thighs, n ah'm lookin at her rows ay chin n ah'm thinkin ay that cover ay *Street Sirens* again, n askin: is this really Claudia Rosenberg?

Now she's got some stuff oot, and man, she's totally chasin some skag wi a foil pipe. Her lungs fill up wi smoke n she goes aw that dozy wey. She offers us the pipe n ah ken ah'm tryin tae be cleanish now, but ah'm that nervous ah take a wee bit, n start coughin, makin her laugh aw loud, but ah dinnae care cause ah'm gaun aw swoony n heavy, n it's pure taken the edge offay the fear, man.

Barry.

Nae nerves at aw now.

So ah start slippin oot ay ma clathes, n ah moves next tae her oan the big bed. She turns her fat wifie face tae mine. — You are a nice boy, she says, runnin her hands ower ma nipples like it wis me thit sort ay hud the tits, likes.

— Ah've . . . eywis . . . kinday . . . admired your . . .

— Shh . . . Again it's the finger ower ma mooth, n her other hand goes doon inside the front ay ma pants, which ah kept oan. Man, it's been that long that even wi that bit ay skag, ah'm still as hard as fuck. — You have a very nice long penis. Very long. Not so wide, but very, very long!

Not so wide . . .

Ah'm pure thinkin aboot what Sick Boy said n ah goes tae pit oan the flunky n opens the lube n rubs it doon the shaft ay ma cock. She's taken oaf her pants n thaire's a leafy smell, it's strong, but ah dinnae say nowt. It's like ye kin tell she's pure chronic oan the skag n sortay gied up a wee bit oan the personal hygiene, ken? Ah wis totally the same before rehab. But it sortay gets us wonderin aboot Janis Joplin or Billie Holiday, what they would've been like in the minge department, ken?

So this Claudia starts tae boom, — Give it to me! Give it to me!

— Awright . . . So ah mounts her, gits in position n pushes they fat legs back, n goes in low against her ersehole, n pushes . . .

Her eyes bulge oot n her body stiffens. — VOT ARE YOU DOING?!

— Ah'm . . . sortay tryin tae . . . gie ye it up the bum, likesay, ah tells her.

Well, man, she pure pushes us oaf her n grabs us by the hair. — GET AWAY FROM ME! GET OUT!

Ah pulls away but ma scalp's pure burnin n she's gone radge, chasin us in slow motion roond the bed, cause we're baith wasted, me in the buff, her naked fae the waist doon but wi a black T-shirt still oan, n ah try n grab ma troosers n miss, n ah'm gaun, — Ah'm sorry . . . ah'm sorry . . . calm doon!

— You think because I am now old you can use me like a toilet?!

— Naw . . . ah jist thoat –

She lunges at us and batters me above the eye wi her fist. — GET OUT! she roars, n ah'm tellin her thit ah'm gaun, jist tae lit us git ma clathes, but she's punchin n kickin us n ah'm movin across the room, ah cannae hit her back cause she's a woman, so ah goes tae lock masel in that big bathroom till she's calmed doon. — Take mair skag . . . ah goes. But she's still shoutin fir us tae go, so ah opens the door, but wi her hasslin us it's the wrong door n it goes oot intae the hotel corridor, n she shoves us through it n slams it shut behind us!

Awww, maaaannnn . . .

Ah'm lookin aroond the deserted corridor, beggin, bangin oan the heavy door, pleadin wi her tae fling oot ma clathes at least, n ah hear her scream fae behind it, — All of your stupid clothes are going out of my vindow!

485

— NAW! DINNAE! ah goes, batterin the door, but a boy fae the next room comes oot n looks at us, n ah goes, — Yuv goat tae help us, ah need a len ay –

The gadge just pulls back intae the room n slams the door shut. Ah looks doon the hall, n aw ah kin think tae dae is tae pick up the metal plate covers ay some cat's room-service trays n pit one in front ay ma nuts n the other yin behind ma erse. Ah'm headin doon the corridor n the lift clicks open n a couple git oot n start gigglin. Ah gits in, but it stops at the next flair n a woman n her young son go tae get oan, then stoap. — That man's not got any clothes on, the bairn says, and his posh ma pills him away. Ah hit the button n the lift goes doon n opens up in the busy lobby.

Ah'm totally done for, man, what am ah gaunny say tae the polis? An auld Dutch singer flung ma clathes oot the windae cause ah tried tae stick ma cock up her erse? Ah'll pure git the jail! So ah jist goes fir it, man, totally bolts across the reception hall, no lookin at anybody, keepin the tin covers held close, n ah kin hear aw the gasps as ah git tae the door.

The doorman boy wi the top hat says, — These dish covers are hotel property!

But ah'm ootside, n ah sees ma jaykit lyin in the wet, oan the pavement by the taxi rank, n thaire's ma Fred Perry in the gutter . . . but whaire's ma jeans? . . . Aw, man; ah looks up n the keks are caught roond the flagpole, but thir gaunny come doon any second . . . Ah hears shriekin lassies' laughter comin fae the boozer across the lane . . . it's the Rutland, man . . . worst place ah kin be . . . but here come the keks . . . there's only one trainer, so ah leave them n drop the dish covers n bundle the clathes up. The doorman, whae's been shoutin aboot polis, comes eftir us n picks up the dish covers, n ah'm runnin bare-ersed doon the side street, clathes bunched in front ay us. One cabbie, whae's been watchin n laughin, shouts some encouragement fae his taxi, as ah bounds doon Rutland Street, doon a flight ay stairs intae a mingin auld basement. Ah'm no bothered but; ah pill masel intae the troosers, ma feet cauld n wet oan the rain-soaked, mucky groond cause its been pishin doon, n ah gits ma shirt n jaykit oan. When ah git back up tae street level, ah cannae face gaun past the Caley or the Slutland tae the bus stoap, so ah heads doon the street taewards Rutland Square. Ma bare feet are freezin as ah walk past aw they snobby solicitors' buildins and posh offices oan the Georgian square wi its big pillars, n ah'm gled that it's late n naebody's aroond. Ma paws are black wi the dirt, and cauld and sair, n ah'm gaunny git pneumonia here n be back in yon hoapsital, ah kin jist pure tell. Ah'm jist lookin at the cracks oan the pavement, mumblin that auld playgroond rhyme:

Stand oan a line n brek yir spine
Stand oan a crack n brek yir back.

Never goat the difference between the two cause yir snookered either wey, but mibbe that's what it's aboot; sortay pure life in Scotland, likesay. Ah gits roond the corner tae Shandwick Place n ah cross ower the road at the Quaich Bar n stand at the bus stoap ootside that big church, St Dodes, people lookin at ma bare feet like ah'm some kind ay community-care radge. A 12 bus comes and thank God that ah've got enough change in ma poakit, that it never fell oot when she flung the keks oot the windae. The bus stoaps n ah pit ma dosh in the slot. The driver looks doon at ma feet. — Bad night?
    — Aye.
N as ah'm sittin oan the bus, ah git tae thinkin, mibbe it's sortay karma. Mibbe God never intended for birds' erses tae be used fir that sortay thing. *In Through the Out Door* as Zeppelin might huv pit it. So ah gits back doon tae Monty Strasse n up the stair, n intae the hoose. Sick Boy, they nice burds fae backstage at the gig n the guitarist boy ur there, chasin broon. Rents is thaire n aw; he looks bombed n gies us a lazy wave. He's wi Hazel, whae isnae touchin the gear n doesnae look awfay happy.
    Sick Boy's pittin some mair skag oan the foil. — You're back early, superstud. Still, ah kin see why ye didnae want tae stey the night! Gory details then, cunt, he snaps.
    — Heard ye goat a result . . . Mark slurs, laughin softly.
    — Hi, man . . . how wis rehab?
    — Ye see it aw, he shrugs, lookin aw apologetically tae Hazel, whae turns away.
    — Not a kisser n teller, eh? Ah admire that. Shows class in a man, Sick Boy says, comin up tae me wi the foil pipe. — Have some ay this, buddy. Whaire's yir fuckin shoes, ya radge?
    — Long story, man, ah goes, takin the pipe, cause ah'm no really in the mood tae refuse anything, ken?

In Business

It had been a long, disquieting drive, visibility hampered by the lashing rain against his windscreen. Now fatigue hit him, rapid and unforeseen; his awareness that the thump and swish of the rubber wipers was having a lulling, heavy-eyed effect only became apparent when a series of yawns tore through him. He shook his head, blinked rapidly, and tightened his grip on the wheel. A road sign, flashing luminous green under his headlights, told him he was close to his destination.

Russell Birch had never been to Southend before, and he'd heard it could get lively, but as he came into the Essex seaside town, it was evident that the bad weather had dampened weekend festivities. As he left the A13, drove past the railway station and down onto the Western Esplanade, the world's largest pier still flashed its attractions, but it was almost deserted. It seemed that people had largely reached where they wanted to go and had holed up in the pub or club of their choice. Only a few brave, underdressed revellers, lashed by rain, scurried down the streets, stoically heading for another port of call.

Russell was driving slowly along the esplanade, looking for his turn-off, stopping at some lights, when two girls, like saturated tea bags hoisted from a pot, suddenly swung from the wet darkness out in front of him, forcing him to brake. — Giz a lift, one shouted, her bottle-blonde hair cascading down her face in soaked ringlets. He was almost tempted; had he not been in a hurry or carrying his disturbing cargo, he probably would have. Instead, he moved on, forcing them over to the side in their heels. — You cunt, he heard one of them screech into the grim night, as he sped away from them.

It took him a while to find the rendezvous point. It was a little out of town, a rather prim alehouse with the rustic pretensions characterising many such places in suburban England. He turned into a small car park at the back of the pub, surrounded by trellis fencing which struggled to hold back the encroaching hedges and trees of the neighbouring gardens. A few lights cut through the almost pitch blackness, showing him only one other car, a black BMW. Russell parked a discreet distance from it.

It had to be them, and they would be inside. He opened the door and stepped out into the rain, aware that his hands were shaking.

Would, these men he was preparing to meet be hardened criminals or, more likely, just dogsbodies like him, burdened with someone fearsome on their backs, compelling them to do this, just as he was with the ex-brother-in-law?

He walked into the pub via the rear doors, going through a narrow conservatory and coming into a large, low-ceilinged lounge bar. Although comfortably shy of six foot, Russell still had to duck to avoid some over-head beams. The pub was practically deserted. Even with the monstrously inclement weather, it seemed inconceivable that a bar could survive such minimal trade on a weekend night. The only other people he could see were two men, standing by a roaring fire, and a barman engrossed in the mounted television, who, in profile, looked the double of the actor who played Arthur in *On the Buses*.

Russell decided not to approach or acknowledge the men by the big stone fireplace straight away. It might be bad form, if there was any eti-quette in this sort of thing. He assumed there would be; everything else had its codes, so why should this business be different?

When the barman turned face on to take his order, the Arthur effect was reduced, but not completely dispelled. Russell ordered a pint of Lon-don Pride, and was disappointed to note the man's north of England accent, rather than Arthur's rasping cockney. He tried to think of the actor's name: nothing came to mind.

The two men were looking over at him. One of them, thin, with a duck's-arse haircut, approached him, moving in a jerky manner. This puppet-like wretch seemed to have been sent by the other man; a portly, menacing figure who smiled at him with gleefully psychotic bonhomie. Russell briefly thought he knew him from somewhere, but realised it was just the grin. It belonged to every thug and bully he'd ever met.

Neither of them seemed to be carrying anything, making him glad he'd left his own package in the car boot. It would be sensible to make this transaction outside, in the dark, secluded car park. He began to feel a bit pleased with himself, growing in confidence as the first man drew alongside him.

— How d'ya do, the man lisped, in a soft but metallic voice. His accent was slightly camp, and the sickly weakness he exuded bolstered Russell's morale further.

— Not bad. Yourself?

— Can't complain. You come far?

— Edinburgh.

The man's face twitched slightly in register. It was evidently some test, as meagre as it was. The man introduced himself as Marriott, making Russell immediately think of Steve Marriott from the Small Faces, a band he'd always liked. — Join us for a drink.

He could see no good reason, after that drive, not to do so. The fire was inviting, though on Russell's approach, the other man gave out mixed signals. He didn't extend his hand, merely acknowledged Russell with a mean smile, then moved up to the bar. He returned with three large whiskies. — Scotch. Scotch for a Scotchman, he observed, seeming pleased with himself as he settled them down on the mantelpiece.

Russell could have done with a brandy, but as he sipped the amber fluid, realised it was a decent malt, the smoky, peaty aroma perhaps indicating Islay. It warmed him, like the fire that roasted at his legs. His pint sat on the bar; he wasn't bothered about it. — Cheers.

The stocky man finally introduced himself as Gal. — Some say it ain't professional, this socialising lark, but I don't agree. It's nice to put a face to a name. Ya gotta know who yer dealing with. You need trust in this business. A covert menace bubbled under the surface of his tone. His lively tongue didn't match his deep-set eyes, slanted at the extremity of the brows as if to suggest inbreeding. Being in his very presence caused Russell to silently curse his ex-brother-in-law, his stupid sister and his own weakness, for once again putting him in this situation. He knew his parents now regarded him as a loser like Kristen, rather than a mover and shaker like Alexander. But, and Russell gained succour from the notion, they didn't know what he did. The other week he'd been driving up Leith Walk and he'd seen that young girl his brother was fucking, heading up into town. She'd looked different; scruffy, damaged, an obvious junky, like this Marriott character. Perhaps that was curse of his family: fatally drawn to lowlife.

After the relatively effusive welcome, Marriott now seemed to be cold-shouldering him, like he'd decided Russell wasn't important enough to try and keep on the good side of. Then he suddenly announced, — I ain't all that keen on people from Edinburgh. I had a bad experience with some people from Edinburgh once.

Russell looked at him, unsure of how to respond, but Gal was definitely the one calling the shots, and he gazed coldly at Marriott. — We're talking about Seeker. He's a friend of mine.

Marriott fell silent.

Gal kept his stare trained on him for a couple of seconds, before turning to Russell, the smile of genial menace back on his face. — You know The Man then?

— He's my brother-in-law, Russell said. It seemed sensible to omit the 'ex'.

Gal looked him up and down, seeming disappointed, certainly in Russell, and perhaps also, he fancied, in Seeker. — You poor sod.

Russell kept his face neutral, feeling that either a collusive smile or disapproving frown might be taken the wrong way.

— Anyway, Gal went on impatiently, — we can't sit here jawing all night. Let's get it over with, and he downed his whisky in a single gulp that strong-armed the others into doing the same. Russell noted that Marriott was struggling, his hand shaking, but Gal's raptorial leer wouldn't leave him till he'd finished. — That's good Scotch, he said accusingly to his associate, who was painfully trying to fight back a gagging reflex.

The walk outside to the car park was torturous. Russell felt a creeping dread that the next thing would be a skull-splitting blow to the back of his head, the prelude to him being bundled into the boot of the BMW like a sack of coal. He'd lie briefly alongside the package in the holdall that had been gift-wrapped in birthday paper (a touch he'd almost felt moved to comment to Seeker about, but had resisted), en route to the bleak wasteland that would be his final resting place. Or perhaps he'd have Seeker's money taken from him with force, and have to explain it all. Every heartbeat-measuring step across the dark, barren parking area seemed part of a doomed procession to the grave.

But Gal just casually went to his car, returning with a box, wrapped up in identical gift paper, and made the exchange. Russell wasn't going to open it up and check the contents; there could have been anything in either of the packages. Both parties behind this transaction evidently held each other in a high degree of confidence.

— Safely home now, but don't spare the horses. I hear ya got a lot of customers waiting for ya back in Edinburgh, Gal smiled again, now reminding Russell of a jaunty travelling salesman, — and tell Seeker that old Gal said hello. Then he turned to the hapless-looking Marriott. It was soul-destroying to Russell how much he empathised with this broken figure, another fellow stooge who had overstepped the mark. — Right, you cunt, let's farking move.

Russell walked stiffly to his car with the package, leaving it on the passenger seat. He watched the BMW pull off and roll out of the car park. His hands were wet on the wheel and trembling, but elation quickly took over him. It was finished. He'd done it. It was a triumph. Now

Seeker really owed him, surely. He'd get his cut and they would be all square.

He started the car up and drove out of the car park, heading away from town, north towards Cambridgeshire. He stopped at an old phone box, outside a garage it pre-dated. He put the package in the boot, lest a potentially fatal temptation to examine its contents grip him.

On the Buses.

The star was obviously Reg Varney. Stan. Who played his sidekick, Jack? Blakey, that bus inspector, that actor's name was Stephen somebody, he was sure of it. And Olive, Arthur's wife, was played by Anna Karen. This stuck in his mind, unusual in that it was two female first names. He dialled a number on the old, black Bakelite phone, a device from another era, grimly hanging on to its tenuous commission. His ex-brother-in-law picked up. — Aye?

— It's me. It all went okay. I mean, I never checked what was in it, I just picked up the package, like you said.

There was an unnerving silence on the other end of the line.

— Eh, Gal sends his regards.

— Fuck Gal. Get back up here, right now, wi that gear.

He spoke as if Russell was just down the street instead of over four hundred miles away. He was exhausted; he had to rest. It was dangerous, he'd be sure to draw police attention in this condition . . . — Look, I'm knackered. If I get pulled over or in an accident, it isn't going to do either of us any good, he protested.

— Just get the fuck back up here now. Or thi'll be an accident awright. Dinnae make us repeat masel again.

The alcohol burning in his gut and brain, Russell wanted to shout, 'Fuck you! Fuck you, ya fucking ignorant bag ay shite!' But it somehow came out as, — Okay, I'll be as quick as I can, as the line went dead, and in tears of exasperation, Russell Birch contemplated the exhausting drive back up to Edinburgh. As he rested the phone down on the cradle, the name of the actor who'd played Arthur in *On the Buses* tauntingly popped into his head.

Junk Dilemmas No. 4

*A*h *know that ah'm the one. Ah can take these circumstances and transcend them. Ah ken this because no only can ah conceptualise everything, ah can also feel it in my fibre, emotionally. Emotional and rational intelligence: ah can dae that shite. Ah'm no a fuckin junky, ah'm just playin at it. Real junkies are mugs like Swanney or Dennis Ross, or even dirty wee Matty Connell. Mingers whae've been intae it since the year dot. Tom's right, it's a phase, and ah'm jist a young gadge, fuckin aboot. Ah will grow oot ay it.*

Ah'll be okay.

Ah'm too brainy, too fuckin clued-up tae faw intae that sort ay trap. It sounds arrogant, aye, but it's fuckin true. Ah ken that a certain kind ay bird fancies me and that ah can — if ah choose tae try hard enough — make other types be bothered.

This shite is nothing tae me. Ah ken everybody says that; that's the allure, aye, but in ma case it's true, cause ah'm the real deal. Ah can fuckin well dae this and dae it easy. Ah can stop aw this at any time, through the sheer fuckin exercise ay my will.

Just end it.

But no right now.

Soft Cell

The cunt tried tae say thit he wis jist inside fir a fuckin traffic offence, bit ye ken they fuckers, they lie through thair fuckin teeth cause thir no gaunny fuckin well turn roond n say thit it wis fir noncin a fuckin bairn. Ken what they'd fuckin well git, the cunts. Bit thaire's eywis weys n means ay findin oot aboot they cunts, fuckin surein thaire is. N ah goat the info fae a fuckin reliable source, a real fuckin mate. It wisnae jist jail gossip. Ah dinnae pey any fuckin heed tae yon shite.

N ah wisnae the only cunt thit thought he wis fuckin well dodgy; whin ah fuckin telt that wee fuckin Weedgie cunt, Albo, thit he wis sharing a cell wi a nonce, he fuckin well set it right up fir us, quick style. Aye, naebody took that much fuckin convincin aboot that cunt. Tae me that fuckin well tells ye somethin right away, fuckin right it does.

It wis easy. We'd arranged it wi the screws thit they'd turn a blind eye, they fuckin well hate nonces n aw. So ah slips intae Albo's cell eftir dinner, n sees the Beast jist sittin thaire oan that fuckin bunk readin a book; cunt looked as plausible as fuck. Well, he wisnae foolin me, fuckin well tell ye that fir nowt. N ah kent awright, cause it wis Rents thit telt us aboot the cunt, n Rents widnae make up a fuckin tale like that, he's no that sort ay a gadge.

So ah says tae this cunt, 'So yir in here fir a traffic offence, aye?' N he looks up n goes, 'What? What d'ye want . . . what is this?' his face aw that wey cunts look as if thir gaunny fuckin well try n catch flies in thir mooths, n he pits his fuckin book doon. Ah lits um stand up n ah goes, 'Tamperin wi fuckin bairns, yir ain wee lassie n aw,' n rams the nut oan um. Goat the cunt a fuckin beauty; ah hears the bone crack n that squeal like ye kin imagine a fuckin pig must make whin it gits its fuckin throat slit in the slaughterhoose. Well, ah wanted tae damage the cunt, tae slash his fuckin chops n carve up his fuckin noncey coupon, but withoot a chib ah jist hud tae stomp n stomp at that stoat heid, hearin the cunt still squealin, but then the noise changin intae a soft groan as he passed right oot. Ah took a pish oan the cunt, then ah felt bad aboot perr Albo's fuckin cell so ah sais tae him oan the wey oot, cunt's only went n pished hissel but, eh.

So that wis me fuckin well chuffed; ma good deed fir the day, giein a bairn-shaggin cunt a dose ay thair ain medicine. It wis only later oan thit ah fuckin well found oot thit the cunt's name wis *Albert* McLeod, no *Arthur* McLeod, whae wis the cunt that Rents meant, but whae seemingly goat huckled the other month by some wide cunt n sent up tae Peterheid nick for his ain safety.

So, ah suppose, well, aye, ah fuckin well goat the wrong fuckin gadge but, eh. It wis an easy mistake tae make wi McLeod bein a common enough fuckin name n that. But that cunt ah done, ah mean, the radge jist *looked* like a fuckin short-eyes n aw, hud stoat written aw ower um. But whin ah git oot ah'll tell Rents thit ah battered the wrong gadge. Still, every cunt makes mistakes n at least wi'll aw be able tae sit doon wi a fuckin peeve n huv a good laugh aboot it later oan but, eh.

Notes on an Epidemic 7

Lothian Health Board
Private and Confidential
Instances of Reported HIV+ Cases in March

Alasdair Baird, 28, Edinburgh North, teacher of English, father of one, intravenous drug use.

Christopher Ballantyne, 20, Edinburgh North, unemployed furniture maker, intravenous drug use.

Michelle Ballantyne, 18, Edinburgh North, hairdressing apprentice, intravenous drug use.

Sean Ballantyne, 23, Edinburgh North, unemployed, former British Army solider, father of one, intravenous drug use.

Donald Cameron, 26, East Lothian, part-time barman, father of two, intravenous drug use.

Brinsley Collins, 17, Edinburgh North, school student, track and field and rugby player, intravenous drug use.

Matthew Connell, 22, Edinburgh North, unemployed, father of one, intravenous drug use.

Andrew Cuthbertson, 19, Edinburgh North, unemployed, father of one, intravenous drug use.

Bradley Davidson, 17, Edinburgh South, YTS Edinburgh Council, intravenous drug use.

Alex Foulis, 19, Edinburgh North, unemployed, haemophiliac, blood transfusion.

George Frenchard, 20, Edinburgh North, unemployed, intravenous drug use.

Andrew Garner, 23, Edinburgh South, unemployed, intravenous drug use.

Colin Georgeson, 16, Edinburgh North, school student, intravenous drug use.

David Harrower, 26, Edinburgh North, actor, intravenous drug use.

Douglas Hood, 17, West Lothian, YTS bricklayer and building trades, intravenous drug use.

John Hoskins, 30, Edinburgh North, unemployed waiter, intravenous drug use.

Derek Hunter, 42, West Lothian, unemployed merchant seaman, father of four, intravenous drug use.

Nigel Jamieson, 18, Edinburgh South, unemployed, intravenous drug use.

Colin Jefferies, 22, Edinburgh South, clerical officer in GPO and singer/guitarist in rock 'n' roll band, intravenous drug use.

David McLean, 20, Edinburgh North, unemployed, intravenous drug use.

Anna McLennan, 23, Midlothian, state registered nurse, intravenous drug use.

Lillian McNaughton, 22, Edinburgh North, seamstress, intravenous drug use.

Michael McQuail, 28, Edinburgh North, unemployed labourer, father of two, intravenous drug use.

Lewis Manson, 21, Edinburgh North, unemployed, intravenous drug use.

Deborah Marshall, 25, Edinburgh North, primary school teacher, sexual contact with intravenous drug user.

Derek Paisley, 26, Edinburgh North, unemployed engineer, Ferranti's electronics, student on part-time computer programming course, father of two, intravenous drug use.

Greg Rowe, 18, Edinburgh North, YTS carpentry trainee, intravenous drug use.

Scott Samuels, 27, Edinburgh South, karate instructor, unprotected sexual contact with intravenous drug user.

Brian Scott, 19, Edinburgh North, YTS Edinburgh Council Direct Labour Organisation, intravenous drug use.

Kenneth Stirling, 24, Edinburgh South, unemployed, intravenous drug use.

Michael Summer, 20, Edinburgh North, pipe-fitter, intravenous drug use.

George Thake, 22, Edinburgh South, University of Edinburgh accountancy student and Duke of Edinburgh Award recipient, intravenous drug use.

Eric Thewlis, 27, Edinburgh North, unemployed heating and ventilating engineer, intravenous drug use.

Angela Towers, 20, Edinburgh South, retail worker, British Home Stores, route of transmission undisclosed.

Andrew Tremenco, 21, Edinburgh North, BA business studies student at Heriot-Watt University, intravenous drug use.

Norman Vincente, 45, Edinburgh South, wine bar proprietor, father of three, unprotected sexual contact with intravenous drug user.

Susan Woodburn, 20, Edinburgh North, Whisky Bonds worker, mother of one, unprotected sexual contact with intravenous drug user.

Kylie Woodburn, 6 months, Edinburgh North, antibodies through birth.

Keith Yule, 22, Edinburgh North, unemployed bricklayer and amateur drummer, intravenous drug use.

Trainspotting at Gorgie Central

E ven in sleep's domain, Renton sensed the onset of withdrawal, that point where his slumbering body gave notice of the critical imbalance in his junk-deprived cells. Through his fatigue he was experiencing his essence's now unstoppable rise to the surface, from somewhere within the fabric of the mattress, or, deeper still, under the floorboards of the building, buried in the warm, soft earth, coming up, up up, into that wrecked, peeled body.

He'd been dreaming (or was it thinking?) about heroin. About being blissed out, staring at walls, his thoughts slowly ebbing all over the place, like golden syrup spilling from an upturned tin. The sudden realisation of how unconnected those ruminations were was followed by the appearance of that one detested itch: the solitary twinge in a previously relaxed body, graciously satiated by a tranquil night's sleep. Yet to scratch this itch would merely bring more, then the torture would begin in earnest. Still desperately tired, he can't get comfy. The prickle is displaced by a severe cramp; the legs first, then the back. When the shivers arrive he knows for sure that it's not his imagination, the gear is leaving him.

He wakes up in the bed, trembling, next to another body. It's Hazel. — What fuckin time . . . ? he hears his hesitant, croaky voice plead.

His next thought: *we huvnae shagged. No way.* At least that was impossible. For three weeks he's been battering into the gear, having lasted about eight hours since his discharge from St Monans. On two occasions they managed the usual tense, unsatisfying couplings. But that was over a fortnight ago. Since then it's been the 'tap me, fix me, ninety-six me' scenario that he and Sick Boy had come up with in gallows response to the 'wine me, dine me, sixty-nine me' slutty T-shirt that was doing the rounds.

But she's still here. Coming in from time to time, sometimes with food, occasionally more welcome paracetamol. In fleeting awe he looks at her asleep; beautiful, serene, temporarily removed from the source of her haunting.

He smells her hair. It merges into less worthy scents in the bed that he and Sick Boy or Spud often share, feet to head. Considers how Hazel in some ways prefers him as a desexualised junky, no threat to her. Recalling that terrible conversation when she came round the first night he was bombed after rehab; how she'd probably have said nothing if he wasn't.

— Sex isnae good for me. It's no you, or laddies . . . it's just that my dad . . . he used to —

Him hearing, but not wanting to: the information coming from miles away through drug and psychic mufflers. Saying to her repeatedly, — It's okay. I'm sorry . . .

— It's no you. As long as you know that. I've tried tae like it but I cannae. I'm just sayin that cause ah ken you see other lassies.

— Right . . . well, no really, he said, grateful for the out. She made him sound like some sort of stud, like Sick Boy. But he did meet more girls than, say, somebody like poor Spud. At that point he thought of Charlene, her pinched features contrasting with the extravagant generosity of the locks that framed them. Fiona, with that oily patch on her forehead he'd loved, and how she got rid of it when she got rid of him. The way he'd been too scared to accept the love she'd offered him.

A coward and a waster.

— So what happened wi her in Aberdeen? Youse seemed really close.

— Oh, you know . . . drugs, he lied. *A coward and a waster.* — She wisnae intae it. He looked at Hazel's sad, pale green eyes. You'd think they'd be brown, he always thought. Maybe it was her hair, she might have been born with a thick head of brown hair. That sudden thought made him almost physically sick: her mother presenting the baby to the smiling nonce father, who'd perhaps observed, 'She's got lovely brown hair. We should call her Hazel.' Renton felt his throat constrict, and quickly asked her, — Why do you see me, ah mean, keep hangin aboot wi us?

Now he watches the shaft of light laser across her face from between those dark blue curtains that never quite pull together. Her eyes shut, her small, slightly protruding teeth glinting. — I really like ye, Mark, she told him.

— But how *can* you like me, he pressed, pained and confused.

— You're a nice guy. Always were.

This had given Renton cause to contemplate that no matter how shite you felt about yourself, some people would never play the game. He said to her that night, — Sleep here wi me. Ah willnae touch ye.

She knew he meant it.

And they'd lain in bed together most nights since then, the junky and the incest victim, the voluntary and conscripted recruits to the army of the sexually dysfunctional, and helped themselves to sleep. They didn't know if they were in some kind of love. They certainly knew they were gripped by a sort of need.

Renton fills his nostrils. Silvikrin, Vosene or Head & Shoulders? He recalls, in grim shame, how he once tried to encourage her to take heroin. He thought it would be something they could share. She point-blank refused and he was actually quite offended at the time. Not now though. Now he'd give nobody a single thing. There was nothing to give.

He gently strokes her hair, marvelling at how fine it feels. Remembering the first time Hazel approached him; she was in first year, he in second. She'd kept smiling at him in the corridors, playground and street. Then, through a friend in his registration class, she'd slipped him a note:

Mark,
Be my boyfriend.
Hazel xxx

After this, she and her mates would giggle in nervy conspiracy whenever he passed them. His own pals started laughing, and took the pish out of him. People began saying that they were boyfriend and girlfriend; that they were 'going out' together.

Mark n Hazel, up a tree, K-I-S-S-I-N-G . . .

This mortified him; they'd barely spoken. Hazel was a sweet, slight wee lassie with specs, who at thirteen looked aboot nine.

— Fuck the erse of it, he recalled Sick Boy threatening, – or I will.

But the infatuation passed. He didn't see her much again till the end of her second year. She'd changed physically; tits, make-up, cooler specs, ones which set up the horn in him (the contact lenses would come later), had all been acquired, and her legs had achieved that definition at the calves that re-routed the flow of blood from brain to cock. But she'd lost something as well. Gone was the sass, and she didn't seem to want a boyfriend any more. Instead, she wanted a friend. And that was what they'd become. They made tapes for each other, went to gigs, developed an emotional intimacy, while pretending to the outside world that they were conventional girlfriend and boyfriend; eighteenth-birthday parties, twenty-firsts, weddings, funerals, they attended together in a strange closeness and awkward resentment. That fucking animal had wrecked her, his own child. Renton was so glad he'd put that call into Begbie. That stoat would be feeling real pain now.

Renton crawls out the bed. Hazel's started to do little whistle-snores. He grabs his jeans like a bouncer would a renegade, windmilling youth in a disco, pinning them down and interrogating them, addressing each pocket with lunges like blows. The first produces some change, a crumpled fiver and a Hibs fixture list, the second a wrap, which causes his spirits

501

to soar, before he sees that it's not only empty, but licked clean. He looks back to Hazel; now he's too sick to be a friend to anybody. He'll have to go, to find gear.

He pulls himself into the discarded clothes and goes through to the front room to be confronted by the crumpled presence of Sick Boy, shivering under a duvet, an instant visual memo of his own condition. As is his mysterious habit, when denied the bed, he's sleeping on the floor rather than the couch, angled across the ripped beanbag that has scattered its polystyrene beads over the worn brown carpet; they're like maggots spilling from him. In case there has been any doubt, Simon Williamson's eyes instantly flick open into an alert rage, taking in Renton's form for a beat, before demanding, — Call Seeker again!

— It'll be the same fuckin story as last night. Renton picks his overcoat from the back of the door and places its weight around his protesting shoulders. The electric bar fire, obtained following the cutting off of the gas for unpaid bills, has been on all night, chucking out a dry heat into the fusty room. But he's shivering.

— Jist call um!

Sick Boy's words are unnecessary; Renton's nerves are singing the same song more effectively. Ghosting across the room, he picks up the plastic phone and stabs out the number. His astonished relief when Seeker's harsh voice growls in his ear: — Aye?

— Seeker. It's me: Mark. Nowt happenin yet?

The long exhalation down the line; Renton can almost see it rising from the holes in the receiver, scalding his ear. — Look, ah telt ye ah'd phone ye soon as ah kent. Ah'm no fuckin hudin oot oan ye. This is my livelihood. There is nothing at aw in this fuckin toon. Goat that?

— Aye . . . sorry. Jist thought ah'd gie ye a wee tinkle –

— Skreel says Glesgey's the same. Phone who ye like, it's no fuckin go. Ah'll tell ye when ah git some news. Now dinnae bug me, Mark, right?

— Sound. See ye.

The line clicks dead.

It's okay for that cunt, Renton considers; he really has stuck with the programme and stopped using. With the cash he's salted away, he's buying an apartment in Gran Canaria. His plan is to head there from November to March, to avoid the weather's assault on his body. Since leaving rehab, Seeker dismissively describes skag as a fool's game and does his best to make it so; selling well-cut gear to boys for cash and bartering it to lassies for fucks and blow jobs.

One night when Renton shakily traipsed along to his flat in Albert Street to score, he disturbed Molly, rattling around in the kitchen in a vesty top and washed-out knickers, scrambling eggs. Her edgy vivaciousness was gone; scattered into dark places even way beyond those desolate, practically deserted streets. She looked old and worn out, curly hair stretched to a limp frizz by whatever greasy substance was in it, face pale but sweaty; she glanced at him with tombstone eyes, before proffering a faint smile of recognition. He averted his gaze, mindful that if you stare for too long into an abyss, it will reciprocate. Anyway, Seeker's icy smile told him that there was a new sheriff in town. To ensure there was no misunderstanding, he informed Renton that he'd 'had a wee word' with her ex-pimp/dealer boyfriend. Once his fractured cheekbones had healed up, he'd come to work for Seeker.

Seeker was more of a gym-hewn mountain than ever. He squeezed Renton's vanishing biceps and told him he should get off the gear and back onto the weights. Although he'd become a valued customer, Seeker made Renton feel as if he was somehow disappointed in him for being on junk, that he was better than that. — Mark Renton, he smiled, — you're a strange yin. Can never quite figure you oot.

Like everything Seeker said, Renton was aware it carried a barely suppressed element of threat. But this, he supposed, was as close to friendship and respect as it was possible for Seeker to get. Renton declined his offer of some business with Molly, and was relieved that Hazel had refused the gear. He didn't want her around any of them. Her wounds might have been made for skag but would only be deepened by it; he'd strive to keep her away.

Sick Boy stands up, pulling the duvet around him like a cape. Then he falls onto the couch, issuing a miserable plea of despair: — What are we gaunny dae?

— Fuck knows. I'll try Swanney again . . . Renton picks up the phone, dials, hearing nothing but the same empty ring. Replaces the receiver on the cradle.

— We go roond there!

— Okay . . . Hazel's asleep . . .

— Leave her, Sick Boy says, — naebody's gaunny bother her here, and he looks at Renton acerbically. – *Cavoli riscaldati*, or reheated cabbage, as we say in Italy. It never works oot.

— Ta for the advice, he cheerlessly replies, heading through to the bedroom. Hazel's still asleep, though her soft snores have ebbed into silence, and he scratches out a note for her:

Hazel,

Had to go out with Simon on a wee message. Don't know when we'll be back, so see you later.

Thanks for taping all those records for me. It means a lot. You've given me back something precious, that I lost through my own stupidity. I used to think that I loved albums as artefacts, for their gatefold sleeves, the track listings, production notes, artwork, etc. But now I realise that a cassette tape with the tracks written out in your hand with one of your drawings and your wee reviews is what I love owning more than anything.

Love

Mark xxx

PS I really do think that you are the most beautiful person I've ever known.

He drops it on the pillow by her head, and goes back to Sick Boy with a crushed, jagged heart. They're embarking on a quest both recognise as futile, but it seems preferable to doing nothing. They take two Valium each and leave the flat, walking down towards Leith. It's daunting but they find a grim, mute stride, which they don't even break with a giggle or ironic nod as they pass the Bendix.

They go to Alison's flat in Pilrig. She looks terrible; minus her make-up and wearing a long blue dressing gown, her increasingly gaunt features heightened by her hair pinned tightly back, with dark circles under her eyes, Renton has to look twice to ascertain it's actually her. She sniffles, unable to stop the thin trickle of snot running out of one nostril, and is compelled to wipe it on her sleeve. — Got a stinkin cauld, she protests, in response to their cynical, hungry scowls. They request that she call Spud at his mother's, reasoning that neither of them would be a welcome voice should Colleen Murphy pick up. — Danny's fell oot with her again, Alison tells them. — He stayed here on the couch the other night, now he's at Ricky Monaghan's.

They call Ricky's, and Spud picks up the phone. Before Sick Boy can ask, he blurts out, — Simon, any skag? Ah'm seek as a poisoned rat, cat-boy.

— Nup, we're aw in the same boat. Ye hear anything, make sure they ken we're in the frame. Call ye later. He puts the phone down. During the conversation, his eyes have never left Alison. — Are you sure thaire's nowt gaun aroond, he asks her, tones both pointed and pleading.

— Nup. Nowt, she says with a final, vapid shrug.

— Right . . . Sick Boy's lip curls south, and he and Renton depart briskly. Alison's glad to see them go, even Simon, as she'd come within an ace of disclosing her mother's morphine stash. Fuck them all: you never know how long this drought would last for and she craves her dead mother's silver needle, can envision one last drop of maternal blood lodged there sliding into her own hungry veins. *Mum would want me to have it.*

Renton and Sick Boy find themselves once more on the well-worn path towards Tollcross. They head up the Walk and then the Bridges and across the Meadows without exchanging a single word and barely looking at each other. Their silence is a serious pact; they're still at the stage where, with mental effort, they can try and negate the worst of their personal misery. They get to Swanney's and it looks as lifeless as an empty film set.

— What now? Sick Boy says.

— We keep movin till we see something or think ay *something*, or we just lay doon and die like dugs.

Walk on through the wind . . .

Walk on through the rain . . .

Billy and me were bored oan that drizzly early-morning walk, n cauld wi waiting oan wheezy auld Granda. It was farcical. He couldnae dae this any mair. Then, just beyond the tower, he suddenly stopped, standing rigid and sucking in a huge breath. It was as if he was trying to pull the shrapnel lodged inside him towards his core. A strange smile played on his lips, then it was obliterated by a spluttered cough as he keeled over, crumpling in a kind ay slow motion tae the tarmacked esplanade. — Stey here! Billy commanded. — Ah'll get help! He ran off down the prom, talked tae two teenagers who looked aw awkward, then left them, bolting ower the road. He was only going tae the shops tae get somebody tae phone, but at the time I thought he'd just run away, leaving me tae deal wi the embarrassment.

Though your dreams be tossed and blown . . .

So I watched my grandfather die, sometimes glancing oot tae the sea, when the witnessing of that grotesque, bewildering event got too much. Because, as he struggled for air, his florid face burning, his rolling amphibious eyes being squeezed from his skull, I had the sense he'd come from the ocean, was caught ashore with the tide out. Ah wanted to tell them tae get him tae the water, even though it made no real sense. Ah felt the woman before ah saw her, ages with my mum, perhaps a bit younger, comforting me, her bosom muffling the sobs ah hudnae realised ah'd been making, as two men tried to help Granda. But he'd gone.

Walk on . . .

Billy ran back down the prom, glaring at me accusingly like he wanted to batter me, like ah'd failed tae keep Granda Renton alive till the ambulance came. Ah mind that woman wanted me tae go wi her, and ah kind ay wanted tae cause she was nice, but Billy gied her a black look n tugged oan ma hand. But when they took Granda away, he put his airm roond ma shoodir, and then bought us baith a cone, for that silent walk back tae the guest hoose. Ma and Dad and Grandma Renton had gone, but Auntie Alice was there and took care ay us.

Oan the bus gaun back up, while Granny Renton sat in shock, my ma and dad kept lookin at me as ah pit my Shoot *fitba stickers intae their album. Manchester City: Colin Bell, Francis Lee, Mike Summerbee, Phil Beal, Glyn Pardoe, Alan Oakes. Kilmarnock: Gerry Queen, John Gilmour, Eddie Morrison, Tommy McLean, Jim McSherry. — Why does he no say anything, Davie? ah mind ay Ma asking, gurgling doolally Wee Davie in her lap. My dad just sat in a trance, occasionally squeezing his mother's hand. — Shock . . . he'll be fine . . . he croaked out.*

Walk on . . .

They walk for what seems like an age, shivering, dropping coins in phone boxes with spirits rising each time in anticipation, but the same grim message prevails: nothing doing, no room at the inn. Those tired, beaten voices on other end of the line: groaning as if in recognition that Death is already chalking their doors with crosses. Still they walk; walking for the sake of walking, unthinking blood and bone and breath, stripped of volition, walking themselves into inertia, a dullness of intellect, sensibility, hope and consciousness. All calculations purely biological.

Glancing sideways at his reflection in the passing shop windows, Renton is reminded of an orang-utan; arms swinging pendulously like he's wearing lead bracelets, greasy tufts of red hair spiking up through a nest of matted sweat and dirt.

After a while, they realise they're in Gorgie. This part of the city makes them feel like intruders. They seem to smell the Hibernian off you over here, Renton reflects; not just the gadges coming out the bookies and boozers, but the young mothers in trackies wheeling the pushchairs, and strangely, worst of all, the auld wifies with gobs like feline ringpieces, who glower witchlike as they shamble by, sick and paranoid.

Who are these people, these aliens, that we move among in such sadness?

Renton thinks their walking has been aimless, with no pattern. But fragments of information and supposition have been coalescing in his fevered brain, guiding his tired legs. Sick Boy senses it from him, following like a hungry dog in pursuit of a jakey master who still might be able to provide some sort of a meal. They steal down Wheatfield Road into a deathly stillness, which spells H-E-R-O-I-N to him, as Renton scents the same desolate skag reek of Albert Street. — What are we daein here?

He strides on, Sick Boy still following in psycho-puppy mode, sinews bulging in his neck. The grass grows thick and coarse between the cobblestones on the street. Yet the Victorian tenements seem to escape any sun as they head past them, looking over at Tynecastle Stadium towards the back of the Wheatfield shed, recalling derby-day battles of old under its long roof, back in the pre-segregated times. The distillery stands at the bottom of the deathly quiet street, and there's a narrow slip road to the left that snakes under the railway bridge, easily missable, he thinks, if you weren't aware of its presence.

— This is it, Renton says, — this is where they make it.

They shuffle under it, and just a few yards ahead a second railway overpass towers above them. Sandwiched between the two bridges, on the right, a three-storey, Victorian building of red sandstone bears the sign: BLANDFIELD WORKS.

This building is the first part of the pharmaceutical manufacturers, the offices where company sales reps are greeted and enquiries dealt with. The subsequent ones, past the next set of railway tracks, are less welcoming, surrounded by high perimeter fences and topped with razor wire. Renton immediately clocks the plethora of security spy cameras, pointing out at them into the street. He notes that Sick Boy is doing the same, his large protruding eyes, scanning and his fevered brain processing information. Employees mill around, coming and going to and from different shifts.

As they walk, Renton gives voice to his thoughts. — This has tae be where the likes ay Seeker n Swanney got their original skag supply, that fabby white stuff. Seeker obviously put the bite on some poor cunt workin here.

— Yes! It all has tae come fae here, Sick Boy twitches. — Let's phone him again!

Renton disregards his prompt, his heated mind trying to piece things together. Seeker and Swanney would each have some poor sucker on the inside and they'd be getting the boys to take big risks by bringing the shit out. But no longer: their contacts are either in jail, have taken off, or worse. The company had cottoned on to the scam, and increased the security, making it impossible for employees to smuggle gear out of the complex. Now Swanney and Seeker are down the pecking order in a national pyramid that brings in the brown from Afghanistan and Pakistan, instead of being local top dogs selling pure product. Renton looks grimly through the fortified chain fence into the plant. — It's aw in there. The best, purest shit we ever hud, or will ever get. Behind those gates, fences and waws.

507

— So what do we dae? Ask the cunts in thaire tae sort us oot? Sick Boy scorns.

Once again, Renton ignores him, continuing his brisk walk around the site, pressing Sick Boy to string along. The latter's busy eyes follow his friend's sight line, opening a window to the thoughts ticking over in his head.

This cunt can't be fucking serious . . .

But Renton has never been more serious. The logical side of his brain has given way to the imperative of sickness. The strained muscles, the throbbing bones and the shredded nerves keep screaming: YES YES YES . . .

The opium factory. Those railway lines seeming to define the place, one set dividing the plant from the distillery, the other bisecting it. They walk past the employee car park, looking over the big fence to the most startling building in a site made up of many disparate examples of industrial architecture: a large silver box with a multitude of gleaming pipes and tubes spilling out from one side, some of them rising skywards. — That looks like chemical processing taking place in there, Renton says.

— That's goat tae be where they make the fuckin skag!

— Aye . . . but . . . we cannae fuckin brek in!

The next thing that catches Renton's eye is a loading bay, with large plastic box containers piled on top of each other. — Storage. Wonder what the fuck's in they boaxes?

They gape in awe at those receptacles, stacked up behind the barbed-wire fences and security cameras. Just the contents of one of them would last them for such a long, long time. — But ye cannae jist . . . Sick Boy begins in feeble protest.

As they prowl past the adjacent wasteland, which a billboard informs them is designated for a new supermarket, they try to think things through. — Where they make it, n where they store it, Sick Boy ruminates, realising that he's converted. They are sick and there's simply no option.

— First, there's how to get in, Renton nods, — second, how tae get access tae the morphine.

— This plant probably manufactures aw sorts ay pharmaceuticals, no just skag. It could be like looking for a fucking three-figure IQ in Tynecastle, Sick Boy spits. — If only we had inside info!

— Well, we're no gaun tae Swanney or Seeker tae get it, Renton says.

— No way.

Still slowly circumnavigating the edge of the plant, they move round to the busy, submerged Western Approach Road, watching the cars shoot into the city. It was once yet another old railway line, which led to the now defunct Caledonian Station at the West End of Princes Street. *I'm a fucking trainspotter*, Renton thinks, as he looks up and watches a goods train pass overhead. The two lines that go through the plant must be part of the old Edinburgh suburban system, now just used for freight rather than passengers. This part of the line, though, hadn't been made into a public cycle path, nor did it house a new development of flats like most of the old Edinburgh rail network. And the embankments were fortified. Why did the circular south suburban line remain intact while the rest of the local Edinburgh urban railway had been ruthlessly ripped up under the infamous Beeching cuts of the sixties? It had to be the skag plant. They wanted people kept away from it.

— That's the way, Renton says, — we get in through the railway line.

— Aye, it's well barricaded roond here, but they cannae protect the whole fuckin line. We'll find a way. Sick Boy's chin juts out in defiance.

But Sick Boy's confidence instantly releases Renton's inner doubts. — This is too much. We bottled it gaun through customs in Essex wi a couple ay poxy wee packets, now we're gaunny brek intae a fortified plant?

— Aye, we are. Sick Boy looks up into the clear blue sky, and back at the overhead railway lines. — Cause we have tae!

They see no plant entrance or egress from the Western Approach Road, as the sun-glinted cars rush by. Crossing over towards Murrayfield Stadium, which stands imposingly opposite the manufacturing complex, they scramble up a pathway that curls up by the railway embankment. From this elevated vantage the dominant building in the plant is a red-bricked, corrugated-roofed Victorian structure which backs onto the road, with a huge barbed-wire fence on top of a stone perimeter wall; the railway line access is prohibited by a similar barrier. A group of tin-hatted railway workers, standing outside a Portakabin, regard them with suspicion. — Fuck this, we'd better nash, says Sick Boy.

— Stay cool. Leave the talking tae me, Renton says as a man advances towards them.

— What are you wantin?

— Sorry, mate, is this private property?

— Aye, it's the railway's property, the man explains.

— Too bad, Renton says wistfully, looking over at the old part of the plant that backs onto the Western Approach Road. — I'm an artist. There's some fascinating Victorian architecture there, great buildings.

— Aye, the man concedes, seeming to warm to him.

— Would've been great tae dae some sketches. Well, sorry to intrude.

— Nae bother. If ye want tae apply tae the railway's PR at Waverley Station, they'll mibbe sort ye oot wi a pass.

— Great! I'll probably go and do just that. Thanks for your help.

Sick Boy is feeling way too poorly to enjoy Renton's performance. A groan rises from his crushed bowels, his deadened flesh crying for heroin, his brain swollen as he gets a whiff of a rank-rotten stench coming from his own body and clothes. He picks some dried, crusted slime from the corner of his eyes.

He's relieved beyond words when the small talk ends and they move back down the path, onto the road, crossing over to the wasteland, heading back round the perimeter of the plant. Renton stops again, just to look down at the railed space between the Victorian office buildings and the embankment and overhead bridge. That's when he sees it; points it out to Sick Boy.

It's a mundane red-bricked outbuilding, topped with what looks to be a felt roof. It has a small rectangle of a door, painted green. It sits by the detritus of an older building, now a pile of algae, silt-and-weed-covered bricks and rotting boards. They stall to peer through the fence at it, then quickly move on as two suits emerge from the offices, heading to the car park over the road, lost in business-speak. But they know what they're going to do. Getting back down to Gorgie Road, they walk into the city, stopping at Bauermeister's on George IV Bridge to shoplift the Ordinance Survey map covering this segment of inner-city west Edinburgh that now obsesses them.

When they get back to the flat in Montgomery Street, Hazel has gone. Renton says nothing. They've barely settled when there's a timorous knock on the door. They open it to be confronted by Spud and Keezbo, a tearful Laurel and Hardy, ailing and shaky through lack of skag. In the front room, Renton and Sick Boy start to outline their proposition, when there's another sudden, disquieting knock on the door. It's Matty, looking completely destroyed. Renton notes that he hasn't even bothered to try and disguise the receding bits at the side of his hairline by blowing the front central section into a bouffant spread. He smells like an exhumed corpse might, and one side of his face twitches in semi-permanent spasm. He looks sicker than any of them. They glance at each other and decide that they can't leave him out. So Renton continues with the rundown.

— It's mental man, never work, we will dae *big time*, telling ye, and we will dae it *big time*. Tellin ye, no way, man, no way . . . Spud gasps.

— Wey we see it, we've nae choice, Renton shrugs. — Ah've been oantae people in Glesgay, London and Manchester. The polis n customs made a lot ay big seizures lately and thaire's jist nae fuckin broon. It's a proper drought. So it's either take a punt oan this pawkle or dae cauld turkey. It's as simple as that.

— I've been daein too much gear tae try that, Sick Boy shakes his head. Sweat seeps from his pores, his body revolting at the very notion. — It'll kill us. And I don't fucking well think that Amelia n Tom in St Monans are gaunny be too keen tae welcome us back intae rehab. And how long is it gaunny take till some cunt has the confidence tae bring another shipment in, or till the polis start puntin it back oot oantae the streets? Too long for me, that's a fucking cert!

— What dae youse think but, boys? Renton looks around the taut faces, into jittery eyes.

— If it looks a sound plan, ah'm in, Matty says doubtfully.

— Me n aw, Mr Mark, Mr Simon, Keezbo confirms.

Everyone looks at Spud. — Awright, he says in a defeated, barely audible rasp.

Renton shows them two diagrams, which he spreads out on the floor. One is the OS map, supplemented with his felt-tipped pen lines. The other is a drawing they can't make head nor tail of. — Obviously, dinnae mention this tae any cunt, no even mates. He looks round them all. — Thank fuck Franco's inside. He'd caw us aw the cunts under the sun then insist oan takin ower. N he'd tell us that we need tae kick the fuck oot ay the security guards instead ay avoidin thum!

They all force a feeble chortle, except Matty, who Renton notes is already acting the cunt. His face is sour, and contemptuous sighs keep erupting from him. Nonetheless, Renton points to the rail lines on the map. — We get oantae the railway line at the old Gorgie Station, just off Gorgie Road. We park the motor and haul the planks up the embankment and walk wi them doon the line towards Murrayfield –

— Planks? Cunt, what fuckin planks? Matty says.

— Sorry, forgot tae mention that we go tae the timber yard in a bit, n git two fifteen-fit planks ay wid cut.

— Cunt, ah think you're the fuckin plank, Renton.

Renton recalls how they used to be best friends. That summer of 1979 when they went to London as teenage punks. It now seemed a long way away. He fights down his anger. — Bear wi us, mate. The line branches off before Murrayfield. The right-hand fork splits the factory fae the distillery. We take the left, cause it goes right through the chemical plant; there's a point where the fence gets really close tae the railway embankment. He points to the drawing. — Across the fence, a few feet away, there's this outbuilding. We take the plank and lay it fae the railway line back oantae the top ay the fence . . .

— Fuck sake, Matty mumbles.

— . . . then we walk up the plank, tae the top ay the fence. One ay us stalls there, the rest pass the other plank along. Then we push it doon fae the toap ay the fence oantae the roof ay the outbuilding, then walk doon oantae the roof.

— Cunt, like fuckin Spider-Man, Matty sneers.

— It's no too high, is it, likesay? Spud asks, eyes full of fear.

— Naw, it'll be easy. Besides, you're the best climber oot ay aw ay us, Renton says.

Spud holds a trembling hand out in front of him. — But no like this but, man . . .

— Lit's no kid ourselves, it isnae gaunny be a piece ay pish; if it wis some other cunt would've done it by now. But it's far fae impossible, Renton insists, turning back to the map. — There's a drainpipe on the outbuilding that we can scramble doon tae get intae the plant. Then we find the skag, which'll probably be in the containers stored in this loading bay, he points out the area on the map, — or in this building here, which is maist likely where they make it.

Matty looks at Renton, then at the others. Shakes his head. — Cunt, some fuckin plan this!

— Let's hear yours then, Matty, Renton challenges.

— Dinnae be actin the smart cunt cause yuv been tae some daft fuckin sheepshagger college, Mark. Matty dismissively swipes the map with the back of his hand. — This isnae the Great Train Robbery and yir no Bruce Reynolds. Cunt, yir mair like Bruce Forsyth, fruitcakin aboot wi fuckin daft maps n drawins!

Spud and Sick Boy chuckle a little, while Keezbo remains deadpan. Renton sucks in some air, and says, — Look, ah'm no bein Mister Big Time. Ah need gear, he points to the plant on the map, — and it's in there.

— Cunt, it's like a fuckin school project tae you! Well, it'll be like tryin tae find a needle in a haystack. Cunt, ye dinnae even ken whaire the fuckin skag is! They've goat guards, probably dugs . . . Matty looks to the others in appeal.

— First sign ay any bother, we fuckin bolt, Sick Boy says. — Nae dugs or spazzy cunts in uniforms are coming up a plank eftir us.

— Ah still say it's fuckin mad! Ah mean, cunt, what huv we goat fuckin gaun for us?

Renton sucks in some of the room's fetid air. Matty is driving him crazy. Withdrawal is gnawing at his brain and bones and it's crucial when you feel like this to invest your strength in the correct grains of conversation. — Fine. Dae cauld turkey then, he snaps.

Then Sick Boy turns on Matty. — Ever heard ay the element ay surprise? The Charge ay the Light Brigade? Three hundred Spartans? Bannockburn? History's fuckin littered wi gadges who've upset the odds, just by huvin the fucking bottle tae huv a dash. Did they change the motto ay Leith fae 'persevere' tae 'shite it' when ah wisnae looking?

Matty falls into a silence that's contagious for a few seconds till the shrill ringing of the phone shatters it, searing their nerve endings. Renton and Sick Boy both pounce and Renton gets there first, instantly deflated to hear the voice of his father on the line. — Mark?

The synapses in his brain stumble over one another. — Dad . . . what is it?

— We need skag, he hears Sick Boy say to Matty. — They've goat it and nae cunt else does. Endy story.

— What are you up tae? Are you keeping oaf that dirty stuff? his father asks.

— Nae option. Thaire's nane, he coldly announces as he hears an argument rage behind him.

— Well, dinnae seem sae disappointed aboot it!

— What dae ye want, Dad? Has Ma been on your case?

— This is nowt tae dae wi yir ma! Ah've got Hazel doon here! She's heartbroken, she's telling us that you've been oan that bloody crap again!

Grassin fuckin fucked-up frigid wee hoor . . .

— Look, this is nonsense. Tell us what ye want, or ah pit the phone doon.

— You willnae pit the phone doon on *me*, son!

A surge of welcome adrenalin shoots through Renton, briefly short-circuiting the pain. — In ten seconds, unless you can convince me otherwise.

— You're ruinin everybody's life, Mark . . . your mother n me . . . eftir Wee Davie, it's no been –

— Nine . . .

— . . . what have we ever asked offay ye?

— Eight . . .

— Ye dinnae care, dae ye? Ah used tae think it wis aw a game wi you –

— Seven . . .

— . . . but now ah know, ye jist dinnae –

— Six . . .

— . . . CARE! YE DINNAE CARE!

— Five, what dae ye want?

— Ah want you tae stoap! Tae stoap daein this! Wee Hazel, she –

— Four . . .

— COME HAME, SON! PLEASE COME HAME!

513

— Three . . .

— WE LOVE YE! Please, Mark –

— Two . . .

— Dinnae pit the phone doon, Mark –

— One . . . so if there's nowt else –

— MAAARK!

Renton rests the phone down gently onto the cradle. He turns to face the boys who stand staring at him, open-mouthed like fat goldfish in a botanical pond at feeding time. — The old man's gone vigilante oan us, so it might be a good idea tae git the fuck oot ay here in case he comes roond. Wuv no goat time for aw that shite right now.

Sundown, and the bellies of the clouds flush pink. Renton reflecting that no matter how early you rise or how late you turn in, you never see that point where light begins or the first bruise of darkness bleeds in under its fragile skin; the beauty, and the scary, unfathomable wisdom of transition. They head out from the lock-up in Matty's van, stopping at the Canasta Cafe in Bonnington Road, ostensibly for some food, but really to dispense the Valium that Renton liberated from his mother's medicine cabinet. They wash the pills down with milky coffees.

Renton is watching Keezbo eating two doughnuts and licking the third and fourth free of sugar. *The power of smack: fat cunt actually seems tae be losing weight.* He himself struggles to get down some scrambled egg on soggy toast. It still cramps his guts. Sick Boy is the same. Spud and Matty manage only the coffee and six cigarettes each. The elderly proprietor becomes disturbed by the shaking of Matty's mug on the Formica table. Sick Boy pacifies him with, — *È stanco: influenza.*

— You've been knockin aboot wi Swanney fir years, Renton whispers to Matty. — You must ken whaire he gits his gear.

Matty's tight mouth twists, mean and salty. — He's no gaunny tell the likes ay me anything, is he?

— You've goat eyes n ears. N yir no stupid, Matty.

Keezbo rises and heads to the toilet. Matty looks, then shrugs and moves closer in. — Cunt, this is between us. Right?

— Aye . . . nae worries, likesay, Spud says.

— Swanney's mate, this boy Mike Taylor, he hud a job at the plant. He was in stores. You've seen the cunt, he half challenges Renton, who nods, but can't place the boy. — Mike's mate worked fir a caterin firm deliverin meals tae their canteen. Ken the grub that comes in they big aluminium trays?

— Like school dinners? Spud asks.

514

— The very same, Matty grants, but evidently annoyed at the interruption. — Well, the skag came oot in they trays. Mike set it up for Swanney, n some other cunts were involved. But he goat huckled, n basically, they sacked him without prosecutin the cunt. Kept it quiet, cause it's bad publicity fir them. But now the security for the staff is meant tae be unbelievable; cameras everywhere, random searches, the lot. Cunt, ye cannae git a fart oot in yir troosers now.

— What aboot Seeker? Sick Boy asks.

— Cunt, ye dinnae want tae ken aboot him, Matty shivers. He clamps his yellow and brown teeth together to stop them chattering. — He's a law untae hissel. Even the likes ay Fat Tyrone huvnae been able tae git thair hooks intae that cunt.

Keezbo returns from the toilet, and Matty pointedly clams up. They settle up and head outside into the street. A newsagent's billboard for the local paper declares:

CITY STREETS 'AWASH WITH HEROIN'

They look at it in grim, derisive laughter. – If only, Sick Boy sneers.

They go round to the timber yard, where they have two planks of wood cut into fifteen-foot lengths. Vince, a chunky operative with dark, spiky hair, can tell that they're up to no good, but he knows Renton, Matty and Keezbo of old from the Fort and won't grass. The noise and relentless power of the saw distresses Spud. He imagines the wood as his limbs, being violently sheared off. Matty is fucked; he stands outside in the yard, frantically trying to light a cigarette, wasting match after match. He gives up and begs Sick Boy for his lighter. As they load the planks in the back, and over the front passenger seat, he reveals he's too fucked to drive. The Vallies have had no impact. — Ah cannae dae it.

Everybody looks to each other, then Keezbo sticks out a doughy hand. Matty hesitates, but after the prompting of the others, drops the keys into it. He gets in the front with Keezbo, while the others climb in the back, cramped and awkward with the diagonally placed planks. They are still unable to shut the back doors and Keezbo has to get out and tie them together. – Gaunny git fuckin well huckled before we get anywhere near there, Matty complains.

Sick Boy flicks a V-sign at the back of his head as Keezbo returns, starts up the van and drives. Renton watches the sweat beads grow and spot his shaved dome and neck like he was a cold bottle of beer. As they pull up onto Ferry Road they see Second Prize out running, and most look away in some sort of shame. As he passes the van, lost in his own world, Renton notes how good he looks.

They turn off Gorgie Road, onto a path by some wasteland, parking the van against a wall. They can hear the rumble of traffic on the street, but are out of sight as they exit, Renton and Sick Boy emerging from the back of the van with two Sealink bags. Although he lost his, Renton's learned that Sick Boy filched a good few from their brief employ. The heavier of the two contains a short crowbar. Sick Boy glances at the thick pieces of wood, and opts for the holdalls. Taking Renton's bag, he bounds ahead, leaving Renton and Matty to each carry an end of the first plank, with Keezbo and Spud taking the second. They are cramping, sweating and shivering as they slowly make their way up the overgrown path towards the embankment.

— Cunt, this isnae a good idea, Matty says again.

— Geez a better yin, then, Renton once more retorts, as they wrestle the wood up towards the fenced-off railway line.

Sick Boy, scurrying ahead along the banking, has found a hole through the patchwork of metal and wooden fencing, shrubbery and barbed wire. He throws the Sealink bags through and scrambles after them. They all squeeze in, although they have to hold up the fence while Keezbo commando-crawls through on his belly. Matty winces as he reaches out and a cluster of nettles brush and spear into his hand. He squeals, watching miserably as it throbs up in white, poisonous spots. — Cunt . . .

— You goat stung by a jaggy nettle, Spud helpfully informs him, as misanthropy burns through Matty like the venom in his hand. But there's a surge of euphoria induced by their meagre success, which he can't help but share in: they are on the railway embankment. They feel a sense of anticipation building, as they look down the tree-and-shrub-lined rail track in the fading light.

They flow like blood from a deep wound, along the gravel-strewn railway banking. After repeatedly stumbling, they give up and take the easier way, striding along the wooden sleepers, as the subtle curving of the rail track draws their laboured steps to the misty vanishing point.

The edge of the world turns dark as the sun sinks behind the broken tenements and the ancient castle, the chilling air now slightly ozone, but augmenting those fumes that the oncoming chemical plant and distillery boak constantly skywards in hazy, almost phantom, tendrils. Ahead is the plant. Why here, Renton asks himself, why in this city? The Scottish Enlightenment. You could trace the line from that period of the city's global greatness, to the Aids capital of Europe, going straight through that mix of processing plants and warehouses within those security fences. It was a peculiarly Edinburgh brainchild of medicine, invention and economics; from the analytical minds of the Blacks and Cullens, filtered through the speculations of the Humes and the Smiths. From the deliberations and actions of Edinburgh's finest sons in the eighteenth century, to its poorest ones poisoning themselves with heroin at the close of this one. A shiver in his eye.

We in Scotland . . .

They move further down the track, the darkness broken up only by the odd lights emanating from the back rooms of tenements. — We have tae watch for freight trains, they take nuclear waste along this line, Renton whispers.

The upbeat vibe doesn't last as they move further down the rail tracks. The planks grow viciously heavy on their shoulders. They're compelled to stop and take a break, sitting on the sleepers protruding from the outside of the rails. Sick Boy, who's been carrying the bags and making them out to be heavier than they are, is urged to take his shift. – Ah've goat a fuckin spel in ma hand, he protests, sucking on a finger.

— How the fuck did you git a spel? You've nivir cairried any wid, Renton bites.

— Ah did it earlier, Sick Boy moans, looking at Renton glaring in doubtful accusation back at him. — What? Ah'll take a fuckin shot!

Matty stretches out, finds some dock leaves and starts rubbing them on his hand. His shoulder aches worse than ever from the plank. He's fucked if he's taking another shift with it. Spud looks nervously at Renton. — Ah feel crap, Mark, this is the worst. His haunted eyes expand. — Dae ye think wir gaunny die?

— Nup, calm doon, mate, we'll be sound. Withdrawal hurts, but it doesnae kill, it's no like OD.

Spud, his eyes like tennis balls, wiping a cascade of snot from under his nose with the sleeve of his ragged yellow sweater, turns to Sick Boy. — What would you dae but, likesay, if ye jist hud a few weeks tae live? Ah mean, we might huv that cowie by now. Tons ay thum's gittin it, likes.

— Shite.

— But what wid ye dae if ye jist hud a few weeks left, ken? Jist sayin.

Sick Boy replies without hesitation: — Ah'd get a season ticket fir Tynecastle.

— Yir jokin!

— Naw, cause at least ah'd die wi the satisfaction of knowing that there would be one less ay these cunts.

Spud forces a dark smile. Keezbo briefly looks at Sick Boy as if he's

517

ready to say something, then turns to contemplate the rails of the track: rusty brown and gleaming silver. He seems deranged with the pain of withdrawal; dislocated and delirious with insomnia. — By rights it's oor skag. It's gittin made in oor toon . . .

— That's right, Keezbo. Sick Boy blows hard, galvanising himself with outrage. — Glaxo's poxy shareholders are minted while we fuckin suffer! We're sick and we fuckin well need it!

— By rights it's the people ay Gorgie's skag but, Spud says, — cause it's in the Jambo end ay toon. Like it's Scotland's oil. If we wir livin in a society ay real socialism, likes.

— Here's the *News at Ten*. Sick Boy hums the tune. — Ding! We urnae!

Renton looks at Spud's disconsolate expression, tries to gee him up. — Keezbo's a Jambo, we're jist helpin um git his share. Try thinkin ay it that wey.

— Dinnae ken how any cunt fae Leith kin support Herts, Matty says.

— Well, ah do, n so does his brar. Keezbo stands up, as he looks to Renton.

— Cunt, they built the skag plant next tae Tyney cause they kent they'd huv a ready supply ay daft fuckers needin somethin for the pain ay livin, Matty sneers defiantly at Keezbo, who is still breathing hard, hands on his hips.

— Ah goat telt by Drew Abbot that Leith wis traditionally Jambo territory, Spud explains, — it's only in the last couple ay generations it's likesay become Hibs, likes cause ay the groond bein near.

— Aye? Sick Boy asks wearily.

— Aye, the dockers were eywis Jambos, cause ye hud tae be a mason tae work oan the docks n shipyards.

— Kin we save this fuckin discussion fir another time?! Renton snaps in exasperation. — If ah wanted a fuckin lecture in history ah'd huv steyed at the university! Let's get movin!

— Ah'm jist sayin, Spud pouts.

— Ah ken, Danny, Renton says, putting his arm round Spud's shoulder. A three-quarter moon, which has inched through the clouds, bathes them in its silvery light. Below, the traffic softly rustles by. — But this is the big yin. We need tae keep focused here or wir fucked. You're ma best buddy, man, sorry ah shouted at ye. He rubs Spud's back. It's so thin and puny he can scarcely believe it belongs to a human being.

— Sorry, Mark, ma bottle just likesay pure went, like crash, smash, tinkle, ken? Ah'm tryin tae sortay distract masel, cause ah'm pure shitein it here, man.

— We'll be fine, Renton says, grabbing a plank and looking at Sick Boy, who tuts, but takes up the other end. Spud and Keezbo get the wood back on their shoulders. They walk slowly down the tracks. This time Matty is taking the break, and picks up the bags.

He walks a few steps behind Renton, then suddenly turns on him. — Cunt, you used tae wear a Rangers strip but, Rents. Primary.

— Look, ah've telt every cunt a hundred times, ma auld man bought me n Billy Rangers tops and took us through tae Ibrox when we were wee laddies, tryin tae make us Huns, Renton puffs, harping on at the disembodied voice behind him. — Billy wanted tae support an Edinburgh team, so my dad took us tae Tynecastle n bought us Herts gear. He turns round and looks at Matty, then Spud who is advancing alongside them, carrying the other plank with Keezbo. — Ah hated gaun thaire, hated that dirty maroon n the smell ay the distillery made us totally fuckin Zorba. So ah asked ma Uncle Kenny tae take us tae Easter Road. Then when ah goat aulder, ah started gaun wi aw youse cunts, he looks across to Spud and back to Sick Boy, — everybody except you, Matty, cause you never fuckin go anyway! Renton shouts towards Matty's face, belligerent and caustic. — Ah fuckin rejected both the Huns and the Jambos through *informed fuckin choice*, so ah'm mair ay a real, genuine Hibby than you'll ever be. So shut the fuck up, ya wee tramp!

Matty drops the bags and steps forward, tensed up. This forces Renton and therefore Sick Boy to do the same with their respectve ends of the plank. — So ah'm a fuckin tramp? Cunt, looked at yersel lately, ya fuckin mingin —

— STOAP IT! Spud shouts, as he and Keezbo drop their plank ends and get in between them. — Stoap aw this shite, youse! Ah hate tae see mates arguin!

— Aye, behave yersels, ya fuckin radges. Sick Boy shakes his head, nods across to the back of an overlooking tenement with kitchen lights burning. — Keep it doon, or they'll have the polis oantae us! Let's pick up the fuckin wid!

— It's aw gaun wrong . . . Spud muses, but Matty, though mumbling to himself, is picking up the wooden plank, taking over from Spud, and they're off again.

— It's aw gaunny be sound, Mr Danny, Keezbo whispers as Spud, in miserable gratitude, grabs the bags. — We git a stack ay gear, keep some ay it tae punt n some tae wean oursels oaf.

— That's it! Renton says in revelation. — Ration ourselves the right amount each day, aw scientific, the reduction cure. Measure it oot *scientifically*.

— Scientifically . . . Spud says blankly.

Matty marches in a silent hell. The rough stave is tearing at his neck, yet to move it from his shoulder is to shred his already poisoned hand. The blue dark sky ahead is now lit with the sinister glow of the plant. He thinks of Shirley, Lisa, and the flat at Wester Hailes. It seemed like a prison, that poky box; now he'd give anything to be there, with them. He suddenly convulses and drops the plank, which makes Keezbo instinctively let go his end.

Renton and Sick Boy follow suit. — What's wrong?

— Cunt, ah cannae . . . ah cannae dae this any mair, Matty crouches, rubbing his gut. — Ah'm crampin up tae fuck!

— We huv tae, it's aw we can dae, Spud goes, and picks up Matty's end. It dawns on him how sick Matty must be; he's used more and for longer than any of them.

Sick Boy, hoisting the plank onto his shoulder, glares at Matty. — Dinnae crap oot on us!

Matty turns and walks a few paces behind them, holding his stomach. He realises he's left the bags, so he stumbles miserably back to retrieve them, then follows. He can't stop scratching his skin, making big scabs, then ripping them off and tearing at the raw, infected flesh with his filthy fingernails. His eyes are red and weary.

They shuffle like constipated penguins towards the spot where the embankment runs close to the fence. They can see the outbuilding, which, to Sick Boy, seems bigger than before. Renton's eyeballs ache; it takes him a while to focus, even though the floodlights shine into the desolate plant. No sign of life. It's like a concentration camp, Renton reflects, and they look like Belsen survivors, trying to *break in*.

The huge silver, box-shaped building comes into view, the pipes spilling from it like spaghetti, the big, lustrous chimney and the other funnels shooting skywards. Then a faint sound, and some wisps of steam coming from one pipe against the dark backdrop. Bar a few isolated dark smudges of cloud, the glowing sky is cavernous and transparent, shimmering with galaxies new, this miracle coming so close to the dirty, crumbling tenements.

— Whoa, man . . . ye think thaire's a night shift? Spud gasps.

— Naw, Matty says breathlessly, — it'll be the machines, like robots, still processin it aw. They cannae shut doon the machinery and restart it every day. They'll keep it gaun through the night.

Sick Boy does an impromptu Begbie impersonation: — Any fuckin robot radge gits fuckin wide they git fuckin chibbed, android or nae fuckin android.

They laugh through their sickness, bonded again, until Spud goes into a dry, hacking coughing fit, almost to the point of seizure. They are concerned about him, after his illness, but he abruptly settles down, his eyes watering, as he forces wispy gasps of air into his shallow lungs. — Aw, man . . . he says over and over again, shaking his head.

— You okay, pal? Renton asks.

— Aye . . . just gittin ma breath back . . . aw, man . . .

Renton looks to Sick Boy, who nods, and they position the plank halfway down the side of the steep embankment and let it fall forward towards the thick mesh wire of the barricade. The end of the stave hits the fence with a crash, provoking a stentorian rustle of chain metal, before coming to rest and nestling on top of the barbed wire. Fearful of detection, they scramble back up to the railway line, where they fall prone, looking from the trackside into the plant.

All is still.

After a few minutes Renton rises and slips down the bank towards the stave. He steps onto it, testing it with his weight, then walks precariously up the forty-five-degree angle towards the barbed wire, which sparkles with starlight, as the razored metal digging into the wood of the plank holds it in place. Cheeks puffed out, Renton ascends to the top of the fence, lit by the resonant white moon, which blasts out briefly from behind layered, murky clouds, then he scurries back down to the embankment. — It's okay, he says to the others, who are now on their feet, marvelling at him like he's a trapeze artist. — The secret is no tae look doon. Gie's the end ay that other plank!

He takes one end and Matty takes the other. With the extra weight of the second body and plank to bear, the first one curves slightly. Renton gingerly makes his way to the top of the fence. He balances precariously in the boxer stance, one foot ahead of the other, as Matty starts to move up towards him, feeding the plank to him.

— Just lay it doon . . . Renton whispers, looking at the zombie faces of his friends, trying to fight off the notion that besets him: we're not human any more. We've slipped out of our skins like lizards, shedding not just our pasts, but our futures. We're shadows. His hands tremble as he looks down the second plank at Matty, and they carry it, balancing on the first one. For a moment it almost slips but Matty keeps a grip. Renton, with a balance and strength he'd never previously conceived of having, holds the end and keeps feeding it through. At the apex he lets the plank fall; his heart seems to fluff a couple of beats as he fears the timber's end will miss the target of the outbuilding roof and fall hopelessly into no-

521

man's-land, aborting the mission, but it smacks onto the tarpaulin roof with a dull whack. The euphoria overcomes fear, and he stays rooted to his perch on top of the fence, waiting for alarms, guards and dogs.

But there's nothing, and the boys are gathering round the base of the plank on the banking. He darts down the other plank, from fence-top onto roof, descending less sharply than the other; it's like the planks form the hands on a clock stuck at twenty minutes to five. — C'mon, he whispers into the night.

Matty, despite his ailments, moves feline-slick, and joins him in seconds. They start to pass over the Sealink holdalls. It's only now, when the plan seems to have at least some prospect of success, that Renton permits himself to think how stupid they've been, taking bags so distinguishable: Adidas or Head would have been better. Praying it won't come to that, he feels the brittle, grainy felt of the roof crack under the thin soles of his worn trainers.

It's Spud's turn to cross into the plant; he starts slowly at first, one foot in front of the other in deliberation, then picks up speed on the incline. Getting to the top of the fence he looks wobbly, before he makes a swift descent down to the roof and into Renton's arms.

Sick Boy follows, looking petulant and disgusted, as if traversing stocking-soled through a field of dog shit, but he negotiates the crossing, and squats on the roof panting nervously. They look below into the deathly still plant, illuminated by the night lights glowing dimly around them. Two metal boxes containing electronic eyes are visible, but face away from them, out towards the gates where workers will come and go. Renton thinks about the unseen men in a box somewhere, charged with looking at the grainy images on those screens. What would you ascertain after a few days but blurred black-and-white static?

— Some fucker tell that fat cunt tae wait there, Matty growls, looking at Keezbo who has got onto the first plank. — He's no gaunny fuckin well make it! Cunt, he'll brek that fuckin plank n trap us aw in here!

The gape at each other in panic.

— He'll slow every fucker doon, Sick Boy agrees, turning to Renton, but Keezbo has already commenced his climb.

— C'mon, Keith, Renton whispers encouragingly. — Wigan's chosen few!

Sick Boy slaps his head, looking to Matty, as the plank buckles under the weight of Keezbo's ascent. But the drummer presses on, like an elephant on a tightrope wire. — When ye git tae the top, dinnae stoap, just run right doon the other side, Matty calls out, rigid with tension, hands balling and unclenching by his side.

522

— Spirit ay Wigan Casino, Keezbo! Renton continues to coax.

Keezbo reaches the apex. Watching his advance, they feel their hearts race towards their mouths as he teeters for a scary two seconds as he changes planks, then power-descends towards them, the plank thrashing on the fence, his mouth open, eyes glaring. — Toughest skiers, Keezbo Yule. Renton plants a smacker of a kiss on Keezbo's sweaty forehead as he comes to rest on the creaking roof. Sick Boy grapples two large buttocks and pelvic thrusts into him in delight.

They are on the outbuilding, a humdrum red-brick structure about fifteen-foot high and twenty-foot square. From this vantage point they look around for security. Nothing. All the cameras point away from them. They look at each other in a kind of childlike wonderment. They are five junkies from Leith, locked inside a compound with the biggest amount of pure morphine on these islands.

Renton scrambles down the drainpipe of the building. It's plastic, not metal, as he'd imagined. He worries about Keezbo's weight on it but says nothing. Matty is down behind him, followed by Spud, then Sick Boy. They again look in horror at Keezbo, then across to the main buildings of the plant, sensing that the pipe will come crashing down, trapping them all inside, helplessly sick in this Venus flytrap, for the morning shift to come and raise the alarm. However, Keezbo shimmies halfway down it, jumping the rest of the distance, landing on his feet with a big grin. — We're in, Mr Mark, Danny, Simon, Matthew.

Renton limits his celebration to a solitary fist beat on his chest. Sick Boy's eyes look as if they are about to pop from his head, and he briefly crouches down against the outbuilding for a second as if in great pain, then springs back to his feet. They go towards the floodlight pylons, making for the loading bay at the side of the processing plant where the plastic boxes are piled up on wooden pallets. — It'll no be skag in thaime, Matty says, — it'll aw be pharmaceuticals. The morphine's gaunny be locked up, he moans.

Acknowledging the logic in what he says, Renton insists, — They're sealed up though, and takes the iron bar from his Sealink bag. — We should make sure before we start brekin intae they labs n warehooses . . .

Keezbo and Spud are holding each other's wrists and jumping around in a circle together, lost in a rabid, strung-out dance. — Here we go, here we go, here we go . . . they gasp in elation, before being silenced with prejudice, as a shrill, severing, turbo-powered alarm shrieks into the night. It seems to erupt from under the ground, vibrating up through their rubber soles, freezing them in the most paralysing shock they've ever experienced. It splits their eardrums, rendering them almost senseless. They can barely hear the shouts of men and barks of dogs above it as fear propels them to bolt through the disabling cacophony, across the concourse towards the outbuilding.

They don't look back, not one of them; Renton gets there first but cups his hands, giving Sick Boy, then Spud, a grateful boost up the drainpipe. By the time he scuttles up onto the roof himself, he can see the moonlit skeleton he assumes is Daniel Murphy, vanishing into heaven, which means that Sick Boy has already crossed over to the embankment.

Renton now allows himself a backward glance. There seem too many pursuers to be feasible, swarming across the shadowy courtyard: dogs and men, barking psychotic encouragement and instruction at each other. Disregarding the shouts and snarls behind him, he launches himself up the plank. At the top, he looks back over his shoulder, shouting for Matty and Keezbo to get onto the roof. Then a flashlight blinds his eyes and he staggers down the board, expecting to fall into the void on the safe side of the barrier, but he makes it all the way to the sloping bank, feeling Spud grab his arm and guide him up to the tracks. Falling recumbent, they watch Sick Boy's ivory silhouette stealing away down the south suburban railway line.

Renton and Spud see Matty coming onto the roof, torches from security guards picking him out. Keezbo is last up the pipe, the guards almost on him, an Alsatian leaping at his foot and missing by an inch. As Matty zooms up the plank towards the fence, Renton and Spud see Keezbo miraculously haul his large frame onto the outbuilding's roof, the dogs snarling at him. It seems that there are around eight men and four dogs, yelping at each other, their handlers screaming into walkie-talkies over the alarm, which squawks like a monster mechanical bird whose eggs are under threat. Keezbo is on the roof. But as Matty hits the top of the fence to begin his descent, a twist of his heel sends the first plank sliding away and crashing down into the black space between the outbuilding and fence. Keezbo is stranded.

As the dogs bark, circling the building, they see Keezbo look first grievously, then sadly up at them from the other side of the fence. His features have contorted in an expression of deep pain and betrayal. Then they suddenly fade into a broken resignation, as he sits down on the roof, like a beaten junky Buddha, surrounded by the shouting men and snarling dogs beneath him.

— Fuck sake . . . Keezbo . . . Spud wheezes as Matty joins them on the track.

Renton suddenly springs to his feet, bellowing into the compound, —

LEAVE UM ALAINE, YA FUCKIN FASCIST CUNTS! IT'S OOR FUCKIN GEAR! WE FUCKIN WELL NEED IT! WE'VE GOAT A FUCKIN RIGHT! He picks up stones from the embankment, hurling them over the fence at the guards and dogs. One strikes a dog in the side eliciting a high yelp. — C'MON THEN, YA FUCKIN SCABBY CUNTS!

Matty pulls him back. — C'mon! Cunt, we goat tae fuckin split, and they see Spud running down the tracks and follow him. Renton looks back a couple of times, then picks up speed to catch up with the others.

— Fat cunt . . . better no . . . grass us up, Matty rasps, as they run breathlessly to the abandoned wreckage of Gorgie Station, where they stop to recover. Sick Boy is waiting in the shadows. Renton feels his head spinning with the decimating effort of the flight as he struggles to get the air into his lungs.

— Nae gadge's gaunny grass any cat up, Spud whines at Matty, taking deep breaths, as Sick Boy's gaze whips from one to the other. — Keezbo's sound.

— What happened tae the fuckin plank? Renton wheezes. — How could he no get up?

— It just fell back in, wi us climbin up it, Matty protests. He sees a judging aspect to Renton's gaze. — It wis an accident! Cunt, what are ye tryin tae say?

Renton turns away, maintaining a pointed silence, but Sick Boy swiftly cuts in. — Tell ye what *ah'm* tryin tae say. A common snowdropper's no in a position tae call any other cunt a grass.

— What? Matty turns to him.

— That sky-blue Fair Isle jumper ah hud. He points at Matty, his mouth buckled tight in accusation. — You ken, the one ye fuckin snowdropped fae the dryin green at the Bannanay flats that time.

— Ah fuckin never stole yir fuckin jumper! Matty turns to Spud in appeal. — Cunt, that was yonks ago, we were just wee laddies, every cunt snowdropped back then!

— Aye, but they didnae *wear* what they fuckin snowdropped! They flogged it, n bought new clathes. Only a fuckin tramp *wears* what they snowdrop, Sick Boy declares, lighting a cigarette, taking a drag. — Ah mind when ah sais tae my ma: 'Matty Connell's nicked that jumper you bought me, he wis wearin it at school,' he smiles thinly. — Ken what she said? She goes: 'Let him keep it, son. The Connells are a poor family, that boy needs it mair than you.' That was what my ma said. My mother was prepared tae pit clathes oan the back ay a tramp, oan a *lice-infested scruff*, he nods gently as he mouths each word, — just cause she felt sorry for him.

— So that's what ye think ay us, then? Eh? That's what you've thought ay me aw they fuckin years?!

— That's right, Sick Boy shrugs, — so go and get aw emotional, as per usual. Poor wee Matty. Poor fuckin *sk-ruff*!

Matty looks plaintively at Spud and Renton in appeal.

— Ye ken what ma take oan this is, Matty, Renton is bent over with his hands on his knees, but is looking sharply up at him, — this fuckin obsession yuv goat wi daein Keezbo doon? It's aboot him being wi Shirley. They wir jist bairns whin they went oot thegither, for fuck sakes! She's wi you now! Git the fuck ower it!

— What . . . ? That's goat nowt tae dae wi anything, Matty protests, wretched and feeble.

Sick Boy turns on him. — Heard it wis a fill-hoose job, her n Keezbo.

— Whaaa . . . ? Matty gasps in disbelief. He looks at his friends, twisted, other-worldly, their cold eyes and zombie-like pallor, and he'd rather have stayed to face the dogs.

— Jist gaun by what I heard, Sick Boy says, mouth tightening.

— Heard fae who? Matty bites back, enraged. — FAE THAT FAT CUNT!?

— Burds talk n aw.

— What're you fuckin well sayin, Williamson?

Sick Boy trains a studied gaze on Matty. — It wis her first time, when she went wi Keezbo. A big, fat ginger-pubed cock up ye, inside ye, burstin yir maidenhood, yir virgin blood trickling doon its shaft; it's bound tae have been memorable for her. It's only natural that she thinks ay that moment *every single time* she sets eyes on Keezbo. So it's bound tae play on *your* mind but, mate, ah kin totally understand that.

Matty stands rooted on the spot, paralysed by a fearful incredulity. — Whaa-aat . . . ? he says again, in disbelief.

Spud is miserably bleating, — Naw, boys, come oan, come oan now . . . this is ootay order . . . this isnae right . . . as Renton and Sick Boy savour Matty's subconscious unspooling before them.

— It. Will. Play. On. Your. Mind, Sick Boy softly mouths.

Matty seems to cook slowly from the inside, then ignites: — FUCK YOU, YA DIRTY FUCKIN PIMPIN TROLL, throwing his sinew-strained neck forward, as snotters fly from his nostrils. Then he glances down to the stones under his feet and goes to pick one of them up. Renton rushes forward and grabs him. — Fuck off wi that –

— CUNT, AH'LL FUCKIN KILL HIM! AH'LL FUCKIN KILL

THAT DIRTY LYIN PIMP BASTARD, and he lunges forward, immediately restrained by Renton and Spud.

Sick Boy stands in a relaxed posture, and takes an exaggeratedly casual drag on his cigarette. — Aye, aye, aye. Sure.

— YOU'RE FUCKIN DEID, WILLIAMSON! Matty half roars and half squeals as he turns on his heel and tears off into the night, as Sick Boy contemptuously feigns getting shot. Matty's retreating shadow is pursued by Spud. — Hey, Matty, wait the now, catboy . . .

— Spud . . . Renton protests weakly.

— Leave the cunts. Sick Boy grabs Renton's wrist to restrain him. — It's better we split up anyway. Four's jist gaunny draw attention.

They watch as Spud scrambles down the banks after Matty, disappearing from their sight onto Gorgie Road and following him not to the van, but down the street, past Stratford's Bar, unsure of why Matty's heading in that direction, even more uncertain as to why Spud's in pursuit.

On the railway line that snakes above the pub and street level, Renton and Sick Boy carry on heading away from the plant. The moon, skulking behind a web of cloud, briefly reminds Renton of Spud's pallid woebegone face as he vanished from his eyeline.

— Matty, fuckin poisonous wee rodent, Sick Boy says as they hurry down the tracks. — Who rattled that cunt's cage? We're aw fuckin seek tae our marrow, but at least try n be a man aboot it.

— Uptight little cunt's eywis the same, seek or no seek, Renton snaps, now wishing he'd punched Matty's pus earlier. — Eywis hus tae pish oan the fuckin pageant. Big Keith's gaunny dae serious jail time for aw ay us, n aw that cunt can dae is slag him oaf!

The pain intensifies, Renton cursing the folly of all that pointless exertion, which has burned off more of the dregs of the junk in their system. They will soon be totally immobilised. They have to get back to the Valium stash. Arms wrapped around themselves, they follow the tracks till they hit the viaduct at the Union Canal, the death's-head energy having preceded them onto this overland wraithlike void that seems parted from the slumbering city streets by dimensions other than mere height. Yet as the canal slopes down to street level, those cold, grey thoroughfares and closes they're expelled onto seem equally hellish, as Renton and Sick Boy sweat and scratch like chickens just broken from the shell.

At Viewforth they leave the waterway, and a cold rain starts to fall. Lurching towards Bruntsfield, they watch the orangey smudges of the sodium lamps splash over the wet streets, before cutting across the Meadows and heading towards the North Bridge. The pavements are lifeless save for the odd stray drunks looking for taxis, late bars or parties. An emergency services siren assaulting the night strikes panic, flushing them like rats down the dimly lit back closes of the Royal Mile, which they descend in agitation towards Calton Road. — I just dinnae get this life gig, Sick Boy says out loud, trembling.

As they walk down the dark and desolate street, memories of Wee Davie assail Renton. The house is empty and soulless without his chaos, the family fragmented. Something can seem to be useless, inefficient or unproductive, but then you take it away and things quickly start to fall apart and get shitey. He finally responds in kind to Sick Boy's statement. — It's weird that we're here one minute, gone the next. In a couple ay generations' time naebody's gaunny gie a fuck. We'll just be some funny-dressed wankers in faded photographs that the one sad descendant wi too much time oan their hands pulls oot a sideboard tae occasionally look at. It's no like some famous cunt's gaunny come along and make a film ay *our* lives, is it?

Renton has scared Sick Boy, who comes to an abrupt halt in the empty street. — You've given up, mate. That's what it's aw aboot. You've given up.

— Mibbe, Renton concedes. Has he? Surely you eventually run out of tears and excuses.

— That bugs the fuck oot ay us. If you gie up, we're aw fucked, he says, finding his stride again, as a lone car rumbles past them. — Ah ken we slag each other off, Mark, but you're the one that's got the goods. That time we broke intae that hoose; you saved that lassie, you n Tommy. Begbie wid've let her croak, n Spud, Keezbo n me, we never had a fucking clue. But you took charge. How did ye ken tae dae that?

Wee Davie . . .

Renton feels a burn, then shrugs, as if to say: fucked if I know. Then he turns to his distressed compadre. — It's you that's the boy but, Si. You're miles ahead the rest ay us. Always have been. Wi birds n that –

— Ah've done so many fucking bad things but, Mark! Sick Boy slaps his head in sudden violence, as they emerge past the back entrance to Waverley Station. — Ah've fucked up big time!

A fissure of pain opens up in Renton and he responds in blind panic, stopping Sick Boy's disclosure instantly. — Me n aw! Ah ken what ye mean!

— Ye mean Olly Curran? We agreed –

— Fuck that cunt! Renton venomously sneers. — Brought it oan hissel wi his uptight, racist shite. Ah've nae sympathy fir that fuckin prick! Ah'm talking aboot Fiona, and he feels something breaking inside him, like a dam crumbling. — Ah loved her n ah fucked it right up! When we were on holiday, ah could see it aw ahead, and he looks up, the Calton Hill towering above them, — me and her, forever. And it scared us . . . scared us fuckin shiteless. When ah got back . . . Renton's eyes are red and puffy, — that lassie ah wis telling ye aboot, her fae Paisley, she was gaun wi ma mate . . . we were drunk, we started muckin aboot, n ah took her up there, he points to the dark, gloomy hill as they emerge onto the slip road leading to Leith Street, — or she took me thaire, cause Fiona must huv telt her that we'd had this shag in that park in East Berlin . . . she used us tae get one up oan her fuckin mate and ah wanted it, so ah fucked her in the park . . . ma mate's bird . . . ah didnae even like the lassie . . .

— Bet the sex was barry, but, Sick Boy says, trying to fuse some enquiry into his voice. After all, he knows this story in all its detail. It was there, in his friend's own handwriting, on that discarded crumpled ball of a journal entry he'd slyly rescued from the litter basket of Renton's room in the St Monans Drug Rehabilitation project, as his friend had drifted off to sleep. He'd been surprised by the detail and fluidity in Renton's prose; how it had all just come out in those unedited sentences, in that thick, flowing scribble. He'd been keeping it back for a laugh, but realises that now isn't the time to mention it, as big dry sobs explode in Renton's chest.

Renton feels miserable and pathetic. He'd betrayed Fiona, so he had to end it. And he'd double-crossed Bisto, he couldn't look at him properly again. There wasn't any excuse. It was how he was, rank rotten to the core, he thinks miserably . . . then he considers Tom Curzon's words, *maybe it's just a phase I'm going through . . .*

And he looks at Sick Boy who now has his head bowed, who seems to understand everything . . . — What? What have *you* done? Renton stops in the dark street and faces his friend.

Sick Boy feels something trying to twist up through his body and escape from his mouth, it has to be fought back. Instead he offers a diversionary gasp. — Matty . . .

— Fuck him.

And now Sick Boy gives relieved thanks for Renton's intervention, preventing his own disclosures. *Thank fuck it always has tae be aboot him.* — But . . . ah think it was that wee cunt . . . that grassed up Janey Anderson wi the benefits fiddle. Ah mentioned it tae him once, it was stupid, just in passing. He looks at Renton, trying the lie for size. — I think he fucking squealed, Mark.

— Naw . . . Renton says shakily, — even he wouldnae stoop that low.

Sick Boy buckles, allowing the will holding his queasy, bilious body and soul together to slacken, in order that he might punish himself with the ensuing rush of nausea. — Ah jist feel so fuckin sick . . .

— Me n aw. But we're nearly thaire, mate. We jist huv tae hud it thegither a bit longer.

Elm Row approaches, followed by Montgomery Street. Outside the stair door, they fight to compose themselves. — Eftir we doss back the last ay they Vallies, Sick Boy says, eyes watering, — that's it. It's over, Mark. Ah've done aw the skag ah'm ever gaunny dae.

With his conviction so powerful and certainty so absolute, Renton is visibly moved. He feels his eyes moisten as the image of Keezbo, stranded in no-man's-land, burns in his skull. — Too right, he says, touching his friend lightly on the shoulder, — we're done here, and they both look up to the sky, unable to enter their stair door, completely drained in fearful anticipation of that cold multitude of steps to their top-floor flat.

We're done here.

And with that realisation, looking up to the munificence and radiance of the stars, Renton feels exalted, like he's been rewarded with a kind of eternal childhood; the idea that the whole of the earth was his to inherit, and to share with every human spirit. Soon he'll be free again. He recalls how, at the end of his life, Nietzsche realised that you couldn't simply turn your back on nihilism; you had to live through it and hopefully emerge out the other side, leaving it behind.

Heroin.

That girl at the break-in. How *did* he know what to do?

Wee Davie.

Without being in that house, watching them tend to him, he'd never have made the cold connection: she's taken shit, we need to get it up. How? Salt water. Those neural pathways had been scorched into his brain by the searing cries of his agitated brother, instilling that awareness of how to care for someone in distress. One bright star burns at him in the sky, like an affirming wink. And he can't help it, can't resist the thought: *The Wee Man.*

Sick Boy perceives himself as prisoner of his own lying lips. Standing every day at the shaving mirror, watching those eyes grow colder and more pitiless in face of the drug's dictates and the world's brutal coarseness. But it's the lies he's told to himself and others that permit him this extravagance. Now he feels something poignant stirring in his soul, and this time he realises in elation that it might even be a truth trying to bubble to the surface. He coughs it shakily from his throat. — One thing,

Mark, ah know that whatever happens, whatever stunts either ay us pull, it'll always be you n me, backing each other up, he contends, his chest slowly rising and falling. — We'll get through this thegither, and he walks into the stair, compelling Renton to follow.

— Ah know that, mate, Renton says, almost distracted under the luminosity of the stars, till the heavy door, closing behind them on the spring, extinguishes their light. — Cauld turkey's on the menu and we'll dae it, nae fuckin bother. It's the end ay the line for me, he smiles in the darkness, kicking the stone steps under his feet. — Ah've taken this skag thing as far as it kin go. It wis a nice wee phase but there's nowt new the drug kin show us, other than mair misery, n ah'm fuckin well done wi aw that.

— Too right, Sick Boy agrees. — Toughest skiers.

Guided by the thin glow of a stair lamp, they reach the summit of their landing. As they unlock the front door and enter the cold flat, the phone explodes in a bone-shaking ring.

They look at each other for a frozen second, into which all time collapses.

ACKNOWLEDGEMENTS

Thanks to Emer Martin, for reading an early draft of this novel and providing great encouragement and pertinent criticism.

To Robin Robertson, who kept faith with me on this book's journey – a more convoluted one than we've both grown accustomed to over the years.

To Katherine Fry for her great wisdom and incredibly sharp eye.

To everyone at Random House UK in the publicity, rights, sales and marketing teams, who really have given me phenomenal support over the years.

To Tam Crawford, for splitting Ally and I's sides in the Cenny, with his tales of breasts and budgerigars.

To Kenny McMillan, the original purseman.

To Jon Baird for his Doric.

To Trevor Engleson at Underground management, and Alex, Elan, Jack and everyone at CAA for being in my corner in Hollywood, and Greg and Laura at Independent Talent for the UK representation.

To friends and family in the great cities of Edinburgh, London, Dublin, Chicago, Miami, Sydney and Los Angeles. You keep me going. It really is your fault.

I need and want to thank my friend, the late, great Davie Bryce, of the Calton Athletic Recovery Group in Glasgow. This inspirational man might no longer be with us, but he's the reason that so many people, who otherwise wouldn't be around, now have a life to get on with.

Most of all though, thanks beyond words to Beth, for all her love.

Irvine Welsh, Chicago, October, 2011